Nemesis is forecast for **1984**.
But so are:—

JORROCKS'

JAUNTS AND JOLLITIES.

Surrey Shooting. Mr. Jorrocks upset out of a Go-cart

Jorrocks out with the Surrey foxhounds (now the Old Surrey and Burstow); Jorrocks at Newmarket, Cheltenham, Margate, Paris and Brighton; Jorrocks hunting, shooting, racing, sailing, fishing, feasting, dancing, dining, drinking, drowning; and Jorrocks *redivivus*.

Jaunts and Jollities will be the most lavishly illustrated of all the R. S. Surtees Society's editions. It will include 9 full-page black and white illustrations by **'Phiz' (H. K. Browne)** from the first (1838) edition, 16 coloured plates by **Henry Alken** which appeared in the third and fourth editions, and 6 further coloured plates—5 by **Alken** and 1 by **W. Heath**—which appeared in a later edition. The great illustrators of Jorrocks's era admirably complement the comedy and farce of the hero's adventures.

The text, and the pictorial stampings on the cover, will be reproduced from the 1874 edition. In size and format *Jaunts and Jollities* will be similar to the other Surtees publications.

Michael Wharton, who is also 'Peter Simple' of the *Daily Telegraph*, has agreed to write an Introduction.

Jaunts and Jollities will be available by the end of June, 1984.

Pre-publication prices

The unprecedentedly large number of full-page illustrations (any of which it would be a pity to omit) increases our costs substantially.

For those who subscribe **before 28th February, 1984** the prices will be:

(*a*) **£11·75** per copy for books which are collected from J. A. Allen & Co Ltd, 1 Grosvenor Place, Buckingham Palace Road, London, S.W.1., and

(*b*) **£13·50** per copy for books which are posted, the price including packing and postage.

The post-publication price will be substantially higher.

A list of those subscribing before 28th February 1984 will be printed at the end of the book.

Minimum of pre-publication subscribers and ordering

A minimum of 1500 subscribers for *Jaunts and Jollities* must be obtained by 28th February, 1984. All cheques will be acknowledged. All pre-publication money will be kept in a separate *Jaunts and Jollities* bank account and will be returned in the event of publication not going ahead.

A leaflet, which includes an order form, has been enclosed. If no order form is available, write to **the Hon. Mrs Robert Pomeroy, R. S. Surtees Society, Rockfield House, Nunney, Nr. Frome, Somerset.** Your order should be accompanied by a cheque for the appropriate amount, made payable to the R. S. Surtees Society. Please show your name and address clearly.

INTRODUCTION

Surtees considered *Handley Cross* 'the best thing I have ever written'. Yet it was a failure, first in serial form and then as a three-volume book published without illustrations in 1843. Ten years later, after much rewriting and now marvellously illustrated by Leech, to his publisher's despair it still failed, a failure which Surtees resented as do most authors when they see their own best-loved creation mauled by reviewers and scorned by readers. How are we to account for this initial flop and the subsequent rise of *Handley Cross* as Surtees' most well-known—if not most widely read-book?

Handley Cross failed because it illustrates many of Surtees' worst characteristics as a writer and because it reflects some of Surtees' shortcomings as a human being. But most of all it sold badly because it embodies attitudes which did not chime with Victorian sensibilities and tastes. Belinda and Lucy Glitters apart, his women, for example, are termagants or tarts mostly engaged in the sordid manipulation of the Victorian marriage market—an obsessive subject with Surtees—with mothers pressing their daughters on prospective suitors 'just as old J pressed his hounds on after a fox'. Reviewers found it 'coarse'. When Jorrocks arrives in Handley Cross covered in mud and Mrs. Blash remarks '*Hut!* he's always on his back, that old feller', Jorrocks retorts 'Not 'alf as often as you are, old gal'. If this is a solitary lapse, Jorrocks himself as the book's hero is out of key with Victorian prudery: there is his taste for low company—such as Mr. Bowker, a friend of a murderer who confessed on the scaffold 'I did boil the exciseman'. More than this, everything that Jorrocks stood for as a fox-hunter runs against the mores and style of the mid-Victorian respectable sporting world. Masters were supposed to be gentlemen. Jorrocks is a city grocer not above touting his tea to his field just as Pigg, his huntsman, tries to sell insurance at meets; he is a Post Office Directory as opposed to a Peerage man. He detests lords and his appalling table manners make him unfit for their society. Nor is Surtees, as Dickens was, on the side of the oppressed and injured: his servants are crooks and his farm labourers clodhoppers who head foxes. The morals of Surtees' characters are those of the Regency; the hunting he enjoyed was that of the provincial packs one remove from the trencher-fed packs which the Handley Cross had once been. He was a throwback, the nostalgic chronicler of a vanishing world, a crusader against the snobbery of the 'cut 'em downs' of Leicestershire.

The idol and chronicler of the smart hunting set was the sporting journalist, C.T. Apperley, who wrote under the pen name of Nimrod. By the 1840s Surtees' relationship with Nimrod was at its worst and their unseemly squabbles public property. Surtees' caricature of Nimrod as Pomponius Ego in *Handley Cross* presents his fellow journalist as a liar and a coward. John Welcome has recently argued that Surtees' animus was rooted in envy of Nimrod's prowess as a horseman and of the social success that his 'buttering' of the great of the fox-hunting world had brought him. At the very time Surtees was pillorying Nimrod as afraid of his fences and making up accounts of runs he had never had the courage to witness he was recovering from a bad fall which helped to kill him. Like Jorrocks, his creator Surtees was not a great 'leaper' and despised those who thought leaping the be all and end all of hunting. Nor was Surtees any great shakes as a master of hounds: he got into trouble with his farmers, had to put his pack down and rapidly resigned. Some of the troubles of his mastership are reflected in Jorrocks' own misadventures. I suspect that Surtees. like Jorrocks, preferred bye days with no other company than his huntsman. 'Ah Pigg, let us fraternise,' Jorrocks declares to his huntsman, whom he had earlier decided to sack for drunkenness, after Pigg's skills have provided a wonderful run.

There is in *Handley Cross*—a long book—a good deal of automatic writing. As to Byron writing was, for Surtees, a sort of drug that, once tasted, becomes an addiction as he himself confessed, 'something like smoking—men get into the way of it and can't leave it off'. The famous 'sporting lektors' are, for example, tedious except for a few brilliant flashes and those memorable phrases that have become a part of the repertoire of every speaker at Hunt Dinners. They are palpable padding as is the insertion in the final rewrite of the odd, if amusing, chapter concerning the Assistant Drainage Commissioner whom ambitious mothers court as a prospective match on the mistaken assumption that he is an A.D.C. to a general.

Given these blemishes, why does *Handley Cross* survive, and survive in triumph? As every commentator has insisted, it is because Surtees has created two immortal characters: Jorrocks and his huntsman James Pigg. Their failings—and they are legion—do not outweigh their devotion to fox-hunting and their sheer vitality evident in the best dialogue in Victorian fiction. Pigg is a gambler, a cheat and a drunkard, from whose mouth issues a continuous dribble of chewed tobacco and a stream of incomprehensible, uncouth utterances; but he is the genuine article. Jorrocks is mean and vain; but his endless soliloquies—when he cannot talk to anyone else he talks to himself—reveal him as a 'brick'. Sooner or later both master and man in a world of hypocrisy tell the truth. When his relatives seek to get him legally declared mad Jorrocks touches the borderland of tragedy; Pigg's evidence nearly ruins him; no man, he tells the court, is sane who makes a back cast unless the fox has been headed. Where hunting is concerned, he is a George Washington.

Jorrocks and Pigg are genuine because their creator himself was genuine, in his own fashion a seeker after truth. We know little about him or his life and we must deduce from his works much of what lay behind that austere, monk-like face. Everything in his life—that is apart from his own intimate feelings—provides copy. He was a J.P. and the vicious portrait of Mr. Muleygrubs must be meant to illustrate the pretensions of those he met on the bench. From Charley Stobbs, who ultimately rescues Belinda, Jorrocks' adopted daughter, from the dreadful Mrs. Jorrocks' machinations to marry her off to the seedy Captain Doleful, we recapture Surtees' hatred of his own time in London as an apprentice lawyer copying precedents and experiencing 'the full force of that London loneliness which damps the spirit of many an ardent genius from the country'. Such an 'ardent genius' was Surtees and *Handley Cross* is a great, if misshapen, monument to that genius.

RAYMOND CARR

St. Antony's College, Oxford
  March 1983

Michael Hardey.

HANDLEY CROSS;

OR,

MR. JORROCKS'S HUNT.

BY

THE AUTHOR OF "MR. SPONGE'S SPORTING TOUR,"
"JORROCKS'S JAUNTS," ETC. ETC.

WITH ILLUSTRATIONS BY JOHN LEECH.

LONDON:
BRADBURY AND EVANS, 11, BOUVERIE STREET.
1854.

First published in this edition in 1983 by
The R. S. Surtees Society

Hon. Sec., Mrs Hedy Sumption,
Craddock Cleve,
Craddock, Nr. Cullompton,
Devon, EX15 3LW

© This Edition and Compilation The R. S. Surtees Society, 1983

ISBN 0 9507697 3 8

Printed in Great Britain by Butler & Tanner Limited,
Frome and London

PREFACE.

Mr. Jorrocks, having for many years maintained his popularity, it is hoped that, with the aid of the illustrations, he is now destined for longevity.

The Author, in the present edition, not being tied to space or quantity, has had a better opportunity of developing his sporting hero than before.

The reader will have the kindness to bear in mind, that the work merely professes to be a tale, and does not aspire to the dignity of a novel.

London, *October,* 1854.

CONTENTS.

	PAGE
THE OLDEN TIMES	1
THE RIVAL DOCTORS AND M.C.	12
THE RIVAL ORATORS	18
THE HUNT BALL	25
THE HUNT COMMITTEE	37
THE CLIMAX OF DISASTER	49
MR. JORROCKS	55
CAPTAIN DOLEFUL'S DIFFICULTIES	70
THE CONQUERING HERO COMES	74
THE CONQUERING HERO'S PUBLIC ENTRY	78
THE ORATIONS	84
CAPTAIN DOLEFUL AGAIN	89
A FAMILY DINNER	92
MR. JORROCKS AND HIS SECRETARY	95
THE COCKNEY WHIPPER-IN	107
SIR ARCHEY DEPECARDE	120
THE PLUCKWELLE PRESERVES	124
A SPORTING LECTOR	127
HUNTSMAN WANTED	143
JAMES PIGG	148
A FRIGHTFUL COLLISION! BECKFORD v. BEN	153
THE CUT-'EM-DOWN CAPTAINS	158
THE CUT-'EM-DOWN CAPTAIN'S GROOM	162
BELINDA'S BEAU	165
MR. JORROCKS AT EARTH	176
A QUIET BYE	180
ANOTHER BENIGHTED SPORTSMAN	198
PIGG'S POEMS	209
COOKING UP A HUNT DINNER	218
SERVING UP A HUNT DINNER	223
THE FANCY BALL	235
ANOTHER SPORTING LECTOR	244
THE LECTOR RESUMED	261
MR. JORROCKS'S JOURNAL	268
THE "CAT AND CUSTARD-POT" DAY	271
JAMES PIGG AGAIN ! ! !	280

	PAGE
MR. JORROCKS'S JOURNAL	285
THE WORLD TURNED UPSIDE DOWN DAY	292
MR. MARMADUKE MULEYGRUBS	299
THE TWO PROFESSORS	314
ANOTHER CATASTROPHE	319
THE GREAT MR. PRETTYFAT	325
M.F.H. BUGGINSON	327
PINCH-ME-NEAR FOREST	332
A FRIEND IN NEED, &C.	339
THE SHORTEST DAY	342
JAMES PIGG AGAIN ! ! !	344
MR. JORROCKS'S JOURNAL	346
THE CUT-'EM-DOWN CAPTAIN'S QUADS	349
POMPONIUS EGO	355
THE POMPONIUS EGO DAY	360
A BAD CHURNING	376
THE PIGG TESTIMONIAL	382
THE WANING SEASON	385
PRESENTATION OF THE PIGG TESTIMONIAL	389
SUPERINTENDENT CONSTABLES SHARK AND CHIZELER	397
THE PROPHET GABRIEL	401
ANOTHER LAST DAY	405
ANOTHER SPORTING LECTOR	410
THE STUD SALE	421
THE PRIVATE DEAL	430
WILLIAM THE CONQUEROR; OR, THE A.D.C.	437
MR. JORROCKS'S DRAFT	449
DOLEFUL v. JORROCKS	455
THE CAPTAIN'S WINDFALL	473
JORROCKS IN TROUBLE	475
THE COMMISSION RESUMED	492
THE COURT RESUMES	496
BELINDA AT SUIT DOLEFUL	506
BELINDA AT BAY	509
DOLEFUL PREPARED FOR THE SIEGE	513
MRS. JORROCKS FURIOUS	518
MR. BOWKER'S REFLECTIONS	526
MR. JORROCKS TAKING HIS OTIUM CUM DIGGING A TATY	530
DOLEFUL AT SUIT BRANTINGHAME	533
THE GRAND FIELD DAY	537
A SLOW COACH	540
THE CAPTAIN CATCHES IT	542
THE CAPTAIN IN DISTRESS	544
WHO-HOOP !	547

ENGRAVINGS ON STEEL.

—◆—

	PAGE
MICHAEL HARDEY	1
MR. JORROCKS STARTING FOR "THE CUT ME DOWN COUNTRIES"	57
MR. JORROCKS ENTERS INTO HANDLEY CROSS	81
MR. JORROCKS (LOQ.)—"COME UP! I SAY. YOU UGLY BEAST!"	106
MR. JORROCKS'S LECTURE ON "UNTING"	129
MR. JORROCKS HAS A BYE DAY	187
MR. JORROCKS'S BATH	197
THE HANDLEY CROSS FANCY BALL	243
THE KILL, ON THE CAT AND CUSTARD POT DAY	279
THE MEET AT MR. MULEYGRUBS	325
"MIND THE BULL"	343
THE POMPONIUS EGO DAY	362
MR. JORROCKS WANTS TWENTY	407
SIR THOMAS TROUT AND THE BLOOMER	439
MR. BARÈGE AND THE DRAFT	451
PIGG IN THE MELON FRAME	485
MR. JORROCKS'S RETURN TO HIS FAMILY	532

ENGRAVINGS ON WOOD.

	PAGE
First Day of the Season	7
Old Michael	11
Roger Swizzle	14
Dr. Sebastian Mello	15
Duncan Nevin's Stud	26
Waiting for the Fly	31
Captain Doleful—"Places for a Country Dance"	33
Doleful begins to feel uneasy	42
The Master of the Ceremonies mounted	44
The Committee of Management	50
John Jorrocks of Great Coram Street	55
Miss Belinda Jorrocks	59
Mr. Jorrocks engaged in Correspondence	65
Mrs Barnington, the "Malade Imaginaire"	72
"The Conquering Hero Comes"	75
"'Ow are ye all?"	86
"Send my Sec. here"	96
Mr. Jorrocks thinks he will shoot Doleful	97
The Hounds and the Image Merchant	101
Mr. Jorrocks calling Benjamin	104
Benjamin in the Saddle-room	108
Mr. Jorrocks in Clover	122
Mr. Jorrocks's Supporters	129
A Horse with only one fault	133
"But I doesn't vont a cow!"	139
James Pigg	148
Mr. Jorrocks and his Whipper-in	157
The Cut-'em-down Captains	158
Mr. Jorrocks Pumping the Captain's Groom	162
Belinda's Beau	165
Snug and Comfey	175
"The Biggest Fox whatever was seen"	184
Mr. Jorrocks at Ongar Castle	190
Mr. Jorrocks takes possession of a room	193
Charley and the Maid	201
The Mercurial Old Gentleman	208
A Bye on the Sly	215
Mr. Jorrocks in Consultation with the Cook	225
The Convivial Meeting	233
Captain Doleful attiring for the Masquerade	241
"Ah! it's Talli-ho Back!"	255
Top Sawyers	256
	PAGE
Mr. Jorrocks's Lecture	257
"Hold hard? Easier said than done"	264
Playing at Catch-stirrup	276
James Pigg again!!!	280
Reconciliation of Mr. Jorrocks and Pigg	284
Taking a Double Fence	289
A Werry Windy Day	293
"Dinner is Sarved"	304
Mr. Jorrocks gets a little "My-dearer" down his sleeve	310
The Juvenile Muleygrubs	312
"Pa—a—r Shoots the Fox!"	321
Mr. Bugginson's Bid	328
Mr. and Mrs. Jorrocks	332
Mr. Jorrocks has another Bye-day	337
A Friend in Need	339
Mind his Heels	352
Handley Cross in a Frost	353
"Hurt? no, Sir,—Rather the Contrary"	367
A Rasper	370
Hark—Talliho!	374
There is Pigg holding the Fox above his Head	375
The Waning Season	385
Mr. James Pigg	391
Mr. Jorrocks and Pigg drink "Foxhunting"	402
The Old Customer	409
Mr. Jorrocks examining his hunting attire	410
Testimonial to John Jorrocks, Esq.	420
The Stud Sale	423
A Judge of a Horse	426
Poor Xerxes	433
Counsellor Martin Moonface	481
Mr. Jorrocks in the Inner Circle of the Regent's Park	486
A present to Dr. Mello	491
James Pigg in the Witness-box	504
Mrs. Jorrocks advising Belinda	510
Doleful prepared for the Siege	513
Bowker ejecting Benjamin	518
The taking of Capt. D.	538
Captain Doleful's Mother-in-law	541
The Captain in Distress	544
Benjamin and his Friend exercising Mr. Jorrocks's hunters	548
Mr. Jorrocks's card	550

HANDLEY CROSS;

OR,

MR. JORROCKS'S HUNT.

CHAPTER I.

THE OLDEN TIMES.

"I respect hunting in whatever shape it appears; it is a manly and a wholesome exercise, and seems by nature designed to be the amusement of the Briton.—BECKFORD.

HEN Michael Hardey died, great was the difficulty in the Vale of Sheepwash to devise how the farmers' hunt was to be carried on. Michael, a venerable sportsman of the old school, had long been at the head of affairs, and without paying all expenses, had enjoyed an uninterrupted sway over the pack and country.

The hounds at first were of that primitive sort, upon which modern sportsmen look down with contempt. Few in number, uneven in size, and ill-matched in speed, they were trencher-fed * all the year round, and upon any particular morning that was fixed on for a hunt, each man might be seen

---

* Unkenneled, or kept at farm-houses and cottages.

wending his way to the meet followed by his dog, or bringing him along
in a string.

> "There was Invincible Tom, and Invincible Towler,
> Invincible Jack, and Invincible Jowler."

Day would hardly have dawned ere the long-poled sportsmen assembled
with their hounds. Then they would trail up to puss. Tipler would
give the first intimation of her erratic wanderings o'er the dewy mead.
Then it was, "Well done Tipler! Ah, what a dog he is!" Then Mountain
would throw his tongue, and flinging a pace or two in advance, would
assume the lead. "Well done, Mountain! Mountain for ever"—would
be the cry. Tapster next would give a long-drawn howl, as if in confirmation of his comrades' doings in front, and receive in turn the plaudits
of his master. Thus they would unravel the gordian knot of puss's
wanderings.

Meanwhile other foot-people try the turnips, cross the stubbles, and
beat the hedges, in search of her—

Yon tuft upon the rising ground seems likely for her form. Aye,
Tipler points towards it. Giles Jolter's hand is raised to signal Invincible
Towler, but half the pack rush towards him, and Jolter kicks puss out
of her form to save her from their jaws. "Hoop! Hoop! Hoop!" There
she goes!" What a panic ensues! Puss lays her long ears upon her
back, and starts for the hill with the fleetness of the wind. The pack,
with more noise than speed, strain every nerve, and the further they go
the further they are left behind. Their chance seems out altogether.
The hare crosses over the summit of the hill, and the hounds are reduced
to their noses for the line. "Now, Mountain! Now, Tipler! Now,
Bonnets-o'-Blue. Ah, what dogs they are!"

*   *   *   *   *   *

Puff, puff, puff, go the sportsmen, running and rolling after their
darlings, with little leisure for shouting. Then, having gained the summit
of the hill, the panting pedestrians would stand lost in admiration at the
doings of their favourites down below, while the more active follow in
their wake, trusting to a check to let them in. When a check ensued, how
bipeds and quadrupeds worked! While the latter were sniffling about,
going over the same ground half a dozen times, the former would call
their hounds to them, and either by pricking or lifting over difficult
ground contrive to give them a lead. The hunt is up again, and away
they all go. The hounds strain over the grass, dash through the furze,
making' the spinney resound with their cry, and enter upon the fallow
beyond. Mountain alone speaks to the scent, and hills re-echo his voice.
—Now he's silent.—She's squatted.

The prickers are at work again, trying each furrow, and taking the rigs
across. How close she lies!

*   *   *   *   *   *

"Hoop!" She jumps up in the middle of the pack, and Mountain
gets a mouthful of fur. That was a close shave!—too close to be
pleasant. The hill people view her, and now every move of puss and the
pack is eagerly watched. "That's right! that's right! over the stubble.

Tipler's just going her very line. Ah, he's taken up the hedge instead of down, and Mountain has it. Now, Mountain, my man!"

She runs round the sheep, but Mountain hits her off beyond. Now she doubles and springs back, but they work through the problem, and again puss has nothing to trust to but her speed. Her strength begins to fail. She makes a grand effort, and again leaves her pursuers in the lurch. Slow and sure they ring her funeral knell after her, each note striking terror into her breast as she pricks her long ears and sits listening.

She nears her own haunt but dare not enter. The hill people descend to join the tussle at the end. Poor puss! her large bright eyes are ready to start out of her head. Her clean brown fur is clotted and begrimed, and her strength is all but exhausted. Another view!

"Poor is the triumph o'er the timid hare."

Now what a noise of men and hounds as they view her again. It is a last chance. She passes into the next grass field, and a friendly hedge conceals her from their view. She steals up the furrow, and reaches the wall at the high end. It is high and loose, and a few stones are out in the middle. Puss jumps in.*

* * * * * * *

Up come the hounds. Mountain and Tipler, and Gamester, and Bonnets-o'-blue, Merryman, and Ferryman, and then a long tail, yelping, yapping, puffing, and blowing.

Over they go into the lane. Now up, now down, now backwards, now forwards, now round about, but no puss.

* * * * * * *

Up come the field. " Now, Mountain, my man, hit her off!" cries his master, vaulting over the wall, and stooping to prick the hare on the road. But no prints are there.

" She must have flown!" observes one.

" Or sunk into the ground," says another.

" Or yon tinker man's knocked her on the head," observes a third, pointing to a gipsy camp at the cross roads, and away they all go to demand the body of puss.

* * * * * * *

The tinker man shows fight on having his cauldron searched, and several stout wenches emerging from the tattered cart awning, a battle royal ensues, and further attention is completely diverted from puss.

Well done, puss!

To proceed—

The next step in the Handley Cross Hunt, was getting a boy to collect the hounds before hunting.†

---

* The manœuvres of a hunted hare are truly astonishing.—The author witnessed the above.

† It is only those who have witnessed it that can credit the sagacity evinced by trencher-fed hounds in knowing the hunting mornings, placing themselves ready for the summons, or rushing with joyous cry to meet the messenger.

They lay wide, and sometimes Mountain's master couldn't come, consequently, Mountain was not there ; sometimes Tipler's master was absent,
and the pack lost the services of Tipler's unerring nose.

Next, some of the farmers began to ride. At first they came out with
young horses, just to let them *see* hounds—then as the horses got older
they thought they might as well work them till they sold them, and at
last it ended in their riding as a matter of course. Foremost among the
riders was Michael Hardey. He had always been a great promoter of
the hunt, breeding his hounds as he did his horses, for speed and
substance. Some used to say they were *ray*ther too swift for a hare.
Others, however, followed his example, and in course of time the heavy
towling harriers were converted into quick and dashing hounds.

Time rolled on, and Michael at length became looked upon as the
master or manager of the pack. Having been always more addicted to
fox than to hare, he had infused a spirit into the country which ended in
making the wily animal their quarry.

The hounds were still kept at walks during the summer, but Michael
fitted up a kennel at his farm to which they were brought towards the
autumn. Peter, the pedestrian huntsman, was taken into Michael's service,
clothed and mounted.

Of course all this was done by subscription. Some gave Michael cash,
some gave him corn, some hay, others straw, and all the old horses in the
country found their way to his farm.

They were then called fox-hounds.

The first day of the first season, after their metamorphosis, the hounds
met at Handley Cross—the Godfather of our work. It was a pretty
village, standing on a gentle eminence, about the middle of the Vale of
Sheepwash, a rich grazing district, full of rural beauties, and renowned
for the honest independence of its inhabitants. Neither factory nor
foundry disturbed its morals or its quietude—steam and railroads were
equally unknown. The clear curl of white smoke, that rose from its cottage
chimneys, denoted the consumption of forest wood, with which the outskirts of the vale abounded. It was a nice clean country. The hazel
grew with an eel-like skin, and the spiry larch shot up in a cane-coloured
shoot. Wild roses filled the hedges, and fragrant woodbine clambered
every where. Handley Cross was a picturesque spot : it commanded an
almost uninterrupted view over the whole vale. Far, to the north, the
lofty Gayhurst hills formed a soft and sublime outline, while the rich vale
stretched out, dotted with village spires, and brightened with winding
silvery streams, closed in on either side with dark streaks of woodland
tracts. To the south, it stretched away to the sea. Handley Cross was
a simple, unpretending village ; the white-washed, thatched-roofed
cottages formed a straggling square, round a village green, in the centre
of which, encircled with time-honoured firs, on a flight of rude stone
steps, stood the village cross, the scene of country hirings. Basket-
making was the trade of the inhabitants ; a healthy and prosperous one,
if the looks of its followers, and the vine-clad and rose-covered fronts of
the cottages might be taken as an index. It had but one public-house—
the sign of the Fox and Grapes, and that was little frequented—had it
been otherwise, there would most likely have been two.

Thither our master brought his hounds the first day of the season in which they professedly began to hunt foxes. It was a day of interest in the vale, and people gathered from afar. The morning was beautifully fine, with a slight tinge of frost on the ground, that half-an-hour's sunshine would dissolve. A little before eight, the foot-people on the steps of the Cross descried Michael crossing the vale by a line of hand-gates from his house—the hounds clustered round his horse, and Peter bringing up the rear. On they come at an easy, steady pace, and then the tall hedges below concealed them from their view; presently they rose the hill, and entered the village-green. " The hounds! the hounds!" cried the children, and away they rushed from the Cross to meet them.

Some of the hounds threw their tongues with delight, as they jumped and fawned on the hands that had fed them; Climbank met his master, and rushed to him with joy, while the honest fellow felt in his pocket for the accustomed crust. "Come-by-Chance" recognised his mistress, and nearly threw her down with the vehemence of his salute. All was cheerful and bright—Michael's black horse pawed the ground, and whinnied with delight, as the hounds bayed him, or leapt against his sides. His master had paid a little extra attention to his toilette that morning; his well-brushed broad-brimmed hat, pressed gently on his close-lying nut-brown curls, his whiskers were newly trimmed, and he had evidently had a keen-edged razor to shave with; health was on his brow, and a good-natured smile hovered o'er his swarthy face, displaying the brightness of his eyes and the whiteness and regularity of his teeth. Michael was then about forty; but for the fullness of his limbs one might have taken something off. The elements had rather hardened than sharpened the features of his face. He stood six feet high, with an amazing expanse of chest, and well-proportioned limbs. His hunting costume consisted of a good nut-brown coat, almost matching his complexion, a scrupulously clean white neck-cloth, with a large flap-pocketed red waistcoat, patent cord breeches, and mahogany-coloured top-boots. His undress, or home costume, was the same, with drab gaiters instead of boots; and his full, or evening costume, ditto, without the gaiters. A twisted hunting horn was slung across his shoulder, and he rode with a spare stirrup-leather round his horse's neck. This coal black steed was an animal of amazing speed and power—nearly thorough-bred, with a light, well-set on head, clean flat legs, immense loins and hocks; he stood nearly sixteen hands, though the shortness of his tail made him look somewhat bigger; he was rising seven years old, and that was his first regular season. Peter was dressed like his master—coat, waistcoat, and breeches off the same web, and rode a wiry-looking bay mare, with white hind-legs. He was then about thirty, short light, and active, barely turning nine stone—Michael weighed fourteen.

Horsemen now began to arrive through the various openings among the cottages on the green. First came James Fairlamb, with his merry round face shining with the morning sun—he rode a crop-eared cob with a Roman nose; his dress consisted of a single-breasted plum-coloured coat, with large silver buttons, black boots, and white lambswool stockings drawn over his knees. Stephen Dumpling, the doctor, appeared at the door of the only four-windowed house on the green, followed by his maid with a foaming tankard. The contents being disposed of, he mounted his dun pony, and joined the group. He was dressed in orthodox black, with powder, and a pigtail, drab shorts, and top-boots. The plot thickened— they came by twos and threes. Peter Jewitt and Harry Jones; two Smiths and a Brown, then another Jewitt, then another Jones; Morgan Hains, and John Thomas; next a horse-breaker; after him, Mr. Giles, the brewer, followed by the Exciseman, on a mule; then Mr. Smith, the overseer, and Miss Fidget's young man with the letter-bag, a mole-catcher, and a gamekeeper.

All his comrades having come, Michael looked at his large silver hunting-watch, and seeing it was half-past eight, prepared for throwing off. The couples were taken off the young hounds, master and man cocked forward their legs and tightened their girths, and then turned their horses' heads for the south, amid a chorus of delight from the hounds and the ill-suppressed cheers of the field.

A hazel copse or two were tried just for the sake of the chance, and on they trotted to a warm lying cover of gorse, or brushwood, formed by the junction of two hills. Jolly-boy, Boniface, and Dexterous, feathered as they approached the spot, and the former dashing in with a whimper and a long-drawn howl, Michael took off his broad-brimmed, low-crowned hat, and waving in the pack, cheered them to the echo. His horse pricked his ears, and whinnied with delight, and could scarcely be brought to stand with his head towards the cover as Michael stood erect in his stirrups, with one hand on the cantrel of his saddle, and the other holding his whip and reins, while his eagle-eye roved over every part of the dell. "*Have at him there, my jewel!*" cried he to old Bonny-bell— a favourite white bitch that lived with him, and could scarcely ever be persuaded to quit his horse's heels,—as she stood whining, lifting a foot, and looking him earnestly in the face;—"*Have at him there, my old lass!*" re-echoed he, looking down upon her, and waving his right hand, to induce her to join cry. The old bitch dashed in, and the chorus increased. The gorse was close, or the hounds must have chopped the fox, for he had made two efforts to break up hill so as to fly for the woodland country, and had twice been driven from his point by Michael's voice and the crack of his whip. A momentary silence ensued, as they over-ran the scent, and Michael had just cried, "Look out, Peter!" to his whipper-in, who was stationed on the opposite hill, when the fox dashed over a piece of stone wall between two large ash trees in the high hedge at the bottom of the cover, and with a whisk of his brush, set his head straight down the vale, crossing over a large grazing ground of at least a hundred acres. "Silence!" cried Michael, holding up his hand to the foot people, who were congregated on the hill, as he turned his horse short, and galloped to the point at which the fox broke away, where with a twang of his bugle, he presently had the old hounds at his heels, and hat in hand he waved them over the wall. Jolly-boy feathered for a second on the grass, and then with a long-protracted howl, as if to draw his brethren to the spot, he went away with his head in the air, followed by Dexterous, Countryman, Bonny-bell, and True-boy, and after them went the body of the pack.

" *Gone away!*" cried Michael, "gone away! tally-ho! tally-ho! tally-ho."

"Get away, hounds! get away!" halloaed Peter, cracking his whip as he trotted down the steep hill; and putting his bay mare straight at the fence at the bottom, went crash through it, with a noise that resembled the outbursting of a fire in a straw-yard. Then came the rush: the black threw the stone wall behind him, as a girl would her skipping-rope; and James Fairlamb's cob came floundering after, bringing down the coping stones, with a rattle and clatter that would have been awful if hounds had not been running. The third man was the Doctor on the dun, who made

it still lower; and after him came Peter Jewitt and John Jones (the latter leading over), and impeding the progress of John Thomas, the other Jewitt, the other Jones, Morgan Hains, the overseer, and the parish-clerk of Welford, who all kept holloaing and swearing away—as obstructed gentlemen in a hurry generally do. The foot-people, seeing how hopeless was the case, stood upon the hills, lost in mute astonishment, eyeing Michael on his black, careering over the meadows and hedges in a straight line with the pack, followed by Peter on his bay, and Fairlamb on his cob, until the plum-coloured coat of the latter assumed the hue of the others, and hounds, horses, and men grew

> "Small by degrees, and beautifully less."

" *Gently !* " cried Michael, as the black horse bounded over the fifteenth fence, with all the dash and vigour with which he had cleared the wall, and the hounds threw up upon a fallow, the first check they had come to. "Yon way ! " cried a countryman on a bean-stack, who had headed the fox, extending his arm like a telegraph ; "to the left, past the hurdles." " *Let them alone !* " cried Michael, " *let them alone !* Jolly-boy has it down the furrow ; hoic to Jolly-boy ! hoic ! " and a wave of his hat brought the pack forward, and away they go full cry, making the welkin ring with the music of their deep-toned notes.

> —— "A cry more tuneable
> Was never holloa'd to, nor cheer'd by horn !"

Forward they press; and Conqueror usurps the place of Jolly-boy. Poor dog, nature must not be denied, and age has slackened the vigour of his limbs ! But they come to slow hunting, and the old hound's unerring nose keeps the pack upon the line. The ground is stained with sheep, which scampering in a half circle as the fox went past, complete the ring, now that they hear the hounds. Michael pulls up, Peter is at his side, Fairlamb is in the next field—crack goes a rail, and the Roman-nosed cob is over, and the doctor's dun comes up just as Michael puts his finger in his ear, and screeches the pack forward to old Bonny-bell, who speaks to the villain under the gate. It is a rotten old thing upon one hinge, formed of at least twenty spars and rails, all rattling and jingling out of concert, and is fastened with hazel-bands and pieces of knotted rope. Michael's ponderous iron-headed whip breaks through them at a blow, and, thrusting the remains back with his right leg, he passes through and enters the open common beyond the vale. They are now upon the downs ! all is brightness and space ; Handley Cross appears like a speck in the distance, rendered visible only by the dark firs on the Green, and the vale looks like a web of green cloth stretched out behind.

They approach rising ground, and the pack no longer press forward in eager jealousy, but each hound seems settled in his place ; in truth, the pace has told upon uneven condition, and four hounds alone carry the scent. The ground becomes steeper and steeper, and even the fox has traversed the "mountain's brow" at an angle. Now Climbank's outline stands against the blue sky, and the pack wind after him in long-drawn file. Michael jumps off his horse as he approaches the steep ascent, and runs up, leading ; Peter follows his example, but Fairlamb sticks to the cob, and the Doctor begins kicking and digging the dun with his spurs.

The heights of Ashley Downs are gained, and the scene changes. The horizon is bounded by the sea, upon whose briny bosom float some pigmy vessels, and the white breakers of the shore are just visible to the eye. It may be five miles off, and the space between is undulating and open, save towards a tract of woodland that appears to join the coast. The Doctor reaches the summit of Ashley Downs, and pulls up fairly exhausted. He takes off his hat and mops the perspiration from his brow, as he sits viewing hounds, horses, and men, swinging away down the hill like a bundle of clock pendulums into the vale below. Not a house to be seen! no, not even a cottage, and as the hounds turn to the right, and run the depths of a rocky dell, whose projecting cliffs support venerable yews and red-berried hollies, their music rends the air,

> " As if a double hunt were heard at once."

" It's twenty years since I was here," said Michael to himself, wiping the perspiration from his forehead, " and the fox beat me, I recollect. If we can but press him out, we must kill. That's the very crag!" added he, " just below the crooked oak. He has tried it, but, thank goodness, Jolly-boy carries the scent beyond! *Yooi on, hounds! yooi on!*" hollons Michael from above, with a crack of his whip to some tail-hounds that kept snuffling at his sides; " *Forrard, away, forrard!*"

The dell opens into a broader expanse of better soil, and the whole pack pour forth into the vale beyond with a chorus and a melody " of musical discord and sweet thunder," that makes even Fairlamb's cob, though somewhat distressed, snort and prick up his ears with pleasure. Forward they go, with every hound upon the scent and speaking to it,

> " What lengths they pass! where will the wandering chase
> Lead them bewilder'd?"

" He's close *afoor* you!" cries a shepherd from a straw-thatched hut, whose dog having chased the fox had caused a check, and Michael cast forward at a trot. A flock of sheep wheeling round a field directed him to the line, and old Bonny-bell hits him off at the hedge-row. All the hounds then stoop to the scent and dash forward into the large wood beyond with mischief and venom in their cry. The wood is open at the bottom and they get through it like wild-fire. Michael is with them, Peter outside, with Fairlamb behind. The wood becomes studded with evergreens and gradually opens upon a lake with a bridge of costly structure at the end; Michael views the fox dead beat, with his tongue out, and brush dragging along the ground just turning the corner to cross the bridge; and dashing forward, hat in hand, in another minute ran into him on the mossy lawn by the terrace of Ongar Castle, just as the Earl of Bramber and family were sitting down to breakfast.

Who shall describe Michael's ecstacy, as he picked up the fox and held him high above the baying pack. There he stood on the well-kept lawn, with his fox grinning in grim death in one hand and his low-crowned hat in the other, whooping and halloaing old Bonny-bell and the pack up to him, while the colt in a smoking white lather, kept moving about, stamping and pawing up the mossy bank as he went. Then Michael pulled his bugle round and sounded a blast that brought Peter and

Fairlamb along at the best pace they could muster, just as the Earl of Bramber threw up the breakfast-room window, and the towers of the castle flashed upon Michael's view. All, however, was right, for his lordship having been a sportsman himself, entered into his feelings, and, stepping out upon the lawn, banished the idea of intrusion by congratulating Michael on his sport. The ladies, too, followed his example, and even forgave the trampling of the horse on their mossy carpet. The horses and hounds were then withdrawn from the terrace to a corner of the park close by, where the fox's brush, mask, and pads, being cut off, Peter climbing up a neighbouring oak, extended himself along a strong arm across which he balanced the fox, whooping and holloaing to the hounds, while Michael and Fairlamb did the same below, and the hounds being tantalised by expectation, and baying in full chorus, down went the fox crash into their mouths. "*Tear him and eat him !*" was the cry, and he was riven to pieces in an instant.

Years rolled on with varying sport, but with Michael at the head of the hunt. Time slackened his pace and the pace of his field ; but as they all grew fat, and old, and grey together, no one noticed the change in his neighbour. The hounds got a name, and while in their zenith none could twist up a fox sooner or in better style. With plenty of music and mettle, they seldom over-ran the scent, were never pressed upon or over-ridden. They turned like harriers. Kennel lameness was unknown.

As a huntsman Michael was superexcellent. He knew when to lay hold of his hounds, and when to let them alone. His voice was shrill, clear, and musical, his eye quick and bright, and he saw things that others never noticed. It is told of him that one day having pressed his fox very hard, and lost him most unaccountably in a wood of some ten acres, as he was telling his hounds over preparatory to going home, he all at once rode back to the top of a hill that commanded a view of the other side of the cover and tally-ho'd *away!* The fox being blown, was soon after killed, and when Michael came to account for his movements, he said that knowing the hounds were all out, he heard a blackbird frightened in cover, and supposed it might be by the fox moving, after they were gone. Hundreds of similar stories were told of him.

In his large woodlands with which the outskirts of the vale abounded, many a fox owed his death to the way Michael threw in his tail-hounds at head. He knew his country and the runs of his foxes, and where he gained an advantage one season he did not forget to repeat it in the next. His dog language was peculiar, partaking more of the nature of dialogue than the short monosyllabic cheering and rating of the present day. His hounds were strongly attached to him ; and if by any chance he did not accompany them to cover, they would rush full cry from Peter and his boy to meet him on the road.

Peter was a capital coadjutor, and master and man played into each other's hands with keenness untinctured with jealousy. The whipper-in's nerve continued after his master's began to fail, and he might often be seen boring through a bullfinch to clear the way for old Michael, or stopping at a brook to give him a help over.

Peace to Michael's manes! He died at the good old age of eighty without a groan or struggle. The lamp of life gradually flickered out, and his spirit passed away almost imperceptibly.

"His memory is cherished yet; and many people say,
With this good old English man good old times are gone for aye."

CHAPTER II.

THE RIVAL DOCTORS AND M.C.

WELL, as we said before, when Michael Hardey died, great was the difficulty in the Vale of Sheepwash to devise how the farmer's hunt was to be carried on.

The difficulty was increased by the change that had come over the country itself. After upwards of thirty years' occupancy of it, Michael witnessed one of those magical revolutions that appear to belong rather to fiction than reality.

One Roger Swizzle, a roystering, red-faced, round-about apothecary, who had somewhat impaired his constitution by his jolly performances while walking the hospitals in London, had settled at Appledove, a small market town in the vale, where he enjoyed a considerable want of practice in common with two or three other fortunate brethren. Hearing of a mineral spring at Handley Cross, which, according to usual country tradition, was capable of "curing everything," he tried it on himself, and either the water or the exercise in walking to and fro had a very beneficial effect on his somewhat deranged digestive powers. He analysed its contents, and finding the ingredients he expected, he set himself to work to turn it to his own advantage. Having secured a lease of the spring, he took the late Stephen Dumpling's house on the green, where at one or other of its four front windows a numerous tribe of little Swizzles might be seen flattening their noses against the panes. Roger possessed every requisite for a great experimental (qy. quack) practitioner,—assurance, a wife and large family, and scarcely anything to keep them on.

Being a shrewd sort of fellow, he knew there was nothing like striking out a new light for attracting notice, and the more that light was in accordance with the wishes of the world, the more likely was it to turn to his own advantage. Half the complaints of the upper classes he knew arose from over-eating and indolence, so he thought if he could originate a doctrine that with the use of Handley Cross waters people might eat and drink what they pleased, his fortune would be as good as made. To this end, therefore, he set himself manfully to work. Aided by the local press, he succeeded in drawing a certain attention to the water, the benefit of which soon began to be felt by the villagers of the place ; and the landlord of the Fox and Grapes had his stable constantly filled with gigs and horses of the visitors. Presently lodgings were sought after, and carpeting began to cover the before sanded staircases of the cottages. These were soon found insufficient ; and an enterprising bricklayer got up a building society for the erection of a row of four-roomed cottages, called the Grand Esplanade. Others quickly followed, the last undertaking always eclipsing its predecessor, until that, which at first was regarded with astonishment, was sunk into insignificance by its more pretending brethren.

The Doctor's practice " grew with the growth " of Handley Cross.

His rosy face glowed with health and good living, and his little black eyes twinkled with delight as he prescribed for each patient, sending them away as happy as princes.

"Ah, I see how it is," he would say, as a gouty alderman slowly disclosed the symptoms of his case. " Shut up your potato trap ! I see how it is. Soon set *you* on your legs again. Was *far* worse myself. All stomach, sir—all stomach, sir—all stomach—three-fourths of our complaints arise from stomach ; " stroking his corpulent protuberancy with one hand, and twisting his patient's button with the other. " Clean you well out and then strengthen the system. Dine with me at five and we will talk it all over."

With languid hypochondriacs he was subtle, firm, and eminently successful. A lady who took it into her head that she couldn't walk, Roger had carefully carried out of her carriage into a room at the top of his house, when raising a cry of " *Fire !* " she came spinning down stairs in a way that astonished herself. He took another a mile or two out of town in a fly, when, suddenly pulling up, he told her to get out and walk home, which she at length did, to the great joy of her husband and friends. With the great and dignified, and those who were really ill, he was more ceremonious. " You see, Sir Harry, " he would say, " *it's all done by eating !* More people dig their graves with their teeth than we imagine. Not that I would deny you the good things of this world, but I would recommend a few at a time, and no mixing. No side dishes. No liqueurs—only two or three wines. Whatever your stomach fancies *give it !* Begin now, to-morrow, with the waters. A pint before breakfast —half an hour after, tea, fried ham and eggs, brown bread, and a walk, Luncheon—another pint—a roast pigeon and fried potatoes, then a ride. Dinner at six, *not later mind ;* gravy soup, glass of sherry, nice fresh turbot and lobster sauce—wouldn't recommend salmon —another glass of sherry—then a good cut out of the middle of a well-browned saddle of mutton, wash it over with a few glasses of iced champagne ; and if you like a little light pastry to wind up with, well and good.—A pint of old port and a devilled biscuit can hurt no man. *Mind,* no salads, or cucumbers, or celery, at dinner, or fruit after. Turtle soup is very wholesome, so is venison. Don't let the punch be too acid though. Drink the waters, live on a *regimen,* and you'll be well in no time."

With these and such like comfortable assurances, he pocketed his guineas, and bowed his patients out by the dozen. The theory was pleasant both to doctor and patient, and peculiarly suited the jolly air of the giver. We beg pardon for not having drawn a more elaborate sketch of Mr. Swizzle before. In height he was exactly five feet eight, and forty years of age. He had a long fat red face, with little twinkling black eyes, set high in his forehead, surmounted by fullish eyebrows and short bristly iron-grey hair, brushed up like a hedgehog's back. His nose was snub, and he rejoiced in an ample double chin, rendered more conspicuous by the tightness of an ill-tied white neckcloth, and the absence of all whisker or hair from his face. A country-made snuff-coloured coat, black waistcoat, and short greenish drab trousers, with high-lows, were the adjuncts of his short ungainly figure. A peculiarly good-natured smile hovered round the dimples of his fat cheeks, which set a patient at ease on the instant. This, with his un-affected, cheery, free and easy manner and the comfortable nature of his prescriptions,

ROGER SWIZZLE.

gained him innumerable patients. That to some he did good, there is no doubt. The mere early rising and exercise he insisted upon, would renovate a constitution impaired by too close application to business and bad air; while the gourmand, among whom his principal practice lay, would be benefited by abstinence and regular hours. The water no doubt had its merits, but, as usual, was greatly aided by early rising, pure air, the absence of cares, regular habits, and the other advantages, which mineral waters invariably claim as their own. One thing the Doctor never wanted—a reason why he did not cure. If a patient went back on his hands, he soon hit off an excuse—"You surely didn't dine off goose, on Michaelmas-day?" or "Hadn't you some filberts for dessert?" &c., all of which information he got from the servants or shopkeepers of the place. When a patient died on his hands, he used to say, " He was as good as dead when he came."

The Handley Cross mania spread throughout the land! Invalids in every stage of disease and suffering were attracted by Roger's name and fame. The village assumed the appearance of a town. A handsome Crescent reared its porticoed front at the north end of the green, to the centre house of which the Doctor removed from his humble whitewashed cottage, which was immediately rased, to make way for a square of forty important houses. Buildings shot up in all directions. Streets branched out, and markets, and lawns, and terraces, stretched to the right and the left, the north, the south, the east, and the west. The suburbs built their Prospect Houses, Rose Hill Villas, Hope Cottages, Grove Places, Gilead Terraces, and Tower View Halls. A fortune was expended on a pump room, opening into spacious promenade and ball rooms, but the speculators never flagged, and new works were planned before those in hand were completed.

A thriving trade soon brings competition—another patientless doctor determined to try his luck in opposition to Roger Swizzle. Observing

the fitness of that worthy's figure for the line he had taken, Dr. Sebastian
Mello considered that his pale and sentimental countenance better became
a grave and thoughtful character, so determined to devote himself to the
serious portion of the population. He too was about forty, but a fair
complexion, flowing sandy locks, and a slight figure, would let him pass
for ten years younger. He had somewhat of a Grecian face, with blue
eyes, and regular teeth, vieing the whiteness of his linen.

Determined to be Swizzle's opposite in every particular, he was
studiously attentive to his dress. Not that he indulged in gay colours,
but his black suit fitted without a wrinkle, and his thin dress boots shone

with patent polish; turned-back cambric
wristbands displayed the snowy whiteness of
his hand, and set off a massive antique ring
or two. He had four small frills to his shirt,
and an auburn hair chain crossed his broad
roll-collared waistcoat, and passed a most
diminutive Geneva watch into its pocket.
He was a widower with two children, a boy
and a girl, one five and the other four.
Mystery being his object, he avoided the
public gaze. Unlike Roger Swizzle, who
either trudged from patient to patient, or
whisked about in a gig, Dr. Sebastian Mello
drove to and fro in a claret-coloured fly,
drawn by dun ponies. Through the plate
glass windows a glimpse of his reclining figure

DR. SEBASTIAN MELLO.

might be caught, lolling luxuriously in the depths of its swelling cushions,
or musing complacently with his chin on a massive gold-headed cane.
With the men he was shy and mysterious; but he could talk and flatter
the women into a belief that they were almost as clever as himself.

As most of his fair patients were of the serious, or blue-stocking
school, he quickly discovered the bent of each mind, and by studying the
subject, astonished them by his genius and versatility. In practice he
was also mysterious. Disdaining Roger Swizzle's one mode of treatment,
he professed to take each case upon its merits, and kept a large quarto
volume, into which he entered each case, and its daily symptoms. Thus,
while Roger Swizzle was inviting an invalid to exhibit his tongue
at the corner of a street—lecturing him, perhaps, with a friendly poke
in the ribs, for over-night indulgence, Dr. Mello would be poring
over his large volume, or writing Latin prescriptions for the chemists.
Roger laughed at Sebastian, and Sebastian professed to treat Roger
with contempt—still competition was good for both, and a watering-place
public, ever ready for excitement, soon divided the place into Swizzleites
and Melloites.

Portraits appeared at the windows, bespeaking the character of each—
Swizzle sat with a patient at a round table, indulging in a bee's-winged
bottle of port, while Mello reclined in a curiously carved chair, one be-
ringed hand supporting his flowing-locked head, and the other holding a
book. Swizzle's was painted by the artist who did the attractive window-
blind at the late cigar shop in the Piccadilly Circus, while Sebastian was

indebted to Mr. Grant for the gentlemanly ease that able artist invariably infuses into his admirable portraits.

Just as the rival doctors were starting into play, a third character slipped into Handley Cross, without which, a watering-place is incomplete. A tall, thin, melancholy-looking man made his appearance at the Spa, and morning after morning, partook of its beverage, without eliciting from widow, wife, or maid, an inquiry as to who he was. He might be a methodist preacher, or a music-master, or a fiddler, or a fencer, or a lawyer, or almost anything that one chose to fancy—he might also be any age, from five-and-thirty to fifty, or even more, for strongly indented lines furrowed the features of a square and cadaverous countenance, while intrusive grey hairs appeared among his thin black hair, plastered to advantage over a flat low forehead—straggling whiskers fringed his hollow cheeks, growing into a somewhat stronger crop below the chin.

His costume consisted of an old well-brushed hat, lined throughout with black, a mohair stock, with a round embroidered shirt-collar, an old white-elbowed, white-seamed black dress coat, while a scrimpy, ill-washed buff waistcoat exposed the upper buttons of a pair of much puckered Oxford-grey trowers, and met, in their turn, a pair of square-cut black gaiters and shoes.

The place being yet in its infancy, and many of the company mere birds of passage, the "unnoticed" held on the even tenor of his way, until he eat himself into the President's chair of the Dragon Hotel. He then became a man of importance. The after comers, having never known him in any other situation, paid him the deference due to a man who daily knocked the table with a hammer, and proposed the health of "Her Majesty the Queen," while mutual convenience connived at the absurdity of being introduced by a man who knew nothing of either party. Being of a ferreting disposition, he soon got acquainted with people's histories, and no impediment appearing in the way, he at length dubbed himself Master of the Ceremonies, and issued his cards,

"CAPTAIN DOLEFUL, M. C."

Who, or what he was, where he came from, or anything about him, no one ever cared to inquire. He was now "Master of the Ceremonies," and Masters of Ceremonies are not people to trifle with. The visitors who witnessed his self-installation having gone, and feeling his throne pretty firm under him, he abdicated the chair at the Dragon, and retiring to lodgings at Miss Jelly's, a pastry-cook and confectioner, at the corner of two streets, opened books at the libraries for the reception and record of those complimentary fees that prudent mammas understand the use of too well for us to shock the delicacy of either party by relating.

This much, however, we should mention of Captain Doleful's history, for the due appreciation of his amiable character. He was pretty well off, that is to say, he had more than he spent ; but money being the darling object of his heart, he perhaps saved more than others would have done out of the same income. He had been in the militia—the corps we forget—but he had afterwards turned coal-merchant (at Stroud, we believe), an unprosperous speculation, so he sold the good-will of a bad business to a young gentleman anxious for a settlement, and sunk his money in an annuity. There are dozens of such men at every large watering-place. In this case, a master of the ceremonies was as much wanted as anything else, for the Pump and Promenade Rooms were on the eve of completion, and there would be no one to regulate the music in the morning, the dances in the evening, or the anticipated concerts of the season. It was out of Roger Swizzle's line, and, of course, Sebastian Mello disapproved of such frivolities.

Handley Cross had now assumed quite a different character. Instead of a quiet, secluded village, rarely visited by a stranger, and never by any vehicle of greater pretensions than a gig, it had become a town of some pretension, with streets full of shops, large hotels, public buildings, public houses, and promenades. The little boys and girls left their labour in the fields, to become attendants on leg-weary donkeys, or curtseying-offerers of wild flowers to the strangers. A lovers' walk, a labyrinth, a waterfall, grottoes, and a robber's cave, were all established; and as the controversy between the doctors waxed warmer, Sebastian Mello interdicted his patients from the use of Swizzle's Spa, and diluting a spring with Epsom salts and other ingredients, proclaimed his to be the genuine one, and all others spurious. He then, under the signature of "Galen," entered into a learned and rather acrimonious argument with himself, in the great London Medical Mediator, as to the wonderful virtues of the Handley Cross New Spa.

Galen, who led the charge, while admitting Dr. Mello's great talents, had described the waters as only so so; while Dr. Sebastian Mello, disdaining the paltry subterfuge of an anonymous signature, boldly came forward and stated facts to prove the contrary.

Galen, nothing daunted, quoted other places as superior; but his vehemence diminishing in the ratio of the doctor's eloquent confidence, he gradually died out, leaving the doctor the undisputed champion of a water capable of curing every disease under the sun. Parliament being up, and news scarce, the doctor contrived, through the medium of a brother, a selector of shocking accidents, to get sundry extracts inserted in a morning paper, from whence the evening ones gladly transplanting them, and the country ones rehashing them for their Saturday customers, the name of the waters, and the fame of the doctor, spread throughout the land, and caused a wonderful sensation in his favour.

The effects were soon felt, for lodgings and houses were written for from all parts, and as a crowning piece of luck a railway was just then opened out to Silverley, some twenty miles beyond, for the purpose of supplying London with lily-white sand, which was soon converted into a passenger line, with a station for our rising Spa.

CHAPTER III.

THE RIVAL ORATORS.

THUS, then, matters stood at Michael Hardey's death. A great town had risen in the centre of his country, the resort of the rich, the healthy, the sick, and the idle of the land. Rival doctors divided the medical throne, and Captain Doleful was the self-appointed *arbiter elegantiarum.* The hounds, though originally hardly a feature, had lately been appended to the list of attractions both in the way of newspaper encomiums, and in the more open notice of " Houses to Let." Indeed, such was the fame of Michael and his pack, that several corpulent cob-riding bachelors had taken up their quarters at Handley Cross, for the purpose of combining morning exercise and evening amusements, and several young gentlemen had shown such an anxiety to get the horses out of the flys, that Duncan Nevin, the livery-stable-keeper, had begun to think seriously of keeping a hack hunter or two.

This worthy—a big, consequential, dark-haired, dark-eyed, butler-mar-rying-housekeeper, having run the gauntlet of inn, public-house, and waiter, since he left service, had set up in Handley Cross, as spring-van luggage remover, waiter at short notice, and owner of a couple of flys and three horses, an establishment that seemed more likely to do good than any of his previous speculations. Not that he knew any thing about horses, but having resolved that ten pounds was an outside price, he could not easily lose much. As a seller he was less contracted in his estimates.

He it was who first heard of the death of Michael Hardey, and quickened by self-interest he was soon at Miss Jelly's with Captain Doleful. Roger Swizzle being seen feeling a patient's pulse in a donkey gig, was invited to the consultation, and though none of them saw how the thing was to be accomplished—they agreed that it would be a great feature to have the hounds at Handley Cross, and that a public meeting should be called to take the matter into consideration. Of course, like sensible people, the land-owners would take their tone from the town, it being an established rule at all watering-places, that the visitors are the lords paramount of the soil.

The meeting, as all watering-place meetings are, was most numerously attended ; fortunately some were there who could direct the line of proceeding. On the motion of Captain Doleful, Augustus Barnington, Esq., a rich, red-headed, Cheshire squire, took the chair, and not being a man of many words, contented himself by stammering something about honour, and happy to hear observations. We do not know that we need introduce Mr. Barnington further at present, save as the obedient husband of a very imperious lady, the self-appointed Queen of Handley Cross.

Captain Doleful then squared himself into attitude, and after three or four ghastly simpers and puckers of his mouth, complimented the husband of his great patron, upon the very able manner in which he had opened the business of the meeting. "It would be superfluous in him to waste their valuable time in dilating upon the monstrous advantages of a pack of hounds, not only in a health-giving point of view, but as regarded the prosperity of their beautiful and flourishing town. To what was the prosperity of other inferior places to be ascribed, but to their hunting establishments, for it was well known their waters were immeasurably inferior to what *they* enjoyed, not only in sulphuretted hydrogen, but also in iodine and potash. But that was beside the question. For his own part, he stood there upon public grounds alone (hear, hear). His numerous and arduous duties of regulating the Spas in the mornings, the promenades at noon, and the balls and concerts of an evening, left him but too little leisure as it was to pay those polite attentions to the fashionable world which were invariably expected from a well-bred master of ceremonies. Many of the aristocratic visitors to be sure, he observed by the subscription book at the library, had kindly overlooked his remissness, unintentional and scarcely to be avoided as it was—and he trusted others would extend him a similar indulgence. With respect to the maintenance of the fox-hounds, he confessed he was incompetent to offer any suggestion; for though he had long worn a scarlet coat, it was when in the army—a Militia captain—and hunting formed no part of their *exercise*. Perhaps some gentleman who understood something about the matter, would favour the meeting with his ideas upon the number of dogs and foxes they should keep (laughter); the probable expense of their maintenance (renewed laughter); and then they might set about seeing what they could raise by way of subscription." The conclusion of his speech was greeted with loud applause, amid which the Captain resumed his seat with a long-protracted, mouth-stretching, self-satisfied grin.

Mr. Dennis O'Brian, a big broad-shouldered, black-whiskered, card-playing, fortune-hunting Irishman, after a short pause rose to address the meeting. "Upon his honour," said he, throwing open his coat, "but the last spoken honourable jontleman had made a mighty nate introduction of the matter in its true light, for there was no denying the fact that *money* was all that was wanted to carry on the war. He knew the Ballyshannon dogs in the county of Donegal, kept by Mr. Trodennick, which cost half nothing at all and a little over, which showed mighty nate sport, and that was all they wanted. By the powers! but they were the right sort, and followed by rale lovers of the sport from a genuine inclination that way, and not for mere show sake, like many of the spalpeens of this country (applause). If the company would appoint him manager-giniral, and give him a couple of hundred in hand, and three or four more at the end of the season, by the holy piper! he would undertake to do all that was nadeful and proper, and make such an example of everything that came in his way, as would astonish his own and their wake minds for iver. He would have foxes' *pates* by the dozen. He had no fear; faith none at all. By the great gun of Athlone he would ride in and out of the Ballydarton pound, or fly at a six-foot brick and mortar wall, dashed, spiked, and coped with broken bottles! He had a horse that he would match against any thing that iver was foaled, a perfect lump of elasticity from his shoulder to the tip of his tail—the devil be with him! but when you got on his back it was

ten to one but he sprung you over his head by the mere contraction of his
muscles! Faith! at his castle in Connaught, he had many such, and he
would give any jontleman or man of fortune in the company that would
fetch a few over to England one for his trouble." Thus Mr. Dennis
O'Brian rattled on for ten minutes or more without producing any
favourable effect upon the meeting, for having won or borrowed money
from most of them, no one felt inclined to allow him to increase his
obligations.

When he had exhausted himself, Mr. Romeo Simpkins, a pert, but
simple-looking, pink-and-white, yellow-haired youth, studying the law in
Hare Court, in the Temple, being anxious to train his voice for the bar,
came forward from the crowd that had congregated behind the chair, and
looking very sheepish, after casting his eye into his hat, where he had a
copious note of his speech, set off at a hand gallop with the first sentence
as follows:—" Mr. Chairman and gentlemen, in presuming to introduce
myself upon the notice of the meeting, I assure you I am actuated by no
motive but an anxious desire, such as must pervade the breast of every
free-born Englishman, every lover of his country—every—I mean to
say every—every"—here he looked imploringly round the room, as much
as to say, "What a mess I'm in!" and then casting his eyes into his hat
again, attempted to read his notes, but he had made them so full, and the
novelty of his situation had so bewildered him, that they were of no use,
and, after a long string of stutters, he slunk back into the crowd amid
the laughter and applause of the company. As he left the room, he
dropped his notes, which, as the reader will see from the following
specimen, were framed for rather a *serious* infliction: "*Presume* to
address—love of country—of all out-of-door amusements, nothing like
hunting—encouraged by best authorities—practised by greatest men—
Sacred history—Nimrod of Babylon—Venus took the field—Adonis killed
in chase—Persians fond of hunting—Athenians ditto—Solon restrained
ardour—Lacedemonians and their breed of speedy dogs—Xenophon—
Olympic games—Romans—Aristotle—Oppian—Adrian—Ascanius—
Somerville—Beckford—Meynell—Colonel Cook—Nimrod of Calais—
Thanks—Attentive hearing."

Mr. Abel Snorem next addressed the meeting. He was a grey-headed,
sharp-visaged, long-nosed, but rather gentlemanly-looking, well-dressed
man, who was notorious for addressing every meeting he could get to, and
wearying the patience of his audiences by his long-winded orations.
Throwing back his coat, he gave the table a thump with his knuckles, and
immediately proceeded to speak, lest the Chairman should suffer anyone else
to catch his eye.—" Mr. Chairman and gentlemen," said he, "if I am
rightly informed—for I have not a copy of the proclamation with me—
this meeting has been convened for the purpose of taking into consideration a very important question connected with the prosperity of this
salubrious spot,—a spot, I may say, unrivalled both for its health-giving
properties, and for those rural beauties that nature has so bountifully
lavished around. In bringing our minds to the calm and deliberate consideration of the subject—fraught, as I may say it is, with the welfare,
the happiness, the recreation, the enjoyment, of many of those around—
I feel assured that it would be wholly superfluous in me to point out the

propriety of exercising a sound, impartial, unbiassed judgment—dismissing from our minds all political bias, all party feeling, all invidious comparison, all speculative theories, and of looking at the question in its single capacity, weighing it according to its true merits, apart from all personal consideration, and legislating upon it in such a manner as we shall conceive will be most conducive to the true interest of this town, and to the honour and welfare of the British dominions. (Laughter and loud coughing, with cries of "question.") The question appeared to him to be one of great simplicity, and whether he regarded it in the aggregate, or considered it in detail, he found none of those perplexing difficulties, those aggravating technicalities, those harrowing, heart-burning jealousies, that too frequently enveloped matters of less serious import, and led the mind insensibly from the contemplation of the abstract question that should engage it, into those loftier fields of human speculation that better suited the discursive and ethereal genius of the philosopher, than the more substantial matter-of-fact understandings of sober-minded men of business (loud coughing and scraping of feet). Neither was it tinctured with any considerations that could possibly provoke a comparison between the merits of the agricultural and manufacturing interests, or excite a surmise as to the stability of the lords, or the security of the Church, or yet the constitution of the commons; it was, in short, one of those questions upon which contending parties, meeting on neutral ground, might extend the right hand of fellowship and friendship, when peace and harmony might kiss each other, truth and justice join the embrace, and the lion and the lamb lie down together"— ("*Cock a doodle doo!*" crowed some one, which produced a roar of laughter, followed by cheers, whistles, coughs, scraping of feet, and great confusion.) Mr. Snorem, quite undaunted and with features perfectly unmoved, merely noticed the interruption by a wave of the right hand, and silence returning, in consequence of the exhaustion of the "movement" party, he drew breath and again went off at score.

" The question, he would repeat, was far from being one of difficulty— nay, so simple did it appear to his mind, that he should be greatly surprised if any difference of opinion existed upon it. He rejoiced to think so, for nothing was more conducive to the success of a measure than the unanimous support of all parties interested in it; and he did hope and trust, that the result of that meeting would show to the world how coinciding in sentiment had been the deliberation of the distinguished assembly which he then had the honour of addressing (applause with loud coughing, and renewed cries of "question, question," "shut it up," "order, order.")—He was dealing with it as closely, and acutely, as logic and the English language would allow (renewed uproar). It appeared to him to be simply this—Divest the question of all superfluous matter, all redundant verbiage, and then, let the meeting declare that the establishment respecting whose future maintenance they had that day assembled, had been one of essential service to the place—upon that point, he had no doubt they would be unanimous—("yes, yes, we know all that)." Secondly ; they should declare that its preservation was one of paramount importance to the place and neighbourhood, and then it would necessarily resolve itself into this ("*Cock a doodle doo!*" with immense laughter)—

those who were of opinion that the establishment was of importance would give it their countenance and support, while on the other hand those, who were of a contrary opinion, would have nothing whatever to say to it. He regretted the apparent reluctance of some of the company to grant him a fair and extended hearing, because, without vanity, he thought that a gentleman like himself in the habit of attending and addressing public meetings (laughter) was likely to clear away many of the cobwebs, films, mystifications, and obstructions that hung in the way of a clear and unprejudiced view and examination of the question; but such unfortunately being the case, he should content himself by simply moving the resolution which he held in his hand and would read to the company.

"That it is the opinion of this meeting, that the hounds which have hitherto hunted the vale of Sheepwash and adjacent country, have contributed very materially to the amusement of the inhabitants and visitors of Handley Cross Spa." Mr. Hookem, the librarian, seconded the resolution, which was put, and carried unanimously.

Mr. Fleeceall, the solicitor, a violent Swizzleite, then stood forward to address the meeting.—He was a tallish, middle-aged, very sinister-looking, bald-headed gentleman, with a green patch over one eye, and a roguish expression in the other. He was dressed in a claret-coloured duffle-jacket, a buff kerseymere waistcoat with gilt buttons, drab trousers, with shoes and stockings. After two or three hems and haws, he began— "Very few countries," he said, "were now without hounds—certainly none in the neighbourhood of a town of the size, importance, and population of Handley Cross; a population too, he should observe, composed almost entirely of the aristocracy and pleasure and health-hunting portions of society.—A couplet occurred to his recollection, which he thought was not inapplicable to the question before them, though he must observe that he introduced it without reference to any quarrel he might have had with a certain would-be medical man in the place, and without any intention of injuring that individual in the estimation of those who were inclined to place confidence in his prescriptions; he merely quoted the lines in illustration of his position, and as being better than his great and increasing business, not only as an Attorney at law, and Solicitor in the High Court of Chancery, but also as a Conveyancer, and Secretary of the Board of Guardians, and Clerk of the Mount Zion turnpike road, would allow him time to pen. They were these:

> " ' Better to rove in fields for health unbought,
>   Than fee the doctor for a nauseous draught;'

and he was sure no one there would deny that hunting, of all pursuits, was best calculated to restore or produce health and drive away dull care, the ills and evils of life, whether in mind or body (applause). Exercise, he would say, without invidious allusion, was the best of all *medicines*. They were standing in the garden of England. On every side Nature's charms were displayed around; and Handley Cross was the capital of Beauty's empire (applause). Within her bounds an unrivalled Spa had burst into existence, the health-giving qualities of whose gushing waters would draw people from all nations of the earth cheers). Air, water, and exercise, he contended, would cure anything that was capable of relief (cheers). Let them, then, take measures for inducing people to enjoy the pure atmosphere from other motives than mere change of air, and the day could not be far distant when quackery would fail and hunting flourish. His business, as he said before, was great—almost overpowering; but such was his devotion to the place—such his detestation of humbug and knavery, that he would not hesitate to accept the situation of secretary to the hunt in addition to his other numerous and arduous appointments, and accept it too upon terms much lower than any other man could afford to take it at."

Mr. Smith, a Hampshire gentleman, one of the earliest patrons of Handley Cross Spa, who, from the circumstance of his lodging round the corner of Hookem's library, had acquired the name of "Round-the-corner Smith," next presented himself to the notice of the meeting. He was a smart, genteelly dressed man, apparently about five-and-thirty, or forty, with a tremendous impediment in his speech—so troublesome was it indeed, that it was hard to say whether it was most distressing to his hearers or himself. After opening a very natty single-breasted blue surtout, so as to exhibit a handsome double-breasted shawl waistcoat hung with Venetian chains, he coughed, and commenced—not a speech but a long string of stutters. "He felt con-sid-did-did-did-rable di-di-di-difficulty in pro-no-no-no-no-nouncing an o-p-p-p-p-pinion upon the matter under con-sid-did-did-de-ration, because he was not co-co-co-co-conversant with the c-c-country, b-b-but he t-t-took it to be an establish-lish-lished rule, that all men who h-h-hun-hunted regularly with a p-p-pack of ho-ho-ho-hounds, ought to contribute to their sup-sup-sup-port. He knew something about h-h-h-hun-hunting, and if his hu-hu-hu-humble services would be of any avail, the co-co-co-country might com-mand them. At the same time he thought, that the h-h-h-hunt would be more li-li-likely to pros-pros-prosper if there were more ma-managers than one, and that a co-co-co-committee would be the likeliest thing under existing cir-cir-cir-cumstances to give sa-tis-tis-faction—He therefore be-be-begged to move the following resolution.—That it is expe-pe-pedient that the Vale of She-she-sheepwash ho-ho-ho-hounds should in fu-fu-future be carried on by subscription, by a co-co-co-committee of management, under the name of the Ha-ha-ha-handley Cross ho-ho-ho-hounds."

Captain Doleful begged to "propose as a fit and proper person to be associated with the honourable gentleman who had just addressed them, in the future management of the pack, his worthy, excellent, public-spirited, and popular friend, Augustus Barnington, Esq., of Barnington Hall, Cheshire, who, he felt convinced, would prove a most valuable ally not only in the field but also in superintending the home department, and arrangements, such as hunt dinners, hunt balls, and other entertainments to the ladies, which he felt assured, it would be equally the pride of the hunt to offer, and the pleasure of the fair sex to accept." (Applause.)

Some one then proposed, that Stephen Dumpling, son of the dun-pony riding doctor, should form the third.

Old Dumpling was dead, leaving Stephen a nice farm, and somewhat independent, but the latter had a soul above the plough, and having got a cornetcy in the yeomanry, had started a gig and horse, and drove about with a clown at his side, with a cockade in his hat. Stephen was a goodish-looking, half-buck, half-hawbuck, sort of fellow. He was of middle stature, dark-complexioned, with dark eyes and hair; but there was an unfinished style about him that marred the general effect. If his hat was good, his boots were bad, and a good coat would be spoilt by a vulgar waistcoat, or misfitting trousers. He grew whiskers under his chin—smoked cigars—and rode steeple-chases. Still he was an aspiring youth, and took, as a matter of right, that which was only done to keep the farmers and landowners quiet—namely, adding him to the committee.

All this being carried nem. con., the uniform was next discussed, and great was the diversity of opinion as to colour. Some wanted yellow, some wanted green, others blue, some both blue and green; in short, all gay colours had their supporters, but the old scarlet at length carried it, with the addition of a blue collar.

But the resolutions will best describe the result of the meeting.

The following is a copy :—

At a meeting of the visitors and inhabitants of Handley Cross Spa, held at the Dragon Hotel, in Handley Cross, to take into consideration the circumstances arising out of the lamented death of Michael Hardey, Esq., the late master of the hounds :

AUGUSTUS BARNINGTON, ESQ., in the Chair :

It was resolved,

That it is highly expedient to continue the hunt, and remove the hounds to Handley Cross.

That Augustus Barnington, Henry Smith, and Stephen Dumpling, Esquires, be appointed a committee of management.

That a club be formed, called the Handley Cross Hunt Club, the subscription to be three guineas, to be paid annually in November, to which the first twenty members shall be elected by the committee, and the subsequent members by the club at large—one black ball in ten excluding.

That, in order to meet the wishes of gentlemen desirous of contributing more than the annual subscription of three guineas, the treasurer be fully authorised to take as much as any one will give.

That the morning or undress uniform be a scarlet coat, with a blue collar, and such a button as the masters may appoint, breeches and waistcoat *ad libitum*.

That the evening or dress uniform be a sky-blue coat, lined with pink silk, canary-coloured shorts, and white silk stockings.

That any member appearing at the cover side, or at an evening meeting of the members, in any other dress, be fined one pound one, for the good of the hunt.

Signed, A. BARNINGTON, Chairman.

CHAPTER IV.

THE HUNT BALL.

"Then round the room the circling Dowagers sweep,
Then in loose waltz their thin-clad daughters leap ;
The first in lengthened line majestic swim,
The last display the free unfettered limb."

Joy, universal joy, prevailed at Handley Cross, when it became known that a committee of management had undertaken to hunt the Vale of Sheepwash. The place had not had such a fillip before—Farmers looked at their fields and their stacks, and calculated the consumption of corn.

Duncan Nevin took a six-stalled stable, and putting a splendid sign of a fox peeping over a rock at some rabbits, christened it the

"NIMROD MEWS'
LIVERY AND BAIT STABLES.
HUNTERS, HACKS, AND PERFECT LADIES' PADS.
N.B. A GLASS COACH."

Emboldened by success, he scraped together five-and-twenty pounds, and asked everybody he met, if he could tell him of a horse for the field. No one with money need long want a horse, but Duncan saw so differently when purchasing, to what he did when selling, that he seemed to have two pair of eyes. To be sure, he was a good judge of a tail, and that, for a watering-place job-master, is something—"Dont tell me what Tattersall says about rat-tails," he used to observe, "I like them full, fine, and long. A horse with a full tail looks well in the field, on the road, or in harness, and will always bring his price."

His first purchase was an old Roman-nosed, white-faced, white-stockinged, brown horse, that had carried the huntsman of a pack of harriers for many a year, and was known by the distinguished name of Bull-dog. He was a little, well-shaped, but remarkably ugly horse, and had a rheumatic affection in one of his hind legs, that caused him to limp, and occasionally go on three legs. He was never fast, and sixteen or seventeen years had somewhat slackened the pace of his youth ; but he was a remarkably hard-constitutioned animal, that no one could drive beyond his speed, and he could creep through or leap almost anything he was put to.

The harriers being done up, the subscribers had handsomely presented the huntsman with his horse, which he came to offer Duncan Nevin for his stud. "He's varrar like the field," observed Nevin, eyeing him, "but his tail's shocking shabby, more like a worn-out whitenin-brush than anything else—our customers require them handsome—I fear he would only do for the field—I want them generally useful."

The huntsman declared he would go twice a-week all the season, and offered to leap him over a gate. This he did so well, that Duncan Nevin priced him—fifteen pounds was all he asked, and he bought him for ten.

A sixteen hands bad bay mare, with a very large head, very light
middle, and tail down to the hocks, was his next purchase for the field.
She was a showy, washy, useless beast, that could caper round a corner,
or gallop half-mile heats, if allowed plenty of breathing time, but invariably pulled off her shoes at her leaps, and was a whistler to boot—she cut

behind and dished before—still she had an undeniable tail, and her size,
and great hocks, as she stood well-clothed and littered, gave her the
appearance of a hunter. She was six years old, had never done any
work—because she never could, and in all probability never would. The
wags christened her Sontag, on account of her musical powers.

Fair Rosamond, a little cantering up and down white hack, stood in the
third stall; and when all the three fly-horses were in, which was never
except at night, the six-stall stable was full. The news of the purchases
flew like lightning; the number was soon magnified into ten—crowds
besieged the mews to learn the terms, and the secretary wrote to know
what Nevin meant to give to the hunt.

Everything now looked cheerful and bright—the hounds were the finest
playthings in the world—they furnished occupation morning, noon, and

night. Every man that was ever known to have been on horseback was invited to qualify for wearing the unrivalled uniform. Names came rolling in rapidly—the farmers, to the number of fifteen, sent in their five and ten pound notes, while the visitors were extremely liberal with their names, especially on a representation from Fleeceall, that payment might be made at their convenience—their names, the *honour* of their names, in short, being the principal thing the committee looked to. Dennis O'Brian put his down for five-and-twenty guineas, Romeo Simpkins did the same for five, Abel Snorem promised "to see what he could do," and all wrote, either promisingly, encouragingly, or kindly.

Duncan Nevin converted a stable into a kennel and feeding-house, and gave up his wife's drying ground for an airing yard, into which the poor hounds were getting constantly turned from their comfortable benches, by one or other of the committee showing them off to his friends. Then the make, shape, and colour of every hound was discussed, and what some thought defects, others considered beauties. The kennel was pretty strong in numbers, for all the worn-out, blear-eyed hounds were scraped together from all parts of the Vale, to make a show; while a white terrier, with a black patch on his eye—who was re-christened " Mr. Fleeceall "—and an elegantly-clipped, curled, dressed, and arranged black French poodle, were engaged to attract the ladies, who seldom have any taste for fox-hounds. Every allurement was resorted to, to draw company.

Poor Peter soon began to feel the change of service. Instead of Michael Hardey's friendly intercourse, almost of equality, he was ordered here, there, and everywhere, by his numerous masters; it was Peter here-Peter there, and Peter everywhere, no two masters agreeing in orders. Smith would have the hounds exercised by day-break; Barnington liked them to go out at noon, so that he could ride with them, and get them to know him; and Dumpling thought the cool of the evening the pleasantest time. Then Barnington would direct Peter to go on the north road, to make the hounds handy among carriages, while Dumpling, perhaps, would write to have them brought south, to trot about the downs, and get them steady among mutton; while Smith grumbled, and muttered something about " blockheads"—"knowing nothing about it." Each committee-man had his coterie, with whom he criticised the conduct of his colleagues.

Autumn "browned the beech," but the season being backwardly, and the managers not exactly agreeing in the choice of a whipper-in, the ceremony of cub-hunting was dispensed with, and Peter, with the aid of Barnington's groom, who had lived as a stable-boy with a master of hounds, was ordered to exercise the pack among the deer parks and preserves in the neighbourhood. November at length approached; the latest packs began to advertise; and Kirby-gate stood forth for the Melton hounds on the Monday. All then was anxiety! Saddlers' shops were thronged at all hours. Griffith, the prince of whip-makers, opened an establishment containing every possible variety of hunting-whip; and Latchford appointed an agent for the sale of his " persuaders." Ladies busied themselves with plaiting hat-cords for their favourites, and the low green chair at the boot-maker's was constantly occupied by some gentleman with his leg cocked in the air, as if he had taken a fit, getting measured for " a pair of tops."

How to commence the season most brilliantly was the question, and a most difficult one it was. Dumpling thought a "flare-up" of fireworks over night would be a flash thing; Round-the-corner Smith was all for a hunt dinner; and after due discussion and the same happy difference of opinion that had characterised all their other consultations, Captain Doleful recommended a *ball*, in the delusive hope that it would have the effect of making friends and getting subscribers to the hounds, and be done, as all contemplated acts are, at a very trifling expense. There was no occasion to give a supper, he said; refreshments—tea, coffee, ices, lemonade, and negus, handed on trays, or set out in the anteroom, would be amply sufficient, nor was there any necessity for asking any one from whom they did not expect something in the way of support to the hounds. Round-the-corner Smith did not jump at the proposal, having been caught in a similar speculation of giving a ball to a *limited* party at Bath, and had been severely mulcted in the settling; but Barnington stood in too wholesome a dread of his wife to venture any opposition to such a measure; and Stephen Dumpling merged his fears in the honour and the hopes of making it pay indirectly by gaining subscribers to the hounds. The majority carried it; and Captain Doleful spread the news like wild-fire—of course, taking all the credit of the thing to himself.

What a bustle it created in Handley Cross! The poor milliner-girls stitched their fingers into holes, and nothing was seen at the tailors' windows but sky-blue coats lined with pink silk, and canary-coloured shorts. The thing looked well, for fourteen candidates appeared all ready to owe their three guineas for the honour of wearing the uniform, or for the purpose of getting their wives and daughters invited to the ball. It was fixed for the first Monday in November, and it was arranged that the hounds should meet in the neighbourhood on the following day.

Meanwhile the committee of management and Doleful met every morning for the purpose of making arrangements, sending invitations, and replying to applications for tickets. The thing soon began to assume a serious aspect; the names which at first amounted to fifty had swelled into a hundred and thirteen, and each day brought a more numerous accession of strength than its predecessor. Round-the-corner Smith's face lengthened as the list of guests increased, and Dumpling began to have his doubts about the safety of the speculation. Barnington took it very easily, for he had plenty of money, and the excitement kept his peevish wife in occupation; and she, moreover, had plenty of friends, whom she kept showering in upon them at a most unmerciful rate. Every morning a footman in red plush breeches and a short jacket arrived with names to be put down for invitations. Doleful was in great favour with her, and by her request he took his place every morning at the table of the committee-room to keep her husband "right," as she called it. Of course, with such incongruous materials to work with, the thing was not arranged without great difficulty and dissension. Dumpling put down his cousins, the three Miss Dobbses, whose father was a farmer and brewer; and making pretty good stuff, "Dobbs's Ale" was familiar at Handley Cross, and his name occupied divers conspicuous signs about the town. To these ladies Mrs. Barnington demurred, having no notion of "dancing in a hop-garden;" and it was with the greatest difficulty, and only on the urgent representation of Doleful, that their rejection would cause the secession of Dumpling, that she consented to their coming. To divers others she took similar objections, many being too low, and some few too high for her, and being the daughter of a Leeds manufacturer, she could not, of course, bear the idea of anything connected with trade.

At the adjournment of each meeting, Doleful repaired to her and reported progress, carrying with him a list of invitations, acceptances, and refusals, with a prospectus of those they thought of inviting. These latter underwent a rigid scrutiny by Mrs. Barnington, in aid of which all Doleful's local knowledge, together with Mrs. Fribble's millinery knowledge, Debrett's Baronetage, and Burke's Landed Gentry of England, were called together, and the list was reduced by striking out names with an elegant gold pencil case with an amethyst seal, as she languished out her length on a chaise-longue. One hundred and fifty-three acceptances, and nineteen invitations out, were at length reported the strength of the party; and Mrs. Barnington, after a few thoughtful moments passed in contemplating the ceiling, expressed her opinion that there ought to be a regular supper, and desired Doleful to tell Barnington that he must do the thing as it ought to be, if it were only for her credit. Poor Doleful looked miserable at the mention of such a thing, for Smith and Dumpling had already began to grumble and complain at the magnitude of the affair, which they had expected would have been a mere snug party among the members of the hunt and their friends, instead of beating up for recruits all the country round. Doleful, however, like a skilful militia-man, accomplished his object by gaining Dumpling over first, which he did by pointing out what an admirable opportunity it was for a handsome young man like himself, just beginning life, to get into good society, and perhaps marry an heiress; and Dumpling, being rather a pudding-headed sort of fellow, saw it exactly in that light, and agreed to support Doleful's motion, on the assurance that it made very little difference in the expense whether the eatables were set out lengthways on a table and called "supper," or handed about all the evening under the name of "refreshments." Indeed, Doleful thought the supper might be the cheaper of the two, inasmuch as it would prevent the pilfering of servants, and the repeated attacks of the hungry water-drinking guests.

This matter settled, then came the fluttering and chopping-off of chickens' heads, the wringing of turkeys' necks, the soaking of tongues, the larding of hams, the plucking of pheasants, the skewering of partridges, the squeezing of lemons, the whipping of creams, the stiffening of jellies, the crossing of open tarts, the colouring of custards, the shaping of blanc-mange, the making of macaroons, the stewing of pears—all the cares and concomitants of ball making and rout giving; and Spain, the "Gunter" of the place, wrote off to London for four-and-twenty sponge cake foxes, with canary-coloured rosettes for tags to their brushes.

The great, the important night at length arrived. The sun went down amidst a brilliant halo of purple light, illuminating the sky with a goodly promise of the coming day, but all minds were absorbed in the events of the evening, and for once the poet's "gay to-morrow of the mind" was disregarded. Every fly in the town was engaged nine deep, and

Thompson and Fleuris, the opposition London and Parisian perruquiers, had dressed forty ladies each before five. Towards dusk, young gentlemen whose hair " curled naturally" came skulking into their shops to get the " points taken off ; " after which, quite unconsciously, the irons were " run through," and the apprentice boys made door-mats of their heads by wiping their dirty hands upon them under pretence of putting a little " moisture in ; " while sundry pretty maids kept handling little pasteboard boxes over the counter, with whispered intimations that " *it* was wanted in time to dress for the ball." Master-tailors sat with their workmen, urging their needles to the plenitude of their pace ; and at dinner time there were only three gentlemen in all the place minus the canary-coloured inexpressibles, and one whose sky-blue coat could not be lined until the Lily-white-sand train brought down a fresh supply of pink silk from town.

Doleful began dyeing his hair at three, and by five had it as dark as Warren's blacking. Mrs. Barnington did not rise until after the latter hour, having breakfasted in bed ; and young ladies, having taken quiet walks into the fields with their mammas in the morning to get up complexions and receive instructions whom to repress and whom to encourage, sat without books or work, for fear of tarnishing the lustre of their eyes.

Night drew on—a death-like stillness reigned around, broken only by the occasional joke of a stationary fly-man, or the passing jibe of a messenger from the baker's, tailor's, or milliner's. The lower rooms of all the houses at length became deserted, and lights glimmered only in the upper stories, as though the inhabitants of Handley Cross were retiring to early rest.

     *   *   *   *   *

Again, as if by general consent, the lights descended, and in drawing-rooms where the blinds had not been drawn or curtains closed, those who stood in the streets might see elegantly dressed young ladies entering with flat candlesticks in their hands, and taking their places before the fire, with perhaps a satin-slippered foot on the fender, waiting with palpitating hearts for their flys, anxious for the arrival of the appointed time, dreading to be early, yet afraid to be late. Wheels had been heard, but they had only been " taking up," none as yet having started for the ball. At length the clatter of iron steps, the banging of doors, and the superfluous cry of " Rooms ! " resounded through the town, and the streets became redolent of animal life.

A line of carriages and flys was soon formed in Bramber-street, and Hector Hardman, the head constable, with his gilt-headed staff in his hand, had terrible difficulty in keeping order, and the horses' heads and carriage poles in their places. Vehicles from all quarters and of every description came pouring in, and the greetings of the post-boys from a distance, the slangings of the flymen, with the dictatorial tones of gentlemen's coachmen and footmen, joined with the cries of the rabble round the door, as the sky-blue coats with pink silk linings popped out, resembled the noise and hubbub of the opera colonnade when a heavy shower greets the departing company.

The " Ongar Rooms " were just finished, and, with the exception of a charity bazaar for the purpose of establishing a Sunday school at Sierra Leone, had never been used. They were a handsome suite of rooms on the ground floor, entered from the street by two or three stone steps, under a temporary canopy, encircled with evergreens and variegated lamps.

WAITING FOR THE FLY.

From the entrance-hall, in which at each end a good fire blazed, two rooms branched off, one for gentlemen's cloaks, the other for ladies. Immediately in front of the entrance, scarlet folding-doors with round panes opened into a well-proportioned anteroom, which again led into the ball-room.

Ranged in a circle before the folding doors, stood Barnington, Smith, Doleful, and Dumpling, all grinning, and dressed in sky-blue coats with pink linings, white waistcoats, canary-coloured shorts, and white silk stockings, except Doleful, who had on a crumpled pair of nankeen trousers, cut out over the instep, and puckered round the waist. Dumpling's dress

was very good, and would have been perfect, had he not sported a pair of
half dirty yellow leather gloves, and a shabby black neckcloth with red
ends. There they all stood grinning and bowing as the entrances were
effected, and Doleful introduced their numerous friends with whom they
had not the happiness of a previous acquaintance. The plot soon thickened so much, that after bowing their heads like Chinese mandarins to
several successive parties who came pushing their way into the room
without receiving any salutation in return, and the blue coats with pink
linings becoming too numerous to afford any distinguishing mark to the
visitors, our managers and master of the ceremonies got carried into the
middle of the room, after which the company came elbowing in at their
ease, making up to their mutual friends as though it were a public
assembly.

The fiddlers next began scraping their instruments in the orchestra of
the ball-room like horses anxious to be off, and divers puffs of the horn
and bassoon sounded through the building, but still the doors remained
closed, and Doleful cast many a longing anxious eye towards the folding
doors. Need we say for whom he looked?—Mrs. Barnington had not
arrived. The music at length burst forth in good earnest, and Doleful,
after numerous inquiries being made of him why the ball did not commence,
at length asked Barnington if he thought his good lady was coming;
when most opportunely, a buzz and noise were heard outside—the folding
doors flew open, and in Mrs. Barnington sailed, with her niece, Miss
Rider, on her arm.

Mrs. Barnington was a fine, tall, languishing-looking woman, somewhat
getting on in years, but with marked remains of beauty, "sicklied o'er
with the pale cast" of listlessness, produced by a mind unoccupied, and
bodily strength unexercised. Her features were full-sized, good, and
regular, her complexion clear, with dark eyes that sparkled when lighted
with animation, but more generally reposed in a vacant stare whether
she was engaged in conversation or not. She wore a splendid tiara
of diamonds, with costly necklace and ear-rings of the same. Her
dress of the richest and palest pink satin, was girdled with a diamond
stomacher, and a lengthening train swept majestically along the floor.
Across her beautifully moulded neck and shoulders, in graceful folds, was
thrown a white Cachmere shawl, and her ungloved arm exhibited a
profusion of massive jewellery. Her entrance caused a buzz followed by
silence throughout the room, and she sailed gracefully up an avenue formed
by the separation of the company,—

    "A queen in jest, only to fill the scene."

Doleful and the managers came forward to receive her, and she inclined
herself slightly towards them and the few people whom she deigned to
recognise.

Having, after infinite persuasion, consented to open the ball with
Dumpling, and having looked round the company with a vacant stare, and
ascertained that there was no one who could vie with her in splendour,
she resignedly took his arm, and the ball-room door being at length
thrown open, she sailed up to the top of the room, followed by countless
sky-blue coated and canary-legged gentry, escorting their wives, daughters,

or partners, with here and there a naval or military uniform mingling among the gay throng of sportsmen and variously clad visitors. Most brilliant was the scene! The room was a perfect blaze of light, and luckless were the wearers of second-hand shoes or ball-stained gloves. There was Dennis O'Brian, towering over the head of every body else,

CAPTAIN DOLEFUL. "PLACES FOR A COUNTRY DANCE."

with his luxuriant whiskers projecting from his cheeks, like cherubs' wings on church corners, with an open shirt collar, confined by a simple blue ribbon and a superabundant display of silk stocking and calf from below his well-filled canary-coloured shorts,—for *smalls* would be a libel on the articles that held his middle man. His dark eyes sparkled with vivacity and keenness—not the keenness of pleasure, but the keenness of plunder, for Dennis had dined off chicken broth and lemonade to be ready to

"Cut the light pack or call the rattling main,"

as occasion might offer towards the morning. Snorem, too, had decked himself out in the uniform of the hunt, and this being his usual bed-time, he walked about the room like a man in a dream, or a tired dog looking where to lie down. Then there was Romeo Simpkins, who had just arrived by the last Lily-white-sand train, and had all his friends and acquaintances to greet, and to admire his own legs for the first time protruding through a pair of buff shorts. Fleeceall stood conspicuous with a blue patch on his eye, pointing out his new friends to his wife, who was lost in admiration at the smartness of her spouse, and her own ingenuity in applying the rose-coloured lining of an old bonnet to the laps of his sky-blue coat.

Now the music strikes up in full chorus, and Doleful walks about the room, clapping his hands like a farmer's boy frightening crows, to get the company to take their places in a country dance; and Mrs. Barnington, having stationed herself at the top, very complacently leads off with " hands across, down the middle, and up again," with Stephen Dumpling, who foots it away to the utmost of his ability, followed by Round-the-corner Smith with her niece, Barnington with Miss Somebody-else, Romeo Simpkins, with Miss Trollope, Dennis O'Brian, who looks like a capering light-house, with little old Miss Mordecai, the rich money-lender's daughter, and some thirty or forty couples after them. Mrs. Parlington's train being inconvenient for dancing, and having been twice trodden upon, upon reaching the bottom on the third time down the middle, she very coolly takes Dumpling's arm, and walks off to the sofa in the bay window, where, having deposited herself, she dispatches Dumpling to desire her husband not to exert himself too much, and to come to her the moment the dance is done. The country dance being at length finished, a quadrille quickly followed; after which came a waltz, then a galop, then another quadrille, then another waltz, then a reel; until the jaded musicians began to repent having been so anxious for the start.

Towards one o'clock, the supper-room door was heard to close with a gentle flap, and Doleful was seen stealing out, with a self-satisfied grin on his countenance, and immediately to proceed round the room, informing such of the company as he was acquainted with, from having seen their names in his subscription book at the library, that the next would be the " supper dance ; " a dance that all persons who have " serious intentions " avail themselves of, for the interesting purpose of seeing each other eat. Accordingly Dennis O'Brian went striding about the ball-room in search of little Miss Mordecai; Captain Doleful usurped Stephen Dumpling's place with Mrs. Barnington ; Round-the-corner Smith started after the niece, and each man invested his person, in the way of a " pair-off," to the best of his ability.   Barnington was under orders for Dowager Lady Turnabout, who toadied Mrs. Barnington, and got divers dinners and pineapples for her trouble ; and Stephen Dumpling, being now fairly " let into the thing," was left to lug in the two Miss Dobbses on one arm, and old mother Dobbs on the other.

The simple-minded couples then stand up to dance, and as soon as the quadrilles are in full activity, Doleful offers his arm to Mrs. Barnington and proceeds into the supper-room, followed by all the knowing-ones in waiting. But what a splendid supper it is ! A cross table with two long ones down the centre, all set out with turkeys, chickens, hams, tongues, lobster salads, spun sugar pyramids, towers, temples, grottoes, jellies, tarts, creams, custards, pineapples, grapes, peaches, nectarines, ices, plovers' eggs, prawns, and four-and-twenty sponge-cake foxes, with blue, red, and canary-coloured rosettes for tags to their brushes! Green bottles with card labels, and champagne bottles without labels, with sherry, &c., are placed at proper intervals down the table,—the champagne yielding a stronger crop upon the more fruitful soil of the cross table. Who ordered it, nobody knows, but there it is, and it is no time for asking.

Shortly after the first detachment have got comfortably settled in their places, the music stops, and the dancers come crowding in with their panting partners, all anxious for lemonade or anything better. Then plates, knives, and forks are in request; the "far gone" ones eating with the same fork or spoon, those only "half gone" contenting themselves with using one plate. Barnington is in the chair at the cross table, with a fine sporting device of a fox, that looks very like a wolf, at his back, on a white ground with "*Floreat Scientia*" on a scroll below, the whole tastefully decorated with ribbons and rosettes. Dumpling and Smith are Vice-Presidents. Hark to the clatter! "Miss Thompson, some turkey? allow me to send you a little ham with it?" "Mrs. Jenkins, here's a delicious lobster salad." "Now, Fanny, my *dear*, see you're dropping the preserve over your dress!" "Oh dear! there goes my knife!" "Never mind, ma'am, I'll get you another." "Waiter! bring a clean glass—*two* of them!" "What will you take?" "Champagne, if you please." "Delightful ball, isn't it?" "How's your sister?" "Who'll take some pineapple punch?" "I will, with pleasure." "I've burst my sandal, and my shoe will come off." "Dear, that great awkward man has knocked the comb out of my head." "Go to see the hounds in the morning!" "Susan, *mind*, there's mamma looking." "Waiter! get me some jelly." "Bachelors' balls always the pleasantest." "Barnington is married." "Oh, he's *nobody!*" "Dumpling does it and stuttering Smith, there's no *Mister* Barnington." "There's the captain—I wonder if he sees us." "Oh the *stoopid!* he *won't* look this way. Should like to break his provoking head!" "How's your horse? Has it learned to canter?" "Take some tongue." "Champagne, if you please."

Thus went the rattle, prattle, jabber, and tattle, until Mr. Barnington, who had long been looking very uneasy, being unable to bear the further frowns of his wife, at length rose from his seat for the most awful of all purposes, that of monopolising all the noise of the room,—a moment that can only be appreciated by those who have filled the unhappy situation of chairman in a company of ladies and gentlemen, when every eye is pointed at the unfortunate victim, and all ears are open to catch and criticise what he says. "Barnington! Barnington! chair! chair! order! order! silence!" cried a hundred voices, in the midst of which Mr. Barnington tried to steal away with his speech, but had to "whip back" and begin again.

"Gentlemen and ladies (order! order!), I mean to say, Mr. Vice-Presidents, ladies, and gentlemen (hear, hear), I beg to propose the health of the Queen—I mean to say, the ladies who have honoured us with their presence this evening." Great applause, and every man drank to his sweetheart.

Mrs. Barnington looked unutterable things at her spouse as he sat down, for women are all orators or judges of oratory, and well poor Barnington knew the vigour of her eloquence. Beckoning Doleful to her side, she desired him to tell Barnington not to look so like a sheepish schoolboy, but to hold himself straight, and speak out as if he were *somebody*. This Doleful interpreted into a handsome compliment, which so elated our unfortunate, that he immediately plucked up courage, and rising again, gave the table a hearty thump, and begged the company would fill a bumper to the health of the strangers who had honoured the Handley Cross hunt ball with their company. The strangers then began fidgetting and looking out an orator among themselves, but were put out of suspense by the rising of Dennis O'Brian, who returned thanks in one of his usual felicitous and appropriate speeches, and concluded by proposing the health of the chairman. Barnington was again on his legs, thanking them and giving "Success to fox-hunting," which was acknowledged by Snorem, who, being half asleep, mistook it for the time when he had to propose the healths of Smith and Dumpling, to whom he paid such lengthy compliments that the ladies cut him short by leaving the room. All restraint now being removed, the gentlemen crowded up to the cross table, wnen those who had been laying back for supper until they got rid of the women, went at it with vigorous determination,—corks flew, dishes disappeared, song, speech, and sentiment, were huddled in together, and in a very short time the majority of the company were surprised to find themselves amazingly funny.

CHAPTER V.

THE HUNT COMMITTEE.

"It is our opening day."

ANDLEY CROSS had a very debauched look the morning after the hunt ball. The Ongar rooms being lighted with windows round the top, with covered galleries outside, for the accommodation of milliners, ladies' maids, and such as wish to criticise their masters and mistresses, had no protecting blinds; and a strong party having settled themselves into "threesome" reels—the gentlemen for the purpose of dancing themselves sober, the ladies, like Goldsmith's clown, to try and tire out the orchestra—the ball seemed well calculated to last for ever, when the appearance of day-light in the room made the wax-lights look foolish, and caused all the old chaperons to rush to their charges and hurry them off, before bright Phœbus exposed the forced complexions of the night. All then was hurry-skurry; carriages were called up, and hurried off as though the plague had broken out, and Johns and Jehus were astonished at the bustle of their "mississes."

The last fly at length drove off; the variegated lamps round the festooned porch began glimmering and dying in succession, as Doleful and the remaining gentlemen stood bowing, grinning, and kissing their hands to their departing partners, while their blue coats and canary-coloured shorts exhibited every variety of shade and complexion that the colours are capable of. Doleful's hair, too, assumed a vermilion hue. The town was clear, bright, and tranquil; no sound disturbed the quiet streets, and there was a balmy freshness in the morning air that breathed gratefully on the feverish frames of the heated dancers. The cock, "the trumpet of the morn," had just given his opening crow, in farmer Haycock's yard behind the rooms, and the tinkling bells of the oxen's yoke came softened on the air like the echoing cymbals of the orchestra.

St. George's chapel clock strikes! Its clear silvery notes fall full upon
the listeners' ears. "One! two! three! four! five! six!—six o'clock!"
and youths say it is not worth while going to bed, while men of sense set
off without a doubt on the matter. Some few return to the supper-room
to share the ends of champagne bottles and lobster salads with the
waiters.

Morning brought no rest to the jaded horses and helpers of the town.
No sooner were the Rosinantes released from the harness of the flys, than
they were led to the stable-doors and wisped and cleaned in a manner that
plainly showed it was for coming service, and not for that performed.
Bill Gibbon, the club-footed ostler of the "Swan Hotel and Livery
Stables," had eight dirty fly-horses to polish into hunters before eleven
o'clock, and Tom Turnbinn, and his deaf and dumb boy, had seven
hunters and two flys ordered for the same hour. There was not a horse
of any description but what was ordered for the coming day, and the
donkeys were bespoke three deep.

If Duncan Nevin had had a dozen Bull-dogs and Sontags, they would
all have been engaged, and on his own terms too.

"Oh sir!" he would say to inquirers, "that Bull-dog's a smart horse
—far too good for our work—he should be in a gentleman's stable—Did
you ever see a horse so like the field, now? I'm only axin thirty pound
for him, and it's really givin' of him away—I couldn't let him go out
under two guineas a day, and then only with a very careful rider, like
yourself. Cost me near what I ax for him, in the summer, and have had
to put him into condition myself. Oats is very dear, I assure you.
Perhaps you'd have the kindness not to say that he's hired, and save me
the duty?"

A little before eleven the bustle commenced; the first thing seen was
Peter leaving the kennel with the hounds, Abelard, the black poodle, and
"Mr. Fleeceall," the white terrier with a black eye. Peter was dressed in
a new scarlet frock-coat with a sky-blue collar, buff striped toilanette
waistcoat, black cap, new leathers and boots. His whip, spurs, gloves,
bridle, and saddle were also new, and he was riding a new white horse.
Barnington's groom followed, similarly attired; and this being his first
appearance in the character of a whipper-in, he acted fully up to the desig-
nation by flopping and cracking the hounds with his whip, and crying
"Co'p, co'p, hounds!—Go on, hounds—go on!—Drop it!—Leave it!
To him, to him!" and making sundry other orthodox noises.

Lamp-black was that morning in great request. Broken knees, collar,
and crupper marks had to be effaced, and some required a touch of lamp-
black on their heads, where they had knocked the hair off in their falls.
The saddling and bridling were unique! No matter what sort of a mouth
the horse had, the first bridle that came to hand was put into it.

Stephen Dumpling's horse, having travelled from home, was the first of
the regulars to make his appearance in the street. He was a great,
raking, sixteen hands chesnut, with "white stockings," and a bang tail
down to the hocks. He was decorated with a new bridle with a blue
silk front, and a new saddle with a hunting horn. Stephen's lad, dressed
in an old blue dress-coat of his master's, with a blue and white striped
livery waistcoat, top-boots, and drab cords, and having a cockade in his

hat, kept walking the horse up and down before the Dragon Hotel, while
Stephen, with a feverish pulse and aching head, kept sipping his coffee,
endeavouring to make himself believe he was eating his breakfast. At last
he lighted a cigar, and appeared, whip in hand, under the arched gate-way.
He had on a new scarlet coat with a blue collar, the same old red-ended
neck-cloth he had worn at the ball, and an infinity of studs down an
ill-fitting, badly-washed shirt, a buff waistcoat, and a pair of make-
believe leathers—a sort of white flannel, that after the roughings of
many washings give gentlemen the appearance of hunting in their
drawers. His boots had not been "put straight" after the crumpling
and creasing they had got in his " bags; " consequently there were divers
patches of blacking transferred to the tops, while sundry scrapings of
putty, or of some other white and greasy matter, appeared on the legs.
Independently of this, the tops retained lively evidence of their recent
scouring in the shape of sundry up and down strokes, like the first
coat of white-washing, or what house-painters call " priming," on a new
door.

Dumpling's appearance in the street was the signal for many who were
still at their breakfasts to bolt the last bits of muffin, drink up their tea,
and straddle into the passage to look for hats, gloves, and whips. Doors
opened, and sportsmen emerged from every house. Round-the-corner
Smith's roan mare, with a hunting horn at the saddle-bow, had been
making the turn of Hookem's library for ten minutes and more ; and the
stud of Lieutenant Wheeler, the flash riding-master—seven " perfect broke
horses for road or field," with two unrivalled ponies—had passed the
Dragon for the eight Miss Mercers, and their brother Tom to go out
upon to " see the hounds." Then sorry steeds, with sorrier equipments,
in the charge of very sorry-looking servants, paced up and down High
Street, Paradise Row, and the Crescent; and a yellow fly, No. 34, with
red wheels, drove off with Dumpling's nondescript servant on the box,
and the three Miss Dobbses, and Mother Dobbs, in scarlet silk pelisses,
with sky-blue ribbons and handkerchiefs, inside. Jaded young ladies,
whose looks belie their assertions, assure their mammas that they are not
in the "least tired," step into flys and drive away through High Street,
kissing their hands, bowing and smiling, right and left, as they go.

Abel Snorem, having purchased a pair of new top-boots, appears in
the sky-blue coat, lined with pink silk, and the canary-coloured shorts of
the previous evening, looking very much like a high-sheriff's horse *foot*-
man going out to meet the judges. Not meaning to risk his neck,
although booted, he makes the fourth in a fly with Mr. and Miss
Mordecai, and fat old Mr. Guzzle, who goes from watering-place to
watering-place, trying the comparative merits of the waters in restoring
appetite after substantial meals : he looks the picture of health and
apoplexy. Mrs. Barnington's dashing yellow barouche comes hurrying
down the street, the bays bearing away from the pole, and the coachman's
elbows sticking out in a corresponding form. Of course all the flys,
horses, and passengers that are not desirous of being driven over by
" John Thomas," the London coachman, are obliged to get out of the
way as fast as they can, and he pulls up with a jerk, as though he had
discovered the house all of a sudden. Out rush two powdered flunkeys

in red plush breeches, pink silk stockings, and blue coatees, when, finding it is only their *own* carriage, a dialogue ensues between them and
Mr. Coachman, as the latter lounges over the box and keeps flanking
his horses to make them stand out and show themselves.

A few minutes elapse, and out comes the portly butler, with a " *Now
then !* Missis coming down !" whereupon the Johnnies rush to their
silver-laced hats on the hall table, seize their gold-headed canes, pull their
white Berlins out of their pockets, and take a position on each side of the
barouche door.   Mrs. Barnington sails majestically down stairs, dressed
in a sky-blue satin pelisse, with a sky-blue bonnet, lined with pink, and a
splendid white feather, tipped with pink, waving gracefully over her left
shoulder.   She is followed by Barnington and Doleful, the former carrying her shawl and reticule in one hand, and his own hunting-whip in the
other.   Barnington, as usual, is well-dressed, having on a neat-fitting,
single-breasted scarlet coat, with a blue collar, and rich gilt buttons,
sky-blue cravat, canary-coloured waistcoat, well-cleaned leathers and
gloves, and exquisitely polished boots, with very bright spurs.   Doleful,
who is rather in disgrace, for having introduced a partner to one of the
three Miss Dobbses over night, and has just had a wigging for his
trouble, sneaks behind, attired in a costume that would have astonished
Tom Rounding himself, at the Epping Hunt.   It consists of an old
militia coat, denuded of its facings and trappings, made into a single-
breasted hunting coat, but, for want of cloth, the laps are lined, as well
as the collar covered, with blue ; his waistcoat is pea-green, imparting a
most cadaverous hue to his melancholy countenance, and he has got on a
pair of old white moleskin breeches, sadly darned and cracked at the
knees, Hessian boots, with large tassels, and black heel spurs.   He carries
his hat in one hand, and a black gold-headed opera cane in the other,
and looks very like an itinerant conjuror.   What strange creatures *fine*
women sometimes fancy !

Mrs. Barnington steps listlessly into the carriage, throws herself upon
the back seat, while Barnington and Doleful deposit themselves on the
front one ; the door is shut with a bang, the " Johnnies" jump up
behind, " *whit* " cries the coachman to his horses, off they go, the fat
butler, having followed them up the High Street with his eyes, closes
the door, and away they bowl at the rate of twelve miles an hour, round
the Crescent, through Jireth Place, Ebenezer Row, Apollo Terrace, past
the Archery Ground, and Mr. Jackson's public gardens, and along the
Appledove road, as far as the Mount Sion turnpike-gate—leaving pedestrians, horsemen, and vehicles of every kind immeasurably in the
distance.

At the gate a crowd is ,assembled—Jones Deans, the " pikeman," has
wisely closed the bar, and " *No trust* " stands conspicuously across the
road.   As the carriage approaches, it is thrown wide open, off goes
Jones's hat.   Mrs. Jones Deans drops a hasty curtsey, that almost brings
her knees in contact with the ground, and the little urchins on the rails
burst into an involuntary huzza.   John Thomas cuts on, and turns at a
canter into the grass-field on the left of the road, where poor Peter has
been walking his hounds about for the last hour or more.   What a
crowd!   Grooms of every description, with horses of every cut and

character, moving up and down, and across and around the field; some to get their horses' coats down, others to get their legs down, a few to get their horses' courage down, others to try and get them up : some because they see others do it, and others because they have nothing else to do.

There are thirteen flys full of the young ladies from Miss Prim's and Miss Prosy's opposition seminaries, the former in sky-blue ginghams, the latter in pink; Mrs. Fleeceall driven by her dear Fleecey with a new hunting whip, in a double-bodied one-horse "chay" with four little Fleecealls stuck in behind; Mr. Davey, the new apothecary, with his old wife, in a yellow dennet drawn by a white cart mare; Mr. and Mrs. Hookem of the library in Jasper Green the donkey driver's best ass-cart; farmer Joltem in his untaxed gig, with his name, abode, and occupation painted conspicuously behind; old Tim Rickets, the furniture-broker, in a green garden-chair drawn by a donkey; the post-man on a mule, Boltem, the billiard table-keeper, and Snooks his marker, in an ass phaeton ; Donald McGrath, "Squire Arnold's" Scotch gardener, on "Master George's pony; " and Sam Finch, the keeper, and Thomas, the coachman, on the carriage horses.

Enveloped in a large dirty old Macintosh, in a single-horse fly, with a dirty apology for a postilion on the animal, with hands stuffed into his front pockets, and a hunting whip peeping above his knees, the mighty Dennis O'Brien wends his way to the meet, his brain still swimming with the effects of the last night's champagne. As he diverges from the road into the grass-field, he takes his hunting whip from its place, loosens the thong, and proceeding to flagellate both rider and horse, dashes into the crowd in what he considers quite a "bang-up way." "Now, Peter, my boy!" he roars at the top of his voice, as standing erect in the vehicle he proceeds to divest himself of his elegant "wraprascal," "be after showing us a run; for by the piper that played before Moses, I feel as if I could take St. Peter's itself in my stride.—Och blood and 'ounds! ye young spalpeen, but you've been after giving that horse a gallop,—he's sweating about the ears already," he exclaims to a little charity-school boy, whom the livery-stable keeper has despatched with a horse Dennis has hired for the "sason," warranted to hunt four days a week or oftener, and hack all the rest—a raw-boned, broken-knee'd, spavined bay, with some very going points about him. "Be after jumping off, ye vagabond, or I'll bate you into a powder."

Romeo Simpkins then comes tip-tup-ing up on a long-tailed dun, with a crupper to the saddle, surrounded by the four Miss Merrygoes, all ringlets and teeth, and the two Miss Millers, all forehead and cheeks,— the cavalcade mounted by the opposition riding-master, Mr. Higgs, who follows the group at a respectful distance to see that they do not take too much out of the nags, and to minute their ride by his watch.* Romeo is in ecstasies! He has got on an ill-made, cream-bowl-looking cap, with a flourishing ribbon behind, a very light-coloured coat, inclining more to pink than scarlet, made of ladies' habit-cloth, a yellow neckcloth,

---

* At most watering-places "unfortunates" are let out by the hour—half-a-crown an hour for a three-legged one; three shillings for a horse that has four.

his white waistcoat of the previous evening, and very thin white cord breeches that show his garters, stocking tops, and every wrinkle in his drawers; added to which, after a fashion of his own, his boots are secured to his breeches by at least half a dozen buttons, and straps round the leg. The ladies think Romeo "quite a dear" and Romeo is of the same opinion.

"Now, Barnington, don't ride like a fool and break your neck," says the amiable Mrs. Barnington to her sapient spouse, as he begins to fidget and stir in the carriage, as the groom passes and repasses with a fine brown horse in tip-top condition, and a horn at the saddle; a request that

DOLEFUL BEGINS TO FEEL UNEASY.

was conveyed in a tone that implied, "I hope you may with all my heart." Then turning to Doleful, who was beginning to look very uneasy as mounting time approached, she added, in a forgiving tone, "Now, my dear Captain, don't let Barnington lead you into mischief; he's a *desperate* rider I know, but there's no occasion for *you* to follow him over everything he chooses to ride at."

Mrs. Barnington might have spared herself the injunction, for Doleful's horse was a perfect antidote to any extravagance; a more perfect picture of wretchedness was never seen. It was a long, lean, hide-bound, ewe-necked, one-eyed, roan Rosinante, down of a hip, collar-marked, and crupper-marked, with conspicuous splints on each leg, and desperately broken-kneed. The saddle was an old military brass-cantrelled one, with hair girths, rings behind, and a piece of dirty old green carpet for a saddle-cloth. The bridle was a rusty Pelham, without the chain, ornamented with a dirty faded yellow-worsted front, and strong, cracked, weather-bleached reins, swelled into the thickness of moderate traces—with the head-stall ends flapping and flying about in all directions, and the choak-band secured by a piece of twine in lieu of a buckle. The stirrups were of unequal lengths, but this could not be helped, for they were the last pair in Handley Cross; and Doleful, after a survey of the whole, mounts and sticks his feet into the rusty irons, with a self-satisfied grin on his spectral face, without discovering their inequality.

"Keep a good hold of her mouth, sir," says the fly-man groom, whose property she is, gathering up the reins and placing them in a bunch in Doleful's hands; "keep a good hold of her head, sir," he repeats, an exhortation that was not given without due cause, for no sooner did the mare find herself released from her keeper, than down went her head, up went her heels, off went the captain's hat, out flew the militia coat laps, down went the black gold-headed cane, and the old mare ran wheel-barrow fashion about the field, kicking, jumping, and neighing to the exquisite delight of the thirteen fly-fulls of pink and blue young ladies from Miss Prim's and Miss Prosy's opposition seminaries, the infinite satisfaction of Mrs. Fleeceall, whom Doleful had snubbed, and to the exceeding mirth of the whole field.

"*Help him! save him!*" screams Mrs. Barnington, with clasped hands and uplifted eyes, as the old mare tears past the barouche with her heels in the air, and the loose riding M. C. sitting like the "Drunken Hussar" at the Circus, unconsciously digging her with his black heel-spurs as she goes. "Oh heavens! will nobody save him?" she exclaims; and there-upon the two powdered footmen, half dying with laughter, slip down from behind, and commence a pursuit, and succeed in catching the mare just as she had got the Master of the Ceremonies fairly on her shoulders, and when another kick would have sent him over her head. Meanwhile Mrs. Barnington faints. Fans, water, salts, vinegar, all sorts of things, are called in requisition, as may be supposed, when the queen of Handley Cross is taken ill; nothing but a recommendation from the new doctor that her stays should be cut, could possibly have revived her.

Peace is at length restored. Doleful, sorely damaged by the brass cantrel and the pommel, is taken from the "old kicking mare," as she was called at the stable, and placed alongside the expiring Mrs. Barnington in the carriage, and having had enough of hunting, Mr. John Thomas is ordered to drive home immediately.

Whereupon Peter takes out his watch and finds it exactly five minutes to one, the hour that he used to be laying the cloth for Michael Hardey's dinner, after having killed his fox and got his horses done up. Barnington having seen his wife fairly out of sight, appears a new man, and mounting his brown hunter takes his horn out of the case, knocks it against his thigh, gives his whip a flourish, and trots up to the pack, with one foot dangling against the stirrup iron.

Peter salutes him with a touch of his cap, his groom whipper-in scrapes his against the skies; and Barnington, with a nod, asks Peter what they shall draw? "Hazleby Hanger, I was thinking, sir," replied Peter with

THE MASTER OF THE CEREMONIES MOUNTED.

another touch; "the keeper says he saw a fox go in there this morning, and it's very nice lying."—"Well then, let us be going," replies Barnington, looking around the field.—"No!" roars Stephen Dumpling, taking a cigar from his mouth; "Hoppas Hays is the place; the wind's westerly,"—wetting his finger on his tongue, and holding it up to the air,—"and if we can force him through Badger Wood and Shortmead, he will give us a rare burst over Langley Downs, and away to the sea."— "Well, what you please, gentlemen," replies Peter; "only we have not much time to lose, for the days are short, and my fellow servant here doesn't know the country; besides which we have five couple of young hounds out."—"*I say* Hazleby Hanger," replies Barnington with a frown on his brow, for he was unused to contradiction from any one but his wife. "*I say* Hoppas Hays," replies Dumpling loudly, with an irate look, and giving his boot an authoritative bang with his whip."—"Well, gentlemen, which ever you please," says Peter, looking confused.—"Then go to Hazleby Hanger," responds Barnington. "*Hoppas Hays!*" exclaims Dumpling; "mind, Peter, *I'm* your master."—"No more than myself,'" replies Barnington, "and I find the whipper-in."—"Where's Smith?" shouts Dennis O'Brian, working his way into the crowd, with his coat-pockets sticking out beyond the cantrel of his saddle, like a poor man's dinner wallet. "Here! here! here!" responded half a dozen voices from horses, gigs, and flys.

"No, *Round-the-corner* Smith I mean," replies O'Brian. "Yonder he is by the cow-shed in the corner of the field;" and Smith is seen in the distance in the act of exchanging his hack for his hunter. He comes cantering up the field, feeling his horse as he goes, and on being holloaed to by some score of voices or more, pulls short round and enters the crowd at a trot. "What shall we draw first, Smith?" inquires Mr. Barnington; "I propose Hazleby Hanger." "I say Hoppas Hays," rejoins Dumpling.—"Ha-ha-ha-ha-ha-zleby Ha-ha-hanger, or Ho-ho-ho-ho-hoppas Ha-ha-ha-ha-hays! I should think Fa-fa-fa-farley Pa-pa-pasture better than either." "Well then, let us draw lots," replied Dennis O'Brian, "for it's not right keeping gentlemen and men of fortune waiting in this way. By the great gun of Athlone, but the Ballyshannon dogs, kept by Mr. Trodennick, would find and kill a fox in less time than you take in chaffing about where you'll draw for one. See now," added he, pulling an old Racing Calender out of his capacious pocket, and tearing a piece into slips, "here are three bits of paper; the longest is for Hazleby Hanger, the middle one is Hoppas Hays, and the short one shall be Farley Pasture, and Peter shall draw;" whereupon Dennis worked his way through the crowd, advanced into the middle of the pack, and just as Peter drew a slip, Dennis's spavined steeple-chaser gave Abelard, the French poodle, such a crack on the skull as killed him on the spot. The field is again in commotion, two-thirds of the young ladies in pink ginghams burst into tears, while one of the sky-blue pupils faints, and a second is thrown into convulsions and burst her stays with the noise of a well-charged two-penny cracker. "*Who-hoop!*" cries Dennis O'Brian, "here's blood already!" jumping off his horse and holding the expiring animal in mid air; "Who-hoop, my boys, but we've begun the season gallantly! killed a lion instead of a fox!" and thereupon he threw the dead dog upon the ground amid the laughter of a few pedestrians, and the general execration of the carriage company.

We need not say that the sport of the ladies was over for the day.

There lay poor Abelard, the only dog in the pack they really admired; whose freaks and gambols, in return for buns and queen-cakes, had often beguiled the weariness of their brother's kennel lectures. The sparkling eye, that watched each movement of the hand, was glazed in death, and the flowing luxuriance of his well-combed mane and locks clotted with gory blood—Alas, poor Abelard!

> "Oh name for ever sad! for ever dear!
> Still breathed in sighs, still ushered with a tear."

The hounds alone seemed unconcerned at his fate, and walked about and smelt at him as though they hardly owned his acquaintance, when " Mr. Fleeceall," the white terrier with the black patch on his eye, having taken him by the ear, with the apparent intention of drawing him about the field, Miss Prim most theatrically begged the body, which was forthwith transferred to the bottom of her fly, to the unutterable chagrin of Miss Prosy, who was on the point of supplicating for it herself, and had just arranged a most touching speech for the occasion. Eyes were now ordered to be dried, and the young ladies were forthwith got into marching order. Pink ginghams wheeled off first; and when they got home, those that did not cry before were whipped, and made to cry after; while the sky-blue young ladies had a page of Sterne's Sentimental Journey, commencing " Dear sensibility! source unexhausted of all that's precious in our joys or costly in our sorrows!" &c., to learn by heart, to make them more feeling in future.

The field, reduced one-half, at two o'clock set off for Farley Pasture; the procession consists of five flys, twenty-three horsemen, four gig-men, and a string of thirteen donkeys, some carrying double, and others with panniers full of little folk.

Dumpling and Barnington look unamiable things at each other, but neither having carried his point, they ride along the sandy lane that leads to the cover in pouting sullenness. The cavalcade rides the hill that commands the cover in every quarter, where Peter and the pack wait until the long-drawn file have settled themselves to their liking. The cover is an unenclosed straggling gorse of about three or four acres in extent, rising the hill from a somewhat dense patch of underwood, bounded on the east by a few weather-beaten Scotch firs; the country around being chiefly grass-fields of good dimensions. Dumpling canters round the cover, and takes a position among the firs, while Barnington plants himself immediately opposite; and Smith, determined not to be outdone in importance, establishes himself to the south. " *Yooi in there!*" cries Peter at last with a wave of his cap, his venerable grey hair floating on the breeze; "*yooi in there, my beauties!* " and the old hounds, at the sound of his cheery voice, dash into the gorse and traverse every patch and corner with eagerness: " Have at him there!" cries Peter, as Belmaid, a beautiful pied bitch, feathers round a patch of gorse near a few stunted birch and oak trees: " *have at him* there, my beauty!"—" yooi, wind him!" "yooi push him!"

" *Talli-ho!*" cries Abel Snorem, in a loud, deep, sonorous voice from his fly, rubbing his eyes with one hand and raising his hat in the air with the other; "*talli-ho!* yonder he goes." "*It's a hare!*" exclaims Peter; "*it's a hare! pray* hold your tongue, sir! pray do!"—It is too late; the mischief is done. Three couple of young hounds that did not like the gorse, having caught view, dash after her; and puss's screams at the corner of the ploughed field are drowned in the horns of the masters, who commenced the most discordant *tootleings,* puffings, and blowings, as soon as Abel Snorem's talli-ho was heard. Meanwhile the whipper-in has worked his way round to the delinquents, and, jumping off his horse, seizes the hind quarters of puss, whereupon Vigilant seizes him *à posteriori* in return, and makes him bellow like a bull. The masters canter round, the field rush to the spot, and all again is hubbub and confusion. "Lay it into them!" exclaims Barnington to his groom whipper-in; "cut them to ribbons, the riotous brutes!" "Don't!" interposes Dumpling, "*I won't* have the hounds flogged;" whereupon the ladies laud his feeling, and mutter something that sounds very like "Barnington and brute." Just as stuttering Smith is in the midst of a long string of stammers upon the question of corporeal punishment, a loud, clear, shrill talli-ho is heard proceeding from the neighbourhood of the fir trees, and Peter on the white horse is seen standing in his stirrups, cap in hand, halloaing his hounds away to their fox.—"Hoic together, hoic!" and the old hounds rush eagerly to the voice that has led them to a hundred glories.— "Yonder he goes by Mersham Hatch, and away for Downleigh-crag," exclaims a lad in a tree, and eyes are strained in the direction that he points.

"Forrard away! forrard." "Crack! crack!" go a score of whips; "talli-ho!" scream a dozen voices. "Away! away! away!" holloas Peter, settling himself into his saddle. "Away! away! away!" echoes the groom whipper-in, as he stands rubbing himself, debating whether to mount or go home to the doctor. Barnington races round the cover, Dumpling takes the opposite side, followed by Smith, and Dennis O'Brian shoves his spavined steed straight through the cover, and goes bounding over the high gorse like a boat off a rough shore. Romeo Simpkins and his tail trot after a fat old gentleman on a black cob, dressed in a single-breasted green coat, with mahogany-coloured top-boots, and a broad-brimmed hat, who makes for Ashley Lane, from thence over Downley Hill, from whence there is a full view of the pack running like wildfire over the large grass enclosure near Ravensdeen village, with no one but Peter within a quarter of a mile of them. Away they speed; and just as Peter's white horse looks like a pigeon in the distance, and the rest diminish into black specks, a curve to the left brings them past Arthing-worth clump, leaving the old tower on the right, and, skirting the side of Branston Wood, far in the distance they enter upon the tract of chalky land beyond. The old gentleman's eye catches fresh fire at the sight; he takes off his low-crowned hat, and mops his bald head with a substantial snuff-coloured bandana, and again bumps off at a trot. He pounds along the lanes, turning first to the right, then to the left; now stopping to listen, now cutting through the backs of farm buildings, now following an almost imperceptible cart-track through a line of field-gates, until he gains Surrenden Lane, where he pulls up short and listens. "Hark!" he exclaims, holding up his hand to Romeo and his female friends, who are giggling and tittering at the delightful canter they have had; "hark!" he repeats, in a somewhat louder voice. A short sharp chirp is borne on the breeze; it is Heroine all but running mute. A deeper note follows,—another, and another, which gradually swell into chorus as the pack carry the scent across the fallow, and get upon turf nearer hand. The old gentleman is in ecstasies. He can hardly contain himself. He pulls his cob across the lane; his hat is in the air, no one views the fox but himself, the hounds pour into the lane; a momentary check ensues. Villager speaks to it in the next field; Dexterous has it too,—and Coroner, Harmony, Funnylass, and Ravenous join cry!—they run the hedge-row—a snap and crack is heard just by the large ash-tree. "*Whoo-whoop!*" holloas the old gentleman, putting his finger in his ear, and Peter comes bounding over the fence, and is among his pack fighting for the fox.

Then up come the field, the horses heaving, panting, and blowing, all in a white lather, and the perspiration streaming off the red faces of riders. There has been a desperately jealous tustle between Barnington and Dumpling which should ride first; and nothing but the badness of the start has prevented their being before the hounds. Dumpling has knocked in the crown of a new eight-and-sixpenny hat; while a strong grower that he bore before him through a stiff bullfinch, returned with a switch across Barnington's nose, that knocked all the skin off the bridge.

"I claim the brush!" exclaimed Dumpling, still in the air. "No such thing!" responds Barnington, as they land together in the deep lane, from the top of the high bank with a strongly pleached hedge on the top. "I say it's mine!" "I say it isn't!" "I say it is!" "Peter, it's mine!" "Peter, it isn't!" "At your peril give it to him!" "You give it to me, or I discharge you!"

"Well, gentlemen," replies Peter, laying the fox before him, "whichever way you please." "Then, give it me." "No, give it me." "Isn't it mine, sir?" says Dumpling, appealing to the gentleman on the cob, "my horse touched ground first, and, according to all the laws of steeple-chasing that ever I've heard, or read of in 'Bell's Life' or elsewhere, that's decisive." "I should say it was Squire Hartley's," observed Peter, looking at the green-coated gentleman on the cob.

"Squire Hartley's!" exclaim Dumpling and Barnington at the same moment; "Squire Hartley's! How can that be? He's not even a member of the hunt, and doesn't give a farthing to it." "It was his cover we found in," replies Peter; "and in old master's time we always gave the brush to whoever was first up." "*First up,*" roars Dumpling, "why, he's never been out of a trot!" "And ridden the road!" adds Barnington. "What do we know about your old master?" rejoins Dumpling, "he was a skirting, nicking, Macadamizing old screw." "He was a better sportsman than ever you will be," replies Peter, his eyes sparkling anger as he spoke. "Let us have none of your impertinence," replies Barnington, nettled at the disrespect towards a member of the committee; "and let me advise you to remember that you hunt these hounds for the amusement of your masters, and not for your own pleasure, and you had better take care how you steal away with your fox again as you did just now." "That he ha-ha-ha-had," exclaims Round-the-corner Smith, as he creeps down the side of the bank, holding by the pommel of his saddle, into the lane, after having ridden the line with great assiduity without seeing a bit of the run; "I never saw such an impudent thing done in all the whole course of my li-li-li-life before."

Poor Peter made no reply. An involuntary tear started into the corner of his eye, when, having broken up his fox, he called his hounds together and turned his horse's head towards home, at the thought of the change he had lived to see. Arrived at Handley Cross, he fed his hounds, dressed his horse, and then, paying a visit to each of his masters, respectfully resigned the situation of " huntsman to the committee of management of the Handley Cross fox-hounds."

CHAPTER VI.

THE CLIMAX OF DISASTER.

" A FELLOW feeling makes us wondrous kind," says the adage, and the present case was no exception to the rule. Our three masters, having slept on their visit from Peter, met the next morning, when all jealousies were merged in abuse of the huntsman. He was everything that was bad, and they unanimously resolved that they were extremely lucky in getting rid of him. " Anybody could hunt a pack of hounds," and the only difficulty they anticipated was the possibility of the groom-whipper-in not being sufficiently recovered from his bite from the hound to be able to take the field on the Friday, for which day the hounds were advertised to meet at Meddingley, three miles down the vale, in the cream of their country. Barnington would have no difficulty in hunting them if any one would whip-in to him; Dumpling was equally confident; and Smith said he had no " he-he-he-he-si-tation about the matter." It was therefore arranged that each should lend a hand, and hunt, or turn the hounds, as occasion required, and let the world at large, and Peter in particular, see what little occasion they had for his services. Meanwhile Beckford, Cook, Scrutator, and others, were perseveringly studied.

Friday came, but like an old "Oaks day" it was very languid and feeble; there was no polishing of hack hunters, no borrowing of bridles or lending of saddles, no bustle or hurry perceptible in the streets; the water-drinkers flocked to the wells as usual, and none but the regulars took the field. Among the number was our old friend Squire Hartley on his black cob, attired in the same green coat, the same brown top-boots, and the same low-crowned hat as before. Snorem and Doleful came in a gig in the inspection style, and Dennis O'Brien smoked three cigars before any one looked at his watch to see how the time went.

At length Squire Hartley ventured to inquire if there was any possibility of the servant having mistaken his way, whereupon it simultaneously occurred to the trio that there might be something wrong. Joe had orders to bring the hounds by an unfrequented lane, so as to avoid

collecting foot people, and after another quarter of an hour spent in
suspense, the field proceeded in the direction they ought to come. On
rising a gentle eminence out of Sandyford Lane, a scarlet-coated man
was seen in the distance standing in the middle of a ploughed field, and a
fustian-coated horseman was galloping about it, endeavouring to turn the
hounds to the former, but in consequence of riding at them instead of
getting round them, he made the hounds fly in all directions. The cavalcade
then pressed on, horns were drawn from their cases, and our three masters
cantered into the field, puffing and blowing most unsatisfactory and discordant blasts.   Joe then disclosed how the pack had broke away on
winding a dead horse hard by, and how, after most ineffectual efforts to
turn them, he had lent a countryman his horse and whip, while he stood
in the field holloaing and coaxing them away.

This feat being accomplished through the assistance of the field, the
hounds, with somewhat distended sides, proceeded sluggishly to the cover.
It was a long straggling gorse on a hill side, with a large quarry hole at
the far end, which, from long disuse, had grown up with broom, furze,
and brushwood. The hounds seemed very easy about the matter, and
some laid down, while others stood gazing about the cover. At length
our masters agreed that it was time to throw off, so they began, as they
had seen Peter, with a whistle and a slight wave of the hand, thinking to
see the pack rush in at the signal,—no such thing, however ; not a single
hound moved a muscle, and three or four of the young ones most
audaciously sat down on the spot. The gentleman on the black cob
smiled.

" *Yooi over there !* " cried Barnington, taking off his hat and standing
erect in the stirrups.

" *Yooi over there !* get to cover, hounds, get to cover ! " screamed
whipper-in Joe, commencing a most furious onset among the sitters,
whereupon some jumped and others crept into cover and quietly laid
themselves down for a nap. Five or six couples of old hounds,
however, that had not quite gorged themselves with horse-flesh, worked
the cover well ; and, as foxes abounded, it was not long before our
friend on the cob saw one stealing away up the brook that girded
the base of the hills, which, but for his eagle eye, would have got off
unperceived.

" Talli-ho ! " cried the old gentleman at last, taking off his hat on
seeing him clear of the cover, and pointing southwards in the direction of
Bibury Wood, a strong hold for foxes.

" Talli-ho ! " responded Barnington without seeing him.   " Talli-ho ! "
re-echoed all the others without one having caught view ! and the old
gentleman, putting the cob's head straight down the hill, slid and crawled
down to the brook followed by the field. Here with much hooping,
holloaing, and blowing of horns, a few couple of hounds were enticed
from the cover, and being laid on to the scent, dribbled about like the
tail of a paper kite, taking precedence according to their several degrees.
First old Solomon, a great black and white hound, with a strong resem-
blance to a mugger's mastiff, gave a howl and a towl ; then Harmony
chirped, and Manager gave a squeak, and old Solomon threw his
tongue again, in a most leisurely and indifferent manner, causing some

of the young hounds to peep over the furze bushes to see what was going on.

The run, however, was of short continuance; after crossing three grass-fields they came to a greasy fallow, across which the hounds were working the scent very deliberately, when up jumped a great thumping hare, which they ran into in view at the well at the corner. Our sportsmen

THE COMMITTEE OF MANAGEMENT.

were somewhat disgusted at this, but made the best of the matter, and laid the mishap to the charge of the horse in the morning.

After consuming another hour or two in drawing hopeless covers, and riding about the country, they entered Handley Cross just in full tide, when all the streets and shops swarmed with bright eyes and smart dresses, and each man said they had had a capital day's sport, and killed. After passing through the principal streets, the hounds and horses were dismissed, and the red coats were seen flitting about till dusk.

The next day, however, produced no change for the better, nor the following, nor the one after; and the oftener they went, the wilder and worse the hounds became. Sometimes, by dint of mobbing, they managed to kill a fox, but hares much more frequently fell a prey to the renowned pack. At length they arrived at such a state of perfection, that they

would hunt almost anything.   The fields, as may be supposed, soon
dwindled down to nothing, and, what was worse, many of the visitors
began to slip away from Handley Cross without paying their subscriptions.
To add to their misfortunes, bills poured in a-pace for poultry and other
damage; and every farmer's wife who had her hen-roost robbed, laid the
blame upon the foxes.   Fleeceall had the first handling of the bills, but
not being a man with a propensity for settling questions, he entered into
a voluminous correspondence with the parties for the laudable purpose of
proving that foxes did not meddle with poultry.

One evening as our masters returned home, quite dispirited after an unusually bad day, without having seen a fox, though the hounds had run
into and killed a fat wether, and seized an old woman in a scarlet cloak,
they agreed to meet after dinner, to consider what was best to be done
under the circumstances.   On entering the room, which they did simultaneously, two letters were seen on the table, one of small size, directed to
" The Gentlemen Managers of the Handley Cross Hunt-Ball and Supper,"
containing, in a few laconic items, the appalling amount of £290 3s. 6d.
for the expenses of the memorable ball-night.   The other more resembled
a Government-office packet than a letter, and was bound with red tape
and sealed; it was addressed to the " Honourable the Committee of
Management of the Handley Cross Fox Hounds."   Barnington, more
stout-nerved than his colleagues, tore off the tape, when out of the
envelope fell a many-paged bill, secured at the stitching part with a
delicate piece of blue silk.   The contents ran thus :—

The Honourable Committee of Management of the Handley Cross Fox-hounds

To WALTER FLEECEALL, Dr.

	£	s.	d.
Sept. Attending you by especial appointment, when you commu- nicated your desire of taking the Hounds	0	13	4
Considering the subject very attentively	1	1	0
Attending Capt. Doleful, M.C., at Miss Jelly's, the Pastry Cook's, conferring with him on the subject, when it was arranged that a Public Meeting of the Inhabitants should be called	0	13	4
Drawing notice of the same	1	1	0
Making two fair copies thereof	0	10	6
Posting same at Library and Billiard Room	0	6	8
Long attendance on Capt. Doleful, M.C., arranging preliminaries, when it was agreed that Mr. Barnington should be called to the chair	0	13	4
Communicating with Mr. Barnington thereon, and advising him what to say	1	1	0
Attending Meeting, self and clerk	1	10	6
Making speech on the merits and advantages of Fox-hunting (what you please)			
Making minute of the appointment of the committee of management	0	6	8
Attending Capt. Doleful, M.C., by especial appointment at Miss Jelly's, when it appeared advisable to conciliate the farmers; writing to Mr. Stephen Dumpling, requesting his attendance	0	6	8
Carried forward . .	£8	4	0

	£	s.	d.
Brought forward	8	4	0
Attending meeting, when Mr. Dumpling's name was added to the committee, and title of hunt changed to "Handley Cross" Hounds	1	1	0
Making special minute thereof, and of appointment of self as secretary	0	10	6
Writing 353 letters soliciting subscriptions, inviting and exhorting gentlemen to become members of the hunt, describing the uniforms—scarlet coats with blue collars in a morning, and sky-blue coats, lined with pink silk, canary-coloured shorts, and white silk stockings in an evening (letters very long and very pressing)	25	0	0
Writing 129 rejoinders to 129 answers from 129 gentlemen who did not readily come into the thing, pointing out the merits and advantages of fox-hunting in general, and of the Handley Cross fox-hunt in particular	10	0	0
Seven gentlemen refusing to subscribe on the grounds that the hounds would hunt hare, drawing long and special affidavit that they were true to fox and would not look at hare . .	2	2	0
Attending swearing same, and paid for oaths	0	6	8
Three gentlemen refusing to become members unless the hounds were allowed to run hare occasionally, writing to assure them their wishes would be complied with	1	1	0
Mr. Spinnage having written to say he could not subscribe unless they occasionally hunted stags, writing to assure him that they were stag-hounds quite as much as fox-hounds . .	0	6	8
Mrs. Margery Mumbleby having sent in a bill of 1l. 8s. 6d. for four hens, a duck, and a goose, stolen by the foxes, consulting sporting records to see whether foxes were in the habit of doing such things, engaged all day, and paid Mr. Hookem, the librarian, for searching through his Sporting Works . .	2	2	0
Writing Mrs. Margery Mumbleby very fully thereon, and stating my firm conviction that it was not the foxes (copy to keep) .	0	13	4
Mrs. Margery Mumbleby not being satisfied with my answer, drawing case for the opinion of the Editor of the "Field; or, Country Gentleman's Newspaper," three brief sheets .	1	11	6
Paid carriage of parcel and booking	0	3	4
Paid him and secretary	2	4	6
Carriage of parcel back, containing Editor's answer, who said he had no doubt the foxes were "two-legged" ones . . .	0	3	0
Fair copy of answer for Mrs. Margery Mumbleby, and writing her fully thereon (copy to keep)	0	6	8
Hearing that Dennis O'Brien, Esq., was going to visit his castle in Ireland, calling at his lodgings to receive the amount of his subscription prior to his departure, when the maid-servant said her master was not at home			
Calling again, same answer			
Ditto ditto			
Ditto ditto			
Ditto ditto			
Ditto ditto, when the servant said Mr. O'Brien had left this morning			
Much mental anxiety, postage, parcels, letters, &c., not before charged (what you please)			
Total	£85	16	2

It is but justice to Mr. Fleeceall's accurate method of transacting business, to state that on the creditor side was 18l. 18s. for six subscriptions received, and a very *promising* list of gentlemen who had not yet found it convenient to pay, amounting in the whole to some 300*l.*

The two bills, however, sealed the fate of the committee of management, and drove the slaughtered wether and scarlet-cloaked old woman of the morning out of their recollections.

Shocked at his situation, Stephen Dumpling took the white-legged chesnut to Duncan Nevin, but though that worthy admitted that he was varry like the field, neither his long tail, nor his flowing mane, would induce him to offer more than twenty-five pounds for him.

"I really have more horses than I can do with," repeated Mr. Nevin; "had you come last week, or the week afore, I had three gentlemen wanting horses for the season, and I could have given you more, for I should have got him kept till April, and there may be a vast of frost or snow before then, but it would not do for me to have him standing eating his head off; you know I've nothing to do with the weather," added he, "when they are once let." Had Duncan known how things stood, he would not have offered him more than ten.

Fortunately for Stephen, Smith and Barnington being both in high credit, the chesnut was saved from the "Nimrod livery and bait stables." Still the committee was at an end, and that soon became known. "Who now was to take the hounds?" was the universal inquiry, which no one could answer. The visitors looked to the townspeople to make the move, and the townspeople wished to give them precedence. With the uninitiated, the main qualification for a master appears to be "plenty of money." With them the great sporting objection of "he knows nothing about hunting," is unheard of.

The case was urgent and the emergency great. None of the committee would touch again, and there was no engagement to hunt out the season. Puff paragraphs were tried in the Handley Cross Paul Pry, a gossiping publication, which enlivened the list of arrivals, departures, changes of residence, parties given, &c., with what it called the "sports of the chase," but without success. Some, to be sure, nibbled, and made inquiries as to expense and subscription, but their ultimatums were always in the negative! Sky-blue coats and pink linings were likely to be at a discount.

In the midst of the dilemma, Captain Doleful's anxious mind, quickened by self-interest, hit upon a gentleman made for the place—rich as Crœsus, a keen and scientific sportsman—an out-and-out lover of hunting—everything in fact that they wanted. His face wrinkled like a Norfolk biffin with delight, and he summoned Fleeceall, Hookem the librarian, Boltem the billiard-table keeper, to Miss Jelly's, where over a tray of hot mutton pies, most magnanimously furnished at his own expense, he arranged the scheme disclosed in the following chapter.

CHAPTER VII.

MR. JORROCKS.

"A man he was to all the country dear."

"WHERE can that be from, Binjimin?" inquired Mr. Jorrocks of his boy of all-work, as the latter presented him with a large double-headed letter, with a flourishing coat of arms seal.

Mr. Jorrocks was a great city grocer of the old school, one who was neither ashamed of his trade, nor of carrying it on in a dingy warehouse that would shock the managers of the fine mahogany-countered, gilt-canistered, puffing, poet-keeping establishments of modern times. He had been in business long enough to remember each succeeding lord mayor before he was anybody—"reg'lar little tuppences in fact," as he used to say. Not that Mr. Jorrocks decried the dignity of civic honour, but his ambition took a different turn. He was for the field, not the forum.

As a merchant he stood high—country traders took his teas without tasting, and his bills were as good as bank notes. Though an unlettered man he had great powers of thought and expression in his peculiar way. He was "highly respectable," as they say on 'Change—that is to say, he was very rich, the result of prudence and economy—not that he was stingy, but his income outstripped his expenses, and money like snow rolls up amazingly fast.

A natural born sportsman, his lot being cast behind a counter instead of in the country, is one of those frolics of fortune that there is no accounting for. To remedy the error of the blind goddess, Mr. Jorrocks had taken to hunting as soon as he could keep a horse, and though his exploits were long confined to the suburban county of Surrey, he should rather be "credited" for keenness in following the sport in so unpropitious a region, than "debited" as a Cockney and laughed at for his pains. But here the old adage of "where ignorance is bliss," &c. came to his aid, for before he had seen any better country than Surrey, he was impressed with the conviction that it was the "werry best," and their hounds the finest in England.

"Doesn't the best of everything come to London?" he would ask, and doesn't it follow as a nattaral consequence, that the best 'unting is to be had from it?"

Moreover, Mr. Jorrocks looked upon Surrey as the peculiar province of Cockneys—we beg pardon—Londoners. His earliest recollections carried him back to the days of Alderman Harley, and though his participation in the sport consisted in reading the meets in a boot-maker's window in the Borough, he could tell of all the succeeding masters, and criticise the establishments of Clayton, Snow, Maberly, and the renowned Daniel Haigh.

It was during the career of the latter great sportsman, that Mr. Jorrocks shone a brilliant meteor in the Surrey hunt—he was no rider, but with an almost intuitive knowledge of the run of a fox, would take off his hat to him several times in the course of a run. No Saturday seemed perfect unless Mr. Jorrocks was there; and his great chesnut horse, with his master's coat-laps flying out beyond his tail, will long be remembered on the outline of the Surrey hills. These are recollections that many will enjoy, nor will their interest be diminished as time throws them back in the distance. Many bold sportsmen, now laid on the shelf, and many a bold one still going, will glow with animation at the thoughts of the sport they shared in with him.

Of the start before day-break—the cries of the cads—the mirth of the lads—the breakfasts at Croydon—the dear "Derby Arms,"—the cheery

Mr. Sorrocks starting for "The cut me down Countries."

Charley Morton then the ride to the meet—the jovial greeting—the glorious find, and the exhilarating scrambles up and down the Surrey hills. —Then if they killed!—O, joy! unutterable joy! How they holloaed! How they hooped! How they lugged out their half-crowns for Tom Hill, and returned to town flushed with victory and *eau-de-vie.*

But we wander—

When the gates of the world were opened by railways, our friend's active mind saw that business might be combined with pleasure, and as first one line opened and then another, he shot down into the different countries—bags and all—Beckford in one pocket—order book in the other—hunting one day and selling teas another. Nay, he sometimes did both together, and they tell a story of him in Wiltshire, holloaing out to a man who had taken a fence to get rid of him, " Did you say *two* chests o' black and *one* o' green?"

Then when the Great Northern opened he took a turn down to Peterborough, and emboldened by what he saw with Lord Fitzwilliam, he at length ventured, right into the heaven of heavens—the grass—or what he calls the "cut 'em down" countries.* What a commotion he caused! Which is Jorrocks? Show me Jorrocks! Is that old Jorrocks! and men would ride to and fro eyeing him as if he were a wild beast. Gradually the bolder ventured a word at him—observed it was a fine day—asked him how he liked their country? or their hounds. Next, perhaps, the M. F. H. would give him a friendly lift—say "good morning, Mr. Jorrocks"—then some of what Jorrocks calls the "hupper crusts" of the hunt, would begin talking to him, until he got fairly launched among them—when he would out with his order book and do no end of business in tea. None but Jorrocks & Co.'s tea goes down in the midland counties. Great, however, as he is in the country, he is equally famous in London, where his "Readings in Beckford" and sporting lectures in Oxendon Street, procured him the attentions of the police.

Mr. Jorrocks had now passed the grand climacteric, and balancing his age with less accuracy than he balanced his books, called himself somewhere between fifty and sixty. He wouldn't own to three pund, as he called sixty, at any price. Neither could he ever be persuaded to get into the scales to see whether he was nearer eighteen "stun" or twenty. He was always "'ticlarly engaged" just at the time, either goin' to wet samples of tea with his traveller, or with some one to look at "an oss," or, if hard pressed, to take Mrs. J. out in the chay. "He didn't ride stipple chases," he would say, "and wot matter did it make ow much he weighed? It was altogether 'twixt him and his oss, and weighin' wouldn't make him any lighter." In person he was a stiff, square-built, middle-sized man, with a thick neck and a large round head. A wooly broad-brimmed lowish-crowned hat sat with a jaunty side-long sort of air upon a bushy nut-brown wig, worn for comfort and not deception. Indeed his grey whiskers would have acted as a contradiction if he had, but deception formed no part of Mr. Jorrocks's character. He had a fine

* "Cut 'em down and hang 'em up to dry!"—*Leicestershire phrase.*

open countenance, and though his turn-up nose, little grey eyes, and rather twisted mouth, were not handsome, still there was a combination of fun and good-humour in his looks that pleased at first sight, and made one forget all the rest. His dress was generally the same—a puddingey white neckcloth tied in a knot, capacious shirt frill (shirt made without collars), a single-breasted high-collared buff waistcoat with covered buttons, a blue coat with metal ones, dark blue stockingnet pantaloons, and hessian boots with large tassels, displaying the liberal dimensions of his full, well-turned limbs. The coat pockets were outside, and the back buttons far apart.

His business place was in St. Botolph's Lane, in the city, but his residence was in Great Coram Street. This is rather a curious locality,—city people considering it west, while those in the west consider it east. The fact is, that Great Coram Street is somewhere about the centre of London, near the London University, and not a great way from the Euston station of the Birmingham railway. Jorrocks says it is close to the two best cover hacks in the world, the Great Northern and Euston stations. Approaching it from the east, which seems the proper way of advancing to a city man's residence, you pass the Foundling Hospital in Guildford Street, cross Brunswick Square, and turning short to the left you find yourself in "Great Coram Street." Neat unassuming houses form the sides, and the west end is graced with a building that acts the double part of a reading-room and swimming-bath; "literature and lavement" is over the door.

In this region the dazzling glare of civic pomp and courtly state are equally unknown. Fifteen-year-old footboys in cotton velveteens and variously fitting coats being the objects of ambition, while the rattling of pewter pots about four o'clock denote the usual dinner hour.—It is a nice quiet street, highly popular with Punch and other public characters. A smart confectioner's in the neighbourhood leads one to suppose that it is a favourite locality for citizens.

We may as well introduce the other inmates of Mr. Jorrocks's house, before we return to our story, premising that they are now going to act a prominent part.

Mrs. Jorrocks, who, her husband said, had a cross of blood in her, her sire being a gent, her dam a lady's maid, was a commonish sort of woman, with great pretension, and smattering of gentility. She had been reckoned a beauty at Tooting, but had outlived all, save the recollection of it. She was a dumpy figure, very fond of fine bonnets, and dressed so differently, that Mr. Jorrocks himself sometimes did not know her. Her main characteristics were a red snub nose, a profusion of false ringlets, and gooseberry eyes, which were green in one light and grey in another.

Mr. Jorrocks's mother, who had long held a commission to get him a wife, had departed this life without executing it; and our friend soon finding himself going all wrong in his shirts and stocking-feet, and having then little time to go a courting, just went, hand over head as it were, to a ball at the Horns at Kennington Common, and drew the first woman that seemed inclined to make up to him, who chanced to be the now companion of his greatness.

No children blessed the union ; and a niece, the orphan daughter of a brother of Mr. Jorrocks, formed their family circle. Belinda Jorrocks was just entering upon womanhood—young, beautiful, and guileless. In person she was of the middle size, neither too slim nor too stout, but just of that plump and pleasantly-rounded form that charms all eyes, whether admirers of the tall or short. Her light-brown silken hair clasped the ivory forehead of a beautiful oval face, while the delicate regularity of her lightly-pencilled eyebrows contrasted with the long rich fringe of her

large blue eyes ; rosy lips and pearly teeth appeared below her Grecian nose, while her clear though somewhat pale complexion brightened with the flush of animation when she spoke. Her waist was small, and her feet sylph-like.

"Where can this be from, Binjimin ? " inquired Mr. Jorrocks, taking the letter before mentioned as he sat in his red morocco hunting-chair in the back drawing-room in Great Coram Street.

"'Andley Cross ! Where is that ? " said he, looking at the post-mark. "Knows no one there, I think," continued he, cutting the paper on each side of the seal with a pair of large scissors kept in the capacious black inkstand before him. Having opened the envelope, a large sheet of white paper and a gilt-edged pink satin-paper note, headed with an embossed stag-hunt, presented themselves. He opened the note first. The writing was unknown to him, so he took up the other, and folding it out, proceeded to read the contents. Thus it run :—

TO JOHN JORROCKS, ESQ.

"Honoured Sir,

"The committee of management of the Handley Cross fox-hounds being under the necessity of relinquishing their undertaking, we, the undersigned keen and determined sportsmen, having experienced the evils of a divided mastership, and feeling fully impressed with the import-ance of having a country hunted single-handed by a gentleman of known talent and experience, who will command the respect and obedience of his followers and the admiration of the world, look up to you, sir, as pre-eminently qualified for the distinguished, honourable, and much coveted situation."

"My vig!" exclaimed Mr. Jorrocks, jumping from his chair, slapping his thigh, and hopping round the table, taking up three or four holes of his face with delight—"My vig! who would have ever thought of such a thing!—O, John Jorrocks! John Jorrocks! you are indeed a most fortunate man! a most lucky dog! O dear!—O dear! Was ever any thing so truly delightful!" Some seconds elapsed ere our worthy friend could compose himself sufficiently to look again at the letter. At last he resumed:—

"When we consider, sir," it continued, "the brilliant position you have long achieved in that most illustrious of all hunts, 'the Surrey,' and the glorious character you have gained as an ardent admirer of field sports, we feel most deeply and sincerely sensible that there is no one to whom we can more safely confide this important trust than yourself."

"Capital! bravo! werry good indeed!" exclaimed Mr. Jorrocks, laying down the letter again for the purpose of digesting what he had read. "Capital indeed," he repeated, nursing one leg over the other, and casting his eyes up at a dirty fly-catcher dangling over his head. Thus he sat for some moments in mute abstraction. At length he let down his leg and took up the letter.

"In conclusion, sir," it ended, "we beg to assure you that you possess alike the confidence and esteem of the inhabitants of this town and neigh-bourhood; and in the event of your acceding to our wishes, and becoming the manager of our magnificent hunt, we pledge ourselves to afford you our most cordial and strenuous support, and to endeavour by every means in our power to make you master of the Handley Cross fox-hounds, at the smallest possible expense and inconvenience to yourself.

(*Signed*)   Miserrimus Doleful, M.C.,
                             Captain half-pay.
                        Duncan Nevin.
                        Alfred Boltem.
                        Simon Hookem.
                        Walter Fleeceall.
                        Judas Turnbill.
                        Michael Grasper"

"Capital, indeed!" exclaimed Mr. Jorrocks, laying down the letter, clapping and rubbing his hands; "werry good indeed—most beautiful, in fact—wot honour I arrive at!—wonder what these chaps are now!" added he; saying which, in taking up the letter his eye caught the pink satin paper note. It was in the same fine lady-like running hand as the letter, and purported to be from Captain Doleful, explanatory of their motives, and vouching for the respectability of himself and brother requisitionists. Mr. Jorrocks was all delight, and being the child of impulse and generous feelings, his joy found vent in stamping on the floor, thereby summoning his servant the aforesaid Benjamin into his presence.

Benjamin, or B*i*nj*i*min, as Mr. Jorrocks pronounced the name, was one of those mischievous urchins that people sometimes persuade themselves do the work of a man without the wages. He was a stunted, pasty-faced, white-headed, ginnified boy, that might be any age from eight to eighteen, and as idle and mischievous a brat as it was possible to conceive; sharp as a needle, and quick as lightning, he was far more than a match for his over easy master, whom he cheated and deceived in every possible way. Whatever went wrong, Benjamin always had an excuse for it, which generally transferred the blame from his own to some one else's shoulders,—a piece of ingenuity that required no small degree of dexterity, inasmuch as the light-porter of the warehouse, Betsey, a maid of all work, and a girl under her, were all he had to divide it among. Not a note came into the house, or a letter went out of it, but Benjamin mastered its contents; and Mrs. Jorrocks was constantly losing things out of the store-room and closets, which never could be traced to anybody.

One unlucky Sunday morning, indeed, Mr. Jorrocks happened to turn back suddenly on his way to church, and caught him sitting in his easy chair at the breakfast table, reading Bell's Life in London, and scooping the marmalade out of the pot with his thumb, when he visited Benjamin's back with a summary horse-whipping; but that was the only time, during a period of three years, that he ever was caught in a scrape he could not get out of. This might be partly attributable to Betsey finding it convenient to be in with Benjamin, who winked at the visits of a genteel young man from a neighbouring haberdasher's. The poor maid under Betsey, and the light porter, who was generally absent, were therefore the usual scape-goats, or somebody else's servant, who had happened to come with a message or parcel. Such was Mr. Jorrocks's domestic establishment, which, like most masters, he either thought, or affected to think, very perfect.

We left our friend stamping for Benjamin, who made his appearance as soon as he could slip down-stairs and come up again, he having been watching his master through the keyhole since delivering the letter.

*　　*　　*　　*　　*　　*

"Now, Binjimin," said Mr. Jorrocks, eyeing him with one of his benevolent looks, and not knowing exactly what to say; "now, Binjimin," he repeated, "are the 'osses all right?"

"Yes, sir, and the wehicle too."

"Werry good," replied Mr. Jorrocks—"werry good," taking a half-emptied pot of Lazenby's marmalade, out of a drawer in his library table. "See now! there's a pot of marmey*lad* for you!" (Mr. Jorrocks had the knack of making the most of what he did, and treated the half pot as a whole one) and mind be a good *bouy*, and I make no doubt you'll rise to be a werry great man—nothing gains man or *bouy* the respect and esteem of the world so much as honesty, sobriety, and cleanliness."

Mr. Jorrocks paused—He would have finished with a moral, wherein his own fortune should have furnished the example, but somehow or other, he could not turn it at the moment, so after scrutinizing Benjamin's dirty face for a second, he placed the marmalade pot in his hand, and said, "now go and wesh your mug."

Uncommonly amiable and consequential was Mr. Jorrocks that morning. As he walked, or rather strutted into the city, he gave twopence to every crossing-sweeper in his line, from the black-eyed wench at the corner of Brunswick Square, to the breechless boy, with the red night cap, at St. Botolph's Lane end; and he entered his dark and dingy warehouse with a smile on his brow, enough to illumine the dial of St. Giles's clock in a fog. Most fidgetty and uneasy was he all the morning—every foot-fall made his eyes start from the ledger, and wander towards the door, in hopes of seeing some member of the Surrey, or some brother sportsman, to whom he might communicate the great intelligence. He went on 'Change with a hand in each breeches pocket, and a strut that plainly told how well he was to do with himself : still some dear-bought experience had given him a little prudence, and all things considered he determined to sleep on the invitation before he answered it.—Perhaps the pro's and con's of his mind will be best displayed by a transcript of what he wrote—

" GENTLEMEN,

"I have the honour to acknowledge the receipt of your favour of the 4th, and note the contents, which I assure you is most grateful to my feelings : in all you have said I most cordially goinside.—It's pleasant to see humanity estimating one's walue at the price one sets on oneself. I am a sportsman all over, and to the back-bone.—'Unting is all that's worth living for—all time is lost wot is not spent in 'unting—it is like the hair we breathe—if we have it not we die—it's the sport of kings, the image of war without its guilt, and only five-and-twenty per cent. of its danger.

"I have no manner of doubt at all, that I'm fully qualified for the mastership of the 'Andley Cross fox-hounds, or any other—'unting has been my 'obby ever since I could keep an 'oss, and long before—a southerly wind and a cloudy sky are my delight—no music like the melody of 'ounds. But enough of the rhapsodies, let us come to the melodies— the £. *s. d.* in fact. Wot will it cost?—In course it's a subscription pack —then say how many *paying* subscribers have you? Wot is the *nett* amount of their subscriptions—how many couple of 'ounds have you? Are they steady? Are they musical? How many days a week do you want your country 'unted? Is stoppin' expensive? What 'un a country is it to ride over? Stiff, or light, or middlin', or what? Enormous, endless woodlands without rides, stiff wales, with small enclosures and unreasonable raspers amid masses of plough; or pleasant copse-like covers, with roomy grass enclosures to reward the adventurous leaper with a gallop? Is it, in short, a country where a man can see 'ounds without zactly ridin' to tread on their tails? Are your covers wide of the kennel? Where is your kennel? I never heard of your 'ounds before—wot stablin' have you? Is 'ay and corn costly? In course you'll have your stock of meal by you? Are there any cover rents to pay—and if so, who pays them? How are you off for foxes? Are they stout and wild, and like to take a deal o' killin', or jest a middlin' sort of hanimal that one may look to who-hoop-in pretty often? Write me fully—fairly—freely—frankly, in fact, and believe me to remain, gentlemen, all your's to serve,

"JOHN JORROCKS,

"*Great Coram Street, London.*

"To MISERRIMUS DOLEFUL, ESQ., M.C.,

   "CAPTAIN HALF-PAY, HANDLEY CROSS."

*   *   *   *   *   *

"Well, come this is more like business than any we have had yet," observed Captain Doleful on reading the epistle—"though some of his questions will be plaguy troublesome to answer. What does he mean by 'are they steady?'—'Are they musical?' and as to the 'stopping being expensive,' of course that must depend a good deal upon how he lives, and whether he stops at an inn or not.—It's a pity but I knew something about the matter, that I might make a satisfactory answer."

Fleeceall had Blaine's Encyclopædia of Rural Sports, but as he was thought rather too sharp, Doleful determined to try what they could do without him; accordingly, he concocted the following epistle, which having copied on to a sheet of sea-green paper, he sealed with yellow wax, and deposited it in the post—

"DEAR MR. JORROCKS,

    "Your kind and flattering letter has just come to hand, and I lose not a moment in supplying you with all the information in my power, relative to our celebrated dogs. Unfortunately the secretary to the hunt, Mr. Fleeceall, is absent on urgent business, consequently I have not access to those documents which would enable me to answer you as fully as I could wish. The dogs, as you doubtless know, are of the purest blood, having been the property for many years of that renowned sportsman, Michael Hardey, and are bred with the very greatest care and attention. It is perhaps not going too far to say that there is not such another pack in the world. There are at present thirty-two couple of old ones, in kennel, besides an excellent white terrier with a black eye. They are very steady and most musical. Their airing yard adjoins the Ebenezer chapel, and when the saints begin to sing, the dogs join chorus. Handley Cross, where the kennel is situated, is in the most beautiful, fertile, and salubrious part of the country, within two miles of the Datton station of the Lily-white-sand railway, and contains a chalybeate spa of most unrivalled excellence. The following is an accurate analysis of the water, taken by an eminent French physician, who came all the way from Rheims for the express purpose of examining it.

ONE PINT (Wine measure).

Sulphate of soda	21 Grains.
Sulphate of magnesia	$3\frac{1}{2}$,,
Sulphate of lime	$4\frac{1}{4}$,,
Muriate of soda	$9\frac{1}{4}$,,
Oxide of iron	1 ,,
Carbonic acid	$1\frac{1}{4}$,,

" To this unrivalled spring, invalids from every part of the world, from every quarter of the globe, flock in countless numbers ; and it is unnecessary to point out to a sportsman like yourself either the advantages that a pack of hounds confer on such a place, or the benefits accruing to the master from having the support of men with whom, to use a familiar phrase, 'money is no object.' Indeed I think I may safely say, that keenness is all that is required, and a gentleman like you would meet with support that would galvanize your most sanguine expectations. You must excuse my saying more at present, as I have been out since day-break, and there is a piece of cold roast beef standing before me at this moment, whose beautifully marbled side, and rich yellow fat with a delicately browned outside, in conjunction with a crisp lettuce-salad in a china bowl, peremptorily order me to conclude, which I do with the earnest exhortation for you at once to declare yourself for the high honour of the mastership of the Handley Cross hounds. Believe me to remain in extreme hunger, dear Mr. Jorrocks, very sincerely your's,

" MISERRIMUS DOLEFUL, M.C.,

Capt. half-pay."

" HANDLEY CROSS."

" Dash my vig ! " exclaimed Mr. Jorrocks, laying down the letter, " what prime beef that must be ! By jingo I almost fancy I see the joint, with the nice, curly, crisp, brown 'orse radish, sticking to it in all directions.— I knows nothing better than *good* cold roast, tinged with red from the gravy in the centre.—Doleful must be a trump—feel as if I knew him. Keen fellow too—Peep-of-day boy.—Dare say he found the fox by the drag—Oh, vot joy is that ! Nothing to compare to it.—Might as well have told me more about the 'ounds too," he observed, as a glimmering of caution shot across his mind.—" Should like to have a fair black and white understanding what they are to cost. I'm rich to be sure, but then a man wot's made his own money likes to see to the spending of it." Thereupon Mr. Jorrocks stuck his hands under his coat-laps and paced thoughtfully up and down the apartment, waving them sportively like the tail of a dolphin. Having pulled his wig about in all directions, he at last composed himself at his table, and drew up the following reply :

" DEAR DOLEFUL,

" Your agreeable favour has come to hand, and werry pleasant it is. It appears to be directed to two points—the salubriosity of 'Andley Cross, and the excellence of the 'ounds. On the first point I'm content. I make no doubt the water's capital. Please tell me more about the 'ounds and country—are you quite certain that people will not be backward in comin forward with the coin? I've lived a goodish while i' the world—say a liberal alf under'd—and I've never yet found money good to get. So long as it consists of pen, ink, and paper work, it comes in like the hocean; many men can't elp puttin their names down in subscription lists, specially when payin time's far off, just as others can't help noddin at auctions, but confound it, when you come to gether in the doits, there's an awful fallin off. Now I think that no one should be allowed to hoop and holloa, or set up his jaw, wot hasn't paid his subscription. Howsomever, you should know best; and suppose now, as you seem full of confidence, you underwrite me for so much, cordin to the number of days you want the country 'unted.

"Turn this over in your mind, and let me know what you think of it; also please tell me more about the 'ounds and the country, for, in fact, as yet I knows nothin. Are there many old ounds in the pack? Are there many young ones to come in? What size are they? Are they level? Do they carry a good head? Have they plenty of bone? Cook says a weedy ound is only fit to 'unt a cat in a kitchen—I says ditto to that. What sort of condition are they in? Can they trot out fifteen miles or so, 'unt and come back with their sterns up, or do they whiles tire afore the foxes? How are you off for foxes? Are they ringers or straight runners? A ringer is only a hare with a tail to it. Do you ever hunt a bagman? Again I say, write to me without reserve—quite freely, in fact, and believe me, &c.,

"Your's to serve,

"JOHN JORROCKS,

"*Great Coram Street, London.*"

'TO MISERRIMUS DOLFFUL, ESQ., M.C.,
"CAPT. HALF-PAY, HANDLEY CROSS SPA."

This letter was a poser, for the worthy M.C. had no notion of running risks, neither had he the knowledge necessary for supplying the information Mr. Jorrocks required ; still he saw the absolute necessity of persevering in the negotiation, as there was no probability of any one else coming forward. In this dilemma, it occurred to him that a bold stroke might be the policy, and obviate further trouble.

Accordingly he wrote as follows :—

"Dear Mr. Jorrocks,
"Your's is just received. I was on the point of writing to you when it came. A rival has appeared for the mastership of the hounds : a great Nabob with a bad liver, to whom the doctors have recommended strong horse-exercise, has arrived with four posters, and an influential party is desirous of getting the hounds for him. Money is evidently no object—he gave each post-boy a half-sovereign, and a blind beggar two and sixpence. I have protested most strongly against his being even *thought* of until your final decision is known, which pray give immediately, and, for your sake, let it be in the affirmative. I can write no more— my best energies shall be put in requisition to counteract the sinister proceedings of others. Pray write immediately— no time is to be lost. In the greatest haste.

"Faithfully yours,

"Miserrimus Doleful, M.C.
"*Capt. Half-pay.*"

"To John Jorrocks, Esq.,
"Great Coram Street,
"London."

This letter was a sad puzzler to our worthy friend. In his eyes a mastership of fox-hounds was the highest pinnacle of ambition, and the situation was the more desirable inasmuch as he had about got all the trade he could in the "cut-me-down" countries, and shame to say, they had rather put him out of conceit of the Surrey. Still long experience had tinctured his naturally ardent and impetuous mind with some degree of caution, and he felt the importance of having some sort of a bargain before entering upon what he well knew was an onerous and expensive undertaking. The pros and cons he weighed and turned over in his mind, and the following letter was the result of his cogitations :—

Dear Doleful,—
"I will candidly confess that to be a master of fox-hounds, or M. F. H., would be a werry high step in the ladder of my hambition, but still I should not like to pay too dear for my whistle. I doesn't wish to disparage the walue of your Nabob, but this I may say, that no man with a bad liver will ever make a good 'untsman. An 'untsman, or M. F. H., should have a good digestion, with a cheerful countenance, and, moreover, should know when to use the clean and when the dirty side of his tongue—when to butter a booby, and when to snub a snob. He

should also be indifferent as to weather; and Nabobs all come from the east, where it is werry 'ot all sunshine and no fogs.

" Again, if I am right, they hunt the jackall, not at all a sportin animal, ⊥ should say, from the specimen in the Zoologicals. Still, as I said before, I doesn't wish to disparage the walue of your Nabob, who may be a werry good man, and have more money and less wit than myself. If he is to have the 'ounds, well and good—I can go on as I 'ave been doing, with the glorious old Surrey, and an occasional turn with the " cut-me-downs." If I'm to have them, I should like to know a little more about the £. s. d. Now, tell me candidly, like a good fellow, without any gammon, wot you think they'll cost, and wot can be raised in the way of subscription. Of course, a man that's raised to the lofty position of an M. F. H. must expect to pay something for the honour; and so far from wishing to live out of the 'ounds, I am well disposed to do what is liberal, but then I should like to know the extent of my liability. Dignity, in my mind, should not be too cheap, but betwixt you and I and the wall I rayther mistrust a water-drinker. To be sure there be two sorts o' water-drinkers : those that drink it to save the expense of treating themselves with aught better, and those wot undergo water for the purpose of bringin their stomachs round to stand summut stronger. Now, if a man drinks water for pleasure, he should not be trusted, and ought to be called upon for his subscription in advance; but if he drinks water because he has worn out his inside by strong libations, in all humane probability he will be a goodish sort of fellow, and his subscription will be underwritten for a trifle. All this may be matter of no moment to a Nabob, but to a man vot's risen from indigence to affluence by the unaided exertions of his own head, it is of importance; and I should like to know werry particularly how many of the subscribers are woluntary water-drinkers, and how many are water-drinkers from necessity.

" I am, as you doubtless know, a great grocer and tea merchant, dealin' wholesale and retail, importing direct from China, which I suppose will be the country your Nabob comes from; and unfortunately at the present writing my junior partner, Simon Simpkins, senior, is on a trading tour, and I can't well be wanted at the shop, otherwise I would run down and have a personal interview with you; but I had a letter this morning from Huddersfield in which he says he will be back as on Friday at farthest; therefore as the season is spending, and the 'ounds should be kept going, I could, should your answer be agreeable, run down on the Saturday and make arrangements for taking the field immediately. Of course I presume there is everything ready for the purpose, and a mounted master is all wot is wanted. I only keep two 'osses—what the lawyers call *qui tam*'ers —' 'osses that ride as well as drive,' and they would only do for my own riding. I have also a sharp London lad, who has been with me in the " cut-me-downs," who might make a second whip; and my establishment consists of Mrs. Jorrocks, my niece, Belinda, Betsay, the maid, and Binjimin, the boy. Of course, Mrs. J., as the wife of the M. F. H., would expect all proper attention.

" I shall want a comfortable house to accommodate this party, and if I could get one with stabling attached, it would be agreeable. Perhaps you may know something of the sort, the willa style would be agreeable. I think that's all I've got to say—indeed, I haven't paper for more, so shall conclude for self and partners,

"Your's to serve,

"JOHN JORROCKS.

"To MISERRIMUS DOLEFUL, ESQ. M.C.
"HANDLEY CROSS SPA."

Doleful was in ecstacies when he got this letter, for he plainly saw the Nabob had told upon Mr. Jorrocks, and that he was fairly entering the meshes of his net. The letter, indeed, was unexceptionable, save the mention of his avocation of a grocer, which Doleful determined to keep to himself, merely announcing him as a gentleman of large fortune, whose father had been connected with trade. Recollecting that Diana Lodge was to let, he forthwith secured the refusal of it at three guineas a week, and calling on Fleeceall, concocted a most flattering list of subscribers and members of the hunt, which he forwarded to Mr. Jorrocks with the following letter :—

"DEAR MR. JORROCKS,

"By the greatest good luck in the world, Diana Lodge, within a stone's throw of the kennel, came vacant this morning, and not having the slightest doubt that on inspection of the accompanying list of subscribers to the hounds and members of our celebrated hunt, which you will see by the letters A. and B. prefixed to their names, contain very few of those most horrible characters water-drinkers from choice, you will immediately accept the honourable office of 'Master,' I have engaged it for you at the very moderate rent of four guineas a-week, *including everything*. It is a cottage ornée, as you say in France, entered by an ivy-covered trellis-work arch, tastefully entwined with winter roses, now in full blow. In the passage is a highly-polished Honduras Mahogany table on claw feet castors, for hats, whips, gloves, cigar-cases, &c. On the right is a dining-room of comfortable dimensions, with another Honduras mahogany table, capable of dining eight people, the orthodox size for a party, with a Honduras mahogany cellaret sideboard with patent-locks, and a dumb-waiter on castors. The carpet is a Turkey one, and the rug a Kidder-minster, of a pattern to match the carpet. On the left of the passage is a drawing-room of the same size as the dining-room, furnished in a style of unparalleled elegance.

"The chairs, ten in number, are of massive imitation-rosewood, with beaded and railed backs and round knobs along the tops, and richly carved legs. In the centre is a beautiful round imitation-rosewood table on square lion-clawed brass castors, and the edge of the table is deeply inlaid with a broad circle of richly-carved, highly-polished brass. Against the wall, below a costly round mirror, supported by a bronze eagle in chains, is a square imitation-rosewood table inlaid with satin-wood in lines, containing two drawers on each side, with ivory knobs for handles. The carpet is a fine flowered pattern, richer than anything I can describe, and the whole is wonderfully complete and surpassingly elegant.

"There are four bedrooms, and a dressing-room which holds a bed, and a kitchen, back-kitchen, scullery, pantry, and other conveniences. To the back is a nice little outlet of a quarter of an acre, laid out in the style of the Jardin des Plantes at Paris; and there is a splendid old patriarch of a peacock, that struts about the walls, spreads his tail, and screams delightfully. In short, it appears to me to have been built with an eye to the residence of a master of hounds.

" And this leads me to tell you that the Nabob has been to the kennel, attended by two Negroes, one of whom held a large green parasol over his head to protect him from the sun, while the other carried a Chinchilla, fur-lined, blue silk cloak to guard him from the cold. I hear he talked very big about tiger-hunting and elephant-riding, and said the waters here had done his liver a vast deal of good. I may observe that it is possible an attempt may be made by a few troublesome fellows to place him at the head of the establishment, particularly if you any longer delay appearing among us. My advice to you therefore is, to place yourself, your amiable lady, and accomplished niece, with your servants, horses, &c., on the mid-day Lilly-white-sand train, on Friday next, and make a public entry and procession from the Datton station into Handley Cross, showering half-pence among the little boys as you go. I will take upon myself to muster and marshal such a procession as will have an imposing appearance, and the Nabob will be a very bold man if he makes any attempt upon the hounds after that.

" I need not say that your amiable lady will receive from me, as M. C. of Handley Cross, all those polite attentions that are invariably paid by all well-bred gentlemen in the dignified situation I have the honour to hold, more particularly from those bearing Her Majesty's Commission in the Army; and in the table of precedence among women that I have laid down for the regulation of the aristocratic visitors of Handley Cross Spa, the lady of the M. F. H. comes on after the members of the Royal Family, and before all bishops' wives and daughters, peeresses, knights' dames, justices' wives, and so forth. Expecting then to meet you at the Datton Station on the Lilly-white-sand Railway, at three o'clock on Friday next, and to have the supreme felicity of making the personal acquaintance of a gentleman who so worthily fills so large a space in the world's eye, I have the honour to subscribe myself, with humble respects to the ladies, dear Mr. Jorrocks,

" Faithfully your's,

" MISERRIMUS DOLEFUL, M. C.

" Capt. Half-pay."

And Jorrocks seeing there was as much chance of getting information by correspondence as there was of getting the truth by interrogatories in the days of old Chancery suits, determined to stand the shot, and wrote to say that henceforth they might append the magic letters, M. F. H., to his name. And forthwith he became so inflated, that Great Coram Street itself could hardly hold him.

CHAPTER VIII.

CAPTAIN DOLEFUL'S DIFFICULTIES.

WHAT a fuss there was preparing for Mr. Jorrocks's reception!—
Captain Doleful was perfectly beside himself, and ran about the town as
though he expected her Majesty. First he went to the proprietary
school, and begged a half holiday for all the little boys and girls; next
he visited Mr. Whackem's mathematical seminary, and did the like by
his; Miss Prim and Miss Prosey both promised to "suspend the duties
of their respective establishments" for the afternoon; and three infant
schools were released from lessons all the day. "Jorrocks for ever,"
was chalked upon the walls, doors, and shutters; and little children
sung out his name in lisping acclamations. Publicans looked cheerful,
and livery stable keepers, ostlers, and helpers talked about the price
of ay and corn. Sebastian Mello called a meeting of the Religious
Freedom Society, who voted eight-and-twenty shillings for placarding
the town with the following comfortable assurance—" FOX-HUNTERS
WILL ALL GO TO ——."

The banner with the fox upon it, and the "Floreat Scientia" scroll
painted for the celebrated ball and supper, was released from the darkness
of Mr. Fleeceall's garret, where it had been deposited after the entertainment, and mounted on poles to lead the way in the procession;
while the milliners, mantuamakers, and tailors were severally called upon
to contribute silk, calico, and bunting for flags, decorations, and ribbons.
Whatever Doleful demanded was necessarily ceded, so absolute was his
sway over the tradespeople at the Spa. He was indeed a very great man.
Did a new cheesemonger, or a new hatter, or a new milk-woman, wish
to settle in the place, the good-will of the M. C. was invariably to be
obtained, else it was to little use their troubling themselves to come; and
the perquisites and advantages derived from these sources made a comfortable addition to his yearly income, arising from the subscription book
at the library. The musicians at the wells were also under his control,
and of course they received intimations to be at the Datton station
before the hour that Mr. Jorrocks had privately announced his intention
to arrive.

The morning sun broke cheerfully through the clouds in a good, downrightly, determined fine day, and as Doleful threw open the latticed case-
ment of his window, and his eye roved to the "sun-bright summit" of
the distant hills, he poured forth an inward ejaculation for the success of
the great enterprise of the day, and for his own especial honour and
emolument. In the midst of his reverie Jemima, the maid of all work
and shop-girl of the house, tapped gently at his door, and handed in
a three-cornered note written on pink satin highly musked paper.
Doleful started as though he had seen an apparition, for in the hand
he immediately recognised the writing of his great patroness, Mrs.
Barnington, and the recollection of Mrs. Jorrocks, the table of precedence

among women, whereby the latter was to supplant Mrs. Barnington, the baits and lures he had held out for the purpose of securing the Jorrocks's, together with the honour he was then instigating the inhabitants to do Mr. J., all rushed upon his mind with terrible velocity. Nor did the contents of the note assuage the anguish of his mind. It was simply this: "Mrs. Barnington will thank Capt. Doleful to wait upon her at twenty-three minutes before eleven."

"Twenty-three minutes before eleven!" exclaimed the Captain, throwing up his hands, looking like a condemned criminal—" How *like* her that is! always peremptory with others and never punctual herself; well, there's no help for it. Jemima," exclaimed he, down the narrow staircase, to the girl who had returned to the shop, "my compliments to Mrs. Barnington, and say I will make a point of being with her at the time she names. I wonder," continued he to himself, pacing up and down his little bedroom in his dressing-gown and slippers, "what she can want—it must be about the Jorrocks's—and yet I could not do otherwise than I have. If she storms, I'll rebel, and trounce her for all her airs; by *Jove*, I will!" saying which, he clenched his fist, and, looking in the glass, brushed up the few straggling hairs that marked the place for whiskers, and felt quite valiant. His courage, however, rather oozed out of his finger ends, as the appointed hour approached, and at twenty-one minutes before eleven by his watch, and twenty-two and a half by the church clock, he arrived at the door of his arbitrary and capricious patroness.

"Mistress is in her boudoir," said the consequential butler on receiving the Captain at the hands of the footman, "but I'll send up your name. Please step into the parlour," and thereupon he turned the Captain into the fireless dining-room, and closed the door upon him.

Towards twelve o'clock, just as the Captain's courage was nearly up again, and he had thrice applied his hand to the ivory knob of the bell-spring to see which way it turned against he wanted to ring, in strutted the butler again, with "Missis's compliments, sir, and is sorry she is indisposed at present, and hopes it will not be inconvenient to you to return at ten minutes before three." — "Ten minutes before three," exclaimed the Captain as a tinge of colour rose to his pallid cheeks, "impossible!" said he, "*impossible!*" Then recollecting himself, he desired the butler to return with his respects to Mrs. Barnington, and say that at any hour next day, he would have great pleasure in waiting upon her, but that his time was completely bespoke for the whole afternoon. The butler forthwith departed, and in about three quarters of an hour, during which time Mrs. Barnington had finished a nap on the sofa, and arranged an elegant negligée toilette wherein to appear, the butler returned, and with a bow and wave of his hand announced that "Missis would see the Captain," whom he preceded up-stairs and handed over to Bandoline, the little French maid, stationed at the door, who ushered the Captain into the presence of Mrs. Barnington in the back drawing-room. She was lying in state on a costly many-cushioned crimson and gold ottoman, dressed in a fawn-coloured robe de chambre, with a rich white Cachmere shawl thrown carelessly about her legs, below which, her elegantly-formed feet in pink swan's-down-lined slippers protruded. Her morning cap of costly

workmanship was ornamented and tied with broad satin cherry-coloured
ribbons, which, with the colour of the ottoman and cushions, imparted a
gentle hue to her clear but delicate complexion, and her bright silky hair
flowed in luxuriant tresses from the sides.   She was a *malade imaginaire*-
ist, having originally come as a patient of Swizzle's; but that roistering

practitioner had grievously offended her by abruptly closing a long list of
inquiries by replying to the question if he thought she might eat a few
oysters, with "Oh, hang it, marm, yes—*shells and all!*"   She was now
pretending to read the Handley Cross Paul Pry, while with her left hand
she kept applying a costly gold vinaigrette to her nose.   The room was a
mass of jewellery, costly furniture, and expensive flowers.

   "Good morning, Captain," said she, with the slightest possible inclination of her head.—"Bandoline, set a chair," which she motioned the

Captain to occupy, and the pretty little maid departed. " Pray," said she, as soon as the door closed, " what is the meaning of all this to do about a Mr. Horrocks, that I read of in the Paul Pry ? "

" Mr. Horrocks," replied the Captain, colouring, " really, marm, I don't know—it's the first time I've heard the name mentioned this long time,— there was a Mr. Horrocks lived in Silenus villa the year before last, but I understood he had gone back to India."

" Oh, no," replied Mrs. Barnington, " that's quite another person— these are Londoners—*trades*-people I hear, and the man Horrocks, the paper says, is to have the hounds."

" Oh," replied the Captain, now blushing to the very tips of his ears, " you've mistaken the name, marm. Yes, marm.—It's *Jorrocks*, marm— Mister Jorrocks of Great Coram Street, marm—a merchant prince, marm —at least his father was. The present Mr. Jorrocks is a mighty sports- man, and hearing the hounds were without a leader, he wrote to offer himself, and some of the sporting gentry of the place have been in treaty with him to take them; but I need not tell you, Mrs. Barnington, that hunting is not an amusement I am partial to, indeed I hope I may never have occasion to go out again; but you know that as Master of the Ceremonies I am obliged to countenance many things that I would gladly avoid."

" True," replied Mrs. Barnington, with a smile of approbation—" I thought *you* would not be likely to encourage vulgar people coming here merely because they don't care for breaking their necks over hedges and ditches—but tell me, isn't there a Mrs. Jorrocks ? "

" I understand so," replied the Captain with a hem and a haw ; " a lady of birth, they say ; but had I known you would have interested yourself in the matter, I should certainly have informed myself so as to have been able to tell you all about her."

" Oh dear no ! *not for the world!*—whether as a lady of birth or a tradesman's wife, it would never do for *me* to concern myself about them. *You* know my position here is not to be controverted by any interlopers, be they who they may,—or come from where they will."

" Undoubtedly not, marm," replied the obsequious M. C.; " there's not a person in the place insensible of the advantages of your presence ; but I should hope,—at least, perhaps I may venture to express a slight wish,—that if those Jorrocks's appear respectable people, you will for the sake of sociability vouchsafe them the favour of your countenance, and condescend to notice them a *little*."

" I don't know what to say about that, my dear Captain," replied Mrs. Barnington thoughtfully. " If they appear respectable people, and if they live in a certain style, and if I thought the matter would rest at Handley Cross, and they would not obtrude their acquaintance upon me elsewhere, and if they appeared sensible of the obligation, I might perhaps call upon them; but where there are so many points to consider, and so many to ascertain, it is almost needless speculating upon how one might act ; all that we can do for the present is to maintain one's own consequence, and *you* know full well the only way to support a place like this, is to uphold the dignity of the chief patroness."

"No doubt," replied Captain Doleful, with a half-suppressed sigh as the table of precedence among women came across his mind. "I am sure, Madam, I have always been most anxious to pay you every respect and attention in my power, and if I have failed it has been owing to the multiplicity of my engagements and duties, and not from any want of inclination on my part."—"I'm sure of it, Captain; and now let us see you back here at dinner at ten minutes past six."—"With pleasure," replied the Captain, rising to depart, with a grin of satisfaction on his melancholy visage.

"Stay one moment," resumed Mrs. Barnington, as the Captain was leaving the room. "The paper says these people arrive to-day. If you chance to see them or can find anything out about them, you know, well and good—perhaps *Mr.* Barnington might like to know."—"By all means," replied the obsequious M. C., backing courtier-like out of the room, and nearly splitting himself up with the now opening door.

CHAPTER IX.

THE CONQUERING HERO COMES.

THE clear bright beauty of the day, combined with the attraction of a stranger coming to fill so important a situation as master of fox-hounds, drew many to the Datton Railway station, who were previously unacquainted even with the name of "Jorrocks;" though it is but right to state that the ignorant portion consisted principally of the fair sex, most men, whether sportsmen or not, having heard of his fame and exploits.

All the flys, hack horses, donkeys, and ponies, were bespoke as usual; and many set out at noon to secure good berths at the station. Precisely at two o'clock Captain Doleful appeared at Miss Jelly's door, attired in a dress that would puzzle the "property man" of a theatre. It was nearly the same as he exhibited himself in on the memorable opening day of the committee of management. The old single-breasted militia coat, denuded of its facings and trappings, with a sky-blue collar and sky-blue linings, and a short, shrivelled, buff-kerseymere waistcoat, with mother-of-pearl buttons, old white moleskin breeches, well darned and patched at the knees, and badly-cleaned Hessian boots and black heel spurs.—His hands were covered with a pair of dirty-white kid gloves; and in his right one he carried a large hunting-whip. An oil-skin-covered hat, secured to a button-hole of his waistcoat by a yard of sky-blue penny ribbon, completed the rigging of this sporting dandy.

Having withdrawn his countenance and custom from Sam Slickem after the affair of the kicking mare, (the effect of which had been considerably to impoverish Mr. Sam,) of course all the other proprietors of hack horses

were on the alert to please the great M. C., and on this day he was
mounted by Duncan Nevin on his white mare, Fair Rosamond, who was
generally honoured by carrying pretty Miss Lovelace, once the head

beauty of the place—but who being unable to ride this day, it came into
the hands of the Captain.

To make the mare more complete, although in winter time, its ears
were decorated with white fly-nets and dangling tassels, and from the
saddle hung a large net of the same colour and texture, with a broad
fringe, completely covering her hind quarters and reaching below her
hocks.

Doleful eyed the whole with a grin of satisfied delight, and never did
field-marshal mount his charger for review with a more self-complacent
air than sat upon the brow of this distinguished character. Having

steadied himself in his stirrups, and gathered up the reins, he cast an eye between the barley-sugar and cake cans in Miss Jelly's window, and hissing at the mare through his teeth with a jerk of the reins, went off in a canter. A rare-actioned beast it was too! Up and down, up and down, it went, so light and so easy, and making so little progress withal, that Ducrow himself might have envied the possession of it.

Thus Doleful went tit-tup-ping along through the silent streets, to the infinite delight of all the Johns and Jennies, who were left to flatten their noses against the windows during their masters' and mistresses' absence, and here and there exciting the anger of a butcher's dog, or farmer's cur, that flew at the mare's heels with an indignant bark as she passed.

Having timed himself to a nicety, our gallant M. C. arrived at the station just as the last fly and flight of donkeys drew up outside the iron railing that runs along the railroad from the station-house, and, in the absence of Mr. Jorrocks, of course he was the object of attraction. "Good morning, Captain Doleful," exclaimed a dozen sweet voices from all sorts of vehicles, for women will toady a Master of Ceremonies, be he what he may ; and thereupon the Captain gave one of his feature-wrinkling grins, and raised his oil-skin-covered hat as high as the yard of penny ribbon would allow, while all the little boys and girls, for whom he had obtained half-holiday, burst into loud acclamations, as they stood or sat on Lily-white-sand barrels, hazel bundles, and other miscellaneous articles, waiting for conveyance by the railway. "Now, children, mind, be orderly, and attend to what I told you," said the Captain, eying his juvenile friends as though he were marshalling them for a quadrille. "It now wants but ten minutes to the coming of the train, so be getting yourselves in order, unfurl the flags ; and you, musicians," turning to the promenade band, who were hard at work with some XX, "be getting your instruments ready, to welcome Mr. Jorrocks with 'See the conquering hero comes!'" As the minutes flew, the scene became more inspiriting. Eyes were strained up the railway in the direction he was to come, and ears were opened to catch the first sound of the engine. All was anxiety and expectation. Hope and fear vacillated on every countenance. "Should he not come, what a bore!" "Oh, but he's certain to arrive, and Mrs. Jorrocks too, arn't they, Captain?" The Captain looked thoughtful and mysterious, as all great men should, but deigned no reply.

Precisely at three-quarters of a minute before three, a wild shrill whistle, that seemed to issue from the bowels of the earth and to run right up into mid-air, was heard at the back of Shavington Hill, and, in an instant, the engine and long train rounded the base, the engine smoking and snorting like an exasperated crocodile. Nearer and nearer it comes, with a thundering sort of hum that sounds throughout the country. The wondering ploughman stops his team. The cows and sheep stand staring with astonishment, while the horses take a look, and then gallop about the fields, kicking up their heels and snorting with delight. The guard's red coat on the engine is visible—next his gold hat-band appears—now we read the Hercules on the engine, and anon it pulls up with a whiff, a puff, and a whistle, under the slate-covered shed, to give the Hercules his water, and set down and take up passengers and goods. Seven first-class passenger carriages follow the engine, all smart, clean, and yellow, with appropriate names on each door panel—The Prince Albert, Queen Victoria, and the Prince of Wales, The Venus, The Mercury, The Comet, and The Star; next come ten second-class ones, green, with covered tops, and half-covered sides, but in neither set is there anything at all like the Jorrocks' party. Cattle-pens follow, holding sheep, swine, donkeys, and poultry; then came an open platform with a broken britzka, followed by a curious-looking nondescript one horse vehicle, containing a fat man in a low-crowned hat, and a versatio or reversible coat, with the preferable side outwards. Along with him were two ladies muffled up in cloaks, and at the back was a good-looking servant-maid. From the bottom of the carriage swung a couple of hams, and a large warming-pan.

"Pray is Mr. Jorrocks here?" inquired the elegant M. C., who had persuaded the station-master to let him in upon the line, riding his white charger near the door of the first-class carriage, and raising his hat as he spoke; but getting no answer, he continued his interrogatory down the whole set until he came to the end, when casting a despairing glance at the cattle pens, he was about to wheel round, when the gentleman in the versatio coat, in a very stentorian voice, roared out, "I say, SIR! Baint this the 'Andley Cross station?"

"It is, Sir," replied Captain Doleful, in his most dignified manner, "the Datton station for Handley Cross at least."

"Then I want to land," responded the same sweet voice.

"Here's a gentleman wants to be down," observed Captain Doleful to the scarlet-coated guard, who came bustling past with a pen of Cochin-Chinas to put upon the train.

"Yes, a gentleman and two ladies," roared our friend; "MISTER AND MISSIS JORROCKS in fact, and MISS JORROCKS!"

"Bless my heart," exclaimed Captain Doleful in ecstacies, "how delighted I am to see you! I really thought you were not coming," and thereupon the Captain raised his hat to the ladies, and offered his hand most cordially to Mr. Jorrocks.

"What, you knows me, do you?" replied Mr. Jorrocks, with the sort of doubtful shake of the hand that a person gives when he thinks the next moment may discover a mistake. "You knows me, do you?" repeated he, "you have the adwantage of me—pray who are *you?*"

"Captain Doleful, M. C.," responded our worthy, presenting his glazed card to the ladies; and thereupon Mr. Jorrocks, with a chuckle on his good-humoured countenance, as he gazed at the Captain's incongruous habiliments, seized his hand and wrung it heartily, saying, "'Ow *are* ye, Doleful? 'Ow do ye do? Werry glad to see you—werry glad indeed; 'ow's the Nabob?"

"Middling, thank you," replied the Captain, with a faint blush on his cadaverous countenance. "But hadn't you better alight and get your carriage and things off the train?" inquired he, glad to turn the conversation, "they'll be off with you if you don't mind," and thereupon the Captain beckoned the guard, and Mr. Jorrocks, standing up in the vehicle, looking very like a hay-stack with a hat on the top, bounded to the ground. Mrs. Jorrocks, in a black velvet bonnet, lined with pink satin,

and her body all shrouded in a sea-green silk cloak, then accepted the
offer of the Captain's arm, and descended with caution and due state;
while Belinda, with the spring of youth and elasticity in her limbs,
bounded on to the foot-way beyond the rail. Benjamin, who was asleep
in the horse-box, being considerately kicked awake by Mr. Jorrocks, the
porters cut off the last joints of the train, when away it went, hissing and
snorting through the quiet country, leaving our party to the undisturbed
observation of the Handley Cross company.

CHAPTER X.

THE CONQUERING HERO'S PUBLIC ENTRY.

APTAIN
DOLEFUL, leav-
ing his charger
in the care of
a porter, now
offered Mrs.
Jorrocks his
arm, and walked
her off to the
station - house,
followed by
Jorrocks and
Belinda, amid
the observa-
tions and in-
quiries of the
numerous party
ranged outside
the barrier.
The ladies being
now left to ar-
range their toi-
lettes, Jorrocks and Doleful joined arms in a most friendly manner, and
strutted back to see about unloading the horses, the sack-like figure of the
one, contrasting with the thin, lathy, mountebank appearance of the other.
This being accomplished, Ben proceeded to strip off his dirty white
great coat, and display his fine new sky-blue postillion jacket, patent
cords and top-boots, while Jorrocks began expatiating to Doleful on the
merits of the animals.

"This 'ere 'oss," says he, rubbing his hand up and down the Roman
nose of a great rat-tailed brown, "I've ridden many seasons, and he's

never given me but one fall, and that was more my fault than his. Indeed I may say it was mine entirely. 'Ow's this country off for foxes! Well, you see, I was chiveyin' this 'ere 'oss along like wildfire, for it was a most special fine scentin' day—breast-high all the way—and Tom Hills, that's our 'untsman, was ridin' wiciously wenomous—by the way that reminds me can you commend me to an honest man to buy my forage of? Well, we blazed down Windy Hill, and past Stormey Wood, just as though it were as level as this rally, when Joe Crane, thinkin' to gain a nick, turned for Nosterly, and Tom and I rode slap for Guilsborough, where he threw a shoe, and I was left alone in my glory. I know'd the country well, and sinkin' the hill, stole down Muddiford Lane, with the pack goin' like beans on my left, with only two men within a mile of them, barrin' a miller with his sacks, who rode uncommon galvanizingly.

"Well, thinks I to myself, if they turn by Gatton steep I'll have a nick, for though his 'oss was never *reglarly* pumped out, yet times are when he'd be better of a little more wind, and so as I rode along peepin' over the 'edge, 'oping every minute to see old Barbican, who was leadin' the pack that day, give a bend to my side, ven vot should occur but a gipsy camp half across the lane, and three donkeys, two jacks and a jinney, huddled together in the other part so as to make a regular barrier, and, by the by, have you read Digby Grand? Grand book it is; but, however, never mind that at present; well, we were close upon the camp and donkeys afore ever we saw them, for it was just at that sharp turn of the road where the waterin' trough is—confound them, they always place pikes and troughs in the hawkwardest places—and this 'oss though with all his eyes about him, was so heager lookin' for the 'ounds, that I'm dashed if he didn't come upon them so suddenly that he hadn't time to change his leg or do no thing, consequentially he dodged first among the gipsy bairns, putting his foot through a *sarce*pan the old father gipsy was a mendin', and then, fearin' mischief, he flew to the left, and cast me right on to the old jinney hass's back, who, risin' at the moment, finished the business by kickin' me off into the dirtiest heap of composition for turnips I ever smelt in my life—haw, haw, haw! I really think I wind it now. Still the 'oss is a good un—an undeniable good un. When he carries me well, I ax's three 'undred for him, at other times I'd take thirty. I never grudges money for 'osses. Des-say if all the money I've spent first and last were equally distributed among them, they wouldn't stand me i' less nor forty pund apiece.

"This too's a *grand* nag!" continued he, taking hold of the ear of a stiff bay with white hind legs, and a bang tail—"good at every thing—rides, drives, 'unts, and carries a 'ooman. I call him Xerxes, cause as how ven I drives two, as I'm a doin' to-day, he goes leader, and in-course the brown, which I calls *Arter*-Xerxes, comes arter him! Both go like the vind—good 'osses! uncommon good! rough and strong as our four-shillin' tea.—Binjamin, mind the traces,—and now be after puttin' too, your Missis will be ready by the time we get all square;" and thereupon Mr. Jorrocks began fussing and busying himself with the horses and harness, and very soon had Xerxes and Arter-Xerxes in their proper places, "tandem fashion." The carriage was an old, low, open, double-bodied one, with red and black wheels, looking as much like a fire-engine as anything else, especially with the Westphalia hams and warming-pan swinging from the bottom like buckets. It held four comfortably, or five on a pinch, and the inmates were Mr. Jorrocks and his wife, Belinda, and Betsey. It was tremendously stuffed and hung about with luggage, and at the back was attached a most sporting package, consisting of two saddles done up in horse-sheeting; and through the roller which fastened them to the carriage, two stout hunting-whips and a new brass horn were thrust. All things being ready, Mr. Jorrocks gave Benjamin a "leg up" on to Xerxes, and gathering up the reins of his wheeler in a most work-manlike manner, stepped into the vehicle, and preceded by Captain Doleful on the white charger, drove up to the station-house door, to the infinite delight of all the spectators outside the rails, amid the puffings, scrapings, and tootlings of the musicians, the pointing of children, the unfurling of flags, and general movement of the meeting.

Mrs. Jorrocks and Belinda had improved the few minutes in the station-house, and with the aid of Betsey and a looking-glass had rectified the little disorders of the journey. Having cast her sea-green wrapper, Mrs. Jorrocks shone forth in a superb scarlet brocade pelisse, so bright and dazzling that even in Great Coram Street, or St. Pancras Church, it acted as a loadstone on the eyes of the beholders, and now in the quiet country was almost overpowering. She looked like a full-blown peony.

Belinda, the young, the fair, the beautiful Belinda, was the picture of innocence and health. Her large lustrous blue eyes, with their long silken lashes, shone "sweetly lambent" from beneath a drab silk drawn bonnet lined with blue, across which a rich black veil was thrown; a smile hovered round her ruby lips, disclosing the beautiful regularity of her pearly teeth; while the late rapid movement through the air, joined with the warmth of the station-house, and the excitement of the scene, had imparted a slight flush to a delicate, but beautifully clear complexion. Her shining brown hair, drawn across her forehead in the Madonna style, was confined with a narrow band of blue velvet, while a rich well-fitting drab silk pelisse displayed the symmetry of her exquisitely rounded figure. Her beautifully-formed feet were enclosed in well-fitting patent leather shoes, whose ties embraced well-turned ankles encased in well drawn up, white gauze silk stockings.

The station-house and buildings concealing our party from view, Mr. Jorrocks had time to make those comfortable dispositions of the persons of his suite as are always desirable in public processions, but which are sometimes driven out of the heads even of the most experienced paraders, by the inquisitive observations of many hundred eyes. He now took Belinda upon the draw-out seat between himself and Mrs. Jorrocks, while Betsey bundled in behind, among Dundee marmalade, sugar loaves, Copenhagen cherry-brandy, and other things. Having given a knowing cast over his left shoulder to see that she was right, Mr. Jorrocks cried out, "Now, Binjimin, follow the Captain," and giving Arter-Xerxes a touch with the point of the whip, passed from the screen formed by the station-house, to the folding iron gates at the side, which being thrown open at the approach of the Captain, they made a splendid turn off the railway line into the crowded space outside. "Huzza! huzza! huzza!

Mr. Jorrocks enters unto Handley Cross.

huzza! huzza! huzza!" exclaimed a hundred voices; "Huzza! huzza!"
responded a hundred more, amid the roll of drums, the puffing of the
horns, the flapping of the flags, and the waving of handkerchiefs from
those whose aristocratic ideas precluded the expression of clamorous
applause. Doleful stopped Benjamin on the leader, and Mr. Jorrocks
pulling short up, stood erect in the vehicle, and taking off his low-
crowned hat, bowed and waved it repeatedly to the company, while
Mrs. Jorrocks acknowledged the compliment by frequent kisses of her
hand, and Belinda's face became suffused with blushes at the publicity and
novelty of her situation.—Having sufficiently exercised their lungs, hats
began to rest upon their owners' heads, handkerchiefs were returned to
their pockets, and amid a general buzz and exclamation of applause, a rush
was made at the carriage to get a closer view of Belinda.

"By Jove, what a beautiful girl!" exclaimed Captain Parkins (a new
comer) to his friend Mr. Dyneley, eyeing Belinda through his glass.

"Did you ever *see* such eyes?" inquired a second.

"Handsomest creature I ever beheld! Fine undulating figure!' observed a third.

"What a quiz the old girl is," remarked another.

"Is she her daughter?" inquired a third of Captain Doleful, who was
busy marshalling the procession.

"Lots of money I suppose!" said another.

"He looks like a rich fellow, with that queer-looking hat of his."

"The servant girl's not bad-looking."

"*Miss* for my money," said another, "I'm in love with her already."

"I wish she'd stand up and let's see her size."

"I lay a guinea she's a clipper."

"There's a hand! I'll be bound for it she has a good foot and ancle.
None of your hairy-heel'd ones."

"He looks like a jolly old dog," observed another. "We shall have
lots of good dinners, I dare say."

Doleful's face wrinkled into half its usual size with delight, for he
plainly saw he had made a hit; and most fortunate were those men who
had cultivated his friendship through the medium of the subscription
books at the libraries, for the two-guinea subscribers were immediately
presented to the trio, while the guinea men were let in at intervals as the
procession moved along the road. Nor should we omit to mention, for
the instruction of all other M. C.'s, that thirteen new names were put down
that evening, so that Doleful's prospects were brighter than ever.

The first burst of applause having subsided, the party got settled into
the order of the day, as laid down in the programme of the worthy M. C.
First went the proprietary school children, eighty boys and a hundred and
nine girls, three a-breast, with sundry pocket-handkerchief banners. Next
came the "Fox and Floreat Scientia" flag, on double poles so as to
stretch across the road; the musicians, two drummers, two horn-blowers,
two fiddlers, and a fifer, were planted behind it; after which came three
glazed calico flags, of various colours in stripes, followed by Whackem's
mathematical seminary, and the rabble at large. Then came another
large double flag, in broad stripes of scarlet and white, with the words
"JORROCKS FOR EVER!" done in blue letters; Doleful's own place was

immediately after this, but of course during the progress to Handley Cross, he kept along-side the carriage of the distinguished strangers. The flys, gigs, ponies, donkeys, chaises, &c., followed on in a long-drawn line, just as they could jostle in, for the Captain knew the high hedges on each side of the narrow road would do more towards keeping them in order than all the injunctions and remonstrances he could lay down or use.

Mrs. Jorrocks was delighted!—Never before did she think anything either of hunting or her husband, but now the former seemed a most delightful amusement, and Jorrocks appeared a perfect hero. He too was charmed with his reception, and grinned and nudged Belinda with his elbow, and cast a sly wink over his shoulder at Betsey, as they jumbled along the road, and the compliments of the crowd came showering among them. Then he turned his eyes up to heaven as if lost in reflection and bewilderment at the honour he had arrived at. Anon he caught the point of his whip and dropped it scientifically along Arter-Xerxes' side, then he began to whistle, when Captain Doleful having resigned the side of the carriage on which Mrs. Jorrocks was sitting to Captain Parkins, came round to say a few nothings to our worthy friend.

"Well, Miserrimus," said Jorrocks, opening the conversation as though he had known him all his life, "you see I'm down upon you as the extinguisher said to the rushlight—always say you carn't be too quick in catchin' a flea.—'Ow's the Nabob?'"

"Middling, thank you," again replied the Captain,—"*you're* looking uncommonly well I'm sure," said he, eyeing Mr. Jorrocks as he spoke.

"Oh *me*!" replied Jorrocks, "bless you I'm never bad—never cept I gets a drop too much, as will happen in the best reglated families, you know, Miserrimus." Whereupon Mr. Jorrocks, with a knowing grin, gave Doleful a dig in the ribs with the butt-end of his whip—saying, "have you got any of that 'cold roast' you told me of in your letter?"

"Why no, Mr. Jorrocks, it's all gone, but there's plenty more in Handley Cross. It's the best place for beef I know.—Indeed for every-thing."

"You'll be desperation fond of 'untin' I s'pose," observed Mr. Jorrocks, after a slight pause, flourishing his whip over his head, and giving a knowing look at Doleful's accoutrements.

"It's the only thing worth living for in my mind," replied Captain Doleful.

"By jingo! so say I," rejoined Mr. Jorrocks; "all time's lost that's not spent in 'untin'.—Give us your hand, Miserrimus, my *bouy*, for you must be a trump—a man after my own 'eart!" and thereupon Jorrocks gave him such a shaking as nearly sent him off his horse.

"That'll be your kiver 'ack I presume," observed Mr. Jorrocks after their hands were released, as he cast an eye at the white. "He goes hup and down like a yard and a 'alf of pump water."

Doleful did not know whether this was meant as a compliment or other-wise, so he "grinned horridly a ghastly smile," and asked Mr. Jorrocks if he was fond of music. "Music!" said Mr. Jorrocks, "*yes*, the music of the 'ounds—none o' your tamboureenin' work. Give me the real *ough, ough, ough,* of a fine deep-toned 'ound in the depths of a rocky dell, as he drags up to old Reynard among the brush-wood," and as he spoke,

Mr. Jorrocks snuffed the air and threw his head about as though he were feeling for a scent himself,—" What sort of fencin' have you ?"

"Fencing!" repeated Captain Doleful thoughtfully—"fencing, why we've had none, I think, since the theatre closed."

"*Humph!*" mused Mr. Jorrocks, "that's queer—never knew a play-actor in my life with the slightest turn for 'untin'."

The foremost in the procession having now reached the outskirts of the town, a halt was made to allow the pedestrians to knock the dust off their shoes, and get their voices ready for shouting. Doleful rode along the line exhorting them to order and regularity, and directing the streets through which the procession should pass, taking particular care to keep wide of the Barningtons. A considerable accession was here made to their strength by numerous groups of ladies and gentlemen, who, attracted by the fineness of the day, and a little natural curiosity, had wandered out to see what sort of an animal a Cockney master of hounds was. Miss Prim and Miss Prosey's seminaries too turned out in their pink and blue ginghams, and came up just at the period of the halt,—all the grooms and helpers of the town who could not get to the station now flocked to swell the throng. The hubbub and confusion was excessive, and they pushed and elbowed, and fought to get near the carriage to have a close view of Mr. Jorrocks. "My eyes but he's a fat un!" exclaimed Mr. Brisket, the butcher, to his foreman, "it would be a downright credit to a butcher to supply such a gent.: can't be less nor three inches o' fat on his rib;" whereupon he thrust a card into Mr. Jorrocks's hand, containing his name, trade, and place of abode. This was a signal for the rest, and immediately a shoal of cards were tendered from persons of all callings and professions. Lucy Sandey would mangle, wash, and clear-starch; then Hannah Pye kept the best potatoes and green-groceries in general; Tom Hardy supplied milk at all hours; George Dodd let donkeys by the day or hour; Samuel Mason offered the card of the Bramber livery stables, where there was a lock-up coach-house; Susan Muddle hoped the ladies would drink with her at the Spa at a shilling a week, and glass found. Then there was a wine-merchant's card, followed by lodging-house keepers' without end, and a chimney-sweep's.

All in advance being now ready, Captain Doleful came grinning and capering through the crowd, and announced to the ladies that they were about to enter the town, and informed Mr. Jorrocks that they would first of all proceed to the Dragon Hotel, from the balcony of which it would have a good effect if he would address the meeting. Without waiting for Mr. Jorrocks's assurance that he "didn't know what to say," he placed himself in advance of Benjamin, and raised his hunting-whip as a signal to the musicians, who immediately struck up "See the conquering hero comes," and the cavalcade proceeded. The boom of the drums, the twang of the horns, and the shouts of the children, brought every human being to the doors, windows, and verandahs, and there was such running, and rushing, and fighting to see the conquering hero, and such laughing among the servant-maids at the ample dimensions of his shoulders, with as many observations upon his retinue, as would fill a chapter of themselves.

After passing the long line of villas that stud the road in the Mount

Sion direction, the cavalcade turned into Arthur Street, where the noise and bustle increased tenfold. Shop-lads, no longer to be restrained, rushed out in defiance of their masters' holloas, some hastily putting up the shutters, others leaving the shops to take care of themselves. Bazaars, fancy shops, jewellers', &c., were drawn of both buyers and sellers; and as the "Floreat Scientia" banner rounded the turn into High Street, an advancing mob from the other end of the town charged with such vigour as sent both poles through Stevenson the hatter's window, damaging a dozen pasteboard boxes, being the principal part of his stock-in-trade. Nothing was heard above the clamour but the boom of the drums, and the occasional twang of a horn, while Captain Doleful's red coat, and his horse's bowing white head, seemed borne upon the shoulders of the multitude. Thus they proceeded in stately array down High Street, and neared the Dragon Hotel.

At length they got the carriage up to the arched door, and the party alighted amid a tremendous burst of applause. Captain Doleful having tendered his arm to Mrs. Jorrocks, Belinda took her uncle's, and no sooner did Betsey get out of the back seat of the carriage than a whole host of little dirty boys scrambled in to obtain a better view, making desperate havoc among the Dundee marmalade, and Copenhagen cherry-brandy, to the infinite indignation of Benjamin, who roared lustily from the leader that he would "oss-vip 'em" all round.

CHAPTER XI.

THE ORATIONS.

SNUBBINS, the landlord, having ushered his distinguished guests into the balconied apartment of the first-floor front, Captain Doleful took a hasty review of his person at the looking-glass, placing his straggling hairs in the most conspicuous manner over his forehead, and, loosening his oil-skin-covered hat from his scarlet coat, he advanced with out-squared toes and elbows to present himself to the notice of the meeting.

His appearance in the balcony was the signal for a universal roar, amid which, the drums and wind instruments did their duty. After bowing and grimacing most condescendingly to the meeting below, silence was at length obtained, and he proceeded to address them as follows :—

"Ladies and gentlemen,—*ladies* and gentlemen," he repeated, laying the emphasis on the word *ladies*, and grinning like an elderly ape on all around, "encouraged by your smiles, by your applause, for, without you, as the poet Campbell'beautifully inquires, 'What is man?—a world without a sun,' I present myself to your notice to perform an act that I verily and conscientiously believe will prove most conducive to the interest, the happiness, and general welfare of this thriving and important town." Here the Captain placed his forefinger on his lip, and, according to previous arrangement with the drummers, they rumbled with their drums, and the children gave some loud huzzas, in conjunction with such of the

mob as were troubled with a turn for shouting. " Ladies and gentlemen,'
he resumed, " I stand not here for the gratification of the paltry personal
vanity of addressing this distinguished assembly, but I present myself to
your notice, in discharge of the high, the onerous, the honourable and all-
important office of Master of the Ceremonies of this renowned Spa, to
introduce to your notice the most distinguished, the most determined, the
most popular, and the most scientific sportsman England, or any other
country, ever saw (loud cheers). Need I say, gentlemen, that this
illustrious individual is the great and renowned Mr. Jorrocks—a name
familiar to our ears as Mr. Dickens's household words—so familiar that it
is even chalked on the walls of our town; and it is indeed a high—a
flattering circumstance to my mind, that I—even I—the humble individual who now stands before you, should have been the means of procuring
for a town that I love so ardently, a man of such unequalled excellence
and such distinguished worth."

Here Doleful being rather blown, put his finger to his lip again, upon
which the drums rumbled, the horns twanged, and a round of applause
was brewed up. He resumed,—" Gentlemen, the temporary cloud that
obscured the brightness of our delightful town has passed away ! another
and a brighter sun has risen, beneath whose fostering rays, prosperity—
bright, unequalled prosperity—shall renovate our homes, and draw forth
blessings from your grateful hearts (cheers). This, gentlemen, is a thought
that repays me for a world of trouble, and believe me that in all the
changes and chances of this eventful life, amid all the frowns of life's
vicissitudes, the bright recollection of this hour will furnish consolation
that a thousand woes will not outweigh (great applause). Let me not,
however, ladies and gentlemen, dwell too long on the part I have happily,
but unworthily played in this transaction. Let me not stand between
that bright constellation of sporting knowledge and the indulgence of your
laudable curiosity. Rather let me withdraw, with a bosom o'erflowing
with heart-felt gratitude for the honours your kindness has heaped upon
me, and introduce to your notice our great and illustrious stranger."
Here Doleful squared out his elbows and bowed most humbly and condescendingly, first to the front, then to the cast and west, and, courtier-
like, backed from the balcony into the room, amid loud and long-continued
cheers.

While he was delivering himself of all this eloquence, Mrs. Jorrocks
was busy inside the room preparing her husband for presentation to the
meeting. Having made him take off his versatio coat, she brushed his
blue under one over, rubbed the velvet collar right, put his wig straight, and
wiped the dust off his Hessian boots with a corner of the table-cover.
Doleful came backing in, and nearly upset Jorrocks as he was standing on
one leg by the table, undergoing the latter operation. "Now, it's your
turn, Mr. Jorrocks," observed the Captain, on the former recovering his
equilibrium, and thereupon they joined hands and advanced into the
balcony, like the Siamese twins, amid the uproarious applause of the
meeting.

"'Ow are ye all?" said Mr. Jorrocks with the greatest familiarity,
nodding round to the meeting, and kissing his hand. "'Opes you are
well. Now my frind, Miserrimus, having spun you a yarn about who I

am, and all that sort of thing, I'll not run his foil, but get upon fresh
ground, and say a few words about how matters are to be managed.

"You see I've come down to 'unt your country, to be master of your
'ounds, in fact,—and first of all I'll explain to you what *I* means by the
word master.   Some people call a man a master of 'ounds wot sticks an
'orn in his saddle, and blows when he likes, but leaves every thing else to
the 'untsman.   That's not the sort of master of 'ounds I mean to be.
Others call a man a master of 'ounds wot puts in the paper Mr. So-and-
so's 'ounds meet on Monday, at the Loin o' Lamb ; on Wednesday, at
the Brisket o' Weal ; and on Saturday, at the Frying-pan ; and after that,
jest goes out or not, as suits his conwenience—but *that's* not the sort of

master of 'ounds I means to be. Again, some call themselves masters of
'ounds, when they pay the difference atwixt the subscription and the cost,
leaving the management of matters, the receipt of money, payment of
damage, and all them sort of partiklars, to the secretary. But that's not
the sort of master o' ounds I means to be. Still, I means to ride with an
'orn in my saddle. Yonder it is, see," said he, pointing to the package
behind the carriage, " a regler Percival, silver mouth-piece, deep cup'd—
and I means to adwertise the 'ounds in the paper, and not go sneakin'
about like some of them beggarly Cockney 'unts, wot look more as if they
were goin' to rob a hen-roost than 'unt a fox, but havin' fixed the meets,
I shall attend them most punctual and regler, and take off my cap to all
payin' subscribers as they come up (cheers). This, I thinks, will be the
best way of doin' business, for there are some men wot don't care a copper
for owin' the master money, so long as the matter rests atwixt themselves,
and yet who would not like to see me sittin' among my 'ounds with my
cap slouched over my eyes, takin' no more notice of them than if they
were as many pigs, as much as to say to all the gemmen round, ' these
are the nasty, dirty, seedy screws wot don't pay their subscriptions.'

" In short, I means to be an M. F. H. in reality, and not in name.
When I sees young chaps careering o'er the country without lookin' at the
'ounds, and in all humane probability not knowin' or carin' a copper
where they are, and I cries, '*old 'ard!*' I shall expect to see them pull
up, and not wait till the next fence fatches them too."

Here Mr. Jorrocks made a considerable pause, whereupon the cheering
and drumming was renewed, and as it died away, he went on as
follows :—

"Of all sitivations under the sun, none is more enviable or more
'onerable than that of a master of fox 'ounds ! Talk of a M.P.! vot's an
M.P. compared to an M. F. H. ? Your M.P. lives in a tainted hatmo-
sphere among other M.P.'s and loses his consequence by the commonness
of the office, and the scoldings he gets from those who sent him there,
but an M. F. H. holds his levee in the stable, his levee in the kennel, and
his levee in the 'untin' field—is great and important every where—has
no one to compete with him, no one to find fault, but all join in doing
honour to him to whom honour is so greatly due (cheers). And oh,
John Jorrocks ! my good frind," continued the worthy grocer, fumbling
the silver in his small clothes with upturned eyes to heaven, " to think
that you, after all the hups and downs of life—the crossin's and jostlin's
of merchandise and ungovernable trade—the sortin' of sugars—the
mexin' of teas—the postin' of ledgers, and handlin' of inwoices, to think
that you, my dear feller, should have arrived at this distinguished post,
is most miraculously wonderful, most singularly queer. Gentlemen, *this*
is the proudest moment of my life ! (cheers). I've now reached the top-
rail in the ladder of my hambition ! (renewed cheers). Binjimin ! " he
holloaed out to the boy below, " Binjimin ! I say, give an eye to them
ere harticles behind the chay—the children are all among the Copenhagen
brandy and Dundee marmeylad ! Vy don't you vollop them ? Vere's the
use of furnishing you with a whip, I wonder ? "

"To resume," said he, after he had seen the back of the carriage cleared
of the children, and the marmalade and things put straight. "'Untin',

as I have often said, is the sport of kings—the image of war without its guilt, and only five-and-twenty per cent. of its danger. To me the clink of the couples from a vipper-in's saddle is more musical than any notes that ever came out of Greasey's mouth (cheers). I dosen't wish to disparage the walue of no man, but this I may say, that no Nabob that ever was foaled, loves 'untin' better than me (cheers). It's the werry breath of my body! The liver and bacon of my existence! I dosen't know what the crazeyologists may say, but this I believes that my 'ead is nothin' but one great bump of 'untin' (cheers). 'Untin' fills my thoughts by day, and many a good run I have in my sleep. Many a dig in the ribs I gives Mrs. J. when I think they're runnin' into the warmint (renewed cheers). No man is fit to be called a sportsman wot doesn't kick his wife out of bed on a haverage once in three weeks! (applause, mingled with roars of laughter). I'm none of your fine, dandified Rotten-row swells, that only ride out to ride 'ome again, but I loves the smell of the mornin' hair, and the werry mud on my tops when I comes home of an evenin' is dear to my 'eart (cheers). Oh, my frinds! if I could but go to the kennel now, get out the 'ounds, find my fox, have a good chivey, and *kill* him, for no day is good to me without blood, I'd—I'd—I'd—drink three pints of port after dinner 'stead of two! (loud cheers). That's the way to show Diana your gratitude for favours past, and secure a continuance of her custom in future (cheers). But *that* we will soon do, for if you've—

> "'Osses sound, and dogs 'ealthy,
> Earths well-stopped, and foxes plenty,'

no longer shall a master be wantin' to lead you to glory (loud cheers). I'll not only show you how to do the trick in the field, but a scientific course o' lectors shall train the young idea in the art at 'ome. I've no doubt we shall all get on capitally—fox 'unters are famous fellows—tell me a man's a fox-hunter, and I loves him at once. We'll soon get quainted, and then you'll say that John Jorrocks is the man for your money. At present I've done—hoping werry soon to meet you all in the field—I now says adieu."

Hereupon Mr. Jorrocks bowed, and kissing his hand, backed out of the balcony, leaving his auditory to talk him over at their leisure.

CHAPTER XII.

CAPTAIN DOLEFUL AGAIN.

HEN Mr. Jorrocks backed from the balcony into the "Moon," after delivering the luminous address reported in our last chapter, Captain Doleful looked at his watch and found it wanted but ten minutes to the time he was to appear at the board of her imperial majesty, Mrs. Barnington; so ringing for Mr. Snubbins, the landlord, he hastily consigned the party to his protection, and, quitting the room, ran through the town like a lamplighter, to re-arrange his toilette at his lodgings. Off went the old militia coat, the white moleskins and Hessians made way with pantomimic quickness for a black coat and trousers, which with a shrivelled white waistcoat, and a pair of broad-stringed pumps, completed the revised edition of the *arbiter elegantiarum* of Handley Cross Spa. The crowded incidents of the hour left no time for reflection, and fortunate, perhaps, it was for the Captain, that he had no time to consider of what had taken place, or even his creative genius might have discovered some little difficulty in reconciling the discrepancies that existed between his professions and performances. So quick, however, were his movements, and the transition of events, that John Trot, the under butler, who was one of the audience before the Dragon, had not time to detail the doings of the day to Mr. Mountford, the butler, to tell Mrs. Stumps, the housekeeper, for the information of Bandoline, to carry in broken English to her mistress, ere Captain Doleful's half resolute tap of a knock announced his arrival at the door.

"Why here's old Wo-begone himself, I do believe!" exclaimed John, breaking off in his narrative at the intrusion of the flag-poles into Stevenson the hatter's window. "It is, indeed," added he, casting his eye up the area-grating at the Captain, as he stood above; "I declare he has pealed off his uniform and come like a Christian. Dirty dog, he can't have washed himself, for I saw him bolt out of the Dragon not three minutes afore I left, and I only looked in at the Phœnix and Flower-pot, and took one glass of hot elder wine, and came straight home;" saying which, John, in the absence of Sam, the footman, settled himself leisurely into his coatee, and proceeded to let the Captain into the house.

"The dog's come to dine," said John, on his return, "and precious hungry he is, I dare say, for he don't allow himself above two feeds a week they say. However, I gave him a bit of consolation, by telling him that missis had laid down at four o'clock, with orders not to be disturbed, and therefore it might be eight or nine o'clock before they dined; but 'Sir,' says I, 'there's the Morning Post,' so I left him to *eat* that, and precious savage he looked. Now, I declare on the honour of a gentleman, of all the shabby screws I ever came thwart of in the whole of my professional career, that Doleful is the dirtiest and meanest. T'other night it was raining perfect wash-hand-stand basins full, and after sitting master out to bed, and missis until she began to yawn, he mustered courage to do the expensive, and asked me to fetch him a fly. Well, never had I seen the colour of his coin, often and often as he has darkened our door, and come with his nasty jointed clogs, dirty cloaks, and wet numbrellas; but thinks I to myself, this surely will be catching time, and it 'ill all come in a heap in the shape of a golden sovereign pound cake; so out I splashed, silks and all, the first day on, too, and brought up Sam Fletcher's yellow with the grey; skipped up-stairs, told him all was ready, handed him his hat, upon which I saw him fumbling in his upper pocket; he stepped into the fly, and just as I closed the door, slipped something into my hand—felt small—half sov., better than nothing, thought I—'thank you, sir, Miss Jelly's,' cried I to Master Sam, off he went, in comes I, looks in my hand—hang me, if it wer'n't a *Joey!*"

"That beats everything!" exclaimed Mr. Mountford, the butler, laying down a handful of spoons he had been counting over; "why do you know he gave *me* one the very same day, and it lies on the entrance table now, to let him see how little we care for Joeys in our house."

"Who's that you're talking about?" inquired Mrs. Stumps, whose room being on the other side of the passage from the butler's pantry, enabled her to hold a dialogue without the trouble of moving herself across, she having been selected on account of her fatness and the volubility of her tongue.

"Only old Lamentable," replied Mr. Trot; "what do you think the fellow's done now?—complimented Mr. Mountford and myself with a Joey a-piece. Stop till I catch him with a decent coat on, and see if I don't dribble the soup or melted butter over it."

"Confound the mean dog," observed Mrs. Stumps, "he's the most miserable man that ever was seen. I do wonder that missis, with all her fine would-be-fashionable airs, countenances such a mean sneak. Master may be dull, and I dare say he is, but he's a prince compared to old Doleful."

"Master's *soft*," replied Mr. Mountford thoughtfully, "and he's *hard* too in some things, but there are many worse men than he. Besides, the wife's enough to drive him mad. *She's a terrible tartar.*"

"She's in one of her tantrums's to-day," observed Mrs. Stumps, "and has had Mademoiselle crying all the morning. She's tried on thirteen dresses already and none will please her. It will be eight o'clock very likely before they dine, and that reminds me she had two notes this morning by post—one was from Lady Gillyfield, and Sam thought he saw something about dining, and staying all night, as he took it up-stairs, so just you keep your ears open at dinner, and find out the day, as I want to have a few friends to cards and a quadrille the first time the family go from home."

"Oh, I dare say I can acquaint you all about it without waiting for dinner," observed Mr. Mountford. "Sam, just step into the clothes-room, and feel in B's brown frock-coat that he had on this morning, and bring me his letters." Sam obeyed, and speedily returned with three. Mr. Mountford took them, and casting an adhesiv'd one aside, as either a "bill or a begging letter," opened a fine glazed note with blue edges, sealed with a transfixed heart on green wax:—"Monday, at ten, at the Apollo Belvidere," was all it contained, and winking at Sam, who winked at John Trot, who passed the wink to Mrs. Stumps, Mr. Mountford refolded the note, and opened the one from Sir Gibeon Gillyfield, which contained a pressing invitation for the Friday following, to make one at a *battu* on the Saturday.

"You must find out whether they go or not," observed Mrs. Stumps; "they will be sure to say something about it at dinner, so mind be on the look-out. There's missis's bell! my stars, how she rings! wouldn't be near her for the world."—A perfect peal!

After Doleful had had a good spell at the Post, beginning with the heading and ending with the printer's name at the end, Mr. Barnington made his appearance from his room below, where he had been deceiving himself into the belief that he was reading, and saluted the M.C. in the way that a man generally takes his wife's friends when he does not like her. After exchanging a few nothings, he looked with an air of easy indifference round the room, then at the French clock on the mantel-piece, next at his watch to see that it was not wrong, and finally composed himself cross-legged into a low douro with massive cushions at the back and sides. Doleful resumed his seat on the sofa. Thus they sat for half an hour, listening to the tickings of the time-piece, looking alternately at each other and the door. Seven o'clock came and no Mrs. Barnington, then the quarter chimed in that concise sort of way, that almost says, "Oh, it's only the quarter!" the half hour followed with a fuller chorus and more substantial music, whereupon Barnington, who was beginning to be hungry, looked indignantly at his watch and the door, then at Doleful, but wisely said nothing. Doleful, who had only treated himself to a penny bun since breakfast, was well-nigh famished, and inwardly wished he had palmed himself off on the Jorrocks's; when just as the time-piece was chiming away at a quarter to eight, a page in a green and gold uniform threw open the door, and in sallied the majestic Mrs. Barnington in lavender-coloured satin. With a slight inclination of her head to the Captain, who was up like an arrow to receive her, and a look of contempt at her husband, she seated herself on an ottoman, and glancing at a diminutive watch in her armlet, and seeing it correspond with the time on the mantel-piece, without a word of apology for keeping them waiting, she hurried off the page to order dinner *instantly*.

CHAPTER XIII.

A FAMILY DINNER.

JUST as Mrs. Barnington was desiring Doleful to ring the bell to see why dinner was not ready, Mr. Mountford, with great state, and an air of the most profound respect, walked into the centre of the room, and announced that it was on the table, when, backing out, and leaving the page in charge of the door, he returned to the parlour to twist a napkin round his thumb, and place himself before the centre of the side-board to be ready to raise the silver cover from the soup tureen, and hand it to John Trot, to pass to Sam, to place on the tray the instant the party were seated. Mrs. Barnington, with an air of languid absence, mechanically placed her hand on Doleful's arm, and sailed down the thickly-carpeted staircase, past the footmen in the entrance, and dropt into a many-cushioned chair at the head of the table. Doleful seated himself at the side opposite the fire, and Barnington of course took his place at the foot of the table. Soup and a glass of sherry passed round amid the stares and anxious watchings of the servants, before anything like a conversation was commenced, for Barnington was not a man of many words at any time, and fear of his wife and dislike of Doleful now sealed his lips entirely. Several indifferent topics were tried during the fish, alternately by Mrs. Barnington and Doleful.—The weather—the Morning Post—the last elopement—somebody's band—the new French milliner, when, gathering up her napkin, and giving her head a toss in the air, she observed, in a careless easy sort of way, " By the by, Captain Doleful, I forgot to ask you if those Horrocks people arrived to-day ? "

" Oh yes, marm, they came," replied the Captain, with uneasiness on his brow, for he saw " Mountford and Co." were all eyes and ears to catch what he said.—" A little malt liquor, if you please. Do you get your malt of Dobbs ? " inquired he of Barnington, making a desperate effort to turn the conversation at the outset, the only chance of effecting it ; "if you don't," observed he, " there's a capital fellow come from Mortlake in Surrey, to establish an agency here for the sale of the same sort of beer the Queen drinks, and apropos of that, Mrs. Barnington, perhaps you are not aware that her Majesty is so truly patriotic as to indulge in the juice of the hop—takes it at luncheon, I understand, in a small silver cup, a present from the Prince, with the lion and the unicorn fighting for the crown, beautifully raised in dead gold upon it, made by Hunt and Roskill, who certainly have more taste in trinkets, and articles of *vertu* than all the rest of London put together,—but this beer is very good—clear—amber and hoppy," added he, drinking it off, hoping to drown old Jorrocks, wife, niece, and all, in the draught.

"Who is Horrocks, that you were asking about, my dear?" inquired Barnington of his wife, for the purpose of letting Doleful see he didn't consider him worth answering, and not from any motives of curiosity,—an infirmity from which he was perfectly free.

"Only some people the Captain and I were talking about this morning, my love, that were expected from London. They are *not* come, you say?" added she, turning to the Captain.

"Oh yes, marm, I said they *were* come. Allow me the honour of taking wine with you? Do you take champagne? Champagne to your mistress," looking at Mr. Mountford. Mountford helped them accordingly, giving the Captain as little as possible.

"Well, and what sort of people are they?" resumed Mrs. Barnington, setting down her glass, and looking at Doleful as much as to say, " come, no nonsense, out with it."

"Upon my word I can hardly give an opinion, for I saw so little of them; but I should say from what little I did see, that they are very respectable—that's to say (haw, ha, hem), people well to do in the world (hem). He seems an uncommonly good-natured old fellow—rattles and talks at a tremendous rate; but really I can hardly fairly give an opinion upon their other qualifications from the very little I saw."

"How many carriages had they?" inquired Mrs. Barnington.

"One, with a pair, but they came by the train; they will probably have more coming by the road."

"Many servants?"

"Not many, I think. Perhaps they are coming by the road too."

"What are the women like?"

"The old lady seems a monstrous good-natured, round-about, motherly sort of body, neither very genteel nor yet altogether vulgar—a fair average woman in fact—charitable, flannel-petticoat, soup-kitchen sort of woman. —This is capital mutton—never tasted better. By the way, Mr. Barnington, did you ever eat any Dartmoor mutton? it certainly is the best and sweetest in the world, and this is as like it as anything can possibly be."

"No," was all the answer Mr. Barnington vouchsafed our hero, who, bent on turning the conversation, and nothing disconcerted, immediately addressed himself to his hostess, with "Beautiful part of the country——fine scenery—should like to live there— people so unaffected and hospitable—ask you to dine and sleep—no puddling your way home through dirty lanes in dark nights. The view from Æther rocks on the edge of Dunmore, most magnificent—there's a fine one also on the road between Exeter and Tiverton—and near Honiton too—what food that country would afford your splendid pencil, Mrs. Barnington. I know no one so competent to do justice to the scenery as yourself," and thereupon the Captain puckered his face into one of his most insinuating grins. Mrs. Barnington went on eating her " *vole au vent*," inwardly resolving to know all about the Jorrocks's, without compromising one jot of her dignity.

The conversation then took a brisk and rapid range over many topics and to divers places—Bath, Cheltenham, Brighton, Tunbridge Wells, were all visited in succession, but at last Mrs. Barnington fairly landed the Captain back at Handley Cross. "I suppose we shall be having a ball here soon, sharn't we, Captain?" inquired she. "That depends upon Mrs. Barnington," replied the obsequious M. C. in the humblest tone. "If *you* are so disposed there's no doubt of our having one. *My* ball at present stands first on the list, and that will take place to-morrow fortnight."

"Oh, I forgot your ball entirely—true—oh dear, no! I shouldn't wish for one before that—it might interfere with yours. Of course you will send me five tickets."

The Captain bowed profoundly, for this as much as said there would be a five-pound note coming. "I hope you will have a good one," added she. "There will most probably be some new comers by that time to amuse one with their strange faces and queer ways.—I wonder if the Horrocks's will go?"

The idea at that moment flashed across the Captain's mind too, and a prophetic thought assuring him they would, he determined to grapple with the subject instead of fighting shy, and ventured boldly to predict they would, and once more essayed to smooth their passage to Mrs. Barnington's patronage.

"Oh, I have no earthly objection to them, I assure you, I *can* have none to people I never either saw or heard of. Of course, if they have letters of introduction I shall call upon them—if not, and you assure me, or rather *convince* me, of their respectability, I shall notice them the same as I do other people who come here as strangers."

"Very much obliged indeed," replied the Captain, feeling all the time that he was "thanking her for nothing."—"They are, I believe, highly respectable. She, I understand, is the daughter of a gentleman who was about the court of King George the Third. The young lady is very pretty, and Jorrocks himself really seems a very excellent old fellow."

"What, you are talking about Mr. Jorrocks, are you?" inquired Mr. Barnington, looking up from his "omelette" with an air of sudden enlightenment on his countenance.

"Why yes, Solomon!" replied his loving spouse, "who did you think we were talking about?"

"Why you called them Horrocks! how was I to know who you meant?"

"How were *you* to know who we meant? why what matter does it make whether *you* know or not? Take the cheese away, Mountford, and don't make this room smell like a beer-shop."

"Stay! I want some," interposed Mr. Barnington.

"Then take it into your master's room," replied Mrs. Barnington. "Go and stuff yourself there as much as you like; and send for your friend Horrocks, or Jorrocks, or whatever you call him to keep you company."

And after an evening of this agreeable dog and cat-ing, varied with occasional intercessions for the Jorrocks family, the gallant Captain at length made his adieus and retired to his confectioner's.

We will now see what our newly arrived friends are about.

CHAPTER XIV.

MR. JORROCKS AND HIS SECRETARY.

"SEND my Sec. here," said Mr. Jorrocks, with great dignity, to Snubbins, the landlord of the Dragon ; who, in compliance with Doleful's directions, was waiting to receive his orders. "Send my Sec. here," he repeated, seeing the man did not catch what he said.

"Your Sec., sir," repeated the landlord, "it'll be your boy, I presume?" turning to the waiter, and desiring him to send the ostler to stand by the horses' heads while Mr. Jorrocks's boy came up-stairs.

"No, not my *bouy*," replied Mr. Jorrocks with a frown, "so you *presumes* wrong."

"Your maid, then?" inquired the sharp waiter, thinking to hit what his master had missed.

"No, nor my maid neither," was the worthy grocer's answer,—"what I want is *my* Sec., the Secretary to *my* 'unt in fact."

"Oh! the Secretary to the hunt, that will be Mr. Fleeceall," rejoined the landlord with a grin of satisfaction.—"Run up to Lavender Lane, and tell Mr. Fleeceall that Mr. Jorrocks has arrived, and wishes to see him."

"Tell him to come *directly*," said Mr. Jorrocks, adding, in a mutter, "I dosen't understand why he's not here to receive me. Fatch me up a glass of cold sherry negus *with*. —Public speakin' makes one werry dry."

Before the *with* was well dissolved, so as to enable our hero to quench his thirst at a draught, our one-eyed friend entered the room, hat in hand, and presented himself to Mr. Jorrocks.

"Now I wants to see you about my 'ounds," said Mr. Jorrocks, with an air of authority.—"Where are they?"

"Some, I believe, are in the kennel, others are in the Vale with the various farmers," replied Mr. Fleeceall.

"Some in the Wale!" repeated Mr. Jorrocks with surprise, "vy arn't they all in kennel? you surely knew I was a comin', and ought not to have had things in this hugger-mugger state.—Whose fault is it? Where's the kennel-book?"

"The kennel-book?" repeated Mr. Fleeceall with surprise.

"Yes, the kennel-book, you know what that is surely—the list of the 'ounds in fact."

"Oh, I beg your pardon—I don't think there is any regular kennel-book—at least I never had one—all that *I* do, is to receive the subscriptions,—write to gentlemen that are in arrear, or are likely to subscribe,—tax poultry bills,—and prevent extortion in general."

"Well, all werry useful in its way," replied Mr. Jorrocks, "but a secretary to an 'unt is expected to know all about the 'ounds too, and everything besides—at least he's no Sec. for *me* if he don't," added he, his eyes sparkling with animation as he spoke.

"Oh, I do," replied Mr. Fleeceall with trepidation, "only Captain
Doleful has had all our people so busy, preparing for your reception, that
we really have not been able at so short a notice to make our arrangements
so perfect as we could wish.   I know all the hounds *well*."

"SEND MY SEC. HERE."

"Then put on your 'at and come with me to the kennel.   It's full
moon to-night, so we needn't mind about time."

Fleeceall hesitated, but seeing Mr. Jorrocks was resolute, he put a
good face on the matter, and boldly led the way.   As he piloted
Mr. Jorrocks through sundry short cuts, he contrived to insinuate, in a
casual sort of way, that things would not be in such apple-pie order as
he might expect, but that a day or two would put everything right.
Calling at Mat Maltby's for the key of the kennel, he enlisted young

Mat into the service, desiring him to stand by and prompt him what to say; he very soon had the new master before the rails of the kennel. The hounds raised a melodious cry as they jumped against the paling, or placed themselves before the door, and anger flew from Mr. Jorrocks's mind at the cheerful sound. "Get *back*, hounds! get *back*! *Bonney-bell*, have a care!" cried Mat, as they pushed against the door, and prevented its opening. "Perhaps you'll take a switch, sir," said he, turning to Mr. Jorrocks, and handing a hazel-rod from a line hanging on the rails beside the door. "Get *back*, hounds!" again he cried, and inserting his right hand with a heavy double-thonged whip through an aperture between the door and the post, he loosened the thong, and sweeping it round among their legs, very soon cleared a space so as to enable the master to enter. Mr. Jorrocks then strutted in.

The kennel was quite of the primitive order, but dry and airy withal. It consisted of two rooms, while the feeding-troughs in the half-flagged yard showed that the hounds dined out of doors. A temporary boiling-house was placed behind, and the whole of the back part adjoined close upon the New Ebenezer Chapel.

Great was Mr. Jorrocks's surprise and indignation at finding that the pack was without a huntsman, whipper-in, or horses.

He was perfectly thunderstruck, and it was some time ere his rage suffered his tongue to give vent to his thoughts.

MR. JORROCKS THINKS HE WILL SHOOT DOLEFUL.

It was a "reg'lar do," and he'd "wesh his 'ands of the concern at once." He'd "shoot Doleful first though—skin him alive in fact."

Fleeccall attempted to soothe him, but finding he was only adding fuel to the fire, he suffered his anger to exhaust itself on the unfortunate and now luckily absent Captain. Mr. Jorrocks was very wroth, but considering how far he had gone, and how he would be laughed at if he backed out, he determined to let it be "over shoes over boots," so he stuck out his legs and proceeded to examine the hounds.

"Plenty of bone," observed he, with a growl.

"Oh, lots of bones!" replied Fleeceall, "that corner's full," pointing to the bone-house.

"Are they steady?" inquired Mr. Jorrocks.

"Middling," replied Fleeceall, anxious to be safe.

"Vot, they're not riotous are they? Never 'unted bagmen or nothin' of that sort?" inquired our master.

"Oh dear no," replied Fleeceall, "ran a boy, I believe, one day."

"Ran a boy!" exclaimed Mr. Jorrocks, "never heard of sich a thing! He must have had a drag."

"They bit his drag," replied Fleeceall, laughing.

"It were a young hound bit an old 'ooman," interposed Mat, anxious for the credit of the pack, "he had a bone, and she would have it from him, and the boy got atween the two."

"*Humph!*" grunted Mr. Jorrocks, not altogether relishing the story whichever way it was. The hounds were a fine lashing-looking lot, chiefly dogs, with a strong family likeness running through the pack. There were few old ones, and the lot were fairly average. Worse packs are to be found in great kennels. Mr. Jorrocks remained with them until he had about mastered their names, and there appearing no help for the matter, he resolved to do the best he could with his boy until he could meet with a huntsman.—Ordering the feeder to be there by day-break, and have the hounds ready for him to take out to exercise, he thrust his arm through Fleeceall's, and desired him to conduct him back to the Dragon.

As they went he lectured him well on the duties of his office. "Now, you see, sir," said he, "I doesn't want one of your fine auditin' sort of Secs., what will merely run his eye over the bills, and write his initials on the back, right or wrong, as many do, but I wants a real out-and-out workin' chap, that will go into them hitem by hitem, and look sharp ater the pence, without leavin' the pounds to take care of themselves. A good Sec. is a werry useful sort of h'animal, but a bad un's only worth 'anging. In the first place you must be werry particklar about gettin' in the subscriptions. That is always uppermost in a good Sec's mind, and he should never stir out of doors without a list in his pocket, and should appear at the coverside with a handful of receipts, by way of a hint to wot hav'nt paid. Now, you must get an account book with ruled columns for pounds, shillings, and pence, and open a Dr. and Cr. account with every man Jack on 'em. You can't do better nor follow the example o' the Leamington lads who string up all the tradespeople with the amount of their subscriptions in the shops and public places. Its clearly the duty of every man to subscribe to a pack of 'ounds—even if he has to borrow the money. 'No tick,' mind, must be the order of the day, and every Saturday night you must come to me with your book, and I shall allow you two glasses of spirit and water whilst we overhaul the accounts. You must be all alive in fact. Not an 'oss must die in the district without your knowin' of it—you must 'ave the nose of a wultur, with the knowledge of a knacker. Should you make an 'appy 'it (hit) and get one with some *go* in him, I'll let you use him yourself until we wants him for the boiler. In the field, a good Sec. ought always to be ready to leap first over any awkward place, or catch the M.F.H.'s 'oss, if he 'appens to lead over. In all things he must consider the M.F.H. first, and never let self stand in the way. Then you'll be a good Sec., and when I dosn't want a Sec. no longer, why you'll always be able to get a good Sec.'s place from the character I shall give you.

"Now, here we are at the Dragon again.—Come up stairs and I'll make you acquainted with your missis," saying which, Mr. Jorrocks led the way, and was met on the landing by the knock-knee'd, greasy-collared waiter, who ushered them into the room, where Mrs. Jorrocks and Belinda, fatigued with the doings of the day, had laid themselves down on a couple of sofas, waiting for the return of Mr. Jorrocks to have their tea.

"This be my Sec.," said Mr. Jorrocks to his spouse, with the air of a man introducing a party for whom there is no occasion to put oneself out of the way. Mrs. Jorrocks, who had bolted up at the opening of the door, gave a sort of half bow, and rubbing her eyes and yawning, very quietly settled herself again on the sofa. Tea passed away, when the ladies having retired, Mr. Jorrocks and Fleeceall very soon found out that they had a taste in common, viz.—a love of brandy and water, wherewith they sat diluting themselves until the little hours of the morning, in the course of which carouse, Fleeceall dexterously managed to possess himself of every particle of his worthy patron's history and affairs. How much he had in the funds, how much in Exchequer bills, how much in railways, and how much in the Globe Insurance Office.

A page or two from Mr. Jorrocks's Journal, which he has kindly placed at our disposal, will perhaps best elucidate the doings of the early days of his reign over the Handley Cross fox-hounds.

"*Saturday.*—Awoke with desperation 'ead ach—Dragon brandy car'nt be good—Dreamed the Lily-vite-sand train had run off with me, and chucked me into the channel—Called to Binjimin—the boy snorin' sound asleep!—only think, snorin' *sound asleep*, the werry mornin' after comin' down to whip into a pack of fox-'ounds—fear he has no turn for the chase. Pulled his ears, and axed him what he was snorin' for. Swore he wasn't snorin'!—Never heard a boy of his size tell such a lie in my life. Rigged for 'unting, only putting on my hat 'stead of my cap,—and on 'orseback by daylight—Xerxes full of fun—Arterxerxes dullish—Bin. rode the latter, in his new tops and spurs—' Now,' said I to Bin. as we rode to the kennel, 'you are hentering upon a most momentous crisis—If you apply yourself diligently and assiduously to your callin', and learn to be useful in kennel, and to cheer the 'ounds with a full melodious woice —such a woice, in fact, as the tall lobster-merchant with the green plush breeches and big calves, that comes along our street of a still

evenin', with his basket on his 'ead, cryin' 'LOB-*sters!* fine LOB-*sters!*'
has, there is no sayin' but in course of time you may arrive at the
distinguished 'onour of readin' an account of your doin's in ' Bell's Life '
or the ' Field ;' but if you persist in playin' at marbles, chuck farthin',
and flyin' kites, 'stead of attendin' in the stable, I'll send you back to the
charity school from whence you came, where you'll be rubbed down twice
a day with an oak towel, and kept on chick-weed and grunsell like a
canary bird,—mark my words if I von't.'

"Found Mat Maltby at the kennel weshin' the flags with a new broom,
and 'issing for 'ard life—werry curious it is, wet or dry, soft or 'ard,
these chaps always 'iss. 'Ounds all delighted to see me—stood up in my
stirrups looking over the rails, 'olloain', cheerin', and talkin' to them.
Yoicks Dexterous! Yoicks Luckey-lass! Yoicks Rallywood! Good dog.
Threw bits of biscuit as near each of them as I could pitch them, calling
the 'ounds by name, to let them see that I knew them—Some caught it
in their mouths like Hindian jugglers—' Let 'em out Mat,' at last cried
I, when back went the bolt, open went the door, and out they rushed
full cry, like a pent up 'urricane, tearin' down Hexworthy Street into
Jireth Place, through Mornington Crescent, by the Bramber Promenade
into the High Street, and down it with a crash and melody of sweet
music that roused all the old water-drinkin' maids from their pillows,
galvanised the watchmen, astonished the gas-light man, who was making
way for daylight, and reg'larly rousing the whole inhabitants of the
place.

" Clapt spurs to Xerxes and arter them, holloain' and crackin' my whip,
but deuce a bit did they 'eed me—On they went! sterns up and 'eads
too, towlin', and howlin', and chirpin',' as though they had a fox afore
them. Butchers' dogs, curs, setters, mastiffs, mongrels of all sorts and
sizes, flew out as they went, some joinin' cry, others worryin' and fightin'
their way, but still the body of the pack kept movin' onward at a splittin'
pace, down the London-road, as wild as hawks, without turning to the
right or the left, until they all flew, like a flock of pigeons, clean out of
sight. ' Oh, dear! oh, dear!' cried I, pullin' up, fairly exhausted, at the
third mile stone, by the cross-roads from Cadger's House and Knowlton,
' I've lost my 'ounds, and I'm ruined for ever.' ' Blow your 'orn!' cried
a countryman who was sittin' on the stone, ' they are not far afore you,
and the dogs not far afore them : ' but blow me tight, I was so blown
myself, that I couldn't raise a puff—easier to blow one's 'orse than one's
'orn. To add to my grief and infinite mortification, Binjimin came
poundin' and clatterin' along the hard road, holloain' out as he went,
' Buy LOB-*ster-r!* fine LOB-*ster-r-r!*'

" The pack had turned down Greenford Lane, and I jogged after them,
sorely puzzled, and desperate perplexed. On I went for a mile or more,
when the easterly breeze bore the 'ounds' cry on its wings, and pushin'
forward, I came to a corner of the road, where the beauties had thrown up
short before an Italian plaster of Paris poll-parrot merchant, who, tray on
head, had the whole pack at bay around him, bellowin' and howlin' as
though they would eat him. ' Get round them, Binjimin,' cried I, ' and
flog them away to me.' and takin' out my 'orn, I blew for 'ard life, and

what with view holloas, and cheerin', and coaxin', with Bin at their sterns,
succeeded in gettin' most of them back to their kennel.   Plaster of Paris
poll-parrot merchant followed all the way, indulgin' in frightful faces and
an unknown tongue."

The Journal then branches off into a mem. of what he did at breakfast
in the eating line, how he paid his bill at the Dragon, after disputing the
brandy items, adding that though attendance was charged in the bill, the
servants all evinced a disposition to shake hands with him at parting,
which he thought was making matters worse instead of better.   He also
recorded how he moved to Diana Lodge, which he did not find quite so
commodious as he expected.   The day's entry closes with a mem. that he
had stewed beef-steaks for dinner.

"*Sunday.*—Up by cock-crow, and into the kennel. Dexterous and Mercury been fightin' about a bone, and Mercury got a bloody ear. Lector'd Bin and Mat upon the unpropriety of leavin' bones about. Made Bin. call over the 'ounds by name, double-thongin' him when he made a mistake.

"Mrs. Jorrocks in a desperation fidget to get to church. Never know'd her so keen afore. Secret out—got a new gown, and a bonnet like a market gardener's flower basket. With all her keenness contrived to start just as the bells gave over ringin'—Beadle, in blue and gold, with a cocked 'at on his head, and a white wand in his hand, received us at the door, and handed us over to the sexton, in deep blue, bound with black velvet, who paraded us up the 'isle, and placed us with much clatterin' in the seat of honour just afore the pulpit. Church desperate full, and every eye turned on the M. F. H.—Mrs. J. thought they were lookin' at her! poor deluded body. Belinda, dressed in lavender, and lookin' werry wholesome. Lessons long—sermon excellent—all about 'onering one's superiors, meaning the M. F. H. doubtless.

"After church, friend Miserrimus came and shook 'ands with us all round. Gave him ' unbounded pleasure' to see us all so bloomin' and well. Mrs. J. delighted, and axed him to dine. Five, and no waitin'. Walked down High Street. Mrs. Jorrocks on one arm, Belinda on t'other. Doleful in the gutter. Fine thing to be a great man. Every body stared—many took off their 'ats.—Country people got off the flags. ' That's Mr. Jorrocks,' said one. ' Which?' cried another. ' Do show him to me,' begged a third. ' Jorrocks for ever!' cried the children. Nothing like being a great man. Kennel at two—feedin'-time—plaster of Paris poll-parrot merchant outside, still in a great rage, but didn't catch what he said. Many people came and wondered how I knew the names of the 'ounds—all so much alike, they said, Take them a lifetime to know them. Miserable ignoramusses.

"*Monday.*—At the kennel by daylight. Binjimin, as usual, to be kicked awake. The bouy seems to take no interest in the thing. Fear all the lickin' in the world von't drive a passion for the chase into him. Threatened to cut his coat into ribbons on his back, if he didn't look lively. Mat Maltby recommended the 'ounds to be coupled this time—condescended to take his advice. Told Bin. not to cry ' boil'd Lob-*sters*' as he did on Saturday, but to sing out in a cheerful woice, rich and melodious, *like* the boiled-lobster merchant. Axed what to sing out? Why, ' get on 'ounds, ven 'ounds 'ang (hang) back, and ' gently there !' when they gets too far forward, said I. Put Xerxes's head towards kennel door this time, instead of from it. Worth a golden sovereign of any man's money to see 'ounds turn out of kennel. Sich a cry! sich music ! old Dexterous jumped up at Xerxes, and the h'animal all but kicked me over his 'ead. Pack gathered round me, some jumpin' up against the 'oss's side, others standin' bayin', and some lookin' anxiously in my face, as much as to say, which way this time, Mr. Jorrocks? Took them a good long strong trot to the pike, near Smarden, and round by Billing-brook, letting them see the deer in Chidfold Park. Quite steady—make no doubt they will be a werry superior pack in less than no time—make them as handey as ladies' maids,—do everything but pay their own pikes in fact. Wonder Doleful don't ride out. Keen sportsman like him, one would think would like to see the 'ounds."

The Journal proceeds in this strain for two or three days more, Mr. Jorrocks becoming better satisfied with his pack each time he had them out. On the Friday, he determined on having a bye-day on the following one, for which purpose, he ordered his secretary to be in attendance, to show him a likely find in a country where he would not disturb many covers. Of course the meet was to be kept strictly private, and of course, like all " strict secrets," Fleeceall took care to tell it to half the place, Still, as it was a " peep-of-day affair," publicity did not make much matter, inasmuch as few of the Handley Cross gentry loved hunting better than their beds.

Fleeceall's situation was rather one of difficulty, for he had never been out hunting but once, and that once was in a gig, as related in a preceding chapter ; but knowing, as Dr. Johnson said, that there are " two sorts of information, one that a man carries in his head, and the other that he knows where to get ; " nothing daunted by the mandate, he repaired to Mat Maltby, the elder, a cunning old poacher, who knew every cover in the county, upon whose recommendation, it was arranged that a bag-fox, then in the possession of a neighbour, should be shook in South Grove, a long slip of old oak, with an excellent bottom for holding a fox. All things being thus arranged, as Mr. Jorrocks conceived, with the greatest secresy, he went to bed early, and long before it was light, he lay tumbling and tossing about, listening to the ticking of the clock below, and the snoring of Benjamin above.

At last day began to dawn, and having sought Ben's room and soused the boy with a pitcher of cold water, Mr. Jorrocks proceeded to jump into his hunting clothes, consisting of a roomy scarlet coat, with opossum pockets and spoon cuffs, drab shags, and mahogany-coloured tops. Arrived at the kennel, he found Fleeceall there, on his old gig mare, with his hands stuck in the pockets of a dirty old mackintosh, which completely enveloped his person. " Is Miserrimus 'ere ? " inquired Mr. Jorrocks, all fuss and flurry on discovering the person of his Secretary. " Well, carn't wait—sorry for it—know better another time ; " and thereupon he ordered out the horses, gave Ben a leg upon to Xerxes, mounted Arterxerxes himself, the hounds were unkennelled with a melodious rush, and desiring Fleeceall to lead the way, Mr. Jorrocks got the glad pack about him, and went away for South Grove, with a broad grin of satisfaction on his jolly face.

The day seemed auspicious, and there was a balmy freshness in the air that promised well for scent. Added to this, Mr. Jorrocks had cut the left side of his chin in shaving, which he always considered ominous of sport.—Bump, bump, jolt, jolt, jog, jog, he went on his lumbering hunter, now craneing over its neck to try if he could see its knees, now cheering and throwing bits of biscuit to the hounds, now looking back to see if Benjamin was in his right place, and again holloaing out some witticism to Fleeceall in advance. Thus they reached the rushy, unenclosed common, partially studded with patches of straggling gorse, which bounds the east side of South Grove, and our sporting master having wet his forefinger on his tongue, and held it up to ascertain which quarter the

MR. JORROCKS CALLING BENJAMIN.

little air there was came from, so as to give the pack the benefit of the wind, prepared for throwing off without delay.   Having scrutinised the wood fence most attentively, he brought his horse to bear upon the rotten stakes and witherings of a low, ill, made-up gap.   In the distance Jorrocks thought of jumping it, but he changed his mind as he got nearer.   "Pull out this stake, Binjimin," exclaimed he to the boy, suddenly reining up short; "Jamp a top on't! jamp a top on't!" added he, "so as to level the 'edge with the ground," observing, "these little places often give one werry nasty falls."   This feat being accomplished, Benjamin climbed on to Xerxes again, and Jorrocks desiring him to keep on the right of the cover, parallel with him, and not to be sparing of his woice, rode into the wood after his hounds, who had broken away with a whimper, ripening into a challenge, the moment he turned his horse's head towards the cover.

What a cry there was! The boy with the fox in a bag had crossed the main ride about a minute before the hounds entered, and they took up the scent in an instant.—Mr. Jorrocks thought it was the morning drag, and screamed and holloaed most cheerily—"Talliho!" was heard almost instantaneously at the far end of the wood, and taking out his horn, Mr. Jorrocks scrambled through the underwood, breaking the briars and snapping the hazels, as he went. Sure enough the fox had gone that way, but the hounds were running flash in a contrary direction. "Talliho! talliho! hoop! hoop! hoop! away! away! away!" holloaed Mat Maltby, who, after shaking the fox most scientifi-cally, had pocketted the sack.

Twang, twang, twang, went Mr. Jorrocks's horn, sometimes in full, sometimes in divided notes and half screeches. The hounds turn and make for the point. Governor, Adamant, Dexterous, and Judgment came first, then the body of the pack, followed by Benjamin at full gallop on Xerxes, with his face and hands all scratched and bleeding from the briars and brushwood, that Xerxes, bit in teeth, had borne him triumphantly through. *Bang*, the horse shot past Mr. Jorrocks, Benjamin screaming, yelling, and holding on by the mane, Xerxes doing with him just what he liked, and the hounds getting together and settling to the scent. "My vig, wot a splitter!" cried Mr. Jorrocks in astonishment, as Xerxes took a high stone wall out of the cover in his stride, without disturbing the coping; but bringing Ben right on to his shoulder— "Hoff, for a fi' pun note! hoff for a guinea 'at to a Gossamer!" exclaimed Mr. Jorrocks, eyeing his whipperin's efforts to regain the saddle.—A friendly chuck of Xerxes's head assists his endeavours, and Ben scrambles back to his place. A gate on the left, let Mr. Jorrocks out of cover, on to a good sound sward, which he prepared to take advantage of by getting Arterxerxes short by the head, rising in his stirrups, and hustling him along as hard as ever he could lay legs to the ground. An open gate at the top fed the flame of his eagerness, and, not being afraid of the pace so long as there was no leaping, Jorrocks sent him spluttering through a swede turnip field as if it was pasture. Now sitting plum in his saddle, he gathered his great whip together, and proceeded to rib-roast Arterxerxes in the most summary manner, calling him a great, lurching, rolling, lumbering beggar, vowing that if he didn't lay himself out and go as he ought, he'd "boil him when he got 'ome." So he jerked and jagged, and kicked and spurred, and hit and held, making indifferent progress compared to his exertions. The exciting cry of hounds sounded in front, and now passing on to a very heavy, roughly ploughed upland, our master saw the hind-quarters of some half-dozen horses, the riders of which had been in the secret, disappearing through the high quick fence at the top.

"Dash my vig, here's an unawoidable leap, I do believe," said he to himself, as he neared the headland, and saw no way out of the field but over the fence—a boundary one; "and a werry hawkward place it is too," added he, eyeing it intently, "a yawnin' blind ditch, a hugly quick fence on the top, and may be, a plough or 'arrow, turned teeth huppermost, on the far side.

"Oh, John Jorrocks, John Jorrocks, my good frind, I wishes you were well over with all my 'eart—terrible place, indeed! Give a guinea 'at to be on the far side," so saying, he dismounted, and pulling the snaffle-rein of the bridle over his horse's head, he knotted the lash of his ponderous whip to it, and very quietly slid down the ditch and climbed up the fence, "*who-a-ing*" and crying to his horse to "stand still," expecting every minute to have him a top of him. The taking-on place was wide, and two horses having gone over before, had done a little towards clearing the way, so having gained his equilibrium on the top, Mr. Jorrocks began jerking and coaxing Arterxerxes to induce him to follow, pulling at him much in the style of a school-boy, who catches a log of wood in fishing.

"Come hup! my man," cried Mr. Jorrocks coaxingly, jerking the rein; but Artexerxes only stuck his great resolute fore legs in advance, and pulled the other way. "*Gently*, old fellow!" cried he, "gently, Arterxerxes my bouy!" dropping his hand, so as to give him a little more line, and then trying what effect a jerk would have, in inducing him to do what he wanted. Still the horse stood with his great legs before him. He appeared to have no notion of leaping. Jorrocks began to wax angry. "Dash my vig, you hugly brute!" he exclaimed, grinning with rage at the thoughts of the run he was losing, "Dash my vig, if you don't mind what you're arter, I'll get on your back, and bury my spurs i your sides. COME HUP! I say, YOU HUGLY BEAST!" roared he, giving a tremendous jerk of the rein, upon which the horse flew back, pulling Jorrocks downwards in the muddy ditch. Arterxerxes then threw up his heels and ran away, whip and all.

Meanwhile, our bagman played his part gallantly, running three quarters of a ring, of three quarters of a mile, chiefly in view, when, feeling exhausted, he threw himself into a furze-patch, near a farm-yard, where Dauntless very soon had him by the back, but the smell of the aniseed, with which he had been plentifully rubbed, disgusting the hound, he chucked him in the air and let him fall back in the bush. Xerxes, who had borne Ben gallantly before the body of the pack, came tearing along, like a poodle with a monkey on his back, when, losing the cry of hounds, the horse suddenly stopped short, and off flew Benjamin beside the fox, who, all wild with fear and rage, seized Ben by the nose, who ran about with the fox hanging to him, yelling, "Murder! murder! murder!" for hard life.

And to crown the day's disasters, when at length our fat friend got his horse and his hounds, and his damaged Benjamin scraped together again, and re-entered Handley Cross, he was yelled at, and hooted, and rid coat! rid coat!—ed by the children, and made an object of unmerited ridicule by the fair but rather unfeeling portion of the populace.

"Lauk! here's an old chap been to Spilsby!" shouted Betty Lucas, the mangle-woman, on getting a view of his great mud-stained back.

Mr. Jorrocks (loq.)—"Come hup! Pray—You ugly Beast!"

"*Hoot!* he's always tumblin' off, that ard chap," responded Mrs. Hardbake, the itinerant lollypop-seller, who was now waddling along with her tray before her.

"Sich old fellers have ne business out a huntin'!" observed Miss Rampling the dressmaker, as she stood staring bonnet-box on arm.

Then a marble-playing group of boys suspended operations to give Jorrocks three cheers; one, more forward than the rest, exclaiming, as he eyed Arterxerxes, "A! what a shabby tail! A! what a shabby tail!"

Next as he passed the Barley-mow beer-shop, Mrs. Gallon the landlady, who was nursing a child at the door, exclaimed across the street, to Blash the barber's pretty but rather wordy wife—

"*A—a—a!* ar say Fanny!—old fatty's had a fall!"

To which Mrs. Blash replied with a scornful toss of her head, at our now admiring friend—

"*Hut!* he's always on his back, that old feller."

"Not 'alf so often as you are, old gal!" retorted the now indignant Mr. Jorrocks, spurring on out of hearing.

CHAPTER XV.

THE COCKNEY WHIPPER-IN.

"WHEN will your hounds be going out again think ye, Mr. Benjamin?" inquired Samuel Strong, a country servant of all work, lately arrived at Handley Cross, as they sat round the saddle-room fire of the Dragon Inn yard, in company with the persons hereafter enumerated, the day after the run described in the last chapter.

Samuel Strong was just the sort of man that would be Samuel Strong. Were his master to ring his bell, and desire the waiter to tell the "Boots" to send his servant "Samuel Strong" to him, Boots would pick Sam out of a score of servants, without ever having seen him before. He was quite the southern-hound breed of domestics. Large-headed, almost lop-eared, red-haired (long, coarse, and uneven), fiery whiskers, making a complete fringe round his harvest moon of a face, with a short thick nose that looked as though it had been sat upon by a heavy person. In stature he was of the middle height, square-built and terribly clumsy.

Nor were the defects of nature at all counterbalanced by the advantages of dress, for Strong was clad in a rural suit of livery, consisting of a footman's morning jacket of dark grey cloth, with a stand-up collar, plentifully besprinkled with large brass buttons, with raised edges, as though his master were expecting his crest from the herald's college. Moreover,

the jacket, either from an original defect in its construction, or from that
propensity to shrink, which inferior clothes unfortunately have, had so
contracted its dimensions, that the waist-buttons were half-way up
Samuel's back, and the lower ones were just where the top ones ought to
be. The shrinking of the sleeves placed a pair of large serviceable-

BENJAMIN IN THE SADDLE-ROOM.

looking hands in nervously striking relief. The waistcoat, broad blue
and white stripe, made up stripe lengthways, was new, and probably the
tailor, bemoaning the scanty appearance of Sam's nether man, had determined to make some atonement to his front, for the waistcoat extended
full four inches below his coat, and concealed the upper part of a very

baggy pair of blue plush shorts, that were met again by very tight drab gaiters, that evidently required no little ingenuity to coax together to button. A six shilling hat, with a narrow silver band, and binding of the same metal, and a pair of darned white Berlin gloves, completed the costume of this figure servant.

Benjamin Brady—or "Binjimin"—was the very converse of Samuel Strong. A little puny, pale-faced, gin-drinking-looking Cockney, with a pair of roving pig-eyes, peering from below his lank white hair, cut evenly round his head, as though it had been done by the edges of a barber's basin. Benjamin had increased considerably in his own opinion, by the acquisition of a pair of top-boots, and his appointment of whipper-in to the hounds, in which he was a good deal supported by the deference usually paid by country servants to London ones.

Like all inn saddle-rooms, the Dragon one was somewhat contracted in its dimensions, and what little there was, was rendered less, by sundry sets of harness hanging against the walls, and divers saddle-stands, boot-trees, knife-cleaners, broken pitchforks, and bottles with candles in their necks, scattered promiscuously around. Nevertheless, there was a fire, to keep "hot water ready," and above the fire-place were sundry smoke-dried hand-bills of country horses for the by-gone season— "Jumper—Clever Clumsy—Barney Bodkin—Billy Button, &c."—while logs of wood, three-legged stools, and inverted horse-pails, served the place of chairs around.

On the boiler-side of the fire, away from the door—for no one has a greater regard for No 1 than himself—sat the renowned Benjamin Brady, in a groom's drab frock coat, reaching down to his heels, a sky-blue waist-coat, patent cord breeches, with grey worsted stockings, and slippers, airing a pair of very small mud-stained top-boots before the fire, occasion-ally feeling the scratches on his face, and the bites the fox inflicted on his nose the previous day—next him, sat the "first pair *boy* out," a grey-headed old man of sixty, whose jacket, breeches, boots, entire person, in fact, were concealed by a long brown holland thing, that gave him the appearance of sitting booted and spurred in his night-shirt. Then came the ostler's lad, a boy of some eight or nine years old, rolling about on the flags, playing with the saddle-room cat ; and, immediately before the fire, on a large inverted horse-pail, sat Samuel Strong, while the circle was made out by Bill Brown, (Dick the ostler's one-eyed helper) "Tom," a return post-boy, and a lad who assisted Bill Brown, the one-eyed helper of Dick the ostler—when Dick himself was acting the part of assistant waiter in the Dragon, as was the case on this occasion.

"When will your hounds be going out again think ye, Mr. Ben-jamin ? " was the question put by Samuel Strong, to our sporting Leviathan.

"'Ang me if I knows," replied the boy, with the utmost importance turning his top boots before the fire. "It's precious little consequence, I thinks, ven we goes out again, if that gallows old governor of ours persists in 'unting the 'ounds himself. I've *all* the work to do ! Bless ye, we should have lost 'ounds, fox, and all, yesterday, if I hadn't rid like the werry wengeance. See 'ow I've scratched my mug," added he, turning

up a very pasty and much scratched countenance. " If I'm to 'unt the
'ounds, and risk my neck at every stride, I must have the wages of a
'untsman, or blow me tight as the old 'un says, he may suit himself."

" What'n a chap is your old gen'leman ? " inquired the " first pair boy
out," who, having been in service himself, where he might have remained
if he could have kept sober, had still a curiosity to know how the world
of servitude went on.

" Oh, hang'd if I knows," replied Benjamin, " precious rum 'un I
assure you. Whiles, he's well enough—then it's Bin this, and Bin that,
and Bin you'll be a werry great man, Bin, and such like gammon ; and
then the next minute, praps, he's in a reg'lar sky-blue, swearin' he'll cut
my liver and lights out, or kind me apprentice to a fiddler—but then I
knows the old fool, and he knows he carnt do without me, so we just
battle on the best way we can together," added Ben with a knowing toss
of his head.

" You'll have good wage I 'spose," rejoined Samuel, with a sigh, for
his " governor " only gave him ten pounds a year, and no perquisites, or
" stealings " as the Americans honestly call them.

" Precious little of that I assure you," replied Benjamin—" at least
the old warment never pays me. He swears he pays it to our old 'oman ;
but I believe he pockets it himself, an old ram ; but I'll have a reckoning
with him some of these odd days, or I'll be off to the diggins. " What'n
a blackguard's your master ? " now asked Ben, thinking to get some
information in return.

" Hush ! " replied Samuel, astonished at Ben's freedom of speech, a
thing not altogether understood in the country.

" A bad 'un I'll be bund," continued the little rascal, " or he wouldn't
see you mooning about in such a rumbustical apology for a coat, with laps
that scarce cover you decently ; " reaching behind the aged post-boy,
and taking up Mr. Samuel's fan-tail as he spoke. " I never sees a servant
in a cutty-coat, without swearing his master's a screw. Now these droll
things such as you have on, are just vot the great folks in London give
their flunkeys to carry coals, and make up fires in, but never to go staring
from home with. Then your country folks get hold of them, and think
by clapping such clowns as you in them, to make people believe that
they have other coats at home. Tell the truth now, old baggy-breeches,
have you another coat of any sort ? "

" Yee'as," replied Samuel Strong, " I've a fustian one."

" Vot, you a fustian coat ! " repeated Benjamin in astonishment, " vy I
thought you were a flunkey ! "

" So I am," replied Samuel, " but I looks ater a hus and shay as well."

" Crikey ! " cried Benjamin, " here's a figure futman wot looks arter
a 'oss and chay—Vy you'll be vot they call a man of ' all vork," a wite
nigger—a wite Uncle Tom in fact ! dear me," added he, eyeing him in a
way that drew a peal of laughter from the party, " vot a curious beast
you must be ! I shouldn't wonder now if you could mow ? "

" With any man," replied Samuel, thinking to astonish Benjamin with
his talent,—

" And sow ? "

" Yee'as and sow."

" And ploo ? " (plough.)

" Never tried—dare say I could though."

" And do you feed the pigs ? " inquired Benjamin.

" Yee'as when Martha's away."

" And who's Martha ? "

" Whoy she's a widder woman, that lives a' back o' the church.—She's a son a-board a steamer, and she goes to see him whiles."

" Your governor's an apothecary, I suppose by that queer button," observed Benjamin, eyeing Sam's coat. " Wot we call a chemist and druggist in London. Do you look after the red and green winder bottles now ? Crikey, he don't look as though he lived on physic altogether, do he ? " added Benjamin turning to Bill Brown, the helper, amid the general laughter of the company.

" My master's a better man than ever you'll be, you little ugly sinner," replied Samuel Strong, breaking into a glow, and doubling a most serviceable-looking fist on his knee.

" We've only your word for that," replied Benjamin, " he don't look like a werry good 'un by the way he rigs you out. 'Ow many slaveys does he keep ? "

" Slaveys," repeated Samuel, " slaveys, what be they ? "

" Vy cook-maids and such like h'animals—women in general."

" Ow, two—one to clean the house and dress the dinner, t'other to milk the cows and dress the childer."

" Oh, you 'ave childer, 'ave you, in your 'ouse ? " exclaimed Benjamin in disgust. " Well come, our's is bad, but we've nothing to ekle (equal) that. I wouldn't live where there are brats for no manner of consideration."

" You've a young Missis, though, haven't you ? " inquired the aged post-boy, adding, " at least there was a young lady came down in the chay along with the old folk."

" That's the niece," replied Benjamin—" a jolly nice gal she is too—often get a tissy out of her—That's to say, she don't give me them herself exactly, but the young men as follows her do, so it comes to the same thing in the end. She has a couple of them you see, first one pays, and then t'other. Green, that's him of Tooley Street, gives shillings because he has plenty ; then Stobbs wot lives near Boroughbridge, gives half-crowns, because he hasn't much. Then Stobbs is such a feller for kissin' of the gals.—' Be'have yourself or I'll scream,' I hears our young lady say, as I'm a listenin' at the door. ' Don't,' says he, kissin' of her again, ' you'll hurt your throat,—let me do it for you.' Then to hear our old cove and Stobbs talk about 'unting of an evening over their drink, you'd swear they were as mad as 'atters. They jump, and shout, and sing, and talliho ! till they whiles bring the street-keeper to make them quiet."

" You had a fine run t'other day, I hear," observed Joe, the deputy-helper, in a deferential tone to Mr. Brady.

" Uncommon ! " replied Benjamin, shrugging up his shoulders at the recollection of it, and clearing the low bars of the grate out with his toe.

"They tell me your old governor tumbled off," continued Joe, "and lost his 'oss."

"Werry like," replied Benjamin with a grin, "he generally does tumble h'off. I'm dashed if it ar'nt a disgrace to an 'oss to be ridden by such a lubber! A great fat beast! he's only fit for a vater carriage." Haw! haw! haw! haw! haw! haw! went the roar of laughter among the party; haw! haw! haw! haw! haw! pealed the second edition.

"He's a precious old file too," resumed the little urchin, elated at the popularity he was acquiring, "to hear him talk, I'm blow'd if you wouldn't think he'd ride over an 'ouse, and yet somehow or other, he's never seen after they go away, unless it be bowling along the 'ard road; — t'other mornin' we had as fine a run as ever was seen, and he wanted to give in in the middle of it, and yesterday he stood starin' like a stuck pig in the wood, stead of ridin' to his 'ounds. If I hadn't been as lively as a lark, and lept like a louse, we should never have seen an 'ound no more. They'd have run slap to France, or whatever there is on the far side of the hill, if the world's made any further that way. Well, I rides, and rides, for miles and miles, as 'ard as ever the 'oss could lay legs to the ground, over every thing, 'edges, ditches, gates, stiles, rivers, determined to stick by 'em,—see wot a mug I've got with rammin through the briars—feels just as if I'd had it teased with a pair of wool-combs; howsomever, I did, and I wouldn't part company with them, and the consequence was, we killed the fox—my eyes, such a wopper!—longer than that," said he, stretching out both his arms, "and as big as a bull —fierce as fury—flew at my snout—nearly bit it off—kept a hold of him though—and worried his soul out—people all pleased—farmer's wife in particklar—offered me a drink o' milk—axed for some jackey—had none, but gave me whiskey instead,—Vill any man here sky a copper for a quartern of gin?" inquired Benjamin, looking round the party. "Then who'll stand a penny to my penny, and let me have a first go?" No one closing with either of these handsome offers, Ben took up his tops, looked at the soles, then replacing them before the fire, felt in his stable-jacket-pocket, which was lying over his own saddle, and bringing out a very short dirty old clay-pipe, he filled it out of the public tobacco-box of the saddle-room, and very complacently crossing his legs, proceeded to smoke. Before he had time to make himself sick, the first pair boy out, interrupted him by asking what became of his master during the run.

"Oh! dashed if I know," replied Benjamin, "but that reminds me of the best of the story—We killed our fox you see, and there were two or three 'ossmen up, who each took a fin and I took the tail, which I stuck through my 'oss's front, and gathering the dogs, I set off towards home, werry well pleased with all I had done. Well, after riding a very long way, axing my way, for I was quite a stranger, I came over a hill at the back of the wood, where we started from, when what should I see in the middle of a big ploughed field but the old 'un himself, an 'unting of his 'oss that had got away from him. There was the old file in his old red coat and top-boots, flounderin' away among the stiff clay, with a hundredweight of dirt stickin' to his heels, gettin' the 'oss first into one corner and then into another, and all but catchin' hold of the bridle, when the nag would shake his head, as much as to say, 'Not yet, old chap,' and trot off to the h'opposite corner, the old 'un grinnin' with h'anger and wexation, and followin' across the deep wet ridge and furrow in his tops, reg'larly churnin' the water in them as he went.

"Then the 'oss would begin to eat, and Jorrocks would take ' Bell's Life ' or ' The Field ' out of his pocket, and pretend to read, sneaking nearer and nearer all the time. When he got a few yards off, the 'oss would stop and look round, as much as to say, 'I sees you, old cock,' and then old J. would begin coxin'—' *Whoay*, my old feller, *who-ay— who-ay*, my old bouy,' (Benjamin imitating his master's manner by coaxing the old post-boy), until he got close at him again, when the 'oss would give a half-kick and a snort, and set off again at a quiet jog-trot to the far corner again, old J. grinnin' and wowin' wengeance against him as he went.

"At last he spied me a lookin' at him through the high 'edge near the gate at the corner of the field, and cuttin' across, he cried, ' Here Binjimin! BINJIMIN, I say !' for I pretended not to hear him, and was for cuttin' away, 'lend me your quad a minute to go and catch mine upon ;' so, accordingly, I got down, and up he climbed. ' Let out the stirrups four 'oles,' said he, quite consequential, shuffling himself into his seat; ' Vot you've cotched the fox 'ave ye ? ' said he, lookin' at the brush danglin' through the 'ead stall. 'Yes,' says I to him says I, 'we've *cotched* him.' Then vot do you think says he to me? Vy, says he to me, says he, ' Then cotch my 'oss,' and away the old wagrant went, 'oss, 'ounds, brush, and all, tellin' everybody he met as how he'd cotched the fox, and leavin' me to run about the ploughed land after his great hairy-heel'd nag—my tops baint dry yet and never will, I think," added Benjamin, putting them closer to the fire, and giving it another poke with his toe.

" What'n 'osses does he keep ? " inquired the return post-boy.

" Oh, precious rips, I assure you, and no mistake. Bless your 'eart, our old chap knows no more about an 'oss than an 'oss knows about him, but to hear him talk—Oh, Crikey ! doesn't he give them a good character, especial ven he wants to sell vun. He von't take no one's adwice neither. Says I to him t'other mornin' as he was a feelin' of my 'oss's pins, ' That ere 'oss would be a precious sight better if you'd blister and turn him out for the vinter.' ' Blister and turn him out for the vinter ! you little rascal,' said he, lookin' as though he would eat me, ' I'll cut off your 'ead and sew on a button, if you talks to me about blisterin'.' Says I to him, says I, ' You're a thorough-bred old hidiot for talking as you do, for there isn't a grum in the world * what doesn't swear by blisters !' I'd blister a cork leg if I had one," added Benjamin, "so would any grum. Blisterin' against the world, says I, for everything except the worms. Then it isn't his confounded stupidity only that one has to deal with, but he's such an unconscionable old screw about feeding of his 'osses—always sees every feed put afore them, and if it warn't for the matter of chopped

---

* Benjamin spoke truth there, for let a groom be ever so ignorant, he can always recommend a blister.

inions (onions) that I mixes with their corn, I really should make nothing out of my stable, for the old 'un pays all his own bills, and orders his own stuff, and ven that's the case those base mechanics of tradesmen never stand nothin' to no one."

"And what do you chop the onions for, Mr. Benjamin?" inquired Samuel Strong.

"Chop inions for!" exclaimed Ben with astonishment, "and is it possible that you've grown those great fiery viskers on either side of your chuckle head and not be hup to the chopped inion rig? My eyes, but you'll never be able to keep a *gal*, I think! Vy you double-distilled fool——"

"Come, sir," interrupted Samuel, again doubling his enormous fist, that would almost have made a head for Benjamin, amid a general roar of laughter, "keep a clean tongue in your head, or I'll knock your teeth down your throat."

"Oh, you're a man of that description, are you!" exclaimed Benjamin, pretending to be in a fright, "you don't look like a dentist either some-how—poor hignorant hass. Vy the chopped inion rig be just this—you must advance a small brown out of your own pocket to buy an inion, and chop it werry small. Then s'pose your chemist and druggist chap gives his 'oss four feeds a-day (vich I s'pose will be three more nor he does), and sees the grain given, which some wicked old warmints will do, you take the sieve, and after shakin' the corn, and hissin' at it well, just take half a handful of chopped inion out of your jacket pocket, as you pass up to the 'oss's 'ead, and scatter it over the who'ats, then give the sieve a shake, and turn the whole into the manger. The governor seeing it there, will leave, quite satisfied that the 'oss has had his dues, and per-haps may get you out of the stable for half an hour or so, but that makes no odds, when you goes back you'll find it all there, and poulterers like it none the worse for the smell of the inions. That, and pickin' off postage-stamps, is about the only parquisite I has."

"Now, Mr. von eye," said he, turning to Bill Brown, the one-eyed helper, "is it time for my 'osses to have their bucket of water and kick in the ribs?"

The time for this luxurious repast not having arrived, Benjamin again composed himself in his corner with his pipe, and the party sat in mute astonishment at his wonderful precocity.

The return post-boy (whose time was precious) at length broke silence, by asking Benjamin if he was living with his first master.

"Deed am I," replied Ben, knocking the ashes out of his pipe, "and had I known as much of sarvice as I does now, I'd have staid at school all my life—Do what they will at school, they carn't make you larn, and there's always plenty of playtime. Crikey, 'ow well I remembers the day our old cock kidnapped me. Me and putty-faced Joe, and Peter Pink-eye Rogers, were laying our heads together how we could sugar old mother Gibb's milk, that's she as keeps the h'apple and purple sugar-stick stall by the skittle-ground at the Royal Artilleryman, on Pentonville Hill; vell, we were dewising how we should manage to get her to give us tick for two pennorth of Gibraltar-rock, when Mr. Martin, the 'ead master,

and *tail* master too, I may call him, for he did all the flogging, came
smiling in with a fat stranger at his 'eels, in a broad-brimmed caster, and
'essian boots with tassels, werry much of the cut of old Paul Pry, that they
used to paint upon the 'busses and pint pots, though I doesn't see no
Paul Prys now a-days.

" Well, this 'ere chap was old Jorrocks, and h'up and down the school
he went, lookin' first at one bye (boy) and then at another, the master all
the while hegging him on, just as the old 'un seemed to take a fancy,
swearing they was *all* the finest byes in the school, just as I've since
'eard old J. himself chaunting of his 'osses ven he's 'ad one for to sell,
but still the old file was difficult to suit—some were too long in the body,
some in the leg, others too short, another's 'ead was too big, and one
whose nose had been flattened by a brick-bat from a Smithfield drover's
bye, didn't please him. Well, on he went, h'up one form, down another,
across the rest, until he got into the middle of the school, where the
byes sit face to face, with their books on their knees, instead of havin' a
desk afore them, and the old cock havin' got into the last line, began
h'examining of them werry closely, fearin' he was not goin' for to get
suited.

" ' Werry rum, Mr. Martin,' said he, ' werry rum, I've been to the
kilt and bare-legged school in 'Atton Garding, the green coat and yellow
breeches in 'Ackney, the red coat and blue vestkits at 'Olloway, the sky-
blues and jockey-caps at Paddington Green, and found nothin' at all to
my mind; must be gettin' out of the breed of nice little useful bo*u*ys,
I fear,' said he, and just as he said the last words, he came afore me,
with his 'ands behind his back, and one 'and was open as if he wanted
summut, so I spit in it.

" ' *Hooi*! Mr. Martin,' roared he, jumpin' round, ' here's a bo*u*y spit
in my 'and! the biggest gog wotever was seen!' showing his mauley to
Martin with it all runnin' off; and Martin seeing who was behind, werry
soon fixed upon me—' You little dirty, disreputable 'bomination,' said he,
seizing of me by the collar, at least wot should have been a collar, for at
the Corderoy's they only give us those quaker-like upright sort of things,
such as old fiery-face there," looking at Samuel Strong, " has on. Says
Martin to me, says he, laying hold on me werry tight, ' vot the deuce and
old Davey, do you mean by insultin' a gen'leman that will be Lord
Mayor? Sir, I'll flog you within half a barley-corn of your life!'

" ' Beg pardon, sir, beg pardon, sir,' I cried, ' thought the gen'leman
had a sore 'and, and a little hointment 'd do it good.'

" ' Haw! haw! haw!' roared Jorrocks, taking out a red cotton
wipe and rubbing his 'and dry, ' haw! haw! haw! werry good, Mr.
Martin, werry good—promisin' bo*u*y that, I thinks, promisin' bo*u*y that,
likes them with mischief—likes them with mischief, poopeys (puppeys)
and bo*u*ys—never good for nothin' unless they 'ave.—Don't you mind,'
said he, pokin' Martin in the ribs with his great thick thumb, ' don't you
mind Beckford's story 'bout the pointer and the turkeys?' Martin
didn't, so J. proceeded to tell it afore all the school. ' Ye see,' said
he, ' a gent gave another a pointer poop, and enquiring about it a short
time arter, the gent who got it said he feared it wasn't a goin' to do him

any good, cos as how it hadn't done him any 'arm. But meetin' him again a fortnight arter, he changed his tune, and thought well on him, for,' says he, ' he's killed me heighteen turkeys since I saw you—haw! haw! haw!—he! he! he!—ho! ho! ho!'—a guffaw in which the saddle-room party joined."

When the laughter subsided, Ben was unanimously requested to continue his narrative.

"And what did the old gent say about you?" asked Sam, expecting to hear that Ben got a good thrashing for his dirty, disrespectful conduct.

"O, why," replied Ben, considering—" O, why, arter he had got all quiet again, and his wipe put back into his pocket, he began handlin' and lookin' at me, and then, arter a good examination, he says to Martin, quite consequential-like—' 'Ow old's the rogue?'

"Now Martin know'd no more about me than I know'd about Martin; but knowin' the h'age that Jorrocks wanted a bye of, why, in course, he said I was just of that age, and knowin' that I should get a precious good hiding for spittin' in the old covey's 'and, if I staid at the Corderoy's, why I swore that I was uncommon fond of 'osses, and gigs, and 'arness, and such like, and after the old file had felt me well about the neck, for he had an ide that if a bye's big in the neck in course o' time he'll get big all over, he took me away, promising Martin the two quarterages our old gal had run in arrear for my larning—though hang me I never got none—out o' my wage, and would ye believe it, the old gudgeon kept me goin' on from quarter to quarter, for I don't know 'ow many quarters, sayin' he hadn't viped off the old score for my schoolin', just as if I had any business to pay it; at last, one day as I was a rubbin' down the chesnut 'oss as he sold to the chap in Tooley Street, he comes into the stable, full of pride, and I thought rather muzzy, for he bumped first agin one stall and then agin another, so says I to him, says I, ' Please, sir, I vants for to go to the Vells this evening.'

" ' To the Vells!' repeated he, staring with astonishment—' To the Vells!—Wot Vells?'

" ' Bagnigge!' said I, and that's a place, Mr. Baconface," observed Ben, turning to Samuel Strong, "that you shouldn't be hung without seeing —skittles, bowls, stalls all around the garding, like stables for 'osses, where parties take their tea and XX—all painted sky-blue with red pannels—gals in shiny vite gowns and short sleeves, bare down the neck, singing behind the h'organ with h'ostrich feathers in their 'eads—all beautiful—admission tup-pence—a game at skittles for a penna—and every thing elegant and quite genteel—musn't go in that queer coat of yours though, or they'd take you for a Bedlamite, and may be send you to the hulks—queer chaps the Londoners—Once knowd a feller, quite as queer a lookin' dog as you, barrin' his nose, which was a bit better, and not so red. Well, he had a rummish cove of a governor, who clapt him into a nut-brown suit, with bright basket buttons, and a glazed castor, with a broad welwet band ' all round his 'at,' and as he was a mizzlin' along Gower Street, where his master had just come to live from over t'other side of the vater, vot should he meet, but one of the new polish (police), who seeing such a b'object, insisted he was mad; and nothin' would sarve him, but that he was mad; and avay he took him to the station 'ouse, and from thence, afore the beak, at Bow Street, and nothin' but a sendin' for the master to swear that they were his clothes, and that he considered them livery, saved the fellow from transportation, for if he'd stolen the clothes he couldn't have been more galvanised than when the new polish grabbed him.

"Well, but that isn't what I was a goin' to tell you about. Blow these boots," said he, stooping down and turning them again, "they never are goin' for to dry. Might as well have walked through the Serpentine in them. I was goin' to tell you of the flare-up the old 'un and I had about the Vells. 'Well,' says I to him, says I, 'I vants for to go to the Vells.'

"'Vot Vells?' said he.

"'Bagnigge,' says I. 'Bagnigge be d—d,' said he,—no he didn't say, 'be d—d,' for the old 'un never swears except he's h'outrageously h'angry. But, howsomever, he said, I shouldn't go to the Vells, for as 'ow, Mrs. Muffin, and the seven Miss Muffins, from Primrose Hill, were comin' to take their scald with him that evening, and he vanted me to carry the h'urn, while Batsey buttered and 'anded round the bread.

"'Well,' but says I to him, says I, 'that don't h'argufy. If I'm a grum, I'm a grum, if I'm a butler, I'm a butler, but it's out of all conscience and calkilation expectin' a man to be both grum and butler. Here 'ave I been a cleanin' your useless screws of hosses, and weshing your hugly chay till I'm fit to faint, in h'order that I might have a night of enjoyment to myself, and then you wants me to carry vater to your nasty old boiler. A man should have double wage, 'stead of none at all, to stand such vork.'

"'Ow do you mean none at all?' said he, grinnin' with anger, 'doesn't I pay your old mother a sovereign annually four times a-year?'

"'Vot's that to me?' said I, 'my mother don't do your work does she?'

"''Dash my vig!' said he, gettin' into a reglar blaze. 'You little ungrateful 'ound, I'll drown you in a bucket of barley water,' and so we got on from bad to worse, until he swore he'd start me, and get another bouy from the Corderoy's.

"''Quite unanimous,' said I, 'quite unanimous, in course you'll pay up my wages afore I go, and that will save me the trouble of taking of you to Hicks Hall.' At the werry word, 'Hicks Hall,' the old gander turned quite green and began to soften. 'Now, Binjimin,' said he, 'that's werry unkind o' you. If you had the Hen and Chickens comin' to take their pumpaginous aqua (which he says is French for tea and coffee) with you, and you wanted your boiler carried, you'd think it werry unkind of Batsey if she wouldn't give you a lift?' Then he read a long lector about doing as one would be done by, and all that sort of gammon that Martin used to cram us with of a Sunday. Till at last it ended in his givin' me a half-crown to do what he wanted, on the understandin' that it was none of my vork, and I says that a chap wot does everything he's bid, like that suckin' Sampson there," eyeing Samuel Strong with the most ineffable contempt, "is only fit to be a tinker's jack-ass." Samuel looked as though he would annihilate the boy as soon as he made up his mind where to hit him, and Benjamin, unconscious of all danger, stooped, and gave the eternal tops another turn.

"We never heard nothin' of your comin' until three days afore you cast up," observed Bill Brown, with a broad grin on his countenance at Benjamin's audacity and Samuel's anger.

"It wern't werry likely that you should," replied Benjamin, looking up, "for as 'ow we hadn't got our own consent much afore that. Our old cove is a reg'lar word-and-a-blow man. If he does, he does, and if he don't, why he lets it alone. Give the old 'un his due, he's none o' your talkin' chaps, wot's always for doin' somethin', only they don't. He never promised me a cow-hidin' yet, but he paid it with interest. As soon as ever he got the first letter, I know'd there was somethin' good in the wind; for he gave me half a pot of his best marmeylad, and then a few days after he chucked me a golden sovereign, tellin' me, go and buy a pair of new tops, or as near new as I could get them for the money."

"And what did you pay for them?" inquired both post-boys at once, for the price of top-boots is always an interesting subject to a stable-servant.

"Guess!" replied Benjamin, holding them up, adding, "mind, they are nothing like now what they were when I bought them; the Jew told me, though it don't do to believe above half what those gents. tell you, that they belonged to the Markiss of Castlereagh's own tiger, and that he had parted with them because they didn't wrinkle in quite as many folds as his Majesty wished. Here was the fault," continued Benjamin, holding one of the boots upon his hand and pressing the top downwards to make it wrinkle. "You see it makes but eight wrinkles between the top and the 'eel, and the Markiss's gen'lman swore as how he would never be seen in a pair wot didn't make nine, so he parted with them, and as I entered 'Olyvell Street from the east, I spied them 'anging on the pegs at Levy Aaron's, that's the first Jew vot squints on the left 'and side of the way, for there are about twenty of them in that street with queer eyes.

"'Veskit!' said he, 'vashin' veskit, werry sheep; half nothin' in fact,' just as these barkers always chaff.

"'No,' said I, passing on—'Yon don't s'pose I wears cast-offs!'

"'Clow for shell,' then said he,—'Bes'h price, bes'h price.'

"'Nor to shell neither,' said I, mimickin' of him. 'I'll swap my shoes for a pair of tops if you like.'

"'Vot vill you give in?' axed Levy Aaron.

"'Nothin',' said I, determined to begin low enough.

"'Valk in then,' said he, quite purlite, ''onour of your custom's quite enough,' so in I went. Such a shop! full o' veskits covered with gold and flowers, and lace, and coats, without end, with the shop sides, each as high as a hay-stack, full o' nothin' but trousers and livery breeches.

"'Sit down, shir,' said he, 'anding me a chair without a back, while his missis took the long stick from behind the door with a hook, and fished down several pairs of tops. They had all sorts and sizes, and all colours too. Mahogany, vite, rose-colour, painted vons; but I kept my eye on the low pair I had seen outside, till at last Mrs. Levy Aaron handed them through the winder.' I pulls one on.

"' Uncommon fit,' said Levy Aaron, slappin' the sole to feel if all my foot was in; 'much better leg than the Markiss o' Castlereagh's tiger; you'll live with a Duke before you die.'

"' Let's have on t'other,' said I.

"' Von's as good as both,' said he. 'Oh!' says I, twiggin' vot he was after,—'If you thinks I'm a man to bolt with your boots, you'r mistaken;' so I kicked off the one I had on, and bid him 'and me my shoes. Well, then he began to bargain—'Thirty shilling and the shoes.' I was werry angry and wouldn't treat. 'Five-and twenty shilling *without* the shoes then.' Still I wouldn't touch. 'Give me my castor,' said I, buttonin' up my pocket with a slap, and lookin' werry wicious. 'You'r a nasty suspicious old warmint.' Then the Jew began to soften. ''Onour bright, he meant no offence.' 'One shovereign then he vod take.' 'Give me my castor,' said I.

"' Good mornin', Mrs. Jewaster,' which means female Jew. 'Seventeen and sixpence!' 'Go to the devil,' said I. 'Come then, fifteen shillin' and a paper bag to put them in.' 'No,' said I, 'I'll give you ten.' 'Done,' said he, and there they are. A nice polish they had when I got them, but the ploughed land has taken the shine off. Howsomever, I s'pose they'll touch up again?"

"Not they," replied Bill Brown, who had been examining one of them very minutely, "they are made of nothing but brown paper!"

"Brown paper be 'anged!" exclaimed Benjamin. "Your 'ead's more like made of brown paper."

"Look there then!" rejoined Bill Brown, running his thumb through the instep, and displaying the brown paper through the liquid varnish with which it had been plentifully smeared.

"*Haw, haw, haw, haw, haw, haw, haw*," pealed the whole of the saddle-room party, in the midst of which Ben bolted with his brown-paper boots.

CHAPTER XVI.

SIR ARCHEY DEPECARDE.

As yet our distinguished friend was in no position for taking the field, for though he had got a pack of hounds—such as they were—he had neither huntsman to hunt them, nor horses for a huntsman to ride if he had one. He was therefore in a very unfinished condition. Horses, however, are soon got, if a man has only money to pay for them, and a master of hounds being clearly the proper person to buy all the horses that other people want to sell, Mr. Jorrocks very soon had a great many very handsome offers of that sort. Among others he received a stiffish, presenting-his-compliments note, from the celebrated gambler, Sir Archibald Depecarde, of Pluckwelle Park, and the Albany, London, stating that he had a very fine bay horse that he modestly said was too good for his work, and which he should be glad to see in such good hands as Mr. Jorrocks's. Sir Archey, as many of our readers doubtless know— some perhaps to their cost—is a very knowing hand, always with good looking, if not good horses, which he is ready to barter, or play for, or exchange in any shape or way that conduces to business. His *recherche* little dinners in the Albany are not less famous for "do's" than his more extended hospitality at Pluckwelle Park, whither he brings such of his flats as require more deliberate preparation and treatment than the racket of London allows. Now our friend Mr. Jorrocks, though not exactly swallowing all the butter that was offered him, had no objection to see if there was anything to be made of Sir Archey's horse, so by way of being upsides with him in dignity, he replied as follows :—

" M.F.H. John Jorrocks presents his compliments to Sir Archibald Depecarde, and in reply to his favour begs to say that he will take an early hopportunity of drivin' over to Pluckwelle Park to look at his quadruped, and as the M.F.H. 'ears it is a goodish distance from Handley Cross, he will bring his night cap with him, for where the M.F.H. dines he sleeps, and where the M.F.H. sleeps he breakfasts."

Sir Archey thought the answer rather cool—especially from a mere tradesman to a man of his great self-importance, but being of opinion that there is no account between man and man that money will not settle, he determined to square matters with the M.F.H. by putting an extra 5*l.* or 10*l.* on the horse. He therefore resolved to pocket the affront and let matters take their chance.

As good as his word, one afternoon a few days after, our plump friend was seen navigating his vehicle, drawn by a Duncan Nevin screw, along the sinuosities of Sir Archibald's avenue, in the leisurely way of a gentleman eyeing the estate, and gaining all the information he could by the way, and having arrived at the Corinthian columned portico, where he was kept waiting longer than he liked, he was shocked to find, by the unlocking and unbolting of the door, that Sir Archey was "from home "

—"just gone to town"—(to look after a gambling-house in which he had a share on the sly).

"*Dash my vig!*" exclaimed Mr. Jorrocks, nearly stamping the bottom of the vehicle out with his foot, and thinking whether it was possible to tool Duncan Nevin's hack back to Handley Cross. "*Dash my vig!*" repeated he, "didn't he know I was a comin'?"

"Beg pardon, sir," replied the footman, rather abashed at the Jorrocks vehemence (who he at first took for a prospectus man or an atlas-monger). "Beg pardon, sir, but I believe Mrs. Markham, sir, has a message for you sir—if you'll allow me, sir, I'll go and see, sir."

"Go," grunted Mr. Jorrocks, indignant at the slight thus put on his M.F.H.-ship.

The footman presently returned, followed by a very smiling comely-looking personage, dressed in black silk, with sky-blue ribbons in her jaunty little cap and collar, who proceeded in a most voluble manner to express with her hands, and tongue, and eyes, Sir Archibald's regrets that he had been suddenly summoned to town, adding that he had left word that they were to make the expected guest as comfortable as possible, and show him every possible care and attention.

"Ah, well, that's summut like," smiled Mr. Jorrocks, with a jerk of his head, thinking what a good-looking woman she was. In another instant he was on the top step of the entrance beside her, giving her soft hand a sly squeeze as she prepared to help him out of his reversible coat. "Take the quad to the stable," said he to the footman, and bid 'em take great care on 'im—adding, with a leer at the lady, "gave a-most a 'underd for him." So saying, hack like, the horse was left to take its chance, while our fat friend followed the fair lady into the library.

"I'll have a fire lighted directly," observed she, looking round the spacious apartment, which, like many bachelors' company rooms, felt pretty innocent of fuel.

"*Fiddle the fire!*" exclaimed Mr. Jorrocks, "fiddle the fire! dessay you've got a good 'un in your room,—*I'll go there.*"

"*Couldn't for the world,*" whispered Mrs. Markham, with a shake of her head, glancing her large hazel eyes lovingly upon Jorrocks. "What! if Sir Archey should hear!"

"Oh, he'll *never* hear," rejoined our friend confidently.

"*Wouldn't he?*" retorted Mrs. Markham, "you don't know what servants are if you think that. Bless ye! they watch me just as a cat watches a mouse."

"Well, then, you must come in to *me*," observed Mr. Jorrocks, adding —"I can't be left mopin' alone, you know."

"It must be after they've gone to bed, then," whispered the lady.

A hurrying housemaid now appearing with a red hot poker, Mrs. Markham drew back and changed the whispering conversation into an audible,

"And please sir, what would you like to 'ave for dinner, sir?"

"Oh, I don't care," shrugged Mr. Jorrocks, "wot 'ave you got?"

"There's soup, and fish, and meat, and game, and poultry; whatever you like to 'ave I dare say."

"*Humph*," mused Mr. Jorrocks, wishing the housemaid further, " I'll 'ave a bit o' fish, with a beef steak, and a fizzant to follow, say—"

" No soup ? " observed Mrs. Markham.

" No ; I doesn't care nothin' 'bout soup, 'less it's turtle," replied he with a toss of his head.

" I'm afraid, there is no turtle, sir," replied Mrs. Markham, well knowing there was not. " Gravy, macaroni, mulligatawney."

" No, jest fish, and steak, and fizzant," rejoined Mr. Jorrocks, " Cod and hoister sauce, say—and p'raps a couple o' dozen o' hoisters to begin with,—jest as a whet you know."

MR. JORROCKS IN CLOVER.

" Any *sweets ?* " asked the lady significantly.

" No, I'll 'ave my sweets arter," winked Mr. J. licking his lips.

"Open tart, apple fritters, omelette, any thing of that sort?" continues she; intimating with her eye that the loitering housemaid might hear his answer.

"No; I'll fill hup the chinks wi' cheese," replied Mr. Jorrocks, stroking his stomach.

"And wine?" asked the housekeeper; adding, "the butler's away with Sir Archey, but I 'ave the key of the cellar."

"That's all right!" exclaimed our friend, adding, "I'll drink his 'ealth in a bottle of his best."

"Port?" asked Mrs. Markham.

"Port in course," replied Mr. J. with a hoist of his eyebrows, adding, "but mind I doesn't call the oldest the best—far from it—it's oftentimes the wust. No," continued he, "give me a good fruity wine; a wine with a grip o' the gob, that leaves a mark on the side o' the glass; not your weak woe-begone trash, that would be water if it wasn't wine."

"P'raps you'd like a little champagne at dinner," suggested Mrs. Markham.

"Champagne," repeated Mr. Jorrocks thoughtfully, "Champagne! well, I wouldn't mind a little champagne, only I wouldn't like it hiced; doesn't want to 'ave all my teeth set a chatterin' i my 'ead; harn't got so far advanced in gentility as to like my wine froze—I'm a Post Hoffice Directory, not a Peerage man," added he with a broad grin.

"Indeed," smiled Mrs. Markham, not exactly understanding the simile.

"Folks talk about the different grades o' society," observed Mr. Jorrocks, with a smile and a pshaw, "but arter all's said and done there are but two sorts o' folks i' the world, Peerage folks, and Post Hoffice Directory folks, Peerage folks, wot think it's all right and proper to do their tailors, and Post Hoffice Directory folks wot think it's the greatest sin under the sun not to pay twenty shillins i' the pund—greatest sin under the sun 'cept kissin' and then tellin'," added he, in an under tone, with a wink, as he drew his hand across his jolly lips.

"Well, then, you'll have it iced," observed Mrs. Markham, in a tone for the housemaid to hear. "Just a few minutes plunge in the pail,—enough to dull the glass p'raps?" continued she.

"Well," mused our friend, "as you are mistress o' the revels, I'll leave that to you, and I makes no doubt," added he, with another sly squeeze of her soft hand, now that the housemaid's back was turned, "I shall fare uncommon well."

And Mrs. Markham, seeing that the maid was bent on out-staying her, sailed away with a stately air, ordering her, in a commanding tone, to "bring some wood to the fire."

And Mr. Jorrocks, we need scarcely say, had a very good dinner, and spent his evening very pleasantly.

CHAPTER XVII.

THE PLUCKWELLE PRESERVES.

EXT morning, in accordance with Sir Archey's injunctions, as Mr. Jorrocks sat at a capital breakfast, Mr. Snapshot, the keeper, sent to know if he would please to go out shooting, or coursing, or rabbiting, and finding that the covers were near the house, and pretty full of pheasants, our M.F.H. thought he might as well have a "blaze among 'em" before he went home. Accordingly he sought Sir Archey's dressing-room, and borrowed a pair of his best thick shoes and leather gaiters, which, with a fustian coat of the keeper's, made him pretty perfect, and the stables being in the way to the kennels, he thought he might as well see how his hack was, and look at his proposed purchase. Accordingly, preceded by Mr. Snapshot, he passed through a lofty, deserted-looking, cobwebby, ten-stalled stable, with a two-stall one beyond, in which were a couple of shooting ponies, of which Mr. Snapshot spoke approvingly; then crossing the central passage, they traversed another two-stall, and entered upon a somewhat better conditioned corresponding stable to the ten.

First there stood Mr. Jorrocks's hundred-guinea horse, with a wretched old rag of a rug over it, then a pair of better-clothed browns that Snapshot alluded to as "our 'cage 'orses;" then, as Mr. Jorrocks passed on to a bright bang-tailed bay beyond, thinking that would be his friend, Snapshot seized him suddenly by the arm, with a "take care of 'im, sir! take care!—*He'll kick ye to a certainty!*"

"Wot, he's wicious is he?" observed Mr. Jorrocks coolly, eyeing the now well laid-back ears and exuberant white of the eye.

"*Most vicious brute alive!*" replied Mr. Snapshot. "If he was to get you off, he'd stand considerin' whether he should kick out your right eye or your left."

"*In*-deed," mused Mr. Jorrocks—"pleasant 'oss to 'ave."

"We're expectin' an old gent from Handley Cross to look at 'im," observed the keeper, "but I think he'll have to be crazier than they say he is afore he buys 'im."

"I think so too," assented Mr. Jorrocks—stumping on out of heels' reach.

They then got the dogs out of the kennel, and proceeded to the pheasants.

Mr. Jorrocks, being out of practice, did not make much of a hand at first, which, coupled with the injunctions all the servants were under to make the stranger as comfortable as possible, induced Snapshot to take him to the home cover, when the pheasants rising in clouds and the hares streaming out like sand ropes, our worthy friend very soon bagged his five brace of pheasants and three hares. Snapshot, now thinking "tipping time" was come, and feeling for his pheasants, proposed a truce, when Mr. Jorrocks, handing him the gun, picked out three brace of the best birds, with which he trudged away, leaving the astonished Snapshot to follow with the rest. Hares he wouldn't take, thinking his riotous hounds would kill him plenty of them. He then very coolly locked the pheasants up in his vehicle, and ordering the horse to be put-to, was ready for a start by the time it came to the door. With a loving leave-taking of Mrs. Markham, he was presently in his rattle-trap and away. A favourable road incline with the horse's head towards home, sent the hundred guinea nag along, and Mr. Jorrocks began to think it "wasn't so bad as it seemed."

As he neared the last unlodged gates in Sir Archey's grounds, he saw another vehicle approaching, and each driver thinking to get the other to open the gate, they timed themselves so as to meet with it between them.

"Sky ye a coppper who opens it!" at length exclaimed Mr. Jorrocks, after a good stare at his much muffled up *vis-à-vis*.

"Eads or tails?" continued he, producing a half-a-crown piece—"Eads I win! tails you lose!"

"Heads!" cried the stranger.

"Its tails!" replied Mr. Jorrocks, pretending to look at it, "so you opens it."

The youth then got out and did so.

"Prop it hopen! prop it hopen!" exclaimed Mr. Jorrocks, adding, "there arn'nt no cattle in either field, and it may as well stand that way as not."

The gentleman did as he was bid, drawing his vehicle—a German waggon with three crests (very symptomatic of money)—alongside of Mr. Jorrocks's.

"You'll be agoin' to Sir Harchey's, I guess," observed Mr. Jorrocks, after scrutinising his fat, vacant face intently.

"I am," replied the stranger.

"Well, I'm jest a comin' from there," continued our friend, stroking his chin complacently, thinking of the pheasants and the fun he had had.

"Indeed," smiled the gentleman.

" He's not at 'ome," observed Mr. Jorrocks.

" At home to *me*," replied the stranger, with a man-of-the-house sort of air.

" *Humph*," mused Mr. Jorrocks, adding, after a pause,—" Well, now blow me tight, I shouldnt be at all s'prised, if they're been a takin' o' me for you. Thought they were sweeter upon me than a mere 'oss-dealin' case required, unless indeed they took me for a most egregius John Ass."

" Hope they've used you well," observed the stranger.

" *Capital*," replied Mr. Jorrocks, " and if it wasn't that I 'ave a 'ticklar engagement, I wouldn't mind returnin' and spendin' the evenin' with you. Independent of a capital dinner, I had just as good a drink as man need wish for. Amost two bottles of undeniable black strap, besides et ceteras, and no more 'ead ache than the crop o' my wip."

" Indeed," observed the stranger, thinking he was lucky to escape such a sand-bag.

" True, I assure you," affirmed Jorrocks—" shouldn't know that I'd taken more nor my usual quantity; shot as well as ever I did i' my life this mornin', and altogether I'm uncommon pleased with my jaunt, and that reminds me," continued he, flourishing his whip bag-man-i-cally over his head, and thinking how he had got to the windward of Sir Archey, " you can do summat for me—I'm Mr. Jorrocks, the M.F.H.— you'll most likely have 'eard o' me—I 'unts the country. Well, I've been to look at an 'oss of Sir Harchey's—a werry nice h'animal he is, but 'ardly hup to my weight—I'm a sixteen stunner you see. Ave the goodness to make my compliments to Sir Harchey, and tell 'im I'm werry much 'bliged by his purlite hoffer on 'im, and that I'm werry sorry he wasn't at 'ome, so that I might 'ave 'ad the pleasure o' makin' his personal 'quaintance, as well as that of his Port ; " so saying, Mr. Jorrocks shortened his hold of the reins, and dropping the point of his whip scienti- fically into the Handley Cross back, bowed to his friend, and bowled away homewards.

And when Sir Archey returned, and found the indignities that had been put upon him, he was exceeding wrath, and vowed vengeance against the grocer.

CHAPTER XVIII

A SPORTING LECTOR.

FOR some days after Mr. Jorrocks's return from Pluckwelle Park, Diana Lodge was literally besieged with people, offering him horses of every sort, size, and description. A man " wanting a horse "—and, confound it ! some people are always " wanting " them, and never buy,— a man "wanting a horse," we say, is always an object of interest to the idle and unemployed, looking out for horses for other people; and Handley Cross being as idle a place as any, everybody seemed bent upon propagating the great M.F.H.'s wants. Even the ladies, who don't generally bestir themselves in such matters, seemed smitten with the mania; and a horse being a horse with them, the curiosities their inquiries produced were very amusing. The horses that came were of all prices, from a hundred guineas down to thirty shillings; indeed, Mrs. Pearlash, the laundress, intimated that she *might* take "rayther" less than thirty for her old woe-begone white Rosinante. Our worthy M.F.H. was indebted to his wife for the offer of it; Mrs. Jorrocks making the subject of "osses" one of her standing topics of conversation, as well with her visitors as to all those with whom she came in contact. Having casually mentioned her great sporting-spouse's wants to Mrs. Pearlash, that useful functionary, sticking her fists in her sides for the purpose of revolving the matter in her mind, said, " Well, now, she didn't know but they *might part* with their horse, and she'd ask her old man; " who readily assented to the sale of an animal that could hardly crawl. Jorrocks was highly indignant when it came, and desired Mrs. J. not to meddle with matters she didn't understand.

Mr. Jorrocks, on his part, having about satisfied himself that hunting a pack of hounds was a very different thing to riding after them, as near to them or as far off as he liked, repelled all inquiries as to when he would be going out again, and when he would begin to advertise, by saying, mysteriously, " that he must get things a little forwarder fust." The fact was, he wanted to pick up a huntsman at whip's wages, and had written to sundry friends in the City and elsewhere, describing what he wanted, and intimating that the whip might occasionally have to " 'unt the 'ounds when he was away, or anything of that sort." His City friends, who didn't approve of his proceedings, and, moreover, had plenty of other matters to attend to of their own, gave his letters very little heed, if indeed they took any notice of them at all. Some of his old cronies shook their heads, and said they "wished any good might come of it ; " while others said " he'd much better have stuck to his shop ; " adding a wish that things might continue " serene " in the " lane."

Altogether Jorrocks's proceedings were not approved of in the commercial world, where hunting and gambling are often considered synonymous. He, however, was all swagger and cock-a-hoop, vowing that he had got "the best pack of 'ounds in the world;" adding, that " they would make the foxes cry 'Capevi!' "

Belinda's beauty and unaffected manners drew Mrs. Jorrocks plenty of callers, who soon found herself a much greater woman at Handley Cross than she was in Great Coram Street.

Belinda might have had an offer every day in the week, but somehow the suitors never could get the old girl out of the room—an error into which ladies, who trade in beauty other than that of their own daughters, are very apt to fall. Mrs. Jorrocks wouldn't admit that she was in any ways indebted to Belinda for her company, and of course sat to receive her own guests. Not that Belinda wanted any of their offers; for, as Ben intimated, she had a young chap in her eye, who will shortly appear in our pages: but Mrs. Jorrocks, like a skilful old mouser, as she was, did not let that out.

So Belinda was talked of, and toasted, and toasted, and talked of, and " set out" for no end of people. The Jorrocks's funds rose ten per cent. at least from having her, and the Barnington ones were depressed to a similar extent.

Our great M. F. H. not finding any responses to his inquiries for a whip, and being dreadfully anxious to be doing, resolved to make known his wants through the medium of the newspapers; and while his bold advertisement for a "huntsman" (not a whip who could 'unt the 'ounds occasionally) was working, he bethought him, instead of exposing his incompetence as a huntsman, to display his sporting knowledge in a lecture, in which he could also inculcate the precepts he wished practised towards himself, both at home and in the field.

Accordingly, he enlisted the assistance of Captain Doleful, to whose province such arrangements seemed peculiarly to belong, and the large room of the Dragon was engaged and tastefully fitted up under their joint superintendence. A temporary platform was placed at the far end, surmounted by a canopy of scarlet cloth, tastefully looped up in the centre with an emblematical sporting device, formed of a hunting-cap, a pair of leather breeches, a boot-jack, and three foxes' brushes. Inside the canopy was suspended a green-shaded lamp, throwing a strong light upon the party below, and the room was brilliantly lighted with wax both from the chandeliers and reflecting-mirrors against the wall. The doors were besieged long before the appointed hour for commencing, and ere the worthy lecturer made his appearance there was not standing room to be had in any part. The orchestra was also full, and in it "we observed many elegantly dressed ladies," as the reporters say.

Precisely at eight o'clock Mr. Jorrocks ascended the platform, attended by Captain Doleful, Roger Swizzle, Romeo Simpkins, and Abel Snorem, and was received with the most enthusiastic cheering. He wore the full-dress uniform of the hunt; sky-blue coat lined with pink silk, canary-coloured shorts, and white silk stockings. His neckcloth and waistcoat were white, and a finely plaited shirt-frill protruded through the stand-up collar of the latter. Bunches of white ribbon dangled at his knees. In his hand he held a roll of notes, while some books of reference and a tumbler of brandy and water, were placed by Benjamin on a table at the

Mr. Corroski's Lecture on "Unting."

back of the platform. Benjamin had on his new red frock with blue collar, cord breeches, and white stockings.

After bowing most familiarly to the company, Mr. Jorrocks cleared his voice with a substantial *hem*, and then addressed the meeting.

"Beloved 'earers!—*beloved* I may call you, for though I have not the pleasure of knowin' many of you, I hope werry soon to make your intimate acquaintance. Beloved 'earers, I say, I have come 'ere this evenin' for the double purpose of seeing you, and instructin' of you on those matters that have brought me to this your beautiful and salubrisome town. (Cheers.) Beautiful I may call it, for its architectural proportions are grand, and salubrisome it must be when it boasts so many cheerful, wigorous countenances as I now see gathered around me. (Loud applause.) And if by my comin', I shall spread the great light of sportin' knowledge, and enable you to perserve those glowin' mugs when far removed from these waters, then shall I be a better doctor than either Swizzle or Sebastian, and the day that drew John Jorrocks from the sugars of retirement in Great Coram Street will henceforth remain red-lettered in the mental calendar of his existence. (Loud cheers.) *Red*-lettered did I say? ah! wot a joyous colour to denote a great and glorious ewent! Believe me there is no colour like red—no sport like 'unting.

"Blue coats and canaries," observed Mr. Jorrocks looking down at his legs, "are well enough for dancin' in, but the man wot does much dancin' will not do much 'unting. But to business—Lectorin' is all the go—and why should sportin' be excluded? Is it because sportin' is its own champion? Away with the idea! Are there no pints on which grey experience can show the beacon lights to 'ot youth and indiscretion?—Assuredly there are! Full then of hardour—full of keenness, one pure concentrated essence of 'unting, John Jorrocks comes to enlighten all men capable of instruction on pints that all wish to be considered conversant with.

"Well did that great man, I think it was Walter Scott, but if it war'nt,

'twas little Bartley, the boot-maker, say, that there was no young man
wot would not rather have a himputation on his morality than on his
'ossmanship, and yet, how few there are wot really know anything about
the matter! Oh, but if hignorance be bliss 'ow 'appy must they be!
(Loud cheers and laughter.)

"'Unting is the sport of kings, the image of war without its guilt, and
only five-and-twenty per cent. of its danger! In that word, ''unting,'
wot a ramification of knowledge is compressed! The choice of an 'oss—
the treatment of him when got—the groomin' at home, the ridin' abroad
—the boots, the breeches, the saddle, the bridle, the 'ound, the 'untsman,
the feeder, the Fox! Oh! how that beautiful word, Fox, gladdens my
'eart, and warms the declinin' embers of my age. (Cheers.) The 'oss and
the 'ound were made for each other, and natur threw in the Fox as a
connectin' link between the two. (Loud cheers.) He's perfect symmetry, and my affection for him, is a perfect paradox. In the summer I
loves him with all the hardour of affection; not an 'air of his beautiful
'ead would I hurt; the sight of him is more glorious nor the Lord
Mayor's show! but when the hautumn comes—when the brownin' copse
and cracklin' stubble proclaim the farmer's fears are past, then, dash my
vig, 'ow I glories in pursuin' of him to destruction, and holdin' him above
the bayin' pack! (Loud cheers.)

"And yet," added Mr. Jorrocks thoughtfully, "it ar'nt that I loves
the fox less, but that I loves the 'ound more, as the chap says in the
play, when he sticks his friend in the gizzard. (Roars of laughter and
applause.)

"The 'oss loves the 'ound, and I loves both; and it is that love wot
brings me to these parts, to follow the all-glorious callin' of the chase, and
to enlighten all men capable of illumination. To-night I shall instruct
you with a lecture on dealin'.

"'O who shall counsel a man in the choice of a wife or an 'oss?'
asks that inspired writer, the renowned Johnny Lawrence. 'The buyer
has need of a hundred eyes, the seller of but one, says another equestrian
conjuror. Who can take up an 'oss book and read 'bout splints, and
spavins, and stringalts, and corns, and cuttin', and farcy, and dropsy, and
fever, and thrushes, and grease, and gripes, and mallenders, and sallenders,
and ring-bones, and roarin', etcetera, etceterorum, without a shudder
lest such a complication of evils should fall to his lot? Who can expect
a perfect 'oss, when he sees what an infinity of hills they are heirs to?
I 'opes I haven't come to 'Andley Cross to inform none on you what an
'oss is, nor to explain that its component parts are four legs, a back-bone,
an 'ead, a neck, a tail, and other etceteras, too numerous to insert in an
'and-bill, as old Georgey Robins used to say.

"'Eavens, wot a lot of rubbish has been written about 'osses!" continued the worthy lecturer, casting up his eyes.

"I took a fut rule t'other night and measured off a whole yard and an
'alf of real down-right 'ard printin' on the single word 'oss; each succeedin' writer snubbin' the last, swearin' he know'd nothin', until one
would expect to arrive at the grand climax of hignorance, instead of
gleanin' wisdom as one went. There was Bartlet, and Bracken, and
Gibson, and Griffiths, and Taplin, and Stewart, and Youatt, and 'Ands,
and Lawrence, and Wite, and Percival, and Hosmer, and Peters, and

Anonymous by 'Ookem, and Wilkinson on Lock-jaw, and Colman, and Sewell, and Happerley, and Caveat Emptier, all snubbin' each other like so many snobs.

"*Away with them all, say I!*" exclaimed Mr. Jorrocks, throwing out his hands, to the imminent danger of his supporters right and left. "Away with them all! Away with all such rubbish, say I! John Jorrocks is the only real enlightened sapient sportsman; and 'ere, '*ere* from this lofty heminence I hurls defiance at the whole tribe of word-manglin', grammar-stranglin', cotation-crammin', cocks! bids them to a grand tilt or tournament of jaw, where hevery man may do his best, and I'll make mince-meat of them all—catermauchously chaw them up, as the Americans say. (Loud cheers.)

"But, gently old bouy," continued he to himself, "you mus'nt be too 'ard on the fools, or you'll kill 'em out-right; curb your wehemence a little; come, I'll give you a drop of brandy and water;" saying which, Mr. Jorrocks retired to the back of the platform, and took such a swig at the tumbler, as left nothing, as he observed, to "carry over."

Presently he returned, smacking his lips, and resumed in a more composed tone as follows:—"Talkin' about writers," said he, "the best informed man to my mind wot ever wrote on equestrian matters, was Mr. Gambado, who held the distinguished post of ridin'-master to the Doge of Wenice. Hosmer may be more learned, and Happerley more latiney, but for real down-right shrewd hobserwation, the Doge's man flogs all t'others, as the Kentucky boy said. Most writers go out of their way to bring in summut wot does not belong to the subject, but Gambado sticks to his text like a leech. Hosmer, for instance, tells us that a hostrich can outstrip an 'oss, but what matter does that make, seein' that no one would like to go cuttin' across country on a hostrich that could get an 'oss. Another tells us how many 'osses Xerxes had in his army after he passed the Hellespont, but it would have been far more to the purpose to have told us how many Mason or Bartley bought at the last 'Orncastle fair.

"Still I don't mean to say that Gambado was all over right, for there are points upon which the Doge's man and I differ, though fashion, in course, has altered things since his time. He writes upon 'osses in general, and says little about those for carrying' a scarlet, without bringin' it to shame, which is wot we most want information upon. Some of his positions too are bad. For instance, talkin' of eyes, he says, some people make a great bother about an 'oss's eyes, jest as if they have anything to do with his haction, and Geoffery says, that if a man chooses to ride without a bridle it may be matter of moment to him to have an 'oss with an eye or two, but that if he has a bridle, and also a pair of eyes of his own, it is p*a*rfect*lie* immaterial whether the 'oss sees or not. Now, from this, I thinks we may infer that the Doge either did not keep 'ounds, or that the country he 'unted was flat and unenclosed, otherwise Gambado would certainlie have felt the inconwenience of ridin' a blind 'un. Indeed, I almost think, from his declining the Rev. Mr. Nutmeg's offer of a mount on his brown 'oss, that Mr. Gambado either was not a sportsman, or had arrived at a time of life when the exertion of 'unting was too great for him.

"The case was this," observed Mr. Jorrocks, taking up the work,

" and the advice is as good now as it was then. Nutmeg says, in his letter
to the ex-ridin' master, who appears to have been actin' as a sort of chamber
counsel on 'oss cases :—' You must know, sir, I am werry fond of 'unting,
and live in as fine a scentin' country as any in the kingdom. The soil is
pretty stiff, the leaps large and frequent, and a great deal of timber to
get over. Now, sir, my brown 'oss is a werry capital 'unter; and though
he is slow, and I cannot absolutely ride over the 'ounds (indeed the

A HORSE WITH ONLY ONE FAULT.

country is so enclosed that I do not see so much of them as I could wish),
yet, in the end, he generally brings me in before the 'untsman goes home
with the dogs.'

"And here let me observe," said Mr. Jorrocks, breaking off, " that
that is neither good sportin' nor good language, and Nutmeg, I should
think, had been one of your Macadamizin' happetite 'unting parsons, or
he would neither have talked of ridin' over the 'ounds, or yet being
content to draggle up after the worry, and just as the *dogs*, as he calls

them, were going home—But let that pass." Mr. Jorrocks then resumed his reading—

" 'Now, sir, my brown 'oss is a noble leaper, and never gave me a fall in his life in that way ; but he has got a hawkward trick (though he clears everything with his fore legs in capital style) of leaving the other two on the wrong side of the fence ; and if the gate or stile happens to be in a sound state, it is a work of time and trouble to get his hind legs over. He clears a ditch finely indeed, with two feet, but the others constantly fall in ; that it gives me a strange pain in my back, very like what is called a lumbago ; and unless you kindly stand my friend and instruct me how I am to bring these hind legs after me, I fear I shall never get rid of it. If you please, sir, you may ride him a 'unting yourself any day you will please to appoint, and you shall be 'eartily welcome.'

" To this letter Gambado replied as follows :—

" ' REVEREND SIR,

" ' Your brown 'oss being so good an 'unter, and as you observe, having so fine a notion of leapin', I should be 'appy if I could be of any service in assistin' you to make his two hind legs follow the others ; but, as you observe, they seem so werry perwerse and obstinate, that I cherish but small 'opes of prewailin' upon them—I have looked and found many such cases, but no cure—However, in examinin' my papers I have found out somethin' that may prove of service to you, in your werry lamentable case—An oat-stealer or ostler has informed me, that it is a common trick played upon bagsters or London riders, when they are not generous to the servants in the inn, for a wicked boy or two to watch one of them as he turns out of the gateway, and to pop a bush or stick under his 'oss's tail, which he instantly brings down upon the stick and 'olds it fast, kickin' at the same time at such a rate as to dislodge the bagman, that bestrides him—Suppose then, when your 'oss has flown over a gate or stile in his old way, with his fore legs only, you were to dismount, and clap your vip or stick properly under his tail, and then mount again ; the puttin' him in a little motion will set him on his kickin' principles in a hurry, and it's ten to one but by this means you get his hind legs to follow the others—You will be able, perhaps, to extricate your stick from its place of confinement when you are up and over (if you arn't down) ; but should you not, it is but sixpence gone. I send you this as a mere surmise ; perhaps it may answer ; perhaps not.

" ' I thank you for your offer, which is a werry kind one, but I beg to be excused accepting it ; all my hambition being to add to the theory with as little practice as possible.'

" ' Add to the theory with as little practice as possible,' " repeated Mr. Jorrocks,—" That's wot a great many writers are anxious to do at the present day—But to proceed—Another circumstance wot leads me to suppose that Jeffery was not an 'unter is this. In some obserwations in his Preface on a portrait of Mr. Gambado that adorns the frontispiece, the editor says that it was done by a friend from memory, and tinctured with the prejudice of friendship. ' Jeffery,' he says, ' was not so slim, nor was his eye so poignant ; nor was he ever known to be possessed of a pair of top-boots himself, though he often mentions boots in his writings.'

" That I think," observed Mr. Jorrocks, " is conclusive. But then

what does it prove? Why, that if Gambado, the best of all sportin'
writers, knew nothin' of 'unting, it is the more incumbent on John
Jorrocks to supply the deficiency.

"But whether Gambado, if I may be allowed to speak of him with
such familiarity, was a fox-hunter or not, it is quite clear that he possessed
a knowledge of 'osses far superior to any man of the present day. 'The
Academy for Grown 'Ossmen,' is a perfect text-book in its way, and when
a man has read Gambado's instructions how to choose an 'oss, how
to tackle him properly, in what sort of dress to ride him, how to mount
and manage him, how to ride him out, and above all how to ride him
'ome again, dull must be the dog wot has occasion to go to a riding-school.

"There is a wast of fancy about dealin'—far more than relates to the
mere colour; indeed some say that colour is immaterial, and there is an
old saw about a good 'oss never being of a bad colour, but the first
question a green 'orn asks is the colour of the prad. Old Steropes
says, if you have no predilection that way, choose a mouse-coloured dun,
for it has the peculiar adwantage of lookin' equally well all the year
round. A black list down the back makes it still more desirable, as the
bystanders will suppose you are ridin' with a crupper, a practice no
finished 'ossmen ought to neglect. This latter point, however, is confuted
by Gambado, who says, ' be werry shy of a crupper if your 'oss naturally
throws his saddle forward. It will certainlie make his tail sore, set him
a kickin', and werry likely bring you into trouble.'

"How perplexin' must all this be to a beginner," exclaimed Mr.
Jorrocks, throwing up his hands.

"The height of an 'oss, Gambado says, is perfectly immaterial, prowided he is higher behind than before. Nothin' is more pleasin' to a
traveller than the sensation of continually gettin' forward; whereas the
ridin' of an 'oss of a contrary make is like swarmin' the bannisters of a
staircase, when, though perhaps you really advance, you feel as if you were
goin' backwards.

"Gambado says nothin' about the size of an 'oss's head, but he says
he should carry it low, that he may have an eye to the ground and see
the better where he steps. Some say the 'ead should be as large as
possible, inasmuch as the weight tends to prewent the 'oss from rearin',
which is a wice dangerous in the highest degree; my idea is, that the
size of the 'ead is immaterial, for the 'oss doesn't go on it, at least he
didn't ought to do I know.

"The ears cannot well be too long, Gambado says, for a judicious rider
steers his course by fixin' his eyes between them. This, however, is a
disputed point, and old Dickey Lawrence recommends that they should be
large and loppin' in a horizontal direction, by which position no rain can
possibly enter, and the 'oss will have no occasion to shake his 'ead, a
habit which he says not only disturbs the brain, but frequently brings on
the mad staggers.

"Here again the doctors differ!

"It seems agreed on all hands that the less an 'oss lifts his fore legs,
the easier he will move for his rider, and he will likewise brush all the
stones out of his way, which might otherwise throw him down. Gambado
thinks if he turns his toes well out, he will disperse them right and left,
and not have the trouble of kickin' the same stone a second time, but

I don't see much adwantage in this, and think he might as well be kickin' the same stone as a fresh one.

"There can be no doubt that a Roman nose like Arterxerxes's adds greatly to the gravity of an 'oss's countenance. It has a fine substantial yeoman-like appearance, and well becomes the father of a family, a church dignitary, or a man in easy circumstances.—A Roman nose and a shovel hat are quite unique.—Some think a small eye a recommendation, as they are less exposed to injuries than large ones, but that is matter of fancy. The nostrils, Lawrence says, should be small, and the lips thick and leathery, which latter property aids the sensibility of the mouth werry considerably.—Some prefer an arched neck to a ewe, but the latter has a fine consequential hair, and ought not to be slighted.

"It may be prejudice, but I confess I likes an 'oss's back wot inclines to a hog bend.—Your slack backs are all werry well for carryin' miller's sacks, but rely upon it there's nothin' like the outward bow for makin' them date their leaps properly. Many men in the Surrey remember my famous 'oss Star-gazer. He was made in that form, and in his leaps threw an arch like the dome of St. Paul's. A long back is a grand thing for a family 'oss.—I've seen my cousin Joe clap six of his brats and his light porter on the back of the old Crockerdile, and the old nag would have carried another if his tail had been tied up.—In the 'unting field, however, one seldom sees more than one man on an 'oss, at a time. *Two* don't look sportin', and the world's governed by appearances.

"Some people object to high blowers, that is, 'osses wot make a noise like steam-engines as they go. I don't see no great objection to them myself, and think the use they are of in clearin' the way in crowded thoroughfares, and the protection they afford in dark nights by preventin' people ridin' against you, more than counterbalance any disconwenience. —Gambado says, a bald face, wall eyes, and white legs, answer the same purpose, but if you can get all four, it will be so much the better.

"There is an author who says the hip-bones should project well beyond the ribs, which form will be found werry conwenient in 'ot weather, as the rider may hang his hat on them occasionally, whilst he wipes the perspiration from his brow, addin' that that form gives the hannimal greater facility in passin' through stable-doors, but I am inclined to think, that the adwice is a little of what the French call *pleasantre,* and we call gammon; at all events I don't follow it.

"Broken knees is nothin'.—Where, let me ax, is the man with the 'oss that he will swear will never tumble down? Geoffry indeed says, 'Be sure to buy a broken-knee'd 'oss whenever he falls in your way; the best bit of flesh that ever was crossed will certainly come down one day or another; whereas, one that has fallen (and scarified himself pretty tightly) never will again, if he can help it.'

"At an American 'oss sale, I read of t'other day, a buyer exclaims—

"'Vy, he's broken knee'd?'

"'Not at all, you mister,' cried the hauctioneer pertly. 'The gen'leman wot sells this 'oss *always* marks his stud on the knee, that he may know 'em again'—*haw! haw! haw!* chuckled Mr. Jorrocks; 'Lofty hactioned 'oss!—struck his knee again his tooth!' I once heard a dealer declare on behalf of a broken-kneed 'un in the city.

"There is an old sayin' in Spain, that a man wot would buy a mule

without a fault must not buy one at all, and faultless 'osses are equally
rare.   Gil Blas's mule, if I recollects right, was ' all faults,' and there are
many 'osses not much better.   To be sure it makes a marvellous difference
whether you are representin' the 'oss's qualities to an expectant purchaser, or are treatin' yourself to a bit of unwarnished truth as we all
must do occasionally.   It is an unpleasant reflection, and says little for
the morality of the age, or the merits of the Reform Bill, that, out of
London, one can hardly get rid of an 'oss without more or less doing
wiolence to one's feelin's of integrity.   ' The purchaser has needs of a
hundred eyes, the seller of but one,' says the authority I quoted before,
but dash my vig, they require the seller to make up in tongue what he
economises in wision.

"Warrantin' an 'oss is highly inconwenient, 'specially when you've
reason to know he's a *screw*, and it requires a good deal of management
to ewade the question so as not to diminish the price.   I generally tries
to laugh it off, sayin', ' Vy really warrantin' is quite out of fashion, and
never thought of at Tat's ; ' or if the buyer is a young un, and apparently
werdant, I says, " Why, faith, *I* should say he's all right, but you can see
the 'oss yourself, and can judge better nor I.'

" Men that have much business of this sort ought to keep a slippery-
tongued grum to whom they can refer a purchaser in a hoff 'and sort of
way, as though it were beneath their dignity to know nothin' of the kind,
and wished the grum to give every possible information, which the
warmint knows a great deal better nor do.

" A respectable lookin' grum wot can lie like truth is truly inwaluable
to gen'lemen of this description.   If a man is rich, he may cheat you
with impunity ; it is only poor men wot suffer in consequence.   Honesty
is of no use to licensed 'oss dealers.   Every man supposes they are
rogues and treat them accordingly.   Who does not remember old bottle-
nosed Richards ?   When any one axed his number, he said, " Oh, you ax
any shop-keeper in Hoxford-street where the biggest rogue lives, and he'll
be sure to send you to me ! '

" But to the warranty, as I said before, it's werry inconwenient warrantin', and if a customer sticks to his point, it is not a bad dodge to try
and puzzle him by makin' him explain wot *he* means by a sound 'oss, and if
he gets any way near the point, ax him if he can lay his 'and on his 'art,
and say that he is not only sound but free from all impendin' disease.   I
once frightened a chap uncommon when we got this far, by exclaimin',
' I'm dashed if there ain't a hectic flush on your mug at this moment that
looks werry like consumption.'   He closed the bargain immediately, and
under pretence of writin' a cheque, went into the 'ouse and had a good
look at himself in the glass.   Tat is werry clever at this work, and when
a Johnny-raw axes him if he warrants an 'oss sound, he exclaims with a
hair of astonishment, ' *Warrant him sound* !   Why sir, I wouldn't
warrant that he's an 'oss, let alone that he's sound '—haw, haw, haw.
My friend Dickey Grunt, who lisps werry much, did a clever thing in this
line t'other day.   He sold an uncommon green 'orn a broken-winded
'oss, *lith*ping out when ax'd if he warranted him sound, ' Oh in courthe
like all men I w-a-a-n-t him thound ; ' whereupon the youth paid the
money and dispersed for a ride.   Presently he comes back with a werry
long wissage, and said, ' Vy, sir, this 'ere 'oss is broken-winded.'

" ' I knows it,' replies Dick, with the greatest effrontery.

" ' Then, sir, you must take him back and return me my swag, for you warranted him sound.'

" ' No thuch thing, my good fellow,' replied Dick, ' you mithtook me altogether; I thaid I *wanted* him thound! not that I warranted him thound.' (Loud laughter).

" Old Joe Smith in Chiswell Street had a wicious nag wot would neither ride, nor drive, nor 'unt, nor do anything that a nag ought. Well, Joe took him to Barnet fair, where he fell in with a swaggerin' chap in tight nankeens and hessians, who axed him in a hoff 'and sort of way, if he knowed of anything that would knock his buggy about, to which Joe conscientiously replied he did, and sold him his 'oss. Having got the tin, Joe left the town, for Barnet is only a dull place of recreation, when what should come past him like a flash of lightenin', but his old nag, with his 'ead i' the hair, kickin' and millin' the splash-board of a tidy yellow buggy, with a cane back, and red wheels picked out with green. Presently, up came the owner on a grey poster, with the traces all danglin' at his 'eels, and jist as he neared Joe, the old nag charged the rails of the new mound, snappin' the jimmey shafts like carrots, and leavin' the rest of the buggy scattered all over the road.

" ' Hooi, you rogue! you willain! you waggabone! ' roared the buyer, gaspin' with rage and fatigue, ' I'll teach you to sell sich nags to family men of fortin! You've all but been the death of Mrs. and Miss Juggins and myself—Where do you live, you complicated abomination of a scoundrel? '

" Now Joe, who is a hoiley little chap, cunnin' as the devil, and not easily put out of his way, 'special ven it's his interest not to be so, let Jug run on till he was fairly blown, when he werry coolly observed, jinglin' the odd pewter in his breeches pocket, ' My dear sir, you are labourin' under a werry considerable mistake. If you call to mind what you axed me, it was, if I knowed an 'oss to *knock* your buggy about, and egad! if he hasn't done it to the letter, (pointin' to the remnants on the road,) I don't know what knockin' about is.'

" Haw, haw, haw! " laughed Mr. Jorrocks, a chuckle in which the majority of the company joined.

" Another chap that I know had an 'oss that was a capital 'unter, and good at everything but 'arness, which his soul disdained. Well, it didn't suit the owner's conwenience to keep anything but what the lawyers call *qui tam* 'osses, that is to say, 'osses wot will ride as well as drive; so he looked out for a customer, and presently found a softish sort of chap in green spectacles, and a shiny wite 'at, who having tried him to ride, axed if he was quiet in 'arness. To this the owner had no hesitation in sayin' yes, for he had seen the nag standin' in 'arness without movin' a muscle, but when the buyer wanted to tack a carriage *to the 'arness*—Oh, my eyes! that was quite a different story; and my lord rebelled, and kicked the *woiture* to bits. The buyer tried to return him, but the owner conwinced him he was wrong, at least he conwinced him he would not take him back, which was pretty nearly the same thing.

" Daddy Higgins in Rupert-street had just such an 'oss as Joe Smith's —one of the reg'lar good-for-nothin's—and sold him to a quaker to draw his cruelty wan, assurin' him, when axed if he was quiet in harness, that it would delight Hobadiah's eyes to see him draw. Well, the quaker tried to tackle him, but the 'oss soon sent his 'eels through the splash board, and when Hobadiah remonstrated, all the Daddy did was to laugh, and assure him it would delight *his* eyes to see him draw, for the 'oss would never bear a pair of shafts in his life.

" But enough of sellin'—It's time I was sayin' somethin' about buyin' —No easy matter either.

"'Speakin' of his time, Gambado said it was immaterial whether a purchaser went to Tattersall's, or Haldridge's, or Meynell's 'unt, or to his Majesty's, for it was probable he would be taken in wherever he went, and things are pretty much in the same state now.

"The less a man knows about an 'oss, the more he expects, and the greater the probability of his thinkin' himself *done*. Oh, my beloved 'earers, 'appy is the day, when brimful of hignorance, the tyro enters on his first 'oss dealin' speckilation—Great may be his greenness, but age and experience will cure all that, and who would not barter grey-'eaded gumption for the joyousness of youthful confidence and indiscretion? For that pure werdancy, wot sends ingenuous youth up back-slums in search of 'osses advertisin' for kind masters rather than high prices, the property of noblemen deceased, or hofficers goin' abroad. (Applause.)

"When I was a *bouy*, clods came to London expectin' to find it paved with gold, and many wot read the newspaper adwertisements, must think it's the real place for humanity and 'oss flesh—sich shape—sich symmetry —sich action—sich temper, the most timid may ride, and sich bargains ! Who would trudge, when for twenty pounds he can have a cob fit to carry a castle, or a canterin' thorough-bred, that a child may ride. The werry trials they hoffer would keep a man goin', *prowided* he could but *get them.*

" No man fit to be at large will ever trouble a puff advertisement. If he does, he will find himself saddled with an 'oss that isn't worth his saddle, or may be, taken to a police-office for stealin' of him. Next, let him awoid choppin' and changin'. We know what we have, but we don't know what we may get, is a werry treasurable truism.

"Whatever may be the risks of out-and-out dealin', there is no doubt but exchangin' is by far the most certain loss ; and it is one of those provokin' uncertain certainties, for a man is never certain wot he loses. ' If he don't suit, I'll take him back,' says a dealer ; no doubt he will, but will he return you the tin ? No such thing ! He'll give you somethin' worse, and make you give him somethin' for doin' so, and the oftener you change, the worse you'll be mounted.

"There's an old sayin' that it's easier to perceive the wrong than pursue the right ; and I reckon it's a vast easier to tell a man wot he should not buy than wot he should. Walk along Piccadilly any summer afternoon, and see the seedy screws shakin' on the cab-stands ; there is age, wice, and infirmity, unaided by blisters or bran mashes. Flesh covers a multitude of sins, but cabby stands forth in the familiar anatomy of high bones, and yet there be good shapes and good pints to admire, but no one would think of buyin' a cab 'oss ! Still there is much good awoidance to be learned by lookin' them over.

"'Who wants to buy an 'oss, wot can walk five, and trot twenty miles an hour ? ' exclaimed a wag among the crowd before the bettin' room at

Doncaster. 'I do!' 'I do!' 'I do!' replied a dozen woices. 'Then if I hears of sich a one, I'll let *you* know,' replied the gentleman; and werry similar is my sitivation with regard to adwisin' you where to purchase. One thing is quite certain, that you can't buy experience with another man's money, but then, havin' to pay for it, he will do best wot gets it for least.

"The first step towards a purchase is to make up your mind what sort of an 'oss you want; 'unter, 'ackney, charger, coach, or 'qui tamer.' This is a most important point, especial where you go to a dealer's, where they never have less than thirty or forty, and as many more comin' from 'Orncastle or 'Owden, or at their farms in the country. For want of this

"BUT I DOESN'T VONT A COW!"

previous arrangement, I once saw a rum scene between Septimus Green, old Verd Antique's ninth son, and Tommy Doem, wot kept the Pelican Livery and Bait Stables in Cripplegate. Old Tommy was on the eve of his perihodical bankruptcy, and jest afore shuttin' up, Septimus arrived flourishin' his cambric, with his white jeans strapped under his chammy leather opera boots, and a tartan Joinville across his neck. Old Tom eyed him as he swaggered down the ride, and having exchanged nods, Septimus began axin' Tommy if he had anything in his line, jest as though he bought an 'oss every other day. Tommy paused and considered, runnin' his mind's eye, as it were, through the seven stalls, and the ten stalls, and the fifteen stalls, and all the loose boxes, and then as usual he called for Joe. Joe was the pictur of a dealer's man; red nose, blear eyes, long body, short legs,—and master and man were one. After a little side talk, in the course of which Tommy heard with regret that the brown was at Greenwich, and the roan at Dulwich, and the white at Blackheath, and half a dozen others of Green's cut away on trial, Tommy exclaimed, with a hair of sudden enlightenment, 'But Joe, there's the cow! jest slip on the 'altar, and bring her hup the ride.'

" ' Cow!' exclaimed Septimus, ' I wants an 'oss!'

" ' Well, but *see her out* at all ewents,' replied Tommy in the sweetest manner possible, 'lookin' costs nothin', added he.

" ' But I doesn't vont a cow!' roared Septimus, bustin' with rage

" Jest then the street gates closed, and hup came Joe, runnin' the cow as he would an 'oss, old Tommy praising her haction, and the way she lifted her leg, swearing she never would come down, takin' no notice of Green stormin' and swearin' he didn't want a cow, he wouldn't take a cow in a gift; and I really believe if I hadn't been there, old Tommy would have talked him into it—for he certain*lie* had the most buttery tongue that ever was hung—and the gates were locked into the bargain.

" But let us narrow the field of 'oss speckilation, and view our buyer on the road to a dealer's in search of an 'unter. No man should go there in black silk stockin's; dress trousers are also out of character. And here I may observe that there be two sorts of fox-'unters—the quiet fox-'unter wot goes out werry swell, but comes home and resumes the appearance of a gemman, and the Tom-and-Jerry fox-'unter wot goes out now and then, to smoke cigars, pick up a steeple-chaser, wear groomish clothes, and be able to talk of the 'ounds. The latter are not the men for the dealer's money. They turn the stables over from end to end, worm out the secrets, and keep a register of the fluctuations in price of each 'oss. Some act as middle-men between the buyer and seller, gettin' wot they can out of each for their trouble. ' I can buy him cheaper than you,' they say, and so they benefit the buyer by pocketin' the difference. These are the bouys to bother a dealer's vig! A vink from them stops many a bargain, while an approvin' nod from such distinguished judges drives ingenuous youth into extempore bargains that they would otherwise bring half their acquaintance to inspect.

" When three men enter a yard, a dealer seldom opens out. Two are plenty for business—if the buyer is *pea*-green, he had better get some riper friend to play first fiddle, and he must be spectator. If he has a button at his 'at and 'olds his tongue, he may pass for a quiet fox-'unter, and so command respect. There's ' masonry ' in fox-'unting, and a loop in at the linin', or a button behind, will do more than all the swagger and bluster in the world.

It is an inwariable rule with the dealers to praise the bad points and let the good 'uns speak for themselves. It is a waste of time observin' that an 'oss is large in the 'ead or light in the carcase, 'cause a contradiction is sure to follow. It is equally useless axin' the age of a dealer's 'oss, because they are all ' six h'off.' If you object to shape, make, or colour, they will tell you it's all fancy! That some folks like a happle others a honion, and Lord So-and-So would give any price for sich an 'oss. As to hargufying with a dealer, that's quite out of the question, because he has his' cut and dried answers to every obserwation you can make, and two or three grums to swear to what he says. Keep, therefore, in mind what Gambado said about being *done*, keep also in view the sort of nag you want, and don't be talked into buyin' a cow, and when an 'oss of your figure makes his appearance, look him full in the face, as though you were used to such interviews. If you have read about sand-cracks, and sallenders, and sit-fasts, and thorough-pins, and quittors, and locked jaws, and curbs, you will save yourself the trouble of enquirin' after any of them by axin' the dealer if he'll warrant him sound. In course he'll say yes, and you may then proceed with your view. The precept 'no fut no 'oss,' is well to be borne in mind perhaps, as also ' no 'ock no 'unter.' Now 'ark forward!

" The dealer, what with his tongue and his whip, will keep you and the nag in a state of trepidation.

" All the good qualities 'oss flesh is heir to will be laid to his charge, and there will be nothin' you can ax but what he will be able to do—'Leap ! Lor bless you, Sir, I vish you'd see'd him last Friday gone a week with the Queen's staggers at Slough. We was a runnin' old Skylark, wot always goes straight, when he planted the field at a six foot vall, dashed and coped with broken bottles—Not another 'oss looked at it, and Davis declared he never see'd sich a lip in his life.'

" *Spooney.*—' Vill he go in 'arness, do you think ? '

" *Dealer.*—' Quietest crittur alive ! Jack's eldest bouy here, a lad o' thirteen, driv him and another to Mile End and back, 'long the Strand, through Fleet Street, Cheapside, and all, busiest time o' day, and he nouther looked to the right nor the left. Lay your leg over him, sir ! '

" Now this latter is an inwitation for the gen'leman to mount, and if so be he of the button has never been much used to ride, he had better let his friend use his leg, or should neither be werry expert, let the dealer's man throw his over. Some 'osses don't like strangers, and nothin' looks so foolish as a man floored in a dealer's yard. Still mountin' is the first step in practical 'ossmanship, and it don't need no conjuror to know that unless a man mount he can have no ride. Should our friend think well of the nag's looks, perhaps he cannot begin his acquaintance too soon. If he sees no wite of the eye or symptoms of wice, no coaxin' or whooain', or shoulderin' to get him to stand, let him march boldly up and mount, like William the Conqueror. 'Osses are queer critturs, and know when we are frightened of them just as well as we do ourselves. Born to be controlled, they stoop to the forward and the bold !

" If Green'orn gets fairly up, the chances are he likes his mount. It is pleasant to find one's self carried instead of kicked off, and some 'osses never ride so well as on trial. Out then Spooney goes, and tries all his paces ; a self-satisfied smile plays on his mug, as rein on neck he returns down the covered ride, and the dealer, with a hair of indifference, axes, ''Ow he likes him ? '

" *Spooney.*—' Why pretty well—but I think he *ray*-ther pulls—I fear he'll be windictive with 'ounds.'

" *Dealer.*—' Pulls ! Vy, if you *pulls* at him, in all humane probability

he'll *pull* at you—-otherwise you might ride him with a thread,' addin'
aside, ' I sells 'osses not 'ands.   Finest mouth'd nag I ever was on ! '

" *Spooney.*—' Well, but you'll take a *lee*-tle less than what you ax ? '

" *Dealer.*—' Couldn't take a fardin' less !—gave within three sovs. of
that myself, and brought him all the vay from 'Orncastle—Squire Smith
will take him if you don't—indeed, here comes his grum.'

" Here the dealer's liveried and booted servant appears.

"The bargain is then closed—the money paid, a warranty included in
the stamped receipt, and Spooney's first ride is to Field's, or the Weteri-
nary College, to have him examined.   One pound one is thus added to
his price.

"Thus, my beloved 'earers," concluded Mr. Jorrocks, " have I conducted you through the all-perilous journey of your first deal, showin' how
warious and conflictin' are the opinions relative to 'osses, and how, as in
many cases, wot is one man's meat is anither man's puzzon.   Far be it
from me to say, that you will be much wizer from anything you have
heard, for the old stager will find nothin' but what he knew before, while
all that can be taught the beginner is not to be too sanguinary in his
expectations.

" ' Turn about is fair play,' as the devil said to the smoke-jack, and it
is only right that those wot have inwested capital in the purchase of experience, should be allowed to get a little back.   By-and-by it will be
Green'orn's turn, and then little Spooney, who now goes sneakin' up the
yard, will swagger boldly in, commandin' the respect and attention of the
world.

" We must all creep afore we can walk, and all be bitten afore we can
bite.   But let not ingenuous youth despair !   If his 'oss is not so good
as he might be, let him cherish the reflection that he might have been far
worse !   Let him apply that moral precept so beautifully inculcated
towards his better 'alf :—

> " ' Be to his faults a little blind,
>   Be to his wirtues ever kind.'

" So shall little Spooney jog on rejoicin' !   Each succeedin' year shall
find him better mounted, and at each fresh deal, he will become a wiser,
and, I 'opes, an 'appier man."

Mr. Jorrocks concluded amidst loud and universal applause.

A loud call being then made on Roger Swizzle, that genius at length
stepped forward, and after a few preparatory hems, declared that " of all
the lectures he had ever listened to, either at Guy's, Bartholomew's, or
elsewhere, he had never heard one so replete with eloquence, genius, and
genuine information. (Cheers.)   " Hunting, and Handley Cross waters "
(the original Spa! some one cried out), "the original Spa, of course," repeated
Roger, " would cure every complaint under the sun, and if he hadn't such
a wash-ball seat, he declared he'd turn sportsman himself.   Before they
dispersed, however, let them pay a tribute of respect to the gentleman to
whom they were indebted for such a great sporting luminary—he proposed three cheers for Captain Doleful."

Captain Doleful returned thanks, and proposed three cheers for Roger
Swizzle, after which the majority of the male portion of the meeting

resolved themselves into a brandy-and-water committee (Jorrocks in the chair), which sat very late, and resulted in our friend being left to pay the greater share of the shot.

CHAPTER XIX.

HUNTSMAN WANTED.

WANTED IMMEDIATELY, for the HANDLEY CROSS FOX-HOUNDS, a strong, active, bold, enterprising young man, in the above capacity. He must be desperately fond of hunting, and indefatigable in the pursuit of it. He must be shrewd, sensible, good-tempered, and sober; exact, civil, and cleanly; a good horseman, and a good groom; his voice must be strong, clear, and musical; and his eye so quick, as to perceive which of his hounds carries the scent when all are running; and he must have so excellent an ear as always to distinguish the foremost hounds when he does not see them. He must be quiet, patient, and without an atom of conceit. Address (post paid), stating full particulars as to age, size, weight, previous service, &c., to M.F.H. JOHN JORROCKS, Diana Lodge, Handley Cross Spa.

Such was the special advertisement that our friend Mr. Jorrocks, with the aid of the editor, drew up for insertion in that gossiping publication the "Handley Cross Paul Pry," from whence it was copied into the "Post," and the London sporting papers generally, producing an immense sensation in the world of servitude.

People whose establishments are regulated with such regard to laziness, that John knows whether it is his business to brush his master's hat, or James's, can have little idea how those in middle life get served at all, or yet the sort of servants that offer themselves for any situation that may be vacant.

Thus, great Herculean ploughmen will offer themselves as postillions, and failing that, will consider themselves equally fit for butlers; while fellows that have never been in a stable, will undertake the charge of horses and carriages, and drive if required.

The above striking advertisement soon caused Diana Lodge to be besieged by all the idle, dog-stealing raffs in the country—flash, slangey-looking scamps in long waistcoats, greasy livery coats with covered buttons, baggy breeches, and square-toed gaiters, buttoning in front of the knee. They all spoke in the highest terms of themselves, and though none of them had ever hunted, they all thought they'd "like it," and one had actually got so far in a hunting establishment, as to have been what he called second pad groom—viz., a helper at twelve shillings a-week. The following sample will show the general character of the correspondence.

"EDGEBASTON.

"SIR,

"I am in whant of a situation, Seeing your advertsment in the Life papey If a greable to you it whould sute me verrey well I have not been in survice be fore I have been A Horse Dealer for my self and with my Father But I have no doubt that I am compident to take the situation for I been used to hunting all my life and have rode in sum of the furst Steeple Chases in the country I can refure you to John Cock's Esq. Cocks' Hall, near Beccles. I have been yoused to hunt with many fine hounds—Stag Hounds, Beagles, and all, and know all about them. I am maried but no famley, onley my self and wife. I am 28 years of age 10 stone wight But as for wage I shall leave for you to state if every other thing meets your approbation I have a friend that is Butler with Captain Boxer, at Bath, you can right to him if you think proper As E knows my self and famely,

" I remain
" Yours
" Obdiaint
" Servant
" Thomas Loggan.

" To John Jorrocks, Esq.,
     " Of the Handley Cross Hunt,
         " Handley Cross."

" Warminster.

" Sir,
          " On hearing you want a huntsman, I take the liberty of writing to enquire after the place I thoroly understand my business either as groom or coachman and have been accustomed with hounds I live at present with John Jones Esq. at Warminster as groom and gardner where I leave on Thursday first if you want a servant I shall be glad to serve you as I am a married man.

" Your obedient servant,
" John Crakethorpe.

" To Mr. Jorrocks, Esq.
     " Handley Cross."

" Dear Sir,
          " I take the liberty of writing those Few Lines to you Hereing that you are In Want of A Servant And I Am in Want of A Situation If you Have No Objections And I have Been in the Racing Stables Seven Years And My Age is 23 And Stands About 65 foot 6½ And My Wages Will be 30£ A Year And If you thought I Should Suit You Direct to Mark Spraggon, North-fleet And for My Caracter Inquire of Major Barns of Horton Hall Near York And My Weight is A bout 9 stone. I am disengaged in the woman way.

" Your humble Servant,
" Mark Puncheon.

" To J. Jorrocks, Esq.,
     " Fox Hunter,
         " Handley Cross."

" Sir,
          " I saw in your advertisement wanted, a single young man as huntsman with a tow days a-week pack of hounds, I should like to know

what the celery will be, as I think I could fulfill this situation very well,
my weight is 9½ stones, Please to write with return of Post about the
Celery and where the situation is, You will much Oblige

" I remain your
" humble Servant,
" JOHN GREEN.

"MR. JORROCKS, M.F.H."

" SIR,

" I write these few lines to inform you that I have seen in the
Field paper that you are in want of a young man as huntsman to your
hounds and I have sent these few lines to say I am a marred man and has
a family but I cannot move my Wife for 4 years to come for I have 8
Boys at trade and they get their meat and lodge at home so if you do not
get one to suet you I should be happy to wait on you if you think that I
will suet you I have been with boath fox Hounds and Harriers to take
care of them in the Kennels and Hunting them in the field and I can
Groom my own Horses to which I like to take Car of my own Horses
allways as for my Age is 52 years and my Weight is 9 stone and has
been 5 years in my last sittuation but I do not wish to give you the
trouble to write back if you get one to suet you for I can be at liberty
in a Week's Notice, so if you think I will suet you my wages is one
Pound per Week and meat in the House likewise, and Close to hunt in so
I remain

" Your humble Servant,
" JOHN COX.

" Please to Direct tc
    Mr. John Cox,
        (Huntsman)
        Epsom."

" To MR. JOHN JORROCKS,
    " MASTER OF HOUNDS, HANDLEY CROSS."

Finding the applications by letter becoming numerous, Mr. Jorrocks
soon discontinued answering those which he did not think held out any
prospect of suiting, but the following from the well-known Dick Bragg
roused his bile into the answer that succeeds :—

" DEAR SIR,

" Seeing that you are in wants of an energetic gent to hunt
your hounds, I beg to represent my qualifications for the appointment.
I've held office Sir in some first rate administrations, yes Sir, in
some first rate administrations Sir ; my Lord Reynards Sir of Turkey-
pont Park Sir, the Duke of Downeybird of Downeybird Castle Sir,
but my precious health not being quite adequate to the mental exertion
and bodily fatigue consequent on a four or five days a week establishment,
I have determined to sink the dignities of life a little in favor of Peace
and quietness and should have no objection to negotiate an alliance with
you for the management of your hounds and country.

I.

" One thing I should stipulate at starting, namely, that if we do not agree, you will have the kindness not mention this application as it would cause me to lose caste in the rank of life in which I have heretofore moved.

"That, I feel assured from your high merchantile reputation I may rely upon—Yes Sir, I feel assured from your high merchantile reputation I may rely upon—To proceed then—In course you would allow me to appoint my own whips, an arrangement that I have always found to be most inducive to sport, for none but a huntsman knows whether his whips play properly into his hands or not, and there is nothing like having the power to turn them off for making them to do as they ought. I don't hold with Beckford that a first whip should be a second huntsman. No Sir, no—I say, a whipper-in can be made, but a huntsman's talent must be born with him—I should basely dissemble if I hesitated to declare that in sporting science my abilities shall yield to none. I will hunt a fox with any man—with the great Lord Elcho himself !

" To descend to particulars however ; perhaps you'll allow me to ask what your salary is—also what the draft hounds may be worth yearly per annum, and what you think the vails will come to—Also if I shall be allowed a boy to brush my clothes and clean my boots, as I shouldn't like to have any dirty work to do—A line to the *Corner* will find me, and hoping to establish a mutually advantageous connection, I beg to subscribe myself

' Yours obediently,
" RICHARD BRAGG.

"P.S. ' *Quick* ' should be the word, as such a chance doesn't offer every day.

"To — JORROCKES, ESQ., M.F.H.,
    " &c. &c. &c.
  " HANDLEY CROSS."

Jorrocks was desperately angry when he got this. He grinned with rage when he read it, to think that any one should think he was such a fool as be taken in by it. At first he was for writing Dick a stiff " M. F. H. John Jorrocks presents his compliments " note, but thinking that would not be sufficient relief to his mind, he turned his attention to an abusive letter calling Dick all sorts of conceited cocktail humbugs, which he sprawled over a sheet of foolscap with his great round school-boy hand, when it occurred to him that the banter tack would be more telling and mortifying, so after a good deal of consideration he concocted the following :—

" SIR,
    " I am werry much obliged by your purlite communication, and much regret that it did not come a little sooner, as I thinks you seem jest the sort of man—I beg pardon—gentleman I want.—I doesn't care a dump about money further nor as it enables one to pursue the pleasures o' the chace, and if you'd shown us the first chop sport you propose, I'd he given you sich a kick at Christmas as would have sent you right hup into

the first class carriage of service, and I makes no doubt my example would have been followed by all the generously disposed.cocks of my 'unt. Unfortunately the appointment is filled up, though perhaps 100*l.* a-year, and perquisites by fair means or foul—which in course I winks at, to the tune of 50*l.* more—might not have been worth your consideration, though Christmas presents would make the salary up good 200*l.* a-year. I does all the dirty work myself, and you might have worn wite kids on non-'unting days.

" Yours to serve,
" JOHN JORROCKS,
" Grocer, Tea dealer, and M.F.H.

"To MR. RICHARD BRAGG,
"MESSRS. TATTERSALL'S,
"HYDE PARK CORNER,
"LONDON."

" Here's a cove vants you," said Benjamin, as he brought in a candle to seal the foregoing.

"Vants me," repeated Mr. Jorrocks, " who can it be ? "

Benjamin.—"Don't know—von't tell me—says his name's Pigg—comes from the north—Scotland, I should think by his tongue."

Mr. Jorrocks.—" Pigg—*humph*—Scotland—*humph*—Shouldn't wonder if he's one of these place-'unting coves—the town's full of them."—Never saw an advertisement work so.—" There," continued he, as he finished sealing the letter, " take that to the Post, and mind you don't pick the 'ead off, and here, Binjimin," continued Jorrocks, " send the Pigg in ! "

" Yez-ur." said Benjamin, taking his departure.

CHAPTER XX.

JAMES PIGG.

SCARCELY had Mr. Jorrocks composed himself in his red morocco audience chair, ere a sledge-hammer sort of blow at the door announced the approach of the stranger.

COME IN ! roared the M.F.H. in a corresponding tone, and the order being obeyed, our friend had a view of his caller.

He was a tall, spindle-shanked man, inclining to bald, with flowing grey-streaken locks shading a sharp-featured, weather-beaten face, lit up with bright hazel eyes. A drop hung at his nose, and tobacco juice simmered down the deeply indented furrows of his chin. His dress was a strange mixture of smart-coloured, misfitting clothes. A blue and white cotton kerchief was twisted carelessly round his scraggy neck—a green-baize jacket, with the back buttons almost between his shoulders, flattened upon a pair of baggy dirty-white cords, between which, and a little red waistcoat, a vast protuberance of soiled linen appeared. His shrunk drab mother-of-pearl buttoned gaiters, dragged upon an ill-shaped leg, making his stooping, lathy figure more ungainly, and the scantiness of his upper garments more apparent. His hands, encased in shiny yellow ochre-coloured gloves, were thrust a long way through the little jacket sleeves, between which and the gloves, coarse dirty wrist-bands appeared—one hand clutched a boy's turned-up hat, and the other rested on a rugged oak staff.

"*Humph!*" grunted Mr. Jorrocks, as he eyed him, observing aloud to himself, "Vot a long-legged beggar it is," inwardly resolving he wouldn't do.

"Your sarvant, Sir," said the figure, shuffling the little hat into the staff hand, while he raised the other to his forehead, and kicked out behind. "Heard tell ye was in wants of a hontsman."

"*Humph,*" grunted Mr. Jorrocks again, "*you* don't look much like one. Vere d'ye come from?"

"Cannynewcassel," replied Pigg. "A, ar's frae Harwich last," added he "but ar's a native of Paradise, aside Cannynewcassel—ye'll ken Canny-newcassel nae doubt," observed he, running the words together.

"Carn't say as 'ow I do," replied Mr. Jorrocks thoughtfully, still eyeing the bird of Paradise. "Is it any way near Dundee?"

"Dundee! no—what should put that i' your head?" snapped Pigg.

"Wot should put that i' my 'ead!" retorted Mr. Jorrocks, boiling up. "Vy, it must be near somewhere!"

"Near somewhere!" now exclaimed Pigg, indignant at the slight thus put on his famous city. "Why, it's a great town of itsel'—ye surely ken Newcassel where arle the coals come frae?"

"You said Candied Newcassel," enunciated Mr. Jorrocks, slowly and emphatically—"you said Candied Newcassel," repeated he, "from which I natterally concluded it was near Dundee, where they make the candied confectionary. I get my marmeylad from there. I'm not such a hignorant hass," continued he, "as not to know where Newcastle is. I've been i' Scotland myself! Durham at least."

They then took a good long stare at each other, each thinking the other a "rum un."

Jorrocks gave tongue first. "Wot 'ounds have you been with?" asked he.

"A, a vast," replied Pigg, "yen way and another."

"Yen way and another," muttered Mr. Jorrocks, still eyeing him intently.

"Aye, ar' ken all the hounds amaist. Tyndale, and D'orm, and Horworth, and arl."

"Ah, but those 'ill be Scotch dogs," observed Mr. Jorrocks, "a country I knows nothin' whatever on—have you been in any civilized country?"

"Aye, civil, aye, they're all civil enough—'gin ye're civil to them. If ye set up your gob, they'll mump it, ar's warn'd."

"No—no—that's not wot I mean," retorted Mr. Jorrocks, getting angry and shuffling about in his seat. "I want's to know if you've ever been in any of the crack countries?"

"Cracked countries," repeated Pigg thoughtfully, scratching his head —"cracked countries, aye—yeas—Warlesend."

"No! no!" growled Mr. Jorrocks, kicking out his legs, "any of the cut 'em down and ang 'em up to dry countries?" asked our master, thinking to exterminate Pigg and be done.

"Why—no—ar' hannut," drawled Pigg, twiddling his hat about.

"Ah then, you'll not do for me," replied our friend, with a supercilious chuck of the chin.

"Why, why, sir," replied Pigg, "ye ken best."

"Ye ken best," repeated Mr. Jorrocks, aloud to himself, adding "what a rum beggar it is to be sure."

They then kept eyeing each other again for a while.

"*Con*-founded nuisance," muttered Mr. Jorrocks to himself, "not being able to get an 'untsman," recollecting the boiled lobster, Plaster of Paris Poll Parrot merchant, and other scenes. "*Con*-founded nuisance indeed." Then he thought he'd sound Pigg again.

"Do you *think* now," continued he, speaking very slowly, and looking very intertly at the applicant.—"do you *think* now you're ekle to my place? first-rate establishment, splendid pack of 'ounds, inwaluable 'osses, swell country, critical field."

"Why, now, it's not for me to say," replied Pigg, turning his quid, "but ar's fond o' hunds, and ar'd de my best te please ye."

"Well," thought Mr. Jorrocks, "that's summut at all events, let me be master, which is agreeable. Wouldn't ha' been so with Mr. Bragg I guess. You can ride I 'spose?" observed he, addressing the applicant in a more conciliatory tone.

Pigg.—"Ride! aye, ar wish ar'd nout else te de."

Mr. Jorrocks.—"And clean an 'oss?"

Pigg.—"Aye, ne doubt,—*grum* him, that's to say."

"You'll be *werry* keen, I s'pose?" said Mr. Jorrocks, brightening as he went.

"Ar's varra hungry, if that's what ye mean," replied Pigg, after a moment's consideration.

"No," said Mr. Jorrocks, "I means, you'll be desperation fond of 'unting.

"Fond o' huntin'! Oh faith is I—there's *nout* like huntin'."

"Dash my vig! so say I," exclaimed Mr. Jorrocks, still brightening up, "so say I! it's the real Daffy's Elixir! The Cordial Balm o' Gilead! The concentrated Essence o' Joy!—Vot weight are you? you're long in the leg," continued Mr. Jorrocks, surveying him from head to foot.

"Ar's lang, but ar's leet," replied Pigg, looking down at his spindle shanks, "ar's sure ar dinna ken what ar weighs—may be elivin stun."

"In course you're a bachelor?" observed Mr. Jorrocks.

"Oh quite," replied Pigg, "ar niver fashes the women folk."

Mr. Jorrocks.—"Vot's your pedigree? 'ow are you bred in fact?"

Pigg.—"A—why—sink"—hesitated the speaker, twisting the hat about hurriedly, "ar dinna ken nout about that. Ar de believe though, gin ar had me dues, ar'd be a gen'lman this day—only ye see, sir, you see," continued he, "mar fore elder John, ye see John Pigg, willed away arle wor brass to the Formory, ye see, and left me wi' fairly nout. Gin ye gan to the Newcassel Formory, ye'll see arle aboot it, in great goud letters, clagged agin the walls. Sink! but he'd better ha gien me it."

"*Humph,*" grunted Mr. Jorrocks, not catching a quarter of this hurried run-together sentence. "*Humph,*" repeated he, looking him over attentively, thinking how to get him to speak English. "Wot d'ye say your father was?" at length asked he.

Pigg.—"Ah, ar dinna ken nout about that; ar's heard tell ar was dropped some where i' Canny Newcassel, but ar niver kenned ne body i' the shape o' father or friend but mar coosin Deavilboger—you'll hav' heard tell of mar coosin Deavilboger, ne doot."

"Can't say as 'ow I have," replied Mr. Jorrocks; "is he a great man for the 'unt?"

"No, deil a bit," laughed Pigg, "it was just that we fell out about. Says Deavilboger to me yen mornin, as I was gannin to Gosforth Gates to see the hunds throw off, says he to me says he, 'If thou doesn't yoke thy cart and gan and lead tormots, thou needn't fash thyself to come back here ony more; ar'll hav' ne gentlemen sportsmen 'bout mar farm.'

"Says ar, to Deavilboger, 'Deavilboger,' says ar, 'thou surely wadn't grudge a man the matter of a hunt, ar that's always i' the way and ready to oblige;' but he's a deuce of a man when he's angered is mar coosin Deavilboger, and he swore and cussed that if ar went ar shouldn't come back—*A, a, a, how he did swear and cuss*—ar really think he didn't leave a part o' me uncussed—'cept my teeth and nails, so ye see we quarrelled and parted ye see.

"But he's a good man i' the main, is mar coosin Deavilboger," continued Pigg, "only he canna bear the hunds, and as sure as iver winter cam round the Deavil an' I were sure to have a dust; but that's all done now and ended, so ar'll always speak well o' the ard Deavil, for he was a good frind to me, and gav' me monny an ard suit o' claes, and monny a half-crown at the Cow Hill and such like times—dare say he gave me this very hat ar hev i' my hand," continued Pigg, thrusting out the little chapeau as he spoke.

"Can you 'unt a pack of 'ounds?" inquired Mr. Jorrocks, wishing to get Pigg on to the old tack.

"Why now it's not for me to say," replied Pigg, "but ar's used to hunds, and ar's fond o' hunds, and have travelled all o'er the world amaist—Bliss ye, all the sportin' gentlemen ken me, King o' Hungary and all!"

"Well, you shall eat as your 'ungry," replied Mr. Jorrocks, not catching the last sentence, "but I wants to know more about you and your pretensions—an 'untsman holds a conspikious place in the world's eye, and it be'oves an M.F.H. to be werry 'tickler wot'un a one he selects. Tell me now can you holloa?"

"Hoop, and holloa, and TALLI-HO!" exclaimed Pigg, at the top of his voice, his eyes sparkling with animation.

"*Gently,*" exclaimed Mr. Jorrocks, partaking of his enthusiasm, "you'll frighten the ladies; tell me now, wot wage do you want?"

"What wage? A ar dinne ken!—we'll not differ 'bout the matter o' wage—What is ar to de?"

"Vy, you'll have to 'unt and feed the 'ounds, clean two 'osses, look arter the tackle; see that all's on the square, in fact."

" Ar can de all that," replied Pigg, " and break yeer 'ard bones into the bargain."

" Humph? *Werry kind*," grunted Mr. Jorrocks.

" Ar mean 'ard kennel bones," explained Pigg, seeing Mr. Jorrocks looked irate.

" Oh, I twig," replied our master, resuming his smile, " break 'em for the farmers—for turnip manure, in fact—We'll go on 'bout the wage."

" Ar'd like to have my vittels i' the house, if you have ne objection," resumed Pigg,

" In the 'ouse," said Mr. Jorrocks, considering, " I doesn't know about that—to be sure you are light i' the girth, and don't look like a great grubber, but 'unting makes one werry 'ungry."

" Bless ye, ar eat nout," replied Pigg, rubbing his hand over his stomach, to show how flat it was, " and ar'd take a vast less wage gin ar were fund in the house."

Mr. Jorrocks.—" S'pose then, we say eighteen pounds, your meat, and a suit of clothes."

Pigg.—" Say twenty, and ar'll find mysel',—ar've a capital cap ar got in a raffle, and a red coat 'ard Sebright gave me."

" No, no," replied Mr. Jorrocks, " none of your cast-offs. The 'Andley Cross 'ounds must be turned out properly.

" Well, then," replied Pigg, " you mun hev it your own way; see gi' us my arles."

" Your wot?" inquired Mr. Jorrocks.

Pigg.—" My arles! we always get arles i' wor country."

Mr. Jorrocks.—" Wot *all* your wittles at once?"

Pigg.—" No, man—sir, ar mean—summut to bind bargain like."

Mr. Jorrocks.—" I twig! See, there's a shillin' for you. Now go and get your dinner—be werry keen, mind."

Pigg ducked his head as he took the money, and slouched joyfully out of the room.

Jorrocks then threw himself back in his red morocco huntingchair, hoping he might answer, and wishing that he hadn't been rather precipitate in the bargain. If Pigg didn't suit, his boots wouldn't fit anybody else. Still he looked more promising than any of the others, and Jorrocks hoped he was keen.

" It might ha' been better p'raps," said he, as he took up a leg to nurse, and entered upon a study of the ceiling—" it might ha' been better if I'd made some inquiries about him—but confound it, wot tradesman can tell anything about an 'untsman, and who else could I ask? Anything's better nor Bin. bellowin' ' boiled lobsters' arter one, or the 'ounds runnin' into Plaster o' Paris Poll Parrot merchant's. Con-found it," continued Jorrocks, shaking his head, " Mr. Payne and Goodhall, and these swells i' the cut-me-downs, do the thing so easy, that it makes us fools o' natur think we can do the same, but dash my buttons, findin' a fox and killin' on 'im are werry different things." Then Jorrocks's run-away imagination carried him right into the cut-me-down countries; to Misterton, to Arthingworth, to Bardon Hall with Sir Richard, to Croxton Park with the Belvoir.

CHAPTER XXI.

A FRIGHTFUL COLLISION!   BECKFORD v. BEN.

S our friend fancied himself luxuriating in a run with the Cottesmore from the top of Ranksborough Hill, he was suddenly disturbed by a loud cry of

"*Murder! Murder! Murder! Here, Sir! Here!*" and Benjamin came bursting into the room with anger and fear depicted in his face, exclaiming, "Please, Sir! here, Sir! that great hugly beast's taken the shoulder o' mutton onto his plate, and swears the taters and gravy are good enough for Betsay and me."

"Taken the shoulder of mutton onto his plate," repeated Mr. Jorrocks in astonishment, "impossible, Binjimin! the man told me he had no appetite at all."

"Oh but he *has*," retorted Benjamin with redoubled energy, "and he swears he'll pick his teeth with the bone, and break my 'ead with it when he's done—I never see'd such a great hugly beast in all my life."

"Vell, I'll go and see arter this," said Mr. Jorrocks, shaking his head, and buttoning up his breeches pockets, as he rose from his chair with the air of a man determined to show fight.

*   *   *   *   *   *   *

"How now!" roared Jorrocks, bursting into the kitchen, to the atonishment of James Pigg, who, knife in hand, was cutting away at the shoulder of mutton to the infinite indignation of Betsay, who seemed about to contend for her share of the prog.

"How now!" repeated Mr. Jorrocks in a still louder voice, which had the effect of making Pigg drop the mutton and jump up from the table.

"Didn't you tell me," said Mr. Jorrocks, speaking very slowly at the commencement, and boiling up as he went on, "didn't you tell me as 'ow that you hadn't no happetite, and yet I finds you seizin' the meat wot's to serve the kitchen for dinner and the parlour for lunch—Vot do you mean by sich haudacity, you great long-legged Scotch sinner?"

"'Ord bliss ye," replied Pigg, "ar was nabbut teasin' yon bit bowdekite," pointing to Benjamin; "mar appetite may be a bit brisker this morn than at most times, for ar had a lang walk, but ar wasn't gannin' to eat all the grub; only that bit bastard wad set up his gob, and say ar was to be in onder him, see ar thought ar'd jist let him see whether or no at startin'."

"Vell, but," replied Mr. Jorrocks, calmly, but firmly, "*fightin' von't do:* I doesn't grudge you the matter o' the mutton, but there must be unanimity and concord, or we shalln't kill no foxes. Binjamin's a fine bouy," continued he, looking at him, " and will fulfil the duties of his station, by which means alone a man can rise to heminence and distinction—*hem!* get fat and rich, werry great things, *hem!*—give satisfaction, and gain unbounded applause, *hem!*—so now jest be'ave and settle yourselves quietly to your dinners, and don't let me have any more nonsense "—saying which Mr. Jorrocks walked deliberately out of the kitchen, and shut the door loudly upon the party. But though our worthy friend had thus apparently settled the difficulty, he was too good a judge not to see the importance of an early understanding between Pigg and Benjamin as to their relative situations ; and, as the latter had to be lowered to the advancement of the former, Mr. Jorrocks had to summon all his dexterity to reduce the one without giving a triumph to the other. Not that Ben would have been difficult to replace, or indeed any loss, but Mr. Jorrocks did not like losing all the training he had given him, and which he still flattered himself would work him into a good and cheap servant. Besides, Jorrocks had committed himself to Ben by ordering him another pair of top boots in lieu of the brown paper ones, and it was hopeless expecting to get another pair of legs that they would fit. Mr. Jorrocks knew the boy too well to suppose that he would easily brook having any one put over him, and the way of doing it occupied our master's thoughts all the afternoon, and through his dinner. As the shades of evening were succeeded by winter's darkness, and Mr. Jorrocks had emptied his third beaker of brandy and water, he stirred his fire, and rang for candles.

Benjamin speedily appeared, but, instead of allowing the youth to depart upon bringing the composites, he ordered him to take a chair on the other side of the table, and listen to what he had to say. Mr. Jorrocks then arranged the candles so that one threw a light on the boy and the other on his book, without their being too near the fire to suffer from the heat. Thus prepared, he gave the fire a finishing poke, and clearing the voice with a substantial hem! addressed the boy as follows :—

"Now, Binjimin," said he, " the 'igh road to fame and to fortin' is open to you—there is no saying what keenness, combined with sagacity and cleanliness, may accomplish. You have all the ingredients of a great man about you, and hopportunity only is wantin' to dewelope them."

"Yez-ir," said Benjamin, assenting to the proposition.

"You must eschew tip cat, and marbles, and takin' backs from bouys i' the streets," continued Mr. Jorrocks, " and turn the main-cock o' your mind entirely on to what Mr. Delmé Radcliffe well calls the Noble Science."

"Yez-ir," assented Benjamin again.

Mr. Jorrocks paused, for it was as far as he had arranged matters in his mind, and the answer rather put him out. "Now, Binjimin," at length resumed he, opening his book apparently at random as he spoke, " this book is the werry best book wot ever was written, and is worth all other works put together. It is the himmortal Peter Beckford's Thoughts upon 'Unting. Thoughts upon 'Unting!" repeated Mr. Jorrocks, casting up his eyes to the ceiling, "My vig, wot a title! Take any page of the book you like, and it's full of reason and genuine substantial knowledge. See!" said Mr. Jorrocks, "I've opened it at page 268, and how his opinions tally with my own.

"'Hegerness and impetuhosity,' says he, 'are such essential parts of this diwersion, that I am never more surprised than when I see a fox-'unter without them.' "Charmin' idea!" exclaimed Mr. Jorrocks, looking up again at the ceiling. "Dash my vig! how true it is. Whoever heard of a lazy fox-'unter? A man may be late for everything—late to bed, late to breakfast, late to the lord mayor's show—but if he's a real out-and-outer, he'll never be late at the kiver side. Vot, I ax, should be done with a man wot is slack? Wot should be done with a man wot is slack, I axes you, Binjamin?" repeated Mr. Jorrocks, after pausing for an answer.

Benjamin was beat for a reply; but seeing his master's glistening optics fixed upon him, he at length drawled out, "Don't know I'm sure."

"Don't *know*, you beggar!" responded Mr. Jorrocks, bristling as he spoke, "I'll tell you then, you warmint. He should be 'ung—choked—tucked up short in fact!"

"Yez-ir," said Benjamin, quite agreeable.

"Now then," continued Mr. Jorrocks, searching in the table of contents for the chapter he wanted, "I wants to tell you wot the great Mr. Beckford says about the vipper-in, and I begs you'll pay 'tikler 'tention to it, for every word deserves to be printed i' letters o' gold, and then, when you understand the duties o' your hoffice, James Pigg and you will go 'and-in-'and together, like the sign of the Mutual Assurance hoffice, and we shall have no more wranglin' about shoulders o' mutton or who's to have the upper 'and.—'Unting is a thing," continued the M. F. H., "wot admits of no diwersity of opinion—no diwision of interests. We must be all on one side like the 'andle of a tin-pot, or like Bridgenorth election. The master, the 'ounds, and the servants, are one great unity, radiatin' from a common centre, like the threads of a Bedfordshire bobbin pillow—hem—and all that sort o' thing—Now," continued Mr. Jorrocks, turning to the book,—"here's the chapter wot I wonts,—No. 9, page one hundred and twenty-two, and again, let me entreat your earnest attention." Mr. Jorrocks then commenced reading as follows:—

"'With regard to the vipper-in, he should be attentive and obedient to the 'untsman;'—attentive and obedient to the 'untsman, you hear, Binjimin, that is to say, always on the look-out for orders, and ready to obey them—not 'anging back, shufflin', and tryin' to shirk 'em, but cheerful and willin'; 'and as his' oss,' says the immortal author, 'will probably have most to do, the lighter he is the better, though if he be a good 'ossman the objection of his weight will be sufficiently counterbalanced.'

"Then mark what he says—

"'He must not be conceited.'—That's a beautiful idee," observed Mr. Jorrocks, fixing his eyes on the boy, and one to which I must 'eartily say ' ditto.'

"'He must *not* be conceited!' No, indeed he must not, if he's to

serve under me, and wishes to 'scape the 'quaintance of my big vip.
No conceited beggar will ever do for J. J.   'I had one formerly,' "
continued Mr. Jorrocks, reading on, " 'who, 'stead of stoppin' the
'ounds as he ought, would try to kill a fox by himself.—This fault is
unpardonable.'

"Dash my vig if it isn't," exclaimed Mr. Jorrocks, " a nasty, dirty,
shabby, selfish trick into the bargain.—'Ow I would trounce a chap wot I
caught at that game—I'd teach him to kill foxes by himself. But 'ark to
me again, Binjimin.

" ' He should always maintain to the 'untsman's holloa, and stop such
'ounds as diwide from it.'

"That's excellent sense and plain English," observed Mr. Jorrocks,
looking at the boy. " ' He should always maintain to the 'untsman's holloa.'
Do ye 'ear, Binjimin ? "

"Yez-ir," replied the boy.

" ' When stopped, he should get forrard with them, arter the 'untsman.'

"Good sense again," observed Mr. Jorrocks.

" ' He must always be content to hact a hunder part.'

"Mark those words, Binjimin, and let them be engraved on your mind's
memory."

" ' He must always be content to hact a hunder part.'

Mr. Jorrocks then omitted the qualifying sentence that follows, and
proceeded in his reading.

" ' You have heard me say, that when there is much riot, I prefer an
excellent vipper-in to an excellent 'untsman. The opinion, I believe, is
new ; I must therefore endeavour to explain it. My meanin' is this—
that I think I should have better sport, and kill more foxes with a moderate
'untsman and an excellent vipper-in, than with the best of 'untsmen
without such an assistant. You will say, perhaps, that a good 'untsman
will make a good vipper-in ; not such, however, as I mean ;—his talent
must be born with him.'

" ' His talent must be born with him,' " repeated Mr. Jorrocks, " that
is to say, he must have the bump of Fox-un-ta-tiveness werry strongly
deweloped ; "—adding to himself, " wonder if that beggar, Binjimin,
has it." He then resumed his reading.

" ' My reasons are, that good 'ounds (bad I would not keep),—Nor I,
nouther,'—observed Mr. Jorrocks,—" ' oftener need the one than the
other ; and genius, which in a vipper-in, if attended by obedience, his
first requisite, can do no 'urt : in an 'untsman, is a dangerous, though a
desirable quality ; and if not accompanied with a large share of prudence,
and I may say, 'umility, will oftentimes spoil your sport and 'urt your
'ounds. A gen'leman told me that he heard the famous Will Dean, when
his 'ounds were runnin' 'ard in a line with Daventry, from whence they
were at that time many miles distant, swear exceedingly at the vipper-in.'

"A werry improper proceedin' on his part," observed Mr. Jorrocks,
without looking off the book.

" ' Sayin', *wot business have you 'ere?*—the man was 'mazed at the
question—*why don't you know,*' said Dean, ' and *be bad worded to you,
that the great earth at Daventry is open?* The man got forward and
reached the earth jest time enough to see the fox go in.'

"Ow provokin'," observed Mr. Jorrocks, "absolutely distressin'—
enough to make a Harchbishop swear. Don't know that I ever read
any thing more 'eart-rendin'. The 'ounds most likely been racin' and
tearin' for blood, and then done out on't. Dash my vig if it hadn't been
a main earth, I'd ha' dug him!" continued he, thinking the case over.

Presently, a loud snore interrupted our friend, and looking up,
Mr. Jorrocks discovered Benjamin sound asleep, with his head hanging
over his left shoulder. Shutting the book in disgust, Jorrocks took a
deliberate aim at his whipper-in's head, and discharged the volume with
such precision, that he knocked the back off the book.

Benjamin then ran roaring out of the room, vowing that Jorrocks had
fractured his skull, and that he would "take the law of him" for it.

CHAPTER XXII.

THE CUT-'EM-DOWN CAPTAINS.

HAVING now got a huntsman, and arranged with Duncan Nevin for
mounting him until he fell in with screws of his own, Mr. Jorrocks felt
if he had business matters arranged in the City, he would be all ready for
a start; "business first, and pleasure arterwards," having always been
one of his prudential mottoes. Accordingly he slipped down by express-
train to the Loopline station, on the Lilywhite and Gravelcoin lines, to
meet his traveller (representative as he calls himself) Bugginson, to wet
samples, and hear how things were looking in the Lane—and the up-train
not fitting cleverly, Mr. Jorrocks repaired to the Imperial Hotel, where,

being as an M.F.H., "rayther above the commercials," he turned into the sumptuously furnished coffee-room. There he found a couple of regular cut-'em-down swells, viz., Captain Arthur Crasher of the Horselydown Hussars, and Captain Blucher Brusher, of the Leatherhead Lancers, carousing after a week's career with Sir Peregrine Cropper's hounds.

Having exchanged their wet hunting things for dry tweeds, and got the week's thorns out of their legs, they had dined and drowned dull care in a couple of bottles of undeniable, Moet-corked, gooseberry champagne, and were now picking their teeth, twiddling their luxuriant moustaches, and stroking their stomachs with the utmost complacency. Mr. Jorrocks's entry rather disturbed them.

"Old boy's made a mistake," whispered the hussar, raising his eyebrows as our creaking-booted friend deposited his reversible coat and writing-case on the side-board—the captain adding aloud, "what shall we have to dwink?"

"Do us no harm, I des-say," replied Brusher, staring intently at Jorrocks, adding, "'spose we say clart?"

"Clart be it," rejoined Crasher, ringing the bell, and presently they had a jug of tolerable St. Jullien, doing duty for Chateau Margaux. The glasses being large, and the measure thick and highly cut, the men of war were not long in discussing its contents, and a second bottle, with an anchovy toast, presently followed.

The captains then began to talk. They were the crack men of their respective regiments, then quartered at Furloughton, each with an admiring knot of his own, and each with the most sovereign contempt of the other's prowess. To hear them talk each other over after mess was peculiarly edifying. "Well, what the deuce anybody sees in that Crasher's equitation, I can't for the life of me imagine!" Brusher would exclaim, amongst his own set, "*Rider!* I really think he's the very worst rider I ever set eyes on!" Then the hussar would express his opinion of Brusher. "Poor Brusher, poor devil!" Crasher would say, "he *is* without exception the greatest humbug that ever got on a horse—greatest tailor I ever saw in my life." And so the gallant men turned out each morning full of envy, hatred, and malice, with the fixed determination of cutting each other down, regardless alike of hounds, master, and field. Hark to their conversation!

"Well I think I never had a better week's work," observed Crasher, throwing himself back in his chair, and eyeing Jorrocks, to see what effect the announcement would have upon him. "Had sixteen falls in five days."

"Sixteen have you?" exclaimed Brusher, doubtingly; "I didn't think you'd had so many. I've had fifteen."

"No, *surely!*" replied Crasher, incredulously.

"Yes I have," asserted Brusher, confidently—"three on Monday, two on Toosday, four on Thursday, three yesterday, and three to-day."

"*Three* to-day!" reiterated Crasher.

"Yes, three," repeated Brusher.

"Ah, but that's reckoning the mill reservoir," observed Crasher.

"Well, surely one's entitled to reckon the reservoir—was deuced near drowned."

"Well, but I was in the reservoir too," observed Crasher, "so that makes me seventeen."

"But, mark! I was in first!" rejoined Brusher, energetically.

"Ah, but you didn't take the stiff post and rail with the yawner out of Cricklewood-spiny though," exclaimed Crasher.

"'Cause I wasn't there, my dear fellow!" replied Brusher; "neither did you take the brook at Waterfield Glen, or the stiff stake and rice-bund on the top of Cranfordheel Hill."

"Oh! didn't I, my dear feller! that's all you know," sneered Crasher. "I took it just after Tom Stot's horse all but came back over at it. Help yourself, and let's dwink fox-hunting," continued he, filling a bumper and passing the claret-jug to his friend, or his foe, whichever he considered him.

"Ah, fox-'untin' indeed," grunted old Jorrocks from behind his Times newspaper—"glad you don't 'unt with me—should 'ave to insure all my ounds' lives and my own too, I should think."

The captains having done honour to the sport that accommodated them with so much jumping, then commenced a more elaborate calculation on their fingers of the number of falls they had each had, in the midst of which they were interrupted by the rushing of a dark-green corduroy-clad porter into the room, exclaiming, pro bono publico, "Please gents! the 'bus for the height-fifteen train 'ill be 'ere in ten minnits!" then addressing Captain Crasher, in a lower tone, he said, "Pleaz zur, your grum wishes to know if you 'ave any horders for 'im afore you goes?"

"Of c-o-o-o-r-s-e, I have," drawled the captain, pompously napkining his moustache with the greatest coolness, adding—"send him here."

The porter withdrew, and presently a stiffly-built, blue-coated, stripe-vested, drab-gaitered groom entered, and with a snatch of his fore-lock, placed himself under the gas-lit chandelier.

The following laconic dialogue then ensued between the captain and him, the captain hardly deigning to look at the man, and treating him quite on the word of command principle :—

Captain.—"Hunt Toosday—Hardriding Hill."

Groom (with another snatch at the fore-lock)—"Yes, sir."

Captain.—"Talavera first—Barrosa second."

Groom.—(as before) "Yes, sir."

Captain.—"Or say Barrosa first—Corunna second."

Groom.—"Yes, sir."

Captain.—"Wednesday, Lubberfield Park, Salamanca first—Talavera second."

Groom.—"Yes, sir."

Captain.—"Thursday, Riddlerough, Toulouse first—Badajoz second."

Groom.—"Yes, sir."

Captain.—"Must send on to the Bull at Lushinger."

Groom, lowly and timidly.—"Please, sir, I shall 'ave to trouble you for some money, sir."

"D——n and b——t!" roared the captain, boiling up furiously, "didn't I tell you you were only to ask me for money once a month?"

Groom, looking confused—"Well, sir,—but if you don't give me enough to last, sir, what *ham* I to do, sir?"

"*Do!*" roared the captain, knitting his brows, and eyeing the man as if he would exterminate him. "*Do!* Do as you did before—go to Mr. Castors," so saying the captain rose from his seat, and dashing his napkin on the floor, bundled the man neck and croup out of the room.

The other captain quickly followed, peeping over the Times as he passed to see whether Jorrocks was laughing, and hurried up stairs, taking three steps at a stride.

Presently the twang of a horn, the rumbling of wheels, with the bumping of portmanteaus on the stairs and in the passage, announced the coming of the 'bus, and then the sound of hurrying footsteps was followed by "r-e-e-it!" and the bang of a door outside, when the renewed thunder of wheels announced that the cut-'em-down captains were gone.

MR. JORROCKS PUMPING THE CAPTAIN'S GROOM.

CHAPTER XXIII.

THE CUT-'EM-DOWN CAPTAIN'S GROOM.

"Got a rummish customer there, I guess," observed Mr. Jorrocks, as the groom now re-entered the room to pick up the waifs and strays.

"Hev that," replied the groom, grinning, and pocketing a pair of dog-skin gloves and a cigar-case his master had left on the mantel-piece. The groom then made a dash at the nearly emptied claret jug.

"Ah, that 'ill do ye no good, my frind," observed Mr. Jorrocks; "that 'ill do ye no good. See," continued he, " 'eres a shillin' for ye—get yourself a glass o' summut warm and comfortable—that 'ill werry likely give you the cholera."

"Thank 'e, sir," replied the man, taking and pocketing the money.

"Are you a stoppin' 'ere?" asked Mr. Jorrocks, who had now arranged himself with a coat-lap over each arm before the fire.

"*I* ham," replied the man, with a knowing leer, adding—"cause why ?—*I can't get away.*"

"'Deed," smiled Mr. Jorrocks.

"Wot, you're i' Short's Gardens, are ye ? " whispered he.

"Just so," nodded the man. "Hup the spout," jerking upwards with his thumb.

"I thought he looked like a fast 'un," rejoined Mr. Jorrocks.

"They'll be 'avin' 'im *fast* afore long, I'm a thinkin'," observed the groom. "Mr. Castor 'ere has wot he calls a lion on his 'osses for I don't know 'ow much."

"Wot you're standin' 'ere are ye ? " asked Mr. Jorrocks.

"Yes, and 'ave been these six weeks, at sixpence a quartern for whoats and all other things in like proportion."

"*In*-deed ! " ejaculated Mr. Jorrocks, thinking he wouldn't like to keep horses on those terms. "Well," continued he, thinking it might lead to something, "'ave ye aught good for anything ? "

"They're not bad 'osses, none on them," replied the groom; "all past mark o' mouth and all done work, but they can go."

"Can they ?" said Mr. Jorrocks, wondering if they would carry Pigg.

"I assure you they can," responded the groom confidently.

"Carry weight ? " asked Mr. Jorrocks in an off-hand sort of way.

"Why, I doesn't know that they'd carry *you*," smiled the man, eyeing our friend's substantial form ; "but they'd carry anything i' moderation."

"Oh, it's not for myself," retorted Mr. Jorrocks, with a frown and a toss of the head ; "I'm a commercial gent, an £ *s. d.* man, not one o' your cut-across country chaps ; only, if I could pick up a thing cheap that would ride and go in 'arness 'casionally, I wouldn't mind a trifle. But I'm not a figurante—not a three figur' man at all," added he,—"far from it—keeps no cats wot don't catch mice."

"Well, either of ours will go in 'arness," replied the groom.

"Vot ! 'ave you only two ! " exclaimed Mr. Jorrocks, "why the man talked as if he 'ad twenty."

"Only two to call our own—our own habsolute own," explained the man—"the rest are jobs—twelve guineas per lunar month, and precious 'ard times they 'ave of it, *I* can tell ye. He *does* knock 'em about, I assure you."

Just then, Castors, the landlord, came to say that Mr. Bugginson had arrived, and availing himself of the introduction, Mr. Jorrocks sought an opportunity, after he got matters arranged with his traveller, for having a little conversation with Castors, beginning on indifferent subjects, and drawing gradually up to the Captain, when, finding the groom's statement pretty well confirmed, Mr. Jorrocks slipped with Castors into the stable to have a look at the nags. Amidst the heaps of clothes and straw in which they were enveloped, our master found pretty good, though abused legs and big hocks, and after observing that he'd "seen wuss 'osses," he quietly withdrew arm in arm with the landlord.

"You see," said Jorrocks, in an under tone, "I'm only a tradesman— a post-hoffice directory, not a peerage man—and I doesn't give extravagant, out o' the way prices for nothin'—least of all for 'osses, but if it so 'appens as you 'spects that these quads o' the captin's come to grief, why

M 2

I wouldn't mind takin' of them at a low moderate figur—twenty, or five-and-twenty pund 'praps—or maybe hup to thirty—jest 'cordin' as they looked out o' doors by day-light, sooner nor they should be degraded i' the 'bus or get into an old ooman's cruelty-wan."

"Just so, sir," replied Castors, thinking it well to have a customer in view.

"As to their 'untin' qualities," continued Mr. Jorrocks, with a pshaw and a pish, I doesn't look at 'em at all i' that light.   It's no commendation to a man wot wants an 'oss for his chay to be hoffered one that can jump hover the moon."

"Certainly not," replied Castors, who sat a horse with firmness, ease, and grace, until he began to move, when he generally tumbled off.

"So," continued Jorrocks, "if you find yourself in a fix, you know where to send to," our friend diving into his pocket as he spoke, and fishing out an enormous steel-clasped, purple-backed, bill-case, from whence he selected one of his city cards, "JORROCKS & CO., GROCERS AND TEA DEALERS, ST. BOTOLPH'S LANE," and presented it to Castors, who received it with a bow.   They then passed by a side-door into the bar, where successive beakers of brandy and water beguiled the time and caused Mr. Jorrocks to be very late, or rather very early (past three A.M.) in getting back to Handley Cross.

CHAPTER XXIV.

BELINDA'S BEAU.

As **Mr. Jorrocks** sat at a late breakfast—his wigless aching head
enveloped in a damp towel—the pawing of 'a horse at the trellised
archway of Diana Lodge, caused him to look up from his well-spread
table to reconnoitre the movement.

"Dash my vig, if here ba'int Stobbs!" exclaimed he, jumping up in
ecstacy, and bolting his bottom piece of muffin.

"Stobbs!" exclaimed Mrs. Jorrocks, rushing to the eagle-topped
mirror.

" Stobbs ! " ejaculated Belinda, almost involuntarily, with a blush and a smile, and Jorrocks ran foul of Betsy in the passage, as she came to announce that " Mr. Stobbs was at the gate."

Charley Stobbs was just four-and-twenty—handsome, lively, and gay, he was welcome wherever he went.   In height he was just five feet ten, full-limbed, but not coarse, with a cleanness of make and shape that bespoke strength and muscular activity.   His dark brown hair clustered in unstudied locks upon a lofty forehead, while bright brown eyes beamed through the long fringes, giving life and animation to an open intelligent countenance.

Charles was the only son of a rich Yorkshire yeoman—of a man who, clinging to the style of his ancestors, called himself gentleman instead of esquire—Gentlemen they had been styled for many generations, and son had succeeded sire without wishing for a change.

The old lattice-windowed manor-house, substantial and stone-roofed, stood amid lofty oaks, upon a gentle eminence above the bend of a rapid river—myriads of rooks nestled in the branches, and the rich meadows around were studded with gigantic oaks, and venerable weather-beaten firs.   The finest flocks and herds grazed in the pastures, ducks were on the pond, pigs and geese revelled in the stubbles, while the spacious yard at the back of the house contained Dorking fowls, the finest turkeys, and the best of cows.   Old Stobbs was in short a gentleman farmer.   His wife had been dead some years, and Charles and a daughter were the only ties that bound him to the world.

The laudable desire of seeing one's son better than one's self, induced old Stobbs to give Charles a good education, not that he sent him to college, but he placed him at a good Yorkshire school, which, just as he was leaving, and the old gentleman was wondering " what to make of him," he happened, while serving at York assizes, to be struck with the easy eloquence or "grand tongue," as the country people call it, of a neighbour's son, whom he remembered a most unpromising boy, that he determined to see if Charles would not train from the saddle and gun and make a grand-tongued barrister too.

Having ascertained the line of study that gentleman had pursued, in due course, old Stobbs and his son started for London, and after a week's sight-seeing, during which they each had their pockets picked half a dozen times while staring into shop windows, they found themselves one fine morning at the chambers of the great Mr. Twister, in Lincoln's Inn Square.

Mr. Twister was one of those legal nuisances called conveyancers, whom it is to be hoped some contrivance will be found to extinguish, and he could find a loop-hole for an unwilling purchaser to creep out at in the very best of titles.   Having plenty to do himself, he took as many pupils as ever he could get, to help each other to do nothing.   Each of these paid him a hundred guineas a year, in return for which they had the run of a dingey, carpetless room, the use of some repulsive-looking desks, and liberty to copy twenty volumes of manuscript precedents, that the great Mr. Twister had copied himself when a pupil with great Mr. somebody else.

The chapel clock was striking nine as father and son entered the dismal precincts of Lincoln's Inn, and before they got to the uncouth outer door that shuts in the chamber set, the great conveyancer had handed his old mackintosh to his bustling clerk, and was pulling a little brown wig straight, preparatory to setting to for the day. The newly-lit fire shed a scanty ray over the cheerless, comfortless apartment, which was fitted up with a large library-table piled with red-taped dusty papers, the representatives most likely of many thousand acres of land, and a rag of a carpet under it, three or four faded morocco chairs, and a large glass book-case, with a twenty year old almanack flopping in front.

"Good morning, gentlemen," said the parchment-faced old man, as the clerk ushered the fresh fly into the spider's web. "Hope to make your better acquaintance," bowing to each.

Old Stobbs would have sat down and told Twister all hopes and fears, but the latter, though a voluminous conveyancer, was a concise conversationalist, and soon cut short the dialogue by looking at his watch and producing a little red volume indorsed CASH BOOK, he politely inquired what Christian name he should enter, and then observing that his clerk would receive the fee, and show Mr. Charles what to do, he civilly bowed them into the outer room.

Contrasting Twister's brevity with his country solicitor's loquacity, old Stobbs told over his hundred guineas to Mr. Bowker, the aforesaid clerk ; and just as he was leaving Lincoln's Inn, his mind received consolation for the otherwise unpromising investment, by seeing the Lord Chancellor arrive in his coach, and enter his court, preceded by the mace and other glittering insignia of office. "Who knows," thought old Stobbs to himself, "but Charles may some day occupy that throne ; " and an indistinct vision flitted across the old man's mind, of stuffing the woolsack with the produce of his own sheep.

Shortly after, with an aching heart and fervent prayers for his son's happiness, the old gentleman returned to Yorkshire ; and Charles, having removed his portmanteau from the Piazza to a first-floor lodging in Hadlow Street, Burton Crescent, made his second appearance at the chambers of Mr. Twister.

*   *   *   *   *   *   *

"Oh, it's *you !*" exclaimed Mr. Bowker, answering the gentle *rat-tat-tat* at the outer door, "come in, Sir, come in—no occasion to knock !— No ceremony !—Paid your footing you know—One of *us*."

Mr. Bowker, or Bill Bowker, as he was generally called, was a stout, square-built, ruddy-complexioned, yellow-haired, bustling, middle-aged man, with a great taste for flash clothes and jewellery. On the present occasion, he sported a smart nut-brown coat, with a velvet collar ; a sky-blue satin stock, secured by numerous pins and brooches ; a double-breasted red tartan waistcoat, well laid back ; with brownish drab stockingnette pantaloons, and Hessian boots. A great bunch of Mosaic seals dangled from a massive chain of the same material ; and a cut steel guard, one passing over his waistcoat, secured a pair of mother-of-pearl-cased eye-glasses, though Bill was not in the least short-sighted.

"You're early," said Bowker, as Charles deposited a dripping umbrella in the stand. "You don't look like a sap either," added he, eyeing

Charles in a free and easy sort of way, for Bill was a real impudent fellow.

"What is the right hour?" inquired Charles, with a schoolboy sort of air.

"Right hour?" exclaimed Bill, "*any time you like*—saps come at opening, others at noon, the honourable not till afternoon. There are two chaps copying precedents now, that the laundress left here at ten last night—(*tinkle, tinkle, tinkle*, went a little hand bell). There's the old file himself," observed Bill, bundling off, adding, as he went, "be back to you directly."

*   *   *   *   *   *   *

"Confound these covenants for quiet enjoyment!" muttered he, returning and opening a pigeon-holed cupboard, labelled like the drawers against a chemist's shop wall with all sorts of titles; "I get no quiet enjoyment for them, I know. One, two, three—there—three and one left," returning a few sheets of manuscript to their hole, "free from incumbrances." "Wish I was," thought Bill—"and for further assurance—one, two, three," counted Bill, "now let's see if he'll have the further assurance to ask for any more to-day."

*   *   *   *   *   *   *

"Well now, what can I do for you?" inquired he, returning from the delivery of his "common forms." There's Squelchback's settlement, that most pupils copy—five hundred pages! Great precedent! produced ten issues, an arbitration, and a Chancery suit.

"But I think I've something in my pee-jacket that will suit you better," observed Bill, taking up a great coarse large-buttoned pilot jacket, and producing a paper from the pocket. "There," said he, opening it out, "there's 'Bell's Life in London;' you'll see a letter from me signed 'Ajax.' Bring it back when you've done, and don't let the Honourable catch it or he'll burn it." Saying which, Bill presented our pupil with the paper, and opening the door of an adjoining apartment, ushered Charles into a room on the right, in which sat two youths in very seedy, out at elbow coats, copying away out of manuscript books.

"Mr. Stobbs, gentlemen!" exclaimed Bill with an air of importance, "Mr. Frost, Mr. Stobbs; Mr. Stobbs, Mr. Frost; Mr. Jones, Mr. Stobbs; Mr. Stobbs, Mr. Jones."

Mr. Frost and Mr. Jones half rose from their chairs, and greeted Mr. Stobbs much in the manner of debtors receiving a chum into their already over-crowded apartment. Frost and Jones were both working men; with their ways to make in the world, they had paid their hundred guineas for a high-sounding name, and betaken themselves to the mechanical drudgery of precedent copying, with an industry worthy of a better direction.

Stobbs's early appearance at chambers inspired hopes that he was going to be a working man, but the sight of "Bell's Life" demolished the idea, and the conversation died out as the pupils gradually resumed their weary occupations.

"The Life" was uncommonly lively that morning; there had been a great fight at No Man's Land, between Big-headed Bob and the Pet of the Fancy, which appeared in the glowing language in which poor Vincent Dowling, as good a man as ever lived, used to clothe his pugilistic accounts. How Big-head was caught, and his nob put in chancery, how he sent the Pet's teeth down his trap in return, how both were floored, and picked up by their seconds with their claret corks out.

Then there was a host of correspondence; complaints against stewards; accounts of races; hints to judges; and Ajax's letter, in which he assumed the toga of his master, and dating from Lincoln's Inn, gave some very queer law respecting landlord and tenant. The challenges too were numerous. Ugly Borrock of Bristol would eat boiled mutton and turnips with any man in England; Tom Jumper had a terrier he would match against any dog of his weight for ten sovereigns, to be heard of at the Jew's Harp, City Road; Joe Scamp could be backed to whistle; Tom King to run on all fours; and the Lord knows what else.

The advertisements, too, were peculiar. In addition to the usual inquiry after hounds, and offers of horses, there were a suit of Daniel Lambert's clothes for sale, a preserved boa constrictor serpent, notice of vocalisation and frontal-frapidigitation, and the meeting of the judge and jury society at the Coal-hole.

Charles kept reading and wondering, amid occasional interruptions from the arrival and introduction of pupils. They were mostly gentlemenly men, somewhat choked into idleness by the prolixity of Squelchback's settlement. Indeed, their chief claims to the title of reading men consisted in the perusal of the newspapers, of which old Twister furnished the "Times," and they clubbed together for the "Chronicle." Bowker's "Life" was well-known, and what with it and a pair of cord trousers Charles had on, they made up their minds that he was a "sporting gent."

Between twelve and one o'clock, all the gentlemen, except the honourable, had arrived, and the old question of "fire" or "no fire" was broached. This had been an open question in the chambers ever since old Twister commenced taking double the number of pupils the room would accommodate, and as it furnished great scope for eloquence and idleness, the debate frequently lasted a couple of hours, during which time the Saps used to sneak out to dinner, generally getting back in time to vote. This day they stayed, expecting the new pupil would "hold forth," but he was so absorbed with "Bell's Life," that when called upon by the chair, he gave a silent vote; and just as Bill Bowker answered the bell, and let off his old joke about issuing a fiery facias, "the honourable" arrived, and the room was full.

The Hon. Henry Lollington, the ninth son of an Earl, was quite a used-up west-end man. He was a tall, drawling, dancing sort of a man, in great request at balls, and had a perfect abhorrence of any thing coarse or common-place. He was a mortal enemy to Mr. Bowker, whom he kept at arm's length, instead of treating as an equal as some of the pupils did.

"Mr. Bowkar," drawled he, as he encountered that worthy in the passage, "bring me a piece of papar, and let me give you orders about my lettars—I'm going to Bath."

"Yes, my Lud!" responded Bill, in a loud tone, to let Charles hear what a great man they had among them.

"Dem you, Mr. Bowkar, I'm not a Lord," responded the Hon. Mr. Lollington.

"*Beg pardon, my Lud!*" replied the imperturbable Bill, bustling out.

Charles at this moment had got into the notices to correspondents, and was chuckling at their humorous originality :—

"'Suppose one man to wilfully fire at another with intention of taking away his life, but accidentally misses his aim and kills another, will the laws of our country find this man guilty of wilful murder?' asked a correspondent.

"'No,' replied the Editor, 'but a jury will, and he will be comfortably hanged.

"'A snake is not a 'barber,' although he 'curls.'' 'The querist is not 'snake-headed,' was the answer to another.

"'We are not aware that a negro boiled, turns white. If *Niger* will boil one of his children and it turns black, the problem will be solved,' he observed to another.

"J. G.—The 'respectable class of servants' alluded to, are very properly employed in turning the mangle; we wish, in their leisure hours, they would turn J. G. inside out.

"The best cure for carbuncles is to rub them with cheese, and sleep in the domicile of mice, who will eat them off in a night.

"The masculine for 'flirt' is cock flirt, if there be such a wretch.

"Apropos.—Hand-shaking is vulgar in polite society upon merely meeting ladies. Pay your respects to the ladies first, married before single.

"Magdalen.—A gentleman may jilt as well as a lady."

The following American story graced the columns of general information :—

"THE NEGRO AND THE CHEESE.—The 'Boston Post' says, that up at the west-end of that city there is a good-natured, fun-making negro, named Parsis, who hovers round the grocery stores in that neighbourhood rather more than is desirable. Like many other gentlemen of colour, he prides himself upon the thickness of his skull, and he is always up for a bet upon his butting powers, and well he may be, for his head is hard enough for a battering-ram. The other day he made a bet in a store that he could butt in the head of a flour-barrel, and he succeeded. He then took up a bet to drive it through a very large cheese, which was to be covered with a crash-cloth to keep his wool clear of cheese-crumbs. The cheese, thus enveloped, was placed in a proper position, and Parsis starting off like a locomotive, buried his head up to his ears in the inviting target. Parsis now began to feel himself irresistible, and talked up 'purty considerable.' A plan, however, was soon contrived to take the conceit out of him. There being some grindstones in the store for sale, one of them was privately taken up, and wrapped up in the same manner as the cheese had been, and looked precisely as if it were a second cheese, and Parsis readily took another bet for 9*d.* that he would butt his head through it as easy as he had sent it through the first. The interest of the spectators in the operation became intense. Everything was carefully adjusted, and upon the word being given, Parsis darted like an arrow at the ambush grind-stone ; he struck it fair in the centre, and in the next instant lay sprawling on the floor, upon which he recoiled. For some minutes he lay speechless, and then he raised himself slowly on his knees, and scratching his head, said, with a squirming voice, 'Bery hard cheese dat, massa ! Dey skim de milk too much altogether before dey make him, dat's a fact.'"

At length, amid many chuckles, having fairly exhausted its contents, in compliance with Bill Bowker's request, Charles left the room for the purpose of returning his paper. As he departed, Mr. Lollington eyed him through his glass, and with an air of well-feigned astonishment, exclaimed, as Charles closed the door,

"Surely, we've got the Tipton Slasher among us!"

"Well," said Bill Bowker, flourishing his great mosaic seals, as he received the paper from Charles, "that's *something like*, is'nt it? And how do you like the Honourable? By the way, I forgot to introduce you! Never mind, soon get acquainted—manner against him—but a good-hearted fellow when you know him. Saw him give a gal half-a-crown once for picking up his glove—noble, wasn't it? Your fiddle-strings will begin to grumble, I guess, for want of your dinner, and by the way, that reminds me, if you havn't got yourself suited for lodging, we have an excellent first-floor disengaged, and Mrs. B. and her sister will be happy to do for you.—Smart gal!—Dances at the 'Cobourg;'" and thereupon Bill, who had exchanged his fine brown coat for a little grey thing that seemed undetermined whether to be a jacket or a coat, kimbo'd his arms, pointed his toe, and pirouetted in the middle of his office.

Charles replied, that he had just taken lodgings in Hadlow Street.

"What, at the feather-maker's?" inquired Bowker, balancing on one leg.

"No," replied Charles; "at Mrs. Hall's, a widow woman's, number twenty something."

"I know her!" exclaimed Bill, resuming both feet, "left-hand side of the way, going up—D—d bitch she is, too (aside); pawned her last lodger's linen—Well, perhaps you'll bear *us* in mind, in case she don't suit—Quiet house—no children—private door—sneck key—social party. You'll find London deuced dull without acquaintance."

This last observation came home with uncommon keenness, for Charles had begun to feel the full force of that London loneliness, which damps the spirit of many an ardent genius from the country. At their own market town of Boroughbridge, he met familiar faces at every turn, while, in London, all hurried on, or looked as they would at an indifferent object—a dog or a post. The style of living too disgusted him.

Instead of the comfortable well-stored table, and cheerful fire, he had been accustomed to at home, he had to stew into hot chop-houses, where they doled out their dinners in portions, and a frowsy waiter kept whisking a duster, to get him away the moment his dinner was done. The dull freedom of manhood did not compensate for the joyousness of boyish restraint.

Mr. Bowker did not give him much time for reflection—"Should have been glad to have taken you to the Cobourg to-night," observed he, "but have a particular engagement, and that reminds me, I must get one of our saps to answer the door when I go, for I must be off before seven. Have to meet a particular friend of mine, a great fox-hunter, to introduce him at the Blue Dragon Yard, where he wants to choose a terrier for the great hunt in Surrey he belongs to. Des say I could take you if you liked?"

Charles had a taste for terriers, and no taste for his own society, and without ascertaining what Bowker's offer amounted to, he gladly accepted it, and just as that worthy had fixed for him to meet him at his snuff and cigar warehouse in Eagle Street, Red Lion Square, old Snarle tinkled the bell for his biscuit, and Charles returned to the pupils' room.

Having settled, on the motion of Mr. Lollington, that Charles was a snob, he met with little encouragement from his brother pupils. They answered his questions, and were civil, but that was all. There was no approach to sociality, and as a dirty, slip-shod straw-bonneted hag of a laundress scattered some block tin candlesticks with thick-wicked candles about the pupils' room, Charles repaired to a neighbouring chop-house, to kill time, until he was due at Mr. Bowker's.

*   *   *   *   *   *   *

At the appointed hour, a fan-tailed gas-light revolving between miniature negroes, stopped his progress up the poverty-stricken region of Eagle Street, and looking up—" BOWKER AND CO'S WHOLESALE AND RETAIL SNUFF WAREHOUSE," figured in gilt capitals above the shop-front, while a further notification of " THE TRADE SUPPLIED," appeared in the window, though the coal-shed, milk shop, pawn-broking, huckstering appearance of the dirty, narrow, irregularly built street, gave a palpable contradiction to the assertion. Large gilt-lettered barrels were ranged along the walls and floor of the shop, and the lower part of the window was strewed with snuff-boxes, Meerschams, loose cigars, and wooden rolls of tobacco.

" Come in ! " exclaimed a female voice, through the sash-door, drawing a green curtain aside, and showing a fire in the little back parlour—as Charley hesitated about entering, on seeing the shop empty—" Oh, it's Mr. Stobbs ! " continued the voice, and a fine fat tawdry woman in ringlets and a yellow gauze gown with short sleeves, made her appearance. The pleasure of being recognised in London was grateful, and Charley readily accepted the lady's invitation to enter and sit down.

" Bill 'll be here presently," observed she, sweeping a handful of filbert shells off the green baize table cover, and throwing them on to the fire. "Take a glass of brandy," said she, handing a tumbler off a side table, and passing the bottle to Charley, to help himself and replenish her glass.

" 'Ot with ? or cold without ? " inquired Mrs. Bowker, pointing to a little black kettle singing on the stand on the upper bar of the fire.

Charles took hot with, and so did Mrs. Bowker ; and the handsome dancer from the Cobourg coming in, they all had hot together.

" Is Stobbs here ? " now exclaimed Bowker, bursting into the shop, with his pea-jacket collar up to his ears, and a low-crowned broad-brimmed hat on his head.—" Ah, you rogue !—what, you've found your way to the ladies, have you ? " continued he, throwing open the sash-door.—" Well, sorry to interrupt you, but my friend's awaiting, so come along and renew your acquaintance here another time. Always happy to see you, you know." Charles bid his fair friends a hasty adieu, and Bowker, thrusting his arm through his, led the way along Eagle Street to the turning down of Dean Street. Under the lamp at the Holborn end, stood a man in shape, make, and dress, the exact counterpart of Bowker. Low-crowned, broad-brimmed hat, pea-jacket up to his ears, tights, and Hessian boots, too.

"Sorry to have kept you waiting, sir," said Bowker, in the most respectful tone, as he approached the figure. "Allow me to introduce my friend Mr. Stobbs—Yorkshire gentleman, sir, of great property—Mr. Stobbs, Mr. Jorrocks; Mr. Jorrocks, Mr. Stobbs," adding, *sotto voce*, to Stobbs, "member of the Right Worshipful Company of Grocers."

Mr. Jorrocks raised his hat, and Mr. Stobbs did the same, and then Bowker, offering an arm to each, they proceeded on their way.

High Holborn, what with its carts, coaches, busses, and general traffic, affords little opportunity for conversation, and it was as much as the trio could do to keep their place on the flags.

"Cross here," observed Mr. Bowker, as they neared the narrower part of the street, and passing under an archway, they suddenly entered upon darkness.

Savage yells, mingled with the worrying, barking, and howling of dogs, issued from the upper part of a building on the right, and Bowker with difficulty made himself heard as he hallooed for Slender Bill.

"I 'opes it's all right," observed Mr. Jorrocks, twisting his watch in his fob, and tripping over a heap of something that lay in his way.

"O, all right, I assure you, sir," replied Bowker, tripping up also. "Confound the rascals," continued he, "near as a toucher broke my neck.

"SLENDER, A-HOOI!" roared he, after three or four ineffectual holloas.

"Coming masters! coming!" exclaimed a voice, and a person appeared on the top of a step-ladder, holding a blacking bottle, with a candle stuck in the neck.

"Come, Billy! come!" exclaimed Mr. Bowker, peevishly, "didn't I tell you to be on the look-out for company, and here you're letting us break our necks in the dark: pretty way to treat gents: show a ligh⁺ come!"

Billy, all apologies, tripped down the ladder, and holding the candle low enough to discover the steps, crawled backwards, followed by Mr. Bowker and his party.

"What's to pay?" inquired Mr. Jorrocks, as he reached the landing, of a forbidding-looking one-eyed hag, sitting in a little curtained corner, partitioned from the scene of action by a frowsy green counterpane.

"O, Mr. Bowker's free here," observed Bill to his gentle wife, drawing aside the curtain, and exhibiting the interior. What a scene presented itself! From the centre of the unceiled hugely rafted roof of a spacious building, hung an iron hoop, stuck round with various lengths of tallow candles, lighting an oval pit, in which two savage bull-dogs were rolling and tearing each other about, under the auspices of their coatless masters, who stood at either end applauding their exertions. A vast concourse of ruffianly spectators occupied the benches rising gradually from the pit towards the rafters, along which some were carelessly stretched, lost in ecstasy at the scene below.

Ponderous draymen, in coloured plush breeches, with their enormous calves clad in dirty white cotton stockings, sat with their red-capp'd heads resting on their hands, or uproariously applauding as their favourite got the turn. Smithfield drovers, with their badges and knotty clubs; huge coated hackney coachmen; coatless butchers' boys; dingy dustmen, with their great sou'-westers; sailors, with their pipes; and

Jews, with oranges, were mingled with Cyprians of the lowest order, dissolute boys, swell pickpockets, and a few simple countrymen. At the far end of the loft, a partition concealed from view, bears, badgers, and innumerable bull-dogs; while "gentlemen of the fancy" sat with the great round heads, and glaring eye-balls of others between their knees straining for their turn in the pit. The yells and screams of the spectators, the baying of the dogs, the growling of the bears, the worrying of the combatants, and the appearance of the company, caused a shudder through the frames of Mr. Jorrocks and the Yorkshireman.

A volley of yells and plaudits rent the building, as the white dog pinned the brindled one for the fourteenth time, and the lacerated animal refused to come to the scratch, and as the pit was cleared for a fresh "set-to," Slender Billy, with a mildness of manner contrasting with the rudeness of the scene, passed our party on, and turned out two coal-heavers and a ticket-porter, to place them advantageously near the centre. This was a signal for renewed uproar.

"Make vay for the real swells wot pay!" roared a stentorian voice from the rafters.

"Crikey, it's the Lord Mayor!" responded a shrill one from below.

"Does your mother know you're out?" inquired a squeaking voice just behind.

"There's a brace of plummy ones;" exclaimed another, as Bowker and Jorrocks stood up together.

"*Luff*, there! *luff! be serene!*" exclaimed Slender Billy, stepping into the centre of the pit, making a sign that had the effect of restoring order on the instant. Three cheers for the Captain were then called for by some friend of Bowker's, as he opened his pea-jacket; and while they were in course of payment, two more bull-dogs entered the pit, and the sports were resumed. After several dog-fights, Billy's accomplished daughter lugged in a bear, which Billy fastened by his chain to ε ring in the centre of the pit.

"Any gentleman," said he, looking round, "may have a run at this 'ere hanimal for sixpence;" but though many dogs struggled to get at him, they almost all turned tail, on finding themselves solus with Bruin. Those that did seize were speedily disposed of, and the company being satisfied, the bear took his departure, and Billy announced the badger as the next performer.

Slender Billy's boy, a lad of nine years old, had the first run at him, and brought the badger out in his mouth, after which it was drawn by terriers at so much a run, during which Mr. Jorrocks criticised their performances, and with the aid of Charley Stobbs succeeded in selecting one for the glorious old Surrey.

But enough of Slender Billy and his bull-dogs. He was a well-known character, but all we have to do with him just now is as the medium of introduction between Jorrocks and Stobbs. That introduction ripened into intimacy, and many were the excursions our friends had together, Jorrocks finding cash, and the Yorkshireman company. But for Jorrocks, and perhaps Belinda, Stobbs would very soon have left the law, whose crotchety quibbles are enough to disgust any one with a taste for truth and straightforward riding; and this lengthened episode brings us back to the point from which we started, namely, Charley's arrival at Handley Cross.

"'Ow are ye, my lad o' wax?" exclaimed Mr. Jorrocks, bouncing out in his sky-blue dressing-gown and slippers, as Charley appeared at the garden-gate, where we have most unceremoniously kept him standing during his introduction.

"Delighted to see you!" continued Mr. Jorrocks, wringing his hand, and hopping about on one leg; "most 'appy indeed! Bed for yourself —stable for your 'oss; all snug and comfey, in fact. Binjimin!—I say, Binjimin!"

"Coming, sir!—coming!" replied the boy, setting himself into a fustian coat.

"Take this 'ere 'oss to the stable, and bid Pigg treat him as one of his own—warm stall—thick blanket—lots o' straw—and crushed corn without end. Now, come in," said he to Stobbs, "and get some grub; and let's 'ear all about it." In then they bundled together.

Pretty Belinda took Charles's proffered hand with a blush, and Mrs. Jorrocks re-entered the room in a clean cap and collar just as the trio were settling into seats. What a burst of inquiries followed!

"'Ow's the dad?" asked Mr. Jorrocks.

"'Ow did you come?" inquired Mrs. Jorrocks.

"How is your sister?" half whispered Belinda.

"Where have you been since we last saw you?" was demanded before Stobbs had answered any of the preceding, and a great cry of conversation was got up.

In the evening Mr. Jorrocks celebrated the event with a couple of bottles of fine fruity port, and a night-cap of the usual beverage—"B. and W." as he briefly designates his brandy and water.

SNUG AND COMFEY.

CHAPTER XXV.

MR. JORROCKS AT EARTH.

MASTER took a cooling draught —a couple of Seidlitz powders —the next morning, intending to lie at earth as he said, and was later than usual in getting down stairs. Stobbs improved his opportunity, and got sixteen kisses of Belinda; according to Ben's reckoning, who was listening outside, ere Mrs. Jorrocks made her appearance either. A voluminous correspondence—a week's St. Botolph's-lane letters, and many private ones, some about hounds, some about horses, awaited our master's descent. The first he opened was the following from our old friend Dick Bragg :—

"*London.*

" DEAR MR. J.,
        " Though I fear it may involve a charge of fickleness, I feel it due to myself to make the following communication :—

" The fact of my having offered my services to you having transpired, I have been so persecuted with remonstrances from those whose judgment and good opinion I value, and representations of the impolicy of accepting office, other than in similar administrations to those I have heretofore co-operated with, that I really have no alternative but most respectfully to request that you will allow me to withdraw my previous communication. It is, I assure you, with great reluctance that I make this announcement, knowing, as I do, by sad experience, the difficulty there is in obtaining talent even under the most favourable circumstances, let alone in the middle of a season, when every body worth having is taken up; but it is one of those casualties that cannot be helped, and, in making this communication, allow me to assure you, Sir, that I shall always speak of you with respect, Sir—yes, Sir, I shall always speak of you with respect, Sir, and esteem you, Sir, as an upright gentleman and a downright fox-hunter. Allow me to subscribe myself,

"Yours very faithfully,

"RICH. BRAGG.

"To —— JORROCKES, ESQUIRE,
"HANDLEY CROSS."

"Ah! Rich. Bragg indeed," grunted Mr. Jorrocks when he read it, "you must think I've a deal more o' the Michaelmas bird i' me than I 'ave to believe you wrote this afore you got my letter. There, Batsay," said he, as the handsome maid now entered with the hissing urn, "take that," handing it to her, "and make curl-papers on't, and don't you be so 'eavy on my witey-brown."

The next letter he selected was from Mr. Bowker.

"*Lincoln's Inn, London.*

"DEAR SIR,
"On calling to pay 'The Life' for your advertisement of 'A hunting-man wanted,' he expressed a wish for you to contribute information respecting the sport with your hounds; and, knowing I had the honour of your acquaintance, he wished me to sound you on the subject. He says he gets lots of pot-house accounts of stag, and bag fox-hunting, with harriers, and such like rubbish; but what he wants is real sporting accounts of runs with superior establishments like yours. An editor, you know, can't be everywhere, or he would like to have a horse in every hunt in the kingdom; but he says if you would have the kindness to furnish off-hand accounts, he would spice them up with learning and Latin. He has 'Moore's Dictionary of Quotations,' and can come the classical quite as strong as the great Mr. Pomponius Ego, whom they reckon the top-sawyer in that line. Some gentlemen, 'The Life' says, send their accounts to a third party, to be copied and forwarded as from an indifferent person; but that consumes time without answering a good end, as the utmost secrecy may be relied upon, and 'The Life' is most particular in combing them into English. In short, gentlemen unaccustomed to public writing may forward their accounts to him with perfect confidence.

"You will be sorry to hear the Slender is in trouble. He had long been suspected of certain spiritual runnings, in the shape of an illicit still, at the back of his horse-slaughtering premises in Copenhagen Fields, and an exciseman was despatched last Thursday to watch, and, if necessary, take him. Somehow or other the exciseman has never cast up again, and poor Billy has been taken up on suspicion of having sent him to 'that bourne from whence no traveller returns.' I hope he has not, but time will show.

"Susan Slummers has cut the Cobourg, and got engaged at Sadlers' Wells, under the name of Clarissa Howard. I said if she was choosing a name, she might as well take a good one: she is to do genteel comedy, and is not to be called upon to paint black or wear tights. Her legs have got rather gummy of late, from too constant strain on the sinews, and the manager wanted to reduce her salary, and Susan kicked in consequence;

N

and this reminds me that I have seen a blister in your stable—James's or Jones's, I forget which—that your groom, Benjamin, told me you applied to horses' legs when they are enlarged. Might I take the liberty of asking if you think it would be beneficially applied in this case ?

"As I presume from a letter I had from Mr. Stobbs the other day that he will be with you by this time, perhaps you will have the kindness to inform him that Mrs. B. will send his 'baccy' by the early train to-morrow, along with your Seidlitz powders, so as to make one parcel do. Old Twist's business is sadly fallen off—my fees have diminished a third —though *my* twist hasn't. We have only half the number of pupils we had. That, however, makes no difference to me, as I never got anything from them but sauce. I hope Mrs. and Miss Jorrocks are enjoying the pure air of Handley Cross. We are enjoying a dense yellow fog here—so thick and so damp, that the gas-lights, which have been burning all day, are hardly visible ; I tripped over a child at the corner of Chancery Lane, and pitched head foremost into an old chestnut-woman's roasting oven.

"By the way, I read an advertisement in a north country paper the other day, of 'the eatage of the fog in a park to let.' I wish some one would take the eatage of it here ; he'd get a good bellyful, I'm sure. Adieu. Excuse haste and a bad pen, as the pig said when he ran away from the butcher ; and believe me to remain,

"Dear Sir,
"Yours most respectfully,
"WM. BOWKER.

"To JOHN JORROCKS, ESQ.
"MASTER OF FOX-HOUNDS, &C. &C.
"HANDLEY CROSS SPA."

Then before Mr. Jorrocks got half through his city letters and made his pencil observations thereupon—who to do business with, whose respectability to inquire into, who to dun, who to decline dealing with, the gossiping Handley Cross Paul Pry, with its list of arrivals, fashionable millinery, dental surgery advertisements, &c., having passed the ordeal of the kitchen, made its appearance with the following important announcement :—

"THE HANDLEY CROSS (MR. JORROCKS'S) FOX-HOUNDS

"Will meet on Wednesday at the Round of Beef and Carrots, Apple-dove-road, and on Saturday at the Mountain Daisy, near Hookey's Hutch, each day at ten o'clock.

"N.B. These hounds will hunt Mondays and Fridays, with an occasional bye on the Wednesdays in future."

"Why you're advertising, I see!" exclaimed Charley, on reading the above.

"I am," replied Mr. Jorrocks, with a grin, "comin' it strong, arn't I ?"

"Very," replied Stobbs, "three days a week—will want a good many horses for that."

"O, I sha'n't be much troubled on the Wednesdays," rejoined Mr. Jorrocks ; "shall jest make that long or short 'cordin' as it suits."

"But you'll go out I s'pose," observed Stobbs.

"In course," replied Jorrocks. "In course—only I shall go out at my own hour—may be height, may be sivin, may be as soon as we can see. Not many o' these waterin' place birds that'll get hup for an 'unt, only ye see as I wants their money, I must give them walue received—or summut like it; but there's nothing like the mornin' for makin' the foxes cry 'Capevi!' " added he, with a grin of delight.

"Nothing," assented Stobbs.

"We'll 'ave some rare chiveys!" exclaimed Mr. Jorrocks, his eyes glistening as he spoke.

"Hope so," replied Stobbs, adding, "let's give them a trot out to-day."

"To-day," mused our master—"to-day," repeated he, thrusting his hands deep in his pockets, and then taking a dry shave of his chin—"couldn't well go out to-day. To-morrow if you like—got a lot o' letters to write and things to do—not quite right nouther—feel as if I'd eat a hat or a pair o' worsted stockins."

"To-morrow will be too near your regular day," observed Stobbs.

"Ah, true, so it would," assented Mr. Jorrocks, thinking he must attend to appearances at first, at all events.

"Better give them a round to-day," continued Stobbs, returning to his point.

"Not prepared," mused Jorrocks—"not prepared. Pigg hasn't got himself 'fettled oop' yet, as he calls it."

"Oh yes he has," replied Stobbs—"saw him trying on his tops as I came down stairs, and his red coat and waistcoat were lying on the kitchen table."

"Indeed," replied Mr. Jorrocks—"wonder 'ow he looks in 'em. Only a hugly beggar out on 'em."

"He's a varmint looking chap," observed Stobbs.

"Yes, he is," assented Mr. Jorrocks; "'ope he's keen."

"How's Ben off that way?" asked Stobbs.

"Oh, Bin's a fine bouy," observed Jorrocks, "and I makes no doubt 'ill train on. Rome wasn't built in a day, Constantinople nouther."

"Certainly not," assented Stobbs, thinking if Ben made a sportsman he was very much mistaken.

After a vigorous attack upon the muffins, kidneys, fried ham, marmalade, and other good things adorning Mr. Jorrocks's breakfast table, our Yorkshire friend again tried to draw the great M.F.H. for a day.

"Couldn't we give the 'ounds a trot out by way of exercise, think ye?" asked he.

"Don't know," grunted Jorrocks from the bottom of his coffee-cup. "Wot good would that do?"

"Make 'em handy," replied Stobbs.

"'Andy enough," replied our master, bolting a large piece of muffin, "'Andy as ladies' maids. Can do everything 'cept pay their own pikes."

Despite this confident assertion, Stobbs still stuck to him. First he proposed that Pigg and he should take the hounds out together. This Jorrocks wouldn't stand. "Be sure to get into mischief." Then Stobbs thought it would do Jorrocks a vast deal of good to have a bump on one of his great rough horses. Our master couldn't quite gainsay this, though he did look out of the window, observing that the sun had risen very red, that he thought it would rain, and he shouldn't like to get wet.

N 2

"Oh, it 'ill not rain," replied Stobbs—"not till night at least,"
ad led he confidently.

"Don't know that," grunted Mr. Jorrocks; "Gabey seems to be of a
different 'pinion," added he, as the noble old peacock now emerged from
under a sun-bright Portugal laurel, and stretching his neck, and flapping
his wings, uttered a wild piercing scream.

"Dash my vig, but that looks like it!" exclaimed Mr. Jorrocks;
adding, as he caught up his right foot with a shake of his head, "Gabriel
Junks is seldom wrong, and my corns are on his side."

Still Stobbs persevered, and, by dint of agitation, at length succeeded
in getting Jorrocks not only to go out, but to have a draw in Newtimber
Forest; Stobbs observing, and Jorrocks assenting, that there would be
very little more trouble in running the hounds through the cover than in
trotting them along the road. And, with some misgivings, Jorrocks let
Stobbs go to make the arrangements, while he applied himself vigorously
to his letters.

CHAPTER XXVI.

A QUIET EYE.

P IGG was all eager for the fray,
and readily came into Stobbs's
suggestion, that they should go
out, and just take their chance
of finding a fox, and of his going
to ground or not as luck and his
courage served.

"Ar'll gan to'ard Duncan's,
and get his grey for wor Ben,"
said Pigg, "gin ye'll set the lad
on to seddle the rest;" adding,
"the Squi-er ar's warned 'ill
ride Arterxerxes."

Off then Pigg went to Duncan
Nevins, and returned with a woe
begone looking horse in a halter,
before Stobbs had made any progress in his department. Ben
was not to be found. Neither
at Mrs. Candy the tart-woman's,
nor at Mrs. Biffin's apple-stall,
nor at Strap the saddler's, nor
at any of his usual haunts, was
anything to be heard of the boy.

The fact was, he had been unable to resist a ride at the back of a return chaise passing along Juniper Street, and being caught by his apron in the spikes, had been carried nearly to Copse Field before he got himself disentangled.

The oracle Gabriel having continued his monitions, Mr. Jorrocks thought to make the absence of the boy an excuse for not going, but now having both Stobbs and Pigg ranged against him, he was soon driven from the attempt. Pigg said "Squi-er Stobbs wad de quite as weal as Ben," and Jorrocks, little loth at heart perhaps, at length hoisted himself on to Arterxerxes with a swag that would have sent a light-carcassed horse over, letting the now smartly-clad Pigg ride the redoubtable Xerxes. So with Stobbs in front, Jorrocks with the hounds, and Pigg behind, they set off at a gentle trot, telling the inquirers that they were only going to exercise, a delusion that Mr. Jorrocks's hat seemed to favour.

Bump, bump,—jog, jog,—on they went; Mr. Jorrocks now chiding, now coaxing, now dropping an observation fore or aft, now looking at the sky, and now at his watch.

"Des say we shall find pretty soon," observed Mr. Jorrocks; "for they tells me the cover has not been disturbed this long time; and there's lots of lyin'—nice, and dry, and warm—foxes like damp beds as little as Christians. Uncommon pretty betch, that Barbara,—like Bravery as two peas,—by Billin'sgate out o' Benedict, I think. 'Opes we may get blood; it'll do them a deal o' good, and make them steady for the Beef and Carrots. Wen we gets the 'ounds all on the square, we 'ill 'ave the great Mr. Pomponious Hego to come and give us a good hoiling. Nothin' like soap.

"Hooi! you chap with the turnip-cart!" now roared our master, to a cartman coming up; "vot do you mean by stickin' your great ugly wehicle right afore my 'ounds!—Mr. Jorrocks' 'ounds, in fact! I'll skin ye alive!" added he, looking at the man, who stood staring with astonishment. And again they went, bump, bump, jog, jog, at that pleasant post-boy pace, that has roused the bile of so many sportsmen, and set so many riders fighting with their horses.

At length they reached the cover side,—a long wood stretching up the sides of a gently sloping hill, and widening towards the summit. On the crown there stood a clump of Scotch firs and hollies, forming a landmark for many miles round. Turning from the high-road into a grass field on the right, the party pulled up to reconnoitre the ground, and make their final arrangements.

"Now," said Mr. Jorrocks, standing erect in his stirrups, and pointing with his whip, which had the effect of making half the pack break towards the cover,—"Now," said he, as soon as he had got them turned, "this is a good big wood—'two 'undred acres or more—and they tells me the foxes generally lie on the risin' ground, towards the clump. The vind's north-vest; so if we puts hin at this point, we shall draw up it, and p'rhaps get close to the warmint at startin', which is a grand thing; but, howsomever, let's be doin'. Draw your girths, Pigg, or your 'oss 'll slip through his saddle. Now observe, there are three rides—one on each side, one hup the middle, *all* leadin' to the clump; and there are cross ones in all directions; so no man need be 'fraid o' losin' himself. Now let's put in. Pigg, open the wicket."

"It's locked," observed Pigg, running the hammer of his whip into the rails, throwing himself off his horse, and pulling a great clasp-knife out of his pocket as he spoke. "Sink, but it aye gars mar knife laugh to see a lock put upon leather," added he, as he drew the huge blade across the stiff band that secured the gate. Open flew the wicket—in went the pack with a dash, a crash, and a little music from the riotous ones, which gradually yielded to the "Have a cares!" and "*Gently*, Wenus;" "Gently, Lousey" (Louisa), with the cracks of the whips of Mr. Jorrocks and his huntsman.

"Now, Pigg, my frind, let's have a touch o' north country science," observed Mr. Jorrocks, bringing his horse alongside of his huntsman's. "I'd like *well* to kill a fox to-day; I'd praise you werry much if we did."

"*Aye, aye*," said Pigg. "Hoic in, Lousey! Solid puddin's better nor empty praise. Have at him there, Statesman, old boy,—ye look like a finder. Deil bon me, but ar thought ar winded him at the crossin' there," added Pigg, pulling his horse short back to a cross ride he had just passed. "Hoic in there, Priestess, ould gal," said he, to an old black and white bitch, feathering round some gorse among the underwood; waving his hand as he spoke. "That's gospel, ar warrant ye," continued he, watching her movements.

"What will't tak for t'ard nag?" inquired Pigg, of a besom-maker, who now came down the ride with a wretched white Rosinante, laden with stolen brushwood.—"Have at him, there, Challenger!" speaking to a hound.

"Twenty shillin'," replied the man.

"Gie ye eight!" was the answer.—"Yooi, push him up!" to the hound.

"Tak' twelve," rejoined the tinker. "Good horse—can get up of hisself, top puller and all!"

"Aye, but we dinna want him to poole; we want him to eat," replied Pigg. "*Had still!*" exclaimed he; "*ar has him!*—TALLY HO!" roared Pigg, cramming his spurs into his horse, and dashing past Jorrocks like a shot. Out went both horns—twang—twang—twang sounded Pigg's; wow! wow! wow! went Jorrocks's in deeper and more substantial notes, and in a very short time, the body of the pack were laid on the scent, and opened the concert with an overpowering burst of melody.

"Oh, beautiful! beautiful!" exclaimed Mr. Jorrocks, in raptures, as each hound put his nose to the ground, and acknowledged the correctness of the scent. "Oh, beautiful indeed!" added he, thumping the end of his horn upon his thigh, as though he were cutting large gun-waddings out of his breeches. "'Ow true to the line! best 'ounds in England, by far—never were such a pack! Shall have a rare Chevy—all alone to ourselves; and when I gets home I'll write an account to 'Bell's Life,' and 'The Field,' which nobody *can* contradict. Hark forrard! hark forrard! hark forrard! away!" continued he, ramming the spurs into Arterxerxes's sides, to induce him to change his lumbering trot into a canter, which having accomplished, Mr. Jorrocks settled himself into a regular home seat in his saddle, and pounded up a grass ride through the centre of the wood in a perfect frenzy of delight, as the hounds worked their way a little to his right with a full and melodious cry.

"Hould hard, ye sackless ould sinner!" now cried Pigg, crossing the main ride at a canter, and nearly knocking Jorrocks off his horse, as he charged him in his stride. "*Had* (hold) *bye, ar say!*" he roared in his master's ear; "or ar'll be dingin' on ye down—fox crossed reet in onder husse's tail, and thou sits glowerin' there and never see'd him."

Out went both the horns again—twang!—twang!—twang; wow! wow! wow!

"Hark together! hark! get forrard, hounds, get forrard!" cried Mr. Jorrocks, cracking his ponderous whip at some lingerers that loitered on the ride, questioning the correctness of their comrades' cry. "*Get forrard, I* say!" repeated he, with redoubled energy. "Confound your unbelievin' souls!" added he, as they went to cry. "Now they are all on him again! Oh, beautiful, beautiful!" exclaimed Mr. Jorrocks, in ecstacies. "I'll lay five punds to a fiddler's farthin' they kill him. Mischief in their cry!—a rare scent—can wind him myself." So saying, he gathered up his reins again, thrust his feet home in the stirrups, crammed the spurs into his horse, and rolled back on the ride he had just come up. "Hark!" now cried our master, pulling up short and holding his hand in the air, as though he had a hundred and fifty horsemen at his tail to check in their career. "Hark!" again he exclaimed; "whoay, 'oss, whoay!" trying to get Arterxerxes to stand still and let him listen. "Now, fool, vot are you champing the bit for?—whoay, I say! He's turned short again! Hoick back! Hoick back! They've overrun the scent," continued he, listening, as the chorus gradually died out; "or," added he, "he *may* have got to ground."

"*Tally ho!*" now screamed Jorrocks, as a magnificent fellow in a spotless suit of ruddy fur crossed the ride before him at a quiet, stealing, listening sort of pace, and gave a whisk of his well-tagged brush on entering the copse-wood across. "*Hoop! hoop! hoop! hoop!*" roared Mr. Jorrocks, putting his finger in his ear, and holloaing as loud as ever he could shout; and just as he got his horn fumbled past the guard, Dexterous, Affable, and Mercury, dashed across the ride, lashing their sterns and bristling for blood, and Pigg appeared a little below cantering along with the rest of the pack at his horse's heels. "*Here, Pigg! there, Pigg!*" roared Mr. Jorrocks; "just by the old hoak-stump.—*Gently* now! ah, ware 'eel—that's not the vay of him; he's hover to the left, I tells ye. That's him! Mercury has him. Hoick to Mercury, hoick! *get away, get away, get away, 'ounds!* hoick together! hoick together! Oh, Pigg, wot a wopper he is!" observed Mr. Jorrocks, as Pigg joined him in the ride. "The biggest fox whatever was seen—if we do but kill him—my vig! I'll eat his tongue for supper. Have it grilled, '*cum grano salis*,' with a *lee*-tle Cayenne pepper, as Pomponius Hego would say."

"Aye," replied Pigg, grinning with delight, his cap-peak in the air and the tobacco-juice streaming down his mouth like a Chinese mandarin. "Ar'll be the *death of a shillin'* mysel'!" Saying which he hustled his horse and turned to his hounds.

Away they go again full cry across the cover to the utmost limits, and then back again to the far side. Now the fox takes a full swing round, but won't quit—now he cuts across—now Mr. Jorrocks views him, and

swears he'll have his brains as well as his tongue for supper. Pigg has
him next, and again comes Mr. Jorrocks's turn.   "Dash my vig, but he's

"THE BIGGEST FOX WHATEVER WAS SEEN."

a tough 'un !" observed Mr. Jorrocks to James Pigg, as they met again
on the rising ground at the top of the ride, where Mr. Jorrocks had been
fifteen times and Pigg seventeen, both their horses streaming with perspiration, and the blue and yellow worsted fronts of the bridles embossed
with foam. "Dash my vig, but it's a million and a half of petties,"
continued Mr. Jorrocks, looking at his watch, and seeing it wanted but
twenty minutes to four, "that we advertised, for there's a wast o' go
left in him yet, and he'll take the shine out of some of our 'ounds
before he is done with them—send them dragglin' 'ome with their sterns
down—make 'em cry capevi, I'm thinking."

   "Niver fear!" exclaimed Pigg—"niver fear!—whativer ye de keep
Tamboreen a rowlin'—yonder he gans! ar wish it mayn't be a fresh un.
Arn't draggled a bit."

"Oh, I 'opes not!" exclaimed Mr. Jorrocks, the picture of despair; "Would eat him, brush and all, sooner than that. Oh, dear! oh, dear! a fresh fox would be cruel—'ounds deserve him—worked him well."

"Now they begin to *chass!*" exclaimed Pigg, listening to the ripening chorus. "Aye, but there's a grand scent!—Ar'll be the death of a shillin' if we de but kill him. How way, ould man, how way," continued Pigg, cheeringly, jerking his arm to induce his master to follow. "Whativer ye de, keep Tamboreen a rowlin'!" continued Pigg, spurring and jagging his horse into a canter.

On man and master go—now they meet Charley, and all three are together. Again they part company for different rides, each according to his fancy. There is an evident improvement in the scent, but whether from a fresh fox, or the hounds having got nearer the hunted one, is matter of doubt. Mr. Jorrocks is elated and excited beyond expression. The hounds are evidently working the fox, but the fear of a fresh one rather mars his enjoyment. The hounds turn short, and Pigg and Charles again join Mr. Jorrocks.

"A! man alive, but they are a dustin' his jacket!" exclaimed Pigg, pulling up to listen;—"iv'ry hund's at him;" saying which he pulled out a large steel box and stuffed his mouth full of tobacco.

    *   *   *   *   *   *   *

A sudden pause ensues—all still as death—not a note—not even a whimper!

"*Who hoop!*" exclaims Mr. Jorrocks in ecstacies—"*Who hoop!* I say —heard the leadin' 'ound crack his back! Old Cruiser for a guinea!"

    *   *   *   *   *   *   *

"*Yonder they gan!*" cried Pigg, pointing to a hog-backed hill on the left, over which three couple of hounds were straining to gain the body of the pack—saying which he clapt spurs to his horse and dashed off at full gallop, followed by Charles.

    *   *   *   *   *   *   *

"Oh, dear! oh, dear!" exclaimed Mr. Jorrocks, the picture of despair —"wot shall I do? wot shall I do?—gone away at this hour—strange country—nobody to pull the 'edges down for me or catch my 'oss if I gets spilt, and there's that Pigg ridin' as if there was not never no such man as his master. Pretty kettle of fish!" continued Mr. Jorrocks, trotting on in the line they had taken. A bridle-gate let him out of cover, and from the first hill our master sees his hounds going like pigeons over the large grazing grounds of Beddington Bottoms, with Pigg and Stobbs a little in the rear, riding as hard as ever their horses can lay legs to the ground.

    *   *   *   *   *   *   *

"'Ow that Scotch beggar rides!" exclaimed Mr. Jorrocks, eyeing Pigg going as straight as an arrow, which exclamation brought him to his first fence at the bottom of the hill, over which both horsemen had passed without disturbing a twig.

"'OLD UP, 'oss!" roared Mr. Jorrocks, seizing the reins and whip with one hand and the cantrel of the saddle with the other, as Arter-xerxes floundered sideways through a low fence with a little runner on the far side. "'OLD UP!" repeated he, as they got scrambled through, looking back and saying, "Terrible nasty place—wonders I ever got over. Should ha' been drund to a certainty if I'd got in. Wouldn't ride at it again for nothin' under knighthood—Sir John Jorrocks, Knight!" continued he, shortening his hold of his horse. "And my ladyship Jorrocks!" added he. "She'd be bad to 'old—shouldn't wonder if she'd be for goin' to Halmack's. Dash my buttons, but I wish I was off this beastly fallow," continued he; "wonderful thing to me that the farmers can't see there'd be less trouble i' growin' grass than in makin' these nasty rutty fields. 'Eavens be praised, there's a gate—and a lane too," saying which he was speedily in the latter, and gathering his horse together he set off at a brisk trot in the direction he last saw the hounds going.

Terribly deep it was, and great Arterxerxes made a noise like the drawing of corks as he blobbed along through the stiff, holding clay.

Thus Mr. Jorrocks proceeded for a mile or more, until he came upon a red-cloaked gipsy wench stealing sticks from a rotten fence on the left.

"'Ave you seen my 'ounds, ould gal?" inquired he, pulling up short.

"Bless your beautiful countenance, my cock angel!" exclaimed the woman, in astonishment at the sight of a man in a scarlet coat with a face to match; "bless your beautiful countenance, you're the very babe I've been looking for all this blessed day—cross my palm with a bit o' siller, and I'll tell you *sich* a fortin!"

"CUSS YOUR FORTIN!" roared Mr. Jorrocks, sticking spurs into his horse, and grinning with rage at the idea of having pulled up to listen to such nonsense.

"I hope you'll brick your neck, ye nasty ugly ould thief!" rejoined the gipsy, altering her tone.

"Opes I *sharn't*," muttered Mr. Jorrocks, trotting on to get out of hearing. Away he went, blob, blob, blobbing through the deep holding clay as before.

Presently he pulled up again with a "Pray, my good man, 'ave you seen my 'ounds—Mr. Jorrocks's 'ounds, in fact?" of a labourer scouring a fence-gutter. "Don't you 'ear me, man?" bellowed he, as the countryman stood staring with his hand on his spade.

"I be dull of hearin', sir," at length drawled the man, advancing very slowly towards our master with his hand up to his ear.

"Oh, dear! oh, dear!" exclaimed Mr. Jorrocks, starting off again "was there ever sich a misfortinate indiwidual as John Jorrocks?—'Ark! vot's that? Pigg's 'orn? Oh, dear, only a cow! Come hup, 'oss, I say, you hugly beast!—there surely never was sich a worthless beast lapped in leather as you," giving Arterxerxes a good double thonging as he spoke. "Oh, dear! oh, dear!" continued he, "I wish I was well back at the Cross, with my 'ounds safe i' kennel.—Vot a go is this!— Dinner at five—baked haddocks, prime piece of fore chine, Portingal honions, and fried plum-puddin'; and now, by these darkenin' clouds, it must be near four, and here I be's, miles and miles away—'ounds still runnin', and adwertised for the Beef and Carrots on Wednesday—never will be fit to go, nor to the Daisy nouther."

"Pray, my good man," inquired he of a drab-coated, big-basketed farmer, on a bay cart-horse, whom he suddenly encountered at the turn of

Mr. Jorrocks has a Bye Day

the road, "'ave you seen anything of my 'ounds? Mr. Jorrocks's 'ounds, in fact?"

"Yes, sir," replied the farmer, all alive; "they were running past Langford plantations with the fox dead beat close afore them."

"'Ow long since, my frind?" inquired Mr. Jorrocks, brightening up.

"Oh, why just as long as it's taken me to come here—mebbe ten minutes or a quarter of an hour, not longer certainly. If you put on you may be in at the death yet."

Away went spurs, elbows, and legs, elbows and legs, Arterxerxes was again impelled into a canter, and our worthy master pounded along, all eyes, ears, and fears. Night now drew on, the darkening clouds began to lower, bringing with them fog and a drizzling rain. "Bad go this," said Mr. Jorrocks, rubbing his hand down his coat-sleeve, and raising his face to ascertain the precise amount of the fall. "Bad go, indeed. Got my Sunday 'at on, too. Hooi, bouys! did you see th' 'ounds?" inquired he of a troop of satchel-slung youths, plodding their ways homeward from school.

"*Y-e-a-s*," at length drawled out one, after a good stare at the inquirer.

"'Ow long since? come, *quick*, bouy!"

"May be twenty minutes; just as we com'd past Hookem-Snivey church we see'd fox, and hounds were close ahint—he was *varra* tired."

"Twenty minutes," repeated Mr. Jorrocks, aloud to himself; "twenty minutes—may be a werry long way off by this; foxes travel fast. Vich way were they a-goin'?"

"Straight for Staunton-Snivey," drawled the boy.

"My vig!" exclaimed Mr. Jorrocks, "vot a run; if we don't kill werry soon, it'll be pitch dark, and then there'll be a pretty kittle o' fish —th' 'ounds will kill all the ship (sheep) i' the country—shall have a bill as long as my harm to pay."

Fear lent fresh impetus to our worthy friend, and tightening his hold of Arterxerxes's head, who now began tripping and stumbling, and floundering along in a most slovenly manner, Mr. Jorrocks trotted on, and reaching Hookem-Snivey, saw by the foot-people standing on the church-yard wall, that the hounds were "forrard;" he turned down a lane to the left of the village stocks, in the direction the people were looking, and catching Staunton-Snivey in the distance, set off for it as hard as ever he could tear. A pretty clattering he made down the stony road.

Night now drew on apace, and heavy darkening clouds proclaimed a fast approaching storm. At Staunton-Snivey, he learned that the hounds had just crossed the turnpike on to the Downs, with the fox "dead beat *close* afore them;" and still unwilling to give in, though every moment increased his difficulties, he groped open a bridle-gate, and entered upon the wide-extending Plain. The wind had now risen, and swept with uncommon keenness over the unprotected open. The drizzling rain too became changed into larger, heavier drops, and thrusting his hat upon his brow, Mr. Jorrocks buttoned his coat up to the throat, and wrapping its laps over his thighs, tucked them in between his legs and the saddle. Dismal and disheartening were his thoughts, and many his misgivings for his rashness. "Oh, dear! Oh, dear!" muttered he, "wot a most momentous crisis—lost! lost! lost!—completely lost! Dinner lost!

'ounds lost, self lost—all lost together! Oh, vot evil genius ever tempted me from the lovely retirement o' Great Coram Street? Oh! why did I neglect the frindly warnin' o' Gabriel Junks? Change, change—storm, storm—was in his every scream, and yet I would go. Cuss the rain, it's gettin' down my werry back, I do declare;" saying which he turned the blue collar of his coat up to his ears, and both laps flew out with a desperate gust of wind. "Ord rot it," said he, "it's not never no use persewerin', may as well give in at once and 'ark back to Snivey; my Berlins are wet through, and I shall be drenched in another second. Who-ay, 'oss! who-ay; stand still, you hugly beast, and let me listen. The ducking-headed brute at length obeyed.

"It *is* the 'orn," exclaimed Mr. Jorrocks, after sitting listening for some time, with his hand to his ear; "it *is* the 'orn, Pigg's not far off! There it goes again, but the 'owling wind carries so many ways, there's no saying whereabouts he is. I'll blow, and see if I can 'ail him." Mr. Jorrocks then drew out his horn, and puffed and blew most lustily, but the raging tempest scattered the notes before they were well out of his mouth, and having exhausted his breath, he again paused, horn in hand, to listen. Between each blast of the raging hurricane, the faint notes of the horn were heard, some coming more fully as the gale blew more favourably, and a fuller one falling on his ear, during a period of partial lull, Mr. Jorrocks determined on advancing and endeavouring to rejoin his lost huntsman. "Come hup, I say, you hugly beast!" exclaimed he, getting Arterxerxes short by the head, and digging the spurs freely into his sides. The lumbering brute acknowledged the compliment with a sort of half hitch of a kick. "Great henterpriseless brute—do believe you'd rayther 'ave a feed o' corn than the finest run wot ever was seen," observed Mr. Jorrocks, cropping him. Night had now closed in, and even the sort of light of darkness that remains so long to the traveller who journeys onward with the closing day, deserted him, and earth and sky assumed the same sombre hue :—

"The dragon wing of night o'erspread the earth."

Scarce a star was visible in the firmament, and the few scattered lights that appeared here and there about the country, seemed like snatches of hope lit up for the moment to allure and perplex the wanderer.

"If ever mortal man catches me in such a quandary as this again," exclaimed Mr. Jorrocks, "I 'opes—*oh, dear!* who's there?—Cus those Seidlitz pooders!—*Speak, I say!—vot are you?*—Come hup, 'oss, I say!" roared he, ramming the spurs into Arterxerxes, who had suddenly shied off with a loud snort. "Now for a murder!" ejaculated Jorrocks, still cramming in the spurs.

"*E-yah! E-yah! E-yah!*" went a donkey, greatly to the relief of Mr. Jorrocks's mind, who had clenched his huge hammer-headed whip by the middle, so as to give an assailant the full benefit of its weight. Out then went his horn again, and the donkey brayed a full accompaniment.

"Oh, the deuce be with the hanimal!" cried Jorrocks, grinning with vexation, "never saw a donkey yet that knew when to 'old his tongue. Oh, my vig, vot a vind! almost blows the 'orn itself; shall be blown to hatoms, I do believe. And the rain too! I really thinks I'm wet to the werry waistband o' my breeches. I'll lay a guinea 'at to a half-crown gossamer I haven't a dry thread upon me in 'alf a minute. Got a five-pund note i' my pocket that will be hutterly ruined. Sarves me right, for bein' such a hass as take these 'ounds—vy wasn't I content with the glorious old Surrey and an occasional turn with the Cut-'em-downs? Well; I thinks this night will be the last of John Jorrocks! Best master of 'ounds wot ever was seen. 'Orrible termination to a hactive life; starved on a common—eat by wolves, or shepherds' dogs, which is much of a muchness as far as comfort's concerned. Why even yon donkey would be 'shamed of such an end. There goes the vind with my 'at—lucky it's tied on," added he, trying to catch it as it dangled at his back, " or I should never have seen it no more. I'd give fifty punds to be back at 'Andley Cross—I'd give a 'underd punds to be back at 'Andley Cross—knows no more where I am than if I was among the Bohea mountains—oh, dear, 'ow it pours! I'd give two 'underd punds to be back at 'Andley Cross—yonder's a light, I do declare—*two* on 'em—come hup, 'oss, I say. The hanimal seems to have no sense! I'll lead you, you nasty hugly brute, for I do believe you'll brick my neck, or my back, or both, arter all;" so saying, Mr. Jorrocks clambered down, and getting on to the sheltered side of the animal, proceeded to plunge and roll, and stagger and stumble across the common, with the water churning in his great boots, in the direction of the distant lights.

After a good hour's roll about the open Downs, amid a most pelting, pitiless storm, our much-respected master at length neared the longed-for lights, which he had kept steadily in view, and found they proceeded from lamps at lodges on either side of handsome gates, betokening the entrance to a large demesne. Mounting his horse, he rode quickly through the gates, and trusting to the sound of Arterxerxes' hoofs for keeping the road, he jogged on in search of the mansion. Tall stately pines, rising like towers to heaven, with sombre yews in massive clumps, now made darkness visible, and presently a sudden turn of the road brought a large screen full of lights to view, some stationary, others gliding about, which acted like sunbeams on our master's mind; more grateful still was the shelter afforded by the lofty portals of the entrance, under which, as if by instinct, Arterxerxes bore his master, and then stood still to be delivered of his load. " The bell 'ill be somewhere here, I guess," observed Mr. Jorrocks, dismounting and running his hand up either side of the door-posts. " Here's as much door as would serve Jack the Giant-killer's castle, and leave a little over." So saying, having grasped the bulky handle of a wall-ensconced bell, he gave it a hearty pull, and paused as they say for an answer.

In an instant, two tall, highly-powdered footmen, in rich scarlet and white lace-bedaubed liveries, threw wide the folding-doors as though they expected Daniel Lambert, or the great Durham ox, exhibiting a groom of the chamber and a lusty porter, laying down the newspapers, and hurrying from a blazing fire in the back-ground.

* * * * * * *

" Perhaps you would like to be shown to your room, sir, as you seem wet?" observed the groom of the chamber, after a mutual stare, which Mr. Jorrocks did not seem likely to interrupt.

"*Seem* vet !" exclaimed Mr. Jorrocks, stamping and shaking himself, "*seem* vet ; I'm just as vet as a man can be and no vetter ; but what shall I do with my 'oss ? The musciful man, you know, is musciful to his quad."

"Oh, there's a stall all ready for him, sir ; your servant's been here this 'alf-hour and more ; I'll send the 'orse round for you, if you'll allow me, sir. Here, Jones, take hold of him, and you, Peters, run down-stairs, and tell Saul to come and take it round."

"Yes," added Mr. Jorrocks ; "and tell Pigg to let him have some warm gruel directly, and to get him well done hup, for he's had a hard day. Werry clever of the chap," continued Mr. Jorrocks, "runnin' to ground here—seems a capital house—wot a passage ! like the Thames Tunnel." Jorrocks then stumped in.

"This way, if you please, sir," said the groom of the chamber,

MR. JORROCKS AT ONGAR CASTLE.

motioning him across a magnificent old baronial hall, and turning short up a well-lit, softly-carpeted winding staircase, he preceded Mr. Jorrocks, with a chamber candle, along a lengthy gallery, all hung with portraits of grim-visaged warriors, and small-waisted, large looming ladies. "This is *your* room, sir," said he, at length, opening a partially closed door, and ushering Mr. Jorrocks into a splendidly furnished apartment, whose blazing fire, gleaming on the rich crimson curtains and hangings of the room, imparted a glow that long exposure to the unruly elements made appear quite enchanting. "'Eavens be praised for these and all other mercies!" exclaimed the grateful Mr. Jorrocks, throwing his hat and whip upon the sofa, and plunging into the luxurious depths of a many-cushioned easy chair.

"Your clothes *are* laid out, I think, sir," observed the groom of the chamber, casting a glance at another sofa, on which clean linen, dress clothes, shiny thin shoes, were ranged in the most orthodox order. 'P'rhaps you'd like some hot water, sir?'"

"Yes, I should," replied Mr. Jorrocks, "werry much—and a little brandy, if you've no objection."

"Certainly, sir, certainly," replied the well-drilled servant, giving the top log on the fire a lift so as to make it blaze, and lighting the toilet-table candles.

All this passed with such extraordinary rapidity—the events of the day had been so numerous and exciting—the transition from the depths of misery to the height of luxury so sudden, and, above all, the perfect confidence of the servant so seductively convincing, that not doubting of the accuracy of every thing, and placing all to the credit of his renowned name and the acuteness of his northern huntsman, Mr. Jorrocks proceeded with the aid of a boot-jack to suck off his adhering boots, and divest himself of his well-soaked garments. The servant presently returned with a long-necked bottle of white brandy on a massive silver tray, accompanied with hot water, lemon, sugar, nutmeg, and a plate of biscuits. Seeing Mr. Jorrocks advancing rapidly to a state of nudity, he placed them on a table near the fire, and pointing to a bell beside the bed, observed that if Mr. Jorrocks would ring when he was ready, he would come and conduct him to the drawing-room. The servant then withdrew.

"Wonder if Pigg's killed the fox," observed Mr. Jorrocks to himself, pouring out half a tumbler of brandy and filling the glass up with hot water. "Capital fun 'unting, to be sure," said he, sipping away; "'specially ven one gets into a good quarter like this," continued he, jerking his head, "but desperation poor fun sleepin' on a common!" and thereupon, after a few more preliminary sips, he drained off the tumbler.

"May as well vet both eyes," observed he, as he felt the grateful influence of the brandy upon his nearly exhausted frame, saying which he poured himself out another half tumbler of brandy, and adding sugar and lemon, drank off a good part of it, and left the remainder till he got himself washed.

"Werry considerate this," said he,—"werry considerate indeed," he repeated, taking a large Turkey sponge out of the handle of a hip bath of warm water, shaded from the fire by a glass screen, inside of which upon a rail hung a row of baked towels. "Kettle too," said he, now attracted

by its simmering, "may as well have a boil;" so saying, he emptied the
contents into the bath, and pulling off his wig, proceeded to wash and
disport himself therein, using the sponge as if it was his own. In the
midst of his ablutions the door opened, and through the glass screen he
saw a servant in a dark coat and scarlet waistcoat enter, and hastily retire
as he caught a glimpse of our white Hottentot-like hero squatting in the
water. Out Mr. Jorrocks got and bolted the door, and hearing something
going on in the passage, he listened for a moment and caught divers
scraps of conversation, apparently between a servant and his master, such
as, "Why, you stupid fool, don't you know the room? You certainly
are the greatest ass ever man encumbered himself with."

"Beg pardon, sir, I could have sworn that was the room."

"Stuff and nonsense! look along the passage; the doors are all so much
alike, no wonder a fool like you is puzzled;" saying which the voices
moved along, and Mr. Jorrocks heard knocking and opening of doors all
along the gallery, until they gradually died away in the distance. Our
hero had just done with his bath, and finished his brandy and water, when
the sound of returning footsteps again drew his attention to his door,
and an angry voice and a meek one sounded alternately through the
panels.

"Now what *are* you staring there about, you great idiot—keeping
me shivering in my wet clothes. If this *is* the room, why don't you
knock?"

"Please, sir, there's a gen'leman in."

"How d'you know?"

"Saw him, sir."

"Then it can't be my room."

"Laid your clothes out in it howsomever, sir."

"How do you know this is it?"

"'Cause I tied this bit of straw round the 'andle of the door."

"Then knock and ask the gentleman to let you in, and get my clothes
out again. You've put them into the wrong room, that's the long and
short of the matter—stupid fool!" The servant then ventured a very
respectful double tap.

"WHO'S THERE?" roared Jorrocks, in a voice of thunder.

"Beg pardon, sir,—but I think I've made a mistake, sir, with master's
clothes, sir."

"NO YOU HAVEN'T!" replied Mr. Jorrocks, in the same sweet tone as
before.

"Oh, beg pardon, sir," rejoined the servant.

"Now ARE YOU SATISFIED?" roared the master in the Jorrockian
strain. "Go along, you fool, and seek a servant."

*   *   *   *   *   *   *

In a few minutes there was a renewed and increased noise outside,
and Mr. Jorrocks now recognised the bland voice of his friend the groom
of the chamber.

"Beg pardon, sir," said he softly through the door, "but would you
allow me to speak to you for a moment?"

"Certainly," replied Mr. Jorrocks; "talk through the door."

"Please, sir, would you 'blige me with your name, sir?"

"Certainly! Mr. JORROCKS, to be sure! The M. F. H.! Who else should it be?"

"Oh, I fear, sir, there's a mistake, sir. This room, sir, was meant for Captain Widowfield, sir. Those are *his* clothes, sir."

"The deuce!" exclaimed Mr. Jorrocks, in disgust. "Didn't Pigg tell you I was a comin'?"

"It was the captain's servant I took for yours, sir."

"*Humph!*" grunted Mr. Jorrocks, "that won't do; at all ewents, I can't part with the garments."

"I will thank you, sir, to let *my* servant remove *my* clothes from *my* room," observed Captain Widowfield, in a slow, determined tone through the door.

"My good frind," replied Mr. Jorrocks, altering his accents, "'ow is it possible for me to part with the garments when I've nothin' o' my own but wot's as drippin' wet as though I'd been dragged through the basin of the Paddin'ton Canal? reg'larly salivated in fact!"

o

"I have nothing to do with that, sir," exclaimed the captain, indignantly; "I'm wet myself. *Will you open the door, I say?*"

"*No, I von't,*" replied Mr. Jorrocks, "and that's the plain English of it!" So saying, he swaggered back to the fire with the air of a man resisting an imposition. He then mixed himself a third tumbler of brandy and water.

It may be well here to mention that the mansion in which Mr. Jorrocks so suddenly found himself was Onger Castle, where Michael Hardy, the founder of the hunt, found himself at the end of his long and successful run. The vicissitudes of many years had thrice changed the ownership of the castle since the day when the good earl greeted our primitive sportsman on killing his fox before the castle windows, and the present possessor was nephew to that nobleman, who having that day attained his majority, was about to celebrate the event among a party of friends and neighbours.

Having waited until half-past six to welcome Captain Widowfield, before dressing, his lordship at length concluded the storm had prevented his coming; and the party, consisting of five or six and twenty, were in the act of retiring to their respective apartments to prepare for dinner, when Walker, the aforesaid groom of the chamber, came hurrying along, pale in the face from the *parley* in the passage, followed by the captain in a high state of exasperation, to announce the appearance of an uninvited guest. No sooner was the name "Jorrocks" announced, than a shout of triumph and a roar of laughter burst from all present; and after learning the particulars of his arrival, which seemed to fill every one with ecstasies, (for during the long wait before dressing, they had talked over and abused all their absent friends,) his lordship begged the gallant captain to be pacified, and put up with a suit of his clothes for the evening.

"It was no use being angry with old Jorrocks," he observed, "whom every body said was mad; and he trusted the amusement he would afford the company would atone for the inconvenience he had subjected his good friend the captain to."

The doctrine, though any thing but satisfactory to a man burning for vengeance, seemed all the consolation the captain was likely to get, so, returning with Walker, he borrowed the roomiest suit of Lord Bramber's clothes, and while attiring himself in them, he considered how best he could have his revenge.

Meanwhile our hero, having disposed of his third tumbler of stiff brandy and water, which contributed materially to the restoration of his usual equanimity, began to appropriate the clothes so conveniently laid out on the sofa.

Captain Widowfield was a stout big fellow, as bulky as Jorrocks, and much taller, and being proud of his leg, was wont to adorn his lower man in shorts on high days and holidays; so having drawn on a pair of fine open-ribbed black silk stockings, over the gauze ones, Mr. Jorrocks speedily found himself in a pair of shorts, which, by dint of tight girthing, he managed to bring up to the middle of his calves. The Captain's cravat was of black satin, the waistcoat a white one, articles, as Mr. Jorrocks observed, that could be reefed or let out to fit any one, and having plunged into the roomy recesses of a blue coat, with Conservative buttons, he surveyed the whole in the cheval glass, and pronounced them

" werry good." He then exchanged the captain's lily and rose worked slippers for his patent leather pumps, and the brandy acting forcibly on an empty stomach, banished all diffidence, and made Jorrocks ring the bell, as though the house were his own.

* * * * * *

" You've got me into a pretty scrape with the Earl," said Walker, entering the room; " I thought you were Captain Widowfield."

" Did you ? " replied Mr. Jorrocks, placing himself before the fire with a coat-lap over each arm.—" You'll know better another time.—But tell me, what Hearl is it you are talkin' about ? "

" The Earl of Bramber, to be sure," replied the servant.

" What ! this is his shop, is it ? " inquired Jorrocks—" Onger Castle, in fact ? "

" Yes ; I thought you had been one of the party when I shewed you in here," replied Walker.

" Oh, never mind," said Mr. Jorrocks, " where there's ceremony there's uo frindship—I makes no doubt I shall be werry welcome—See ; there's five shillin's for you," giving him a dollar. " You mustn't let the captin in here though, mind. Now tell us, is there any grub to get ? "

" Dinner will be served in a quarter of an hour," replied Walker.

" *Dinner !* " exclaimed Mr. Jorrocks, looking at his watch; " ten minutes past seven, and not dined yet; what will the world come to next ? Dead o' winter too !"

Walker then conducted him down stairs, and ushered him into a splendid drawing-room, brilliantly lighted up, whose countless mirrors reflected his jolly person a hundred-fold. The housemaids were just giving the finishing sweep to the grates, and the footmen lighting the candles and lamps, when our master entered ; so making up to a table all covered with pamphlets and papers, he drew an easy chair towards it, and proceeded to make himself comfortable.

Lord Bramber was the first to enter. He was a tall handsome young man, of delicate appearance and gentlemanly manners. He wore mustachios, and was dressed in a black coat and trousers, with a white waistcoat.

Seeing a stranger, he had no difficulty in settling who he was, so he advanced with a bow and extended hand to greet him.

Mr. Jorrocks was up in an instant.

" My Lord, '*necessitas non habet legs*,' as that classical stableman, Mr. Pomponius Hego, would say—or, ' 'unger makes a man bold,' as I would say—I'm werry glad to see you," saying which he shook his lordship's hand severely.

" Thank you," replied Lord Bramber, smiling at his guest's hospitality ; " thank you," repeated he—" hope you left Mrs. Jorrocks and your family well."

" Thank'e," said Mr. Jorrocks, " thank'e, my lordship," as the existence of his better-half was brought to his recollection ; " 'opes I sharn't find her as I left her."

" How's that ? I hope she is not unwell ? " inquired his lordship with well-feigned anxiety.

" Oh, no," replied Mr. Jorrocks, raising his eye-brows with a shrug of

o 2

his shoulders; " oh, no, only I left her in a werry bad humour, and I
'opes I shall not find her in one when I gets back—*haw, haw, haw*,—
he, he, he,—s'pose your 'at (hat) covers your family—wish mine did too;
for atwixt you and I and the wall, my lordship, women are werry weary
warmints.   I say, my lord, a gen'leman should do nothin' but 'unt,—it's
the sport of kings, the image of war, without its guilt, and only five-and-
twenty per cent. of its danger.   You've got a werry good shop here—
capital shop, I may say," added he, surveying the rich orange silk furniture and gilding of the room.   " Wonder how long this room is ?   Sixty
feet, I dare say, if it's a hinch ;—let's see."   So saying, Mr. Jorrocks,
having set his back against the far wall, took a coat-lap over each arm,
and thrusting his hands into Captain Widowfield's breeches pockets, proceeded to step the apartment.   " One, two, three, four, five, six, seven,
eight, nine, ten, eleven, twelve, thirteen, fourteen, fifteen, sixteen,
when he was interrupted in his measurement by the opening of the door,
and entrance of some of the guests.   He was introduced to each in
succession, including Captain Widowfield, a big, red-whiskered, pimply-
faced, choleric-looking gentleman, to whom our worthy master tendered
the hand of fellowship, in perfect ignorance of his being the person with
whom he had held communion sweet through the door.

Dinner was then announced.

We suppose our readers will not care to have the names of the guests
who sat down to the banquet, or yet the wines or viands that constituted
the repast; suffice it to say, that the company consisted chiefly of people
in the neighbourhood, sprinkled with a few idle Honourables, who lend
themselves out to garnish country-houses in the dull season, and the best
French and English cookery furnished the repast.

Despite the prevailing non-wineing fashion, every body, save Captain
Widowfield, drank wine with Mr. Jorrocks, and before the dessert
appeared, the poor gentleman, what from the effects of brandy on an
empty stomach before dinner, and wine on a full one during it, began to
clip her Majesty's English very considerably.   " Never were such 'ounds
as mine," he kept hiccupping, first into one neighbour's ear and then into
another.   "Never were such 'ounds, (hiccup) certainly—hurrah, I say,
(hiccup) Jorrocks is the boy !   Forrard !   hark, forrard, away !   (hiccup.)
You must come and 'unt with me," hiccupped he to the gentleman on the
left.   "Beef and Onions on Wednesday, (hiccup)—Candid Pig—no,
Mountain-Daisy, (hiccup) — Saturday—James Pigg is a real warmint
(hiccup)—a trump, a real trump, (hiccup) and no mistake.   Give me
port, none o' your clarety wines."

The Earl of Bramber's health, of course, was proposed in a bumper,
with " all the honours."   Mr. Jorrocks hooped and holloaed at the top of
his voice—an exertion that put the finishing stroke to his performances,
for on attempting to resume his seat he made a miscalculation of distance,
and fell with a heavy thump upon the floor.   After two or three rolls he
was lifted into his chair, but speedily resuming his place on the floor,
Walker was summoned with two stout footmen to carry him to bed.

Captain Widowfield followed to make sure of his clothes : the gap
caused by Mr. Jorrocks' secession was speedily closed in, and the party
resumed the convivialities of the evening.

Mr. Jorrocks's Bath.

The room to which our master was transferred was the dressing-room, over a large swimming-bath, on the eastern side of the castle, and very cozily he was laid into a little French bed. Walker wound up his watch, Captain Widowfield walked off with his clothes, and our drunken hero was left alone in his glory.

The events of the day, together with the quantity of brandy and wine he had drank, and the fatigue consequent upon his exertions, combined to make Mr. Jorrocks feverish and restless, and he kept dreaming, and tossing, and turning, and tumbling about, without being able to settle to sleep. First, he fancied he was riding on the parapet of Waterloo Bridge with Arterxerxes, making what he would call a terrible fore-paw (*faux pas*), or stumble; next, that he was benighted on the common, and getting devoured by shepherds' dogs; then, that having bought up all the Barcelona nuts in the world, and written to the man in the moon to secure what were there, he saw them become a drug in the market, and the firm of Jorrocks and Co. figuring in the " Gazette."

Next, he dreamt that he had got one of James Pigg's legs and one of his own—that on examination they both turned out to be left ones, and he could not get his boots on. Now that he was half-famished, and chained to a wall in sight of a roast goose—anon that the Queen had sent to say she wanted to dance with him, and he couldn't find his pumps; "No! give him all the world, sir, he couldn't find his pumps." Now that the Prince wanted to look at Arterxerxes, and he couldn't find the ginger. "No: give him all the world, sir, he couldn't find the ginger!" Then he got back to the chase, and in a paroxysm of rage, as he fancied himself kicking on his back in a wet ditch, with Benjamin running away with his horse, his dreams were interrupted by a heavy *crack, bang, splash* sort of sound, and in an instant he was under water. All was dark and still. His dreams, though frightful, had all vanished as he awoke, and after rising to the top he waited an instant to see if this would not do likewise; but the sad reality was too convincing, so he began bellowing, and roaring, and splashing about in a most resolute manner.

" *Hooi ! hooi ! hooi !* " spluttered he, with his eyes and mouth full of water. " *'Eip ! 'elp ! 'elp ! 'elp !* I'm a drownin', I'm a drownin' ! Mr. Jorrocks is a drownin'—oh, dear, oh, dear, will nobody come ?—Oh, vere am I ? vere am I ? Binjimin ! I say, Binjimin ! James Pigg ! James Pigg ! James Pigg ! Batsay ! Batsay ! Murder ! 'elp ! murder ! 'elp !"

" What's happen'd ? what's happen'd ? what's happen'd ? Who's there ? who's there ? Oh, dear ! oh, dear ! oh, dear !" screamed half-a-dozen voices at once, rushing with candles into the gallery of the swimming-bath.

" Vot's 'appen'd ? " replied Mr. Jorrocks, blobbing and striking out for hard life with his white cotton night-capped head half under water ; " Vy, I'm drownin'.—'Elp ! 'elp ! 'elp, I say ! Oh, vill nobody come to 'elp ? "

" Throw out the rope ! throw out the rope !" cried half-a-dozen voices.

" No ; get a boat," responded Mr. Jorrocks, thinking there was little choice between hanging and drowning. " Oh dear, I'm sinkin', I'm sinkin' ! "

"Come to this side," cried one, "and I'll lend you a hand out;" thereupon Mr. Jorrocks struck out with a last desperate effort, and dashed his head against the wall.

They then pulled him out of the bath, and with great care and con-dolence put him to bed again. He was still rather drunk—at least, not quite sober; for when pressed to exchange his wet shirt for a dry one, he hugged himself in it, exclaiming, "No, no; they'll worry it! They'll worry it!"

CHAPTER XXVII.

ANOTHER BENIGHTED SPORTSMAN

"Heard the winds roar, and the big torrent burst."—THOMSON.

"WELL, I can't stand it any longer, so it's no use trying," said Charley Stobbs to himself, turning his horse's head in the direction of a light he saw gleaming past a window on the left of the road.

Having about got through his horse, and lost Pigg and the hounds, he had taken temporary refuge at a small public house, which he had imprudently left, in hopes of regaining Handley Cross that night.

After much casting about in the dark, with the imperfect and contra-dictory directions usually obtained from peasants in remote parts, Charley's perseverance at length failed him, and he resolved to give in.

The night was drear and dark—the wind howled and whistled with uncommon keenness—and the cutting hail drifted with the sharpness of needles against his face. Horse and rider were equally dispirited.

Having formed his resolution, Charley was speedily at a white gate, whose sound and easy swing denoted an entrance of some pretension.

A few seconds more, and he was under the lee of a large house. Having dismounted, and broken his shins against a scraper, he at length discovered a bell-pull in the door-post, which, having sounded, the echoing notes from afar proclaimed the size and importance of the mansion.

All was still, save the wild wind, which swept over the lawn, dashing a few straggling leaves about with uncommon fury. Charley stood dripping and shivering, with his horse in his hand, but no one came—all was still within. Another pull sounded through the house, and a third succeeded that. At length, in a partial lull, a soft female voice was heard through the door, inquiring, "Who was there?"

"Me!" exclaimed Charley; " Mr. Stobbs!—a benighted fox-hunter— been out with Mr. Jorrocks's hounds."

"Master's gone to bed," replied the servant, drawing the bolts and chain as she spoke: and just as she began to open the door, a sudden gust of wind extinguished her candle.

"I'll run for a lantern," exclaimed she, shutting-to the door, leaving Charley stamping and thumping himself with his hands. Presently she returned with a dark lantern, with the slide up, which threw a light over the horseman without discovering the holder.

The sight of a red coat banishing fear, she closed the door after her, and informed Charley that master was gone to bed, and the butler too, but she would show him the stable, and get a man to take charge of the horse. The Yorkshire nag seemed to understand the arrangement, for he immediately gave himself a hearty shake, as if to say that his labours were done at last.

The maid led the way, and on they went to the stable. It formed the wing of the house, and a groom, sleeping above, being roused from his bed, came with the alacrity usually displayed by servants in the service of a red coat.

Indeed, as Mr. Jorrocks says, there's no colour like scarlet. In it, a man winks at the women, rings at your bell, orders your brandy, rides through your garden, and all in the style of doing you a favour. The half-dressed groom would whole-dress the horse, and get him some gruel, and clothe him well up, and litter him well down ; and as he hissed, and pulled at the horse's ears, he paused every now and then and grinned with delight at Charley's account of the sport.

" A', it must have been a grand run! " exclaimed he ; " and where did you kill him ? "

" Don't know that," replied Charles ; " we got upon the Downs, when it became actually racing—the fox going in the teeth of the wind, and no one with the hounds but the huntsman, and a farmer who cut in during the run. I got into a bog, and the hounds ran clean out of sight before I recovered my horse, and night came on without my even being able to hear or see anything more of them."

" Dear ! " exclaimed the groom, " you don't say so—that *was* a bad job ; and was Squire Jorrocks not up ? " thereupon the groom dived elbow-deep into the gruel-pail, and, lifting it up, the horse quaffed off the contents like a basin of soup. Blankets and bandages came warm from the saddle-room fire, and having seen his horse well done by, and told the groom all he could about the run, Charley again sought the shelter of the house.

The little maiden had returned there after providing the gruel, and was ready to open the door as she heard Charley's approach. " She would show him into the parlour," she said, " where there was a good fire ; " and forthwith led the way up a long passage, with a couple of steps in the centre. The parlour was evidently the master's room—the *sanctum sanctorum*—a small snuggery, with book-shelves on two sides— guns, swords, game-bags, powder-tryers, fishing-rods, &c., on the third— and a red-curtained window on the fourth ; a round table, with the fragments of dessert, an empty and a half-empty decanter stood before the fire, while a well used red morocco easy-chair stood on one side of the table.

" A bachelor," said Charley to himself, glancing at the table and chair, and then at the pretty maid whose cork-screw curls dangled down her healthy cheeks, despite the unruly elements to which they had just been exposed ; " clear case that, I think," said he, eyeing the fit of her nicely done-up blue cotton gown, and well-turned ankles, with broadish sandalled shoes ; "no missis would keep such a pretty blue-eyed maid as that," said he to himself.

"Would you like to take any thing, sir ? " inquired she, lighting the wax-candles, and casting a look of commiseration at Charley's wet breeches.

"Nothing, thank you, my pretty dear, except—a kiss," giving her ruby lips a smack that sounded along the passage.

" *Hush !* " exclaimed she, colouring up, in alarm, " Mrs. Thompson will hear."

"And who's Mrs. Thompson ? "

"The housekeeper, to be sure ; she's just gone to bed."

"Well, if that's the case," replied Charles, " I think I should like a little sherry-and-water, or something," lifting up the half-emptied decanter, " if you could get some hot water and sugar ; or never mind the sugar, if Mrs. Thompson's got the keys."

"Oh, I'll get you both," replied blue-eyes, tripping away.

Charles now began to reconnoitre the apartment. Taking a light, he proceeded to examine the book-case. There was a curious mixture :— Burns's Justice and the Gentleman's Magazine ; Statutes at Large and Anderson's Agriculture ; the Tatler and Pope's Homer ; Don Quixote and the Old Sporting Magazine ; Seneca's Morals and Camden's Britannia ; Osbaldestone's British Sportsman ; Calamy's Sermons and Adam's Essays ; Walker's Pronouncing Dictionary and Sidney's Arcadia; Dacier's Plutarch and White's Farriery.

"Sporting parson, perhaps," thought Charles to himself. "No, that can't be," continued he ; " no bachelor parsons—at least, not with such houses as this. Some young man just come to his fortune, most likely, and hasn't had time to pick up a wife yet. No, that won't do ; a young 'un wouldn't be in bed so soon as this." Blue-eyes interrupted the speculation by appearing with a tray containing a nice plate of ham-sandwiches, hot water, sugar, lemon, nutmeg, &c.

"You're a darling ! " exclaimed Charley, squeezing her hand as she placed them on the table : " By Jove, there's no work done with *that*," said he to himself, as she ran out of the room ; " soft as a mowdy-warp ! "

Charley took the red morocco chair, and mixing himself some negus, recommenced his speculation on the probable station of his host. The books and the blue-eyes, and the guns and the soft hand confused him : and the more he thought, the nearer he was falling asleep—and the farther from arriving at a conclusion.

"Master's gone to bed," muttered Charley, recollecting the little maid's first observation. "No mistress, that's clear ; " and thereupon he drained off his tumbler, and filled up another. " Curious assortment of things he has in his room," thought Charley, looking about him. " I don't see a hunting-whip ; " and having satisfied himself on that point, without moving from his chair, he commenced a vigorous attack on the ham-sandwiches.

*   *   *   *   *   *   *

"Shall I show you to bed ? " inquired the little maid, peeping in at the door just as Charley was dropping asleep.

"If you please, my dear!" replied he, starting up, rubbing his eyes, and draining off the tumbler of sherry-and-water that had been cooling at his elbow.

The maiden lighted a bed-candle, and proceeded to lead the way up a wide, black oak stair-case, whose massive, shining banisters were ornamented with carved birds, monkeys, guinea-pigs, and other specimens of zoology, at the turns of the frequent landings. The wind had lulled, and the heavy ticking of a large black-faced time-piece with gilt figures was all that disturbed the monotony of night.

Lightly following his fairy guide, an involuntary hope came over Charley that he might not make the acquaintance of his host through the medium of a horse-pistol cocking at him through one of the black doors as they passed. Turning from the wide passage, up a narrower one on the left, a gleam of light, through a partially closed door, showed the termination of his travels, and throwing it open, a large poker in a downward slant, evinced the activity of the little maid, who had lighted the fire, got the room ready, and all the little arrangements made, while Charles was busy with his negus and speculations.

We need scarcely say that the room was not that bugbear to humble minds—the best one in the house, up whose lofty beds short-legged men swarm, as though they were climbing a tree, but it was one of those betwixt-and-between sort of apartments, that, like the pony in a stable, comes in for most of the work. The bed was exceedingly low, scarcely two feet from the ground, and stood in the centre of the room, with the head against the wall and the feet towards the fire. The curtains were of thick but faded orange damask, and the counterpane was patchwork of many colours. Round the bed was a slip of black and red carpeting ; another piece lay before a dressing-table, on which was a curious old black and gilt Chinese-patterned looking-glass, with many drawers, and the thoughtful little maiden had placed another piece of carpeting under the foot-bath before the fire. The rest of the floor was bare, and there was a large black oak press in the corner, with richly carved festoons above the drawers, and coats of arms emblazoned on the panels.

"Shall I take your coat down to dry ? " inquired the little maiden, slipping the poker out of the fire.

"If you please," replied Charles ; "but first you must help me out of it." Whereupon she put down the poker, and taking hold of the cuff, Charles drew himself out of the adhering garment. "Now," said he, giving her the wet scarlet and a kiss at the same time, which produced a corresponding effusion in her cheeks ; "how shall I know about getting up in the morning ? "

"Oh, Aaron will call you ! " replied the little maid, seizing the poker and tripping away.

"Aaron will call me ! " repeated Charley, returning from chasing her to a green baized door at the end of the passage. "Aaron will call me ! —what a queer name for a servant !—Wonder what the master is ? Aaron !—'Gad he must be a priest, and Aaron is his clerk and valet-de-chambre. No, that can't be either, for here's a boot-jack, a thing one never meets with in a parson's house ; and, as I live ! no end of sporting pictures," added he, holding his candle to the wall.

Sure enough, there were Loraine Smith's famous pictures of the Quorn Hunt, the progenitor of the now innumerable race of sporting prints ; " Bagging the Fox ; " " The Rendezvous of the Smoking Hunt at Braunstone," in which gentlemen appear with great meerschaums in their mouths ; " The Loss of the Chaplain," exhibiting a reverend gentleman somewhat in Mr. Jorrocks' predicament—in danger of drowning, if he were not in equal danger of hanging ; " The Meeting at Grooby Pool ; " " The Victory of obtaining the Brush," &c. ; all stretched on canvass, with broad gilt borders, and ranged round the room. Above the fire-place was a portrait of an old gentleman in a cocked hat, a gold-laced blue coat, with a snuff-box in one hand, and the other resting on the head of a greyhound, whose master seemed to look upon Charley, as he sat up to his knees in hot water, in anything but a patronising way.

"Should this be my host, or even my host's father or grandfather," thought Charley to himself, "perhaps he may not be over glad to see me ; however," added he, "' enough for the day is the evil thereof ; '" so, exchanging his damp shirt for a nice well-aired cotton one, with the initials J. W. F., on one side, and rejecting both a double and single nightcap, laid out for his choice, he put out his candle, and turned into bed.

* * * * * * *

Sound and healthy were his slumbers;—day dawned without his waking, and neither the darting rays of a dazzling sun brightening the moreen curtains through the chinks of the shutters, nor the noisy tick of the passage clock, had any influence on his sleep.

At length he started up, as a sledge-hammer sort of thump sounded on the door.

" Come in ! " exclaimed he, involuntarily, the exertion of which awoke him to a recollection of the past and a sense of his situation. " How deuced awkward ! " thought he to himself, looking at a great bell-tassel hanging above his head, and considering whether he should pull it or not,—

" Thump ! " went the door again, and no mistake.

" Come in ! " exclaimed Charley ; but still no one entered. " Must get up at all events," reasoned Charley ;—" must be eight, at least ; " looking at the rays of sunshine shooting into the room. Just as his hand grasped the bell-pull,

" Thump ! " went somebody at the door again.

" COME IN ! " roared Charles, for the third time, but still the door remained closed. Just as he was debating whether to ring the bell or compose himself for another nap, the door opened, and a slow, heavy foot paced steadily across the room to the window. Drawing aside the window-curtain, the heavy cross-bar swung lengthways in the shutter, which being folded exhibited the person of the intruder.

He was an elderly, clumsily built, middle-sized man, with a brown scratch-wig, surmounting a square, thick-featured, unmeaning countenance. A school-boy's turnip lantern would perhaps convey the best idea of the style of his much-tanned face and features. He was dressed in a snuff-coloured coat, loose buff waistcoat, puddingy-white neckcloth, drab kerseymere breeches ; and his swelling calves and enormously thick ankles were cased in white lamb's-wool stockings ; thick shoes, with leather strings, completed his costume. Having opened the shutters, he stumped to the foot of the bed, and placing himself right in the middle, thus delivered himself in good set Zummerzetzhire,—

" Please, zur, meazter gittin oop."

" Thank you, Aaron ! " exclaimed Charles, never doubting his man. " Pray can you tell me what o'clock it is ? "

" I'll zee, zur," replied Aaron, after a pause, stumping out of the room to consult the passage clock.

" What a man it is ! " exclaimed Charley, burying his face in the pillow, as he roared with laughter at his unmeaning, cast-iron countenance. What *can* his meazter be ! " Presently, creak, creak, creak, announced old heavy-heels returning. Placing himself in his old position, exactly at the centre of the bed, he thus delivered himself,—

" Pleaz, zur, it's nineteen minutes pazt eight. Will you pleaz, zur, to want any thing more, zur ? " at length inquired the stupid old man.

" *More !* " thought Charles, " why, I've got nothing as yet ; " wishing he had his female valet-de-chambre of the previous night back instead of old Aaron. "Yes, I should like some warm water for one thing, and my boots cleaned for another," looking at his mud-stained tops standing against a chair near the foot-bath. Razors, brushes, combs, sponges, and a host of etceteras, flitted across his mind, but considering the slowness of Aaron, and the state of his raiment, Charles thought he had better do with as little as possible. Out, then, Old Aaron stumped, and Charles was left alone to his reflections.

"Confounded awkward!" said he to himself, ruminating on his situation. "Suppose there's a mistress or young misses, what a figure I shall cut at a breakfast-table! Leathers like parchment, boots all dirt, neckcloth spoiled; better start off, and take my chance on the road, or breakfast when I get home." Then the recollection of the previous night deranged his reasoning. The little snuggery, the solitary easy chair, the remnants of dessert instead of tea, and the little blue-eyed maid, all savoured of bachelorism; so dismissing the lady consideration from his mind, he again applied himself to the question of what his host could be. Aaron and the blue-eyed maid were inconsistent. Such a pretty little girl, and such a very ugly old man—one so sharp, the other so slow —"and yet what a stupe I am," continued Charles; "Aaron's just the sort of man to keep in the house with a pretty girl;" and thereupon his host assumed the character of a fox-hunter, and Charles felt as if he knew him already.

"No, that won't do," continued Charles, demolishing the vision he had just conjured up; "she wouldn't have blushed so if she'd been used to kissing;" and thereupon his spirits fell below zero. Stump, stump, stump, creak, creak, creak, came old heavy-heels along the passage, disturbing Charles's reverie as well by his footsteps as his sledge-hammer thumps at the door. Thrice did he thump ere he would enter, and at length, when he did, having deposited a can of hot water on the wash-hand stand, he laid Charley's scarlet coat exactly in the centre of the table, and resuming his old position at the foot of the bed, cast his unmeaning eyes towards the pillows, and drawled out,—

"Pleaz, zur, do you pleaz to want anything elze?"

"Nothing but my boots cleaned!" exclaimed Charles, exhausted by his slowness, "though, perhaps," added he, as Aaron was stumping away, "you may as well make my compliments to your meazter, and say that a gentleman, who lost his way out with the hounds yesterday, wishes to pay his respects to him at breakfast—or rather (aside), to his breakfast."

"Yeaz, zur," replied Aaron, trudging out. Up Charles jumped, and making for the window, surveyed the prospect outside.

Immediately below the terrace was an ill-kept garden, divided by massive clipt yew-hedges, opening by antique white gates upon an undulating park, girded by a river. A few cows stood listlessly to the sun, and two or three mares and yearlings scratched themselves with the lower branches of the trees with which the park was plentifully studded. The tufty grass showed the land was not overstocked. Beyond the river a rich grazing vale stretched to distant hills, whose undulating outline closed the grey horizon.

Having made his survey, Charles proceeded to dress. "Wish I had little blue-eyes to get me what I want," thought he, pulling on a stained stocking, and looking at his shirt where the wet had soaked through his coat. Just then old Aaron was heard plodding back with his boots, which having placed at the door, he gave a loud thump, and asked if Charles wanted anything more.

"Oh, no!" replied Charles, opening the door, and taking in the dingy tops; "but tell me, what did your master say to my message?"

"He said varra well," replied Aaron, stroking his hand over his wig.

"He said varra well," repeated Charles, shutting the door in disgust; "what an inhospitable answer—fear he's no fox-hunter—would have been up with shaving-pot and razors before this; however, never mind, I'll soon be back to old J. and Belinda." So saying, he began handling his leathers; they were tolerably dry, except at the knees, but were desperately the worse for wear—large mud-stains disfigured their creamy colour, and there was a great black patch down one side, where he had rolled in the bog. However, he coaxed himself into them, and pulling on his boots, he made the best he could of his damaged blue neckcloth, while his cord waistcoat and red coat felt grateful for their acquaintance with the fire.

He was now ready for a start; and, the passage-clock striking nine, in an Aaron-like pace Charles made for the sound, and soon got into the gallery he had traversed overnight. Descending the zoological staircase, he found his friend Aaron standing with his ear at a door, listening, like a terrier at a rat-hole; Charley would fain have had a word with him, but Aaron gave him no time for inquiry, by opening the door, and discovering the top of a well-powdered head, with a pig-tail cocking above the red morocco chair.

"*The* gentleman, sir," said Aaron, advancing to the back of the chair.

Up jumped a little red-faced old gentleman, who, depositing a newspaper on the breakfast-table, made a profound Sir Charles Grandison salaam as he presented a full front to the enterer.

He was dressed in a single-breasted high-collared blue coat, with large silver buttons, white cravat, with a black one over it, buff waistcoat, with flap-pockets, cut out over the hips, yellow leather breeches, and rose-coloured top-boots, buckling round his knees with broad leather boot-garters.

Charley bowed his best in return, and thinking what a sorry figure his much-stained clothes must cut by the spotless ones before him, began muttering something about fox-hunting, boldness, benighted, hospitality, hungry—the little old gentleman jerking and bowing all the time, and motioning him into a chair on the other side of the round table.

Glad to hide his dilapidations under the table, Charley sidled to the seat, and tucking his napkin under his waistcoat, cast his eye round the apartment, and then began to reconnoitre the well-furnished breakfast-table.

His host resumed his seat, and jerking out his short legs as though he were on horseback, fixed his little beady black eyes upon Charles, and opened a voluble battery with—"Charming sport fox-hunting!—was a *great* sportsman myself!—one of the fastest of the fast—long since now—days of old Sef. in fact—have often sat up in the saddle-room at Quorn playing cards till it was time to go to cover. Those *were* the days! No such young men now—degenerate race, quite—horses, too, all good for

nothing—bad and weedy—no welters—shall never see such horses or
hunting again as we used then—real science of the thing exploded—all
riding and racing—no such men as old Meynell—or Corbet, or Lambton,
or any of your lasters. Swell masters ruin a country—go a burst, and are
done—foxes now run short and bad—worse than hares—if it wasn't the
grass the thing would be over. Pray make yourself at home. Take tea
or coffee? None of your flagon-of-ale and round-of-beef breakfasts now-
a-days—slip-slop, wishy-washy, milk-and-water, effeminate stuff—spoil
nerves—no such riders as there used to be. Cold fowl on the side-
board—Aaron will bring some hot sausages directly.—Turf seems all
rotten—saw O'Kelly's young Eclipse win the Derby in 1781—horses
were horses then—Eclipse—Florizel—Highflyer—Juniper—men that
might be called sportsmen and gentlemen too—not your half-lord and
half-leg.

"There was Lord Abingdon," continued the old gentleman, telling
them off on his fingers—"Duke of Bolton—Sir Charles Bunbury—
Mr. Bradyll—Lord Clermont—Mr. Jolliff—remember his bay horse,
Foxhuntoribus by Fox-hunter, well. Then there was Lord Milsintown—
Mr. Pulteney—Mr. Panton—Duke of Queensbury—and a host whose
names I forget. Ah! those recollections make an old man of me. Well,
never mind! I've had my day, and the old 'uns must make way for the
young;" then, turning short upon Charley, who was glancing at the
newspaper as it lay on the table, he said, with a jerk, " Allow me
the privilege of inquiring the name of the gentleman I have the honour of
addressing."

This was a poser, and coming after such a string of high-sounding
names, poor Charles's humble one would cut but a poor figure. It so
happened, however, that he was just skimming by a sort of sidelong
glance the monthly advertisement of the heavy triumvirate, wherein well-
known "unknowns" make names for themselves much better than their
own. There was " Shooting, by Ranger," and " Racing, by Rover," and
"Fishing, by Flogger," and in larger letters, as if the great gun of the
number, " A TRIP TO TRUMPINGTON, BY POMPONIUS EGO."

Charles had just got so far as this, when suddenly interrogated as
described, when he unconsciously slipped out the words, " Pomponius
Ego."

"Pomponius Ego!" exclaimed the little gentleman, jumping on to
his short legs as though he were shot, extending his arms and staring
with astonishment, " I never was so out in my life!"

Charley, " I beg pardon——"

"No apologies, my dear sir," interrupted our host, resuming his seat
with a thump that stotted his short legs off the carpet. " No apology!
no apology! no apology! We old men are apt to fancy things, to fancy
things, to fancy things—and I candidly confess I pictured Pomponius
Ego quite a different sort of man to myself."

Charles, " But if you'll allow me to ex——"

"No explanations necessary, my dear Mr. Ego—Mr. Pomponius Ego,
I mean," jabbered the voluble little old gentleman. " Eat your muffin
and sausages, and believe me you're heartily welcome ; I've lived long in
the world—take some more coffee—there's tea if you like it, but I never

was so out before. Lord! if old Q.* could see me!" continued he clasping his hands, and casting his eyes up to the ceiling.

Charley, "Well, but perhaps, sir——"

"There's no *perhaps's* in the matter, my dear sir—no perhaps in the matter; I'll tell you candidly, I pictured Pomponius Ego a prosy old chap, who went the horse-in-the-mill round of his stories from sheer want of originality and inability to move from home in search of novelty. The only thing that ever staggered me was your constant assertion, that second horses were unknown in Leicestershire in Meynell's time. Never was a greater fallacy, saving your presence! Always had a second horse out myself, though I only rode eight stun ten—never took soup for fear of getting fat—a host of others had second horses—Lambton and Lockley, and Lindow and Loraine Smith, and—But never mind! don't assert that again, you know—don't assert that again. Now take another sausage," pushing the dish towards Charley in a friendly, forgiving sort of way, as if to atone for the uneasiness the correction had occasioned him.

"But I never said anything of the sort!" exclaimed Charley, reddening up, as soon as he could get a word in sideways.

"Saving your presence, a *dozen* times," rejoined the little mercurial old gentleman—"*a dozen times at least!*" repeated he, most emphatically. "The fact is, my dear sir, I dare say you write so much, you forget what you say. We readers have better memories. I noted it particularly, for it was the only thing that ever shook my conviction of Pomponius Ego being a very old man. But let that pass. Don't be discouraged. I like your writings, especially the first time over. Few stories bear constant telling; but you've a wonderful knack at dressing them up.

> My father had a jolly knack at cooking up an almanack,
> Yes, he had a jolly knack, at cooking up an almanack.

By the way, *you* once cooked up an almanack! and a pretty hash it was, too!" added the little old gentleman. "I'll tell you what," continued he, tucking his legs up in his chair, and grasping a knee with each hand; "I'll tell you what—I'd like to match you against the gentleman that does the cunning advertisements of Rowland's Odonto or Pearl Dentifrice; I'd lay——"

"Zounds, sir!" interrupted Charles.

"Hear me out!" exclaimed the old gentleman, "Hear me out!" repeated he, throwing an arm out on each side of the chair; "I'd match you to lead one further on in an old story, without discovery, than Rowland's man does with his puffs of paste, or whatever his stuff is."

"But you are on the wrong scent altogether," roared Charles; "I've nothing to do with Pomponius Ego or Pearl Dentifrice either."

"*Blastation!*" screamed the little old gentleman, jumping up frantically into his chair, with a coffee-cup in one hand and a saucer in the other; "*Blastation!* tell me *that*, when it's written in every feature of your

* The sporting Lord Queensbury used to be called old Q.

face!" So saying, he sent the cup through the window, and clapped the saucer on his head.

* * * * * * *

"Come and feed the chuck cocks—pretty chuck cocks," said Aaron, stumping in at the sound of the crash; "Come and feed the chuck cocks —pretty chuck cocks," repeated he soothingly, taking his master down by the arm, and leading him quietly out of the room, observing to Stobbs as they went, "It's your red coat that's raisin' him."

CHAPTER XXVIII.

" 'Bout Lonnun, then, divent ye make sic a rout,
   There's nowse there maw winkers to dazzle :
For a' the fine things ye are gobbin about,
   We can marra in canny Newcassel."—PIGG'S POEMS.

AN ye let us lie i' yere barn, please, canny man?" inquired Pigg of a farmer, at whose door he knocked a long time on the night of this memorable run, before he got him to answer. "Ar's drippin' wet, huss is tired, and hunds can't travel."

"Who are ye?" inquired the farmer, unused to visitors at any time, more particularly after nightfall.

"Ar's Pigg, Squire Jorrocks's huntsman," replied James; "we've had a *desperate* run, and canna get hyem te neet."

"*S-o-o-o!*" replied the farmer in astonishment. "Here, Mary!" holloaing to his wife; "fetch a light, here be the hounds. And hev ye killed him?" inquired the farmer, looking closer at his visitor.

"Aye, killed him, aye. Ar's gettin' his head i' my pocket—if ye can put your hand in you may get it—ar's see numb ar can de nout."

*   *   *   *   *   *

"Sure-*lie* he's a big un!" exclaimed the farmer, pulling out the head, and weighing it by the ears; "Well, I think!—but come, let's get ye put up—it's a tarrible night; not one for standin' out at doors. Here! fetch the lantern, Jane, and help me to put the beast away, so as to make room for the gen'leman's horse;" adding to Pigg, "you are surely very wet."

Pigg.—"Wet, aye! wet as muck. Ar wish ar may ha' getten all my hunds away though. If ye can let us have some clean stree i' the barn, wor ard maister 'ill pay ye liberal for 't i' the mornin'—he's quite the gent."

"A! never mind about the pay, we will do what we can for you," replied the farmer. So saying he led the way with the lantern, and the jaded horse and tired hounds followed on with Pigg.

The farmer's lads took the horse, while Pigg looked over his hounds, and finding only a couple and a half wanting, he shook them down plenty of straw, and returned to the house to see what he could get to feed them on. A tub full of milk, with brown loaves sliced into it, was

P

quickly prepared, but there was little demand for it, the majority of the hounds seeming to prefer a continuance of the rest into which they were quietly subsiding to being disturbed for a meal. At length they had all been coaxed to the pail, and after a hearty shake each nestled into his neighbour, and the pack were soon in a very small compass.

Having seen his horse done up also, Pigg began to turn his attention to himself.

"Sink, but it's wet," said he, giving his cap a dash towards the floor, which sent a shower bath on to the flags; "however, ar's lucky in gettin' housed at all; for ar really thou'ht ar'd ha had to lie out like them poor divils at Chobham;" saying which he followed the farmer into an apartment, in which sat his wife and daughters, round a fire composed of a little coal and a good deal of rubbish-wood.

"Ar think ar'll gan into the kitchen," observed Pigg, looking at the fire.

"This be the kitchen," replied the farmer's wife, setting him a chair by the fire, thinking he was shy.

Pigg sat down, and after contemplating the fire a few seconds, he exclaimed, "Ods wons! but ye keep varry bad fires i' this country."

"Nay, man," replied Mr. Butterfield, his host, "we call that a varra good one."

"Ar doesn't ken what a bad un 'ill be like, then," rejoined James.

"Well," said Butterfield, throwing on another fagot, "you are welcome to it, such as it is. What will you have to eat?"

"Ought ye can give me," said Pigg; "a rasher o' bacon, collops and eggs, or ought," casting his eye up at the flitches and hams hanging from the ceiling, adding, " ar's mortal hungry."

While the rashers of bacon were frying, Butterfield made Pigg exchange his wet coat, waistcoat, and shirt, for dry clothes of his own, and adding a cold pork-pie and a flagon of ale to the hot bacon, Pigg was very soon in his glory. Having at length cleared the decks, he again turned to the fire, which, eyeing for some time with critical amazement, he at length exclaimed, with a laugh, "Sink, if mar cousin Deavilboger see'd sick a fire i' his kitchen, ar wonder what he'd say!"

"You'll keep good fires in your country, then, I presume?" inquired Mrs. Butterfield.

"Aye, fires, aye!" exclaimed Pigg; "nebody kens what a fire is but them as has been i' wor country."

"Whereabouts is it?" inquired Butterfield, puzzled with his dialect.

Pigg.—"A canny Newcassel, where all the coals come frae. You've niver been there, ar's warn'd, or you'd have heard tell o' mar coosin Deavilboger—farms a hundred and nine acres of land aside Kenton. Sink it, frae his loupin on stane ar's seen all the country side flaring wi' pit loues. Mar cousin's kitchen fire niver gans out frae Kirsmas to Kirsmas. A! it *is* a bonny country! By my *soule*, ar's niver been reetly warmed sin ar left the North."

"Indeed!" exclaimed Mrs. Butterfield, in astonishment; "your cousin must spend a fortin i' firin'."

"Deil a bit—coals cost nout—if they did, folks wad warm theirsels at the pit heaps. Iv'ry poor man has his shed full o' coals; great blazin'

fires to come hyem te at night, a nice singin' hinnies, all ready for slicin'
and butterin', swingin' o' the girdle—but ye dinna ken what a girdle is i'
this country, ar's warn'd."

"No," replied Mrs. Butterfield; "we don't."

"Why, ye see," said James, "it's a great round, flat iron broad like,
may be, three times as big as your hat-crown, with a hoop over the top
to hank it on tiv a crook i' the chimley; and then the missis makes
a thing like a spice loaf, which she rolls out flat with a rollin'-pin, till it's
the size o' the girdle, and about as thick as yeer finger, and then she
bakes it on the girdle, and splets it up, and butters it see that the grease
runs right down your gob as ye eat it."

"Nay, then!" exclaimed Mrs. Butterfield, "but that will only be for
gentle folk?"

Pigg.—"Iv'ry man i' the country has a singin' hinnie of a Saturday
night, and many of a Sunday, tee. There wasn't a man on mar cousin
Deavilboger's farm but has his fifteen and sixteen shillin' a-week, and
some up to twenty."

"Wonderful!" exclaimed Mr. Butterfield, who only paid his eight.
"It must be a grand country to live in."

"A, it's a grand country!" repeated Pigg. "Ar's *sure* ar's never been
rightly warm sin' I left it. What they call a fire i' the South, is nabbut
what we wad tak to light one on with i' the North;" rubbing his wet
cords as he spoke. "A, it's a bonny country!—bonny Shiney Raws all
about the pits. Ivery man with his pig and his gairden; sweetbriar i'
the middle, and poseys round about."

"You must have a drop of gin, and see if that will warm you,"
rejoined Mr. Butterfield, unlocking a cupboard as he spoke. "Here,
Mary, get some glasses, and put the kettle on, and let us have a cheerer
to the gentleman's health. It's not every night that brings us a visitor."

A large black bottle of Hollands, labelled "Eye Water," part of a
contraband cargo, was fearlessly placed on the table. More wood and
coal were added to the fire; the wood crackled merrily up the chimney,
shedding a cheerful blaze over the family group circled about. One seat
of honour was ceded to Pigg, the other was occupied by Mrs. Butterfield,
while her two daughters came in between her and their father, who sat in
the centre, and the servant lads kept a little in the rear of their master on
the left. The servant girl bustled about in the background.

"Help yourself, now," said Mr. Butterfield, passing the bottle and
tumbler to Pigg, having poured himself and his wife each out a glass.
"Don't be afraid of it; you're heartily welcome, and there's more in the
cupboard when you've finished that. Here's your good health! I'm fond
of fox-hunters."

"Thank ye," replied Pigg, filling his glass half full of gin, and topping
it with hot water. "Ar wish the country was made o' sic chaps as ye;
we shouldn't hear se much 'war wheat' then, ar's warn'd ye."

Mr. Butterfield did not catch the latter part of the sentence, or he
would have read him a lecture on riding over wheat.

A second half tumber succeeded the first, and Pigg waxed uncommonly
jovial; his eyes twinkled, and his tongue ran riot with all manner of
stories, chiefly about hunting, the importance of his cousin Deavilboger,

and the magnificence of the town of Newcassel. " Mr. Jorrocks was nothing but a good un. If it wasn't for him, he'd never stop i' the South." At the third half tumbler, Deavilboger's farm had grown into nine hundred acres, and Newcassel was bigger than London.

" God sink ar'll sing ye a sang," said he, turning the quid in his mouth. " A ! one o' the bonniest sangs that iver was sung—all about a dog o' wor toon, and when ar stamps wi' my foot, ye mun all join chorus. Now ar'll begin —

> "In a town near Newcassel, a pitman did dwell,
> Wiv his wife named Peg, a tom-cat, and himsel ;
> A dog called Cappy, he doated upon,
> Because he was left by his great uncle Tom.
>> Weel bred Cappy, famous au'd Cappy
>> Cappy's the dog, Tallihò, Talliho !"

" Now, that *last's* chorus," observed Pigg, wiping the tobacco stream from his mouth with his sleeve.

> " His tail pitcher-handled, his colour jet black ;
> Just a foot and a half was the length of his back ;
> His legs seven inches frer shoulders to paws,
> And his lugs like twe dockins, hung owre his jaws."

Hereupon Pigg gave a mighty stamp, and the company joined in with—

> "Weel bred Cappy, famous au'd Cappy,
> Cappy's the dog, Talliho, Talliho !

> " For huntin' of varmin reet clever was he,
> And the house frer a' robbers his bark wad keep free.
> Could baith fetch and carry ; could sit on a stool,
> Or, when frisky, wad hunt water-rats in a pool.
>> Weel bred Cappy, &c.

> " As Ralphy to market one morn did repair,
> In his hatband a pipe, and weel combed was his hair,
> Ower his arm hung a basket—thus onwards he speels,
> And enter'd Newcassel wi' Cap at his heels.
>> Weel bred Cappy, &c.

> " He hadn't got further than foot of the side,
> Afore he fell in with the dog-killin' tribe ;
> When a highwayman fellow slipp'd round in a crack,
> And a thump o' the skull laid him flat on his back !
>> Down went Cappy, &c.

> " Now Ralphy, *extonish'd*, Cape's fate did repine,
> Whilst its eyes like twe little pearl buttons did shine;
> He then spat on his hands, in a fury he grew,
> Cries, ''Gad smash ! but ar'l hev settisfaction o' thou,
>> For knockin' down Cappy,' &c.

> " Then this grim-luiken fellow his bludgeon he raised,
> When Ralphy eyed Cappy, and then stood amazed ;
> But fearin' aside him he might be laid down,
> Threw him into the basket, and bang'd out o' town.
>> Away went Cappy, &c.

"He breethless gat hyem, and when liftin' the sneck,
His wife exclaim'd, 'Ralphy! thou's suin gettin' back;'
'Getten back!' replied Ralphy, 'ar wish ar'd ne'er gyen,
In Newcassel, they're fellin' dogs, lasses, and men.
 They've knocked down Cappy, &c.

"'If aw gan to Newcassel, when comes wor pay week,
Ar' liken him again by the patch on his cheek;
Or if ever he enters wor toon wiv his stick,
We'll thump him about till he's black as au'd Nick,
 For killin' au'd Cappy,' &c.

"Wiv tears in her een, Peggy heard his sad tale,
And Ralph wiv confusion and terror grew pale;
While Cappy's transactions with grief they talk'd o'er,
He creeps out o' the basket quite brisk on the floor!
 Weel done, Cappy!" &c.

Great applause followed, producing another song, "The Keel Row," after which came another stiff tumber of gin and water—then another song, or parts of a song rather—for the vocalist was fast becoming *hors du combat;*—his face turned green—his eye gradually glazed, and at length his chin sunk on his breast; but for the fortunate circumstance of the farmer's boy being on the look-out, his tumbler would have dropped to the ground. They then carried Mr. Pigg off to bed, but not being able to get off his boots, they happed him up as he was.

The next morning when Farmer Butterfield came down-stairs, he found Pigg on his over-night seat, with his legs cocked over the back of a chair, with one of his boys blacking his boots. He had neither cold nor head-ache, and eat as much breakfast as if he had had no supper. His coat was dry, his waistcoat was dry, he was all dry together; the sun shone brightly, the lost hounds had cast up, and taken shelter in an out-house, his horse was freshish, and the pack poured out of the barn bright and glossy in their coats, though somewhat stiff in their limbs.

 *   *   *   *   *   *   *

"If evir ye come to Handley Cross, wor ard maister will be glad to thank ye and pay ye," said Pigg, grasping the farmer's hand as he mounted, "and if evir ye gan to canny Newcassel, cast your eye o'er mar coosin Deavilboger's farm—A! what tormot's he has! Aye, and see his grand pedigree bull—A! what a bull he has!"

"You're *heartily* welcome," replied Farmer Butterfield, shaking Pigg by the hand, "and whenever you pass this way, give us a look in, there'll always be a drop of eye-water in the bottle; stay, let's open the gate for you;" running to the fold-yard from which Pigg emerged with the glad pack at his horse's heels.

Mrs. Butterfield, her daughters and servants, were clustered at the door, to whom Pigg again returned thanks, and touching his cap, trotted down the lane on to the road, the brightness of the morning contrasting with the dark wildness of the hour in which he arrived. What a different place he had got to, to what he thought! On Pigg jogged, now coaxing a weakly hound, now talking to his horse, and now striking up the chorus of—

 "Cappy's the dog, Talliho! Talliho!"

 *   *   *   *   *   *   *

"Your master's just gone through," said Anthony Smith at the Barrow Hill Gate.

"Mar maister!" replied Pigg, "what Squire Jorrocks?"

"Yeas," said the man, "he was axing if I could tell him what become of his hounds yesterday."

"Indeed," replied Pigg, "give me fourpence and a ticket."

On Pigg trotted as well as he could with a pack of hounds without a whipper-in, and catching a view of Mr. Jorrocks' broad red back rounding a bend of the road, he gave a puff of his horn that acted like magic.

Mr. Jorrocks stopped as though he were shot.

Turning short back, he espied his huntsman and the hounds, and great was the joy and exultation at meeting.

"*Killed* him did you say!" exclaimed Mr. Jorrocks, in ecstasies, "*vere's his brush?*"

"A, sink 'em, they'd spoil'd it," replied Pigg, "afore iver I gat te them—but ar's getten his head i' my pocket!"

"*Fatch it out!*" exclaimed Mr. Jorrocks, "vy, man, you should ride with it at your osses' side. Have you never a couple loup to your saddle? —run a bit of vipcord through his snout, and let the world see the wonders we've done—you've no proper pride about you! There now," continued he, having adjusted the head at Pigg's saddle side, "let the world see it—don't let your coat lap hang over it."

Thus Mr. Jorrocks and Pigg proceeded at a foot's pace, relating their mutual adventures. Before they had got to the end of their stories, who but Charles should pop upon them from a by-road, and the three having got together again, they entered Handley Cross in triumphant procession, as though they had never parted. Rumours of the run had been rife all the morning, but in what direction it had been, nobody could tell. The stables and kennel were besieged by inquirers, and Mr. Fribbleton, the man-milliner, who edited the "Paul Pry," having been granted an audience, managed from Mr. Jorrocks's account to manufacture the following article for the second edition of his paper. It was headed—

"BRILLIANT RUN WITH MR. JORROCKS'S HOUNDS!

and proceeded—

"As this unrivalled pack were taking their daily exercise on the Summerton road, accompanied by the huntsman, their worthy master, and his friend, Mr. James Stobbs, a large dog-fox suddenly crossed before them, with which the pack went away in gallant style, despite all efforts to stop them, as they were advertised to meet at the Round-of-Beef and Carrots to-morrow. The place the fox so suddenly popped upon them was just at the four-mile-stone, near the junction of the Appledove road, and as there were some coursers on Arthington open fields, it is conjectured bold Reynard having been suddenly disturbed by the long dogs, had come upon the hounds in a somewhat ruffled state of mind, without dreaming of his danger. However, he was quickly convinced that there was some, by the cry of his redoubtable pursuers, and the shortness of his start caused him to put his best leg foremost; and setting his head for

Wollaton Plantations, he went straight as an arrow towards them, passing near the main earths on Thoresby Moor, and going through the low end of the plantations, where they run out into a belt.

" Here he was chased by a woodman's dog, and the hounds came to a momentary check; but Mr. Jorrocks, being well up, made a scientific cast forward, and getting upon grass, they hit off the scent at a meuse, and went at a racing pace down to Crowland, through Lady Cross Park, leaving Bilson a little on the right, and so on to Langford Plantations, from thence by King's Gate to Hookem-Snivey, and on by Staunton-Snivey to the Downs, crossing at Depedean, leaving the Windmill to the right, and the Smugglers' Cave on the left. Night and a hurricane now came on; but, despite all impediments, this truly gallant pack realised their fox at the foot of Gunston Crags. A few more minutes would have thrown the mantle of protection over the varmint, for the crags are strongholds, from whence foxes are seldom or ever dislodged. It was the biggest Reynard that ever was seen, and the tag of his tail was uncommonly large.

"The distance gone over could not have been less than five-and-twenty miles; and altogether it was the very finest run ever encountered in the annals of fox-hunting. Mr. Jorrocks went like a bird, and earned a title to a niche among the crack riders of England.

"The hounds lay out all night, but have arrived at Handley Cross in very fair order; and we trust this run is a prelude to a long career of brilliant sport that we shall have the good fortune to record under the auspices of their most sporting master, and his equally renowned and energetic Scotch huntsman—Charles Pigg."

Mr. Jorrocks wrote the following letter to Bill Bowker :—

"DEAR BOWKER,

"Your's to hand, and note the contents. We've had a *buster!* Three hours without a check and a kill! Should have been 'appy to have sent old 'Nunquam Dormio' * an account, but it was a bye on the sly, and no one being out, there are no names to bring in. It's soapin' chaps cleverly wot makes a run read. Howsomever, I hopes to have lots of clippers for him to record before long. Not that I cares about fame, but it's well to let the 'ounds have the credit of what they do. You say Dormio will spice the articles up with learning and Latin. Latin be 'anged!—Greek too, if there's any grown now-a-days. Now for the run.

"It's an old sayin', and a true 'un, that a bad beginnin' often makes a good endin'. We lost Binjamin at startin'; the little beggar was caught in the spikes of a po-chay, and carried a stage out of town—teach him to walk up street for futur'. Howsomever, off we set without him, and a tremendious run was the result. I send you the 'Pry,' and you can judge for yourself; the first part, about the find, must be taken 'cum grano salis,' with a *leetle* Quieanne pepper, as Pomponius Ego would say. We meant to have a private rehearsal as it were, and got a five-act comedy instead of a three. Indeed, it were like to have been a tragedy.

"Somehow or other I got to the Earl of Bramber's, where there was a great spread, and I had a good blow-out, and a solemnish drink. Either I walked in my sleep and fell into a pond or some one pitched me into one, and I was as near drowned as a toucher. Howsomever, I got out, and werry attentive people were to me, givin' me brandy, and whiskey, and negus, and all sorts of things. I slept pretty well after it, nevertheless; but when I awoke to get up, I seemed to be in quite a different room—no bell, no lookin'-glass, no wash-hand, no towels, no nothin', but my 'unting clothes were laid nice and orderly. I dressed, and found my way to the breakfast-room, when sich a roar of laughter greeted my entrance! Still, they were all werry purlite; but I observed, whenever a servant came in he nearly split his sides with laughin'. Well, jist as I was goin' away, I caught a sight of myself in a glass, and, oh, crikey! my face was painted broad red and yellow stripes, zebra-fashion! I couldn't be angry, for it was so werry well done; but it certainly was werry disrespectful to an M.F.H. Have no great fancy for lords—

* An eye, with "nunquam dormio" round, is the crest and motto of "Bell's Life"

werry apt to make first a towel, and then a dish-clout on one. But enough of that.

"I hope the Slender has not been silly enough to shoot an exciseman; they are clearly not game. It will be haukward for them both if he has: of course he has too many legal friends not to get the best advice. I'm sorry to hear about Susan's legs—they were a pair of uncommon neat ones, certainlie; all the symmetry of Westris's, without the smallness. I don't think blisterin' would do them any good; rest—rest—with occasional friction: hand-rubbin', in fact, is the best thing.

"Charley's quite well, and slept last night at a lunatic's, a poor chap wot went mad about 'unting. You needn't send him none of your nasty 'baccy down here, for I don't stand smokin'. As you say Snarle's business has fallen off, you'll have fewer common forms to copy, and more time for letter-writing. Tip us a stave when you've nothin' to do, and believe me yours to serve,

"JOHN JORROCKS.

"P.S. 1. I enclose you 5*l*. for the Slender. Tell him to buy a good hard-mouthed counsel with it. I fear Billy's only a 'lusus naturæ,' or 'loose 'un by natur',' as Pomponius would say. J. J.

"P.S. 2. Tell Fortnum and Mason to send me a dozen pots of marmeylad; also Gilbertson to send me three quartern loaves—two brown and a wite—every other day. Can't get sich bread as his 'ere, and neither Alum nor Branfoote subscribe a dump to the 'ounds, so its no use puzzonin' oneself on their account. Also see Painter, and tell him if his turtle's first chop, to send me six quarts, with a suitable quantity of punch. J. J."

CHAPTER XXIX.

COOKING UP A HUNT DINNER.

CAPTAIN DOLEFUL, ever anxious for the prosperity of the town and his own emolument, conceived that a hunt dinner on the night of his ball would have the effect of drawing divers rural parties to the town who might not otherwise honour him with their presence, and he lost no time in communicating the idea to the worthy master, Mr. Jorrocks.

Of course the *éclat* it would confer on the hunt, and the brilliancy it would reflect on Mr. Jorrocks's mastership, were the main points Captain Doleful urged on behalf of his proposal; and Mr. Jorrocks, nothing loth to indulge in a good dinner, at which he was to play first fiddle, readily came into the proposition, and the following notice was inserted in the " Paul Pry : "—

" MR. JORROCKS'S FOX HOUNDS !

" There will be a HUNT DINNER, at the Dragon Hotel, on the night of the Master of the Ceremonies' Ball, at which Members of the Hunt and the public in general, are invited to attend.

" MR. JORROCKS IN THE CHAIR!

" Tickets, twelve shillings each, to be had at the bar of the Dragon Hotel up to five o'clock on Monday evening, after which none can possibly be issued."

Never was a happier device, or one more eminently successful. Not only did the visitors of the place hasten to secure tickets, but people from all the neighbouring towns showered in their orders by the post, and it soon became apparent that a bumper would be the result. The longest long room at the Dragon was soon declared inefficient for the accommodation of the party, and the masons and joiners were summoned to lay the adjoining bed-room to the end, which would afterwards be restored to privacy by the usual means of folding-doors. Then came the joining and fitting of tables, the measuring of cloths, the borrowing of knives, forks, glasses, salt-cellars, decanters, and waiters. Captain Doleful flew about the town like a lost dog in search of its master. When Mr. Snubbins, the landlord of the Dragon failed in accomplishing a loan, the Captain exerted his authority in compelling one. What with his ball and the dinner he scarcely had time for his meals.

On the Monday he bespoke an audience with Mr. Jorrocks to put the finishing stroke to his arrangements. He was duly received in the dining-room of Diana Villa, where pens, ink, and paper were laid for his coming. The dinner, he assured the worthy master, was calculated to make him eminent in the eyes of all men, and most materially to aid the financial department of the hunt. "There will be," said he, "a gathering from all quarters. Men from every point—sportsmen of every shade and grade are about to assemble, and if you can manage to tickle the fancy of each with a speech, so as to make him believe his favourite sport is the best, there is no saying but in the happy mood that most men are in when pleased and half-drunk, you may draw a good many into becoming members or subscribing."

"Well, there can be no difficulty whatsomever at all," replied Mr. Jorrocks, "in making them a werry 'andsome speech—beautiful speech, I may say, but in course they can't expect me to tell them that I consider any sport better than 'unting."

"Why as to that," rejoined Captain Doleful, "it makes little odds what a man says on an occasion of this sort, especially a chairman, whose first care should be to put every one in good humour with himself; and if you were to outstep the real facts a little for once, no one would ever think of throwing it in your teeth on a future occasion. For instance now, Captain Couples, the great courser, has written for tickets for three,—himself, his son, and a friend,—in order that he may have the honour of making your acquaintance, and then of presenting his son in due form. Of course you will take an early opportunity during the evening of buttering him by introducing as a toast the beautiful sport of coursing, which you may say is one of the most classical and elegant of field-sports, and say that it is one which you feel a peculiar pleasure in proposing, inasmuch as you have been given to understand that one of the most distinguished patrons of the leash has honoured the Handley-Cross Hunt dinner with his presence, which affords you an opportunity of coupling with the sport the name of the gallant Captain Couples, and of course the toast will be responded to with a heavy round of cheers, which will lay the Captain open to the insinuating applications of Mr. Fleeceall, and you may reckon him, if not his son also, a member of your hunt for a year at all events, especially if you get him to pay the money down on the nail."

"Humph!" said Mr. Jorrocks, turning it over in his mind whether he could do such violence to his feelings as to praise the sport of coursing, or call it *sport* at all, for the sake of the three sovereigns he would get by Captain Couples becoming a member of the hunt. Nothing daunted, Captain Doleful proceeded with his enumeration and recommendations. "Mr. Trippitt, the famous cricketer, will most likely come. He was the founder of the Winwicket Cricket Club, which beat all London at Lord's the year before last; you should toast him and his club together, and of course you would string a lot of sentences together in praise of the game of cricket, which you are doubtless aware is most popular all over England. Then there is Mr. Ringmore, the quoit-player, and loads of people who keep some hobby or other for their private riding, who should all be toasted in turn."

"Werry well," said Mr. Jorrocks, "werry well, there cannot be not never no objection whatsomever at all to sayin' somethin' pleasant and soapy of all the warious amusements, but it is werry difficult and inconwenient to have so many cut and dried speeches, as well as one's dinner aboard at the same time. If I could manage to couple two or three of them together, such as coursin', fishin', and fiddlin', for instance, it would suit my constitution better."

"Oh no! that would not do," replied Captain Doleful, "because one of the objects in singling out a sport or diversion to give as a toast is the circumstance of some patron or follower being at table, who will make a speech in reply; but if you club two or three together, not only will you fail in getting any one to consider the toast as a compliment, but no one will rise to acknowledge it; because, though he may be a keen follower of one branch of sport, he may care nothing about the thing you couple with it—You understand?"

"Then we must jest dot down wot we think should be given," observed Mr. Jorrocks, "and also wot I should say, for it is far more than probable, indeed I should say most likely, that in the heat and noise, and lush and flush, and one thing and another, I shall forget one half o' the toast, and possibly give the coursin' man to the fiddlin' feller, or the cricketer instead of the quoit-player." Thereupon Mr. Jorrocks took pen, ink, and paper, and proceeded to draw out his list of toasts.

"In course, ' the Queen, and her stag 'ounds,' will come first," observed he, writing the words at the head of a long slip of paper—adding, "bumper toast. Cheers. Do you think there will be any staggerin' sinner there to acknowledge the toast?"

"Probably there will," replied the Captain, "at all events, if there isn't, I would say a few words in return, as it would not look well to let the toast pass without saying something on behalf of our young and virtuous queen. I can acknowledge it as Vice-president, and also as holding her Majesty's commission."

"Well, then," said Mr. Jorrocks, "let's see what should come next? Shouldn't it be the 'Andley-cross Fox-'ounds, and my werry good health?"

"No—that will be too soon. The Chairman's health should never be given until the company have had a few glasses of wine to elate them for shouting. Besides, your health will be the toast of the evening, and things always become flat after that is given, and perhaps the company will begin to disperse."

"Werry well—any thing for a quiet life—what shall we put then?"

Captain Doleful.—"Prince Albert, to be sure! and his harriers."

"With all my 'eart," replied Mr. Jorrocks, placing the Prince's name after her Majesty's.

"We must have the Prince of Whales next, in course," observed our master, "and all the rest of the Royal family," putting it down, and asking the captain what should follow.

"Mr. Strider, the great racing man of these parts, will most likely come; and if so, you should give the Turf," observed Captain Doleful. "Besides, he is a very likely man to become a member of the Hunt, if not to subscribe, now that there is a regular master, his only excuse for not doing so when the committee had the hounds being that he didn't like partnership concerns in any thing but race-horses."

"The Turf, and Mr. Strider's good health!" Mr. Jorrocks wrote

down—adding the words—"improve breed of 'osses—promote sport—
amuse lower orders—mount cavalry—lick the world," as the headings for
his speech.

"Come now, jog on," said Mr. Jorrocks, looking at the nib of his
pen, "we've only got five toasts ready as yet: shouldn't we give Fox-
'unting?"

"Oh, certainly," replied Captain Doleful; "that is a general toast, and
acceptable to all; besides, Mr. Yarnley will be at the dinner," observed
Captain Doleful. "He has two capital covers, and one capital speech,
which he likes letting off. Write down 'Mr. Yarnley, and Promoters of
Fox-hunting!' for he doesn't hunt himself, and only preserves foxes in
order that he may have his health drunk at ordinaries and public dinners,
when he tells the company how he has always preserved foxes, and does
preserve foxes, and will preserve foxes, and so forth."

Mr. Jorrocks then added Mr. Yarnley's name to the list of toasts, adding
the words, "proprietors of covers and promoters of fox-'unting," and the
following headings for a speech, "Considerate gentleman—free from
selfishness—good example." "We should cheer this toast, I think,"
added Mr. Jorrocks, "'specially as I s'pose the gemman takes no rent for
his covers."

"I believe not," replied Captain Doleful, upon which Mr. Jorrocks put
the word "cheers" after "good example."

"Now Coursing should come, I think," remarked Captain Doleful,
"and Captain Couples's health. He's a great man at the Deptford
meeting, and thinks coursing the only sport worth living for."

"He must be a werry big blockhead, then," replied Mr. Jorrocks,
laying down his pen, and stretching out his legs as though he were going
to take "the rest." "A werry remarkable jackass, indeed, I should say.
Now of all slow, starvation, great-coat, comforter, worsted-stockin', dirty-
nose sort of amusement, that same melancholy coursin' is to me the most
miserably contemptible. It's a satire on racin'."

"Never mind," said Captain Doleful, "Couples's guineas will be as
good as any other man's; and, as I said before, a chairman is not
expected to swear to all he says—your business is to endeavour to please
every one, so that they may go home and tell their wives and daughters
what a jolly, delightful, at-all-in-the-ring sort of gentleman Mr. Jorrocks is."

"Aye, that's all werry good," grunted our master, "but conscience is
conscience arter all, and coursin' is coursin'. It's as bad as drinkin' the
'Andley-Cross waters to have to praise what one doesn't like. I'll give
the Merry 'Arriers afore Coursin', howsomever," said Mr. Jorrocks,
putting down the words Hare-'unting; "Will there be any currant-jelly
boy to return thanks?—I'm sure there will, indeed, for I never knew a
mixed party yet without a master of muggers among them."

To this toast Mr. Jorrocks added the words—"nose—fine music—
pleasant—soup." "Now," said he, "we've got the Queen and the
Staggers—Prince Halbert—Prince of Whales—Strider and the Turf—
Fox-'unting—Yarnley and Proprietors of Covers—the Merry 'Arriers."

"Put 'Coursing' next, then," said Doleful; "it will follow hare-
hunting very well, and be all in the soup line."

" Well, if you must have it, you must," replied Mr. Jorrocks, writing down the word : " coursin'." " Who acknowledges the toast ?—ah, Couples—*Captain*, I think you said he is ? Captain Couples—a werry good man too—blow me tight though if I knows what to say in givin' on it."

" Oh, say it's classical, and a fine bracing amusement." Mr. Jorrocks added the words " fine amusement."

" Well, that's eight bumpers from the chair," observed Captain Doleful; " and now we'll let you take your breath a little—unless Mr. Snapper comes, when you must give pigeon-shooting and the triggers generally. I'll now toast the Chair."

" The Chair," wrote Mr. Jorrocks, " that's me.   Cheers in course."

" In course," replied Captain Doleful, adding, " I shall butter you uncommon."

" With all my 'eart—I can stand a wast of praise," replied Mr. Jorrocks.

" Well, then, after that, and after your speech, which of course will be highly complimentary to the company, and full of promises of what you will do, you must propose my health—as master of the ceremonies of Handley Cross Spa."

" And as a great sportsman ! " added Mr. Jorrocks.

" No, no, I'd rather not," exclaimed Doleful in alarm ; " the fact is, I only hunt on the sly.   If the Dowagers thought I did not devote my whole time and energies to the town amusements, they would grumble, and say I was always out hunting instead of attending to the important duties of my post.   No ; just confine yourself to the M. C. department, not forgetting to insinuate that it is my ball-night, and to express a hope that all the company will honour it with their presence ; you might say something, apparently half-facetiously, in the way of a hint about giving guineas for their tickets ; for some people are getting into the dirty trick of paying at the door."

" Werry good," said Mr. Jorrocks, writing down " Capt. Doleful, M. C., not sportsman—pleasant feller—nice ball—pumps in pocket—tickets at bar—guinea.   You'll be ' cheer'd,' I s'pose ? "

" Of course," said the Captain—" all the honours—one cheer more if you can get it."

Cricketing, quoit-playing, shooting, badger-baiting, steeple-chasing, hurdle-racing, crow-shooting, and divers other sporting, extraordinary, and extravagant toasts were then added ; some to fit people that were known to be coming, others put down to take the chance of any amateur of the amusement presenting himself unexpectedly at the table.

" Werry well now," said Mr. Jorrocks at last, dotting up the column of toasts with his pen, " that's two, four, six, seven, eight, ten, twelve, fourteen, sixteen.   Sixteen bumper toasts, with speeches both goin' and returnin', to say nothin' of shoutin', which always tells on weak 'eads. Wot shall we say next ? "

" Oh ! " said Captain Doleful, in an indifferent sort of way, as much as to say the important business of the evening would be finished on drinking his health ; " why just pass the bottle a few times, or if you see a gentle-man with a singing face, call on him for a song ; or address your neighbour right or left, and say you'll trouble him to give a gentleman and his hounds.

"A gen'lman and his 'ounds," said Mr. Jorrocks, "but they'll have had a gen'leman and his 'ounds when they've had me."

"Ah, but that's nothing—'a gentleman and his hounds,' is a fine serviceable toast at a hunt-dinner. I've known a gentleman and his hounds—a gentleman and his hounds—a gentleman and his hounds—serve chairman, vice-chairman, and company throughout the live-long evening, without the slightest assistance from any other source. Fox-hunters are easily pleased, if you do but give them plenty to drink. Let me, however, entreat of you, above all things, to remember my ball, and do not let them oversit the thing, so as not to get to it. Remember, too, it's a fancy one, and they'll take more dressing."

"Aye, aye, I'll vip them off to you when I think they've had enough," replied Mr. Jorrocks.

CHAPTER XXX.

SERVING UP A HUNT DINNER.

THE important night drew on, and with it the cares and excitement of a double event. The interests of all hearts and minds were centred in that day. None looked beyond. The dinner and dance formed the boundary of their mental horizon. At an early hour in the afternoon numerous rural vehicles came jingling into Handley Cross, with the mud of many counties on their wheels. Here was Squire Jorum's, the chairman of quarter sessions, green chariot, with fat Mrs. Jorum and three fat little Miss Jorums crammed inside, young Mr. Jorum having established himself alongside a very antediluvian-looking coachman, in dark drab, with a tarnished gold-band on a new hat, who vainly plied the thong and crop of a substantial half pig-driver, half horse-breaker's whip, along the ribs and hind-quarters of a pair of very fat, square-tailed, heavy, rough-coated, coarse-headed, lumbering nags, to induce them to trot becomingly into the town. Imperials, a cap-box, a maid in the rumble, all ensconced in band-boxes, proclaim their destiny for that day. Captain Slasher, with a hired barouche and four black screws, all jibbing and pulling different ways—the barouche full of miscellaneous foot cornets in plain clothes (full of creases of course), dashes down East Street, and nearly scatters his cargo over the road, by cutting it fine between Squire Jorum's carriage and the post. A yellow dennet passes by, picked out with chalk, mud, and black stripes : two polar bear-looking gentlemen, in enormous pea-jackets, plentifully be-pocketed, with large wooden buttons, are smoking cigars and driving with a cane-handled hunting-whip. Then a "yellow," with the driver sitting on the cross-bar, whose contents, beyond a bonnet and a hat, are invisible, in consequence of the window having more wood than glass in its composition, works its way up, and in its turn is succeeded by another private carriage with a pair of posters.

Then there was such a ringing of bells, calling of waiters, cursing of chambermaids, and blasting of boots, at the various hotels, in consequence of the inability of the houses to swell themselves into three times their size, to accommodate the extraordinary influx of guests. "Very sorry, indeed," says Mr. Snubbins, the landlord of the Dragon, twisting a dirty duster round his thumb, "very sorry, indeed, sir," speaking to a red-faced big-whiskered head, thrust out of a carriage window, "we are full to the attics—not a shake-down or sofa unoccupied; can get you a nice lodging out, if you like—very comfortable.

"D— your comfortables, you lying thief!—do you suppose I can't do that for myself? Well, if ever you catch me coming to your house again I hope I may be ——" The wish was lost by some one pulling the irate gentleman back into his chaise, and after a short parley inside, during which three reasonable single gentlemen applied to Mr. Stubbins for the accommodation of a room amongst them to dress in for dinner, the boy was ordered to drive on, and make the grand tour of the inns.

Weary, most weary were the doings at the Dragon. *Ring a ding, ding a ding dong,* went the hostler's bell at the gate; "Room for a carriage and pair?"

"Whose o' it?"

"Mrs. Grout's!"

"No, quite full!" The hostler muttering to himself, "Mrs. Grouts and two feeds—sixpence for hostler." *Ring a ding, ding a ding, ding a ding dong.* Hostler again—"Coming out!" "Who now?" "Squire Gooseander! four posters, piping hot, white lather, boys beery, four on to Hollinshall, bait there, back to hall—sixpence a mile for good driving—out they come—there's your ticket—pay back and away."

Tinkle, tinkle, tinkle, tinkle, tinkle, tinkle, tinkle, went a little bell, as though it would never stop.

"WAITER!" roared a voice from the top of the house, that came like a crash of thunder after the insignificant precursor, "am I to ring here all day? Where's the boots? I sent him for a barber an hour ago, and here I've been starving in my shirt-sleeves ever since."

"Now, Jane, Miss Tramp wants her shoes."

"Where's the chambermaid?" exclaimed a gentleman, rushing half frantic down-stairs; "here's a man got into my room and swears he *will* dress in it."

"Oh! I begs pardon, sir," replied the chambermaid, trying to smooth him over, "we really are *so full*, sir, and I didn't think you'd be coming in so soon, sir."

"Waiter! somebody has changed my place at dinner! I was next Mr. Walter Dale, and now they've put me below Mr. Barker—between him and Mr. Alcock: who the devil's done it?"

"Boots! Porter! Boots! run down to Mr. Ingledew the tailor's—you know him, don't you? Corner of Hill Street—just as you turn off the esplanade; and tell him he's sent me the wrong coat. Not half the size of my own—more like a strait-jacket than any thing else. And here! desire Mrs. Kirton to send some ball gloves for me to try on—lemon colour or white—three and sixpenny ones."

"Lauk, I've come away and left Miss Eliza's stockings, I do declare!"

exclaims Jemima Thirlwell, Miss Eliza Rippon's lady's maid, pale with fear, "what *shall* I do? Never was any thing so unlucky—just took them to run my hand through and see they were all right, and left them hanging over the back of the chair. Know as well where they are as possible—but what's the use of that when they are ten miles off?"

"Waiter, what time's dinner?"

"Five o'clock, sir, and no waiting—Mr. Jorrocks swears he'll take the

chair at five precisely, whether it's served or not," adds the waiter, with a grin.

Then there was such work in the kitchen—Susan Straker, the cook, like all the sisterhood, was short in her temper, and severe and endless were the trials it underwent in consequence of the jingling and tinkling of the bells calling away the chambermaids who were to have assisted her in the kitchen. Then Mr. Jorrocks deranged her whole system by insisting upon having a sucking pig and roast goose that she intended for centre dishes, right under his nose at the top of the table; added to which, the fish was late in coming, and there was not half as much maccaroni in the town as would make an inn dish.

"Now, Jun," said Mrs. Jorrocks to her loving spouse, taking a finishing look of our hero as he emerged from his bed-room in the full dress uniform of his hunt, "see and conduct yourself like a gen'leman and with dignity, and, above all, keep *sober*—nothing so wulgar or ungenteel as gettin' intosticated. Belinda and I will call for you at ten minutes before ten, to take you on to the ball; for, in course, it carn't commence till we come, and it won't be politeful to keep people waitin' too long."

"Jest so," replied Mr. Jorrocks, adjusting a capacious shirt-frill in the glass. "Binjimin, I say, run and fatch the fly."

Mr. Jorrocks was uncommonly smart. Sky-blue coat lined with pink satin, finely starched white waistcoat, new canary-coloured shorts, below

Q

which stood a pair of splendid calves, encased in gauze white silk stockings, and his feet appeared in shining shoes with silver buckles.   At
either knee a profusion of white riband dangled in graceful elegance,
looking for all the world like wedding favours.   Benjamin, notwithstanding his boasting and taunting to Samuel Strong, knew his master
too well, and the taste of his whip also, to attempt any of the exclusive
tricks in the way of service, he gave himself credit for acting; so settling
himself into his frock-coat, and drawing on a pair of clean white Berlins,
sufficiently long at the fingers to allow the ends to dribble in the soup-
plates, he wiped his nose across his hand, and running away down to the
stand, very soon had a fly at the door.   Jorrocks stepped in, and
Benjamin mounted behind with all the dignity of a seven-foot figure
footman.   Away they dash to the Dragon.

Notwithstanding the descent of a drizzling rain, and the "inclement
season of the year," as newspapers phrase it, there was a crowd of servants,
post-boys, beggars, and loiterers hanging about the arched gate-way of
the Dragon to get a sight of our renowned hero alighting from his fly;
and great was the rushing and jostling to the door as it drew up.
Mr. Snubbins, the landlord, a choleric round-faced little man, with a snub
nose and a pimple on the end of it, had put himself into a white waistcoat, with his best blue coat and black kerseymere shorts, to officiate
behind Mr. Jorrocks' chair, and hearing our master's name bandied about
on his arrival, met him at the foot of the stairs with all becoming respect,
and proceeded to conduct him into the waiting-room.   There was a
strongish muster; but two melancholy mould-candles, in kitchen candlesticks, placed on the centre of a large table, shed such a dismal ray about
the room, that little was distinguishable, save a considerable mass of
white, and an equally large proportion of a darker colour.   Some thirty
or forty members of the Hunt, strangers and others, were clustered about,
and there was a dull, funeral sort of hum of a conversation, interrupted
every now and then by the recognition of friends, and the entrance of
another arrival into the dingy apartment.   Then there was the usual
hiding of hats and cloaks—the secretion of umbrellas, goloshes, and
sticks, and the expression of hopes that they might be forthcoming when
wanted.

Meanwhile the savoury smell of dinner fighting its way up the crowded
staircase, in the custody of divers very long-coated post-boys turned
waiters, and a most heterogeneous lot of private servants, some in top-
boots, some in gaiters, some few in white cotton stockings, and the most
out-of-the-way fitting liveries, entered the waiting-room, and the company
began to prepare for the rush.   All things, soup, fish, joints, vegetables,
poultry, pastry, and game, being at length adjusted, and the covers taken
off to allow them to cool, Mr. Snubbins borrowed a candle from the low
end of the table, and forthwith proceeded to inform Mr. Jorrocks that
dinner was served.

Great was the rush!   The worthy citizen was carried out of the waiting-
room across the landing, and half-way up the dining-room, before he
could recover his legs, and he scrambled to his seat at the head of the
table, amidst loud cries of "Sir, this is my seat! Waiter, take this person
out."—"Who are you?"—"You're another!"—"Mind your eye!"

—" I *will* be here ! "—" I say you won't though ! "—" That's my bread ! "

Parties at length get wedged in. The clamour gradually subsides into an universal clatter of plates, knives, and forks, occasionally diversified by the exclamation of " *Waiter !* " or, " Sir, I'll be happy to take wine with you." Harmony gradually returns, as the dinner progresses, and ere the chopped cheese makes its appearance, the whole party is in excellent humour. Grace follows cheese, and the " feast of reason " being over, the table is cleared for the " flow of soul."

A long web of green baize, occasionally interrupted by the inequalities of the various tables, succeeds, and clean glasses with replenished decanters and biscuit plates, for they do not sport dessert, are scattered at intervals along the surface. The last waiter at length takes his departure and eyes begin to turn towards the chair.

" Mr. Wice ! " roars Mr. Jorrocks, rising, and hitting the table with an auctioneer's hammer, " Mr. Wice-President, I say ! " he repeats, in a louder and more authoritative tone, amid cries of " Chair ! chair ! order ! order ! silence ! silence ! " " I rises," says he, looking especially important, " to propose a toast, a bumper toast in fact, that I feels confident you will all drink with werry 'earty satisfaction—it is the health of our young, wirtuous, and amiable Queen (applause), a werry proper toast to give at a great sportin' dinner like this, seein' as how she is a werry nice little 'ooman, and keeps a pack of stag-'ounds. Gentlemen, I need not tell you that stag-'unting is a sport of great hantiquity, as the curiosity shop-keepers say ; but they couldn't do it in nothin' like the style in former days that they do now, so in that respects we have the better of the old hancients. Who hasn't seen Frank Grant's grand pictor of the meet of the stag-'ounds on Hascot 'Eath ? That will tell you how it's done now—French polish, blue satin ties, such as Esau never could sport. That's a pictor, my bouys, and when I've 'unted your country to the satisfaction of you all, as I've no manner of doubt at all that I shall, then you subscribe and get Frank to paint me and my 'ounds. And now for the toast," added Mr. Jorrocks, raising a brimming bumper high in hand : " The Queen and her Stag-'ounds ! " Drank with a full and heavy round of applause. After resuming his seat for a few seconds, during which time he conned the next toast in his mind, Mr. Jorrocks, rose and called for another bumper, just as Captain Doleful was rising to return thanks on behalf of her Majesty.

" Mr. Wice ! " he roared out, " I rise to propose another bumper toast, as big a bumper as the last in fact, and one that I feel conwinced you will all be most 'appy to drink. We have just had the honour of drinking the health of the Queen ; there is one near and dear to her Majesty, who, I feels assured, you will not be the less delighted to honour (applause). I need not say that I alludes to the great patron o' the Woods and Forests, Prince Halbert, the best-looking man i' the country." (Drank with immense applause—one cheer more—HUZZAH !)

Mr. Jorrocks being an expert chairman, from frequent practice at " free-and-easys," went on pretty briskly at starting, and the company had hardly drained their glasses, and got settled after cheering, before his hammer was at work again, and he called for another bumper toast.

Having given "The Prince of Whales," as he called him, and "the rest of the Royal Family," "Gentlemen," said he, rising, glass in hand, "I have now to propose to your favourable consideration an important branch o' British diwersion, and one for which this country long has, and ever will, stand most howdacious conspicuous (cheers). I allude to the noble sport of racin' " ("hear, hear, hear," from Mr. Strider, and a slight jingling of glasses from friends in his neighbourhood). "Gentlemen, racin' is a sport of great bantiquity, so old, in fact, that I carn't go back to the time when it commenced. It is owin' to racin' and the turf, that we now possess our superior breed of 'osses, who not only amuse the poor people wot carn't afford to hunt, by their runnin', but so improve our breed of cavalry, as enables us to lick the world (cheers). I am sure, gentlemen, you will all agree that racin' is one of the noblest and most delightful sports goin', and honoured as we are, this evenin', by the presence of one of the brightest hornaments o' the British turf," (Mr. Jorrocks looking most insinuatingly down the table at Strider, as much as to say, "That will do you, my boy.") "I feels assured I need only couple with the turf the popular name of Strider (loud cheers), to insure a burst of hearty and enthusiastic applause." Jorrocks was right in his surmise, for no sooner was the name pronounced, than there was such a thumping of the baize-covered tables, such a kicking of the floor, and such a shouting and clapping of hands, that the concluding words of his speech were audible only to the reporter, who was accommodated with a small round table and a large bottle of port immediately behind the chair.

Strider was rightly named Strider, for he was an immensely tall, telescopic kind of man, so tall, that he might pass for the author of Longfellow's poems, who now drew himself out from under the table as though he was never going to end. He had a frightful squint, so that when meant to look at the chair, one eye appeared settled half-way down the table, and the other seemed to rest upon the ceiling. He was dressed in a round, racing, cut-away coat, with basket buttons, drab trousers, and a buff waistcoat, with a striped neckcloth. He had made money by racing —if honestly, he was a much belied man—but as he spent it freely, and not one man in a hundred cares to ask how it comes, Strider was popular in his neighbourhood.

"He felt deeply sensible of the honour that had been done him by their distinguished chairman and that great meeting, not only by the manner in which his health had been proposed, but for the handsome compliment that had been paid to the great national and all-enjoyable sport of racing, which he felt assured required no recommendation from him, as no one could partake of it once without being fully convinced of its infinite superiority and worth. He was happy to see that his humble exertions in the great and good cause had not been altogether thrown away, for, in the list of races for next year, he saw many names that had never been put down before, and having now got a master of hounds whose name was closely associated with everything that was sporting and popular, he made no doubt things would proceed in a true railway style of progression, and the name of Jorrocks would be followed by every well-wisher to that noble animal, the horse. The list of Hashem races for the next year, he would take the liberty of handing up to the chair," producing, as he spoke, a long, half-printed, half-manuscript sheet from his coat-pocket, "and, in conclusion, he had only to repeat his most grateful thanks for the very distinguished honour they had conferred upon him."

Thereupon three-quarters of the orator disappeared under the table—the list passed quickly up, for no one ventured to look at it, lest a subscription should be inferred, and on its reaching the president, he very coolly folded it up, and put it in his pocket. Mr. Strider looked all ways except straight at Mr. Jorrocks, who very complacently proceeded with his list of toasts. "Gentlemen," cried he, getting up again, "Mr. Wice-President and gentlemen!" he exclaimed; "the next toast is one that I feels assured you will drink with werry great satisfaction, and in a full bumper, with all the honours—it is the health of a gentleman now present, who, though no fox-'unter himself—the more's the pity—is nevertheless a real friend to the sport, and not one of your selfish warmints wot destroys foxes because he does not care about Talli-hoing himself, but, with most trumpish consideration, does his best to promote the sport of his friends and neighbours, thereby settin' an example worthy of imitation by all, both great and small (cheers). When I say it's the health of a gentleman wot gives a brace of covers, free gratis, all for nothin', to our 'unt, your percussion imaginations will readily supply the name of Yarnley (loud applause); and I propose we drink in a full bumper the health of Mr. Yarnley, and proprietors of covers, and promoters of fox-'unting." This toast was drunk with very great applause, and some seconds elapsed before silence was restored. Mr. Yarnley then rose.

He, too, was a tallish man, but coming after Strider he looked less than he really was, added to which, a frock-coat (sky-blue, with pink lining) rather detracted from his height; his face was long and red, his nose very short and thick, and his hair very straight. "Mr. President and gentlemen!" said he, very slowly, fixing his eyes steadily on a biscuit-plate before him, "for the honour you have done me—hem—in drinking my health—hem—I beg—hem—to return you—hem—my most sincere thanks—hem—and gentlemen, I can only say—hem—that I have always been a friend—hem—to fox-'unting—hem (cheers)—and I always shall be a friend to fox-'unting, gentlemen (cheers)—which I am sure is a most agreeable sport (cheers)—hem, hem—and, gentlemen, I hope you will always find foxes in my covers—hem (applause)—for I can only say, gentlemen, that I do preserve foxes, gentlemen—hem (renewed applause) —and I always have preserved foxes, gentlemen—hem, hem—" when Yarnley, seeming about brought up, the company cheered, and drinking off his heel-taps, he concluded with saying, "and, gentlemen, I always *will* preserve foxes!"

"Mr. Wice-President," roared Mr. Jorrocks, above the clamour that now began to prevail, as tongues became loosened with the juice of the grape, "Mr. Wice-President, having drank the first of all sports, let us not forget another werry pleasant branch of 'unting that many delight in who cannot partake of the other, and which is useful as well as pleasant, I mean 'are-'unting; it is a werry nice lady-like amusement; and though we had no 'are-soup at dinner, I makes no doubt we have some werry keen 'are-unters at table for all that. I begs to give you ''Are-'unting, and the merry Dotfield 'Arriers.'"

While Mr. Jorrocks was delivering himself of this eloquence, an evident uneasiness prevailed among divers fat, ruddy-faced members of the Dotfield hunt, chiefly dressed in single-breasted green coats, with bright buttons, and drab breeches, with woollen stockings, who were scattered among the company, as to who should acknowledge the honour that was done their calling, and gradually they turned to a sportsman near Mr. Jorrocks, one of the many masters who, bolder than the rest, returned thanks in a dribbling, cold-hunting sort of speech, while some dozen stood up to signify their approbation of the sentiments of the speaker, and their sense of the honour that had been individually done them.

Coursing followed hare-hunting, according to previous arrangement, which Mr. Jorrocks described as a fine useful sport, and expatiated largely on the merits of " 'are-soup," and "jugged 'are."

Captain Couples briefly acknowledged the honour.

Doleful now began twisting his face into a variety of contortions as the time approached for him to let off his cut-and-dried speech. He had it in notes under his biscuit-plate, at least all the long words he was likely to forget, and now was the time for pouring them upon the company. " Gentlemen ! " said he, in a shrill, penny-trumpet sort of voice, hitting the table with his knuckles ; " Gentlemen ! " he repeated, without drawing the attention of the company to his upright position.

" SILENCE ! " roared Mr. Jorrocks, like Jupiter himself, and the noise was quelled on the instant.

" Gentlemen ! " shrieked Captain Doleful, for the third time, " often as it has fallen to my lot to address meetings of my friends and fellow-citizens, never, no never, did I rise with feelings of such unmitigated embarrassment and trepidation as I do upon the present occasion, for I rise to take upon myself the high and important honour of offering to one of the most distinguished and enlightened assemblies human being ever addressed (loud cheers) a toast that no tongue can do justice in proposing, for it is the health of a man whose worth is superior to any form of words the English language is capable of supplying" (immense cheers). " 'Ookey Valker," said Mr. Jorrocks in an under tone. " Gentlemen," continued Captain Doleful, " deeply conscious as I am of my own unworthiness and incapacity, I would infinitely prefer comprising the toast in the magic name of the gentleman whose health it is, were it not for the honourable and important office of master of the ceremonies of this unrivalled town, which renders it imperative upon me to attempt, however feebly and defectively, a slight portraiture of his unrivalled and surpassing worth (cheers). Gentlemen, whether I regard our great master in his private relation as a friend and delightful companion, or look at him in that resplendent cynosure, formed by the mastership of the Handley Cross fox-hounds, I know not in which character I feel the greatest difficulty and barrenness of expression—the greatest paucity of words, of simile, of fitting comparison (loud cheers). In the one, our estimable chairman is all mildness, like the blessed evening-star ; and in the other, all energy and daring, like the lion lord of the forest, rampant for his prey ! " (Renewed cheers.) " 'Ookey Valker," again said Mr. Jorrocks, blowing his nose. " Unbounded in his liberality—unbounded in his hospitality—unbounded in his urbanity, his private character is equalled only by his public one (loud cheers). They are like rival moons!—opposition suns! (Immense cheers.) But, gentlemen, what boots it for an humble individual like myself to occupy your valuable time (cries of "Go on," "Go on,") in attempting to do justice to a subject that, as I have already said, is beyond the reach of praise,—above the powers of words to accomplish; let me rather resume the place I humbly occupy at this festive board—resume it at least until my important avocations call me, and *you* I hope I may add," grinning like a death's head upon the company, "to another and equally enchanting scene; but before I sit down, let me utter the magic words, ' Health and long life to John Jorrocks!' "

The latter words were delivered in something between a screech and a yell, but fortunately the unearthly sound was immediately quelled by the instantaneous rising of the company, who, in the most uproarious manner—some standing on their chairs, others with one leg on a chair and another on the table—roared forth the most deafening discharge of applause that ever was discharged in the Dragon, while Mr. Jorrocks sat wondering how long it would last. After a lapse of some minutes, order began to be restored, the company gradually got shuffled into their seats, and, filling himself a brimming bumper of port, Mr. Jorrocks at length rose to return thanks.

"Well, now, dash my vig," said, he, sticking his thumbs into the armholes of his waistcoat, "but frind Miserrimus has buttered me uncommon (laughter and cheers). Never was so reg'larly soaped i' my life (renewed laughter). A werry little more might have made one doubt his sincerity. I'm the man for all sorts of larks, and no mistake—one that goes the *extreme* animal—the entire pig—without a doubt. 'Untin' is the foremost passion of my 'eart! compared with it all others are flat and unprofitable (cheers and laughter). It's not never of no manner of use 'umbuggin' about the matter, but there's no sport fit to hold a candle to fox-'untin' (cheers from the blue-coated party). Talk of stag-'untin'! might as well 'unt a hass!—see a great lolloppin' beggar blobbin' about the market-gardens near London, with a pack of 'ounds at its 'eels, and call that diwersion! My vig, wot a go! (laughter). Puss-'untin' is werry well for cripples, and those that keep donkeys (renewed cheers from the blues, with angry looks from the green-coated gentry). Blow me tight! but I never sees a chap a trudgin' along the turnpike, with a thick stick in his 'and, and a pipe in his mouth, but I says to myself, there goes a man well mounted for 'arriers! (immense laughter and uproar continuing for some minutes, in the midst of which many of the green party left the room). I wouldn't be a master of muggers for no manner of money! renewed laughter). Coursin' should be made felony! Of all daft devils under the sun, a grey'ound's the daftest! (renewed uproar, mingled with applause.—Captain Couples looked unutterable things). Racing is only for rogues! (Strider squinted frightfully). I never goes into Tat.'s on a bettin'-day, but I says to myself as I looks at the crowd by the subscription-room door, there's a nice lot o' petty-larceny lads! I'd rayther be a black-faced chimley sweep nor a white-faced blackleg!" (hisses and applause).

Strider now drew himself from under the table, and shaking a fist towards Mr. Jorrocks, while his eyes looked across, and down, and round the room, everywhere but at the chairman, he stalked off, followed by Couples, and Couples's son, and a gentleman for whom Couples had paid, and brought in the chaise, amid ironical cheers from the blues, who encouraged Mr. Jorrocks by the most vociferous applause. " Believe me, my beloved bouys," continued Mr. Jorrocks, perfectly unconscious of the movement or the mischief he was doing, "that 'untin', 'untin', 'untin', is the sport ! Oh," said he, with up-turned eyes, " vot a martyr I am to the chase ! It makes me perfectly mad,—I dreams about it night after night, and every night. Sometimes I'm tormented with foxes ; I fancy I sees them grinnin' at me from all parts of the bed-curtains, and even sittin' upon the counterpane ! then I kicks them off, and away we all go to the tune of 'eads up and sterns down. Presently I sees Binjimin a ridin' on a whirl-wind, and directin' the chase ; next minute I fancies myself on a pumped-out 'oss, a 'eavin' and sobbin' i' the heavy, not a soul with the 'ounds, who are going away with a fresh fox, jest as I sees the 'unted one dead beat, a crawlin' down an 'edge-row ; I outs with my 'orn, and, blow me tight, I carn't sound it ! At another time, a butcher's bouy, without an 'at, comes tearin' on a runaway tit, right among the 'ounds, who have thrown up in a lane, and the crashin' and yellin' is hawful. Again, I dreams, that jest as the darlin's are runnin' into the warmint all savage, and bristlin' for blood, a flock of sheep cross their line, when every 'ound seizes his mutton ; and then I sees a man with a long bill in his 'and, with a lawyer in the distance, makin' towards me, and then I avakes.

"Oh, gen'lemen ! gen'lemen ! none but an 'untsman knows an 'unts-man's cares ! But come, never mind ; care killed the cat ! sha'nt kill me—vot's the toast ? " said he, stooping, and looking at his list ; " Ah ! I sees," reading to himself in a pretty loud voice, "Doleful, M.C.—great sportsman—pleasant feller. Gen'lemen ! " roared he, resuming an erect position, " gen'lemen ! pray charge your glasses—bumper-toast—no 'eel-taps, no sky-lights, but reg'lar downright brimmin' bumpers to the 'ealth of a man wot shall be himmortal ! oh, gen'lemen, if ever it was hutterly unpossible to do the right measure of genteel by any one, it is upon the present most momentous crisis, when I rises to butter a man that is superior to butter—to hoil a man that is Macassar itself. Oh ! surely Doleful there," looking at the vice-chairman, " is a trump, and no mistake (laughter). Whether I looks at him as chief of the fantastic toers, or a leading sportsman of our brilliant 'unt, I doesn't know which character is the brightest (immense laughter, for all who knew Doleful knew how per-fectly innocent he was of sporting ; Doleful himself began to make wry faces). I loves him as a sportsman, though we all know he only 'unts on the sly ! but then what a brilliant boy he is in a ball-room ! Talkin' of that, gen'lemen, this is his benefit ball-night, and after we have had our twelve shillings' worth of liquor, I vote we should each spend a guinea with Miserrimus ; no one will grudge that trifle to such a werry pleasant trump—such a werry agreeable cock ; and though guineas don't grow upon gooseberry-bushes, still you must all fork out one to-night, for nobody goes in for less." Doleful, on hearing Jorrocks put this finishing stroke to his hash, wrung his hands in agony, and rushed out of the room, vowing, as he went down-stairs, that Jorrocks was the biggest ass—the greatest fool—the stupidest sinner, that ever came to Handley Cross. " Talliho !

gone away!" roared Mr. Jorrocks, as he saw Doleful bolt. "Hark back!
hark back!" cried the company; but Doleful was deaf to the rate, and
cut away home, half frantic with rage.

"Well," said Mr. Jorrocks, "as the gen'loman's hoff, it's no use i'
finishin' my oration; so, 'stead of the 'ealth of Old Doleful, I begs to
propose, most cordially, that I sit down."

Our friend then resumed his seat amidst great applause from the blues,

THE CONVIVIAL MEETING.

and was considering how he could introduce a limping song he had composed in honour of Doleful, when a sudden rush of green and dark coats,
headed by Strider, poured noisily into the room, and elbowed their way
back to their places. The malcontents had held a consultation, and,
advised by Doleful, were come to put their decision into execution.

"Gentlemen!" roared Strider, who had now reached his seat, "gentle-men!" repeated he, standing like the monument, and squinting frightfully, amid cries of "Hear, hear—chair, chair—order, order—go it l ong 'un!" from adverse parties.—"I rise to propose a resolution," roared Strider, holding a slip of paper upside down; "I rise to propose a resolution," now getting the paper the right way for reading, "that I feel assured will be acceptable to the majority of this meeting—I move (reading) that Jorrocks John is the shabbiest fellow and greatest humbug we ever had at Handley Cross!" And Jorrocks, who had been crouching like a tiger for his spring, immediately rose amid immense uproar, and declared that he would move as an amendment, that "JORROCKS WAS A BRICK!" and putting the amendment, he declared that "the 'bricks' had it," whereupon a scene of indescribable confusion ensued, the green coats going in at the blues like bulls, and upsetting some half dozen of them before they knew where they were, while Jorrocks, getting hold of Strider, dealt a heavy blow in his ribs, and then split his coat up to the collar, just as a green biscuit dish grazed our master's head and knocked off his wig.

Lights were then extinguished, and the company fought their way out of the room as best they could. Jorrocks lost a coat-lap, which now flaunts as a banner-screen in the drawing-room of Mrs. Royston of the Dotfield hunt. And so ended what the veracious Paul Pry called "a most convivial evening"

CHAPTER XXXI.

THE FANCY BALL.

E must here indulge in a little retrospection — Although Mr. Barnington hunted with the hounds, his lady took no notice of the Jorrockses, and dashed past their one-horse chaise with the air of an ill-bred woman drawn by well-bred horses. On foot, she never saw them; and if she admitted a knowledge of their existence, it was in that casual sort of way that one speaks of a horse or a dog.

Still she could not disguise from herself that they were thorns in her side. Mr. Jorrocks' popularity, with Belinda's sweetness and beauty, went far to undermine the throne Mrs. Barnington had set up for herself. Not only were her evening parties less sought after, but she had reason to suspect that even Captain Doleful had declined a dinner invitation in favour of the Jorrockses!

As yet they had never met, save in the streets; but Captain Doleful's ball involved a crisis that could not be got over without a collision. This had been changed, by Mrs. Barnington's desire, into a fancy one, in order that she might triumph in the number and brilliance of her diamonds. The costume she fixed upon was that of Queen Elizabeth— not an ill-chosen one for her height and haughty bearing. The dress was ordered in London, as well for the purpose of having it unexceptionable in style and richness, as to enable her to blaze a splendid and unexpected meteor in the assembled host of Handley Cross. It was also expected to have a beneficial influence on Captain Doleful, should any doubt exist as to who was the fittest person for honour.

Notwithstanding Mrs. Barnington's precautions, the secret of her dress transpired. Mrs. Jorrocks's Batsay having established an intimacy with our friend John Trot, the footman, the fact descended from the exalted region of upper servitude, and was communicated to Mrs. Jorrocks with the slight addition, that the Queen had graciously lent Mrs. Barnington her crown and sceptre.

*   *   *   *   *   *

"Nay, then!" exclaimed Mrs. Jorrocks, thinking it was all over with her, and fancying she saw Mrs. Barnington sailing into the room with Captain Doleful, her head in the air and her eyes on the ceiling. Long did she muse ere the table of precedence flashed across her mind. No sooner did it occur to her, than off she darted to Mr. Jorrocks's drawers, where, amid a goodly collection of letters, she succeeded in finding Captain Doleful's one, stating that "the Lady of the M.F.H. came on after members of the royal family, and before all bishops' wives and daughters, peeresses, knights' dames, justices' wives, and so forth."

*   *   *   *   *   *   *

"Mischievous 'ooman!" exclaimed Mrs. Jorrocks, conning the passage attentively; "nasty, mean, circumwenting hanimal, I *sees* what she's after!—wants to steal a march on me as a member of the royal family. Come in as a queen, in fact! I'll be hupsides with her though!"

Thereupon Mrs. Jorrocks took a highly ornamented sheet of notepaper out of her envelope case, and concocted the following epistle to Captain Doleful :—

"Mrs. Jorrocks' Comp^ts Cap^n Doleful, and I will feel much obliged if he will have the kindness to lend her your table of Precedence for a few minutes, as she wishes to see how things stand in Handley Cross.

"*Diana Lodge.*"

*   *   *   *   *   *   *

Captain Doleful was sitting on the counter in Miss Jelly's shop, in deep consultation with her about his fancy dress, when the note arrived. Having to be the great man of the ball, it was incumbent upon him to have something better than the old militia coat, or even the dress-hunt one, revised. Time pressed, or he would have tried what the Jew clothesshops in London could do for him, but Miss Jelly, having a fertile imagination, and his interest at heart, he summoned her to his councils, to invent something showy without being expensive.

Many costumes were talked over. Spanish would not do, because the captain would have to show his legs; Swiss entailed a similar objection; and the old English costumes were equally objectionable. Some were too costly, others too complex.

*   *   *   *   *   *   *

"I have it!" at length exclaimed Miss Jelly, clapping her hands,— "I have it!" repeated she, her face beaming with exultation. "You shall be the great Mogul!"

"The Great Mogul!" repeated Captain Doleful, thoughtfully.

"Yes, the Great Mogul!" rejoined Miss Jelly. "A turban, with a half-moon in front, petticoat trousers, shell-jacket, moustachios, and so forth."

"That will do, I think," replied Doleful, squeezing her hand. "Sound well, and not cost much—will it?"

"Oh, *very* little!" replied Miss Jelly. "Let me see! One of your scarlet pocket-handerchiefs will make the crown of the turban, and the folds can be formed of white neckcloths. I have a bird of paradise feather in my Sunday hat, and a string of large blue beads that will ornament the front. You want some summer trousers, so if you buy as much stuff as will make two pair, it will only be the making and alter-ing, and you can get Nick Savoy into the house at three-and-sixpence a-day and his meals, who can cut out the jacket, and I will make and trim it myself."

"Excellent!" exclaimed Captain Doleful, rubbing his hands, and putting a whole penny tart into his mouth. Just then Benjamin entered, and after having been refused credit for an ounce of paragoric, he put Mrs. Jorrocks's note into Captain Doleful's hand.

* * * * * * *

"I'll bring it immediately," said the Captain to Benjamin, bolting out of the shop by the side-door, winking at Miss Jelly as he went.

* * * * * * *

Presently a stamp over-head announced that the Captain wanted Miss Jelly, who imprudently leaving the shop in charge of Benjamin, our friend filled his pockets with macaroons and his hat crown with sponge-biscuits, while she was getting her message up-stairs.

* * * * * *

"Captain Doleful's compliments to Mrs. Jorrocks," said Miss Jelly, returning, "and is very sorry that the table of precedence has not been returned from the Heralds' College, where it was sent to be enrolled, but immediately it comes Mrs. Jorrocks shall have it."

"Yes, *marm*," said Benjamin, hurrying off.

* * * * * *

"Please, *marm*, the Captain's compliments, and his table is at the joiner's gettin' rolled, but as soon as it comes 'ome you shall have it," was the answer Benjamin delivered to his mistress.

The Captain was shy for a day or two, and Mr. Jorrocks, being more intent upon hunting than etiquette, the poor lady was left to her own devices. Belinda did not appreciate the point, and, moreover, was too busy with her dress to enter upon the question as she should do.

Mrs. Jorrocks, mistrusted the Captain, and thought he might be inclined to shuffle her off, under pretence of Mrs. Barnington being a queen.

"I'll be a queen, too!" at length exclaimed she, after a long gaze at the fire, thinking the thing over; "I'll be a queen, too!" repeated she, snapping her fingers, as though she were meeting Mrs. Barnington; "I'll be a queen!—the Queen of 'Earts;" exclaimed she, looking at herself in the eagle-topped mirror.

That evening she wrote the following letter to Miss Slummers, or Miss Howard, as she was now called:—

"DEAR MISS,—We are agoing to have a fancy ball here, and I want your assistance in a dress. Was you ever the Queen of 'Earts? If so, please lend me your robes. If not, pleaze lend me a crown as like the Queen of 'Earts' crown as you can get it. You know it's not exactly a

crown, but something like a crown stuck on a cap. The sceptre seems
like a wand with a rose at the end. Pleaze let me know how I should be
dressed behind, as the cards give one no idea. Should like the full
robes, if you have them; but, in course, will be happy to take what I
can get. Excuse haste and a werry bad pen. Yours, in haste,

" JULIA JORROCKS.

" *Diana Lodge, Handley Cross Spa.*

"Miss Clarissa Howard,
" Sadlers' Wells Theatre, London."

Miss Slummers had never been the Queen of Hearts, but had enacted
one of the rival Kings of Brentford, in the popular pantomime of that
name, and, after a conference with the property-man of the theatre, she
thus answered her distinguished friend :—

" HONOURED MADAM,—Your commands have been received; and I
much regret that, never having appeared in the distinguished part of the
Q. of Hearts, I have not the necessary properties to send you. I am not
aware that the character has ever appeared upon the stage other than in
pantomime, and never at either of the theatres to which I have been
attached; but our property-man thinks the accompanying crown, fixed on
a Swiss cap, 'Canton de Berne,' will come as near the card as we can get
it. I also send a sceptre, to which is attached a large rose, that we used
for the 'two Kings of Brentford' to smell at, which comes as near the
spirit of the thing as anything can be. The sceptre is our best, and
triple gilt. The robes should be of brocaded satin, and a large reticule of
red silk, in the shape of a heart, dangling negligently on your left arm,
will at once proclaim your character. The back of your dress is not
material, as crowned heads are only looked at in front. Any further
assistance I can be of will be extremely gratifying to me; and I beg to
subscribe myself, with great respect, your most obedient and very
humble servant,

" C. HOWARD.

" *Theatre Royal, Sadlers' Wells.*

" Mrs. Jorrocks,
" Diana Lodge, Handley Cross Spa."

So far, so good. The crown did admirably. It was studded with false
brilliants, and looked splendid by candle-light. The sceptre, too, was
imposing; and, regardless of expense, Mrs. Jorrocks had the richest
brocade cut into the requisite shapes, to wear over a red satin gown she
had by her. Nor was the heart-reticule forgotten; and, altogether,
Mrs. Jorrocks succeeded in making herself a very fair representative of
her Majesty of Hearts. Belinda's pretty blue and white petticoat, with
the scarlet body of a Valencian peasant, was changed for a plain white
satin dress, with a court plume, for her to attend as maid of honour on
her majesty. Charley was converted into a blue-bodied, white-legged
page, with a Spanish hat and feathers.

The Great Mogul's dress progressed favourably, too. His wide sleeve and great trousers were done, and Miss Jelly had got a bargain of tarnished lace for braiding his red jacket. A splendid beard, whiskers moustache, and all, were hired for the night, and a pair of five-and-sixpenny red leather slippers were bought, to act the part of shoes at the ball, and supersede a pair of worn-out pumps afterwards.

Mrs. Barnington having set the fashion of mystery about her dress, it was followed by the *élite* of the place, and each tried to mislead his neighbour. Swiss peasants said they were coming as Turks, Turks as Chinese, Charles the Seconds as Napoleons, and Huntsmen as Hermits. Still secrets will transpire, and Mrs. Barnington and Mrs. Jorrocks knew all about each other's dresses as well as if they were together every day. The former talked at Captain Doleful instead of to him, sometimes pretending to doubt whether the Jorrocks' would go, fearing they would not, for vulgar people seldom liked getting so completely out of their element. For her part, she hoped they would, for she had a taste for natural curiosities—heard, too, their daughter was pretty, and should like to see her; and she closed her last interview by presenting Captain Doleful with ten pounds for her tickets.

Mrs. Jorrocks was less mealy-mouthed, and finding the table of precedence was not likely to come, she called at Miss Jelly's on the morning of the ball, and asked the Captain what time she should be there to go into the room with him. This was a poser, that even the skilful Captain found difficult to parry ; but, while bustling his turban and trousers under the sofa, and fussing a greasy-covered arm-chair towards Mrs. Jorrocks, the dinner occurred to him, and, after looking vastly wise, he declared that that was the only thing he had any difficulty about. "You see," said he, "I am vice-president—then, Mr. Jorrocks is rather a sitter— not that I mean to say he gets drunk, but you know he is fond of society, gay and careless about time, and there are so many toasts to propose and so many speeches to make, that I fear it is utterly impossible to say what time we may get away, and I——"

"Well, but," interrupted Mrs. Jorrocks, "the dinner has nothin' to do with the dance; if Jun chooses to lower 'imself by gettin' drunk, that's no reason why you should, and one wice can always appoint another wice, and wicey wersey, I suppose."

"True," replied Captain Doleful, assenting to the position ; "but, then, if all the dancing men are at the dinner, what use will a master of the ceremonies be of to the ladies ? "

"Fiddle the ladies ! " exclaimed Mrs. Jorrocks ; "it's not dancin' men wot 'ill go to the dinner—not your 'air-curlin', arm-squarin', caperin' swells, but old-season'd casks, wot 'll never think o' the dance."

"I hope not," replied Captain Doleful ; "why, there will be Mr. Stobbs, for one."

"He'll not go to the dinner," rejoined Mrs. Jorrocks—"stays at 'ome with me."

  *   *   *   *   *   *   *

Just then, Miss Jelly, judging her lodger was in a dilemma, adroitly resealed three or four old notes, and bringing them up on a tart-plate, apologised for intruding, but said the servants were all urgent for answers ; and Captain Doleful, availing himself of the excuse, set to work most assiduously, and what with apologising, scribbling, and mistaking, Mrs. Jorrocks found she might as well go away.

* * * * * * *

Thus matters stood on the eventful evening whose progress we have so far described. Mrs. Jorrocks was right as to the formation of the dinner-party, few dancing men, and scarcely any fancy dressers, being there. Most of the young gentlemen were corking their eyebrows, fixing on moustache, or drawing on dresses that made them look as unlike themselves as possible. Rear-admirals, who had never had a shave; colonels, who didn't know how to fasten on their swords; grandees, who didn't know how to get on their breeches; and fox-hunters, who did not know how to put on their spurs,—stood admiring themselves before their sisters' mirrors, thinking the ball hour would never arrive. Young ladies laced themselves extra tight, and a little more *tournure* was allowed for setting off the gay bodices and swelling drapery of their dresses. Neat ankles availed themselves of the license for wearing fancy dresses requiring short petticoats, while sweeping trains concealed others that were less fortunate in their make. Old dresses were metamorphosed into new, and new fancy ones were made for re-conversion into plain ones another time.

Confused with wine and anger, Captain Doleful rushed hurriedly home to his lodgings, and threw himself into the easy chair by the fire. He was not done abusing Mr. Jorrocks, when Miss Jelly entered with a bed-candle, and a little jug of warm water. She had laid his dress out on the bed; his red and white turban, beaded and feathered, with a barley-sugar half-moon, surmounted his baggy trousers; the red jacket was airing before the fire, and scarlet and white rosettes appeared on the insteps of the slippers. Seeing he was disturbed in his mind, Miss Jelly merely intimated that it wanted ten minutes to nine, and withdrew quietly below.

There was no time to lose; so hastily doffing his hunt-coat, &c., Captain Doleful was soon in his baggy trousers; and having stamped over-head, Miss Jelly was speedily with him, assisting him into his drawn linen vest, over which came the embroidered scarlet jacket, with baggy linen sleeves, tightening at the wrist; a long blue scarf encircling his waist, displaying the gilt handle of his militia sword. When he had got on his beard, moustaches, and whiskers, and surmounted the whole with his turban, his black eyes assumed a brightness, and his whole appearance underwent a change that elicited an involuntary expression of admiration from Miss Jelly. "The captain," she really thought, "looked splendid!" Thereupon, regardless of the increasing ratio of fare, he liberally offered her a ride in his fly to the rooms.

The Queen of Hearts commenced her toilette immediately after tea, and had no little trouble in fixing her crown, and her cap, and her front on her head. The rustling robes required much adjusting, and Belinda got little of Betsy's services that night.

Mrs. Barnington's robes being accurately made, were easily adjusted. Her great ruff rose majestically; her pink satin jewelled stomacher, piqued in the extreme, glittered with diamonds and precious stones, and her portentous petticoat of white satin, embroidered with silver, stood

imperiously out. Round her neck she wore a costly chain, and her black
coif was adorned with ropes and stars of jewels, with an enormous diamond
brilliant in the centre. She rustled at every move.

By half-past nine, all Handley Cross was in masquerade. Brothers
met sisters in the drawing-rooms, and were lost in astonishment at each
other; the servants came openly forward to inspect their young masters

and missises. The rain had ceased and been succeeded by a starlight
night; the populace turned out to congregate about the ball-rooms, or at
the doors where carriages waited to take up. The noise inside the Dragon
kept a crowd up outside; and as the Queen of Hearts drove up for her
husband, rival cheers announced her arrival.

"It's a man!" exclaimed one, putting his face close to the window, as Mrs. Jorrocks lowered the glass of the fly, to give her orders to the fly-man.

"It's not!" replied another.

"I say it is!" rejoined a third. "It's a beef-eater—what they stick outside shows to 'tice the company up." Then a fresh round of cheers arose, which might either be in answer to applause within, or in consequence of the discovery made without, for a mob is never very particular what they shout for. Meanwhile Mrs. Jorrocks drew up the glass protecting her maid of honour, her page, and herself, from the night air.

The Queen of Hearts was in a terrible fidget, and every moment seemed an hour. Flys drove up for gentlemen that were "not ready," and cut away for those whose turn came next. Shouts sounded in the various streets as befeathered and bespangled dresses darted through the crowds into the carriages; and as the vehicles fell into line by the rooms, there was such gaping, and quizzing, and laughing among the spectators, and such speculation as to what they were.

People generally go early to fancy-balls; it is one of the few things of life that a person is not ashamed of being first at. Indeed the order of things is generally reversed, and instead of people telling their friends that they mean to be there earlier than they do, they are apt to name a somewhat later time, in order to arrive first themselves. Some thirty or forty people had got there before Captain Doleful, chiefly door-payers, who came to see the fun, without regard to benefiting him. Three Bohemian brothers, a Robin Hood, a Mail Guard, and a Rural Policeman were not a little puzzled at the Great Mogul's *empressement*, for though they knew him as Captain Doleful, M.C., they had no idea who the gentleman was in the turban and trousers.

The red folding-doors now kept flapping like condors' wings, as Highlanders, and archers, and deputy-lieutenants, and Hamlets, and sailors, and Turks, and harlequins, and judges, and fox-hunters, came shouldering and elbowing in with variously-dressed ladies on their arms,—Russians, Prussians, Circassians, Greeks, Swiss, and Chinese — a confusion of countries all speaking one tongue. Captain Doleful was pushed from his place before the doors, and nobody ever thought of asking for him, so intent were they on themselves and each other. "Bless me, is that you?"—"Who'd have thought?"—"Mar, here's James!" "Oh, dear, and William Dobbs!"—"What's your dress?"—"Beautiful, I declare!"—"Your pistols arn't loaded, I hope?"—"Splendid uniform!"—"French chasseur!"—"They told me you were coming as a post-boy."—"Oh, dear, look there!"—"What a rum old lass!"—"The Queen of the Cannibal Islands!"—"Mrs. Hokey Pokey Wankey Fum!"

We need scarcely say that this latter exclamation was elicited by the entrance of the Queen of Hearts, followed by her page in Spanish costume of spangled purple velvet and white, with black hat and feather; and Belinda in white satin, with a court plume of feathers. A slight flush of confusion mantled over her lovely brow, imparting a gentle radiance to her languishing blue eyes, contrasting with the fixed and stern determination of her aunt's. Her majesty's appearance was certainly most extraordinary. The free-masonish sort of robes, the glittering crown on the sombre cap, the massive sceptre held like a parasol, were ludicrous

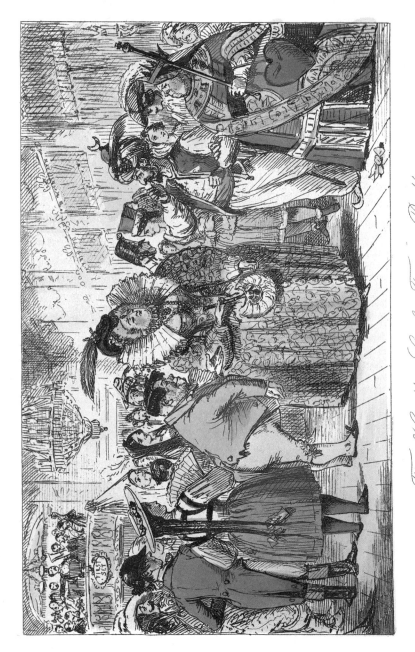

The Handley Cross Fancy Ball.

enough; but in addition to this, her majesty had forgotten to put off her red and white worsted feet-comforters, and was making her way up the room with them draggling about her ankles.

Captain Doleful, all politeness, informed her of the omission, and unfortunately discovered himself, for no sooner did Mrs. Jorrocks find out to whom she was indebted, than keeping her arm in the Great Mogul's, where it had been placed while she drew the things off, she made a movement towards the ball-room door, which being seconded by the crowd behind—all anxious to get in and scatter themselves for inspection—they were fairly carried away by the tide, and the Queen of Hearts and the Great Mogul entered the room with people of all nations at their heels.

Great was Mrs. Jorrocks' gratitude. " Oh, dear, it was so werry kind —so werry engagin'. If it hadn't been the captin announcin' himself, I should never have guessed it was him ; " and the captain bit his lips and cursed his stupidity for getting himself into such a mess. Still the Queen of Hearts stuck to him, and, sceptre in hand, strutted up and down the well-lit room, fancying herself " the observed of all observers."

For the first time in his life, the captain's cunning forsook him. He didn't know how to get rid of his incubus,—and even if he did, he knew not whether to station himself in the ante-room to receive Mrs. Barnington, or to let the ball begin, and brazen it out. As he walked about, half frantic with rage, his turban pinching, and his beard and whiskers tickling him, an opposition Mogul gave the signal to the musicians, and off they went with a quadrille, leaving the couples to settle to the figure as the music went on.

Then as Turks *balanced* to Christians, and Louis Napoleon wheeled sweet Ann Page about by the arms, two highly-powdered footmen threw wide the doors, and in sailed Mrs. Barnington catching poor Doleful with Mrs. Jorrocks on his arm. One withering look she gave, and then drawing herself up into a sort of concentrated essence of grandeur, towered past, followed by old Jorrocks minus his coat-tail ; and our worthy master, thinking to do all proper honours to the wife of a gentleman who subscribed so liberally to his hounds, immediately asked her to dance, which being indignantly refused, he consoled himself by taking all the pretty girls in the room by turns, who unanimously declared that he was a most agreeable, energetic old gentleman, and an excellent dancer.

And owing to the spirit with which Mr. Jorrocks kept it up, that ball was productive of a most prolific crop of offers, which, we need scarcely say, sent the Jorrocks funds up very considerably

CHAPTER XXXII.

ANOTHER SPORTING LECTOR.

MR. JORROCKS's tongue being now well laid in for talking, he determined to keep it going, by giving another sporting lecture. Being, however, of opinion that a lecture that was worth listening to, was worth paying for, he determined to charge a shilling a head entrance, as well for the purpose of indemnifying himself against the expenses of the room, &c., as of giving Pigg the chance of any surplus there might be over for pocket-money, of which useful article James was rather short.

Our master's fame being now widely established, and occupation uncommonly slack at Handley Cross, a goodly muster was the result.

Precisely as the clock was done striking seven, Mr. Jorrocks ascended the platform, attended by a few friends, and was received with loud cheers from the gentlemen, and the waving of handkerchiefs from the lady part of the audience. Of these there was a goodly number, among whom was Mrs. Jorrocks, in a great red turban, with a plume of black feathers, reclining gracefully on one side; Stobbs sat between her and Belinda, who was dressed in a pale pink silk, with a gold cord in her hair: Belinda looked perfectly happy. When the applause had subsided, Mr. Jorrocks advanced to the front of the platform (which was decorated as before), and thus addressed the audience :—

"Frinds and fellow-countrymen! Lend me your ears. That's to say, listen to wot I'm a goin' to say to you. This night I shall enlighten you on the all-important ceremony of takin' the field." (Loud applause.)

"TAKIN' THE FIELD!" repeated he, throwing out his arms, and casting his eyes up at the elegant looping of his canopy. "TAKIN' THE FIELD! glorious sound! wot words can convey anything 'alf so delightful?

"In my mind's eye I see the 'ounds in all their glossy pride a trottin' around Arterxerxes, who stamps and whinnies with delight at their company. There's old Pristess with her speckled sides, lookin' as wise as a Christian, and Trusty, and Tuneable, and Warrior, and Wagrant, and Workman, and Wengence, and all the glorious comrades o' the chase.

"But to the pint. Ingenious youth, having got his 'oss, and learned to tackle him, let me now, from the bonded warehouse of my knowledge, prepare him for the all-glorious ceremony of the 'unt.

"How warious are the motives," continued Mr. Jorrocks, looking thoughtfully, "that draw men to the kiver side. Some come to see, others to be seen; sòme for the ride out, others for the ride 'ome; some for happetites, some for 'ealth, some to get away from their wives, and a few to 'unt. Ah! give me the few—the chosen few—' the band o' brothers,' as the poet says, wot come to 'unt!— men wot know the 'ounds, and know the covers, and know the country, and, above all, know when 'ounds are runnin', and when there're hoff the scent—men wot can ride in the fields, and yet 'old 'ard in the lanes—men wot would rayther see the thief o' the world well trounced in cover, than say they took a windmill in the hardour of the chase. Could I but make a little country of my own, and fill it with critturs of my own creation, I'd have sich a lot o' trumps as never were seen out o' Surrey. (Loud cheers.)

"Bliss my 'eart, wot a many ways there is of enjoyin' the chase," continued Mr. Jorrocks, "and 'ow one man is led into folly and extravagance by another! Because great Sampson Stout, who rides twenty stun', with the nerves of a steam-hengine, keeps twelve 'unters and two 'acks, little Tommy Titmouse, who scarcely turns nine with his saddle, must have as many, though he dare 'ardly ride over a water furrow. Because Sir Yawnberry Dawdle, who lies long in bed, sends on, Mr. Larkspur, who is up with the sun, must needs do the same, though he is obliged to put off time, lest he should arrive afore his 'oss. Because Lady Giddyfool puts a hyacinth in her lord's button-'ole, every hass in his 'unt must send to Covent-Garden to get some. I werily believes, if a lord was to stick one of my peacock Gabriel Junks's feathers in his 'at, there would be fools to follow his example; out upon them, say I: unting is an expensive amusement or not, jest as folks choose to make it.

"There's a nasty word called 'can't,' that does an infinity of mischief. One can't 'unt without eight 'osses; one can't do without two 'acks; one can't ride in a country saddle; one can't do this, and one can't do that— hang your can't's! Let a man look at those below him instead o' those above, and think 'ow much better hoff he is nor they. (Applause) Surely the man with one 'oss is better off than the man with none! (Renewed applause.)

"Believe me, my beloved 'earers, if a man's inclined for the chase, he'll ride a'most anything, or valk sooner than stay at 'ome. I often thinks, could the keen foot-folks change places with the fumigatin' yards o' leather and scarlet, wot a much better chance there would be for the chase! They, at all events, come out from a genuine inclination for the sport, and not for mere show-sake, as too many do.

"Dash my vig, wot men I've seen in the 'unting-field! men without the slightest notion of 'unting, but who think it right to try if they like it, jest as they would try smokin' or eaten' olives after dinner.

"'You should get a red coat, and join the 'unt,' says a young gen'le-man's old aunt; and forthwith our hero orders two coats of the newest cut, five pair of spurs, ten pair of breeches, twenty pair of boots, waist-coats of every cut and figure, a bunch of whips, diachulum drawers, a cigar-case for his pocket, a pocket siphonia, a sandwich-case for one side, and a shoe-case for t'other, and keeps a hair-bed afloat agin he comes 'ome with a broken leg. (Laughter and applause.)

"But I lose my patience thinkin' o' sich fools. If it warn't that among those who annually take the field, and are choked off by the expense, there are ingenuous youths who, with proper handlin', might make good sportsmen and waluable payin' subscribers, I'd wesh my 'ands of sich rubbish altogether. If any such there be within the limits of this well-filled room, let him open wide his hears, and I will teach him, not only how to do the trick, but to do it as if he had been at it all his life, and at werry little cost. Let him now pull out his new purchase, and

learn to ride one 'oss afore he keeps two. We will now jog together to
the meet. And mark! its only buoys in jackets and trousers that are out
for the *first* time.—Viskers, boots, and breeches, are 'sposed to come from
another country. First we must dress our sportsman ;—no black trousers
crammed into top-boots—no white ducks shaped over the foot, or fur-
caps cocked jauntily on the 'ead ;—real propriety, and no mistake!

"That great man Mr. Delme Ratcliffe, says in his interestin' blue-
book, 'that there's nothin' more snobbish than a black tye with top-
boots.' It was a werry clever remark, and an enlargement of Mr. Hood's
idea of no one ever havin' seen a sailor i' top-boots. Bishops' boots
Mr. Radcliffe also condemned, and spoke highly in favour of tops cleaned
with champagne and abricot jam. 'Hoganys 'owever, are now all the go,
and the darker the colour, the keener the wearer expects to be thought. I
saw a pair i' the Cut-me-Downs last year, that were nearly black.

"Leather-breeches Mr. Radcliffe spoke kindly of, but unless a man
has a good many servants, he had better have them cleanin' his 'oss than
cleanin' his breeches. Leathers are werry expensive, though there's a
a deal of wear i' them. I have a pair that were made by White o'
Tarporley, in George the Third's reign, and though the cut is summut
altered, the constitution of them remains intact. In those days it was
the fashion to have them so tight, that men used to be slung into them
by pulleys from their ceilings; and a fashionable man, writin' to his
tailor for a pair, added this caution, 'Mind, if I can get into them, I
won't have them.' Leathers were once all the go for street-work, and
werry 'andsome they looked.

"I've heard a story, that when George the Fourth was Prince, a swell
coveted the style of his leathers so much that he bribed the Prince's valet
largely for the recipe. 'You shall have it,' said the man pocketin' the
coin, and lookin' werry wise; 'the fact is,' added he, 'the way his Royal
'Ighness's royal unmentionables look so well is, because his Royal
'Ighness sleeps in them.'" ("Haw, haw, haw," grunted Mr. Jorrocks, in
company with several of his audience.) "Some chaps affect the dark
cords as well as the 'hogany boots, but there's as much haffectation i' one
as the other. Blow me tight, if it were'nt for the bright colours there
would'nt be many fox-'unters.

"The custom of riding in scarlet is one it becomes me to speak upon ;
—I does'nt know nothin' about the hantiquity of it, or whether Julius
Cæsar, or any other of those antient covies, sported it or not; but, like
most subjects, a good deal may be said on both sides of the question.
There's no doubt it's a good colour for wear, and that it tends to the
general promotion of fox-'unting, seeing that two-thirds of the men wot
come out and subscribe would'nt do so if they had to ride in black. Still
I think ingenuous youth should not be permitted to wear it at startin',
for a scarlet coat in the distance, though chock full of hignorance, is quite
as allurin' as when it encloses the most experienced sportsmen.

"I remembers dinin' at a conwivial party in London, where there was
a werry pleasant fat 'M. F. H.,' who told a story of wot 'appened to him
in the New Forest. This, I need scarcely say, is a great wood of many
thousand hacres, (a hundred thousand p'raps), and unless a man looks
sharp, and keeps near the 'ounds, he stands a werry good chance of losin'

of them. Well, it so 'appened that this 'ere fat gen'lman did lose them, and castin' about, he saw a red coat flyin' over a flight o' rails i' the distance. In course he made for it, but afore he got up, what was his extonishment at seein' red-coat pull up and charge back! He found the gen'l'man knew nothin' about the 'ounds, and was gettin' on capital without them.

" A Yorkshire frind o' mine went to a union 'unt, where men from three countries attended.—The field was frightful! Three 'underd and fifty 'ossmen, all determined to ride, and as jealous as cats. Now my frind being a true-born Briton, and not to be made to ride over nothin' on compulsion, started away in quite a different line to wot the fox broke, followed by an 'underd 'ossmen, or more. The 'arder he went, the 'arder they rode, and fearin' he might fall, and be flummox'd, he made for a windmill on a neighbouring 'ill, and stuck his 'oss's tail to the sails.

" Up came his followers, puffin' and blowin' like so many grampuses. ' Vich vay? vich vay? vich vay are th' 'ounds gone? ' gasped they.

" ' 'Ounds!' exclaimed my frind; 'I've been ridin' away from you all the time; 'ounds be gone t'other way?'" (" Haw, haw, haw!" a laugh in which the whole room joined, till the mirth got up into a roar, which Mr. Jorrocks availed himself of to pay his respects to a stiff tumbler of brandy and water that now began to send forth its fragrance from the table at the rear of the platform).

Smacking his lips, he thus resumed—

" So much for the force of example, gen'lemen;—had my frind been in black, the crowd wouldn't have come. Still the colour's good, and it ar'n't the use, but the abuse, that I complains on. For my part I likes a good roomy red rag, that one can jump in and out of with ease. These fine tight things," continued he, taking hold of his sky-blue coat, lined with pink silk, and looking at his canary-coloured shorts, "are all well enough for dancin' in, but for real scrimmagin' out-door work, there's nothin' like room and flannel;—good long-backed coats, with the waist-coat made equally warm all round, and the back to come down in a flap, and plenty of good well-lined laps to wrap over one's thighs when it rains."—Mr. Jorrocks suiting the action to the word, and describing the cut of each article as he went on. " Berlin gloves are capital for 'unting in," continued he; " they keep your 'ands warm, and do to rub your nose upon in cold weather.

" Youngsters should be cautious o' spurs;—they may use them wot is called incontinently, and get into grief. I disagree with Geoffry Gambado, who recommends the free use of them, as tendin' to keep the blood in circulation, and preventin' one's toes catchin' cold. He recommends spurrin' i' the shoulder, where he says an 'oss has most feelin', because he has most weins; adding, that by spurrin' at his body, five times in six your labour is lost; for if you are a short man, you spur the saddle-cloth only; if a leggy one, you never touch him at all; and if middlin', the rider wears out his own girths, without the 'oss being a bit the better for it ; but my own opinion is, that the less ingenuous youth uses them the better.

" A slight knowledge o' farmin' promotes the true enjoyment of the chase. What so 'umiliatin' as to see a big farmer bullyin' a little man in leather and scarlet for ridin' over his seeds, when the innocent is ignorant

of havin' done nothin' o' the sort. Seeds, my beloved 'earers, are what
grow into clover, or new-land hay; they come hup arter the corn-crop,
and when that is reaped, if an inquiring sportsman will examine the
ground, he will see little green herbs, like crow's feet, shootin' hup 'mong
the stubble, which rear themselves into stalks with expandin' leaves; and
those glorious pink and white balls, called clover, wot smell so fragrantly
as one loiters pensively along the shady dusty lanes.

"Now, if the iron-shod 'unter careers over these young and tender
plants, leavin' his copyright behind him, and it comes wet shortly arter,
the standin' water perishes the plants, and leaves the farmer to water his
bed with tears and lamentation.   Oh, miserable bunch-clod!

"So it is with wheat. If you see a field nicely laid away, the surface
all smooth, and the furrows all open, you may conclude that is wheat,
even though the tender green blades—the promissory notes of life's
comin' year, are not yet apparent. Some labour 'ard to make themselves
believe that it increases the crop to ride over it, and many a hargument
I've held with farmers in favour of that position myself, but no man, who
treats himself to a little undisguised truth, can make himself believe so,
unless, indeed, he is satisfied that a drove of hoxen would improve the
prospects of a flower-garden by passin' a night in frolicsome diwersion.
The wheat-field is the farmer's flower-garden!—It is to it that he looks
for the means of payin' his rent, and giving his hamiable wife and accomplished darters a new piannet, and a scarlet welwet bonnet a-piece, with
a black feather drooping over the left hear (Mr. Jorrocks looking slyly at
Mrs. J. as he said this); and young and heedless men, if even they have
no compassion on the old cock-farmer, should think what distress they
will cause to the hens if they lose their scarlet welwet bonnets with the
appurtenances. Some wags say that wheat is called 'ard corn, because it
stands a wast of ridin' over; but I maintains that it no more means that,
than that 'ard-money currency means 'money 'ard to get at,'—or that an
'ard rider means a man wot will trot down 'Olborn 'ill on a frosty
mornin'. Let every feelin' man, then, consider, when he is about to ride
over wheat, that he is about to trample under foot scarlet welwet bonnets,
and with them the farmer's darters' best and tenderest 'opes.

"And here let me observe, that I cannot help thinkin' that that that
celebrated man, Gambado, has been the unconscious means of many a
field of wheat being trampled down. When such great men talk lightly
on a subject, little minds catch the infection, and far outstrip the author's
most sanguinary conceptions.

"Speaking in laudatory terms of the merits of the dray 'oss—merits
that no one will deny—Gambado talks of the figure they are calculated
to made on the road or in the field. 'Scarce any of them,' says he, 'but
is master of thirty stone and hupwards!' (Roars of laughter.) 'What a
sublime scene would it be,' continues he, 'to see fourscore or a 'underd
of these hanimals on the full stretch over a piece of wheat, to catch sight
of an 'ound!' (Roars of laughter.)

"Gentlemen," continued Mr. Jorrocks, looking very irate, "I'm sorry
for your mirth—(hisses and laughter)—shocked at your immorality, in
fact!—Dash my vig if I arn't!" (Renewed laughter and cheers.)

"Such undecent mirth would disgrace a Cockney! A Cockney looks upon a farmer as an inferior crittur !—a sort of domestic conwict, transported far beyond the bills o' mortality, and condemned to wander in 'eavy 'ob-nailed shoes amid eternal hacres o' dirt and dandylions. I 'opes such is not your opinion.—(Loud cries of " No, no," and cheers.) I'm glad sich wickedness finds no response here." Mr. Jorrocks again retired, and recomposed himself with another draught of brandy and water.

* * * *

" Now," said he, licking his lips, as he returned to the front of the platform ; " let ingenuous youth suppose himself at the meet, and that he has been presented to the M.F.H., to whom the greatest respect and reverence should always be paid, for there's no man to compare to him i' point o' greatness. The meet is the place for lettin' off the fulminatin' balls of wit ; but unless young green'orn be a tolerably jawbacious sort of chap, he had better be a listener at first. There are a few stock jokes that do for any country, the ready appliance of which stamps the user as a wag or a sportsman among those who don't know no better. ' Dear sir,' says one man to another, ridin' a wite-faced 'oss, ' I fears your nag is werry bad ! '

" ' 'Ow so ? ' inquires t'other, all alarm.

" ' Vy, he's all vite in the face ! ' ("Haw ! haw ! haw ! ")

" ' Yours is an expensive nag, I see,' observes a second.

" ' Not more than other people's,' is the answer.

" ' Yes, he is ; for I see he wears boots as well as shoes,' pointing to speedy-cut boots.

" ' 'Ave I lost a shoe in coming ? ' inquires a gentleman, who with a late start has come in a hurry.

" ' They're not all on before ! ' exclaims half-a-dozen woices, ready with the joke.

" ' Does you're mother know you are out ? ' is a familiar inquiry that may be safely hazarded to a bumptious boy in a jacket. ' More dirt the less hurt ! ' is a pleasant piece o' consolation for a friend with a mud mask ; and ' One at a time, and it will last the longer ! ' is a knowin' exclamation to make to a hundred and fifty friends waiting for their turns at an 'unting-wicket. ' Over you go ; the longer you look the less you'll like it ! ' may be 'ollo'd to a friend lookin' long at a fence. ' Hurry no man's cattle ! you may keep a donkey yourself some day ! ' is the answer to the last. When you see a lawyer floored, sing out, ' There's an 'oss a layin' down the law ! ' If a chap axes if your nag will jump timber, say, ' He'll leap over your 'ead.' These, and sich as these, are your tickets for soup, as the cook said when she basted the scullion with the hox-tail ! (Loud laughter.)

" Flattery is easier accomplished than wit, and the meet is a place where butter, with a little knowledge, will go a long way. All masters of 'ounds like praise. Some are so fond on it, that they butter themselves. If you see 'ounds' ribs, and their loins are well filled and flanks hollow, you may say they look like their work ; if they're fat, say they are werry even in condition ; if lean, that they look like goin' a bust ; if jest noways in 'ticklar, you can't get wrong if you say, you never saw a nicer lot. If you see some with clips on the hears, or along the backs, you may conclude they are new comers, and ax where they are from.

Rich coloured 'ounds you may liken to the Belvoir, and then you can talk
of Goodhall and Guider, or of the Quorn Trueman, or even go back as
far as Furrier and Hosbaldeston; and swear you never saw sich legs
and feet; in short, let legs and feet, or legs and loins, be the burthen o'
your song. Beware of callin' 'ounds dogs, or sterns tails. Sich a slip
would make the M.F.H. turn tail on you directly.

"It looks werry knowin' to take a bit o' biscuit out of your pocket, as
you are lookin' over the 'ounds, and make them rise on their hind legs to
receive it, while you scrutinise them werry attentively. This is a most
scientific proceedin' and will immediately stamp you as a werry knowin'
'and, if not for an M.F.H. himself. Still let your talk be of legs and
loins, with an occasional mention of helbows and shoulders. Perfection!
symmetry! 'andsome! level! bone! breedin'! condition! Lord Enry!
Sir Richard, Sir Tatton, Mr. Jorrrocks,—are terms that may be thrown in
at random, jest as the butter seems to go down. If, however, ingenuous
youth's afraid o' bein' tempted out of his depth, it's a safe wentur to
look werry approvinly at the pack generally, and then say that 'they're
larger nor some he has seen, and not so large as others.' (Laughter.) In
sayin' this, it may p'raps be well jest to feel his 'oss with the spur, so as
to make him wince, which will give him an excuse for withdrawin' on the
score o' being afear'd o' kickin' the 'ounds, and save him from bein'
axed to name the larger or smaller packs he's seen, which might be
inconwenient.

"'Untsmen are either 'eaven-born or hidiots—there's no medium.
Every schoolboy can criticise their performance. It's 'stonishin' how
quickly 'untsmen are run up and down, jest like the funds, with the bulls
and the bears. As no M. F. H. keeps what he considers a fool, it may
be well to commence in the soapy line; for even though a master may
abuse a servant himself, he may not fancy his field doing so too.

"At the meet, every man's time is accordin' to his own conwenience.
Should he have been too early, the 'ounds have come late; and should he
be late, the 'ounds were there afore their time. The last man always
says that there's no one else comin', as in course he does not see the wit
of waitin' after he arrives.

"Among the many followers of the chase, there be some men wot start
with wot seems like a good mould-candle passion for the chase, but, somehow or other, after a few seasons, it simmers down to little better nor a
fardin' rushlight. After the first brush of the thing is over, they begin to
economise their 'osses in November, that they may have them fresh
about Christmas; or they don't work them much in February, as they
wish to save a couple to take to town in the spring; or tool their
missesses about in the Booby Hutch. Ven I hear chaps talk this way,
I always reckon upon seein' their coats nailin' the happle-trees up afore
long.

"Some are much greater 'oss coddles than others. When Tat wrote
to Ferguson to know vot he wanted for 'Arkaway, and whether the 'oss
was in work, Ferguson replied, 'The price of 'Arkaway is six thousand
guineas, and I 'unts him twice and thrice a-week!' (roars of laughter.)

"Some men keep servants to be their masters.

"'I shall ride the roan, to-morrow, Jones,' says a gen'lman to his
grum.

" ' Can't, sir ; just given him a dose o' physic.'

" ' Well, then, the black. He's not been out since yesterday week.'

" ' His turn's not till Toosday.'

" ' Oh, never mind! Just let me have a look at him.'

" ' *Can't*. Stable's done up—not to be hopen till four; so mizzle, master.'

"In course these chaps have 'igh wages," continued Mr. Jorrocks, " or they could'nt 'ave such himperence. They are the bouys wot won't let their masters buy osses o' men o' my woracity and judgment, unless they 'ave their ' reglers,' five per cent. on the price, or as much more as they can get. A man wot would be master of his stable, must never consult his grum about a quad. Consult 'im forsooth! " exclaimed Mr. Jorrocks. " Why, there is not one grum i' fifty that knows when an 'oss he has the care on is lame. They'll go slouchin' to cover on 'osses that their masters pronounce lame the moment they mount. A man with a strong bouy and a hash-plant is generally master of his stud; a master with a bouy and no hash-plant is like a fiddle without a stick.

" More 'osses are ruined from want o' work than from the excess on't. Take a season through, and 'ow werry few days there are on which there is really any thing for gen'lmen's 'osses to do; though, to be sure, such days generally come in a heap; yet, as no one can say how long a run o' luck will last, my adwice is, to keep goin' as long as ever you can. A man can get but six days a-week if he labours ever so, and there are werry few wot would not rayther have four, or maybe two. The flash o' ridin' long distances to meet one pack of 'ounds, when another's at 'and, arises from the pleasure of sportin' a red coat through a longer line o' country, and vinkin' at the gals on the road, or from a desire to be talked of as havin' done so, and as being werry keen 'ands. I generally find them werry great fools!

" There is another way that would-be sportsmen have of showin' their keenness. Durin' a storm it is not unusual for the M.F.H. to advertise that th' 'ounds will meet at the kennel the first day the weather permits. Well, as soon as ever the eves begin to drop, the would-bes put on their red coats and go to the kennel, continuin' the process day after day until the thaw really arrives; they throw up, and swear they von't 'unt with him any more.

" ' Not hung yourself yet, Gilhespie?' suitin' the haction to the word by feelin' your neck and cockin' your thumb under your hear, is a fine sportin' interrogatory to put to a frind in the street durin' a frost. All these mendacious means let ingenuous youth despise. It's one thin' to cover your hignorance and another to help you to imperance. I does the former only.

" And now," continued the worthy lecturer, casting his eyes up to his canopied curtain, as he jingled the silver in his canary-coloured shorts, " And now, if I had a few words 'bout cost, 'bout old £ *s. d,,* I think I'd be ready for a start. The cost of 'unting, my beloved 'earers, like all other things, depends a'most entirely on 'ow you go about it. The only really indispensable outlay is the subscription to the 'ounds, which ought always to be paid punctual in adwance, jest like you 'ave to pay the stakes at a race. Whoever wants, the

M.F.H. should be paid. Prudence and 'conomy are all right and proper in everything 'cept 'unting. For 'unting there must be a liberal outlay, and no grumblin'. Mus'nt do like dirty Harry Tight who, when Fleecy axed wot he would subscribe to my 'ounds, exclaimed, ' Subscribe ! I wouldn't insult Mr. Jorrocks by offerin' of him money !" (Laughter and hisses.) " Insult," exclaimed Mr. Jorrocks, looking very irate, " jest as if I was a likely man to be insulted with the hoffer of money. Much more likely to insult 'im for *not* offerin it." (Laughter and applause.)

" Well, then, the requirements o' the master bein' satisfied," continued Mr. Jorrocks, buttoning up and slapping his breeches'-pocket, " let ingenuous youth turn his 'tention to the stable. It's no use givin' a publican and sinner a guinea or five-and-twenty shillings a week for keepin' your quadrupeds, when you can rent a stable and keep-them yourself for ten or twelve shillin'. There's not even the benefit of any flash i' the thing, which is wot moves many men to the 'orrors o' the chase. Still less use is it wastin' your substance on old Bonnyface's 'ouse, with his sixpenny breakfasts for 'alf-a-crown, and dinners i' like proportion, when you can get a comfey rumph lodgin' and find yourself for 'alf or a third o' the money. There are no people want puttin' to rights so much as the innkeepers. Kiver 'acks are all gammon for men wi' short studs. An 'ack can do nothin' but 'ack, while he will cost as much as a third 'oss wot will both 'ack and 'unt. Let ingenuous youth then learn to dispense with the useless appendage. I often think," continued Mr. Jorrocks musingly, " that it would be a capital thing to pass ingenuous youth generally through a sort of Chobham camp to learn 'em wot they can really do without."

" Ingenuous youth, 'aving now got all the implements o' the chase scraped together, and the early rains of dear delightful November—the best and plisantest month i' the year—'avin well salivated the ground, forthwith let 'im put all my precepts in practice, istead o' sneakin' off to Boulogne or Paris for the winter, arter talkin' 'bout the delights of 'unting all the summer.

" ' Time trieth troth,' says the proverb, but ' November trieth truth ' i' the 'unting line, and men that don't like 'unting, had much better not give themselves the trouble of pretendin' they do, for they're sure to be found out, and branded for 'umbugs for their trouble. It's a werry rum thing 'ow few men there are who candidly say they don't like it. They've all been keen sportsmen at some time or other o' their lives. Every man," continued Mr. Jorrocks, sententiously, " wot prefers his 'ealth to the interests o' the Seidletz pooder makers, will get as much 'unting as ever he can afore Christmas. (Great laughter and applause.) So now let's be doin' !" added he, rubbing his elbows against his sides as if anxious for the fray.

" Let us s'pose the last, *last* fumigatin' piece o' conceit has cast up, and the M.F.H. gives the hoffice to the 'untsman to throw off. 'Osses' 'eads turn one way, th' 'ounds brisk up at the move, the coffee-room breaks up, frinds pair off to carry out jokes, while the foot people fly to the 'ills, and the bald-'eaded keeper stands 'at in 'and at the gate, to let th' 'ounds into cover.

" *Eleu in !* " at length cries the 'untsman, with a wave of his 'and. and in an instant his 'osses' 'eels are deserted. The vipper-in has scuttled round the cover, and his rate and crack are 'eard on the far side. 'Gently, Conqueror! *Conqueror, have a care!* Ware are! ware are!'"

*   *   *   *   *

Here Mr. Jorrocks paused, apparently for the purpose of recollecting something.

"There's a bit o' potry due here," observed he; "but somehow or other it von't come, to halloo!

> 'Great, glorious, and free,
> First flower o' the hocean, first——' "

continued he. "No, *that* von't do, that was old Dan's dodge. Yet it's somethin' like that, too; can no one help me? Ah, I have it :—

> 'Delightful scene!
> When all around is gay, men, 'osses, dogs;
> And in each smilin' countenance appears
> Fresh bloomin' 'ealth, and uniwersal joy.'

And yet that's not exactly the place it should have come in at nouther," observed Mr. Jorrocks, recollecting himself; "that scrap is meant for the meet; throwin' off is thus described by Peter Beckford, or some other gen'l'man wot described it to him. Howsomever it von't do to waste a cotation, so you can jest joggle t'other one back in your minds to the right place. This is throwin' off :—

> 'See! ow they range
> Dispersed, 'ow busily this way and that,
> They cross, examinin' with curious nose
> Each likely 'aunt. 'Ark! on the drag I 'ear
> Their doubtful notes, preludin' to a cry
> More nobly full, and swelled with every mouth.'

"Now that's poetry and sense too," observed Mr. Jorrocks, smacking his lips! "which is more than poetry always is; for a poet, you see, has to measure his words, and werry often the one that would best express vot he vonts von't fit in with t'others, so he's obliged to halter his meanin' altogether, or mount a lame steed. For my part I likes prose best, and I reckon Peter's prose better nor most men's werse. Hear 'ow he finds his fox." Mr. Jorrocks then took his newly-bound Beckford from the table at the back of the platform, and read as follows :—

"'Ow musical their tongues! And as they get near to him, 'ow the chorus fills! 'Ark! he is found. Now, vere are all your sorrows and your cares, ye gloomy souls! or where your pains and aches, ye complainin' ones! one holloo has dispelled them all. Vot a crash they make! and hecho seeminly takes pleasure to repeat the sound. The 'stonished traveller forsakes his road; lured by its melody, the listenin' ploughman now stops his plough, and every distant shepherd neglects his flock, and runs to see him break. Vot joy! vot heagerness in every face!'

"Now," said Mr. Jorrocks, smacking his lips again, "that's what I call *real prime stuff*—the concentrated essence of 'untin'—the XXX of sportin', so different from the wire-spun, wishy-washy yarns of modern penny-a-liners, who smother their meanin' (if they have any) in words. If I've read Peter once, I've read him a hundred times, and yet I finds somethin' fresh to admire every time. Wernor and Hood, Birchin Lane, published this edition in 1796; and on the title-page is pasted a hextract from a newspaper that would adorn a monument. ' Monday, 8th March, 1811, at his seat, Stapleton, in Dorsetshire, Peter Beckford, Esq., aged 70. Mr. Beckford was a celebrated fox-'unter, and hauthor of ' Letters on 'Unting.' There's an inscription for a marble monument ! ' Multum in parvo,' as Pomponius Ego would say. Blow me tight ! but I never looks at Billy Beckford supplicatin' the king on his marble monument in Guildhall, but I exclaims, ' Shake Billy from his pedestal and set up Peter ! ' (Hisses and applause.)

" I once wrote my epitaph, and it was werry short,—

' Hic jacet Jorrocks,'

was all wot I said ; but the unlettered 'untsman, or maybe M.F.H., might pass me by, jest as he would a dead emperor. Far different would it be should this note follow,—' Mr. J. was a celebrated fox-'unter, and lectorer upon 'unting.' Then would the saunterin' sportsman pause as he passed, and drop a tribute to the memory of one who loved the chase so well. But I'm gettin' prosaic and off the line. Let us 'ark back into cover ! The chase, I sings ! Let's see.

" We had jest found our fox. Well, then, let's at Peter again, for there's no one boils one hup into a gallop like him. Here's a description of the thief o' the world afore he breaks."   Mr. Jorrocks reads :—

" ' Mark 'ow he runs the cover's hutmost limits, yet dares not wentur forth ; the 'ounds are still too near ! That check is lucky ! Now if our frinds 'ead him not, he will soon be off ! '

" Talli-ho ! " screamed Mr. Jorrocks, at the top of his voice. ' Dash my vig, that's the cry ! " continued he, holding his hand in the air. " See 'ow pale the gen'leman in light scarlet and bishop's boots is turnin', and how delighted old Jack Rasper, in the cut-away olive, broad cords, and hoganys is ; his low-crowned 'at's in the hair, for he sees the warmint, a sight more glorious nor the lord mayor's show ; yet he 'olloas not ! Ah, it's talli-ho back ! The fox is 'eaded by yon puppy in purple, strikin' a light on the pommel of his saddle. 'Ope he'll soon be sick ! Th' 'ounds turn short, and are at him again. Have at him, my beauties ! Have at him, my darlins' ! Have at him, I say ! Yonder he goes at t'other end !—now he's away ! Old Rasper has him again ! ' Talli-ho, away ! ' he cries. The old low-crowned 'at's in the hair, and now every man 'oops and 'ollows to the amount of his superscription. Twang ! twang ! twang ! goes the Percival ; crack ! crack ! crack ! go the whips ; 'ounds, 'osses, and men, are in a glorious state of excitement ! Full o' beans and benevolence ! "

" So am I, my beloved 'earers," observed Mr. Jorrocks, after a pause ; " and must let off some steam, or I shall be teachin' you to over-ride the 'ounds." So saying, Mr. Jorrocks retired to the back of the platform, and cooled himself with a fresh glass of hot brandy and water. Presently he returned, and thus resumed his discourse.

"Oh! my beloved 'earers, if I'd been at the great Mr. Pomponius Hego's helbow when in describin' this critical period of the chase he penned the words, '*go along*, there are three couple of 'ounds on the scent,' I'd ha' seen if I could'nt ha' got him to put in 'now 'old your jaws, and

"AH! IT'S TALLI-HO BACK!"

'old 'ard! and let em settle quietly to the scent.' Believe me, my beloved 'earers, the words '*go along*, there are three couple of 'ounds on the scent,' have lost many a run and saved the life of many a warmint. 'Ow I likes to see the 'ounds come quietly out, settlin' and collectin' together, gradually mending their pace as they go, till they brew up a reg'lar bust. That's the way to make the foxes cry 'Capevi!'" added he. (Laughter and applause.)

"Here let me hobserve," continued Mr. Jorrocks, "that it's a grand

thing for ingenuous youth to get a view of the warmint at startin'; by so
doing he gets a sort of wested interest in the fox, and rides arter him as
he would arter a thief with his watch.   There's a knack in doin' this, and
some men are cleverer at it than others, but half the battle consists in not
being flurried—'Yonder he goes! yonder he goes!   Talli-ho! talli-ho!'
exclaim a dozen people, pointin' different ways—and hearin' that a fox is
a quick travellin' beast, ingenuous youth begins to look some half-a-mile
a-head; whereas, if the people were to cry 'Here he is! here he is!'
pointin' downwards, Spooney would take a nearer range, and see that a
fox travels more like a cat nor a crow.   Folks overlook the fox, jest as
one overlooks a mustard-pot under one's nose.

   "Well, then, my beloved 'earers, glorious talli-ho! talli-ho!—whose
very echo kivers me all over with the creeps—is holloaed and repeated,
and responded and re-echoed, and th' 'ounds are settlin' to the scent.

TOP SAWYERS.

As soon as ever you 'ear the cry, make up your minds either to go on or
go 'ome.   But I won't s'pose that any man will stop stirrin' till the
puddin's done; at all ewents, not till he sees a fence, so thrust your
'eads well into your 'ats, tighten your reins, 'arden your 'earts, and with

elbows and legs, elbows and legs, get forrard to the 'ounds."   Mr. Jorrocks
suiting the action to the word, straddling and working an imaginary horse
with his arms.

" Now we are away !   The cover's wacated, and there's not another

within four miles, which courtesy will call fourteen !   Vich vay's the
vind ?   South-east, as I live.   Then he's away for Brammelkite Brake !
Now for your topographical dictionaries, or, vot is still better, some
gemman with a map of the country in his 'ead.   The field begins to
settle into places, like folks at the play.   If there's no parson to pilot the
way, gen'l'man with 'osses to sell take the first rank.   Every one now
sees who are there, and many may be wantin' at the end to tell who
come in so ; a rasper well negotiated at this time o' day has sold
many a screw.   After the gen'l'man with 'osses to sell comes the
'untsman, entreatin' the gen'l'men with 'osses to sell not to press upon
the 'ounds ; but as he only talks to their backs, they regard the
exhortation as a mere figure o' speech.   The top-sawyers of the 'unt
will be close on the 'untsman.   There will not be many of these ; but
should there be a barrack in the neighbourhood, some soger officers
will most likely mex up and ride at the 'ardest rider among 'em.
The dragon soger officer is the most dangerous, and may be known

by the viskers under his nose. A foot soger officer's 'oss is generally better in his wind than on his legs. They generally wear chin wigs, and always swear the leaps are nothin' compared with those in the county they come from—Cheapside, p'raps.

"In the wake of the top-sawyers and soger officers will come your steady two 'oss men, their eyes to the 'ounds, their thoughts in the chase, regardless of who crams or who cranes. These generally wear cords, their viskers are greyish, and their brown top-boots look as if they have never been wite.

"The 'safe pilot' is generally a man with a broad back, clad in bottle-green, with plain metal buttons, white neckcloth, striped veskit, drab kerseys, with ribbons danglin' over a 'hogany top; or may be in the scarlet coat of the 'unt, with a hash-plant, to denote that he is a gate-opener, and not a leaper: a man of this sort will pilot a youngster all day without ridin' over a fence. He knows every twist, every turn, every gate, every gap, in the country, and though sometimes appearin' to ride away from the 'ounds, by skirtin' and nickin', will often gain Reynard's p'int afore them—p'raps afore Reynard himself!

"We must not follow him, but 'streak it' across the country a bit, as brother Jonathan would say, and this is the time that, if ingenuous youth's 'oss has any monkey in him, he will assuredly get his dander up and show it. The commonest occurrence in all natur' is for him to run away, which is highly disagreeable. Geoffrey Gambado well observes, that when a man is well run away with, the first thing that occurs to him is how to stop his 'oss. Some will run him at a ditch, which is a werry promisin' experiment, if he leaps ill, or not at all: others try a gate-post, but it requires a nice eye to hit the centre with the 'oss's 'ead, so as not to graze your own leg. Frenchmen—and Frenchmen ride as well now as they did in Gambado's time—will ride against one another; and Geoffrey tells a good story of an ingenious Frenchman he saw make four experiments on Newmarket Heath, in only one of which he succeeded. His 'oss ran away with him whilst Gimcrack was runnin' a match, and the Count's 'opes of stoppin' him being but small, he contrived to turn him across the course and rode slap at Gimcrack, 'opin' to effect it by a broad-side; but Gimcrack was too quick for the Count, and he missed his aim. He then made full at Lord March, but unluckily only took him slantin': baffled in this second attempt, the Count relied on the Devil's Ditch as a certain check to his career, but his 'oss carried him clean over; and had not the rubbin'-house presented itself, the Count asserted he werily believed he should soon have reached London. Dashin' at the rubbin'-'ouse, with true French spirit, he produced the desired effect; his 'oss, not being able to proceed, stopped, and that so suddenly that Ducrow himself would have kissed his own saw-dust. The count, it is true, came off but tolerably well; the 'oss broke his 'ead and the count's likewise, so that, accordin' to the opinion of two negatives makin' an affirmative, little or no 'arm was done, an ingenious, if not a satisfactory, mode of disposin' of damage.

"And here let me observe, that to 'unt pleasantly two things are neces-sary—to know your 'oss and to know your own mind. An 'oss is a queer critter. In the stable, on the road, or even in a green lane, he may be all mild and hamiable—jest like a gal you're a courtin' of—but when he gets into the matrimony of the 'unting-field among other nags, and sees th' 'ounds, which always gets their danders up, my vig! it's another pair of shoes altogether, as we say in France. Howsomever, if you know your 'oss and can depend upon him, so as to be sure he will carry you over whatever you put him at, have a good understandin' with yourself afore ever you come to a leap, whether you mean to go over it or not, for nothing looks so pusillanimous as to see a chap ride bang at a fence as though he would eat it, and then swerve off for a gate or a gap. Better far to charge wiggorously, and be chucked over by the 'oss stoppin' short, for the rider may chance to light on his legs, and can look about unconsarnedly, as though nothing particklar had 'appened. I'm no advocate for leapin', but there are times when it can't be helped, in which case let a man throw his 'eart fearlessly over the fence and follow it as quick as ever he can, and being well landed, let him thank Providence for his luck, and lose no time in lookin' for the best way out. Thus he will go on from leap to leap, and from field to field, rejoicin'; and havin' got well over the first fence, it's 'stonishin' 'ow fearlessly he charges the next. Some take leapin'-powder—spirits of some sort—but it's a contemptible practice, unworthy of ingenuous youth.

"The finest receipt, however, for makin' men ride is shakin' a sportin' hauthor afore them at startin'. Crikey! 'ow I've seen 'em streak across country so long as he remained in sight! Coves wot wouldn't face a water-furrow if they had had their own way, under the impulse of glory, will actually spur their steeds!

"Gentlemen wot take their ideas of 'unting from Mr. Hackermann's pictor-shop in Regent's Street must have rum notions of the sport. There you see red laps flyin' out in all directions, and 'osses apparently to be had for catchin'. True, that in 'unting men will roll about—but so they will on the road; and I'd rayther have two bumps in a field than one on a pike. Danger is everywhere! An accomplished frind o' mine says, 'Impendet *omnibus* periculum'—Danger 'angs over an omnibus: and 'Mors *omnibus* est communis,'—You may break your neck in an *omnibus:* but are we, on that account, to shun the wehicle of which the same great scholar says, 'Wirtus parvo pretio licet ab omnibus,'— Wirtue may ride cheap in an omnibus? Surely not!

"Still, a fall's a hawful thing. Fancy a great sixteen' and 'oss lyin' on one like a blanket, or sittin' with his monstrous hemispheres on one's chest, sendin' one's werry soul out o' one's nostrils! Dreadful thought! Vere's the brandy?" Hereupon Mr. Jorrocks again retired to the back of the platform to compose his nerves.

"Now, my beloved 'earers," continued he, returning and wiping his mouth on the back of his hand,—"Now, my beloved 'earers, let's draw on old Peter for a run, for I really think a good suck of 'im is a'most as good as a tuck out at the Ship and Turtle Tavern.

"Here we 'ave 'im," continued Mr. Jorrocks, opening at the place, and proceeding to read with all due energy and emphasis; "'Mind, *Galloper*, 'ow he leads them? It's difficult to 'stinguish which is first, they run in such good style; yet *he* is the foremost 'ound. The goodness of his nose is not less excellent than his speed:—'ow he carries the scent! and

when he loses it, see 'ow eagerly he flings to recover it again! There—
now he's at 'ead again! See 'ow they top the 'edge! Now, now they
mount the 'ill!—Observe wot a 'ead they carry ; and show me, if thou
canst one shuffler or shirker 'mongst 'em all : are they not like a parcel
of brave fellows, who, when they 'gage in an undertakin', determine to
share its fatigue and its dangers equally 'mongst 'em ?'

"Capital!" exclaimed Mr. Jorrocks, smacking his lips. "Excellent
indeed. That's jest precisely like my 'ounds.

"Dash my vig, if I could but get a clever feller like Leech to draw
me a panorama o' the chase, with all my beauties goin' like beans—'eads
up and sterns down, and a lot o' trumps ridin' as they should do—near
enough to 'ear their sweet music, but not too near to prevent their
swingin' and spreadin' like a rocket to make their own cast, I'd—I'd
—I'd—bowl Halbert Smith and his wite mountain and his black box
right down Sin Jimses street into the Thames, and set hup i' the
'Giptian 'All myself." (Great laughter and applause.) When it subsided,
Mr. Jorrocks, returning to his volume, said,

"Peter now does a little potry, and we'll do ditto. Here it is :—

> ———" 'Far o'er the rocky 'ills we range,
> And dangerous our course ; but in the brave
> True courage never fails. In wain the stream
> In foamin' eddies whirls, in wain the ditch
> Wide gapin' threatens death. The craggy steep,
> Where the poor dizzy shepherd crawls with care,
> And clings to every twig, gives us no pain ;
> But down we sweep, as stoops the falcon bold
> To pounce his prey. Then hup the opponent 'ill
> By the swift motion slung, we mount aloft ;
> So ships i' winter seas now slidin' sink
> Adown the steepy wave, then tossed on 'igh
> Ride on the billows and defy the storm.'

"That's capital, too," observed Mr. Jorrocks, conning the matter
over, "werry superior readin', indeed, but some 'ow or other, I thinks I
likes old Peter better ; it comes more nattural like. 'Ere, for instance,
is a bit o' fine sportin' scenery, that makes one feel all over, 'unting
like."

Mr. Jorrocks then read as follows :—

"'It was then the fox I saw, as we came down the 'ill ;—those crows
directed me which way to look, and the ship ran from 'im as he passed
along. The 'ounds are now on the werry spot, yet the ship stop them
not, for they dash beyond them. Now see with wot heagerness they
cross the plain!—*Galloper* no longer keeps his place ; *Brusher* takes
it—see 'ow he flings for the scent, and 'ow impetuously he runs! 'Ow
heagerly he took the lead, and 'ow he strives to keep it. Yet Wictor
comes hup apace. He reaches 'im! See wot an excellent race it is
between them! It is doubtful which will reach the cover first. 'Ow
equally they run! 'Ow heagerly they strain! Now Wictor—Wictor!—
Ah Brusher you are beaten ; Wictor first tops the 'edge. See there!
See 'ow they all take in their strokes! The 'edge cracks with their
weight, so many jamp at once.'

"Capital, indeed," exclaimed Mr. Jorrocks; "most excellent, I may say. All sheer 'unting—no nasty jealous stipple chase ridin', 'urryin' 'ounds a mile beyond the scent. No '*go alongs!* there are three couple of 'ounds on the scent,' but real ' Fox et preteria nihil,' as Hego would say. Blow me tight, if such readin' doesn't parfectlie bust me," added he again, retiring to the brandy, amidst the loud and long-continued applause of the company.

CHAPTER XXXIII.

THE LECTOR RESUMED.

"WELL now," continued Mr. Jorrocks, returning, rubbing his lips preparatory to resuming his reading, "Peter does a bit o' cunnin', and I'll elucidate it. The fox you know's i' cover—Rashworth or 'Igh Wood Grove, let us say, and the thing is to take care that he doesn't slip away unseen—upon this Peter says, 'Now 'astes the wipper-in to the other side o' the cover; he is right unless he 'ead the fox.' That's capital," observed Mr. Jorrocks,—"he's right unless he's wrong; right one day p'raps, and wrong another, for he can't control the fox who may fancy to break at one pint one day and another the next. Howsomever," mused our master, "that shows the adwantage o' havin' some one to blow hup when things go wrong, and Cook—I think it is who tells of an M.F.H., who kept a wip on purpose to be blown hup, and who he used to make ride along side any '*go-along*'—there are three couple of 'ounds on the scent cove, while the M.F.H. lectord the man as if he had committed the 'forepaw,' adding at the end, with a frown and a shake of his vip, (bad word), 'ye, sir, I may (bad word) *you*, at all ewents!' (Laughter and applause).

"But come, let's see wot our hauthor makes on 'im in cover," resumed Mr. Jorrocks, returning to his Beckford—"Peter's at the potry again, I declare," said he, clearing his throat for the following :—

> "''Eavens! wot melodious strains! 'ow beat our 'earts
> Big with tumultuous joy! the loaded gales
> Breathe 'armony; and as the tempest drives
> From wood to wood, thro' ev'ry dark recess
> The forest thunders, and the mountains shake.'

"Werry fine!" exclaimed Mr. Jorrocks, turning up his eyes to the sporting looping of his canopy, "werry fine indeed! 'The forest thunders, and the mountains shake.' That's jest wot my beauties make them do. Dash my vig, but they kick hup a pretty dust when they once begin. But let us follow Peter into cover, for if his country was anything like wot it is now, he'd be pretty much at 'ome in one I reckon." Mr. Jorrocks then read as follows :—"'Listen! the 'ounds have turned. They are now i' two parts: the fox has been 'eaded back.' The wip's been wrong," observed Mr. Jorrocks, with a shake of his head, "or," continuing his reading, " ' we have changed at last.' Changed at last," repeated Mr. Jorrocks, sorrowfully, " bad luck to those changes," observed he, they are the werry deuce and all in 'unting. Arter one's ridden oneself red 'ot, and nearly galloped one's oss's tail off, and think it's full time to be 'andlin' the warmint, to 'ave a gen'lman goin' away as fresh as a four-year-old. Dash my buttons, but I remembers a desp'rate cunnin' Charley," observed Mr. Jorrocks, " that used to go away from Ticklefield-gos, in Crampshire, and, arter runnin' a wide ring, would return and pashin' hup another fox, would lie quiet hisself. As it happened, 'owever, his substitute was a mangey one, and desp'rate disgusted we used to be at findin' we were ridin' arter a thing like a rat 'stead of a beautiful clean-furred Reynard.

" But Peter," says Mr. Jorrocks, " 'opes to 'old on with the 'unted fox, and this is wot he says to his Ben"—Mr. Jorrocks reading—" ' Now, my lad, mind the 'untsman's alloo, and stop to those 'ounds which he encourages,'—which doesn't mean that the vip's to make a haffidavit that that's the 'untsman's alloo," continued he, looking knowingly at Ben, for a reason which will appear in Mr. Jorrocks's Journal, " but that he's to stop all such 'ounds as are not runnin' the way the 'untsman's ollooin'; he's to maintain to the 'untsman's olloo in short, and stop sich 'ounds as diwide from it," explained Mr. Jorrocks.

" Well, let's 'ave that sentence over again," said he, referring to his volume.

" ' Now, my lad, mind the 'untsman's halloo, and stop to those 'ounds which he encourages.' He is right! that doubtless is the 'unted fox; —that doubtless is the 'unted fox," repeated Mr. Jorrocks, thoughtfully, —" ay," added he, " they're all the 'unted foxes that anybody sees. Howsomever, we'll take Peter's word for it, and at 'im again. Well now," continued the worthy lecturer, conning the page, " 'ere's a reg'lar yard and a 'alf o' potry, describin', wot Pomponious would call the ' second bust amost as terrible as the fust'—the difference atwixt Peter and Pompey, ye see, bein' " added Mr. Jorrocks, looking off the book, " that Peter is all for the pack, and Pompey for the performers, or ' customers,' as they call the crack riders i' the cut-me-downs. Howsomever," continued Mr. Jorrocks, reverting to the poetry, " it's a prime sample of a sportin' scurry, and if I shalln't be fatiguein' on ye, I'll spout it." (Cries of " No, no, go on ; go on," and applause.)

Our great master then read as follows :—

" Wot lengths we pass ! were will the wanderin' chace
Lead us bewildered ! smooth as swallows skim,
The new shorn mead, and far more swift we fly.
See my brave pack; 'ow to the 'ead they press,
Jostlin' i' close array, then more diffuse
Obliquely weel, wile from their hopenin' mouths
The wollied thunder breaks—
——————————Look back and view
The strange confusion of the wale below,
Where sore wexation reigns;————
—————————— Old age laments
His wigour spent; the tall, plump, brawny youth
Cusses his cumbrous bulk and envies now

> The short pygmean race, he whilom kenn'd
> With proud insultin' leer. A chosen few
> Alone the sport enjoy, nor droop beneath
> Their pleasin' toils."

Great applause followed the reading of the above. When it subsided, our master, taking the " Chase and Road " volume from the table at the back of the platform, said " let us jest take a peep at frind Pomponious under similar circumstances. ' The squire's 'ounds are runnin' with a brest-'igh scent over the cream of the cut-me-down country, and most musically do the light notes o' Wocal and Wenus fall on the ear of those who may be within reach to catch 'em. But who is so fortinate i' this second bust 'nearly as terrible as the fust?' asks Hego. ' Our fancy supplies us again,' says he, ' and we think we could name 'em all. If we look to the left, nearly abreast o' the pack, we see six men goin' gallantly, and quite as straight as the 'ounds themselves are goin'; and on the right are four more, ridin' equally well, though the former 'ave rayther the best of it, owin' to 'avin' 'ad the inside o' the 'ounds, at the last two turns, which must be placed to the chapter of haccidents. A short way i' the rear, by no means too much so to enjoy this brilliant run, 'are the rest o' the *élite* o' the field, who had come hup at the fust check; and a few who, thanks to the goodness o' their steeds, and their determination to be with the 'ounds, appear as if dropped from the clouds. Some, 'owever, begin to show symptoms o' distress. Two osses are seen loose in the distance —a report is flyin' 'bout that one o' the field is badly 'urt, and somethin' is 'eard of a collar-bone bein' broken, others say it is a leg; but the pace is *too good* to inquire. A crackin' o' rails is now 'eard, and one gen'l'man's oss is to be seen restin', nearly balanced, 'cross one on 'em, his rider bein' on his back i' the ditch, which is on the landin'-side. 'Who is he?' says Lord Brudenel to Jack Stevens. ' Can't tell, my lord; but I thought it was a queerish place when I came o'er it afore 'im.' It is evidently a place o' peril, but the case is *too good* to 'ford 'elp.'

" So," continued Mr. Jorrocks, closing the volume with a clap, and chucking it to Pigg in the background, "they cut 'im down, but *don't* 'ang 'im up to dry." (Laughter and applause.)

" 'OLD 'ARD!'" now exclaimed Mr. Jorrocks at the top of his voice, advancing to the front of the platform, causing silence throughout the room. " 'OLD 'ARD!" repeated he, holding up his hand; " appallin' sound!" added he mournfully, "fearful to the forrard, and dispiritin' to all. Now's the time that the M.F.H., if he has any mischief in him and 'appens to be hup, will assuredly let drive at some one.

" ' 'OLD 'ARD,' explained the worthy lecturer, " means that gen'l'men are to stop their 'osses, a thing easier said than done, sometimes. Then if any troublesome stranger, or unpunctual payer, appears to be forrard, he is sure to catch it.

" ' Thank you, Mr. Red Veskit!' or, 'I'm much obleged to that gen'l'man with the big calves for over-ridin' *my* 'ounds!—werry *much* 'bleged to him!—most *'tick*larly 'bleged to him!—most confoundedly 'bleged to him!—G—d d——d 'bleged to him!—*Wish the devil had him*, big calves and all!'

" Meanwhile the 'untsman makes his cast, that's to say, trots his 'ounds in a circle round where they threw up : 'threw up' doesn't mean womitin' mind, but standin' starin' with their 'eads up, instead of keepin' them down, tryin' for the scent. As this is a critical moment, young gen'l'men should refrain from inwitin' the 'untsmen or whips to follow

"HOLD HARD? EASIER SAID THAN DONE."

them over gates or dangerous leaps. All should be 'tentive. A cast is a thing to criticise, on the principle of the looker-on seein' the most of the game. If there are no big fences in the way, and the 'untsman knows how far the 'ounds ran with a scent, he will probably hit it off pretty soon. That will be science.

"If the leaps are large, he may not be so lucky, and then Mr. Red Veskit, or the gen'l'man with the big calves, will catch it again.

"Should any one 'int that they have seen a better cast, little buoys will go home and tell their ma's they don't think much of Jack Jones, and Jack's character will begin to go. A fish-fag's ware isn't more perishable than an 'untsman's fame ; his skill is within the judgment of every one—'Cleverest feller alive !'—'Biggest fool goin' !'

"But to the run! The *Chass* I sing! A run is either a *buster*—elbows and legs throughout—or it is sharp at first, and slow arterwards; or it is slow at first and sharp arterwards. The first is wot most frequently finishes the fox; and when every 'ound owns the scent, unless Old Reynard does the hartful dodge, by lyin' down in an 'edge-row, or skulkin' among cattle or ship, in all humane probability his life arn't worth twenty minutes purchase from the find.

"The second class run—sharp at first, and slow arterwards—is the most favourable to the fox; for the longer it lasts, the slower the 'ounds go, until they get to wot the old Agony coachmen used to call Parliament-pace—that is to say some six miles an 'our, when they are either run out o' scent, or a big 'are jumps up afore them, and leads them astray. It's then, '*Ware are Wenus! Wictory, for shame!*' and off 'ome.

"The third class—slow at first, and sharp arterwards—is hawkward for the fox, but good for beginners, for they get warm in the progress, instead of being choked at the start. The thing improves, jest like a hice-cream i' the eatin'.

"No two men 'gree upon the merits of a run, 'less they 'appen to be the only ones to see it, when they arrange that wot one says t'other shall swear to; your real jealous buoys can't bear to see many at the finish. In relatin' a run to an absent friend, it is always allowable to lay on fifty per cent. for presence.

"Talking of a run, ingenuous youth should speak in praise of the 'ead the 'ounds carried. This doesn't mean that they ran with an 'ead of no sort in their mouths, but that they packed well together, and each strived to be first. It is this wot distinguishes a real pack of fox-'ounds from your trencher-fed muggars, and constitutes the charm o' the chase. If the death of a fox be all that's desired, a gun will do the business much cleaner and better than Muggins and Co.'s towlers.

"What looks so contemptible as a stringin' lot o' towlin' beggars toilin' in long line over the 'eavy fallows, and the fox gettin' knocked on the 'ead because the dogs are too tired to kill him themselves? Out upon sich outrages! say I. But to the legitimate run.

"Not bein' in at the death is reckoned slow, and numerous are the excuses of defaulters—losin' a shoe is one of the commonest; assistin' a friend in trouble, another; oss fallin' lame, a third; thrown out in turnin' 'ounds, a fourth; anything but the real one—want o' nerve. Nerve means pluck: in Alderman Harley's time, they called it courage. Still it's quite lawful for men to 'unt, even though they won't ride over the moon. 'Deed you might as well say that a man has no business at Hepsom who can't ride a race as that a man has no business at an 'unt that won't undertake to be in at the death. Let every man do his best, and grind away as long as he can; at all ewents, until either he or his 'oss tire, or he gets thrown out, in which latter calamity let 'im remember the mustard pot, and not go ridin' straight an end, as if it were unpossible for the 'ounds to turn to the right or to the left. Let him pull hup a bit on a risin' ground, and as he sits moppin' his nob, let 'im examine the landscape, and see wot cattle are starin' or scamperin' about, and rely upon it, the 'ounds are not far off. If ingenuous youth, after ridin' the line, sees 'osses bein' led about a green field, and red coats standin' in a ring, he may conclude bold Reynard is capevi'd, and, by quickenin' his pace, may steal quietly in afore the worry.

"But we'll let old Peter kill his fox, for dash my vig, there's nobody can do it like him. Let's see, where was I?" continued Jorrocks, resuming that volume—"Ah, I have it, the fox has been 'eaded or they have changed at last.—' Now for a moment's patience!' cries Peter,—' We press too close upon the 'ounds! 'Untsman, stand still! as they want you not. 'Ow admirably they spread! 'Ow wide they cast! Is there a single 'ound that does not try? if there be, ne'er shall he 'unt again. There *Trueman* is on the scent—he feathers, yet still is doubtful—'tis right! 'ow readily they join 'im! See those wide-casting 'ounds, 'ow they fly forrard to recover the ground they 'ave lost! Mind *Lightnin'*, 'ow she dashes; and *Mungo* 'ow he works! Old *Frantic*, too, now pushes forrard; she knows as well as we, the fox is sinkin':—

> ————'Ah! he flies, nor yields
> To black despair. But one loose more and all
> His wiles are wain. 'Ark! thro' yon willage now
> The rattlin' clamour rings. The barns, the cots,
> And leafless elms return the joyous sounds.
> Thro' ev'ry 'ome-stall, and thro' ev'ry yard,
> His midnight walks, pantin', forlorn, he flies.'

"And, dash my vig, he makes me pant too," continued Mr. Jorrocks, holding his obese sides. "However, judicious Peter gives one a little breathin' time here, in these conwenient words:—

"' 'Untsman! at fault at last? 'Ow far did you bring the scent? 'Ave the 'ounds made their cast? Now make yours—you see that ship-dog as coursed the fox; get forrard with your 'ounds, and make a wide cast,' during which time," continued the worthy lecturer, "we are all 'sposed to be sittin' quietly givin' our quads the wind, and all 'oldin' our tongues — a most desirable thing," observed Mr. Jorrocks, looking knowingly round the room.

"Peter, who 'as his ears well cocked with an 'and behind the right one," continued the worthy lecturer, "gives tongue with,—

"' 'Ark! that halloo is indeed a lucky one. If we can 'old 'im on, we may·yet recover 'im; for a fox, so much distressed, must stop at last. We shall now see if they will 'unt as well as run; for there is but little scent, and the himpendin' cloud still makes that little less. 'Ow they enjoy the scent! see 'ow busy they all are, and 'ow each in his turn prewails!'

"Capital writin'!" exclaimed Mr. Jorrocks; "feels for all the world as if I was there. Now for a bunch of 'ints for an 'untsman!

"' 'Untsman! be quiet! Whilst the scent was good, you pressed on your 'ounds; it was well done; when you came to a check, you stood still and interrupted them not: they were arterwards at fault; you made your cast with judgment and lost no time—you now must let 'em 'unt; —with such a cold scent as this you can do no good; they must do it all themselves; lift 'em now, and not an 'ound will stoop again. Ha! a 'igh road at sich a time as this, when the tenderest nosed 'ound can 'ardly own the scent; 'ave a little patience, and let 'em, for once, try back.'

"Oh, that weary scent!" exclaimed Mr. Jorrocks, "that weary incomprehensible, incontrollable phenomenon! 'Constant only in its inconstancy!' as the hable hauthor of the noble science well said. Believe me, my beloved 'earers," continued Mr. Jorrocks, "there's nothin' so queer as scent, 'cept a woman! (Hisses, mingled with laughter and applause.)

"''Ark to Beckford!'' exclaimed Mr. Jorrocks, resuming his reading as the noise subsided. ' We now must give 'em time:—see where they bend towards yonder furze brake. I wish he may 'ave stopped there! Mind that old 'ound, 'ow he dashes o'er the furze; I think he winds 'im. Now for a fresh *en tapis!* 'Ark! they 'alloo! Aye, there he goes.'

" Pop goes the weasel again!" exclaimed Mr. Jorrocks, straddling and working his arms, as if he were riding. He then resumed his reading.

" ' It is nearly over with 'im; had the 'ounds caught view, he must ha' died. He will 'ardly reach the cover; see 'ow they gain upon 'im at every stroke! It is an admirable race! yet the cover saves 'im.

" ' Now be quiet, and he cannot 'scape us; we 'ave the wind o' the 'ounds, and cannot be better placed : 'ow short he runs! he is now in the werry strongest part o' the cover. Wot a crash! every 'ound is in, and every 'ound is runnin' 'im. That was a quick turn! Again, another! he's put to his last shifts. Now *Mischief* is at his 'eels, and death is not far off. Ha! they all stop at once; all silent, and yet no hearth is hopen. Listen! now they are at him agin! Did you 'ear that 'ound catch 'im! they overran the scent, and the fox had laid down be'ind 'em. Now Reynard look to yourself! 'Ow quick, they all give their tongues! Little *Dreadnought,* 'ow he works 'im! the terriers, too, they are now squeakin' at 'im! 'Ow close *Wengeance* pursues! 'ow terribly she presses! it is jest up with 'im! Gods! wot a crash they make; the 'ole wood resounds! That turn was werry short! There! now! aye, now they 'ave 'im! WHO-HOOP!' "

Here Mr. Jorrocks put his finger in his ear, and gave a " Who-hoop!" that shook the very rafters of the room, which being responded to by the party, a noise was created that is more easily imagined than described.

Three cheers for Mr. Jorrocks were then called for, and given with such vehemence as to amount to nine times nine, and one cheer more, during which the worthy master kept bowing and scraping on the platform, until he got a crick in his neck from the exercise.

CHAPTER XXXIV.

MR. JORROCKS'S JOURNAL.

A FEW more extracts from our distinguished friend's journal will perhaps best put our readers in possession of the nature of the sport with his hounds, and doings generally, though being written on loose sheets of paper, and sometimes not very legible, we have had some little difficulty in deciphering it. Indeed, what appear to have been the best runs —especially those with a kill—are invariably the worst written, owing perhaps to our friend indulging in a third pint of port on what he calls "qualified days."

On one occasion he seems to have been writing his journal and a letter to his traveller, Mr. Bugginson, together, and to have put into the journal what was meant for the traveller, and most likely sent to the traveller what was meant for the journal. However, our readers shall have it as we find it, and we will endeavour to supply any little deficiencies from such other sources as are open to us.

Mr. Jorrocks would seem to have had another bye-day with Ben while Pigg's clothes were making, when Ben did not cut any better figure than he did on the boiled lobster one. Having got the hounds into cover, as soon as ever Mr. Jorrocks began to yoicks and cheer, and crack his whip, exhorting the hounds to "*rout 'im out !*" and "*pash 'im hup !*" Ben stood erect in his stirrups, and made the following proclamation, to the great amusement of the field:—

"*I maintain that's the old un's holloo !*" "*I maintain that's the old un's holloo !*" repeated he. "*I maintain that's the old un's holloo !*" he added for the third time, as he re-seated himself in his saddle, and scuttled away to astonish another group of sportsmen with a similar declaration.

Mr. Jorrocks adds to his confused note of the transaction:—"Incorrigible bouy ! Good mind to stuff him full o' Melton dinner pills, and see if they will give him any knowledge o' the chase."

He also seems to have had several "bye " and other days at " Pinch-me-near " forest, when a light-coloured fox beat him so often as to acquire the name of the "old customer." We see on chronicling his losings generally, he adds the words—"the musciful man is musciful to his fox "—just as if he could have killed him if he chose. That, of course, our readers will believe as much of as they like. We shouldn't like to be a fox with old J. at our brush.

Some of his runs appear to have been severe, at least if we may judge by the entries of money paid for "catchin' my oss "—"stoppin' my oss "—and " helpin' me on to my oss "—which our worthy friend enters with the most scrupulous accuracy.

The following is our master''s minute of his opening day :—

" *Wednesday.*—Round of beef and carrots—momentous crisis—first public day as an M. F. H.—morning fine, rather frosty—there betimes—

landlord polite—many foot-folks—large field—Romeo Simpkins on Sontag—Captain Slack on Bull Dog—Miss Wells on Fair Rosamond— great many captains—found soon—ringin' beggar—ran three rounds, and accounted for him by losin' him—found again—a ditto with a ditto finish—good for the foot-folks—home at four—musciful man is musciful to the foxes. Paid for catching my 'oss, 6d.·

"Found two petitions. One from Joshua Peppercorn prayin' his honour the M. F. H. to subscribe to reinstate him in a cart 'oss, his own havin' come to an untimely end of old age. Says the M. F. H.'s always subscribe. Replied as follows:—

"'M. F. H. John Jorrocks presents his compliments to Mr. Joshua Peppercorn, and is sorry to hear of the death of his prad, but the M. F. H. 'as enough to do to mount himself and his men without subscribin' to find other folks i' quads.

"'DIANA LODGE.'

"Margaret Lucas had her patent mangle seized for rent and arrears of rent, and 'opes the master of the fox-dogs will do somethin' towards redeeming it. Wrote as follows:—

"'M. F. H. John Jorrocks presents his compliments to Mrs. Margaret Lucas, and is sorry to 'ear of the sitivation of her patent mangle, but the M. F. H. having laid it down as a rule never to subscribe to redeem patent mangles, can't depart from it in her case.'

"People seem to think M. F. H.'s have nothin' to do but give away tin. You know one a'n't quite sure her mother mayn't have *sold* her mangle! Besides, if I mistake not, this is one o' the saucy jades wot laughed at me when I came 'ome with a dirty back.

"*Mountain Daisy.*—Saturday, and few farmers out.—Not many pinks, but three soger officers, two of them mounted by Duncan Nevin—a guinea and a 'alf a day each, and 'alf a guinea for a hack.—Drew Slaughterford, and up to the Cloud Quarries.—Priestess seemed to think she had a touch of a fox in the latter, but could make nothin' on't.— Trotted down to Snodbury Gorse—wants enclosin'—cattle get in. No sooner in, than out came a pig, then came a fox, then another pig—then another fox.—Got away with last fox, and ran smartly down to Coombe, where we was headed by a hedger, and we never crossed his line again.— Found a second fox in Scotland Wood—a three-legger—soon disposed of him.—Found a third in Dulverton Bog, who ran us out of light and scent; stopped the 'ounds near Appledove.—Pigg says Charley Stebbs 'coup'd his creels' over an 'edge.—Scotch for throwin' a somersault, I understands.—Paid for catchin' my oss, 6d."

We also glean from the journal that Mr. Jorrocks allowed Pigg to cap when they killed; but Pigg, not finding that process so productive as he wished, hit upon the following novel expedient for raising the wind:— Seeing that a great many young gentlemen appeared at the meet who never attempted to get to the finish, Pigg constituted himself a sort of Insurance Company, and issued tickets against hunting accidents—similar to what

railway companies issue against railway ones. By these he undertook for
a shilling a day, or five shillings the season, to insure gentlemen against
all the perils and dangers of the chase—broken necks, broken backs,
broken limbs, broken heads, and even their horses against broken knees.

Indeed, he went further than this, and we have been told by parties
who were present and heard him, that he would send Ben among the
outsiders at the meets, singing out, "Take your tickets, gents! please
take your tickets! goin' into a hawful country—desperate bull finchers!
yawnin' ditches! rails that'll nouther brick nor bend! Old 'un got hi?
monkey full o' brandy!" by which means, and occasionally by dint of
swearing he'd "ride over some of them if he caught them down," Pigg
managed to extract a good deal of money.

Mr. Jorrocks, we may observe, seems to have been in the habit of
filling his sherry flask with brandy when going into a stiff country—a
thing of very frequent occurrence with our friend.

The following is the mixed entry between the traveller and the tres-
passer, if we may so call the fox—which we present as a true copy—
"errors excepted," as they say in the city :—

"When you go to 'Alifax, you'll most likely see Martin Proud-
foote, of Sharpset-hill. This cove's father bit me uncommon 'ard,
a'most the first journey I ever took, when a great stupid flock o' sheep
made slap for the gate, and reg'larly stopped the way, there being no
way out 'cept over a most unpossible, 'eart-rendin' 'edge, with a
ditch big enough to 'old a cathedral church, which gave the infatuated
fox considerable adwantage * * (illegible) * * for he had got
early information that sugar had riz. * * (illegible) * * there
bein' only 3000 and odd bags of Mauritius, at from 29s. to 32s. for
brown, and summut like the same quantity o' wite Benares, and though
* * (blot, and illegible) * * we found 'im at the extremity of our
wale country, and ran 'im for more nor an hour at a rattlin' pace
through the entire length o' the grass-land, and then away for the open
downs, crossin' the river near the mill at Floaterheels, the 'ounds castin'
hup and down the banks to satisfy themselves the fox was not on their
side, then returnin' to the point to which they 'ad carried the scent,
they all dashed in like a row o' buoys bathin', so (something wiped out
with his finger—then half a line illegible). You must just do as
you can about coffees, for I can't possibly be always at your helbow to
cast you, but be careful o' the native Ceylon, and don't give above 48s.
per cwt. for good ordinary . . I'd be sweeter on either Mocha or
Rio, for it isn't possible to see a better or truer line 'unter than old
Factor, or one that I should 'ave less 'esitation in usin' as a stud-'ound,
though some may say his flat feet are agin 'im, but 'andsome is wot
'andsome does, and I'll always speak well o' the bridge wot carries me
over, so tell Fairlips it's all gammon sayin' the last sugars we sent him
were not equal to sample—and that his customers can be no judges of
quality or they wouldn't say so. Tell him always to show an inferior
sample first, and always to show wite sugars on blue paper—but if the
man's to be taught the first rudiments of his trade, it's time he gave hup
'unting the country, for things can't be done now as they used in old
Warde and Sam Nichol's time, when men fed their osses on new oats,

and didn't care to look into their pedigrees, and nothin' but a fiat i'
bankruptcy will teach sich a chap wisdom, and in course the lighter we
ride in his books the better, for givin' away one's goods is a most
absurd prodigality, seasoned foxes bein' as necessary to sport as experienced 'ounds—for you may rely upon it if we seek for comfort here
below, it will only be found in a 'ound and a pettikit; and wotever they
may say about the merits of a slight dash o' chicory in coffee, there's
more wirtue in the saddle than in all the doctors' bottles put together, so
I'd have nothin' wotever to do with cheap tea—and beware of supplyin'
any of the advertisin' chaps, for scent of all things is the most fluctuatin',
and * * (illegible) there's nothin' so queer as scent 'cept a woman,
and tradesmen undersellin', and 'ounds choppin' foxes in cover is more a
proof of their wice "—(Inkstand apparently upset, making a black sea on
the paper.)

CHAPTER XXXV.

THE "CAT AND CUSTARD-POT" DAY.

HE above day
deserves a more ex-
tended notice than
it receives in Mr.
Jorrocks's journal.
He writes that
" somehow or other
in shavin', he
thought they'd 'ave
mischief," and he
went into the gar-
den as soon as he
was dressed to con-
sult the prophet
Gabriel Junks, so
that he might take
his pocket Siphonia
in case it was likely
to be wet, but the
bird was not there.
Then just as he had
breakfasted and was
about ready for a
start, young May,
the grocer, sent him
a horse to look at,
and as "another
gen'l'eman" was waiting for the next offer of him Charley and Mr.

Jorrocks stayed behind to try him, and after a hard deal, Mr. Jorrocks bought him for £30—which he makes a mem. : "to call £50."

Meanwhile Pigg and Ben trotted on with the hounds, and when they reached the meet—the sign of the Cat and Custard-Pot, on the Muswell road, they found an immense assemblage, some of whom greeted Pigg with the familiar enquiry "what he'd have to drink ? "

"Brandy ! " replied Pigg, " brandy ! " and tossing off the glass with great gusto, a second horseman volunteered one, then a third, then a fourth, then a fifth ; for it is observable that there are people in the world will give away drink to any extent, who yet would be chary of offering either money or meat. Pigg, who as Mr. Jorrocks says in his journal, is only a *lusus naturæ*, or loose 'un by natur', tosses off glass after glass, smacking his lips and slapping his thigh, getting noisier and noisier with each succeeding potation. Now he would sing them a song, now he would take the odds ag'in Marley Hill, then he would tell them about Deavilboger's farm, and how, but for his foreelder John, John Pigg, ye see, willin' his brass to the Formary ye see, he'd ha been a gen'l'man that day and huntin' his own hunds. Then as another glass made its appearance, he would take off his cap and halloo out at the top of his voice, making the hounds stare with astonishment, " *Keep the tambourine a rowlin'!* " adding as he tossed it off, " *Brandy and baccy 'ill gar a man live for iver !* " And now when he was about at the noisiest, with his cap turned peak-backwards, and the tobacco juice simmering down the deeply indented furrows of his chin, our master and Charley appear in the distance, jogging on, not too quickly for consequence, but sufficiently fast to show they are aware they are keeping the field waiting.

"Here he comes ! here's Jorrocks ! here's the old boy ! here's Jackey at last ! " runs through the meeting, and horsemen begin to arrange themselves for the reception.

"*A—a—a* sink ! " exclaims Pigg, shaking his head, blinking and staring that way, "here's canny ard sweetbreeks hissel ! " adding with a slap of his thigh as the roar of laughter the exclamation produced subsided, " *A—a—a*, but ar de like to see his feulish 'ard feace a grinnin' in onder his cap ! "

" How way, canny man ; how way ! " now shouts Pigg, waving his hand as his master approached. " How way ! canny man, how way ! and give us a wag o' thy neif," Pigg extending his hand as he spoke.

Mr. Jorrocks drew up with great dignity, and placing his fist in his side, proceeded to reconnoitre the scene.

"*Humph !* " grunted he, " wot's all this about ? "

" Sink, but ar'll gi' thou a gob full o' baccy," continued James, nothing daunted by his master's refusal of his hand. " Sink, but ar'll gi' thou a gob full o' baccy," repeated he, diving into his waistcoat pocket and producing a large steel tobacco box as he spoke.

Mr. Jorrocks signified his dissent by a chuck of the chin, and an ominous shake of the head.

"*A—a—a* man ! " exclaimed Pigg, now changing his tone, " but ar'll tell thee of a lass well worth her licks ! "

" You deserve your *own*, sir, for gettin' so drunk," observed Mr Jorrocks, haughtily.

Pigg.—"Ar's as sober as ye are, and a deal wizer!"

Jorrocks, angrily.—"I'll not condescend to compare notes with ye!"

Pigg, now flaring up.—"Sink! if anybody 'ill had mar huss, ar'll get off and fight him."

Jorrocks, contemptuously.—"Better stick to the shop-board as long as you can."

Pigg, furious.—"Gin ar warn't afeard o' boggin mar neif, ard gi' thou a good crack i' thy kite!"

Jorrocks, with emphasis.—"*Haw—da—cious* feller. I'll 'unt the 'ounds myself afore I'll put hup with sich himperence!"

Pigg, throwing out his arms and grinning in ecstacies.—"Ar'll be death of a guinea but arl coom and see thee!"

Jorrocks, looking indignantly round on the now mirth-convulsed company.—"Who's made my Pigg so drunk?"

Nobody answered.

"Did'nt leave his sty so," muttered our master, owering himself jockey ways from his horse.

"Old my quad," said he to Charley, handing him Arterxerxes, "while I go in and see."

Our master then stumped in, and presently encountering the great attraction of the place—the beautiful Miss D'Oiley—asked her, with a smiling countenance and a hand in a pocket, as if about to pay, "Wot his 'untsman 'ad 'ad?"

"Oh, sir, it is all paid," replied Miss D'Oiley, smiling as sweetly upon Jorrocks as she did on the generality of her father's customers, for she had no more heart than a punch-bowl.

"Is all paid?" muttered our friend.

"Yes, sir; each gentleman paid as he sent out the glass."

"*Humph!*" twigged Mr. Jorrocks, adding, with a grunt, "and that's wot these critters call sport!"

Our master then stumped out. "Well, gen'l'emen," exclaimed he, at the top of his voice off the horse-block, "I 'opes you're satisfied wi' your day's sport!—you've made my nasty Pigg as drunk as David's sow, so now you may all go 'ome, for I shalln't throw off; and as to you," continued our indignant master, addressing the now somewhat crest-fallen Pigg, "you go 'ome too, and take off my garments, and take yourself off to your native mountains, for I'll see ye at Jericho ayont Jordan afore you shall 'unt my 'ounds," giving his thigh a hearty slap as he spoke.

"Wy, wy, sir," replied Pigg, turning his quid; "wy, wy, sir, ye ken best, only dinna ye try to hont them thysel'—*that's arle!*"

"There are as good fish i' the sea as ever came out on't!" replied Mr. Jorrocks, brandishing his big whip furiously; adding, "I'll see ye leadin' an old ooman's lap-dog 'bout in a string afore *you* shall 'unt 'em."

"No ye won't!" responded Pigg. "No ye won't! Arve ne carle te de nothin' o' the sort! Arve ne carle te de nothin' o' the sort!—Arle gan back to mar coosin Deavilbogers."

"You may gan to the devil himself," retorted Mr. Jorrocks, vehemently—"you may gan to the devil himself—I'll see ye sellin' small coals from a donkey-cart out of a quart pot afore you shall stay wi' me."

"Thou's a varra feulish, noisey, gobby, insufficient 'ard man!" retorted

T

Pigg, and " ar doesn't *regard thee!* No; AR DOESN'T REGARD THEE!" roared he, with a defiant flourish of his fist.

"You're a hignorant, hawdacious, rebellious rascal, and I'll see ye frightenin' rats from a barn wi' the bagpipes at a 'alfpenny a day, and findin' yoursel, afore I'll 'ave anything more to say to ye," rejoined Mr. Jorrocks, gathering up his big whip as if for the fray.

"Sink, arle tak' and welt thee like an ard shoe, if thou gives me ony mair o' thy gob!" rejoined the now furious Pigg, ejecting his baccy and motioning as if about to dismount.

Jorrocks, thinking he had done enough, then took his horse from Charley Stobbs, and hoisting himself on like a great crate of earthenware, whistled his hounds away from the still stupified Pigg, who sat blinking and staring and shaking his head, thinking there were two Jorrocks's on two Arterxerxes', two Ben's, two Charley Stobbs's, and something like five-and-forty couple of hounds.

The field remained behind praising Pigg and abusing Jorrocks, and declaring they would withdraw their subscriptions to the hounds if Pigg "got the sack." None of them would see Pigg want; and Harry Capper, more vehement than the rest, proposed an immediate subscription, a suggestion that had the effect of dispersing the field, who slunk off different ways as soon as ever the allusion to the pocket was made.

Jorrocks was desperately angry, for he had had an expensive "stop," and came bent on mischief. His confusion of mind made him mistake the road home, and go by Rumfiddler Green instead of Muswell Hill. He spurred, and cropped, and jagged Arterxerxes—now vowing that he would send him to the tanners when he got 'ome—now that he would have him in the boiler afore night. He was very much out of sorts with himself and everybody else—even the hounds didn't please him—always getting in his way, hanging back looking for James Pigg, and Ben had fine fun cutting and flopping them forrard.

Charley, like a wise man, kept aloof.

In this unamiable mood our master progressed, until the horrible apparition of a great white turnpike-gate, staring out from the gable end of a brick toll-house, startled his vision and caused him to turn short up a wide green lane to the left. "Take care o' the pence and the punds 'ill take care o' theirsels," muttered our master to himself, now sensible that he had mistaken his road, and looking around for some land-mark to steer by. Just as he was identifying White Choker Church in the distance, a sudden something shot through the body of the late loitering indifferent hounds, apparently influencing them with a sort of invisible agency. Another instant, and a wild snatch or two right and left, ended in a whimper and a general shoot up the lane.

"*A fox!* for a 'underd!" muttered our master, drawing breath as he eyed them. "*A fox!* for two-and-twenty 'underd!" continued he, as Priestess feathered but spoke not.

"*A fox!* for a million!" roared he, as old Ravager threw his tongue lightly but confidentially, and Jorrocks cheered him to the echo.

"*A fox!* for 'alf the national debt!" roared he, looking round at Charley as he gathered himself together for a start.

Now as Jorrocks would say, Beckford would say, "where are all your sorrows and your cares, ye gloomy souls! or where your pains and aches, ye complaining ones! one whimper has dispelled them all."

Mr. Jorrocks takes off his cap and urges the tail-hounds on. A few more driving shoots and stops, producing increased velocity with each effort, and a few more quick snatchey whimpers, end in an unanimous outburst of downrightly determined melody.

Jorrocks, cocking his cap on his ear, seats himself plump in his great saddle, and, gathering his reins, gallops after them in the full grin of delight. Away they tear up the rutty grassy ride, as if it was a railway. "*F-o-o-r-rard on! F-o-o-r-rard on!*" is his cry.

"*H-o-i-c cry! h-o-i-c cry! h-o-i-c!*" squeaks Ben, wishing himself at home at the mutton, and delighted at having got rid of James Pigg, who always would have the first cut.

It is a long lane that never has a turn, and this one was no exception to the rule, for in due course it came to an abrupt angle. A convenient meuse, however, inviting the fox onward, he abandoned the line and pursued his course over some bare, badly-fenced pastures, across which Mr. Jorrocks cheered and rode with all the confidence of a man who sees his way out. The pace mended as they went, and Jorrocks hugged himself with the idea of killing a fox without Pigg. From the pastures they got upon Straggleford Moor, pretty much the same sort of ground as the fields, but the fox brushing as he went, there was a still further improvement of scent. Jorrocks then began to bet himself hats that he'd kill him, and went vowing what he would offer to Diana if he did. There was scarcely any promise too wild for him to make at this moment. The fox, however, was not disposed to accommodate Jorrocks with much more plain sailing for the purpose, and seeing, by the scarlet coats, that he was not pursued by his old friends the Dotfield harriers as at first he thought, and with whom he had had many a game at romps, he presently sunk the hill and made for the stiffly-fenced vale below.

"Blow me tight!" exclaimed Jorrocks, shortening his hold of Arterxerxes, and putting his head straight as he used to do down the Surrey hills, "Blow me tight! but I wish he mayn't be gettin' me into grief. This looks to me werry like the Ingerleigh Wale, and if it is, it's a bit of as nasty ridin' grund as ever mortal man got into—yawnin' ditches with himpracticable fences, posts with rails of the most formidable order, and that nasty long Tommy bruk, twistin' and twinin' about in all directions like a child's rattle-snake. 'Owever, thank goodness, 'ere's a gap and a gate beyond," continued he, as his quick eye caught a gap at the corner of the stubble field he was now approaching, which getting through, he rose in his stirrups and cheered on the hounds in the line of the other convenience. "*For-r-a-r-d! For-r-a-r-d!*" shrieked he, pointing the now racing hounds out to Charley, who was a little behind; "*for-rard! for-rard!*" continued Jorrocks, rib-roasting Arterxerxes. The gate was locked, but Jackey—we beg his pardon—Mr. Jorrocks—was quickly off, and setting his great back against it, lifted it off the hinges. "*Go on!* never mind me!" cried he to Charley, who had pulled up as Jorrocks was dancing about with one foot in the stirrup, trying to remount.—"*Go on! never mind me!*" repeated he, with desperate energy, as he made another assault at the saddle. "Get on, Ben.

you most useless appendage ! '' continued he, now lying across the saddle,
like a miller's sack.   A few flounders land him in the desired haven, and
he trots on, playing at catch-stirrup with his right foot as he goes.

"*Forrard on !   forrard on !*" still screamed he, cracking his ponderous
whip, though the hounds were running away from him as it was, but he
wanted to get Charley Stobbs to the front, as there was no one to break
his fences for him but him.

The hounds, who had been running with a breast-high scent, get their
noses to the ground as they come upon fallow, and a few kicks, jags, and
objurgations on Jorrocks's part, soon bring Arterxerxes and him into the
field in which they are.   The scent begins to fail.

"*G—e-e-e-nt—ly* there !" cries Jorrocks, holding up his hand and
reining in his horse, inwardly hoping the fox might be on instead of off

to the right, where he sees his shiny friend, long Tommy, meandering smoothly along.

" *Yo dote !* Ravager, good dog, *yo dote*, Ravager!" cheers Jorrocks, as the sage feathers and scuttles up the furrow. " *Yo-o dote !* " continued Mr. Jorrocks, cheering the rest on—adding as he looks at them scoring to cry, "wot a petty it is we can't put new legs to old noses ? " The spurt, however, is of short duration, for the ground gets worse as it rises higher, until the tenderest-nosed hound can hardly own the scent. A heavy cloud too oppresses the atmosphere. Jorrocks sees if he doesn't look sharp he'll very soon be run out of scent, so getting hold of his hounds, he makes a rapid speculation in his mind as to which way he would go if he were the fox, and having decided that point, he loses no time in getting the pack to the place.—Jorrocks is right!—Ravager's unerring nose proclaims the varmint across the green head-land, and the next field being a clover ley, with a handy gate in, which indeed somewhat influenced Jorrocks in his cast, the hounds again settle to the scent, with Jorrocks rolling joyfully after them, declaring he'd be the best 'untsman under the sun if it warn't for the confounded lips. Away he now crams, up the field road, with the hounds chirping merrily along on his right, through turnips, oat stubble, winter beans, and plough. A white farm onstead, Buckwheat Grange, with its barking cur in a barrel, causes the fox to change his course and slip down a broken but grassy bank to the left. "Dash his impittance, but he's taken us into a most unmanageable country," observes Mr. Jorrocks, shading his eyes from the now out-bursting sun with his hand as he trotted on, eyeing the oft occurring fences as he spoke. "Lost all idee of where I ham, and where I'm a goin'," continued he, looking about to see if he could recognise anything. Hills, dales, woods, water, were equally new to him.

Crash ! now go the hounds upon an old dead thorn-fence, stuck on a low sod-bank, making Jorrocks shudder at the sound. Over goes Stobbs without doing anything for his followers.

"*Go on, Binjimin! go on !* Now," cries Jorrocks, cantering up, cracking his whip, as if he wanted to take it in stride, but in reality to frighten Ben over to break it. " *Go on !* ye miserable man-monkey of a boy ! " repeats he, as 'Xerxes now turned tail, nearly upsetting our master—"Oh you epitome of a tailor ! " groaned Jorrocks ; " you're of no more use wi 'ounds than a lady's-maid,—do believe I could make as good a wipper-in out of a carrot ! See ! you've set my quad a refusin', and I'll bet a guinea 'at to a 'alf-crown wide awake, he'll not face another fence to-day—Come hup, I say, you hugly beast ! " now roared Jorrocks, pretending to put Arterxerxes resolutely at it, but in reality holding him hard by the head,—"Get off, ye useless apology of a hosier and pull it down, or I'll give you sich a wopping as 'll send you to Blair Athol for the rest of the day," exclaimed our half-distracted master, brandishing his flail of a whip as he spoke.

Ben gladly alighted, and by dint of pulling away the dead thorns, and scratching like a rabbit at the bank, he succeeded in greatly reducing the obstacle.

"Now lead him over ! " cried Mr. Jorrocks, applying his whip freely to 'Xerxes, and giving Ben a sly, accidental cut. 'Xerxes floundered over, nearly crushing Ben, and making plain sailing for Jorrocks. Our master then followed and galloped away, leaving Ben writhing and crying and vowing that he would " take and pull him off his 'oss."

The hounds had now shot a few fields ahead, but a flashey catching scent diminishing their pace, Mr. Jorrocks was soon back to them yoicking and holding them on. " *Yooi, over he goes !* " cheered he, taking off his cap, as Priestess endorsed Ranger's promissory note on a very wet undrained fallow—" *Yooi, over he goes!*" repeated he, eyeing the fence into it, and calculating whether he could lead over or scuttle up to the white gate on the left in less time, and thinking the latter was safer, having got the hounds over, he rose in his stirrups, and pounded away while Charley took the fence in his stride. They were now upon sound old pasture, lying parallel with tortuous Tommy, and most musical were the hounds' notes as each in turn prevailed—Mr. Jorrocks had lit on his legs in the way of gates, and holloaed and rode as if he didn't know what craning was.

" Forrard on, Priestess, old betch ! " cheered he, addressing himself to the now leading hound, "forrard on!—for-rard ! " adding " I'll gie ye *sich* a plate o' bones if we do but kill."

On the hounds went bustling, chirping, and whimpering, all anxious to fly, but still not able to accomplish it. The scent was shifty and bad, sometimes serving them, and then as quickly failing, as if the fox had been coursed by a dog. Jorrocks, though desperately anxious to get them on better terms with their fox, trots gently on, anxiously eyeing them but restraining his ardour, by repeating the old couplet,—

> " As well as shape full well he knows,
> To *kill* their fox they must 'ave nose."

" Aye, aye, but full well he knows also," continued our master, after he had repeated the lines three or four times over, " that to kill their fox they must press 'im, at some period or other o' the chase, which they don't seem at all inclined to do," continued he, looking at their indifferent slack mode of proceeding. " *For-rard on !* " at length cries our master, cracking his whip at a group of dwellers, who seemed inclined to reassure every yard of the ground—" For-rard on ! " repeated he, riding angrily at them, adding " cus your unbelievin' 'eads, can't you trust old Priestess and Ravager ? "

To increase our worthy master's perplexities, a formidable flock of sheep now wheel semicircularly over the line, completely obliterating any little scent that remained, and though our finest huntsman under the sun, aided by Charley as whip, quickly got the hounds beyond their foil, he was not successful in touching upon the line of the fox again.

" *Humph,*" grunted our master, reviewing his cast, " the ship must ha' heat 'im, or he's wanished into thin hair;" adding, " jest put 'em on to me, Charley, whilst I makes one o' Mr. Craven Smith's patent all-round-my-'at casts, for that beggar Binjimin's of no more use with a pack of 'ounds than a hopera-box would be to a cow, or a frilled shirt to a pig." So saying, Mr. Jorrocks out with his tootler, and giving a shrill blast, seconded by Charley's whip, proceeded to go down wind, and up wind, and round about wind, without however feeling a touch of his fox. At

The Kill, on The Cat & Custard Pot Day.

length scarce a hound would stoop, and old black Lucifer gave unmistakeable evidence of his opinion of matters by rolling himself just under Jorrocks's horse's nose, and uttering a long-drawn howl, as much as to say, "Come, old boy! shut up! it's no use bothering: let's off to dinner!"

"Rot ye! ye great lumberin' henterpriseless brute!" roared Jorrocks, cutting indignantly at him with his whip, "rot ye! d'ye think I boards and lodges and pays tax 'pon you to 'ave ye settin' up your 'olesale himperance that way?—g-e-e-t-e away, ye disgraceful sleepin' partner o' the chase!" continued he, as the frightened hound scuttled away with his tail between his legs.

"Well, it's nine 'underd and fifty thousand petties," muttered our master now that the last of the stoopers had got up their heads, "it's nine 'underd and fifty thousand petties that I hadn't got close away at his brush, for I'd ha' killed 'im to a dead certainty. Never was a fox better 'unted than that! Science, patience, judgment, skill, everything that constitutes an 'untsman—Goodhall, himself, couldn't ha' done it better! But it's not for mortals to command success," sighed our now greatly dejected master

CHAPTER XXXVI.

JAMES PIGG AGAIN !!!

JUST as Mr. Jorrocks was reining in his horse to blow his hounds together, a wild, shrill, view holloo, just such a one as a screech-owl gives on a clear frosty night, sounded through the country, drawing all eyes to Camperdown Hill, where, against the blue sky, sat a Wellington-statue-like equestrian with his cap in the air, waving and shouting for hard life.

The late lethargic hounds pricked their ears, and before Mr. Jorrocks could ejaculate the word "Pigg!" the now-excited pack had broke away, and were streaming full cry across country to where Pigg was perched.

"*Get away hooic! Get away hooic!*" holloaed our master, deluding himself with the idea that he was giving them leave. "*Get away h-o-o-ick! Get away h-o-o-ick!*" repeated he, cracking his ponderous whip.

The hollooing still continued—louder if possible than before.

"Blow me tight!" observed Mr. Jorrocks to himself, "wot a pipe the feller 'as! a'most as good as Gabriel Junks's!" and returning his horn to his saddle. he took a quick glance at the country for a line to the point, instead of crashing after Charley Stobbs, who seemed, by the undue elevation of his horse's tail on the far side of a fence, to be getting into grief already. "There 'ill be a way out by those stacks," said Mr. Jorrocks to himself, eyeing a military-looking line of burly corn stacks drawn up on the high side of a field to the left: so saying he caught Arterxerxes short round by the head, and letting in the Latchford's, tore away in a desperate state of flutter and excitement, the keys and coppers in his pockets contributing to the commotion.

Mr. J. was right, for convenient gaps converged to these stacks, from whence a view of the farm-house (Barley Hall) further on was obtained. Away he next tore for it, dashing through the fold-yards, leaving the gates open as if they were his own, and catching Ben draining a pot of porter at the back-door. Here our fat friend had the misfortune to consult farmer Shortstubble, instead of trusting to his own natural instinct for gaps and gates, and Shortstubble put him on a line as wide of his own wheat as he could, which was anything but as direct a road as friend Jorrocks could have found for himself. However, Camperdown Hill was a good prominent feature in the country, and by dint of brisk riding, Jorrocks reached it in a much shorter time than the uninitiated would suppose he could. Now getting Arterxerxes by the mane, he rose in his stirrups, hugging and cramming him up the rugged ride to the top.

When he reached the summit, Pigg, whose sight was much improved, had hunted his fox with a very indifferent scent round the base of the hill, and having just got a view, was capping the hounds on as hard as ever his horse could lay legs to the ground, whooping and forcing the fox away into the open.

"Wot a man it is to ride!" ejaculated Jorrocks, eyeing Pigg putting one of Duncan Nevin's nags that had never seen hounds before at a post and rail that almost made him rise perpendicularly to clear. "Well done you!" continued Mr. Jorrocks, as with a flounder and scramble James got his horse on his legs on the far side, and proceeded to scuttle away again as hard as before. "Do believe he's got a view o' the varmint," continued Mr. Jorrocks, eyeing Pigg's cap-in-hand progress.

"Wot a chap it would be if it could only keep itself sober!" continued Mr. Jorrocks, still eyeing James intently, and wishing he hadn't been so hard upon him. "Of all 'bominable vices under the sun that of hintemperance is the most degradin' and disgustin," continued our master emphatically, accompanying the assertion with a hearty crack of the whip down his leg.

Jorrocks now gets a view of the varmint stealing away over a stubble, and though he went stouter than our master would have liked if he had been hunting himself, he saw by Pigg's determined way that he was master of him, and had no doubt that he would have him in hand before long. Accordingly, our master got Arterxerxes by his great Roman-nosed head, and again letting the Latchford's freely into his sides, sent him scrambling down hill at a pace that was perfectly appalling. Open went the gate at the bottom of the hill, down Jorrocks made for the Long Tommy ford, splash he sent Arterxerxes in just like Johnny Gilpin in Edmonton Wash,—

" —— throwing the water about,
    On both sides of the way,
    Just like a trundling mop,
    Or a wild goose at play."

Then having got through, he seized the horse by the mane, and rose the opposing bank determined to be in at the death if he could. " Blow me tight ! " ejaculated he, " do believe this hungry highlander will grab him arter all ! " And then rising in his stirrups and setting up his great shoulders, Jorrocks tore up the broken Muggercamp lane, sending the loose stones flying right and left as he went.

" If they can but pash him past Ravenswing-scar," observed Mr. Jorrocks, eyeing the leading hounds approaching it, " they'll mop 'im to a certainty, for there's nothin' to save 'im arter it. Crikey ! *they're past!* and its U. P. with old Pug ! Well, if this doesn't bang Bannager I doesn't know what does ! If we do but kill'un, I'll make sich a hofferin' to Bacchus as 'ill perfectly 'stonish 'im," continued Mr. Jorrocks, setting Arterxerxes agoing again. " *Gur-r-r along !* you great 'airy 'eeled 'umbug ! " groaned he, cropping and rib-roasting the horse with his whip.

Arterxerxes, whose pedigree, perhaps, hasn't been very minutely looked into, soon begins to give unmistakeable evidence of satiety. He doesn't seem to care much about the whip, and no longer springs to the spur. He begins to play the castanets too in a way that is anything but musical to Mr. Jorrocks's ear. Our master feels that it will very soon be all U. P. with Arterxerxes too.

" Come hup, you snivellin', drivellin', son of a lucifer match-maker ! " he roars out to Ben, who is coming lagging along in his master's wake. " Come on ! " roared he, waving his arm frantically, as, on reaching the top of Ravenswing scar, he sees the hounds swinging down, like a bundle of clock pendulums into the valley below. " Come hup, I say, ye miserable, road-ridin', dish-lickin' cub ! and give me that quad, for you're a disgrace to a saddle, and only fit to toast muffins for a young ladies' boardin' school. Come hup, you preter-pluperfect tense of 'umbugs ! " adding, " I wouldn't give tuppence a dozen for such beggarly boys ; no, not if they'd give me a paper bag to put them in."

Mr. Jorrocks, having established a comfortable landing-place on a grassy mound, proceeded to dismount from the nearly pumped out Arterxerxes, and pile himself on to the much fresher Xerxes, who had been ridden more as a second horse than as a whipper in's.

" *Now go along !* " cried our master, settling himself into his saddle, and giving Xerxes a hearty salute on the neck with his whip. " *Now go along !* " repeated he, " and lay yourself out as if you were in the cut-me-downs," adding, " there are twenty couple of 'ounds on the scent ! "

" By 'eavens, it's sublime ! " exclaimed he, eyeing the hounds, streaming away over a hundred-acre pasture below. " By 'eavens, it's sublime ! 'ow they go, screechin' and towlin' along, jest like a pocket full o' marbles." Ow the old wood re-echoes their melody, and the old castle seemingly takes pleasure to repeat the sound. A Jullien concert's nothin' to it. No, not all the bands i' the country put together."

" How I wish I was a heagle ! " now exclaimed Mr. Jorrocks, eyeing the wide stretching vale before him. "How I wish I was a heagle, 'overin over 'em, seein' which 'ound has the scent, which hasn't, and which are runnin' frantic for blood."

"To guide a scent well over a country for a length of time, through all the changes and chances o' the chase, and among all difficulties usually encountered, requires the best and most experienced abilities," added he, shortening his hold of his horse, as he now put his head down the steep part of the hill. Away Jorrocks went wobbling like a great shape of red Noyeau jelly.

An accommodating lane serves our master below, and taking the grassy side of it, he pounds along manfully, sometimes hearing the hounds, sometimes seeing Pigg's cap, sometimes Charley's hat, bobbing over the fences; and, at more favoured periods, getting a view of the whole panorama of the chase. Our master is in ecstacies! He whoops, and shouts, and grins, and rolls in his saddle, looking more like the drunken Huzzar at the circus, than the sober, well-conducted citizen.

"*F-o-r-rard on!*" is still his cry. Hark! They've turned and are coming towards him. Jorrocks hears them, and spurs on in hopes of a nick. Fortune favours him, as she generally does the brave and perse-vering, and a favourable fall of the land enables our friend to view the fox still travelling on at an even, stealthy sort of pace, though certainly slower than the still pressing, squeak, squeak, yap, yap, running pack. Pigg and Charley are in close attendance, and Jorrocks nerves himself for a grand effort to join them.

"*I'll do it,*" says he, putting Xerxes at a well broken-down cattle-gap, into Wandermoor common. This move lands him well inside the hounds, and getting upon turf he hugs his horse, resolved to ride at whatever comes in his way. Another gap, not quite so well flattened as the first, helps our friend on in his project, and emboldened by success, he rams manfully at a low stake and rice-bound gateway, and lands handsomely in the next field. He thus gains confidence.

"Come on, ye miserable, useless son of a lily-livered besom-maker," he roars to Benjamin, who is craning and funking at the place his master has come so gallantly over. "Rot ye," adds Jorrocks, as the horse turns tail, "I'll bind ye 'prentice to a salmon pickler."

The next field is a fallow, but Jorrocks chooses a wet furrow, up which he spurts briskly, eyeing the country far and near, as well for the fox, as a way out. He sees both. The fox is skirting the brow of the opposite heathery hill, startling the tinkling belled sheep, while the friendly shepherd waves his cap, indicating an exit.

"Thank 'ee," cries Jorrocks, as he slips through the gate.

There is nothing now between him and the hounds, save a somewhat rough piece of moorland, but our master not being afraid of the pace so long as there is no leaping, sails away in the full glow of enthusiastic excitement. He is half frantic with joy!

The hounds now break from scent to view and chase the still flying fox along the hill side—Duster, Vanquisher, and Hurricane have pitched their pipes up at the very top of their gamut, and the rest come shrieking and screaming as loudly as their nearly pumped-out wind will allow.

Dauntless is upon him, and now a snap, a turn, a roll, and it's all over with reynard.

Now Pigg is off his horse and in the midst of the pack, now he's down, now he's up, and there's a pretty scramble going on !

"*Leave him! leave him!*" cries Charley, cracking his whip in aid of Pigg's efforts. A ring is quickly cleared, the extremities are whipped off, and behold the fox is ready for eating.

"O Pigg, you're a brick ! a fire brick !" gasps the heavily perspiring

RECONCILIATION OF MR. JORROCKS AND PIGG.

Mr. Jorrocks, throwing himself exhausted from his horse, which he leaves outside the now riotous ring, and making up to the object of his adoration, he exclaimed, "O Pigg, *let us fraternise!*" Whereupon Jorrocks seized Pigg by the middle, and hugged him like a Polar bear, to the mutual astonishment of Pigg and the pack.

"*A—a—a* wuns man, let's hev' him worried!" roared Pigg, still holding up the fox with both hands high above his head. "*A—a—a* wuns man, let's hev' him worried," repeated James, as Jorrocks danced him about still harder than before,

"*Tear 'im and eat 'im !*" roars Pigg, discharging himself of the fox, which has the effect of detaching Jorrocks, and sending him to help at the worry. Then the old boy takes a haunch, and tantalises first Brilliant, then Harmony, then Splendour, then Vengeance, all the eager young entry in short.

Great was Mr. Jorrocks's joy and exultation. He stuck his cap on his whip and danced about on one leg. He forgot all about the Cat and Custard-Pot, the gob full of baccy, and crack in the kite, in his anxiety to make the most of the victory. Having adorned the head-stall of his own bridle with the brush, slung the head becomingly at Pigg's saddle side, and smeared Ben's face plentifully with blood, he got his cavalcade in marching order, and by dint of brisk trotting re-entered Handley Cross just at high change, when everybody was abusing him for his conduct to poor Pigg, and vowing that he didn't deserve so good a huntsman. Then when they saw what had happened, they changed their tunes, declaring it was a regular preconcerted do, abused both James and Jorrocks, and said they'd withdraw their subscriptions from the hounds.

CHAPTER XXXVII.

MR. JORROCKS'S JOURNAL.

WE learn from the above veracious record, that when our worthy friend arrived at home after the foregoing memorable day, he found how it was that the prophet, Gabriel Junks, the peacock, was not in the garden when he went to consult him about the weather. Among other letters, a highly musked, superfine satin cream-laid paper one lay on his table, from no less a man than Doctor Sebastian Mello, complaining in no measured terms of Gabriel having killed Mello's fine white Dorking cock.

"*Humph !*" grunted Mr. Jorrocks, throwing it down, " that 'counts for the bird not bein' forthcomin' this mornin'. Wot business has he out of his own shop, I wonder." Fearing, on second thoughts, that Mello might try to make him pay for him, and that too at the rate of the mania price for poultry, Mr. Jorrocks thought it best to traverse the killing altogether, which accordingly he did by the following answer.

" M.F.H. John Jorrocks presents his compliments to Dr. Sebastian Mello, and is much surprised to receive a note complaining of the M.F.H.'s peacock, Gabriel Junks, havin' slain the Doctor's dung-ill cock. The M.F.H. thinks the Doctor must be mistaken. The M.F.H. cannot bring himself to think that Gabriel, with his 'igh and chivalrous feelins, would condescend to do battle with such an unworthy adwersary as a dung-'ill cock.　Nevertheless, the M.F.H. begs to assure the Doctor of his distinguished consideration.

"DIANA LODGE."

And having despatched Ben with it, and given him instructions to find out, if he could, whether any one saw the bird at work, Mr. Jorrocks proceeded to make the following entry in his journal :—

"Letter from Bowker, requesting the loan of a 50*l*. Stock been seized for rent and arrears,—seems to be always gettin' seized ;—no interest paid on former fifty yet.　Queer chap, Bill, with his invoices, and flash of supplyin' the trade, when 50*l*. was all he set up with, and that I had to lend him.—Never chop-fallen, seemingly, with all his executions and misfortunes.—Writes,

"'I had a rum go in a 'buss on Saturday.　Streets being sloppy, and wantin' to go to my snuff-merchant in the Minories, I got into a 'buss at the foot of Holborn Hill, and seated myself next a pretty young woman with a child in her arms.　Stopping at Bow Church, she asked if I'd have the kindness to hold the babby for a minute, when out she got, and cut down the court as hard as ever she could go.　On went the 'buss, and I saw I was in for a plant.　A respectable old gentleman in black, shorts and a puddingey white tie, sat opposite ; and as the 'buss pulled up at the Mansion-house, I said, ' Perhaps you'd have the kindness to hold the babby for a minute, while I alight ; ' and popping it into his lap, I jumped out, making for Bucklersbury, threading all the courts in my line till I got back to Lincoln's Inn.'

"Sharp of Bill ;—deserves 50*l*. for his 'cuteness.　May as well lend it on an ' I. O. U.,' for it's no use throwin' good money after bad by usin' a stamp."

While our master was thus writing, Ben returned with the following minute account of the Gabriel Junks' transaction from the refined Mr. Sebastian Mello himself :—

"Sir,—I am surprised that you should contradict my assertion respecting your cock having killed my white Dorking fowl, on no better grounds than mere supposition. *I tell you he did kill my cock.* He passed through the Apollo Belvidere gardens and perched on one of the balls at my back gates, as if the place were his own.　When my maid, Maria, fed the fowls, he flew among them, and because my cock resented the intrusion he killed him on the spot ; and then his master adds insult to injury, by saying he does not believe it.　These sort of manners may be very well for the city, but they won't do for civilised life.　I may take this opportunity of observing that you are very indecorous in your general proceedings.　The day before yesterday you walked your hounds and your servants in scarlet before my windows, and stood there, a thing that I, as a religious man, would not have had done for ten sovereigns. I desire you will not do so again.

"Your obedient servant,
"SEBASTIAN MELLO.

SULPHUR WELLS HALL."

To which Mr. Jorrocks makes a "Mem.—To take 'orns as well as 'ounds next time, and blow before his house—a beggar."

The next entry of importance is the following ·—

"Had Fleecey to see how the cat jumps in the money department. Sharp chap, Fleecey—manages to keep the expenses up to the receipts, what with earth-stoppin', damage, cover rent, and law bills. Wanted to take credit for receivin' no salary. Axed him what his bills were? Said public officers always had a fixed salary besides their bills. Had twenty-five pounds a-year from the Mount Sion Turnpike-road. Told him I knew nothin' about 'pikes, but if he did not get me all arrears of subscription in by New Year's Day I'd be my own sec., and save both his law bills and his salary.

"Read the *Life*—good letter on bag foxes.

"'BAG FOXES.

"'*To the Editor of Bell's Life in London.*

"'Sir,—as your journal is a sporting one, and unquestionably the first in the kingdom, I am very sorry frequently to see in it accounts of runs with *bagged foxes*. You, sir, who are so well acquainted with the sports of the field, must know what a very difficult thing it is to show sport with fox-hounds, and that very much of that difficulty arises from the almost entire impracticability of preserving foxes, occasioned in great measure by their being stolen and sold to hunters of bagged foxes. It matters not if the animal is turned out before hounds in a country where no regular fox-hounds are kept, the crime (in a sporting sense) and the evil done are always the same. I am sure you will acknowledge that fox-hunting is, of all others, the noblest of English sports, and cannot doubt that a moment's consideration will show you, that your publishing accounts of runs with bagged foxes is giving a tacit approval of that practice (I will not term it sport). Should you, upon consideration, decline publishing accounts of any more of these runs, you will have the hearty thanks of every real sportsman, and you will show that you are determined that the character of your journal shall be that of *The Sporting Chronicle of England*.

"'A FOX-HUNTER,
"'BUT NOT A MASTER OF HOUNDS.'

"*Waterbury Turnpike.*—'Pikes are better for meetin' at than publics. Gabriel Junks began screamin' at day-break; so put on my old hat and coat, ditto boots, and breeches.—Began to drop just as we left kennel. Useful bird Junks, to be sure,—no pack perfect without a peacock;—the most 'arden'd minister dirsn't tax a peacock. Reg'lar down-pour by the time we got to the 'pike. Duncan Nevin's screws out as usual; and a groom in twilled fustian, with a green neckcloth, and a cockade in his 'at, leadin' some rips up and down the road for soger officers. Home at one—wet as water. Paid for catchin' my oss 1s.

"Turtle soup day. Roger Swizzle dined and got glorious;—says the true way to be healthy is to live freely and well.—Believes he has cured more people of indigestion than any man goin'.—Thinks Mello a cantin' humbug.—Wishes he could ride, that he might hunt : subscribes twenty-five guineas to the 'ounds since I got them—*pays too*.—Showed him Mello's letters.—Says the open in front of Sulphur Wells Hall is public property, and I may kick up whatever row I like upon it.—Will write to Bowker to send a company of mountebanks down to perform there."

Passing over some intermediate matter, chiefly about horses that people sent for him to look at, believing on the strength of his lecture that he would not require them to be warranted—a supposition that they found themselves mistaken in, we come to the following entry about a gentleman with whom we shall presently have the pleasure of making the reader acquainted.

"Most purlite letter from a gentleman signin' himself Marmaduke Muleygrubs, J.P., sayin' that being a country gentleman, and anxious to do wot is right, he should be 'appy to encourage the 'unt, and would be glad if I would fix a day for dinin' at Cockolorum Hall, and let the hounds meet before it the next mornin'."

To which Mr. Jorrocks replied as follows :—

"M.F.H. John Jorrocks presents his compliments to Mr. Marmaduc Muleygrubs, and in reply to his purlite favour duly received, begs to say that he will be 'appy to dine and sleep at Cockolorum Hall as soon as ever his other 'unting arrangements will enable him to meet on that side of the country ; and that with regard to the subscription so 'andsomely promised to his 'ounds, it can be paid either to his credit at Bullock and Hulker's in the Strand, or to the M.F.H.'s account at Stumpey and Co.'s here—

"HANDLEY CROSS SPA,
   "DIANA LODGE."

The few next days disclose no feature of general interest—found, lost, killed, lost, found, killed, &c., being the burthen of the journal, so we omit them altogether.

"Letter from Bowker, brimful of gratitude for the loan of 50*l*." This letter being pasted into the journal, we give the greater part of it, containing, as it does, some further particulars of Bowker's badger-baiting friend.

"You will be sorry to hear," says he to Mr. Jorrocks, "that the Slender is found guilty, and ordered to be scragged on Monday morning, for though they have not found the exciseman, the jury found Billy guilty. Poor Slender ! I've known him long, and safely can I aver, that a nobler fellow never breathed. He combined many callings : bear and badger-baiter, dog-fancier, which has been unhandsomely interpreted into fancy gentlemen that fancy other people's dogs, horse-slaughterer, private distiller, and smasher.* About five years ago he was nearly caught at the latter work. Sitting, as 'was his custom always in an afternoon,' at a public-house in the Hampstead-Lane, upon ' his secure hour,' two policemen stole. The energetic firmness of Billy's character was manfully displayed. Seizing a handful of bank-notes, which he had

* Coiner, or passer of forged notes.

in his pocket, he thrust his hand into the fire, and held them there until
they were consumed. The flesh peel'd off his fingers.

"He once had a turn with the excisemen before. With his intimates
Billy had no deceit, and used to boast that there was summut running
under his heaps of old horse-bones that was the marrow of his existence.
Well, the Excise strongly suspecting this, sent down a *posse comitatus*

to Copenhagen-fields to bring up Billy's body. He was busy with a
bunch of sporting men at a dog-fight when Miss Aberford * came to give
the office. Billy's mind was soon made up. Sending all his sporting
friends into the house, and locking the doors, he unmuzzled his two
bears and turned them loose among the officers. The scramble that

---

* Billy's daughter. The name of this singular man was Aberford.

ensued beggars description.   In less than five minutes the red-breasts *—
for it was before the crusher times—-were flown.   It is a singular fact and
says much for the influence of female charms, that *Mrs. Aberford* could
hold and fight the dogs when they were too savage for Billy.

" I always feared Billy's illegitimate pursuits would lead him into
trouble.   ' Master Bowker,' said he to me one day, ' Do you want to buy
an 'oss cheap ? '   ' Where did you get him, Billy ? ' said I.   ' *Found him,*
master,' said he.   ' As I was coming home on foot from Chiswick, I sees
a gig and 'oss a standing all alone in Chiswick-Lane—says I, Billy, my boy,
you may as well ride as walk—so I driv it home, and now the body o' the
gig's in the black ditch, the wheels are on my knacker-cart, and I've hogged
the 'os's mane and cut his tail, so that his own master wouldn't know him.'

" Altogether, Billy has been a queer one, but still hangin's a hard
matter, especially as they have not found the exciseman.   Billy may now
sport his own joke to Jack Ketch, of ' Live and let live, as the criminal
said to the hangman.'

" Your second letter about the mountebanks is just received—strange,
that I should be writing about rope-dancing just as it came.   I'll see
what I can do about sending you a *troop*.   *We* of the sock and
buskin do not call them companies.   I rather think Polito is down in
your part of England, perhaps his wild beasts would answer as well ;—
beef-eaters, tambourine, &c., would make a grand row before Sanctity
Hall.   Mello wants flooring.   I'll send him a broken dish by this post,
requesting his acceptance of a piece of plate from his London patients.
A basket of cats by coach would be a nice present, labelled ' game.'

" Your much obliged and very humble servant,

" WM. BOWKER."

The following seems to have been a good run ; we take it verbatim
from the journal, omitting some matters of no interest :—

" *Candid Pigg.*—Went with the 'ounds for fear of accidents.   Large
field, and many strangers.   Lots o' farmers.   Mr. Yarnley in a yellow
gig.   Told us to draw his withey bed first.   Trotted down to it, and no
sooner were the 'ounds in than out went Reynard at the low end.   Sich a
fine chap !   Bright ruddy coat, with a well-tagged brush.   One whisk of
his brush, and away he went !   Pigg flew a double flight of oak rails, and
Bin began to cry as soon as ever he saw them.   'Ounds got well away,
and settled to the scent without interruption.   Away for Frampton End,
and on to Pippen Hall, past Willerton Brake, and up to Snapperton
Wood.   Here a check let in the roadsters ; it was but momentary.
Through the wood and away for Lutterworth Bank.   Earths open, but
Reynard didn't know them, or hadn't time to try them—headed about a
mile to the north of Lutterworth Spinney by people at a foot-ball match,
and turned as if for Hollington Dean, taking over the large grass
enclosures between that and Reeve's Mill, bringing the deep race into the
line.   Pigg blobbed in and out like a water-rat ; out on the right side
too.   Barnington went over head, and his 'oss came out on one side, and
he on t'other.   Stobb's little Yorkshire nag cleared it in his stride ; and

---

* The Bow Street officers of former days wore red waistcoats.

Captain Shortflat went in and came out with a cart-load of water-cress on his back; lost his hat too. Duncan Nevin piloted his pupils down to the bridge, followed by the rest of the field. Fox had run the margin of the race, and we nicked the 'ounds just at the bridge. Man on Stoke Hill holloa'd, and Pigg lifted his 'ounds, the scent bein' weak from the water. Viewed the fox stealin' down to the walley below, and Pigg capped them on and ran into the varmint in Tew Great Fields, within a quarter of a mile of Staveston Wood. Finest run wot ever was seen! Time, one hour and twenty-five minutes, with only one check. Distance, from pin't to pin't, twelve miles. As they ran, from fifteen to twenty. Many 'osses tired. Pigg rode young May's 'oss, Young Hyson, and went well—worth his 30*l.* I think;—shall ax 60*l.* at the end of the season. Barnington got up before the worry, wet, but quite 'appy. Felt somethin' movin' in his pocket; put in his hand and pulled out a pike! Fishin' as well as 'unting. Paid for catchin' my 'oss twice two shillings.

" *Grumble Corner.*—Drew the gorse blank, then to Finmere Diggin's, crossin' two or three turnip fields in our line. All blank; smelt werry strong of a trap. Barrack Wood. Found immediately. Away for Newtimber Forest; but headed within a quarter of a mile by coursers. Field rather too forrard, or Pigg rather too backward, havin' got bogged comin' out of cover. Came up in a desperate rage, grinnin' and swearin' as he went. Barnington in front, swore at him just as he would at a three-punder. The idea of swearin' at a gen'l'man wot gives 50*l.* a year to the 'ounds! Made nothin' more of the fox. Came on rain, and give in at two. Lectored Pigg for swearin' at a large payin' subscriber. Paid for catchin' my 'oss 6*d.*"

The following bunch of anathemas seem to have been produced by Mr. Jorrocks being brought up short by a double ditch, with a fence most unjustifiably mended with old wire-rope, whereby our energetic master lost another of the " finest runs wotever was seen," from Screecher Gorse to earth at Sandford Banks—time and distance, anything that anybody liked to call it!

Con—found all farmers say I, wot deal in double ditches!

Con—found all farmers say I, wot mend their fences with old wire-rope!

Con—found all farmers say I, wot don't keep their gates in good order!

Con—found all farmers say I, wot are unaccommodatin' about gaps!

Con—found all farmers say I, wot arn't flatter'd by 'avin' their fields ridden over!

Con—found all farmers say I, wot grumble at the price o' grain, and then plough out their grass!

Con—found all farmers say I, wot hobject to 'avin' a litter of foxes billeted upon them!

Con—found all farmers say I, wot hobject to walkin' the M.F.H. a pup!

Con—found all farmers say I, wot don't keep their stock at 'ome, when the 'ounds are out!

Con—found all farmers say I, wot let their 'erds keep a cur!

Con—found all farmers say I, wot 'aven't a round o' beef or a cold pork pie to pull out, when the 'ounds pass!

Con—found all farmers say I, wot 'aven't a tap of good " October" to wash them down with

CHAPTER XXXVIII.

THE WORLD TURNED UPSIDE DOWN DAY.

"WAS that the vind, or a dream?" exclaimed Mr. Jorrocks, starting out of his sleep at something like thunder over-head—*rumble, rumble, tumble,* went a stack of chimneys, and Mr. Jorrocks was on the floor in an instant. *Blast* went the wind, and in came his window—"Vot next? as the frog said when his tail dropped off," exclaimed Mr. Jorrocks, wondering what was going to happen—over went the looking-glass, which was dashed to atoms, two five-pound notes were whisked about the room, and the clothes-horse came clattering among the jugs.

"It's a *con*founded wind," said Mr. Jorrocks, running after the five pound notes, "wonder wot's the meanin' of it all—fear th' 'ounds will be werry wild," recollecting that they were to meet at the "World Turned Upside Down," on the Hookem-Snivey road.

It was a terrific morning—the wind blew a perfect hurricane—chimneys were toppling and tumbling, slates falling, tiles breaking, and here and there whole roofs taking flight—family washings were whisked away, or torn to tatters on the drying lines—children were lifted off their legs, and grown-up people knocked against each other at the corners of the streets.

"This is summut new at all ewents," said Mr. Jorrocks, eyeing a large laurel torn up by the roots in the garden, "that tree never had such a hike afore in its life," and as he looked, the back-door flew open with a crash that split it from top to bottom.

"Wish there mayn't be mischief," said he, huddling on his dressing-gown and running down-stairs, recollecting there was something about repairs in his agreement. Here he found the soot covering the drawing-room carpet, and the kitchen floor strewed with bricks and mortar—"Oh dear! oh dear," exclaimed he, "here's a terrible disaster, five punds worth of damage at least, and, ord rot it! there's my Jerry Hawkins mug broke:" gathering the fragments of a jug representing that renowned Gloucestershire sportsman.

The wind was cuttingly keen, and swept up and down with unrestrained freedom. There was not a fire lighted, and the whole place smelt of soot, and was the picture of misery.

"Shall never get to the World Turned Upside Down to-day," said Mr. Jorrocks, eyeing the scene of desolation, and wishing what he saw might be the extent of the mischief. "Pity to lose a day too," added he, thinking it might only be a squall.

He now sought the refuge of the parlour, but oh! what greeted him there!—the window wide open—chairs huddled in the centre of the room, the table in the corner, and Betsey with up-turned gown, scrubbing away at the grate.

"Now blast it, Batsay," roared Mr. Jorrocks, as a gust of wind swept a row of china off a chiffonier, "Now blast it Batsay, vot in the name of all that's hugly are you arter now?"

"Only polishing the grate!" exclaimed Betsey, astonished at seeing her master walking about in his night-cap and dressing-gown.

"But vot in the name o' badness are you workin' with the winder open for?"

"To air the house, to be sure!" replied Betsey, tartly.

"Hair the 'ouse!" screamed Mr. Jorrocks, whisking his dressing-gown round as he spoke; "Hair the 'ouse, it's hairy enough already!— ord rot it! you 'ousmaids have no sort o' compassion about you—the colder the day, the hairier you are! See vot you've done now! Belinda's pet-lambs, your misses's Cupid, and my model of the Saracen's 'Ead on Snow 'Ill, all dashed to spinnage! Enough to make the Harch-bishop o' York swear!" saying which, Mr. Jorrocks whisked his dressing-gown the reverse way, and bounced out of the room, lest he might be tempted into the indiscretion of an oath.

Our master ran up-stairs, but little consolation greeted him there. His dressing-table was covered with blacks—his looking-glass was on the swing—his soap was reduced to a wafer—there was nothing but cold water to shave with, and his beard being at all times rather untrac-table, rough enough to light a lucifer match upon, he inflicted sundry little gashes on his chin, as he jagged a blunt razor over the stubborn stubble; altogether his toilette was performed under most discouraging disheartening circumstances. Still he dressed for hunting, the hounds being advertised, and there being a possibility of the wind lulling.

Batsay had got the parlour "haired" before he made his second appearance, but she had had to borrow a neighbour's kettle, and was making some toast in the room when he entered. The wind having abated, Mr. Jorrocks thought he might as well make up with her, as a sort of peace-offering to Æolus.

"Now, Batsay," said he, in a mild agreeable tone, "I've never had cause to find fault with you afore, but really on a vindy day like this, it does seem rayther unkind lettin' old Boreas take the run o' the 'ouse in ——"

"It warn't old Borus," replied Betsey, colouring brightly.

"Oh, dash my vig!" exclaimed Mr. Jorrocks, hurrying out, "that confounded young carpenter's been here again! That's the way they hair one's 'ouse."

Whish—Wha-s-s-sh—blash—roar went the wind, as Mr. Jorrocks left the room.

*　　*　　*　　*　　*　　*　　*

Stobbs wouldn't get up, and Mr. Jorrocks got through breakfast alone under very chilly disheartening uncomfortable circumstances. The kettle had only half-boiled, and the tea was little better than water— blacks floated on the cream, and the butter was similarly ornamented— the eggs were cold in the middle, and the sausages only done on one side, added to which, the baker's oven was blown down, and there was nothing but stale rolls; altogether, it was a very sorry affair. "Well, better luck next time," said Mr. Jorrocks to himself, hurrying away from the scene of discomfort.

*   *   *   *   *   *   *

"Can we 'unt, think you, Pigg?" inquired he of James, who he found turning the horses round in their stalls, preparing for a start.

Pigg.—"Yeas, ar should think we may, towards noon; the wind's uncommon kittle now, though,—maist had mar head smashed with a pantile comin' past ard Tommy Trotter's Biar."

"It's werry cold," observed Mr. Jorrocks, thumping his right hand across his chest. "Now, Binjimin, wot's 'appened to you?" looking at the boy all bathed in tears.

"*So-o-o cold*," drawled the boy.

"COLD! you little warmint!" repeated Mr. Jorrocks briskly; "wot business have *you* to be cold?—Think o' ginger. I'm froggy myself, but I doesn't cry! Think o' ginger, I say."

The boy still went on blubbering, wiping his eyes with the back of his hands, imparting a little of their dirt to his face.

It was ten o'clock before they got started, and the wind still blew with unabated fury. Pigg and Benjamin turned their cap's peak backwards, and Mr. Jorrocks shortened his string two holes. The hounds set up their backs, and the horses shied at every thing they came near,—indeed, they were not wholly without excuse, for the broken and uprooted trees, the prostrate walls, demolished barns, and flying stacks, they encountered in their progress, were enough to startle less observing animals than they are. Here was half an elm tree rolling about the country—there a thrashing-machine lifted to the skies. Our party made slow progress in their journey. The wind veered about, now catching their coats, now taking them in the rear, and now nearly blowing them over their horses tails. The hounds, too, took advantage of the scrimmage; some cut away home, while others hung back, or hurried before the horsemen. Had Mr. Jorrocks guessed it was any thing but a high wind, he would never have gone.

There were few people astir, and the Borrowdale Turnpike-gate was still shut. "Gate! gate! gate!" roared Pigg. "Gate! gate! gate!" shouted Mr. Jorrocks, but the wind scattered their voices in all directions. They were kept there for ten minutes at least, when Mr. Jorrocks had recourse to his horn, and gave it a twang that brought Tom Take-ticket out in a hurry.

"Bliss my heart!" exclaimed he; "is it you, Mr. Jorrocks?—I thought it was the mail. Sure-*lie* you arn't goin' to hunt such a mornin' as this?"

"But I am," replied Mr. Jorrocks; "and I'll thank you to hopen the gate.—Kept me here quite long enough.—Got to meet at the World Turned Hupside Down, and been bellerin' here for 'alf an hour and more. Here, take your pay; I harn't got no copper, but there are three postage-stamps instead."

Having got his stamps, Tom turned the key in the lock, and a blast blew the gate against the post with a crash that shivered it to splinters.—The party then jogged on.

*   *   *   *   *   *   *

The "World Turned Upside Down" was one of those quiet way-side inns out of whose sails the march of railroads has taken the wind. It was a substantial old stone mansion, standing a little off the road, approached by a drive round a neatly cultivated oval-shaped garden, where, amid well-rolled gravel walks, and fantastically cut yews, swung a blue and gold sign bearing its name—"THE WORLD TURNED UPSIDE DOWN." A clustering vine covered one end of the house, and reached nearly up to the latticed windows in the stone roof, while luxuriant Irish ivy crept up to the very chimney-pots on the other; rose-bushes and creepers were trained upon trellises in front, and altogether it was as pretty an *auberge* as any in the land.

It was a posting-house, though not exactly a first-rate one, inasmuch as the stage on either side was short, and four-horse people generally went through; but it was a favourite resort for newly-married couples, and was equally esteemed by stage-coachmen, who always made an excuse for pulling up at its honeysuckled porch. Its charges too were quite within comfortable compass, and one set of visitors recommended another set, instead of flying to the columns of the "Times" for consolation under the infliction of spurious, unrequired wax, and other enormities. Venerable elms sheltered the ends of the house, and the side from the road opened into a spacious garden overlooking rich meadows, sloping away to a smoothly gliding stream, while distant hills closed the scene in circling greyness of romantic form.

That was its summer aspect. On this eventful day things wore a different garb. As the hounds approached, Flash Jim's swell Talliho coach was seen resting against the bank, while the purple stream of life was fast flowing from a dying horse. The huge elms at the east end of the house were all uprooted, while one on the west had fallen with destructive crash upon the house, bearing down a whole stack of chimneys, and stripping the ivy off the wall.

The blue and gold sign creaked and flapped in the wind, while the pride of the road, a yew-tree equestrian, was torn up by the roots, and dashed against the railing beyond.

"Bliss my 'eart!" exclaimed Jorrocks, eyeing the fallen horseman, "*that's too bad!* Those great helms I wouldn't care about, but to ruin such a triumph of the h'art is too bad—cruel in the extreme." A cutting sleet came on, and a passer-by put up an umbrella, which was immediately turned inside out, and carried over the house-top. Mr. Jorrocks's horse swerved, and nearly capsized him.

"Let's get shelter," said he, making for the yard, "or ther'll be mischief, I'm blow'd if there won't."

"Mine host," Jemmy Lush, or the "Old World,"—as he was familiarly termed—was almost frantic. He, poor man, had retired to rest early, and almost the last thing he did, was to arrange some twigs in the yew-tree horse-tail, and train a couple of shoots at the rider's heels for spurs. For twenty years the Old World had loved and nursed that tree; it was the pride of the country! Not a stage-coachman passed, but jerked his elbow at it; and its image was engraven on the minds of hundreds of husbands and wives, now cultivating little olive-branches of their own, who had admired its symmetry in connexion with each other.

"Oh, Mr. Jorrocks!" exclaimed Jemmy, waddling out of the house in his shirt-sleeves, his tapster's apron flying up to his bottle nose, displaying the substantial form of his garterless legs, and his breeches open at the knee; "Oh, Mr. Jorrocks, *I'm ruined, sir!—I'm ruined!—I've lost my bush!*" and the poor man put his hand before his eyes to avert the sad calamity.

"Never mind, old cock!" replied Mr. Jorrocks, cheeringly grasping his hand as he spoke, "plant another, and I'll warrant you'll see it grow."

"*Never! never!*" responded the Old World, sobbing as he spoke. "That man and hoss——" and here his feelings choked his utterance. He would have said that Mrs. Jemmy and he planted it on their wedding-day, and had long regarded it as their first-born.

The wind blew, the hail beat, the trees creaked, and seemed inclined to follow their leaders, and our party, half benumbed, gladly sought the shelter of the Old World's barn. The poor hounds shivered, as if in the last stage of distemper; and the horses' coats stared like Friesland hens' feathers.

"Surely no man in his senses will come to 'unt such a day as this," observed Mr. Jorrocks, slackening his horse's girths as he spoke; "would deserve to have a commission of lunacy taken out again him for his pains if he did."

Leaving Benjamin in the barn, Mr. Jorrocks and Pigg sought the shelter of the house. The wind had stove in the back door, and a venerable elm was prostrate before it. Scrambling through the branches, they at length gained admission, but the inside was almost as cheerless as the out. No fire—no singing kettle, for hot stopping, as was wont, and the elder wine-bottle remained in the cupboard. Bricks, soot, lime, dust, and broken furniture, strewed the house, and the "little Worlds" were huddled together in a corner, not knowing whether to be frightened or pleased.

The "Old World" had thrown himself into an easy chair in the parlour, having taken the precaution of wrapping his wife's red petticoat about his shoulders to prevent his catching cold. "I shall never get over it," exclaimed he, as Mr. Jorrocks entered, whip in hand: "ruined, sir!—beggared!—nothing left for me but the onion—the bastille!"

"Vy the vind has certain*lie* paid you a hawful wisit," observed Mr. Jorrocks, looking at the trees lying across each other outside; "but it would have been worser if it had broke them."

"Oh, it's not *them* I cares about," exclaimed Jemmy, pulling the petticoat about his ears; "it's not them, nor the great oak at the bottom of the field—kept the sun off the grass; those are my landlord's. It's my bush I'm bad about;" and thereupon he pulled the petticoat up to his bottle nose, and burst into tears.

"What ails the 'cull man?" inquired Pigg, with a fine stream of tobacco, all clotted with dust, running from his mouth.

"It's his beautiful bush," replied Mr. Jorrocks, in a whisper. "Didn't you see that the yew-tree 'oss and rider were torn up by the roots? The Old World loved that bush."

Pigg.—"Ord sink! what's the use o' blubberin' about that? there are plenty o' bushes left. There be twe fine hollins, he may cut into what he likes, shot towers, steeples, or ought;" saying which, Pigg left the room.

"Come, cheer up, old buoy," said Mr. Jorrocks, soothingly, " and let's have a drop o' comfort. I declare I'm perfectly perished. Let's have bottoms of brandy. 'Ot with——"

At the word brandy, the Old World brightened up. He dived into his apron pocket, and ringing the bell, ordered his misses to bring glasses and the bottle.

Drink brings comfort to some minds, and Jemmy Lush's mind was of that description. With the first glass he said little ; the second, not much more, but the petticoat began to droop trom his ears ; and at the third, he had it upon his shoulders.

"It's an ill wind that blows nobody good," at length observed he, with a sigh. " That great oak at the bottom of my meadow has been an eye-sore to me these twenty years. Its great ugly branches covered half an acre of land, and our squire never would have it lopped or cut down. Said he, ' There's the finest view in the country from it—you see the river, and the ruins of the abbey, and the Gayhurst hills in the distance,' and I don't know what ; the silly man forgetting, all the time, that he would see just the same things whether the tree was there or not ; and it spoiled as much grass as would have kept me a calf."

"Great humbrageous beggar ! " observed Mr. Jorrocks ; adding, " I s'pose the tree would be worth summut ? "

"No doubt," replied Jemmy. " But nothing like so valuable as my bush ; " and thereupon he heaved a sigh, and pulled the petticoat about his ears.

Just then a man passed the window, with a couple of horses, and Mr. Jorrocks ran to look at him. He was dressed in a very old hat, with a new cockade in it, a faded green neckcloth, a stained red waistcoat, a fustian frock and trousers, with thick shoes and worsted stockings, and wore moustachios. He rode a weedy chesnut, and led an unhappy-looking grey, the latter decorated with a running martingale and a nose-band, and sundry rings and contrivances.

"Whose be those ? " inquired Mr. Jorrocks, with great importance.

"Captain Smith and Lieutenant Brown," replied the soldier-groom saluting him.

"Foot-captins, I presume ? " replied our master, looking at their horses.

"Grenadier company," replied the man.

"It's all the same to me," replied Mr. Jorrocks. " They don't expect I'm agoin' to 'unt sich a day as this—do they ? "

"Don't know," replied the man ; " got my orders last night, and in course I came on."

"Then you'd better cut away and meet them, and say that unless good *payin'* subscribers, to the amount of thirty pounds, cast up, I shallnt' cast off ;" adding, as he wheeled about, "Don't think any man with thirty pence he could call his own would turn out such a day as this."

Mr. Jorrocks returned to the parlour, and was beginning a dissertation upon hunting, when Pigg entered the room, with a spade over his shoulder, and addressed Jemmy Lush with—

"Now gan and water your buss with your tears, 'ars gettin' it oop again."

"No ! " exclaimed Jemmy, running to the window ; sure enough it was up, and two horse-keepers were busy securing it with ropes and strong posts.

Jemmy Lush was half-frantic. He threw the petticoat into the
corner, and ran to the garden to embrace his old friend. Little mischief
had ensued from its excursion. The rider's hat had got a cast on one
side, and the bit of the horse's bridle was broken; but there was nothing
that Jemmy's fatherly care would not easily rectify.

Great was Jemmy's gratitude. He placed all the cold meat in his
larder at Pigg's disposal, and as the storm abated and the party were
about to set off, he insisted upon putting a bottle of brandy into each of
Pigg's pockets. One of them, we are sorry to say, was broken on its
journey home, by bumping against the back of his saddle.

The "Paul Pry" of that week contained a long list of damage and
disasters, and Mr. Jorrocks learnt from the heading of the article that he
had been out in a "terrible hurricane."

In his mem. of the day's doings in his Journal, he adds this passage
from his friend Beckford :—

"Take not out your 'ounds on a werry windy day."

CHAPTER XXXIX.

MR MARMADUKE MULEYGRUBS.

TOWARDS the close of a winter's day, a dirty old dog-cart, with "JOHN JORROCKS, M.F.H." painted up behind, whisked from the turnpike up the well-laurelled drive of Cockolorum Hall.

The hounds were to meet there in the morning, and Mr. Jorrocks had written to apprise his unknown host of his coming. Being rather late, and having a hack, Mr. Jorrocks had driven a turn faster than usual, and as he cut along the sound drive, the Hall was soon before him.

It had originally been a large red-fronted farm-house, converted by a second owner into a villa! increased by a third into a hall; while under the auspices of its present more aspiring master it was fast assuming the appearance of a castle. Massive stone towers, with loop-holed battlements, guarded the corners—imitation guns peered through a heavy iron palisade along the top—while a stone porch, with massive black nailed folding oak doors, stood out from the red walls of the centre. A richly-emblazoned flag, containing the quarterings of many families, floated from the roof.

Mr. Marmaduke Muleygrubs had been a great stay-maker on Ludgate Hill, and, in addition to his own earnings (by no means inconsiderable), had inherited a large fortune from a great drysalting uncle in Bermondsey. On getting this he cut the shop, bought Cockolorum Hall, and having been a rampant Radical in the City, was rewarded by a J. P.-ship in the country. Mr. Jorrocks knew all about him, though Mr. Muleygrubs did not know he did.

"Quite genteel, I declare," said Mr. Jorrocks, eyeing the mansion as he pulled up at the door, and clambered down his vehicle to give the massive bronze helmet-handled bell a pull. "Perfect castle," added he; "'opes I shalln't get soused," recollecting his last adventure in one.

The spacious folding-doors were presently opened by an ill-shaped, clumsy-looking youth, in a gorgeous suit of state livery, and a starched neck-cloth, so broad and so stiff as perfectly to pillorise him. A quantity of flour concealed the natural colour of his wild matted hair, while the ruddiness of a healthy complexion was heightened by a bright orange-coloured coat, with a white worsted shoulder-knot dangling at the side. His waistcoat was a broad blue and white stripe, breeches of scarlet plush, and white silk stockings, rather the worse for wear, as appeared by the darning up the calf; stoutish shoes, with leather strings, completed the costume of this figure footman.

"Now, young man!" said Mr. Jorrocks in his usual free-and-easy way, "Now, young man! jest stand by my nag while I takes out my traps, for I harn't brought no grum.—See, now," continued he, pulling out the gig-scat, "put that i' my bed-room, and jest give them 'ere tops a rub over for the mornin'," producing a pair of mud-stained boots that

he had worn the last day's hunting; "it wern't no use bringin' a clean
pair," observed he, half to himself and half to the servant, "for they'd
a' got crumpled i' the comin' and those won't take no more cleanin'.
Now, where's the stable? Love me, love my 'oss," continued he,
adjusting the reins in the territs, and preparing to lead round.

"That way," said stiff-neck, extending his left arm like the wand of a
telegraph, as he stood with the dirty top-boots in the other, saying which
he wheeled about, and re-entered the house, leaving Mr. Jorrocks to find
his way as he could.

"Ah, never mind," said the worthy man to himself, seeing he was
gone, "if I could find the 'ouse, be bund I can find the stable;"
saying which he turned his vehicle round, and following the old wheel-
marks on the gravel, was very soon in the stable-yard at the back of
the castle.

Here he found another youth in red plush breeches and white silk
stockings, washing his face at the cistern, purifying himself from the
stable preparatory to appearing in the parlour.

"Here, young man," said Mr. Jorrocks, "jest put up my 'oss afore
ever you start to adorn yourself; and if you take well care of him, I'll
give you 'alf-a-crown i' the mornin'. He's a clipped 'un, and won't take
no cleanin'," continued he, eyeing the smoking, curly-coated brute, and
wondering whether the chap would believe him or not.

This matter being arranged, Mr. Jorrocks ferreted his way back to the
front, and, opening the door, passed through the green folding ones of the
porch, and entered a hall beyond. This was fitted up in the baronial
style. Above a spacious mantel-piece, occupying about a third of the
apartment, branched an enormous stag's head, hung round with pistols,
swords, cutlasses, and warlike weapons of various kinds, and the walls
were covered with grim-visaged warriors, knights in armour, and ladies of
bygone days. Many had their names painted in white at the bottom of
the pictures, or done in black on the various patterned frames: there
was Sir Martin Muleygrubs, and Dame Juliana Muleygrubs, and Darius
Muleygrubs, and Erasmus Muleygrubs, and Memnon Muleygrubs, and
Pericles Muleygrubs, and Demosthenes Muleygrubs, and John Thomas
Muleygrubs.

"Such a lot of stay-makers!" as Mr. Jorrocks observed.

A full-length figure of Nemesis, the goddess of justice, with her balance
in one hand and whip in the other, hung over a richly-carved, high-back,
old oak chair; and on a table near were ranged Burns's "Justice,"
"Statutes at Large," Archbold's "Magistrate's Pocket-book," and other
emblems of the law.

"The chap must be a *beak!*" said Mr. Jorrocks aloud to himself, as
he glanced them over.

The fire threw a cheerful gleam over the baronial hall, and our master,
having hung his hat on the stag's horns, and deposited his Siphonia on
the table, took a coat-lap over each arm, and, establishing himself with
his back to the fire, proceeded to hum what he considered a tune. His
melody was interrupted by the partial opening and closing of a door on
the right, followed by a lisping exclamation of—"Oh, ma! here's Kitey
come again!" A "*Hush*, my dear," and scuttling along the passage,

reminded Mr. Jorrocks that he was not at home, so, dropping his tails, and pulling his wig straight, he made for the recently opened door.

This let him into a passage, lighted with flickering, ill-established lamps, along which he kept till he came to a pink sheep-skin mat before a door, at which he paused, and presently turning off, he entered a room, in which he found a lady and a bunch of excited children. The former rose, and concluding she would be the "missis," Mr. Jorrocks tendered the hand of fellowship, and then gave each child a chuck under the chin; nor was he wrong in his conjecture, for Mrs. Marmaduke Muleygrubs immediately began apologising for the absence of her lord.

"Duke," she said, "was unfortunately engaged at that moment with some important justice business"—(decanting the wine).

Mr. Jorrocks "'Oped his grace wouldn't 'urry himself."

"It was very provoking," she continued, without regarding Mr. Jorrocks's observation; "but the whole county came to him for justice, and Duke could hardly be said to have a moment to himself. Every Saturday he was engaged the whole day on the bench, and at the Poor-Law Guardians, but she hoped before long they would find some more people fit to make magistrates of, for really it was taxing ability rather too highly. Not but that Duke's affection for the Queen would prompt him to serve her as long as he could, but——" Just as she had got so far, the door opened, and Duke himself appeared, smoothing down his cuffs after the exercise of his magisterial functions.

He was a little, round-about, pot-bellied, red-faced, bald-headed, snub-nosed, chattering chap, who, at first sight, would give one the idea of being very good-natured, if it were not notorious that he was the most meddling, officious, ill-conditioned little beggar in the county.

He was dressed in one of the little nondescript jackets of the day, with a "ditto" waistcoat, drab kerseymeres, and leather leggings. Over his waistcoat he sported a broad mosaic gold chain, made to resemble a country mayor's as much as possible.

"Mr. Jorrocks, I presume," said he, rubbing his fat hands as he advanced up the room.

"*Right!*" replied our Master, extending his hand.

"Beg ten thousand pardons for not being here to receive you," said Duke, intending to be very gracious.

"Make no apology," interrupted Mr. Jorrocks; "where there's ceremony there's no frindship."

"Been bored with justice business all the afternoon," continued Mr. Muleygrubs; "bailing a bull that was unjustly put in the pound. You are not in the Commission of the Peace, perhaps?"

"Not I," replied Mr. Jorrocks carelessly; "never was in any commission, save one, as agent for Twankay's mexed teas, and a precious commission it was—*haw! haw! haw!*—lost three 'underd pund by it, and more. But, however, *n'importe*, as we say in France. Werry glad to come here to partake o' your hospitality,—brought my nightcap with me, in course,—a rule o' mine, that where I dine I sleep, and where I sleep I breakfast. Don't do to churn one's dinner up,—'ow long does't want to feedin' time?"

Mr. Marmaduke was rather posed with his guest's familiarity. He intended to patronise Mr. Jorrocks, whereas the latter seemed to think himself on a perfect footing of equality. Not in the Commission of the Peace, either! But then Duke didn't know that Mr. Jorrocks knew about the stays.

Pulling out a great gold watch, our host asked his wife what time they dined. (Duke included the kitchen department in his magisterial functions.)

"Half-past six, my dear," replied his wife, with great humility.

"Wants twenty minutes to six," observed Mr. Marmaduke, striking the repeater. "Perhaps you'd like to take something before dinner—sandwich and a glass of sherry?"

"Never touch lunches," replied Mr. Jorrocks, disdainfully. "Never know'd a chap good for nothin' wot did. Wonder you don't dine at a reasonable hour, though," added he.

"Faith, we think half-past six rather early," replied Mr. Muleygrubs; "seven's our usual hour—same as my friend Onger's—but we have some neighbours coming, and made it a little earlier on their account."

"Well, it'll be so much the worse for your grub when it does come," observed Mr. Jorrocks; "for I'm well-nigh famished as it is. Howsomever that reminds me that I've a letter to write; and if you'll let me 'ave a peep at your 'Directory,'" continued he, advancing towards a round table well garnished with gilt-edged books, "I'll look out the feller's address, for there's nothin' like doin' things when they're in one's mind, and"——

"'Directory!'" exclaimed Mr. Muleygrubs, "that's a 'Peerage!'"

"Bother your Peerages!" muttered Mr. Jorrocks, chucking the costly volume down; adding, aloud to himself, "Wot business ha' you wi' Peerages, I wonder?"

Mrs. Muleygrubs looked at our Master with an air of commiseration. She wondered what her husband was making such a fuss about such a man for.

"Well, now then," said Mr. Jorrocks, turning short round and buttonholeing his host, while he looked at him as Muleygrubs would at an unwilling witness; "Well, now then, tell me 'bout the foxes—'ave you plenty on 'em?"

"*Plenty!*" replied Muleygrubs, with the utmost confidence, for he had just received a very fine dog one from the well-known Mr. Diddler, of Leadenhall Market, who, by dint of stealing back as fast as he supplies, manages to carry on a very extensive business with a very small stock in trade.

"*Plenty!*" repeated Muleygrubs, with the same confident tone.

"That's *good*," said Mr. Jorrocks, winking and poking him in the ribs; "that's *good*—for though I'm 'appy to dine wi' people, yet still the 'unt is the real thing I comes for; and I always says to folks wot ask me to stir hup their covers, 'Now, don't let us 'ave any 'umbug. If you haven't foxes,' say I, 'don't pretend that you 'ave, for the truth must out, if my 'ounds come, and it will only be addin' the wice o' falsehood to the himputation o' selfishness, sayin' you 'ave them if you 'aven't.'"

"Just so," assented Mr. Muleygrubs, congratulating himself on having excused himself from either charge.

Mr. Jorrocks, having thus broken the ice, proceeded, in a most energetic manner, to give Mr. Muleygrubs his opinions upon a variety of subjects connected with the chase, the breeding and rearing of hounds, the difference of countries, the mischief of too much interference, killing above ground and digging, uncertainty of scent, signs and indications, with a glance at the impositions of keepers, all of which, being Hebrew to Mrs. Muleygrubs, and very nearly Hebrew to her husband, caused her to slink quietly away with her chicks, leaving her husband to the mercy of the "extraordinary man" he had been so indiscreet as invite.

Poor Mr. Muleygrubs couldn't get a word in sideways, and was sitting the perfect picture of despair, when *rumble, dumble, dumble, dumble*, went a great gong, startling Mr. Jorrocks, who thought it was another hurricane.

"An old-fashioned custom we still preserve," said Mr. Marmaduke casually, observing Mr. Jorrocks's astonishment; "that gong was brought by one of my ancestors from the holy wars—shall I show you to your room?"

"If you please," said Mr. Jorrocks.

Our Master, of course, had the state room. It was a large gloomy apartment, with a lofty four-post bed, whose top hangings were made of green silk, and curtains of green moreen.

"Here's a fine twopenny 'ead and farthin' tail," observed Mr. Jorrocks, whisking his candle about as he examined it.

The absence of fire, and the coldness of the apartment holding out little inducement for dallying, Mr. Jorrocks was soon in his blue coat and canaries, and returned to the drawing-room just as the stiff-necked boy announced Mr., Mrs., and Miss Slowan, who were quickly followed by Mr. and Miss De Green, who apologised for the absence of Mrs. De Green, who was suffering under a violent attack of tic-doloreux.

The Rev. Jacob Jones having combed his hair and changed his shoes in the entrance, announced himself, and Professor Girdlestone, a wandering geologist, having dressed in the house, the party was complete, and Mr. Muleygrubs gave two pulls at the bell, while the party sat staring at each other, or wandering moodily about as people at funerals and set parties generally do.

"Dinner is sarved!" at length exclaimed the stiff-necked foot-boy, advancing into the centre of the room, extending his right arm like a guide-post. He then wheeled out, and placed himself at the head of a line of servants, formed by the gentleman Mr. Jorrocks had seen in the yard; a square-built old man, in the Muleygrubs livery of a coachman; Mr. De Green's young man in pepper-and-salt, with black velveteens; and Mr. Slowan's ditto, in some of his master's old clothes. These lined the baronial hall, through which the party passed to the dining-room. Muleygrubs (who was now attired in a Serjeant's coat, with knee-buckled breeches and black silk stockings) offered his arm to Mrs. Slowan, Mr. De Green took Miss Slowan, the Professor paired off with Miss De Green, and Mr. Jorrocks brought up the rear with Mrs. Muleygrubs, leaving Jacob Jones and Mr. Slowan to follow at their leisure. This party of ten was the result of six-and-twenty invitations.

* * * * * * *

"Vot, you've *three* o' these poodered puppies, have you?" observed

Mr. Jorrocks, as they passed along the line; adding, "You come it strong!'

"DINNER IS SARVED."

"We can't do with less," replied the lady, the cares of dinner strong upon her.

"*Humph!* Well, I doesn't know 'bout that," grunted Mr. Jorrocks, forcing his way up the room, seizing and settling himself into a chair on his hostess' right; "Well, I doesn't know 'bout that," repeated he, arranging his napkin over his legs, "women waiters agin the world, say I! I'll back our Batsay, big and 'ippy as she is, to beat any two fellers at waitin'."

Mrs. Muleygrubs, anxious as she was for the proper arrangement of her guests, caught the purport of the foregoing, and, woman-like, darted a glance of ineffable contempt at our friend.

Our Master, seeing he was not likely to find a good listener at this interesting moment, proceeded to reconnoitre the room, and make mental observations on the unaccustomed splendour.

The room was a blaze of light. Countless compos swealed and simmered in massive gilt candelabras, while ground lamps of various forms lighted up the salmon-coloured walls, brightening the countenances of many ancestors, and exposing the dullness of the ill-cleaned plate.

The party having got shuffled into their places, the Rev. Jacob Jones said an elaborate grace, during which the company stood.

"I'll tell you a rum story about grace," observed Mr. Jorrocks to Mrs. Muleygrubs, as he settled himself into his seat, and spread his napkin over his knees. "It 'appened at Croydon. The landlord o' the Grey-

'ound told a wise waiter, when a Duke axed him a question, always to say Grace. According the Duke o' Somebody, in changin' osses, popped his 'ead out o' the chay, and inquired wot o'clock it was.—' For wot we're a goin' to receive the Lord make us truly thankful,' replied the waiter."

Mrs. Muleygrubs either did not understand the story, or was too intent upon other things ; at all events, Mr. Jorrocks's *haw ! haw ! haw !* was all that greeted its arrival.—But to dinner.

There were two soups—at least two plated tureens, one containing pea-soup, the other mutton-broth. Mr. Jorrocks said he didn't like the latter, it always reminded him of " a cold in the 'ead." The pea-soup he thought werry like oss-gruel ;—that he kept to himself.

*   *   *   *   *   *   *

" Sherry or *My*-dearer ? " inquired the stiff-necked boy, going round with a decanter in each hand, upsetting the soup-spoons, and dribbling the wine over people's hands.

While these were going round, the coachman and Mr. De Green's boy entered with two dishes of fish. On removing the large plated covers, six pieces of skate and a large haddock made their appearance. Mr. Jorrocks's countenance fell five-and-twenty per cent., as he would say. He very soon despatched one of the six pieces of skate, and was just done in time to come in for the tail of the haddock.

*   *   *   *   *   *   *

" The Duke 'ill come on badly for fish, I'm thinkin'," said Mr. Jorrocks, eyeing the empty dishes as they were taken off.

" Oh, Marmaduke don't eat fish," replied Mrs. M.

" Oh, I doesn't mean your Duke, but the Duke o' Rutland," rejoined Mr. Jorrocks.

Mrs. Muleygrubs didn't take.

" Nothin' left for *Manners*, I mean, mum," explained Mr. Jorrocks, pointing to the empty dish.

Mrs. Muleygrubs smiled, because she thought she ought, though she did not know why.

" Sherry or My-dearer, sir ? " inquired the stiff-necked boy, going his round as before.

Mr. Jorrocks asked Mrs. Muleygrubs to take wine, and having satisfied himself that the sherry was bad, he took My-dearer, which was worse.

" Bad ticket, I fear," observed Mr. Jorrocks aloud to himself, smacking his lips. " Have ye any swipes ? "

" Sober-water and Seltzer-water," replied the boy.

" 'Ang your sober-water ! " growled Mr. Jorrocks.

" Are you a hard rider, Mr. Jorrocks ? " now asked his hostess, still thinking anxiously of her dinner.

" *Ardest in England*, mum," replied our friend confidently, muttering aloud to himself, " may say that, for I never goes off the 'ard road if I can 'elp it."

*   *   *   *   *   *   *

After a long pause, during which the conversation gradually died out, a kick was heard at the door, which the stiff-necked foot-boy having

x

replied to by opening, the other boy appeared, bearing a tray, followed by all the other flunkeys, each carrying a silver-covered dish.

" Come *that's* more like the thing," said Mr. Jorrocks aloud to himself, -eyeing the procession.

A large dish was placed under the host's nose, another under that of Mrs. Muleygrubs.

" Roast beef and boiled turkey ? " said Mr. Jorrocks to himself, half inclined to have a mental bet on the subject. " May be saddle o' mutton and chickens," continued he, pursuing the speculation.

Four T. Cox Savory side-dishes, with silver rims and handles, next took places, and two silver-covered china centre dishes completed the arrangement.

" You've lots o' plate," observed Mr. Jorrocks to Mrs. Muleygrubs, glancing down the table.

" Can't do with less," replied the lady.

Stiffneck now proceeded to uncover, followed by his comrade. He began at his master, and, giving the steam-begrimed cover a flourish in the air, favoured his master's bald head with a hot shower-bath. Under pretence of admiring the pattern, Mr. Jorrocks had taken a peep under the side-dish before him, and seeing boiled turnips, had settled that there was a round of beef at the bottom of the table. Spare ribs presented themselves to view. Mrs. Muleygrubs's dish held a degenerate turkey, so lean and so lank that it looked as if it had been starved instead of fed. There was a rein-deer tongue under one centre dish, and sausages under the other. Minced veal, forbidding-looking *Rissoles*, stewed celery, and pigs' feet occupied the corner dishes.

" God bless us ! what a dinner ! " ejaculated Mr. Jorrocks, involuntarily.

" Game and black-puddings coming, isn't there, my dear ? " inquired Mr. Muleygrubs of his wife.

" Yes, my dear," responded his obedient half.

" ' Murder most foul, as in the best it is ;
But this most foul, base, and unnattaral,' "

muttered Mr. Jorrocks, running his fork through the breast of the unhappy turkey. " Shall I give you a little *ding dong ?* "

" It's turkey," observed the lady.

" True ! " replied Mr. Jorrocks ; " *ding dong's* French for turkey."

" Are yours good hounds, Mr. Jorrocks ? " now asked the lady, thinking how awkwardly he was carving.

" *Best goin'*, mum ! " replied our friend. " Best goin', mum. The Belvoir may be 'andsomer, and the Quorn patienter under pressure, but for real tear-'im and heat-'im qualities, there are none to compare wi' mine. They're the buoys for making the foxes cry Capevi ! " added our friend, with a broad grin of delight on his ruddy face.

" Indeed," mused the anxious lady to whom our friend's comparisons were all gibberish.

" Shall I give anybody any turkey ? " asked he, holding nearly half of it up on the fork preparatory to putting it on his own plate. Nobody claimed it, so our friend appropriated it.

Munch, munch, munch was then the order of the day. Conversation was very dull, and the pop and foam of a solitary bottle of 40s-champagne, handed round much after the manner of liqueur, did little towards promoting it. Mr. Jorrocks was not the only person who wondered "what had set him there." Mrs. Muleygrubs attempted to relieve her agonies of anxiety by asking occasional questions of her guest.

"Are yours greyhounds, Mr. Jorrocks?" asked she with the greatest simplicity.

"No; greyhounds, no: what should put that i' your 'ead?" grunted our Master with a frown of disgust; adding, as he knawed away at the stringy drumstick, "wouldn't take a greyhound in a gift."

The turkey being only very so-so, and the rein-deer tongue rather worse, Mr. Jorrocks did not feel disposed to renew his acquaintance with either, and placing his knife and fork resignedly on his plate, determined to take his chance of the future. He remembered that in France the substantials sometimes did not come till late on.

Stiffneck, seeing his idleness, was presently at him with the dish of mince.

Mr. Jorrocks eyed it suspiciously, and then stirred the sliced lemon and meat about with the spoon. He thought at first of taking some, then he thought he wouldn't, then he fixed he wouldn't. "No," said he, "no," motioning it away with his hand, "no, I likes to chew my own meat."

The *rissoles* were then candidates for his custom.

"Large marbles," observed Mr. Jorrocks aloud to himself—"large marbles," repeated he, as he at length succeeded in penetrating the hide of one with a spoon. "Might as well eat lead," observed he aloud, sending them away too.

"I often thinks now," observed he, turning to his hostess, "that it would be a good thing, mum, if folks would 'gree to give up these stupid make-believe side-dishes, mum, for nobody ever eats them, at least if they do they're sure to come off second best, for no cuk that ever was foaled can do justice to sich a wariety of wittles."

"O! but, Mr. Jorrocks, how could you send up a dinner properly without them?" exclaimed the lady with mingled horror and astonishment.

"Properly without them, mum," repeated our master, coolly and deliberately; "properly without them, mum—why that's jest wot I was meanin'," continued he. "You see your cuk 'as sich a multitude o' things to do, that it's hutterly unpossible for her to send them all in properly, so 'stead o' gettin' a few things well done, ye get a great many only badly done."

"*Indeed!*" fumed the lady, bridling with contempt.

"The great Duke o' Wellington—no 'fence to the present one," observed Mr. Jorrocks, with a low bow to the table—"who, I'm proud to say gets his tea o' me too,—the great Duke o' Wellington, mum, used to say, mum, that the reason why one seldom got a hegg well biled was, 'cause the cuk was always a doin' summut else at the same time, and that hobservation will apply purty well to most cuking hoperations."

"Well, then, you'd have no plate on the table, I presume, Mr. Jorrocks?" observed the irascible lady.

"Plate on the table, mum—plate on the table, mum," repeated Mr. Jorrocks, with the same provoking prolixity, "why I really doesn't know that plate on the table's of any great use. I minds the time when folks thought four silver side-dishes made gen'lmen on 'em, but since these Brummagem things turned hup, they go for a bit o' land—land's the ticket now," observed our Master.

While this unpalatable conversation—unpalatable, at least, to our hostess was going on, the first course was being removed, and a large, richly-ornamented cold game-pie made its appearance, which was placed before Mr. Muleygrubs.

"Large tart!" observed Mr. Jorrocks, eyeing it, thinking if he could help himself he might yet manage to make up his lee-way: "thought there was dark puddins comin'," observed he to his hostess.

"*Game* and *black* puddings," replied Mrs. Muleygrubs. "This comes between courses always."

"Never saw it afore," observed Mr. Jorrocks.

Mr. Marmaduke helped the pie very sparingly, just as he had seen the butler at Onger Castle helping a *pâté de fois gras;* and putting as much on to a plate as would make about a mouthful and a half to each person, he sent Stiffneck round with a fork to let people help themselves. Fortunately for Mr. Jorrocks, neither Mr. nor Miss De Green, nor Miss Slowan nor Mr. Muleygrubs took any, and the untouched plate coming to him, he very coolly seized the whole, while the foot-boy returned to the dismayed Mr. Muleygrubs for more. Putting a few more scraps on a plate, Mr. Muleygrubs sent off the pie, lest any one should make a second attack.

By dint of playing a good knife and fork, our friend cleared his plate just as the second course made its appearance. This consisted of a brace of partridges guarding a diminutive snipe at the top, and three links of black pudding at the bottom—stewed celery, potato chips, puffs, and tartlets forming the side-dishes.

"*Humph!*" grunted our friend, eyeing each dish as it was uncovered. "*Humph!*" repeated he—"not much there—three shillins for the top dish, one for the bottom, and eighteen-pence say for the four sides—five and six—altogether—think I could do it for five. Howsomever, never mind," continued he, drawing the dish of game towards him. "Anybody for any *gibier*, as we say in France?" asked he, driving his fork into the breast of the plumpest of the partridges.

Nobody closed with the offer.

"Pr'aps if you'd help it, and let it be handed round, some one will take some," suggested Mr. Muleygrubs.

"Well," said Mr. Jorrocks, "I've no objection—none wotever—only, while these clumsey chaps o' yours are runnin' agin each other with it, the wittles are coolin'—that's all," said our Master, placing half a partridge on a plate, and delivering it up to go on its travels. Thinking it cut well, Mr. Jorrocks placed the other half on his own plate, and taking a comprehensive sweep of the crumbs and bread sauce, proceeded to make sure of the share by eating a mouthful of it. He need not have been alarmed, for no one came for any, and he munched and cranched his portion in peace. He then eat the snipe almost at a bite.

"What will you take next, Mr. Jorrocks?" asked his hostess, disgusted at his rapacity.

"Thank 'ee, mum, thank 'ee," replied he, munching and clearing his mouth; "thank 'ee, mum," added he, "I'll take breath if you please, mum," added he, throwing himself back in his chair.

"Have you killed many hares, Mr. Jorrocks?" now asked his persevering hostess, who was sitting on thorns as she saw an entering dish of blancmange toppling to its fall.

"No, mum, *none!*" responded our Master, vehemently, for he had an angry letter in his pocket from Captain Slaughter's keeper, complaining bitterly of the recent devastation of his hounds—a calamity that of course the keeper made the most of, inasmuch as friend Jorrocks, as usual, had forgotten to give him his "tip."

Our innocent hostess, however, never listened for the answer, for the blancmange having landed with the loss only of a corner tower, for it was in the castellated style of confectionery, she was now all anxiety to see what sort of a savoury omelette her drunken job-cook would furnish, to remove the black puddings at the other end of the table.

During this interval, our Master having thrust his hands deep in the pockets of his canary-coloured shorts, reconnoitered the table to see who would either ask him to take wine, or who he should honour that way; but not seeing any very prepossessing phiz, and recollecting that Mrs. J. had told him the good old-fashioned custom was "wulgar," he was about to help himself from a conveniently-placed decanter, when Stiffneck, seeing what he was at, darted at the decanter, and passing behind Mr. Jorrocks's chair, prepared to fill to his holding, when, missing his aim, he first sluiced our Master's hand, and then shot a considerable quantity of sherry down his sleeve.

"Rot ye, ye great lumberin' beggar!" exclaimed Mr. Jorrocks, furiously indignant; "Rot ye, do ye think I'm like Miss Biffin, the unfortunate lady without harms or legs, that I can't 'elp myself?" continued he, dashing the wet out of his spoon cuff. "Now, that's the wust o' your flunkey fellers," continued he in a milder tone to Mrs. Muleygrubs, as the laughter the exclamation caused had subsided. "That's the wust o' your flunkey fellers," repeated he, mopping his arm; "they know they'd never be fools enough to keep fellers to do nothin', and so they think they must be constantly meddlin'. Now, your women waiters are quite different," continued he; "they only try for the useful, and not for the helegant. There's no flash 'bout them. If they see a thing's under your nose, they let you reach it, and don't bring a dish that's steady on the table round at your back to tremble on their 'ands under your nose. Besides," added your Master, "you never see a bosky Batsay waiter, which is more than can be said of all dog un's."

"But you surely couldn't expect ladies to be waited upon by women, Mr. Jorrocks," exclaimed his astonished hostess.

"I would though," replied our Master, firmly, with a jerk of his head— "I would though—I'd not only 'ave them waited upon by women, but I'd have them served by women i' the shops, 'stead o' those nasty dandified, counter-skippin' Jackanapes's, wot set up their himperences in a way that makes one long to kick 'em."

"How's that, Mr. Jorrocks?" asked the lady with a smile, at his ignorance.

MR. JORROCKS GETS A LITTLE "MY-DEARER" DOWN HIS SLEEVE.

"'Ow's that, mum?" repeated our Master—"'Ow's that? Why, by makin' you run the gauntlet of pr'aps a double row o' these poopies, one holloain' out—'Wot shall I show you to-day, mum?' Another, 'Now, mum! French merino embroidered robes!' A third, 'Paisley and French wove shawls, mum! or Russian sables! chinchillas! hermines!' or 'Wot's the next harticle, mum?' as if a woman's—I beg pardon—a lady's wants were never to be satisfied—Oh dear, and with Christmas a comin' on," shuddered Mr. Jorrocks, with upraised hands; "wot a lot o' squabbles and contentions 'ill shortly be let loose upon the world— bonnets, ribbons, sarsnets, bombazeens, things that the poor paymasters expected 'ad come out of the 'ouse money, or been paid for long ago."

While Mr. Jorrocks was monopolising the attention of the company by the foregoing domestic "lector" as it may be called, the denounced domestics were clearing away the sweets, and replacing them with a dish of red herrings, and a very strong-smelling, brown soapey-looking cheese.

Our Master, notwithstanding his efforts, being still in arrear with his appetite, thought to "fill up the chinks," as he calls it, with cheese, so he took a liberal supply as the plate came round—nearly the half of it in fact.

He very soon found out his mistake. It was strong, and salt, and leathery, very unlike what Paxton and Whitfield supplied him with.

"Good cheese! Mr. Jorrocks," exclaimed his host, up the table; "good cheese, eh?"

"*Humph!*" grunted our Master, munching languidly at it.

"Excellent cheese, don't you think so, Mr. Jorrocks?" asked his host, boldly.

"C-h-i-e-l-dren," drawled our Master, pushing away his unfinished plate, "would eat any q-u-a-a-n-tity of it."

The clearing of the table helped to conceal the ill-suppressed titter of the company.

And now with the dessert came an influx of little Muleygrubs, who had long been on guard in the passage intercepting the return viands, much to the nurse's annoyance, lest they should stain their red-ribboned white frocks, or disorder their well-plastered hair. The first glare of light being out of their eyes, they proceed to distribute themselves according to their respective notions of good-natured faces; Magdalene Margery going to Mrs. Slowan, Leonora Lucretia to Miss De Green, and Victoria Jemima to Mr. Jorrocks, who forthwith begins handling her as he would a hound.

"And 'ow old are you, Sir?" asks he, mistaking her sex.

"That's a girl," explained Mrs. Muleygrubs; "say four, my dear."

Mr. Jorrocks—"Charmin' child!" (aloud to himself) "little bore."

"And wot do they call you, my little dear?" asked he; "'Gravity,'—'Notable,'—'Habigail,'—'Mischief,' p'r'aps?" added he, running over the names of some of his lady hounds.

"No: Victoria,"—"Victoria, what?" asked mamma.

"Victoria Jemima," lisped the child.

"Ah, Wictoria Jemima," repeated Mr. Jorrocks. "Wictoria Jemima—Wictoria arter the Queen, I presume; Jemima arter who? arter mamma, I des say."

Mrs. Muleygrubs smiled assent.

"Werry purty names both on 'em," observed Mr. Jorrocks.

"And 'ow many pinches did the nus give your cheeks to make them this pretty pink?" asks our Master, making a long arm at the figs.

"*Thre-e-e,*" drawled the child.

"*Hush! nonsense!*" frowned Mrs. Muleygrubs, holding up a forefinger.

"She *d-i-i-i-d!*" whined the child, to the convulsion of the company.

"*No, no, no,*" responded Mrs. Muleygrubs, with an ominous shake of the head, and trying to direct her attention to a dish of sticky sweets that were just placed within reach.

"How many children have you, Mr. Jorrocks?" now asked the lady thinking to pay him off for some of his *gaucheries*.

THE JUVENILE MULEYGRUBS.

"'Ow many chi-e-l-dren 'ave I, mum," repeated Mr. Jorrocks, thoughtfully. "'Ow many chi-e-l-dren 'ave I. Legally speakin', mum, *none*."— "Chi-e-l-dren," continued our Master, dry-shaving his stubbly chin, "are certain cares, but werry uncertain comforts, as my old mother said when I hupset her snuff-box into the soup."

"Oh dear, I'm afraid you've been a sad mischievous boy, Mr. Jorrocks," observed the lady, motioning Stiffneck to put the almond-backed spongecake rabbit straight on the table.

"Poopeys and buoys never good for nothin' unless they are—'Opes yours are well found that way?"

The enquiry was lost upon the lady, who was now in a state of desperate tribulation at seeing Stiffneck secundus bent on placing a second course sweet on the table instead of the dessert dish. A significant cough, and a slight inclination of the head drew Stiffneck's attention to the mistake, and our hostess has at length the satisfaction of seeing all things in their right places. Apples, pears, foreign grapes, all sorts of unwholesome fruit, having been duly handed round, the wine next set out on its travels; and Mr. Jorrocks, who had looked in vain for a water-biscuit, again turned his attention to the now lip-licking child.

"Well, my little dear," said he, stroking down her head, and then tempting her to rise to a piece of sponge-cake held above her nose, " well, my little dear," repeated he, giving her it, " do you like barley-sugar? "

" Yeth, and thugar candy," lisped the child.

Mr. Jorrocks—" Ah, sugar candy; sugar candy's grand stuff. I sell sugar candy."

Victoria Jemima (in amazement).—" Thell thugar candy! I thought you were a gempleman! "

Mr. Jorrocks—" A *commercial* gen'leman, my dear."

Victoria Jemima—" Not a great gempleman like Pa? "

Mr. Jorrocks (with humility)—" No; not a great gempleman like Pa. He's a Peerage man, I'm only a Post Hoffice Directory one," Mr. Jorrocks looking slyly at his host as he said it. "Howsomever, never mind," continued our Master, helping himself liberally as the fleet of bottles again anchored before him, " Howsomever, never mind, when you comes to see me at Andley Cross, I'll give you a pund o' sugar candy, and show you my 'ounds," added he, passing the bottles.

" *And the bear!* " exclaimed the delighted child.

"Bear, my dear! I've no bear," replied Mr. Jorrocks soberly.

Mrs. Muleygrubs (with a frown, and a fore-finger held up as before)— " *Hush, Victoria Jemima!* don't talk nonsense."

Victoria Jemima (pouting)—" W-a-l-e m-a-a-r, you know you said Mr. Jonnocks was next *door* to a bear."

Mrs. Muleygrubs, whose quick apprehension saw the mischief her daughter was drawing up to, cannoned a smiling glance at Mrs. Slowan off on Miss De Green on the opposite side of the table, and rose, vowing as she drove the party out before her, that one ought " *never* to say any thing before children."

CHAPTER XL.

THE TWO PROFESSORS.

THE ladies being gone, the usual inquiries of " Are you warm enough here, sir? " " Won't you take an arm-chair? " " Do you feel the door? " having been made and responded to, the party closed up towards Mr. Muleygrubs, who now assumed the top of the table, each man sticking out his legs, or hanging an arm over the back of his chair, as suited his ease and convenience. Mr. Jorrocks being the stranger, the politeness of the party was directed to him.

" Been in this part of the country before, sir? " inquired Professor Girdlestone, cornering his chair towards Professor Jorrocks.

" In course I 'ave," replied Mr. Jorrocks; " I 'unts the country, and am in all parts of it at times—ven I goes out of a mornin' I doesn't know where I may be afore night."

" Indeed! " exclaimed the professor. " Delightful occupation! " continued he: " what opportunities you have of surveying nature in all her moods, and admiring her hidden charms! Did you ever observe the extraordinary formation of the hanging rocks about a mile and a half to the east of this? The ——"

" I ran a fox into them werry rocks, I do believe," interrupted Mr. Jorrocks, brightening up. " We found at Haddington Steep, and ran through Nosterley Firs, Crampton Haws, and Fitchin Park, where we had a short check, owin' to the stain o' deer, but I hit off the scent outside, like a workman as I am, and we ran straight down to these werry rocks, when all of a sudden th' 'ounds threw up, and I was certain he had got among 'em. Vell, I gets a spade and a tarrier, and I digs, and digs, and houks as my Scotch 'untsman calls it till near night, th' 'ounds got starved, th' 'osses got cold, and I got the rheumatis, but, howsomever, we could make nothin' of him; but I——"

" Then you would see the geological formation of the whole thing," interposed the professor. " The carboniferous series is extraordinarily developed. Indeed I know of nothing to compare with it, except the Bristol coal-field, on the banks of the Avon. There the dolomitic conglomerate, a rock of an age intermediate between the carboniferous series and the lias, rests on the truncated edges of the coal and mountain limestone, and contains rolled and angular fragments of the latter, in which are seen the characteristic mountain limestone fossils. The geological formation——"

" Oh, I doesn't know nothin' about the geo-nothin' formation o' the thing," interposed Mr. Jorrocks hastily, " nor does I care; I minds the top was soft enough, as most tops are, but it got confounded 'ard lower down, and we broke a pick-axe, a shovel, and two spades afore we were done, for though in a general way I'm as indifferent 'bout blood as any one, seein' that a fox well fund w'c me is a fox as good as killed, and there is not never no fear o' my 'ounds bein' out o' blood, for though I says it, who p'raps shouldn't, there's no better 'untsman than I am, but some'ow this begger had riled me uncommon, 'avin' most pertinaciously refused to brik at the end o' the cover I wanted, and then took me a dance hup the werry steepest part o' Higham Hill, 'stead o' sailing plisantly away over Somerby water meadows, and so on to the plantations at Squerries——"

"That's the very place I've been cudgelling my brains the whole of this blessed day to remember," exclaimed the Professor, flourishing his napkin. "That's the very place I've been cudgelling my brains the whole of this blessed day to remember. A mile and a half to the east of Squerries—no, south-east of Squerries, is a spring of carbonic acid gas, an elastic fluid that has the property of decomposing many of the hardest rocks with which it comes in contact, particularly that numerous class in whose composition felspar is an ingredient, it renders the oxide of iron soluble in water, and contributes to the solution of calcareous matter; I——"

"*You don't say so!*" interrupted Mr. Jorrocks, "I wish I'd 'ad a bucket on it wi' me, for I really believe I should ha' got the fox, for though I holds with Beckford, that 'ounds 'ave no great happetite for foxes longer nor they're hangry with 'em, yet in a houk, as we expects each dig to be the last, one forgets while one's own hanger's risin, that theirs is coolin', and though we worked as if we were borin' for a spring——"

"That's *very* strange!" now interrupted Mr. Marmaduke, who had been listening attentively all the time, anxious to get a word in sideways. "That's *very* strange! Old Tommy Roadnight came to me one morning for a summons against Willy Udal for that very thing. He would have it that Willy had bored the rock to draw the water from his well. Now I as a justice of the peace of our sovereign lady the Queen—perhaps you are not in the Commission of the Peace, are you, Mr. Jorrocks?" inquired Mr. Muleygrubs again.

"*Not I,*" replied Mr. Jorrocks, carelessly.

"Well, never mind, perhaps you may get in some day or other," observed the consoling justice; "but as I was saying, I as a county magistrate, with the immense responsibility of the due administration of the laws, tempered always with mercy, without which legislation is intolerant and jurisprudence futile,—I, I say, did not feel justified in issuing my summons under my hand and seal for the attendance of the said William Udal, at the suit of the said Thomas Roadnight, without some better evidence than the conjecture of the said William, besides, perhaps, you are not aware that the trespass act, as it is termed, should rather be called the wilful damage act, for the J. P. has to adjudicate more on the damage actually sustained by the trespass, than on the trespass itself, indeed without damage there would seem to be no trespass, therefore I felt· unless the said Thomas Roadnight could prove that the said William Udal really and truly drew off the said water——"

"*Con-*found your water!" interrupted Mr. Jorrocks; "give us the *wine*, and let's have a toast: wot say you to fox'-unting?"

"With all my heart," replied Mr. Muleygrubs, looking very indignant, at the same time helping himself and passing the decanters. "Upon my word," resumed he, "the man who administers justice fairly and impartially has no easy time of it, and were it not for the great regard I have for the Lord-Lieutenant and my unbounded loyalty to the Queen, I think I should cease acting altogether."

"Do," exclaimed Mr. Jorrocks eagerly, "and take to 'unting instead, —make you an honorary member of my 'unt,—far finer sport than sittin' in a 'ot shop with your 'at on;

> "'Better to rove in fields for 'ealth unbought,
> Than fee the Doctor for a nauseous draught.'"

Mr. Muleygrubs did not deign a reply.

The wine circulated languidly, and Mr. Jorrocks in vain tried to get up a conversation on hunting. The professor always started his stones or Mr. Muleygrubs his law, varied by an occasional snore from Mr. Slowan, who had to be nudged by Jones every time the bottle went round. Thus they battled on for about an hour.

"Would *you* like any more wine?" at length inquired Mr. Muleygrubs, with a motion of rising.

"Not any more I'm obleged to you," replied the obsequious Mr. Jacob Jones, who was angling for the chaplaincy of Mr. Marmaduke's approaching shrievalty.

"*Just another bottle!*" rejoined Mr. Jorrocks, encouragingly.

"Take a glass of claret," replied Mr. Muleygrubs, handing the jug to our Master.

"Rayther not, thank ye," replied Mr. Jorrocks, "not the stuff for me.—By the way now, I should think," continued Mr. Jorrocks, with an air of sudden enlightenment, "that some of those old ancient hancestors o' yours have been fond o' claret."

"Why so?" replied Mr. Muleygrubs, pertly.

"Doesn't know," replied Mr. Jorrocks, musingly, "but I never hears your name mentioned without thinking o' small claret. But come, let's have another bottle o' black strap—*it's good strap*—sound and strong—gót wot I calls a good grip o' the gob."

"Well," said Mr. Muleygrubs, getting up and ringing the bell, "if you must, you must, but I should think you have had enough."

"PORT WINE!" exclaimed he, with the air of a man with a dozen set out, to his figure footman as he answered the bell.

"Yes, sir," said the boy, retiring for the same.

"Letter from the Secretary of State for the HOME Department," exclaimed Stiffneck, re-entering and presenting Mr. Muleygrubs with a long official letter on a large silver tray.

"Confound the Secretary of State for the Home Department!" muttered Mr. Muleygrubs, pretending to break a seal as he hurried out of the room.

"*That's a rouse!*" (*ruse*,) exclaimed Mr. Jorrocks, putting his forefinger to his nose, and winking at Mr. De Green—"*gone* to the cellar."

"Queer fellow, Muleygrubs," observed Mr. De Green.

"What a dinner it was!" exclaimed Mr. Slowan.

"'Ungry as when I sat down," remarked Mr. Jorrocks.

"All flash," rejoined Professor Girdlestone.

"I pity his wife," observed Jacob Jones, "they say he licks her like fun."

"Little savage," rejoined Mr. Jorrocks, "should like to make a drag of him for my 'ounds."

The footboy at length appeared bringing the replenished decanter. Mr. Muleygrubs returned just as the lad left the room.

Having resumed his seat, Mr. Jorrocks rose and with great gravity addressed him as follows :—" Sir, in your absence we have 'ad the plissur o' drinkin' your werry good 'ealth, coupled with the expression of an 'ope that the illustrious 'ouse of Muleygrubs may long flourish in these your ancestral and baronial 'alls," a sentiment so neat and so far from the truth, as to draw down the mirth-concealing applause of the party.

"Mr. Jorrocks and gentlemen," said Mr. Muleygrubs, rising after a proper lapse of time, and holding a brimmer of wine in his hand, "Mr. Jorrocks and gentlemen," repeated he, "if any thing can compensate a public man for the faithful performance of an arduous and difficult office—increased by the prolixity of the laws and the redundancy of the statute-book, it is the applause of upright and intelligent men like yourselves (hear, hear). He who would administer the laws faithfully and impartially, needs the hinward harmour of an approving conscience, with the houtward support of public happrobation (hear, hear). I firmly believe the liberal portion of the unpaid magistracy of England are deserving of every encomium the world can bestow. Zealous in their duties, patient in their inquiries, impartial in their judgments, and inflexible in their decisions, they form a bulwark round the throne, more national and more noble than the coronetted spawn of a mushroom haristocracy."

Mr. M. waited for applause, which, however, did not come. He then proceeded :—

"I feel convinced there is not a man in the commission who would not prefer the tranquillity of private life to the lofty heminence of magisterial dignities, but there is a feeling deeply implanted in the breasts of English gentlemen which forbids the consideration of private ease when a nation's wants have been expressed through the medium of a beloved Sovereign's wishes,—England expects that every man will do his duty!" continued Mr. Muleygrubs, raising his voice and throwing out his right arm.

"Bravo, Grubs!" exclaimed Mr. Jorrocks ; "you speak like Cicero!" an encomium that drew forth the ill-suppressed mirth of the party, and cut the orator short in his discourse.

"Gentlemen," said Mr. Muleygrubs, looking very indignantly at Mr. Jorrocks, "I thank you for the honour you have done me in drinking my health, and beg to drink all yours in return."

"And 'ow's the Secretary o' State for the 'Ome Department ?" inquired Mr. Jorrocks, with a malicious grin, after Mr. Muleygrubs had subsided into his seat.

"Oh, it was merely a business letter—official ! A Fitzroyer in fact."

"Ah !" said Mr. Jorrocks, "that's the gent to whom we're so much indebted for reformin' our street cabs. A real piece o useful legislation that, for the most hexperienced man in London could never tell what a cab would cost." Mr. Jorrocks then proceeded to compare the different expense of town transit, and, with the subject apparently well in hand, was suddenly done out of it by the stone-professor on his mentioning the subject of water-carriage.

"If geologists are right in their conjecture," cut in the professor, "that this country has been drained by large rivers, which were inhabited by gigantic oviparous reptiles, both bivorous and carnivorous, and small insectivorous mammifera, one may naturally conclude that out-of-doors gentlemen like you will often meet with rare specimens of animal antiquity."

"*No, we don't,*" retorted our Master snappishly. "When a man's cuttin' across country for 'ard life, he's got summit else to do than look out for *mammas*. That's 'ow chaps brick their necks," added he.

"*True,*" jerked in Mr. Muleygrubs. "Then comes the coroner's inquest, the jury, the finding, and the deodand," observed the host. "I regard the office of coroner as one of the bulwarks of the constitution. It was formerly held in great esteem, and none could hold it under the degree of knight, third of Edward the First, chapter ten, I think; and by the fourteenth of Edward the Third, if I recollect right, chapter eight, no coroner could be chosen unless he had land in fee sufficient in the same county, whereof he might answer to all manner of people. My ancestor, Sir Jonathan Muleygrubs, whose portrait you see up there," pointing to a bluff Harry-the-Eighth-looking gentleman in a buff jerkin, with a red-lined basket-handled sword at his side, "held it for many years. He was the founder of our family, and ——"

"Then, let's drink his 'ealth," interposed Mr. Jorrocks, finding the wine did not circulate half as fast as he could wish. "A werry capital cock, and every way worthy of his line;" saying which he seized the decanter, and filled himself a bumper. "I wish he'd been alive, I'd have made him a member of our 'unt; and who's that old screw with the beard?" inquired Mr. Jorrocks, pointing to the portrait next Sir Jonathan, a Roman senator-looking gentleman, wrapped in a loose pink and white robe.

"That," said Mr. Muleygrubs, "is my great-grandfather, an alderman of London and a member of Parliament for Tewkesbury."

"I thought you said it was Shakespeare," observed Mr. Jones, somewhat dryly.

"Well," said Mr. Jorrocks, knowingly, "that's no reason why it should not be his great-grandfather too; I should say our 'ost's werry like Shakespeare, partiklar about the 'ead—and, if I recollects right, Shakespeare said summut about justices o' the peace too."

"Tea and coffee wait your pleasure in the drawing-room," observed the stiff-necked footman, opening the door and entering the apartment in great state.

"Cuss your tea and coffee!" muttered Mr. Jorrocks, buzzing the bottle. "Haven't had half a drink; Here's good sport for to-morrow" said he, sipping his wine. "You 'unt with us, in course," observed he to the professor.

" Oh, indeed, no," said Professor Girdlestone, "that is quite out of my line; I am engaged to meet Mr. Lovel Lightfoot, the eminent geologist, to examine the tertiary strata of ——"

" Well, then," interrupted Mr. Jorrocks, " all I've got to say is, if you meet the fox, *don't 'ead him;*" saying which he drained his glass, threw down his napkin, and strutted out of the room, muttering something about justices, jackasses, and fossil fools.

Tea and coffee were enlivened by a collision between the footboys. Stiffneck with the tea-tray made a sudden wheel upon No. 2 with the coffee-tray, and about an equal number of cups and saucers were smashed. The crash was great, but Muleygrub's wrath was greater. "Stupidest beggars that ever were seen—deserve a month a-piece on the treadmill! "

" Weary of state without the machinery of state," Mr. Jorrocks gladly took his chamber-candle to retire to his twopenny head and farthing tail.

CHAPTER XLI.

ANOTHER CATASTROPHE.

No reproving nightmare censured Mr. Jorrocks for over-night indulgence, and he awoke without the symptoms of a headache. His top-boots had got the mud washed off, and his red coat and drab shags stood invitingly at the bed-foot. He was soon in them and downstairs. The active magistrate was before him, however, and they met in the baronial hall.

Mr. Muleygrubs' costume was very striking. A little brown coat with filagree buttons, red waistcoat, white mole-skins, and Wellington boots with wash-leather knee-caps. His Britannia-metal-looking spurs, with patent leather straps were buckled inside. A large breast-pin representing Justice with her scales, secured the ends of a red-striped white neckcloth.

" Good morning, Mr. Jorrocks! " exclaimed our J. P., with extended hand; " I fear you've not slept well, you are down so early ; hope the bed was comfortable, best in the house, barring ——"

" O, quite comfey, thank ye," replied Mr. Jorrocks; "only I have had as much of it as I want, and thought I'd have a turn round your place afore breakfast. It seems a werry fine mornin'."

"Beautiful morning," replied Mr. Marmaduke.

> " ' There is a freshness in the mornin' hair,
>   And life, what bloated ease can never 'ope to share; ' "

replied Mr. Jorrocks. " Let's have a look at your stud."

They then got their hats. First they went to the stable, then to the cow-bier, next to the pig-sty, and looked into the hen-house.

" You haven't a peacock, have ye ? " inquired Mr. Jorrocks.

" No," replied Mr. Muleygrubs.

" Wonders at that—finest birds possible; my Junks is as wise as most Christians. A peacock on each of those towers would look noble," observed Mr. Jorrocks, turning to the castle as they sauntered along the garden.

Two or three men in blue trousers were digging away; but a garden in winter being an uninteresting object, Mr. Muleygrubs merely passed through it (by the longest way, of course), and striking into a gravel walk by the side of a sluggish stream, made a *détour*, and got upon the carriage-road. Here they suddenly came upon two mechanic-looking men in white aprons and paper caps.

" Holloa, there, you sirs ! where are you going ? " exclaimed Mr. Muleygrubs.

" Poor men out of work, sir," replied the foremost, touching his cap. " Weavers, your honour—been out of work all the winter."

" Poor fellows ! " said Mr. Muleygrubs, soothingly.

" True, I assure you, your honour," rejoined the other. " My comrade's wife's just lying-in of her tenth child, and I've a wife and six bairns all lying ill of the fever."

" Poor fellows ! " repeated Muleygrubs again. " You don't look like common beggars—S. Vs., sturdy vagrants—I. R. incorrigible rogues."

" Necessity's driv us to it, yer honour—never begged afore."

" You'd work if you could get it, I dare say," continued the J. P., in the same consoling strain.

" *Oh, that we would, yer honour !* " exclaimed both. Mr. Muleygrubs smiled, for he had them.

" Come along, then," said he, leading the way to a heap of stones by the side of the carriage-road. " Now," said he, slowly and solemnly, " mark what I say. I am a justice of the peace of our sovereign lady the Queen, charged with the preservation of the peace and the execution of the laws of this great kingdom—hem ! " (The men looked blank.) " There is a hact called the Vagrant Hact," continued Mr. Muleygrubs, " which declares that all persons who, being able to work and thereby maintain themselves and their families, shall wilfully refuse or neglect so to do, shall be deemed rogues and vagabonds, within the true intent and meaning of the hact, and may be committed to hard labour in the house of correction—hem !—Now, gentlemen," said he, " there are two heaps of stones, hard and soft, you are both out of work—there are two hammers, and when you have broken those stones, my bailiff will measure them off and pay you for them, and thus you will get employment, and save a trip to the mill. Take the hammers and set to work."

*   *   *   *   *   *   *

" *Down upon them*, I think," chuckled Mr. Muleygrubs to Mr. Jorrocks, as they returned to the house. " That's one of the few pulls we magistrates have—I keep my avenue in repair and my walks weeded by the vagrants."

" But not for nothin' ? " observed Mr. Jorrocks, inquiringly.

" Oh, yes—they never work long—generally sneak off at the end of an hour or two, forfeiting what they've done. All these heaps," pointing to sundry heaps of stones among the trees, "have been broken by beggars. Shall be able to sell some to the surveyors this year. Working beggars, and employing the new police about one's place occasionally are really the only pulls we justices have."

"Dress the poliss up as flunkeys, I s'pose," observed Mr. Jorrocks.

"Just so," replied Mr. Muleygrubs, "or work them in the garden.

"P-A-A-R *shoots* THE FOX!"

It's by far the best way of disposing of the force," continued Mr. Muleygrubs; "for you see, in a thinly populated district, where each man has a considerable range, you never know where to lay hands on a policeman whereas, about here, they know they have only to send to his worship's to get one directly."

"No doubt it is," replied Mr. Jorrocks, adding, aloud to himself, as the bearings of the case crossed his mind, "and the best thing for the

Y

thief too. Wonders now if the beggar would let one make earth-stoppers on them—stop the thief o' the world."

In the present instance the police were not of much avail, for the weavers, having seen the justice into his castle, pocketed the hammer-heads and cut their sticks.

Among the group who stood in the baronial hall waiting Mr. Muleygrubs' return was Mr. Macpherson, the wily churchwarden of the neighbouring parish. "Taken the liberty of calling upon you to request your countenance to a subscription for repairing our organ," said he.

"Confound your subscriptions!" interrupted the justice—"my hand's never out of my pocket. Why do you all come to me?"

"We always go to the people of the first consequence first," replied the churchwarden, in a tone more directed to Mr. Jorrocks than to Mr. Muleygrubs.

"Very *kind* of you," replied he, satirically—"kind and considerate both."

"The example of gentlemen in high stations has great influence," replied Mr. Macpherson.

"Then why not go to Sir Harry Martin?"

"Because you are the largest landowner in the parish," replied the Scotchman, in the same "talk-at-him" tone as before.

This was a clencher—proclaimed in his own baronial hall, in the presence of Mr. Jorrocks, as the greatest man and largest landowner in the parish, was something.

"Well," said he, with a relaxing brow, "put me down for a couple of guineas."

"Thank you kindly," replied Mr. Macpherson, taking a horn inkstand out of his pocket, and writing the name Marmaduke Muleygrubs, Esq., J.P., 2l. 2s., at the head of the first column.

"You'd like it put in the papers, I suppose?" observed Mr. Macpherson.

"*Papers!* to be sure!" replied Mr. Muleygrubs, ruffled at the question; "what's the use of my giving if it isn't put in the papers?"

A Jew picture-dealer next claimed the justice's ear. He had a kit-cat of a grim-visaged warrior, with a lace-collar, and his hand resting on a basket-handled sword.

"Got a match for your dining-room por——"

"I'll speak to you after!" exclaimed Mr. Muleygrubs, hastily pushing the purveyor of ancestors aside, and drawing Mr. Jorrocks onward to the breakfast-room.

There was a great spread in the way of breakfast, at least a great length of table down the room. A regiment of tea-cups occupied one end of the table, coffee-cups the other, and the cold game-pie was in the middle. Four loaves, two of white, and two of brown bread, guarded the corners, and there were two butter-boats and four plates of jelly and preserve.

"Come, there's plenty to eat, at all ewents," observed Mr. Jorrocks aloud to himself, as he advanced to greet Mrs. Muleygrubs, and give the little Muleygrubs the morning chuck under the chin. "S'pose you've a party comin this mornin'," continued he, looking at the cups, and then pulling out his watch; "five minutes to ten by 'Andley Cross," said he : "'ounds will be here in twenty minutes—Pigg's werry punctual."

Mrs. Muleygrubs said, "That being a county family, they wished to make themselves popular, and would give a public breakfast to the Hunt."

Mr. Jorrocks said, "Nothin' could be more proper."

*   *   *   *   *   *   *

Five minutes elapsed, and he looked again at his watch,* observing, "that the 'ounds would be there in a quarter of an hour."

"Hadn't we better be doin', think ye?" asked Mr. Jorrocks, impatiently, as Mr. Muleygrubs entered the room after his deal for the ancestor; "'ounds 'll be here in no time."

"I suppose there's no great hurry," observed Mr. Muleygrubs, carelessly.

"'Deed but there is," replied Mr. Jorrocks; "punctuality is the purliteness o' princes, and I doesn't like keepin' people waitin'."

"Well, then," said Mr. Muleygrubs, "we'll ring for the urn."

*   *   *   *   *   *   *

In it came, hissing, for the footmen wanted to be off to the Hunt.

Dry-toast, buttered-toast, muffins, twists, rolls, &c., were scattered down the table, and two stands of eggs flanked the cold game-pie in the centre.

There is no greater nuisance than making a feast and no one coming to eat it,—even Gog and old Magog complained when William the Fourth disappointed the guzzlers in Guildhall:—

> "Said Gog to old Magog, ' Why, fury and thunder !
> There surely is some unaccountable blunder,' " &c.

In vain Mr. Marmaduke played with his breakfast, and pretended to enjoy everything. His eye kept wandering to the window in hopes of seeing some one, even the most unwelcome of his friends, cast up. Still no one arrived, and the stiff-necked boy sat in the baronial hall without being summoned to open the doors. A group of children first ventured to enter the forbidden field in front of the Justice's, emboldened by a mole-catcher, who was combining business with pleasure. A boy on a pony next arrived, and was the object of attention until two grooms appeared, and began to fuss about the stirrups, and rub their horses down with handkerchiefs. Presently more arrived ; then came more ponies, then a few farmers, and at last a red-coat, to the delight of the youngsters, who eyed the wearer with the greatest reverence. Meanwhile Mr. Jorrocks worked away at his breakfast, first at the solids, then at the sweets, diversified with a draught at the fluids.

Four red-coated gentry came cantering into the field, smoking and chattering like magpies. Out rushed the figure footman to enlist them for the breakfast, but the hard-hearted mortals ask for cherry-brandy out-

---

* Reader, if you are a non-fox-hunting housekeeper, and ever entertain fox-hunters, *never let them wait for their breakfasts*. The most sumptuous repast will not compensate for the loss of ten minutes, or even five, at this time of day.

side.   Mr. Jorrocks looked at his watch, and the children raise a cry of
" Here they come ! " as James Pigg and Benjamin were seen rounding a
belt of trees, with the hounds clustered at Pigg's horse's heels, while a
Handley Cross helper on Mr. Jorrocks's horse assisted to whip in.   As
they come towards the front, up goes the window, and Mrs. Muleygrubs
and the children rush to the view.

Pleased with the sight, Mr. Muleygrubs desired the footboy to give the
men a glass of claret a-piece.

" Thank ye, no ! " exclaimed Mr. Jorrocks ; " I'll give them a Seidlitz
pooder a-piece when they gets 'ome."

" Do you love your huntsman, Mr. Jonnocks ? " asked Magdalene
Margery, who was now a candidate for the great man's favour.

" I loves everybody, more or less, my little dear," replied our Master,
patting her plaistered head.

" Well, but would you kith him ? " demanded Victoria Jemima.

" Would you pay for his shoes ? " asked Albert Erasmus, who sported
a new pair himself.

" He wears bouts, my dear," replied our ready friend.

" Do you hunt well, Mr. Jonnocks ?—Are you a good hunter ? " asked
Master Memnon.

" Capital, my dear !—Best in England ! " replied our Master.

" Why don't you shoot the fox, Mr. Jonnocks ? " now demanded
Darius, astonished at the size and number of the pack.   " P-a-a-r shoots
the fox," added he, in a loud tone of confident superiority.

" *Nonsense, Darius ! nothin' of the sort !* " exclaimed the guilty
Muleygrubs.

" You *d-o-o-o,*" drawled Darius, eyeing his parent with a reproving
scowl.

" *Hush !* you foolish boy ! " stamped Marmaduke, looking as if he
would eat him.

" Be bund to say he does," grunted Mr. Jorrocks, aloud to himself,
with a knowing jerk of his head.

" Bless us ! what a many dogs you have ! " exclaimed Mr. Muleygrubs,
anxious to turn the conversation.

" 'Ounds ! if you please," replied our Master.

" Well, *hounds !* " aspirated Mr. Muleygrubs, as if correcting Mr.
Jorrocks's pronunciation :   " Is it possible you know all their names ? "

" Quite possible," replied Mr. Jorrocks, making for the window that
had just been opened.

Giving one of his well-known shrill gallery whistles, the pack caught
sight of their master, and breaking away, dash through the windows,
demolishing the glass, upsetting the children, and seizing all the dainties
left on the breakfast-table of Cockolorum Castle.

Mr. Muleygrubs' was knocked under the table, Mrs. Muleygrubs and
all the little Muleygrubs' hurried out, and the stiff-necked foot-boy had a
chase after Priestess, who ran off with the cold rein-deer tongue.   Three
or four hounds worried the pie, and Ravager—steady old Ravager—
charged through the coffee-cups to get at the rolls.   Altogether, there was
a terrible crash.

Mr. Jorrocks bolted out of the window, and, by dint of whooping and

The Meet at Mr. Muleygrubs.

holloaing, aided by the foot-boy's endeavours, succeeded in drawing off the delinquents, and sending Ben in for his cap, desired him to apologise for not returning to bid his hostess adieu, on the plea that the hounds would be sure to follow him.

The commotion was not confined to the house, and Ethelred the gardener's nerves were so shook, that he forgot where to enlarge the bag fox, which he did so clumsily, that the animal, as if in revenge, made straight for his garden, followed by Jorrocks, and the whole train-band bold, who made desperate havoc among the broccoli and winter cabbages. The poor, confused, half-smothered brute took refuge up the flue, from whence being at length ejected, our "indifferent man about blood" celebrated his obsequies with " ten miles straight on end " honours. He then made a show of drawing again but as " P-a-a-r shoots the fox," we need not state the result.

CHAPTER XLII.

THE GREAT MR. PRETTYFAT.

MR. JORROCKS'S introduction to the "old customer" originated in a very bumptious, wide-margined letter from the great Mr. Prettyfat, deputy surveyor of the wretched forest of Pinch-me-near. Luckily it was a royal forest, for it would have ruined any one else. It had long been " administered " by Mr. Prettyfat, formerly butler to the great Lord Foliage, when that nobleman was at the head of the Woods and Forests; and twenty years had not diminished the stock of ignorance with which Prettyfat entered upon the duties of his office. He had, however, forgotten all about "napkins," and was now a most important stately stomached personage, with royal buttons on a bright blue coat. It was always "her Majesty and I," or, "I will consult with her Majesty's Ministers," or "my Lords Commissioners of her Majesty's Treasury, and I think there should be a new hinge to the low gate," or, "the Secretary of the Treasury and I differ about cutting down the shaken oaks on the North-east Dean, as I think they will recover." Indeed, he would sometimes darkly hint that her Majesty was likely to pay him a visit to inspect his Cochin China and Dorking fowls, for which he was justly famous.

Now the foxes, with their usual want of manners, had presumed upon the Royal forest poultry, and though Prettyfat had succeeded in trapping a good many of them, there was one audacious old varmint that seemed proof, as well against steel, as against the more deadly contents of his blunderbuss barrels. Prettyfat could neither catch him nor hit him. The oftener he blazed at him, the more impudent the fox seemed to become, and the greater pleasure he seemed to take in destruction, generally killing half-a-dozen more fowls than he carried away. Prettyfat then tried poison, but only succeeded in killing his own cat. At length he was fairly at his wit's end. In this dilemma, it occurred to him that Jorrocks was the proper person to apply to, and hearing that he was a grocer in the city, who took a subscription to his hounds in the country, he concluded Jorrocks was a better sort of rat-catcher, who they might employ by the day, month, or year, so with the usual contempt of low people for those who make money, he concocted the following foolscapped sheet of impertinence, which he directed " On her Majesty's service," and sealed, with royal butter-pat sized arms :—

" Pinch-me-near Forest House.

" Sir,

" I am directed by the Right Honourable the Commissioner in charge of her Majesty's Woods and Forests to desire that you will inform me, for the information of the Right Honourable the Lords Commissioners of her Majesty's Treasury, what you will undertake to exterminate the foxes in the Royal Forest of Pinch-me-near for ? Their ravages have been very detrimental to the growth of naval timber, for which purpose alone these royal properties are retained.

" You will, therefore, please to inform me,—

" 1st. What you will undertake to keep the foxes down for by the year ;

" 2ndly. What you will undertake to catch them at per head.

So that the Right Honourable the Commissioner in charge of her Majesty's Woods and Forests may be enabled to give the Right Honourable the Lords Commissioners of her Majesty's Treasury their choice as to the mode of proceeding.

" I am, Sir,
" Your most obedient Servant,
" John Prettyfat,
" Deputy Surveyor.

" To Mr. Jorrocks,
" Handley Cross Spa."

To which Mr. Jorrocks, after a little inquiry, replied as follows :—

" Diana Lodge, Handley Cross

" Dear Prettyfat,

" Yours to hand, and note the contents. I shall be most 'appy to do my possible in the way of punishin' the foxes without any bother with your peerage swells, who would only waste the season, and a great deal of good letter paper in needless correspondence. Life's too short to enter into a correspondence with a great official; but as they tells me it is a most frightful beggarly sort o' country, to which none of the water-drinkers here would go, I must just dust the foxes' jackets with a short pack on bye days, which will enable me to begin as soon as ever you like in a mornin', which arter all is said and done, is the real time for makin' them cry ' Capevi ! ' I does it all for the love o' the thing, but if there are any earths, I shall be obliged by your stoppin' them. Don't stop 'em in mind, or I'll have to inform the Right Honourable the Commissioner in charge of her Majesty's Woods and Forests, for the information of the

Right Honourable the Lords Commissioners of her Majesty's Treasury.
So no more at present from

"Yours to serve,
"JOHN JORROCKS.

"To John Prettyfat, Esq.,
"*Deputy Surveyor,*
"Pinch-me-near Forest House."

And there we will leave Mr. Prettyfat for the present, in order to
introduce another gentleman.

CHAPTER XLIII.

M.F.H. BUGGINSON.

Now, Mr. Jorrocks's bagman, Bugginson, or "representative," as he
calls himself, had, since his master's elevation to the fox-hunting throne,
affected the sportsman a good deal, dressing in cut-away coats, corduroy
trousers, and sometimes even going so far as gosling-green cords and very
dark tops, and talking about our 'ounds, our country, and so on, and this
great swell strayed incautiously, at half-cock (for it was after luncheon),
into Mr. Chaffey's repository at Muddlesworth, in company with a couple
of local swells, when, as bad luck would have it, the worthy auctioneer
was dispersing the " splendid hunting establishment " of Sir Guy Spanker,
under a writ of execution from the Sheriff of Fleetshire. He had got
through the valuable collection of screws, and was just putting up the
first lot of hounds, ten couple of dogs, in the usual flourishing style of
the brotherhood beginning at an outrageous price, and gradually getting
down-stairs to a moderate one, when booted Bugginson and Co. entered.

"What will any gen'leman give for this superb lot of hounds?"
demanded Chaffey, throwing his voice towards Bugginson, "what will
any gen'leman give for this superb lot of hounds, unmatched and
unmatchable?"

"Doubt that," winked Bugginson to Jim Breeze, one of his chums,
intimating that he thought " theirs " were better.

"What will any gen'leman give!" repeated the auctioneer, flourishing
his little hammer, "five 'underd guineas — will any gen'leman give
five 'underd guineas for them?" asked he hastily, as if expecting them
to be snapped up in a moment.

"Four 'underd guineas!

"Three 'underd guineas!

"Two 'underd guineas!

"One 'underd guineas!

"Will any gen'leman give a 'underd guineas for this splendid lot of
dog-hounds—the fleetest, the stoutest, the gamest hounds in England! *No*
gen'leman give *one* 'underd guineas for them!" exclaimed he, in a tone
of reproach. Then apparently recovering his mortification, he proceeded,

" Fifty guineas !

" Forty guineas !

" Thirty !

" Ten !   Will any gen'leman give ten guineas ? " inquired he.

" *Shillings !* " exclaimed Bugginson, knowingly, knocking off the end of his cigar.

" Thank'e, sir ! " exclaimed the auctioneer, glad of an offer.

MR. BUGGINSON'S BID

Bugginson felt foolish.   He wished he " hadn't "—still he thought there was no chance of their going for that.   Chaffey hurried on.

" Ten shillings is only bid !—any advance on ten shillin's ?—going for ten shillin's—any body give more than ten shillin's ! *can't dwell ! must* be sold—*only* ten shillin's bid—third and *last* time for ten shillin's, goin' (tap), *gone.*"

" Going (tap), gone ! "   Ominous words !   What a thrill they send through one's frame. "Going (tap), gone." Oh, dear, who shall describe the feelings of poor swaggering Bugginson thus let in for ten couple of hungry-looking hounds—four or five and twenty inch dogs!— Bugginson, who had never had to do with a dog of any sort in his life, suddenly becoming the owner of a pack of hounds—an M.F.H. like his master. "M.F.H. Bugginson presents his compliments to M.F.H. Jorrocks," &c.

"Deuced cheap," "dog cheap!" exclaimed his now exalted companions.

"Very," simpered Bugginson, wishing he was well out of them.

"Where to, yer 'oner?" now demanded a ragged Irishman, who had seized the great bunch of dogs from the man of the yard as they came from the rostrum.

"Stop," muttered the man of the yard, "the gen'lman 'ill be buyin' some more."

"*Will he*," thought Bugginson, eyeing the unruly lot pulling away in all directions, adding to himself, "catch me at that game again."

"Take them to the 'Salutation,'" said Bugginson pompously, "and tell the ostler to put them into a stable."

"Half a croon, yer 'oner!" demanded the man.

"Half a crown!" retorted Bugginson, "why I only gave ten shillin's for the lot."

"So much the better! Sure, then, yer 'oner can afford to pay me liberal and bountiful."

"But half a crown's out of all reason," retorted Bugginson, angrily; "why it's not fifty yards," shortening the distance one half.

"Raison or no raison," replied Pat, "I'll not take them for less;" and, Bugginson seeing, by the desperate rush some of the hounds made to get at a bunch of comrades now coming to the hammer, that he could do nothing with them himself, was obliged to submit to the extortionate demand.

Though Bugginson was too knowing a hand to exhibit symptoms of mortification at the mess his swagger had got him into, he was not to be persuaded into bidding for any more; and in vain Mr. Chaffey expatiated on the merits of the next lots, intimating his opinion that Bugginson ought at least to make up his twenty couple.

Bugginson simpered, chucked up his chin, haw-haw'd, and thanked him, but was "only making up his number;" and having remained sufficiently long to look as if he was quite unconcerned, he repaired to his hotel, to take another look at the animals, which he thought of turning loose upon the town during the night, when an unfinished letter to his master—we beg pardon, his "principal"—stating who he had seen, who he had "drawn," who he had been told was "respectable," and who the reverse, caused him to alter his plans, and to add a P.S., saying he hoped Mr. Jorrocks would allow him to offer him a Christmas box, in the shape of ten couple of very fine fox-hounds, late the property of Sir Guy Spanker, Baronet, which he had had the good fortune to meet with, and which he would forward by the 9·30 A.M. luggage train, with directions to be passed on to the Lily-white Sand Line, by the 11·20.

"*Con*-found all presents wot eat!" exclaimed Mr. Jorrocks, on reading the announcement. "*Con*-found all presents wot eat!" repeated he, with a hearty slap of his thigh. At first he was half inclined to work the wires, and bid Bugginson keep them himself. On second thoughts, however, he recollected that rope was cheap enough, and as he was drawing some of his hounds rather fine (being desperately addicted to bye-days), with the Pinch-me-near proposal in hand, he thought they might be worth looking at, perhaps. Accordingly, he despatched Pigg to the station, who in due time arrived with what James called "a cannyish lot o' hunds, only they hadn't getten ne neames," names being a thing Bugginson never thought of asking for, or the Sheriff of Fleetshire of supplying. In truth, they looked better than they were; for, like most first lots at a sale, they were anything but the pick of the pack. There were skirters, mute runners, and noisy ones, besides a few worn-out old devils, that could evidently do nothing but eat. These Jorrocks condemned without a hearing, and so reduced the lot to eight couple. Mr. Jorrocks told Pigg they were a draft from the Quorn, with a good deal of the Trueman blood in them; and though James did say he was "warned they'd be good for nout, or they wadn't ha' parted with them at that time of year," still the announcement had a very favourable effect in ingratiating them in Pigg's favour. Thus reinforc'd, Mr. Jorrocks ventured to broach the subject of another bye-day, against which Pigg had lately been protesting, vowing that Jorrocks would have both "husses and hunds worked off their legs afore he knew where he was." To our master's surprise, Pigg didn't make any objection to the forest.

"Wy, wy, sir," replied James, scratching his head and turning his quid, "it winna be a bad place, ar dinna think."

"Vot, you know it, do you?" asked Mr. Jorrocks.

"Why now, ar canna say as how ar ken this forest, but ar kens what a forest is weal enough, and this 'll be gay like arle others, ar's warned."

"All bog and bother," suggested Mr. Jorrocks.

"Arle bog and bother, no! what should put that i' yer head?"

Mr. Jorrocks. "They tell me this one is—"

Pigg. "It winna be like wors, then. When canny ard Lambton hunted our country, arve been i' Chopwell wiles, and the rides were jest like race-coourses."

Mr. Jorrocks (in astonishment). "You don't say so! That'll be a well kept place, then, with great trees growin' as they ought?"

Pigg. "Deil a bit! Deil a bit! The rides was arle they minded. The man o' the woods gat the grass for his cows, and so he kept the rides varra canny. The woods was just like bad nursery grunds—nothin' but switches. They tell me," continued Pigg, "sin' ar come'd away, that they've had the 'Marican reapin' machine at work, mowin' them down."

"You don't say so!" exclaimed Mr. Jorrocks, "wot an age of impruvment this is!"

"Aye," continued Pigg, turning his quid, "and now they're gannin' to growin' a crop o' pea-sticks on the same grund."

"I wish they'd grow faggot sticks," observed Mr. Jorrocks, "for Batsey uses an uncommon lot lightin' the fires; but 'owsomever, never mind, that's not the pint—the pint is, that we'll go to the forest, and take this new lot of 'ounds, and see wot they're made on."

"Wy, wy," replied Pigg, "wy, wy, ar's quite 'greeable."

"Jest you and I," observed Jorrocks; "it's no use takin' Ben."

"Deil a bit!" replied Pigg, with disdain, "deil a bit!"

"You on young Hyson, me on Arterxerxes," continued Mr. Jorrocks.

"Ye'd better ride t'other," replied Pigg; "ye're niver off t'ard husses back."

"Do the great rumblin'-stomached beggar good," replied Mr. Jorrocks; "goes jest as if he 'ad a barrel o' milk churnin' in his inside."

"Wy, wy, sir," replied Pigg, "ye ken best; only, ye see, if ye brick him down, ye see ye'll not can git such another—not i' these parts, at least."

"Oh, never fear," replied Mr. Jorrocks, carelessly, "there are as good fish in the sea as ever came out on it. No man need want a quad. long, wot 'ill pay for one," he continued, hustling the silver vigorously in his pantaloon pocket.

"Wy, wy, sir," replied Pigg, "ye ken best, ye ken best. Then we'll fix it so, and ar'll tak these new hunds i' couples, and a few of our own to show them the way like."

"Jest so," assented Mr. Jorrocks.

And so master and man parted.

CHAPTER XLIV

PINCH-ME-NEAR FOREST.

S if Mr. Jorrocks's hunting appetite grew by what it fed upon, he passed a very restless, feverish night, dreaming of all sorts of hunting casualties, and greatly diturbing Mrs. Jorrocks's repose by his evolutions. At length, thinking he was throwing down a stone wall, to pick up his fox, he set his feet against her with such force as sent her flying out of bed, and so finished the performance. Mrs. J. went off to Belinda's room, and our master got up, though it was only five o'clock. Early as he was, however, Pigg, who had not gone to bed at all, was before him, and when Mr. Jorrocks got down-stairs, he found him at a sumptuous breakfast with Batsey in the back kitchen. Setting Pigg off to the stable, Mr. Jorrocks took his place at the table, and rated Batsey soundly for encouraging a man of Pigg's "unsteady 'abits."

Batsey justified herself on the score of promoting her master's sport. "Pigg," she was "sure was nothin' to her." *She* didn't want to be Mrs. Pigg. Not she, indeed! She could do better than that any day, she 'oped! "*Pigg, forsooth !*" and she bounced about, and banged the butter upon the muffins and toast, as if her feelings were outraged in the extreme. How the dispute might have ended is doubtful, for in the midst of it Batsey gave Mr. Jorrocks a kidney so hot off the fire, that he burnt his mouth, and as he danced about the kitchen floor, unable to retain it, yet unwilling to give it up, she took advantage of the opportunity and slipped quietly away, to have a cry in her own room. Our master then finished his breakfast with a blistered mouth, as best he could, and then followed Pigg to the stable.

It was so dark when Pigg gave Mr. Jorrocks his horse, that our master was obliged to feel along his back to his tail, to be sure that he hadn't got hold of Xerxes instead of Arterxerxes; for though if our friend had been selling him, he would have sworn that Xerxes was far the best of the two—finest oss wot ever was seen, in fact—yet an inconvenient jerk he had with his hind-quarters in his jumps, more than counter-balanced any little additional speed he had over Arterxerxes. It took Mr. Jorrocks more time to get shuffled back into his saddle after a leap on Xerxes, than Arterxerxes would have lost by his steady laborious plodding, to say nothing of the inconvenience of riding on a horse's neck, instead of on his back. But to our story. Pigg, like a prudent man, had coupled the strange hounds with some of their own, or they would have been all over the town in no time. Master and man spurred briskly on, Jorrocks acting whipper-in, and Pigg yoicking and coaxing the hounds to him as best he could. They cleared the town, and got to the Whickenby Gate before the 'pike-man was up; and violent was the clattering, and dread the denunciations that Jorrocks hurled at his white cotton night-capped head, when at length he popped it out to inquire the cause of the row.

Our friends didn't get much use of the hard road for their money, for Pinch-me-near Forest being quite a back-slum sort of place, that nobody ever wanted to see, the roads all seemed to shun it, and it was only by very vague conjectures and speculative cuts that our friends managed to steer towards it at all. Not that the forest itself was worse than any of its Royal brethren; indeed, it was better than some, for Prettyfat neither stole the wood himself, nor knowingly suffered others to steal it, his being the easy do-nothing style of management, that let the trees grow if they liked, or if they didn't like, let them stand still and die, or be blown down and rot at their leisure. He made his reports regularly and fairly, and so long as he got as much money as paid his own salary and the wages of his labourers, he felt he fulfilled all the duties of a faithful servant of the Crown, and did all that a grateful nation could require.

A very rubicund sun at length began to struggle through the dull leaden clouds, gradually revealing hill and dale, fields, fences, and enclosures, the whole paraphernalia of a landscape, just like a child's puzzle-map getting put together.

"Yon's it!" exclaimed Mr. Jorrocks after a careful survey of the now developed scene. "Yon's it!" repeated he, pointing with his ponderous whip towards a dark mass in the distance.

"Ar's warn'd ye, is't," replied Pigg, replenishing his mouth with tobacco. "Ar's warn'd ye is't. It's a gay bit off though."

"*Trot on!*" retorted Mr. Jorrocks anxiously, spurring Arterxerxes vehemently, an insult that the animal resented by a duck of his head and a hoist of his heels.

Bump, bump, trot, trot, squash, splash, swosh, they went through the open fields, over the commons and heaths of a wet, sterile, Pewitey country, which gradually got worse as they neared the stunted brushwood of the straggling forest. At length they came upon a nest of forest squatters, with their wretched mud cabins and rolling fences, by whom they were directed to a smart, well-hung green gate, with a cattle-gap on either side, as the commencement of Mr. Prettyfat's inattentions. Some well-used horse trods, converging towards a gently rising hill on the right, from whence a curl of clear smoke was now rising, favoured the supposition that the representative of Royalty was not far off. Though the morning was in its pride, yet when our friends got to the front of the neat rose-entwined house,—the windows were as white as the rough cast walls—there were no signs of animation of any sort. "The beggar's not hup yet I do believe," observed Mr. Jorrocks, spurring the great splaw-footed Arterxerxes right on to the trimly shaven grass-plot in the centre of the carriage ring. Rising in his stirrups, and clearing his throat with a prolonged *y-e-a-u-u-p !* as he prepared his big whip for execution, he gave such a cannonade of a crack, as sounded through the house and reverberated in the forest.

"Sink, but that's a good 'un!" grinned Pigg, listening to the oft-repeated echoes.

Scarcely were the words out of his mouth, before, bang, went a lattice window up above, and a rival of the red-faced sun appeared beneath the night-capped head of the Deputy-surveyor.

"What are you doin' here?" roared a stentorian voice.

"Rum, ar say! rum!" exclaimed Pigg, thinking he was asking what he would have to drink.

"Doin' 'ere!" replied Mr. Jorrocks, whose ears had served him better. "Doin' 'ere! vy I be come to 'unt the foxes to be sure!"

"Hunt the foxes," retorted Prettyfat, indignantly—"Is *this* a time to come and hunt foxes—none but chimney-sweeps would disturb one at this hour."

"Sink, gin ye'll had mar hus ar'll get off and fight 'im!" exclaimed Pigg, furious at the comparison.

"*Hush !*" said Mr. Jorrocks, "let me talk to 'im."

"Vy, didn't I tell ye I'd come hearly?" asked our Master, rising in his stirrups and speaking in a conciliatory tone.

"Come early," repeated Prettyfat, recollecting the wide margined official, "come early, yes, but you don't call tramplin' on a gen'l'man's grass-plot comin' early, do ye? You don't 'spect to find a fox there."

"Hoot, thou 'ard feul, what's thou grumblin' 'bout thy grass plat for?" demanded Pigg, in a tone of derision.

"Treasonous, traitrous rogues," exclaimed Prettyfat. "I'll hand you over to the law-officers of the Crown."

"Let's off!" ejaculated Jorrocks, catching Arterxerxes short round by the head—"Lets off!—I've no relish for law, still less for hornamentin' the top o' Temple Bar with my 'ead;" so saying our Master spurred through the pack, and treading on a couple of hounds, raised such a clamour as drowned the further observations of the Sylvan Viceroy. Down they dived into the wood again. They had not got very far before they met Prettyfat's perspiring drab-turned-up-with-grease flunky, panting along with a pitchfork in his hand, who exclaimed, on seeing them—"Oh gen'l'men! gen'l'men! you should ha' been here a bit sooner (puff), that tarnation fox has been at the (puff) poultry again."

"You don't say so!" grinned Mr. Jorrocks, pulling short up and standing erect in his stirrups. "You don't say so! Show us the way on 'im, and I'll sarve 'im out. Off with the couples, Pigg," added he, turning to James, who was already on the ground disengaging the draft.

Away they tear in all directions, howling and towling like mad. A shrill blast of the horn gets them into a smaller compass, and Mr. Jorrocks trots on preceded by the man, to show him where he last saw the fox. Old Ravager first drops his stern, feathers, but speaks not, when one of the new noisy ones immediately gives tongue, and the sage taking a fling in advance, gave something between a squeak and a note, which being immediately endorsed by the rest, they drive with an echoing crash into the thick of the forest.   Now our friend's misfortunes commence, for the further they get from the seat of government, the worse the riding becomes.   Impervious thickets, through which hounds meuse, but horses can make no way, soon separate them from the pack, whose music falls fainter and fainter on the ear; our anxious Master pushes on, through the wet sterile sand, or slobby quagmires, impeded ever and anon by a fallen tree—in hopes that a favourable turn may again land him with the pack— "Dash my vig," says he, shortening his hold of Arterxerxes, who all but falls over a fern-concealed log—"Dash my vig, I wish I mayn't brick my neck in this terrible desert—most outlandish place I ever was in."

" It *is* a rum place," observed Pigg, doing the like.

" Ark ! where are they ? " asked Mr. Jorrocks, pulling short up, with his hand to his ear.

" They seem arle oour," replied Pigg; " wish these Quorn dogs may be quite what they oout."

" It's the confounded hecho," observed Mr. Jorrocks, still listening attentively.

" Ar tell ye, they've divided," asserted Pigg.

" Then turn them," rejoined Mr. Jorrocks.

" Torn them thysel'," retorted Pigg, dropping his elbows and starting off at a canter.

" Now where's the man goin' to ! " exclaimed Mr. Jorrocks, eyeing his fast receding huntsman diving into the thicket—" Wot's he a leavin' me 'ere fore ? " continued he, feeling the desolation of his position.   " Wish I may ever find my way out," continued he, looking around on the grey unhealthy scene of stunted desolation.

Thinking to stick to Pigg, at all events, our master set Arterxerxes agoing again, and blobbed on in his deep, black imprints.   Sorry work it was for old Arterxerxes, who was no great hand at going through deep. Jorrocks spurred him, and jagged him, and cropped him, and called him all the great lumberin' henterprizeless beggars he could think of.   In the excess of his energy—he overshot the mark, and kept right on, instead of turning short up a track on the left.   The one he kept, from a uniformly rotten surface, now became alternately soft and hard, the water standing in the hollows like baths, and these, Arterxerxes, as if suspicious of treachery, commenced leaping, but possibly finding the trouble greater than he expected, he soon took to blundering through them, squirting the muddy water about in all directions.   The forest still continued the same forlorn, unprosperous-looking place ; where the wet stood, moss grey, aguish-looking trees were dying by the middle, while higher up, the oaks battled with the briars and other smothering rubbish.   Our Master however was too busy to observe anything of the sort—all he knew was, that it was werry bad riding.   The sound of the horn on the left first

caused him to pause and ponder whether he was on the track of Pigg.
There were footmarks, but not so fresh as his should be. Another
unmistakable twang, and Mr. Jorrocks determined to alter his course.
Where all was so bad, there was nothing to choose. Accordingly he
swung Arterxerxes short round, and turned him up another rushy,
waterlogged track, that seemed to lead in the direction of the horn.
Desperately bad the riding was. The nature of the ground seemed to
change, and from hop-pole-like ash and alder, to be stocked with nothing
but stunted birch. The soil was black and peaty, with here and there
the outline of a long-subsided drain.

"Blow me tight," muttered Mr. Jorrocks, shortening his hold of his
horse, "I wish I mayn't be gettin' bogged," and scarcely were the
words out of his mouth ere Arterxerxes floundered up to the shoulders in
a moss hag, shooting our friend softly over his head on to his side.

"*W-o-a-y oss! W-o-a-a-y!*" roared our Master, now kicking on his
back like a lively turtle, expecting to have the struggling animal a top of
him every moment.

"W-o-a-y oss! w-o-a-a-y!" repeated Jorrocks, jerking himself off to
the side. The horse beat and plunged, and groaned and heaved,
still stemming the black slough of despond, until he got fairly through,
when after standing a second or two to shake himself, he set off at an
unprovoked trot, leaving our master in a most unhappy state of bewilderment as to how he should ever catch him, or get home without him.

"Dash the beggar," groaned Jorrocks, as he saw him rolling his great
hind quarters away in the distance—"Dash the beggar, but I wish I was
a top on 'im, I'd give 'im summut to run for," so saying, our Master
gathered himself together, and skirting the moss hag, commenced the
unpleasant performance of running in top-boots. Squish, squash, splash,
he floundered, now over the insteps, now up to the ankles, now almost up to
the knees. He soon began to sob and sigh—"Oh dear! oh dear!" groaned
he, "did ever mortal man see sich a road—might as well try to run in a
river. And that confounded quad.," continued he, eyeing Arterxerxes
still on the move. "Dash my vig, but I'd give ye summut to run for if I
had 'old on ye—I'd make ye cry 'Capevi!' my frind. Drot the road!"
exclaimed he, as he plunged into a rush-concealed rut, and squirted the
dirty water up into his face. "Well this is a pretty performance,"
continued he, mopping himself with a great crimson bandana—"Beats
all others into fits. *Con*-found these bye-days. They're always gettin'
on me into grief. And now the brute's gone altogether," as the vista
closed without Arterxerxes on the scene. "Ark! I 'ear 'ounds. No,
they're crows. Well, if this isn't a sickener, I don't know wot is—might
as well try to run i' the mud off 'Ungerford stairs, as in this sludge.
Shouldn't like to clean these bouts I know," continued he, looking down
on his black, and all black, tops. A bit of sound ground again tempted
him into a trot, and at length brought him to the rising ground up which
great Arterxerxes had disappeared. "Oh dear! oh dear!" groaned
Mr. Jorrocks, as a stitch in his side suddenly stopped him. "Oh dear!
oh dear! I'm regularly floored. Might as well try to follow Halbert
Smith hup Mont Blanc as Arterxerxes hup this incorrigible mountain;"
so saying our heavily-perspiring Master sought the support of a fallen

willow, and distributing himself equitably among its branches, sofa
fashion, proceeded to bewail his lamentable condition. "Oh dear! oh
dear!" groaned he, "was there ever sich an misfortunit indiwidual as
John Jorrocks! was there ever an independent British grocer made sich a

MR. JORROCKS HAS ANOTHER BYE-DAY.

football on by fortin? Tossed about the world like an old 'at. Tempted
from the 'olesomest, the plisantest, the most salubrisome street i' London,
to take these 'ounds, and then be drawn into this unpardonable wilderness. Nothin' but rushes, and grass that Nebuchadnezzar 'imself would
turn up his nose at. Oh dear! oh dear!" continued he, as his thoughts
reverted to home and Handley Cross, "shall never see my dinner this day.
Torbay soles with Budle cockle sauce, Dartmoor forest mutton, puddin',
and taturs under the meat, 'stead of starvin' in a dreary desert—happed

z

up by cock robins or other benevolent birds ;" a thought that so distracted
our master as to cause him to start and turn in his couch, when the rotten
main prop to his back giving way, he came crashing and smashing to the
ground.

"*There!*" ejaculated Mr. Jorrocks, "*there!*" repeated he, as he lay
among the rotten fragments. "Fallen a 'underd feet from the grund!
Broke every bone in my skin, I *do* believe. Bet a guinea 'at to a 'alf-
crown gossamer I 'aven't a 'ole bone i' my body." So saying our
master having carefully shaken first one limb and then ano..her, to
ascertain the amount of the mischief, rose slowly from the wet ground,
and after anathematising the deceptive unfriendly tree, resumed the tracking
of his horse up the hill. His boots were now well "salivated" as he would
say, and the cold bog-water poached and churned as he went. But if
his feet were cold, his temper was warm, and various were the recreations
he promised Arterxerxes. He would ride "his tail off," then recollecting
how little he had, he "would ride him till he dropped." Then he would
"skin him alive, and make his hide into a hair trunk"—then he would cut
it into whip thongs—next into shoe-strings—finally he would give him to
"the first mugger he met."

As Mrs. Glasse would say, however, "first catch your horse," and this
seemed a remote possibility, for though our master in the course of a two
miles tramp, which he called ten, did get a view of him once, the grass
was of too coarse and uninviting a character to induce the animal to take
more than a passing snatch as he went, which he did at a pace that
seemed well calculated to last for ever. At length our Master was fairly
exhausted, and coming to a part of the forest that ran out into rocks and
sandy heathery hills, he threw himself upon his back on a large flat stone,
and kicking up first one leg and then the other, to let the bog-water out
of his boots, moaned and groaned audibly. Beginning at a guinea, he
bid up to a hundred and twenty, to be back at Handley Cross, and two
hundred and fifty to be back in Great Coram Street, clear of the 'ounds
and all belonging to them. And he vowed that if Diana would only
'ave the kindness to come to his assistance that once, he would never
trouble her with any more of his vagaries. No, *indeed* he wouldn't, he
would sell his 'ounds and his 'osses, burn his boots and his Beckford,
and drive about in a pill-box the rest of his life.

CHAPTER XLV.

A FRIEND IN NEED, &c.

UR Master was interrupted in the midst of his groans and lamentations by a low voice dropping down upon him with a "are you hurt, sir?" and starting up, he encountered the sinister gaze of a haggard-looking man, dressed in a cap and complete suit of dirty grey tweed.

"Are you hurt, sir?" repeated the man, not getting an answer to his former inquiry.

"Hurt, sir!" replied Mr. Jorrocks, eyeing him as though he expected an immediate stand and deliver; "Hurt, sir! No, sir!" clutching his formidable hammer-headed whip, "*I've lost my 'oss.*"

"Oh, that's all, is it?" sneered the man.

"D'ye call that nothin'?" retorted Mr. Jorrocks, bridling up.

"My little gal said she thought you'd broke your back by the noise you were makin'," replied the man.

"Did she?" rejoined Mr. Jorrocks, feeling he had been making a great fool of himself. "Did she? Then tell your little gal she'd made a mistake."

"Then I can't do nothin' for you?" observed the man, after a pause.

"In course you can," replied Mr. Jorrocks; "you can catch my 'oss for me."

"Is he near at hand?" asked the man.

Mr. Jorrocks.—"That I don't know. Far or near, I'll give ye 'alf-a-crown for bringin' 'im to me."

z 2

"Doubt I daren't ventur," replied the man reluctantly.

Mr. Jorrocks.—"Huts, there's nobody to 'urt ye."

"Can't go so far from home," rejoined the man.

Mr. Jorrocks, brightening up—"Wot! you live near 'ere, do ye?"

"Not far off," replied the man, with a jerk of his head, as much as to say "I'm not going to tell you."

Mr. Jorrocks.—"Well, but p'raps you could get me summut to drink, for my 'oss has run away with my monkey, and I'm fit to die of habsolute unquenchable thirst."

The man eyed him suspiciously, and at length drawled out, "What, you've been hunting, have you?"

"'Deed, 'ave I," replied our Master; "started afore daylight."

"It 'ill be Mr. Jorrocks, I dessay," observed the man, with an air of enlightenment.

"Wot, you knows me, do ye!" exclaimed our Master, brightening up.

"Yes, sir—no, sir—that's to say, sir, I know your huntsman, sir—Mr. Pigg, sir."

"Indeed," mused Mr. Jorrocks.

"Mr. Pigg and I are very old friends, sir," continued the man, "very old friends, indeed—most respectable man, Mr. Pigg, sir—most fortunate in having such a servant."

"Humph," grunted Mr. Jorrocks, not being quite so sure of that.

"Finest sportsman in the world, sir," continued the man—"finest sportsman in the world, sir—can do a'most anything—sing a song, dance a jig, grin for baccy, play dominoes, prick i' the belt, or thimble-rig. If that man could have got a spirit license he'd ha' made a fortin. He'd ha' bin the first man o' the day."

"*In*-deed," mused our Master.

"Most accomplished gentleman," continued the speaker—"most accomplished gentleman. I'd rayther have James Pigg for a partner than any man I ever saw."

"And pray may I ax your name?" inquired our Master, curious to know something more of his huntsman's friend.

"O, my name's Turveylow, Tom Turveylow, but he won't know me by that name. Whiskey Jim," added he, dropping his voice with a knowing leer, "is the name he'll know me by."

"I twig," winked our Master. "You 'aven't a drop o' the cretur with ye, 'ave ye?"

"Hard-bye," replied the man, "hard-bye," jerking his thumb over his shoulder.

"Let's at it," said Mr. Jorrocks, brightening up.

"You're safe, I s'pose," hesitated the man.

"Honour bright," replied Mr. Jorrocks; "wouldn't peach if it was ever so—"

"Well, I don't think any friend of Pigg's would," said the man, gaining courage; so saying, he wheeled about, and beckoning Jorrocks to follow him, led the way, across the sharp sandy heath, towards a precipitous range of rocks, whose heights commanded an extensive view over the forest and surrounding country. It was towards their rugged base that they now directed their steps. Passing some large upright stones, that guarded the entrance to a sort of outer court, they came all at once upon the smuggler's cave.

"Bow your head and bow your body," said the man, turning and suiting the action to the word as he reached the frowning portcullis-like rock that guarded the entrance.

"Come on! come on! you've nothin' to fear," cried he, seeing Jorrocks stood irresolute, "there's no honester man in the world than your humble servant."

"Self-praise is no commendation," muttered our Master, going down on all-fours preparatory to creeping under the beetling rock. This let him into the smuggler's ante-room, a cold, damp, dropping den, formed from a natural cavity in the rock. Beyond was a larger, loftier cave, and over a bright wood fire, illuminating the hard walls, was a fine Venetian-shaped girl, in a tight blue bodice and red flannel petticoat, chucking the savoury contents of a frying-pan up in the air.

Her back being turned, she was not aware of the enterers, until her temporary lord and master exclaimed, "Sally! here's old keep-the-tambourine-a-roulin's master."

"Lawk, Jim! 'ow could you bring a gent when I 'aven't got my stockin's on?" exclaimed the lady, whisking round and showing the beautiful symmetry of her delicate white legs. She then turned her lustrous eyes upon our friend and basilisked him with a smile. Mr. Jorrocks stood transfixed. He thought he had never seen a greater beauty. Sir Archy Depecarde's housekeeper was nothing to her.

"Take a seat, sir, take a seat," said the smuggler, sweeping a bundle of nets and snares off a stool—for of course he combined the trade of poacher with that of smuggler—and placing it behind our Master. Mr. Jorrocks did as he was bid, and sat lost in the novelty of the scene, the beauty of the lady, and the savouriness of the pig's-fry she was cooking.

"You'll take your dinner with us, sir, I hope," said the smuggler, possessing himself of our Master's hat and whip. "You'll take your dinner with us, sir, I hope," adding, as he chucked them into a corner, "any friend of Pigg's is welcome here."

"Much plissur," replied Mr. Jorrocks, who all of a sudden waxed "uncommon hungry."

"Get the gent a plate and things, Ann," said the smuggler to the little girl who had reported J.'s vagaries on his back.

The implements of eating were quickly placed on the already set-out table, and our party were presently at work at the fry, which was followed by roast potatoes and a jugged hare, late a tough old denizen of the forest; oat-cake, cheese, and bottled ale completed the repast. Mr. Jorrocks played a most satisfactory knife and fork, declaring, as he topped up with a heavy cannonade of whiskey, that he couldn't have dined better with the Grocers' Company.

"Good stuff that," said the smuggler, with a knowing wink at the bright sparkling whiskey.

"Capital," replied Mr. Jorrocks, replenishing his glass.

"I toast you, sir," said the smuggler, bowing, glass in hand to our master.

"You do me proud," said Mr. Jorrocks, returning the salute.

"Not at all, sir," replied the condescending host. "I believe you to be a most respectable man."

Mr. Jorrocks next looked towards the lady, who acknowledged the compliment with a sweet glance.

The smuggler then, as in duty bound, gave the health of his royal partner, the Queen, after which other loyal and patriotic toasts followed, and Mr. Jorrocks gave the ladies generally, adding, as he leered at his hostess, that he "liked a fine well-flavoured ooman." He then began to get noisy. It was the old story.

"You must (hiccup) with my 'ounds (hiccup), best 'ounds goin' (hiccup), best 'ounds in (hiccup) England. Best 'ounds in (hiccup) Europe—best 'ounds in (hiccup) Europe, Hasia, Hafrica, 'Merica— (hiccup)." Then, as he rolled about on his stool, forgetting there was no back to it, he lost his balance, and kicking up the ricketty table with his toes, came heavily down on his back. What happened after, is matter of uncertainty, for the next thing our Master remembers was finding himself getting transferred from a light-tilted cart on a bright frosty night into a Handley Cross fly, at Rosemary-lane gate; but when he came to pay the man his fare, he found his purse was gone, which he might have thought had dropped out of his pocket into the cart, were it not that his watch was wanting too. However, being at home, he just told Betsy to pay the fare, and clambered up-stairs to bed as if nothing "'ticklar" had happened. And next day Pigg gave such a wonderful account of the run, and how he would have killed the fox half-a-dozen times if he had only had Jorrocks to help him, that our Master, forgetting all his promises to Diana, very soon had another turn at the forest.

CHAPTER XLVI.

THE SHORTEST DAY.

MR. JORROCKS's next adventure in the hunting line originated in a very furious letter from a gentleman, signing himself "John Gollarfield, farmer, Hardpye Hill," complaining bitterly of the devastation of his hen-roost, and calling loudly for vengeance against the foxes. Accordingly our Master made a meet for Hardpye Hill, instead of Langton Pound, as he intended.

The road to the hill lying through some roomy inclosures, and Christmas having let loose its enterprise upon the country, great was the spurting and racing that marked the line there. Mr. Jorrocks, arrayed in his best pink, jogged pompously on with his cavalcade, receiving the marked attention of the country. Arrived at the hill, he turned into a grass field to give his hounds a roll and hear the news of the day—how Miss Glancey was after Captain Small—how Mrs. Buss had captivated old Frill. Then, when the cantering, smoking cover hack

"Mind the Bull."

swells came up, they resolved themselves into a committee of taste, scrutinising this hound and that, passing their opinions on the pack generally, and on the Bugginson hounds in particular. Some thought they were coarse, some thought they were common, but when they heard they were drafts from the Quorn, they were unanimous in thinking they must be good—especially when Mr. Jorrocks broadly hinted he had given Day ten guineas a couple for them. The noise the party made prevented their hearing sundry ominous moans and lows in the neighbourhood, which gradually rose to a roar, until a simultaneous crash, and cry of "Mind the bull!" drew all eyes to the bank of the adjoining fence, where, with head down and tail up, a great roan bull was seen poising himself preparatory to making a descent upon the field. Down he came with a roar that shook the earth to the very centre, and sent the field flying in all directions. Mr. Jorrocks, who was on foot among his hounds, immediately rushed to his horse, which Ben had let loose, but making a bad shot at the stirrup, he became a *point d'appui* for the bull, who after him with a vigour and determination that looked very like a finisher. Our Master was carried, clinging to the neck, half across the field in a "now on, now off" sort of way that would have made any one feel very uncomfortable who had an annuity depending on his life. At last he got fairly into his saddle, and setting himself down to ride, he threw his heart boldly over a stiff "on and off," and shoved Xerxes at it in a way that proved too many for the bull. Ploughing up the pasture with his feet, in his effort to stop himself as he neared it, he tossed his great wide-horned head in 'the air, and uttering a frightful bellow that thundered through the valley and reverberated on Hardpye Hill, he turned, tail erect, to take a run at some one else. And having succeeded by the aid of gates in placing a couple more inclosures between them, Mr. Jorrocks sought a rising ground from which he thought over the magnitude of his adventure, and how he would like to have Leech to draw him taking the leap. And having gained breath as he magnified it, and having duly congratulated himself upon his escape, he out with his horn and blew his hounds together, leaving Hardpye Hill as he came, and entering among the anathemas in his Journal the following :—

" *Con*-found all farmers say I, wot don't tie up their bulls ! "

A bad beginning in this case did not make a good ending, for though our Master drew on till dark, which it was at half-past two, he never had a touch of a fox, and he sent word to Gollarfield, by the mole-catcher, that he was a " reg'lar 'umbug," and Pigg desired the man to add that he would fight him for what he pleased.

CHAPTER XLVII.

JAMES PIGG AGAIN ! ! !

THE smuggler was right in his estimate of Pigg's abilities, for, in addition to his great talents for hunting, he had a turn for low gambling, which the uninitiated sometimes confuse with legitimate sporting. Among other things, he was in the habit of betting on the weight of people's pigs, backing his own opinion as to what they were, or would feed up to, against the opinions of others; quite as useful and praiseworthy a pursuit, by the way, as people backing horses they have never seen, and over whose running they can exercise no control : be that as it may, however, Pigg was in the habit of exercising his judgment in that way, and had been highly successful at Handley Cross. He had come nearer the weight of Giles Jollyjowle's pig than eleven others, and had completely distanced all competitors in his estimate of Blash, the barber's, Hampshire hogs. He had also carried off the sweepstakes at two goose clubs, and received the second prize in a race for a hat. In addition to all this, his "cousin," Deavilboger, who, notwithstanding their little differences about hunting, had still a sort of sneaking regard for "wor James," had marked his appreciation of the festive season of the year, by sending him a large grey hen of whiskey, so that, what with his winnings and it, James was generally in a state of half fuddle. He would take as much as he could manage if kept quiet, and more than he could manage if put into motion. Now, as bad luck would have it, our uneasy, insatiable Master, wishing to retrieve his blank day before the usual stoppage of the season, thought to get something out of the fire, by a quiet "bye" at Newtimber Forest, the scene of his former misfortunes. Pigg, who had just paid his second morning visit to the hen, did not make any decided objection to the proposal, backed as it was by Mr. Jorrocks's plausible observation, that at that critical season of the year it "be'oved them to get every day they possibly could," and it was not until they reached the Copperchink Gate, and Pigg pressed a sovereign on the woman's acceptance for the toll, desiring her, when told to wait for his change, to "keep it," adding, that their "'ard maister had plenty o' brass," that Jorrocks was aware how matters stood. Recollecting, however, the "Cat and Custard-pot" scene, Mr. Jorrocks did not make any observation, but quietly getting his silver, trotted on as if it was "all right," hoping Pigg would sober as he went. When they got to Foggythorpe Green, where the road diverges through the fields, another scene occurred. Pigg wanted to pay the field-gates, and holloaed at a woman who happened to be passing, to "tak' her money," tendering a shilling, as if he had been kept waiting at a turnpike-gate for an hour. Next, as he was making, as he thought, a most sagacious steer through a gate, his eye deceived him as to the number of posts, and, catching by his toe, he was swept head foremost off into a complete hip-bath of mud. He

was too wise, however, to let go his hold of the bridle, and as the horse
kept smelling at him as he lay under his nose, Pigg kept vociferating,
"Sink, they dinna mak their yets hafe wide enough! They dinna mak
their yets hafe wide enough, ar say!" At length Mr. Jorrocks got him
raised and scraped, and stuck straight on his horse, and they proceeded
on their course together. Arrived at the wood, Mr. Jorrocks, thinking
the best plan would be to humour him, said if Pigg would go one way,
he would go the other, which James assenting to, the hounds dashed
into cover, and master and man proceeded to "yoicks" and crack their
whips, having the hounds in a widening space between them. The wood
was thick and rough, and as Jorrocks proceeded, Pigg's unearthly notes
gradually died out, and our Master had all the noise to himself. Being
fond of the sound of his own voice, he proceeded, yoicking and cracking
his whip, exhorting the hounds to "find 'im," and keeping a good look-
out a-head, when, to his surprise, at a cross ride, Pigg's horse came
snorting and cantering towards him. Pigg, feeling uncomfortable, had
laid down to sleep, and left his horse to his own devices. "W-o-a-y, my
man! W-o-a-y!" cried Jorrocks, fishing at him with his whip as he
approached, which only caused the horse to start and rush past him at a
gallop. "W-h-o-a-y, my man," roared Jorrocks, as the horse went
scuttling down the ride without rhyme or reason. "*Con*-found the
hanimal," continued Mr. Jorrocks, as he eyed him staring about from
side to side with the reins all dangling about his feet. "*Con*-found the
hanimal," repeated he, "was there ever sich a daft divil as that?—was
there ever sich a misfortunit indiwidual as John Jorrocks? Cus that
Pigg, I wish I'd never seen 'im—worst warmint I ever knew. Yoicks,
Lavender, good betch! Bet a guinea 'at we find a fox, and the 'ounds
run clean away from me. Lose either them or my dinner, or both.
Well," continued Mr. Jorrocks, spurring on to where Lavender was
feathering,—"well, needs must when a certain old gen'lman drives, but
if I 'ad my own way, it would be ''ome, sweet 'ome,' for me. Dublin
bay 'addocks, with appropriate sauce, goose, and happle pye. Oh dear!
A fox! for a 'underd, *a fox!* for anything that any body likes to say,"
continued our Master, staring his eyes out as he gets his horse short by
the head. "Now for ten miles as the crow flies with ten bottomless
brucks, and Berwickshire doubles without end. Ah! thank 'eavens its
not!" continued he, as a great banging hare bounced out of the wood,
and took down the ride with Lavender full cry after her, and Jorrocks
cracking his whip full cry after Lavender. At length he stopped her, and
taking advantage of the partial scoring to cry off the hounds, he out with
his horn and blew a shrill reverberating blast that drew out the rest, and
away he rode with the hounds all clustering about his horse's heels as if
he was going to lay them on to a scent, but in reality to get them out of
cover. The horn operated doubly, for a smock-frocked countryman,
having caught Pigg's horse, came cantering up to its sound, and Jorrocks
and he were presently on the Woodford and Handley Cross road.
Promising the man half a crown and his dinner for seeing him safe
home, Mr. Jorrocks started away at a brisk trot, hoping he was getting
rid of Pigg for good. And when "wor James" awoke, and learnt from
a tape-selling tramp what had happened, he was very wrath, and vowed

"he wadn't stand such work—he wadn't be robbed in that sort of way—no, he wadn't. He'd hev redress. He'd hev justice—yis, he'd hev justice—he wadn't be treated in that sort of way;" and he talked and fretted himself into believing that he had been most infamously used. Finding there was a magistrate in the neighbouring village of Yelverton, thither he directed his steps, and gaining an audience, boldly accused his master of stealing his horse, and applied for a warrant for his apprehension. The justice, seeing the maudlin state he was in, humoured the application, but pretending it would be necessary, in consequence of a recent decision, that a man may help himself to a horse to forward him on a journey, to see that Mr. Jorrocks had not taken it for that purpose, he got Pigg into his dog-cart and had him driven over to Handley Cross.

And when Mr. Jorrocks reproved him for his improprieties, he replied that he (Jorrocks) "had ne business out a hontin' on a drinkin' day."

CHAPTER XLVIII.

MR. JORROCKS'S JOURNAL.

WE will again have recourse to our worthy friend's journal for an outline of such proceedings as are not of sufficient importance to demand separate chapters to themselves. The following seems an original idea.

"Notice from the churchwardens and overseers, that in consequence of several mad dogs havin' made their appearance, all dogs were to be muzzl'd, and requirin' me to see that the 'ounds were properly muzzl'd before they went out to hunt. Wrote and told them I didn't believe there were such a set of jackasses in Her Majesty's dominions as to suppose an M. F. H. would go out with a pack of muzzl'd hounds.—Absurd! This is Mello's doing. Will pay him off."

"New Year's Day.—Sich a crowd! Sich compliments of the season, and sich screws. Old Doleful grinnin' about on Fair Rosamond like Death on the Pale 'Oss. Found in the Cloud Quarries, but might as well have been in the clouds, the field surrounded it so, and drove the fox into the mouth of the 'ounds. A young gentleman in nankeens and patent leather boots, rode over old Barbara. 'That's right!' exclaimed Pigg, 'ride amang em!—ride amang em! Kill a hund or two; we've plenty mair at hyem! It mun be a poor concern that wont stand a hund a-day.' Differ from Pigg there though. Howsomever, old Barbara ain't worth much. Declared she was the best in the pack notwithstandin'.

"*Staunton Snivey.*—Batsay brought up shavin' water, saying Binjimin wished to be excused 'unting, havin' got the gout. All moonshine, I dare say! Boy has no passion for the chase. Have a good mind to stuff him full of Hunter's pills, and see if they will have any effect upon him. Wot business has a boy like him with the gout? Only for rear admirals, town counsellors, and such like cocks. Caught Charley pinchin' Belinda under the table. Mounted him on Xerxes, as Ben couldn't go. Largish field. Captain Thompson (who never pays his three pounds) observed he never saw a pack of foxhounds without a whip before, and muttered somethin' about Master livin' out of the hounds. Shall set Fleecey at him.

"Drew Longford Plantations; then on to Fawsley Wood. Found immediately, but Reynard inclined to hang in cover. No great scent either, but cover surrounded with foot people and little holiday boys. Bin useful in coaxin' them into crowds, to listen to his 'hallegations,' as he calls his lies. At length Reynard broke from the West end, and made straight for Iver Heath, runnin' a wide circuit by Staunton Snivey, and over the hill, up to Bybury Wood. Scent poor and pace bad. All the holiday hobbledehoy boys treadin' on the 'ounds' tails. A short check at Farmer Hayband's, and thought all was over, when Priestess hit it off in a grass field behind the barn, and away they went with the scent improvin' at every yard. Pace changed from an 'unting run to a reg'lar bust, and quite straight over the cream of the country.

"How the tail lengthened! A quarter of a mile, increasin' as they went. Young gen'lemen charged to bring home the brush, found their grass ponies beginnin' to gape. Captain Shortflat made Duncan Nevin's mare cry Capevi on Hutton Bank top, and many bein' anxious to give in, great was the assistance he received. Major Spanker would bleed her in the jugular, Mr. Wells thought the thigh vein, and another thought the toe, so that the mare stood a good chance of bein' bled to death, if Duncan's man who was cruising about hadn't fortinately cast up and saved her from her frinds.

"On the hounds went for Crew, passing Limbury, leaving Argod Dingle to the right, over the Lily-white Sand Railway near the station at Stope, pointing for Gore Cross, the fox finally taking refuge in a pig-sty behind the lodge of Button Park. Piggy at home and unfortunately killed, but who would grudge a pig after such a werry fine run?

"Pigg rode like a trump!—seven falls—knocked a rood of brick-wall down with his 'ead. What a nob that must be! Charley left one of his Yorkshire coat-laps in a hedge—Barnington lost his hat—Hudson his whip—Mr. Ramshay a stirrup, and Captain Martyn his cigar-case. Only seven up out of a field of sixty—day fine and bright—atmosphere clear, as if inclining for frost—hope not.

"*Jan. 7th.*—Reg'lar decided black frost — country iron-bound — landscape contracted—roads dry as bones—mud scrapins like granite— never saw so sudden a change; thought yesterday it looked like somethin'; the day changed, and hounds ran so hard in the afternoon; Pigg thinks it won't last, but I think it will; 'opes he'll be right.

"*8th.*—Frost *semper eadem*, 'arder and 'arder as Ego would say: windows frost fretted—laurels nipped—water-jugs frozen—shavin'- brush stiff—sponge stuck to water-bottle, and towel 'ard. Pigg still says it won't last—wish he may be right—little hail towards night.

"*9th.*—Alternate sun and clouds—slight powderin' of snow on cold and exposed places—largish flakes began to fall towards afternoon, and wind got up—purpleish sun-set—walked hounds before Sulphur Wells Hall, after feedin', but they had a cold, dingy look, and I hadn't heart to blow my 'orn. Gabriel Junks doesn't seem to care about the cold, and gives no indication of a change—Oh for one of his screams!

"10*th*.—Awoke, and found the country under two feet of snow. Well, it's always somethin' to know the worst, and be put out of suspense. Wind high, and drifted a large snow-wreath before the garden-gate—tempestersome day—Can't stir out without gettin' up to the hocks in snow. Desired Binjimin to sweep the way to the stable and kennel. Boy got a broom, and began 'issing as if he were cleanin' an 'oss. Letter from Giles Shortland, requestin' the M. F. H. to subscribe to a ploughin' match at Tew. Answered that I should be werry 'appy to subscribe, and wish I could see them at work. Old Dame Tussac came with eight turkey-heads in a bag—fox had killed them last night, and she wanted pay. The bodies were at home—told her to bring the bodies —will make werry good stock for soup : one doesn't know but she may have sold the bodies. Wrote Bowker to go self and wife to sleep in my bed in Great Coram Street, to get it well haired. Shall run up to town and see the pantomime, and how things go on at the shop.

"Old Doleful called with a requisition for me to give a sportin' lector · —axed wot I should lector upon—said he thought 'scent' would be a very good subject. Told him, all that could be said about scent was that it was a werry queer thing. Nothin' so queer as scent 'cept a woman. Told him to compose an oration upon it himself if he could. He then said summering the 'unter would be a good subject. Told him that corn and a run in the carriage was the true way of summering the 'unter. Riding to 'ounds he then thought would do. Told him I wasn't a 'g-u-r-r along! there are three couple of 'ounds on the scent' man at all, and ridin' arter 'ounds wouldn't draw. Didn't seem to take the difference but took his departure, which was just as well.

"*Letter from Bowker.*

"'Honoured Sir,—Yours is received, and Mrs. B. and I will be proud to act the part of warming-pans. I suppose we may expect you in a day or two. You will be sorry to hear that poor Billy was hung this morning. *He died game.* As it was strongly suspected he had accomplices, a mitigation of punishment was offered if he would disclose his confederates. Billy listened sullenly to the offer, and passing his fingers through his thick curly hair, he said, 'Look here, masters, if every hair on this head was a life, I wouldn't peach to save a single one.' At length he confessed—'*I did boil the exciseman!*' said he. Poor Billy! All the little beggarly boys, and hoarse-throated scoundrels in the town, are screaming his dying *speech* and confession about, when '*I did boil the exciseman,*' was all that he said. I am greatly distressed at poor Billy's fate.

> 'Take him for all and all,
> We ne'er shall look upon his like again.'

"'London is suicidically gloomy to-day—I feel as if I could cut my throat—would that I could leave it !—But

> 'The lottery of my destiny
> Bars me the right of voluntary choosing.'

"'I'm about tired of old Twist. Our business is fast falling off, and an old man's trade never rallies. Might I take the liberty of asking if you think a snuff and cigar shop would answer at Handley Cross? I have a splendid new nigger, five feet six, with a coronet full of party-coloured feathers on his head, a sky-blue jacket with gold lace, and a pair of broad red-striped trousers, leaving half his black thighs bare, that I thought of setting at the door in Eagle Street, but would reserve him for the Cross, if you thought it would do. Of course, I would carry on business in Eagle Street as well—at least for the present; but I have plenty of canisters, wooden rolls of tobacco to stock a branch establishment, and Mrs. Bowker fancies a change of air would do her asthma good. Pray excuse the freedom, and believe me to remain,

" ' Dear Sir,

" ' Yours most respectfully,

" ' WM. BOWKER.

" ' To J. Jorrocks, Esq.' "

CHAPTER XLIX.

THE CUT 'EM DOWN CAPTAIN'S QUADS.

CHRISTMAS, that withering, relentless season, that brings so many people short up, having exercised its blighting influence on our cut-em-down Captain, the following hand-bill, having paid a visit to St. Botolph's Lane, arrived in due course at Handley Cross, "with Mr. Castor's comp^{ts}." written inside the envelope :—

HUNTERS FOR SALE.

TO BE SOLD BY AUCTION, AT TWELVE O'CLOCK ON WEDNESDAY NEXT,

BY MR. TAPPINGTON,

IN THE IMPERIAL HOTEL YARD, LOOPLINE,

(The property of an Officer going Abroad), the following very superior

HORSES,

well known with Sir Peregrine Cropper's and Mr. Slasher's hounds.

1st.—TALAVERA, a brown bay, with black points, 7 years old, nearly thorough bred ;

2nd.—CORUNNA, a bright chesnut, or bitter beer colour, 8 years old, also nearly thorough bred.

Loopline is at the Junction of the Lily-White Sand with the Gravelsin and Boodler Railways, and Trains stop there every hour.

Loopline.

" Humph," said Mr. Jorrocks, reading it at breakfast as he dry-shaved his chin, "Humph—got to the end of his tether has he? thought 'ow it would be—not 'zactly the time for buyin' quads though, with a yard and a 'alf of snow on the ground ; 'owsomever that 'ill make 'em easier bought praps.—All the swells will be hup in town seeing their aunts or

gettin' their 'airs cut. May as well 'ave a ride in the rail as poke about
i' the snow—shall go second class though," adding—

> X. was expensive and soon became poor,
> Y. was the wise man and kept want from the door.

Accordingly on the appointed day, our Master having filled one pantaloon
pocket with sovereigns and five pound notes, and the other with samples
of tea, proceeded on his destination, telling Mrs. Jorrocks he was going
to meet Bugginson. Screech—hiss—whistle, roll, rattle, roll, porter !
what's this station ?—whistle—hiss—screech—roll, rattle, roll, "tickets
ready, please, Loopline station ! Loopline station ! change here for the
Boodler line," and he was there.

Loopline, with its piles of dirty snow and yards of icicles, looked very
different to what it did on Mr. Jorrocks's former visit, and even Castors
seemed greatly the worse for wear. The Captain's horses having in his
judgment, nearly completed the awkward exploit of eating their heads
off before the storm came, he felt morally certain that it would last for
six weeks or two months, which would leave him desperately in the lurch.
The consequence was he had taken it uncommonly to heart, and his
buff waistcoat and drab shorts and continuations were a good deal
roomier.

"Well, old bouy, 'ow goes it ? " asked Jorrocks, greeting him familiarly
as he found him pacing restlessly up and down the stable yard.

"Oh ! sir, mister, mister, mister," replied Castors, not being able to
hit off the name, "Oh ! sir, I've been hill, desperate hill. I've 'ad the
lumbago, sir, to an extent, sir, that's 'ardly creditable, sir."

"You don't say so," observed Mr. Jorrocks compassionately, "why
don't you take a leetle o' the old remedy—'ot with—"

"Ah, 'ot with," sighed Castors with a shake of his head, as he fixed
his watery grey eyes earnestly on Jorrocks, to see if he was not one of
the many customers with whom he drunk for the "good of the house."
"Ah, 'ot with, indeed ! " repeated he, as if nothing loth to try the
remedy.

"You don't want to buy any tea ? " said Mr. Jorrocks, producing a
sample as he spoke.

"Oh, it's Mr. Jorrocks ! " now exclaimed Castors brightening up,
"It's Mr. Jorrocks,—you'd get a bill from me, sir, didn't ye ? a bill
'bout the Capting's 'osses, ye know. You told me to send you one, you
know."

"Ah, 'osses, indeed," replied Mr. Jorrocks. "No time this for
buying 'osses, old bouy—glass down to fecit—country bund hup in a
hiron frost and like to continue under snow for the next two months;"
Mr. Jorrocks breathing heavily on the bright pure atmosphere as he
spoke.

"Too 'ard to last, too 'ard to last," retorted Castors, fidgeting at
the observation. "Never know'd it stand when it was so *desp'rate*
'ard," added he, with a heavy emphasis on the " *desp'rate*." How he
wished the Captain had gone to the Cross Keys, the White Hart, any
house but his.

"You'd better look at the tea," observed Mr. Jorrocks, still holding the sample out on the palm of his hand, "Tea 'ill be hup you'll see, and you'd better buy afore it rises. This is a first chop article—Lapsang Souchong."

"Well, but I'm busy just now, I'm busy just now," retorted Castors testily, "Come after the sale, sir, come after the sale, and we'll see if we can do business."

"Well," replied Mr. Jorrocks, pocketing the sample, and buttoning his brown bear cloth jacket comfortably up to the throat, "I'll go into the town and see what I can do with the grocers there;" so saying he swaggered off, without noticing Castors' exclamation of "You'll be back to the sale then! you'll be back to the sale!"

Twelve o'clock came, but brought with it no symptoms of a start.— Half-past, and still the same. Time is of little value in the country. At length as one o'clock drew near, a lank-haired seedy-looking half boots, half waiter sort of youth appeared with what at first sight might have been taken for a Punch and Judy show, but which, on being placed on the ground, proved to be the auctioneer's rostrum. This was a signal for sundry indolent looking, sportingly attired but horseless youths, and small dealers with their slangey attendants to turn in, and some dozen drab coated farmers, for it was market day, and general idlers mingling with the rest, the auctioneer swigged off the remains of his tumbler of brandy and water, and attended by a brilliant staff, consisting of the aforesaid seedy one, swaggered imposingly upon the scene. He was a burly, big-faced, impudent fellow, with a round of whisker, a consequential sort of hat, and a corporation so large as to look as if he had thriven in all the occupations he had turned his hand to—Hatter, Wine Merchant, Coal Merchant, Accountant, Land Agent, Temperance Hotel Keeper, Stationer, Broker, and General Negotiator.

He seemed to be a sort of character, for his appearance was hailed with a round of jokes and coarse salutes, which gradually subsided into inquiries after the health of Mrs. Tappington and the little Taps. Having replied to these, he ascended the rostrum, and clearing his throat with a substantial *hem!* commanded *silence*, and proceeded to read the conditions of sale; after which Talavera came trotting up to the hammer.

"Now," said the auctioneer, "will any gentleman with the wit in his head and the money in his pocket, favour me with an offer for this proud animal, whose worth is far beyond the reach of my 'umble imagination!"

"Make a ring, gentlemen, make a ring," continued he, motioning with his hand, adding to the ostler, "trot him round, and he'll soon enlarge the circle of our acquaintance," whereupon crack went the circus-whip of the man in the middle, and round spun the horse with his heels in the air, snowballing the shrinking company with the greatest precision.

That feat being accomplished, he was again trotted up to the rising ground by the rostrum, where he stood panting and snorting with a watchful eye, wondering what was going to happen. "Now, gentlemen," continued the auctioneer, "perhaps some of you will favour me with an offer for this proud animal—a horse, as far as my 'umble judgment goes, as near perfection as it is possible to imagine. What will any gentleman say for a beginning?"

"Ah! to be sure," to a dirty-looking anything-arian, who now approached him, "ah! to be sure, examine him, sir! examine him attentively, sir! examine his mouth! examine his eyes! examine his legs! examine his nose! Well, what d'ye make of his age?"

"Seventy-two," replied the man coolly.

"Old enough for anything!" retorted the auctioneer, amid the laughter of the company. "What will any gentleman say for this grand animal, with the high courage of a gentleman, and all the docility—this

MIND HIS HEELS.

noble viewly beast, with the neck and chest described in the book of Job? Look at his chest! look at his loins! look at his bellows, *but mind his heels!*" added he, as the horse began plunging and kicking from the cold.

"Ten guineas," now offered the man who had examined him.

"Ten guineas?" retorted the auctioneer, angrily, "ten guineas! you must be joking; ten guineas for a proud animal like this! You astonish him! you insult him! you degrade him! Ten guineas for such a horse as this! It's a downright insult to the whole animal creation. And ten guineas are only bid," continued the auctioneer, adopting the offer, and proceeding to force, and screw, and coax, and exhort, and dwell, in a way that would take Tattersall at least a week to get through an ordinary Monday's sale. At length the hammer fell on both the proud animals, and on Flaps, the saddler of Loopline, declaring his principal, Mr. Jorrocks

was found to be the purchaser of both Talavera at twenty-eight, and Corunna at thirty pounds. Mr. Jorrocks then adjourned to inaugurate his purchase with brandy and water, and let Castors know what a great man he really was. And Castors was much chagrined to find that Flaps was not bidding for Martin Greenwood, of the Triumphant Chariot Livery Stables, where he had occasional dealings, for, by very little management, he could have made the cut-em-down Captain's bill cover a good deal more purchase-money. Mr. Jorrocks, however, mollified him with the old specific, and also succeeded in selling him a couple of chests of tea, Lapsang Souchong and strong Congou—which he managed to deduct from the price of the horses. And Handley Cross being reduced to a state of perfect torpor by the frost, the news that old Jackey, as they profanely called Mr. Jorrocks, had bought some new nags, was a great accommodation, and drew divers parties to the station to criticise them as they came. Among others was our old friend Mr. Barnington, who, being struck with the looks and action of bitter-beer-coloured Corunna asked our master if he would sell him?

A A

"Oh! why, faith, Barney," replied Mr. Jorrocks, raising his eyebrows, puffing out his cheeks, dangling his seals, and looking the very essence of good-natured innocent simplicity; "oh! why, faith, Barney, I've never thought o' nothin' o' the sort, but you're a good sort o' feller, and subscribes liberal to my 'ounds : I doesn't care 'bout the lucre o' gain, nobody cares less 'bout money nor I do, and you may take him for sixty—take him for sixty, and no more 'bout it." So saying, Mr. Jorrocks passed his purchase to his friend, who felt flattered by the favour, and complimented Pigg with a sovereign.

Pigg too was pleased with the horse that went into his stud, so that altogether our master did pretty well—cleared his railway expenses, as he said. The thing now was, to get a little work out of his establishment, for he was no man for keeping things to look at.

The storm weighed heavily on Mr. Jorrocks's spirits, and James Pigg d——d the south country, and swore "they never had seck weather i' the north." Often did our worthy, warming himself at Batsay's pittance of a kitchen fire, wish himself at Deavilboger's never-failing grate.

*   *   *   *   *   *   *

"Ar think we're gannin' to have fresh," observed Pigg to his master one day, as the latter was paying his usual lengthy visit to the stable.

"Have what?" inquired Mr. Jorrocks.

"*Fresh*," repeated Pigg, with an emphasis; "ye ken what fresh weather is, dinnat ye?"

"Vy, no," replied our master thoughtfully; "you don't mean a thaw?"

"Yeas, a thow," replied Pigg.

"I vish we may!" exclaimed Mr. Jorrocks, brightening up; "somehow the day feels softer; but the hair generally is after a fall. Howsomever, *nous werrons*, as we say in France : it'll be a long time afore we can 'unt, though—'edges will be full o' snow."

"Ay, dike backs," replied Pigg, "lies lang i' them; but one can always loup in, or loup o'er."

"Ah, that's all werry good talkin'," observed Mr. Jorrocks, shaking his head, and jingling the silver in his breeches-pocket; "that's werry good talkin'," repeated he, "but there are sich things as 'osses' necks to be considered."

"A! but if ar'll risk mar neck, ye surely may risk yeer 'osse's," observed Pigg.

"Don't know," replied Mr. Jorrocks, smiling at his huntsman's keenness. "Fear we shalln't have a chance in a hurry : have you seen Junks?"

"No, ar's not; the missis was on the house-end as I came to stable, but Gabriel wern't there."

"Ah, the missis is nothin'," replied Mr. Jorrocks, "had Gabriel been there it would have been summut like ; good bird Mrs. Junks, but has'nt Gabey's delicate perception 'bout the weather—follows—never takes a lead. A scream from Gabey would give one 'opes of getting the Jenny Linds to work again." So saying, our master drew on his American overshoes, and returned to the consolations of the cupboard.

Despite Mr. Jorrocks' opinion of her, Mrs. Junks was a true prophet. The next day, Gabriel himself descended from the stable top into the garden with a loud and piercing scream. His crest was erect, his neck feathers slightly ruffled, and as he lifted one foot and then the other out of the snow, there was an air of comfort in his walk that told of other feelings than that of frost—Mr. Jorrocks went out at the back-door in his slippers, and poking his finger into the snow, proclaimed it was a thaw—a large drop splashing on his wig confirmed the judgment—spouts began to trickle, then to run, sewers to overflow, streets stood in snow-broth, and the prospect of a return to verdure and animation was the only consolation for wet-footed walkers. It was a decided thaw. There was a gentle wind, and the rain fell soft and warm—laurels expanded to the more genial atmosphere, the leafless trees seemed to increase in size, and the lately distinct distant objects resumed their gray dimness in the landscape.

Mr. Jorrocks soon began to wax uncommonly eager, and he, who had reproved Pigg's ardour, now in turn proposed a day—a quiet bye, just by their two selves to see "'ow the country looked and when they could begin to advertise." And as luck would have it, they fell in with a high-conditioned old flyer, who led Pigg such a dance as never was seen, and left Mr. Jorrocks stuck in a snow wreath in Eastfield-lane, out of which he had to be dug at an expense of seven shillings, the tinkers who found him refusing to put in a spade until he said what he'd give. That cooled our master's courage for a week, at the end of which time, things got into working order, and the establishment soon assumed such a form as tempted Mr. Jorrocks into the indiscretion disclosed in the following chapter.

CHAPTER L.

POMPONIUS EGO.

THE great Mr. Ego having exalted the horns of the principal hunts in the kingdom, was now spending his time pleasantly between London and Paris—living at Calais—from whence he emerged at short notice to attend buttering matches in England ; and the glowing account he gave of some great man's establishment, caused Mr. Jorrocks to pant for that enduring fame which statuary and stationary best can give. Accordingly he made the overture contained in the following letter :—

" DEAR MR. HEGO,

" If your intercourse with Dukes and other great guns o' the world, leaves any margin for the doin's of the pop-guns o' the chase, I shall be werry 'appy if you will come here and take a look at our most provincial pack. In course I needn't tell you that my 'ouse is not large enough to require a kiver 'ack to canter from the dinin' to the drawin'-room, neither is the pack on a par with many you have seen; but I can give you a good blow-out, both in the way of wittles and drink, and shall be 'appy to 'put you up,' as they say in the cut-me-downs, on as good a quad as I can, and show you sich sport as the country will afford. *Entre nous,* as we say in France, I want to be famous, and you know how to do it. In course *mum's* the word.

"Yours to serve,
"JOHN JORROCKS.

"P.S.—Compts. to Julius Seizeher and all the ancient Romans when you write."

"*Diana Lodge, Handley Cross Spa.*
"To Pomponius Ego, Esq., Calais.

The following is Mr. Ego's answer :—

"DEAR MR. JORROCKS,—
"You remind me of Catullus! None but the old Latian could have put the point as you do. D—m all dukes! I'm for mercantile life—£. *s. d.*—I shall have great satisfaction in inspecting your pack, on Thursday next, which I have no doubt I shall find all I can desire. Pick me out an easy-going, sure-footed, safe-leaping horse, with a light mouth, and let him have a Whippy-saddle on—I can't ride in any other. I like a bed-room with a southern aspect,—the feathers above the mattress, if you please ; wax-candles and Eau de Cologne, will pitch the tune for the rest. Compliments to Mrs. Jorrocks, from, dear Jorrocks,

"Yours very truly,
"POMPONIUS EGO.

"P.S.—What would you like to be done in? The 'Q. R.,' * the 'H. T.,' 'Fraser,' 'Blackwood,' 'New Monthly,' 'Encyclopedia,' 'Life,' 'Field,' 'Era,' or what?

"To John Jorrocks, Esq.,
"Master of Fox-Hounds,
"Diana Lodge, Handley Cross Spa."

This point being arranged, great preparations were made for the important event. Hounds may go on for centuries without being known beyond the limits of their country, but the one day that brings the Inspector-General lives for ever in the page of history. Where, then, is the master of hounds, where the huntsman, where the whip, where the member of a hunt, whose heart does not beat responsive with Mr. Jorrocks', on this trying occasion? Who, in the familiar language of low life, does not wish him well out of it?

*   *   *   *   *   *

"Now, James," said our master to his huntsman, as they stood in the kennel-yard looking over the hounds, a few days before the appointed visit, "you must get all on the square ; the great Pomponius Hego is a comin', and we shall be all down in black and wite."

---

* "Q. R." stands for "Quarterly Review ;" "H. T," for "Heavy Triumvirate," which carries the lead, known in the trade as the "Old and New Sporting Magazines," and the "Sporting Review."

" Whe's he ? " inquired Pigg, scratching his head.

" Vot ! not know Pomponius Hego ! " exclaimed Mr. Jorrocks, in astonishment; " you sure*lie* don't mean to say so."

" Ar' dinna ken him, ar's sure," replied Pigg, with the greatest indifference. " Is he a skeulmaister ? "

" A *skeulmaister !* " repeated Mr. Jorrocks, with a sneer and an indignant curl of his lip; " a skeulmaister ! *No !*—a master of 'unting—not an M.F.H., like me, but a man wot makes hobserwations on M.F.H.'s, their packs, their 'osses, their 'untsmen—their every thing, in fact."

" What's he de that for ? " inquired Pigg, with surprise.

" Vy that the world at large may know what he thinks on 'em, to be sure. He prints all he sees, hears, or thinks, in a book."

Pigg.—" Ye dinna say se ! "

" Quite true, I assure you," replied Mr. Jorrocks; " and if by any unlucky chance he blames an 'untsman, or condemns a pack, it's all dickey with them for ever; for no livin' man dare contradict him, and every one swears by wot he says."

" Woons man," replied Pigg, in a pucker, " we maun be uncommon kittle then ar' guess."

" You must exert your hutmost powers," replied Mr. Jorrocks, most emphatically; " for dash my vig, if we fail, I, even I—John Jorrocks himself, will go perfectly mad with rage and wexation."

" He'll ken all aboot the hunds and huntin' then, ar's warn'd," replied Pigg, catching the infection of fear.

Mr. Jorrocks.—" Oh, yes !—at least he writes about them; and no one disputes print. Oh, dear ! oh, dear ! I almost fear I've made a mess o' myself, by axin' of him to come. I question if the world would not have been as 'appy without the mighty Hego. Hoil, butter, sugar, soap, all that sort o' thing is werry pleasant; but then—oh, 'orror ! the idea of being rubbed the wrong way by Hego ! *Death itself would be better !* "

Pigg.—" Hout, tout !—fear nout ! there's nout to boggle a man ! Gin I were ye, with all yeer brass, ar' wadn't care for neone."

Mr. Jorrocks.—" Ah ! but, Pigg !—think of hambition !—think of fame !—think of that summut arter life wot prompts men to great hactions ! Here, for five-and-thirty years, have I been a hardent follower of the chase—loved it, oh, 'eavens ! for its own sake, and not from any hanxious longins arter himmortality ! and now, when greatness has been thrust upon me—when I shines forth an M.F.H.— to think that all may be dashed from me, and 'stead of reignin' King of 'Andley Cross —'stead of bein' the great and renowned John Jorrocks—I may be dashed t' oblivion ! Oh, Pigg !—hambition is a frightful, a dreadful thing ! "

Pigg.—" *Hout, tout,* fear nout. Does he ride, or nabbut looks at pack at cover-soide loike ? "

Mr. Jorrocks.—" Both, both—fust, he'll come and look us all over, ax the name of this 'ound and that—call 'em level—enquire 'ow each is bred—talk of Hosbaldeston's Furrier, Lord Enry's Contest, or Sutton's Trueman—look at this nag—then at that—ax their pedigrees—their hages—their prices—their every things—vether we summers them in the 'ouse or in the field—do a little about 'ard meat—'ow much corn they get—if we bruise it—vether we split our beans, or give them whole— then when we throws off he marks each motion—sees whether we put in at the right end of the cover or the wrong—observes whether the men have 'ands equal to their nerves, or nerves equal to their 'ands; books their seats and their names—not their seats by the coach, mind—but their seats in the saddle. To read his accounts of the runs you'd fancy he was every where at once, both before, behind, and above—with the fox—with the 'ounds—with the first, and with the last man in the field—so knowin'ly does he describe every twist, every turn, every bend of the run. Oh Pigg! my excellent, my beautiful Pigg! now that the fatal day 'proaches, and I sees the full brightness o' my indiscretion starin' me i' the face, I begins to repent havin' axed him to come. Wot can fame do for Jorrocks? I have as much tin as I wants, and needn't care a copper for no man. Would that I was well out o' the mess!"

"Never fear," replied Pigg, "here be good like h'unds, and yeer husses can gan; if we de but find, the deuce is in it if we don't cook him up a run."

"Oh, Pigg! my buck of a Pigg!" exclaimed Mr. Jorrocks, "those *ifs* are the deuce and all in 'unting—There's nothin' so difficult to ride as an 'if.' *If* we find a fox, then there's the difficulty of gettin' well away with him; or *if* we do get well away, then there's the chance of his bein' 'eaded back; or of there bein' no scent, or of his takin' a bad line, or of his bein' chased by a cur, or of his gainin' an earth we don't know of, or of a great banging 'are misleadin' the 'ounds, or of the fox beatin' us disgracefully at the far end—these things are dreadful to the anxious mind of a M.F.H. at all times, but *'orrible*, most *'orrible*, at a time like the prisent."

"Dinna fear," replied Pigg, "dinna fear—you'll see he'll be nowt but mortal man after all. If you want to kill a fox, gan to big wood, and have somebody there with black bitch."

"Black bitch," said Mr. Jorrocks, thoughtfully, "black bitch—Wot should we want with black bitch when we have all the 'ounds out?"

"*Hout*, thou fondy!" said Pigg, "doesn't thou ken what black bitch is?"

"No I doesn't—unless it's a dog's wife."

"Dog's wife!" roared Pigg; "Ne sike thing. It's a *gun*, man! Just pop a few shot corns into fox's hint-legs, and h'unds 'ill soon catch him."

"My vig!" exclaimed Mr. Jorrocks, with an air of sudden enlightenment, "I've often seen chaps in welweteen with guns at cover sides, but never knew what they were there for. Ah, but," added he, with a shake of his head, "Hego will be up to the black-bitch rig—No, no, that wont do—no use tryin' to 'oax him—it must be summut genuine. Oh, Pigg, if you could but manage to give him a *real* tickler, so that he might have summut good to put in his book, the gratitude of John Jorrocks should rest with you for ever and ever—you should drink brandy out of a quart pot for breakfast dinner and supper."

"You dinna say se!" exclaimed Pigg, with delight. "Let's see—

dang'd if ar ken—yes, ar de tee—run a drag and sheck a bag fox at far
end loike."

Mr. Jorrocks.—" That von't do—*no not it.* He'll be sure to find out,
and trounce us to all eternity ; besides, if any of the Bell's Lifers were
to catch us, they'd never let us 'ear the end on't."

" Not they," replied Pigg : " nebody 'ill find out if ye de but had
your gob—start i' big wood—run drag round—bother him well—then
out o'ur big loup—give him summut to glower at, instead o' h'unds."

" No, Pigg, no," replied Mr. Jorrocks, shaking his head and jingling
a handful of silver in his pantaloon pocket ; "it must be summut more
genuine—*Tally ho! yonder he goes!* then elbows and legs—elbows and
legs ; " Mr. Jorrocks suiting the action to the word, by straddling and
working an imaginary horse with his arms.

" Give him that tee," replied Pigg ; " stick chap up a tree to holloa
away—another on a hill to had up hat, and so on."

" Ah, but so many cuks will spoil the broth, Pigg ; so many cuks will
spoil the broth. S'pose, for a moment, one should peach ! S'pose Hego
should find us out ! I should sit on pins—on wool-combers—with nothin'
but summer drawers on, till the account appeared, and then I question
I should have courage to cut the pages. Oh, hambition ! hambition !
wot a troublesome warmint you are ! Wish I'd let the great man alone."

Pigg.—" A, man alive niver fear; he cannot de thee ne harm. Let
me manish him,—ar'll give him summut to bragg on."

Mr. Jorrocks.—" I vish I dirst—you Scotchmen are cliver fellers ; but
s'pose he should smell a rat, 'ow he would trounce us, as much to how
his own 'cuteness, as to punish us for our imperance ! "

" Ye've nout to fear, ar tell ye," replied Pigg, confidently ; " ye've
nout to fear ; just leave it arl to me, and had your jaw about it, and
dinna call me a Scotchman, and keep thy bit bowdekite quiet—ar'll
manish matters."

With much fear, and many misgivings for his rashness in asking Ego
to come, Mr. Jorrocks at length consented to intrust the management of
the day's sport to his northern huntsman, and the feeder.

By these it was arranged to run a drag of aniseed and red-herring
over some of the best of their country, and to turn down a fox at the
far end, in some convenient unsuspicious-looking place. The evening
before Mr. Ego was to arrive, James Pigg communicated the find, the
run, and the finish, to Mr. Jorrocks, with such other information as
would enable our master to ride to points without exciting suspicion, and
Mr. Jorrocks undertook to say as much to Benjamin as would put the
boy on his mettle, without letting him too much into the secret.

Accordingly, when Stobbs left the dining-room to play his usual game
of beggar-my-neighbour with Belinda, Mr. Jorrocks rang the bell, and
desired Betsy to send in the boy. The latter entered in his usual
sneaking way, knowing that he had been guilty of several " piccadillies,"
as his master would call them, for which he deserved to be well
bastinadoed.

" Now, Binjimin," said Mr. Jorrocks, eyeing his whipper-in with one
of his most scrutinising looks ; " now, Binjimin," repeated he, with great
dignity, "you are on the eve of a most mo-men-tous crisis ! "

"Yez-ir," replied Benjamin, wondering what sort of a shaped thing it was.

"That renowned man, Mr. Pomponious Hego, 'unts to-morrow with our unrivalled 'ounds, and I would fain give him a stinger."

"Yez-ir," replied Benjamin.

"Now, then, you see, Binjimin, James Pigg is a mighty 'unter—keen and game to the backbone, and thinks he can 'stonish him. Now, Binjimin, you must lend us a hand."

"Yez-ir," replied Benjamin.

"You are werry fond o' marmeylad," observed Mr. Jorrocks, after a short pause, during which he considered how he had best put the point.

"*Uncommon!*" exclaimed Ben, with a grin of delight.

"Well then, now you see, Binjimin, if you hact well your part, obey James Pigg, and do all wot he tells you—if all goes on smoothly and well on your part—wen you comes 'ome, I'll give you a pot o' marmeylad as big as your 'ead!"

"Crikey, oh!" exclaimed Benjamin, in ecstasies.

"But, 'ark to me again, Binjimin," continued Mr. Jorrocks, holding up his finger, and knitting his brow at the boy; "'Ark to me again, Binjimin, if by any chance you bitch the thing, if all does not go on smoothly and well on your part, so far from givin' of you any marmeylad, I'll take you to one of the new-fangled matrimony-shops, and tie you hup with a stout gipsey wench, with sich a small hindependence of her own, as 'ill find you in tons of misfortin' and black language, fresh from the pit's mouth, and make you miserable from now till the first Monday arter eternity."

"*Oh-o-o!*" groaned Benjamin, inwardly, at the thought.

"So now make yourself scarce, and mind wot you're at," said Mr. Jorrocks, dismissing him. Our master then adjourned to the parlour, and endeavoured to compose himself for bed with a couple of very stiff glasses of B. and W., and got through the night better than might have been expected.

CHAPTER LI.

THE POMPONIUS EGO DAY.

A THICK white rind powdered the face of nature, and Mr. Jorrocks found himself with a beautiful silver-foliaged window in the morning. Still the evergreens in the garden exhibited no symptoms of a nipping, and as the night-clouds cleared off and the sun stood forth all lurid in the firmament, he congratulated himself on the appearance of opening day. Mrs. Jorrocks, Belinda, Stobbs, Betsy, and Benjamin, were up with the lark, all busy preparing for the great, well-known unknown. A fly was despatched to the Datton station of the Lily-white-sand railway to meet him, and punctual to his time, Ego turned out at Diana

Lodge, enveloped in shawls, numerous great coats, and a pair of French-jointed clogs to keep his feet warm.   Mutual salutations being over, and having got rid of his husks, breakfast was attacked with a true railway appetite—kidneys, chops, eggs, muffins, crumpets, toast, red herrings, all the delicacies of the season in short, that make one's mouth water to write, vanished in succession, aided by large draughts of undeniable tea and coffee from "the Lane," as Mr. Jorrocks calls his place of business. At length they completely topped up, and after begging some brandy to put in his flask, Ego rose from his seat and began pacing about the room and looking out of the window, as men are in the habit of doing who want to be commencing a "New Series" of the periodical occupations of life.   Stobbs had a bad headach—or pretended to have one, not wanting to be butter'd.

Ten o'clock came, and as it struck, James Pigg and Benjamin appeared outside the white rails before Diana Lodge, clad in their best habiliments, mounted, and each leading a horse.   Uncommonly *spicy* they all looked, for Pigg, regardless of expense, had generously divided a penny's-worth of ginger among the four, so that their tails stuck up like hat-pegs, and, as if in sympathy with the horses, Gabriel Junks flew on to the summit of the gateway arch, and expanded a glorious tail to the rays of the sun, at the same time setting up a scream that startled the horses.   Forth sallied Ego and Jorrocks; up went the bed-room window for Betsy to look out, Mrs. Jorrocks appeared framed in the lower one, with a face of most rubicund hue, while Belinda peeped past the green and white chintz curtain, and had her glimpse of the scene.

"There!" said Mr. Jorrocks, pulling up short at the gate, seizing Ego by the arm as he pointed to his stud; "there! there are a lot of nags for you—none of your cat-legged, tumble-down, kick-me-off, brik-my-neck, split-my-skull beggars; but real seasoned 'unters, sure and steady, with an eye for each foot, and one over.   Binjimin," said he, turning to the boy, "take up those stirrups three 'oles, and don't let me catch you ridin' like a dragon.   Now, Mr. Hego, be arter mountin'—time's precious, and punctuality is the purliteness of princes.   There," said he, as Ego got himself into his saddle on Talavera, "you are mounted—delightful! make a pictor for Leech!   Gave a mint o' money for that 'oss, but I doesn't care a dump 'bout money, further nor as it enables one to pursue the plisurs o' the chase.—Pigg, put Arterxerxes next the rails, so that I may get on easy.   *Whoay, 'oss! Whoay!*" roared Jorrocks, as the horse began fidgetting and hoisting, on feeling his foot in the stirrup.   "*Whoay!* I say, you hugly brute!" adding, "rot ye, but I'll take the gay insolence out o' your tail afore night."   A bold effort lodged him in the first floor of the saddle, and, gathering up his reins, Jorrocks turned Arterxerxes' head from the house, the horse walking with his fore legs, and kicking with his hind ones, an example immediately followed by the other three.   Away they all go, kicking and snorting, amid the renewed screams of the peacock and the shouts of the little boys who had congregated about.

> " And one and all aloud declare
> Twas a fit sight for country fair,
> Far better than a dancing bear."

The kennel reached, the pack were soon round Pigg's horse's heels, and after a few consequential cracks of his whip, and cries of " Go on, hounds ! go on ! *to him! to him!* " from Benjamin, as they proceeded through the streets, which, as usual, were all commotion to see them pass, they cleared the town and entered upon the hedge-rows of the country.

Jorrocks now began to feel the full force of his situation, and inwardly wished himself well out of it.

" A nice*ish* lot of hounds," observed Ego, casually, as he brought his horse alongside James Pigg, " to look him over," as he calls it ; and Pigg, who was rather sprung, instead of capping him, gave him a most unceremonious stare.

" A dom'd *nice* pack ! ar should say," replied Pigg.

" Humph ! " said Ego to himself, " a rummish genius this, I guess—I am POM-PO-NIUS EGO," observed he, with an air of annihilation.

" Sae they say," replied Pigg, turning his quid. " What's your cracks ? "

" What's your *whats ?* " repeated Ego to himself, without being able to hit off the scent. " Who told you I was Ego ? " inquired he, after a pause, during which he kept scrutinising Pigg.

Pigg.—" Whe tell't me ? Why, Jorrocks, to be sure ! Whe else should ? "

" *Whe else should ?* " repeated Ego, in disgust, " you're a pretty fellow for a huntsman."

" Ye'll be wantin' a ticket, ar's warn'd," observed Pigg, pulling one of his 5*s*. pink pasteboards out of his waistcoat pocket and tendering it to him.

Ego looked unutterable things.

" Well, my frind, and vot do you think of the 'ounds ? " inquired Mr. Jorrocks, who had had a suck at his monkey, riding up at this critical period. " Some of the real sort for makin' them cry ' Capivi '—all workmen—no skirtin', babblin' overrunnin' beggars kept for show merely because they are 'andsome—'andsome is wot 'andsome does, is my happhorism ? "

" A very good motto, Mr. Jorrocks," observed Ego; " a very good motto. We shall see presently what they are made of. They seem a goodish sort of hound—level—if anything, rather full of flesh."

" A werry good fault, too, at this time o' year, we shall soon work them fine enough," replied Mr. Jorrocks.

" As fine as Sam Nichol had his, eh ?—that poor John Warde used to say a man had only to take his shaving-pot into the kennel, lather his face, and scrape his face with the back of a hound—*he, he, he !* good joke that, Mr. Jorrocks, eh ? "

" Haw ! haw ! haw'! werry good joke, Mr. Hego, werry good joke, indeed—have laughed at it *werry* often—werry old friend o' yours and mine, that joke. S'pose it will be due again soon ? Shall be ready to laugh at it again when it appears."

" Mixed pack, I see," now observed Ego, who had been scrutinizing the hounds as they trotted quietly along.

Mixed pack," repeated Jorrocks, gaily, adding: "dogs I thinks correct the wolatile natur' o' the betches. I 'old wi' Mr. Craven Smith," continued

John Leech

The Pompuous Eye Dims.

he, "that though the betches are quicker nor the dogs, they do not always show the same sport, or kill the most foxes—another thing is, I likes plenty o' music, and the betches are not so free wi' their tongues as the dogs, and sometimes slip away without one's knowing it, which is inconwenient, as it doesn't look well for a gen'l'man, 'specially for an M.F.H., to go gallopin' 'bout the country, exclaimin', "'Ave you seen my 'ounds? 'ave you seen my 'ounds?'"

"That will not often happen with you, Mr. Jorrocks, I should think," observed Ego, smiling at our friend's substantial form.

"Not often," replied our master, with a chuck of the chin; "not often—still it *might,* and one doesn't like bein' left i' the lurch."

"Certainly not," assented Ego; "certainly not—nothing like being on good terms with your hounds and your banker."

"Nothin'," replied Jorrocks, "'specially wi' sich beauties as mine," looking lovingly down upon the pack.

"Some fairish looking animals among them," observed Ego, with up-turned lip.

"Fairish lookin' hanimals 'mong 'em," retorted Jorrocks; "fairish lookin' hanimals 'mong 'em; I tells ye wot," continued he, drawing breath, "if they're not 'zactly the 'andsomest pack o' 'ounds i' the kingdom, they're the steadiest—the wisest—and the best!"

"*In-deed!*" bowed Ego, with a supercilious smile.

"True guiders of a scent in 'ard runnin', close, patient 'unters with a cold scent, and as stout as steel."

"*In-deed!*" bowed Ego again.

"I'm not a conceited hass," observed Jorrocks, boiling up, "wot thinks every thing I 'ave is the best, and if I 'ears of good blood anywhere, I'll 'ave it—as I said afoor, I doesn't care twopence 'bout tin, further nor as it enables me to pursue the plisures o' the chase."

"That's your ticket!" exclaimed Ego.

"Sink ye, ye wadn't ha' it just now," observed Pigg over his shoulder, thinking the great man had changed his mind, and wanted his insurance ticket against hunting accidents.

"To hobtain a good run," continued Mr. Jorrocks, vehemently, without noticing either of these interruptions, "to hobtain a good run, your 'ounds should not only 'ave good abilities, but they should be hexperienced and well 'quainted with each other. To guide a scent well over a country for a length o' time, through all the hintricacies and difficulties o' the chase, requires first chop abilities," added he with a hearty slap of his thigh.

"So it does," assented Ego.

"Keep the tambourine a roulin'!" exclaimed Pigg, who had been reining in his horse to hear his master bounce.

"*Yooi doit!* there, Warrior!" added he, with a crack of his whip to a hound that was leading others out of ear-shot.

"There's a fine 'ound," observed Mr. Jorrocks, again arresting the great man's attention, by pointing out old Ravager, now trotting singly along the footpath.

"You'll most likely be wishin' to say summut soapey and plisant 'bout the pack, and you can't lay it too thick on to him—Ravager, by

Lord Yarborough's Rallywood out of his Ringlet. Would gladly give fifty guineas a couple for a few more sich. That's a nice dog too, Fugleman," pointing a speckled black and white one out. "Fugleman,* by the Beaufort Potentate out of Foljambe's Frantic; so's that," pointing to a mealy coloured hound; "Dorimont, by Drake's Duster out of the Belvoir Blameless. Dorimont! old bouy!" continued Mr. Jorrocks, rising in his stirrups, and chucking him a bit of biscuit for answering to his name. "Dorimont, old bouy! mind the heyes of Hengland are 'pon you! In fact," continued Mr. Jorrocks, sousing himself into his great saddle, and dropping his voice as he took Ego confidentially by the elbow, "in fact, you can't say too much in praise o' the pack—Quads neither. I'm not a wain man," continued Mr. Jorrocks, "far from it—but merit should be noticed, and it's not never of no manner of use keepin' one's candle under a bushel. *Is it?*" asked he, anxiously.

"Not a bit!" replied Ego, with another slight upward curl of his lip.

Our friends then bumped on for some time in silence, Jorrocks wondering what Ego thought of him, and Ego wondering if Jorrocks was really the liberal indifferent man about money he represented himself to be. Jorrocks was half inclined to ask Ego how he proposed buttering him, lest there might be any mistake, but just as he was going to pop the tender question, Arterxerxes gave such a terrible stumble, as nearly sent him out of his saddle. He then took to jagging and objurgating the horse, which put it out of his head, and by the time he got himself and his horse appeased, he was thinking of his dinner.

As they proceeded, the spangled hedges dropped their jewels—the fields gradually resumed their pristine hue—and on reaching Bumpmead Heath, all nature smiled with the sweetness of premature spring. What a concourse was there! Flys, carriages, gigs, hunters, hacks, donkeys, all to see an author on horseback!

"There!" said Mr. Jorrocks, pointing to the field as they turned from the road and entered the wide expanding common, "wot an 'unt mine is! Shall present them to you in reg'lar rotation—largest subscribers fust, and so on, down to the three-guinea coves. This little podgy cock on the cob is Latitat the lawyer. Bein' a werry thick-winded little sinner, they call him Whezey, junior. Yon bouy on the brown, that is fidgetin' about as though he didn't like his load, is Squire Barnington, the man wot wanted to be master; he gives fifty. My missis and his don't 'it it, but we are werry good friends. He buys 'osses like a brick, without bringin' all the relations and frinds of this world to 'sist 'im. Barnington!" holload Jorrocks to him, "come and be presented to the mighty Hego. This be him, with the bird's-eye fogle round his squeeze—coolish mornin' you see, and Hegotists † are scarce—keeps his throat warm." Mr. Barnington and Ego made mutual salutations with their hats. "Hooi, Fleecy!" roared Jorrocks to his secretary, who was poking about among the group on a long-tailed rat of a pony, with a slip of paper in his hand and a pencil between his teeth, "come and pay your devours to Hego, the man wot makes us all famous. This be my sec.," observed Mr. Jorrocks to Ego,

---

* All gammon! They were some of Bugginson's lot.
† Nothing of the sort; we wish they were.—AUTHOR.

adding, in a lower tone, "Does a little word-combin' himself at times—signs himself Junius Secundus—*you twig !* "

"Proud to make the personal acquaintance of Junius Secundus," observed Ego, bowing and laying his hand upon his breast. " Often heard of him." Fleeceall brings his hat in contact with his heel.

"This be old Barleycorn," observed Mr. Jorrocks, stopping a jolly-looking farmer, in dark clothes, on a good-looking brown horse; "a werry good friend to 'unting—always goes fust over his own wheat."

Pomponius Ego vouchsafed him a bow.

"Here comes a cove now," observed Jorrocks, laying hold of Ego's arm. "Jest look at this chap i' the cap and cut-away coat, with the bridle all over buckles. 'Dis arter six,' I calls him. His mother gets her tea o' me, and when this young blade came to settle the bill, he wanted dis arter six. Dis arter six !" exclaimed Mr. Jorrocks, with an emphasis. "As if anybody ever 'eard o' dis arter six ! The dirty-looking dog in the plum-coloured coat and dingy Napoleons wot's jest joined 'im, we call ' Two upon Ten '—they 'unt in couples, Dis arter six and Two upon ten. They took poor Two for a thief, and wen he went into the shops, they used to sing out ' *Two upon ten ! two upon ten !* ' meanin', two eyes on ten fingers—haw, haw, haw !" chuckled our master, adding, " I won't inter-duce neither o' them. But 'ere comes a good chap," continued he, "Ridge the slater, gives ten pund, and pays it too. Slates, old bouy !" continued Jorrocks, beckoning him, come this way, and let me be the makin' on you. Let me interduce you to the great Mr. Hego, King o' the Chase, I may call 'im." Ridge made as bountiful a bow as though he expected an order to roof in a palace.

"'Ere's another good chap," continued Mr. Jorrocks, "Pigott the master plasterer—M.P., as he calls himself. 'Ere, Piggy !" continued Jorrocks, hailing him, "let me do the splendacious by you. Mr. Hego, let me interduce a reg'ler brick—fire-brick, in fact—gives sivin pund to the 'ounds, and pays it too."

" Most praiseworthy character," observed Ego with a salaam.

"And 'ere's another good cove," continued Jorrocks, " Sugar the grocer. He's a payin' subscriber too, gives ten pund."

" *Five,*" observed Sugar, whose real name was Smith, with a smile.

"Five, is it ?" growled Mr. Jorrocks, adding aloud to himself, " shalln't interduce you, then. Yon chap trottin' along as if his wite choker wouldn't let him look either to the right or the left, is the Reverend Titus Cramcub, a learned man like yourself—reads Lord Bacon's works, and eats fat bacon for breakfast. He teaches the young idea 'ow to shoot, but prefers 'unting himself, and as soon as 'ounds 'ave shaken off the crowd, and settled to a run, he drops into the front rank, and goes as if he couldn't 'elp himself. This is not a bad chap," continued Mr. Jorrocks, nodding towards a square-built man in white moleskin breeches, an olive-coloured coat, and boots to match, who now turned a well-shaped gray upon the heath. "This is not a bad chap, Haimes the saddler, and I'll tell ye a story 'bout him that may come into your palarvarment, if you like. His trade lies a good deal 'mong the saints, who wouldn't 'prove of his 'unting, so he always christens his 'oss Business, and when any on 'em call when he's out, his foreman says his master's away on ' business '

—*haw, haw, haw! he, he, he!*"—a chuckle in which the great journalist joined. " This is a shabby screw," said Mr. Jorrocks, pointing to a man in a rusty Bath-bricky scarlet, riding a badly-clipped ewe-necked dun. " He's 'unted all his life, they say, and never given a copper to 'ounds, always declarin' that each season was to be his last. And, by the way, reminds me," continued Mr. Jorrocks, turning short on his secretary, " 'ow do the chaps buck up now that they've got wot they want in the way of an 'untsman ? "

" Why, only very middling, I'm sorry to say, Sir," replied Mr. Fleeceall. " Somehow or other, I never can find a man with any money in his pocket. It's always, ' Oh, I'll pay you next time we meet,' or, ' I s'pose you'll be out on Monday, when I will bring my subscription,'—but the happy day never comes."

" Well, but that's all nonsense," ejaculated Mr. Jorrocks, "that's all nonsense. Won't ᴐo in a commercial country like this, at least only for landowners, and folks wot don't understand 'ow money makes money. I'll tell ye wot ye must do," continued Mr. Jorrocks, " I'll tell ye wot you must do," repeated he, boiling up, " you must get a set of hinterest tables, and charge every man Jack on 'em five per cent. from the day the subscription becomes due."

" Well, Sir, what you think right," replied Mr. Fleeceall.

" Well, I thinks that right," retorted Mr. Jorrocks, adding : " if I was to get over the left wi' Bullock and Ulker, d'ye s'pose they wouldn't charge me five per cent., or may be more ? They'd be werry unlike bankers i' general if they didn't. Why should I give tick wi' the 'ounds ? "

" Certainly not, Sir ; certainly not," replied Fleeceall. " The misfortin is, that every man thinks what he owes is of no importance. Now, there is Mr. Gillyflower coming up, as though the county was all his own," pointing to a stylish young gentleman cantering along on a white cover hack, attired in a spic and span new scarlet coat, with patent leather fisherman boots coming half up his thighs, and puffing large clouds of smoke as he went ; " he is down for twenty guineas, and I carn't get a halfpenny of it." Just then Mr. Gillyflower spying the master as he cantered along, pulled short up, and taking his cigar from his lips, accosted Mr. Jorrocks with—

" Holloa ! good morning—how are ye, old boy ? "

Mr. Jorrocks deigned no answer.

"Here's a fine hunting morning, Mr. Jorrocks," he continued in a somewhat subdued tone, seeing our distinguished stranger.

"A werry *bad* 'untin' mornin',' I should say," replied Mr. Jorrocks, looking very irate, and unconsciously spurring his horse, who was still fidgetting about, from the effects of the ginger.

"A good scenting one, at all events, I should think," resumed the youngster, looking rather disconcerted.

"A werry *bad* scentin' one, I should say," rejoined Mr. Jorrocks, ramming the spurs into his horse, which the animal acknowledged by a sudden and desperate kick, which fairly shot our master over its head.

Great was the consternation ! Ego, Fleeceall, Gillyflower, Barnington, Dis arter six, Two upon ten, and half-a-dozen more, all leaped off their horses at once, while Gillyflower caught the hat and wig, and was loud in his hopes that Jorrocks wasn't hurt.

"*Hurt!*" exclaimed Mr. Jorrocks, his eyes sparkling with rage, as he scrambled up and replaced his lost head-gear, "*hurt*, Sir," he repeated, looking as though he would eat him, "*no, Sir—not at all—rather the contrary!*"

HURT! NO, SIR—RATHER THE CONTRARY.

Our hero, however, having fallen both clean and soft, and having vented his anger upon his non-paying subscriber, things soon resumed their right course, while Pigg turned the accident to account by sending Ben about with the insurance tickets, singing out "Take your tickets, gents? please take your tickets! goin' into a *hawful* country—bottomless brooks! Old 'un got brandy in his bottle! Reg'lar cut-em-down-and-'ang-'em-up-to-dry country!"

This traffic was in turn interrupted by an extraordinary Hyena-looking cap and scarlet-coated youth, with a cane-coloured beard and moustache,

cantering furiously about on a long-tailed cream-coloured hack, dashing
at every group of grooms and dark-coated horsemen, with the inquiry—
"*Have you seen my fellow ? Have you seen my fellow ?*" At last
he made for the pack, and hazarding the same enquiry of Pigg, that
distinguished observer, after a careful though somewhat impertinent
scrutiny, exclaimed,

"*N—o—r, ar'm d—d if iver ar did !*" and Mr. Jorrocks seeing the
stranger arranging his whip as if for action, and knowing Pigg's pugnacious disposition, immediately gave the signal for throwing off, and in an
instant the glad pack were frolicing over the greensward of the heath,
with the now contracting crowd pressing on after them.

South Grove, as our readers may remember, was the scene of
Mr. Jorrocks's former bag-fox exploit, and was well adapted for such
experiments. It was a long wood of stately oaks, running parallel with
the Appledove Road, for about a mile, the wood widening into something
like twelve acres towards the middle. The other side was bounded by
Bumpmead Heath, and the country around was of that undulating nature,
that requires a man to ride close with hounds, or run a chance of losing
them. From South Grove to Doitwich, the nearest cover, was four
miles, as the crow flies, but a judicious winding of certain irregularities
of surface would not only lengthen it into five or six miles, but also draw
a bottomless brook twice into the run. Another great advantage it
possessed for Mr. Jorrocks was, that sundry bridle-roads all made for the
next cover, and yet each by itself appearing to lead in a different direction,
no one who did not know them would think of following him.

"But where's Mr. Hego?" inquired he, looking round, expecting to
find him at his elbow.

"O, he's just trotted back to the Cock-and-Bottle," replied Mr.
Fleeceall, "he will be here directly."

"Wot can he want at the Cock-and-Bottle?" inquired Mr. Jorrocks.
"He doesn't need any more jumpin' powder than he has in his pocket,
surely !"

"No," replied Mr. Fleeceall, "but in looking into his silver sandwich-
box just now, he found they had not put any mustard between the beef
and bread, and he can't eat it that way he says. He will be back
directly, I dare say—yonder he comes, indeed !"

"Then let's be doin', Pigg !" exclaimed Mr. Jorrocks, as Ego neared
them ; adding, "now Binjimin, *mind your eye !* Marmeylad, you
know !"

"*Gently,* hounds !" roared Pigg, as they approached the cover, and
wanted to dash at the spot they took the scent up on the former occasion.
"*Have a care,* all on ye !" added he, with a crack of his whip, as they
reached the hedge.

"*Yooi, over in then !*" cheered Pigg, cap in hand, seeing they
were bent upon breaking away. "*Yooi, over in !*" and every hound
dashes into cover, with rather more music than strict etiquette would
allow.

"*Beautiful !*" exclaimed Mr. Jorrocks, fist in side, hoping Ego might
not hear the riot. "Unkimmun heager certain*lie.* Now, Mr. Hego,
look out for the find. They'll drag up to him with all this rind, or

whatever you call the stuff," knocking some of it off the bushes with his whip. "*Have at him* there, Manager, old man! Undeniable 'ound that," turning to Ego, and pointing out a black and tan dog; "ven he begins to speak, you may look arter your silver sandwich-box,—haw! haw! haw!"

"*Hoic in! hoic in!*" cheered Pigg along the ride, chuckling at the trick he was going to play. "Have at him, Crowner! good dog! Yooi! wind him, Lousey!" (Louisa) "good bitch! Have at him there, all on ye, and mind skeulmaister's lookin'," turning to Pomponius Ego with a grin, and saying, "Bain't that *industry?*"

*   *   *   *   *   *   *

"*Tally-ho! tally-ho! tally-ho!*" screamed Ben, from the thickest part of the cover, as though he were getting murdered.

"*Hoic, holloa! hoic, holloa! hoic, holloa!*" exclaimed Ego, in the most orthodox style.

"*A, how-way, canny man! how-way!*" roared Pigg, gathering up his reins and ramming his spurs into his horse. "*How-way, ar say!* dinna stand blairin' there! Whativer ye de, keep the tambourine a roulin'."

Away tore Pigg to the holloa, through bogs, briars, bushes, and brambles, followed by Ego; and now the full music of the pack proclaims the finding of the drag. There is a tremendous scent, for though it has lain an hour it is strong enough to last a week. Round they go, full swing, every hound throwing his tongue, and making the old wood echo with their melody.

"They'll kill him in cover," observed Ego, taking out his watch. "Beckford's wrong about scent never lying with a white frost. I'll write an article to prove it." A momentary check ensues—the drag has been lifted.

"Killed for a crown!" exclaimed Ego, with delight.

"Niver sick a thing;—niver sick a thing!" retorts Pigg with a grin.

*   *   *   *   *   *   *

Now they are on him again, and the old oaks seem to shake with the melody.

*   *   *   *   *   *   .   *

"Is he a big 'un, Ben?" asks Pigg, as they meet at the junction of the rides.

"*Uncommon!*" exclaims Benjamin, gasping for breath.

"Aye, but we'll bucket him," responded Pigg, turning his quid in his mouth; adding, "ar'll be the death of a shillin', ony how! Sink it!" added he, "brandy and baccy 'ill gar a man live for iver!"

It's now near leaving time, and Mr. Jorrocks and the field come up in long drawn file. The worthy M.F.H. all excitement and agitation.

"Oh!" exclaims he, dropping his ponderous whip down his leg with a heavy crash, "if we do but manish it, 'ow 'appy I shall be! My vig, they're away!"

Affable and Mercury top the fence out of cover, and the whole pack follow with desperate velocity. One twang of his horn is all Pigg gives, and then sticking it into his boot, he gets out of cover, hustles his horse, and settles himself into his seat. Away they go, up a long grass field by

B B

the side of the cover, scent breast high, the pack running almost mute, and the slow ones beginning to tail.

Pomponius Ego having got a good start, begins to spur, and passes Pigg in his stride, singing out,

> "When Greek meets Greek, then comes the tug of war!"

A stiff fence, with a strongly made-up gap, brings him up short, and turning to Pigg, he hollos out,—

"I'll hold your horse if you'll pull it down!"

"*Ar niver gets off!*" replies James, flying over the fence.

A gap at the end by the wood lets Ego through, and away he strides

after Pigg, as hard as ever his horse can lay legs to the ground. Three or four more large enclosures are sped over without any change of position, the hounds going best pace all the time.

"Sink him, but he's made it o'er strang!" exclaimed Pigg to himself, thinking of the drag; "ar wish they main't beat us," looking at the hounds running away from them.

* * * * * * *

A hat held against the clear blue sky proclaims the line over the hill.

"That's the way on him," exclaims Pigg, pointing to the holloa.

"Curse the fellow!" replies Ego; "he'll have headed him to a certainty," inwardly rejoicing at the thoughts of a check.

On they go, at a pace truly awful. The drag has never been lifted till within a few yards of the halloa on the hill, and the rising ground tells on the heaving horses. Now they have a check, and on ploughed land, too. The hounds dash towards the fence beyond, and swing their cast without a whimper.

Pigg sits like a statue, giving his horse the wind, his eagle eye fixed upon the pack. They throw up; and now he takes out his horn, gives one blast, and in an instant the pack are with him.

"I'll lay my life he's headed back!" exclaims Ego. "That confounded fool on the hill did all the mischief. Do for once try back, as Beckford says."

"Forroard yonder, to the left of the harrow," whispers a confidant to James Pigg, "then along the bottom of the next grass field, and straight over Ulverstone Pasture and Bysplit, to the back of the red house yonder."

"That can *never* be the line!" exclaims Ego, wiping the perspiration from his brow. "None but a born idiot would make such a cast—in the very teeth of the wind, too!"

"How-way, canny man! How-way!" exclaims Pigg, waiving his arm and pointing to Priestess hitting off the scent; "*how way*, ar say; what! hast getten *ne mair ink i' pen!*"

Away they go, at best pace as before, but a lane at the bottom of a turnip-field, a mile or two farther on, again brings them up.

This check joins heads and tails. Mr. Jorrocks, who has come pounding along, in a state of desperate perspiring excitement, all eyes, ears, and fears through his pet line of gates, jumps with his man at the point in the lane where the drag has crossed. Both are in such a stew, that Jorrocks can only articulate, "Headies! 'ow they go!" and Pigg, all anxiety to get his hounds across before the tail comes up, exclaims, "*Had bye, ard man! Sink! ar'll be dingin on ye down!*" adding, "*ye've* ne carle to ride for raputation!" The tobacco-juice streams down either side of his chin, and his lank hair floats on the breeze as, bare-headed, he caps the hounds over into the field. They are now upon grass again. The scent lies parallel with the lane, and Mr. Jorrocks, whose horse and whose self are nearly pumped out, keeps on the hard road, followed by a heterogeneous tail of mud-stained, elbowing horsemen. The aspirants for fame stick to the hounds, and follow them into every field, Cramcub, who cast up as the hounds broke cover, leading.

Nothing can be finer than the line! Large grazing grounds, some forty, none less than twenty acres, are sped over, and twice Dribbleford Brook comes in the way for those whose ambition is waterproof. What a scene!—what blobbings in and scramblings out; what leavings of hind legs and divings for whips, sticks, and cigar-cases!

Jorrocks, who is well laid in on the road for a view, screeches and halloas them on. " Now, Sugar! now Slates! now Dis arter six!" Then up came Whezey, Junior, looking very like " enough." " Hover ye go!" roars our master, cracking his ponderous whip. " O, Mr. Jorrocks! (puff) I must enter a (pant) *nolle prosequi*," gasps the exhausted lawyer. " Enter it then," exclaims our master, delighted at the symptoms of distress, and saying to himself. " If this don't 'stonish old Hego, there arn't no halligators! Come hup,·you hugly beast!" he adds to his horse, again spurring and kicking him into a canter.

The hounds bend again to the right, the stain of cattle rather slackens their pace, and some heavy sticky fallows at length bring their noses to the ground. " 'Eavens be praised!" exclaimed Mr. Jorrocks, easing his horse, and eyeing them topping the fence between the pasture and arable land : " we may now have a little breathin' time, and see if they can 'unt as well as run. Oh, the beauties, 'ow they spread! one, two, three, and now altogether—oh, beautiful! beautiful! He's up the furrow. Where's Hego?"

And echo answered, " Where?"

Mr. Jorrocks is right. The mock "thief o' the world" has gone up the wet furrow, to the injury of the firm of Herring and Aniseed, who carry on business very languidly. Old Priestess's unerring nose alone keeps the pack on the line. Pigg, however, is at hand, with a good idea of the run of his fox, and now carries away a rood of fence as he crashes into the field to his hounds. His horse's neck begins to stiffen, and there have been one or two ominous throat-rattles, but Pigg hustles him along, and casts his hounds forward to Sywell Wood. What a crash! The feeble whimper that barely owned the scent, is changed into a full and melodious chorus ; every hound throws his tongue, and echo answers them a hundred-fold! *There's a rare scent!*

The cover being open at the bottom, the hounds are quickly through, and Pigg, catching Benjamin at the far end, pulls him off his horse, and makes a fresh start on the boy's.

Grass again greets the pack. The red-topped house is neared, and the scent improves. The hounds run stout, though, perhaps, not carrying quite so good a head as might have been desirable, had Ego been near. On they go ; and now a sudden check ensues at the corner of the stack-yard. The music that lately rent the air is lulled, the hounds having swung a rocket-like cast, stand staring with their heads in the air.

" *Who-hoop, gone to ground!* " exclaims some one in the rear, anxious for a termination of the enjoyment.

" *Not a bit of it*," replies Mr. Jorrocks, knowing better. " OLD 'ARD!" roars he to the forward roadsters, who are now getting among the hounds. " You 'air-dresser on the chesnut 'oss!" holloaing to a gentleman with very big ginger whiskers ; " PRAY 'OLD 'ARD!"

" HAIR-DRESSER!" exclaims the gentleman, in a fury, turning short round ; " *I'm an officer in the ninety-first regiment!* "

" Then you hossifer in the ninety-fust regiment, wot looks like an 'air-dresser, 'old 'ard," replied Mr. Jorrocks, trotting on, adding most unconcernedly, " *Cast 'em forrard, Pigg! Cast 'em forrard!* or make a patent all round my hatter."

On goes Pigg, making good the line the warmint should have gone. Not a hound speaks!—all mute as death.

"*Werry rum, Pigg,*" said Mr. Jorrocks winking significantly to his huntsman, as the latter trotted round with his hounds; "werry rum—for once cast back—clear the way there, gen'lemen, if you please, clear the way, who knows but you are right upon the line o' scent!" cried Mr. Jorrocks to the horsemen who were clustering about, thinking of any thing but what they ought.

That would not do.

"Oh dear! oh dear! that's bad," muttered Mr. Jorrocks to James Pigg; "where the deuce can the fool ha' gone?"

We may here state that Giles Gosling the farmer having seen Pigg and his comrade setting out the line, and not exactly relishing their progress over his wheat a little farther on, had watched Maltby's coming, and seizing him, drag and all, had stowed him away in his cellar.

"Ar mun just try to cross the line on him," observed Pigg, pulling his horn out of his boot, and giving it a twang; "put hunds forrard 'ard, man," said he to his master, trotting on, and blowing as he went.

"Who ever saw such a cast?" exclaimed Ego, who had now got draggled up; "your huntsman must be mad, Mr. Jorrocks!"

"Ill lay a guinea 'at to a 'alf-crown wide awake he recovers his fox for all that," replied Mr. Jorrocks, with a good deal more confidence than he felt.

"If he does I'll eat him!" rejoined Pomponius Ego, with an air of importance.

This prediction, coming from so high an authority, combined with the state of the steam had the effect of stopping the majority of a pretty well exhausted field, who all clustered round Ego to relate their daring leaps, in hopes of monthly immortality. "I leapt Dribbleford Brook." "I charged the ox-fence on the far side." "I never left the hounds." "I did this—I did that!" Ambitious men!

With fear and anxiety on their faces, Pigg and his master bumped on, in hopes of hitting off the scent. Mr. Jorrocks was in a desperate stew.

"Oh, Pigg!" exclaimed he, as they got out of hearing, "I'd give the world to finish wi' blood. If you could but manish to kill him, 'ow gratefully obleged I should be to you and your heirs for ever! You shall drink brandy out of a pint-pot for breakfast, dinner, and supper!"

"Ye said a *quart!*" observed the man of the north, eyeing his hounds.

Jorrocks.—"Did I? I'll be as good as my word."

Pigg.—"Ords wuns, ard man, fetch hunds on; does think, thou ard gouk, ar can hit him off o' mysel'?" looking back at the hounds all straggling behind Mr. Jorrocks's horse.

Mr. Jorrocks pockets the rebuke, and bestirs himself to get the hounds on to his huntsman; Pigg trots on, letting them feel for the scent as they go.

Mr. Jorrocks bumps on, vowing all sorts of vows to Diana, if she will only 'ave the kindness to assist him that once. He would give her a hat and feather! He would give her a swan's-down muff and tippet! Nay, he would stand a whole rig-out at Swan and Hedgar's; pettikits, bustle, and all!

Pigg's eagle-eye lights up, as a hat is waved near the windmill on the rising ground.

"Yonder he is!" exclaims James, grinning with delight.

"Vere?" inquires Mr. Jorrocks, all eyes, like Gabriel Junks's tail.

Pigg spurs his horse, and trots on to the holloa.

It *is* the man, who has been waiting in anxious expectation, and has just shook the fox.

After staring about, Reynard proceeds from a crawl to a trot, and then sets his head for the vale, from which the hounds have just come.

Pigg views him stealing past a plantation end, and lays his hounds quietly on; they quickly take up the scent.

A stranger in the land, the fox goes stoutly down wind, with the hounds too near to give him much chance for his life. As if anxious for the promotion of the sport, he makes for the vale, and the pack come swinging down the hill in the view of the field planted below. Fresh ardour is

caught at the sight! Those who ridiculed the cast are now loudest in its praise. They reach the bottom, and fox and hounds are in the same field. Now they view him! How they strain! It's a beautiful sight. Old Priestess is tailed off, and Rummager falls into the rear. Ah, age! age! Now Vanquisher turns him, and races with Dexterous for the seize! Who-hoop! Fox and hounds roll over together!

Now Pigg crushes through the Bullfinch at the far end, followed by Mr. Jorrocks, who doesn't even ask "What there's on t'other side?" Master and man race for the brush, but Pigg throws himself from his horse, and has the fox high in air just as the field come up in the opposite direction. What delight is in every countenance! There is Pigg holding the fox above his head, grinning and gaping, with his cap on one side, his white neckcloth ends flying out, and a coat-lap torn to ribands. Mr. Jorrocks gets off his horse, and throwing his hat in air, catches it again, and then kicks the crown out, while his heaving horse stretches and shakes himself after his unwonted exertion. Lather! lather! lots of lather! Even dribbling Ben catches the infection, and whoops and holloas at the top of his voice.

Up comes Ego, and Mr. Jorrocks, with brush in one hand and crownless hat in the other, greets him on one leg, waving the proud trophy about, and hurraying at the top of his voice, "*Hurrah! hurrah! hurrah!* Allow me, Mr. Pomponius Hego," says he, "to present you with the brush of the werry gamest old thief o' the world whatever was seen. Time, one hour and twenty minutes, with only one check—distance, wot you please to call it. Am sorry you wern't hup to see the darlin's run into the warmint! Did it in style!

"Never were sich a pack as mine; best 'ounds in England!—best 'ounds in Europe!—best 'ounds in Europe, Hasia, Hafrica, or 'Merica!" So saying, Mr. Jorrocks, resuming his equilibrium, presented Ego with the brush, who received it with laudable condescension.

"Now, vot will you do?" inquired Mr. Jorrocks; "eat your sandwiches and find another fox, or eat your sandwiches and cut away 'ome?"

THERE IS PIGG HOLDING THE FOX ABOVE HIS HEAD.

"Why, for my part, I should like to try again," replied Ego; "but I fear your horse's condition is hardly equal to another burst; added to which, there's a frost in the air that will harden the ground, and, perhaps, damage your hounds' feet. I think, perhaps, we had better leave well alone."

"So be it," replied Mr. Jorrocks. "Here, then, you chap with the dandy legs!" calling to a knock-kneed lad on the other side of the ring; "fatch me my 'at-crown, the cold strikes through my cocoa-nut."

Having got it, Mr. Jorrocks stuck the crown in the best way he could, and, remounting his horse, returned to Handley Cross in state, and great exultation.

In the evening he entertained Mr. Ego to a sumptuous banquet, the particulars of which are recorded by him in the following chapter.

CHAPTER LII.

A BAD CHURNING.

AFTER many prefatory twangs of his trumpet, the following account of the visit at length appeared in the " Heavy Triumvirate."

"A DAY WITH MR. JORROCKS'S HOUNDS:

BY

POMPONIUS EGO.

" All the world has heard of the renowned John Jorrocks—renowned as a citizen—renowned as a wit—and renowned as a sportsman ; but all the world may not know, until I have the pleasure of proclaiming it, that I have lately done Mr. Jorrocks the honour of paying him a visit at Handley Cross Spa. But a few words by way of introduction : I first became acquainted with Mr. Jorrocks at a soapey-tailed pig-hunt at Moulsey Hurst, which I attended for the purpose of furnishing an original article on our great national sports and pastimes for the ' Encyclopedia,' the ' Quarterly Review,' the ' Heavy Triumvirate,' ' Fraser,' and ' Blackwood's ' Magazines; and liking Mr. Jorrocks's looks, I entered into conversation with him, without his having the slightest idea who I was. I subsequently met him at our excellent friend Ackermann's, when, on a regular introduction, he fully developed those feelings of reverential awe that necessarily pervade even the most obtuse when suddenly ushered into the presence of transcendent genius, that—means—*me*. Of Mr. Jorrocks's early life, habits, tastes, pursuits, &c., I would gladly furnish the numerous and intelligent readers of the ' Heavy Triumvirate ' with some account, but unfortunately it does not lie in my power to accomplish so desirable an object. Many of my readers will doubtless ask why not ? I answer them, because I do not know any thing ! Of his present fame, however, there is no doubt ; and if he owes his position in the commercial world solely to the efforts of his own head, who will deny that it does him very great credit ? An English merchant, in my eyes, is one of the most honourable and enviable of men. ' *Stat nominis umbra*,' as the elegant Junius writes, for his name is in a blaze of light. Though some may affect to decry the lustre of civic honour, such sentiments meet with no response in the breast of Ego, who knows what is estimable in commerce as well as in cover. But to my point.

" One day, as I was polishing off, and weaving the quotations into an admirable article on the breed of the unadulterated ' Genuine Jack-Ass,' which many of the readers of the ' Heavy Triumvirate ' will doubtless anxiously look for, I received an invitation from Mr. Jorrocks to inspect the Handley Cross hounds, of which I need hardly inform my readers he is the master. Now, this offer was very kind, and I will briefly explain why it was so. In the first place, Mr. Jorrocks, being a master of hounds, will naturally be supposed to have to mount his own men, and offering me the loan of a horse under such circumstances, converted such a favour into a double obligation. But have I no other reason for expressing myself in this manner ? Undoubtedly I have. He accompanied the offer with an invitation to stay with him. Could I be so unwise as to neglect such an invitation ? No; for in the language of the classic moralist—I feel

'Nemo mortalium omnibus horis sapit !'

I regret that it was not in my power to go to him overnight, or I should doubtless have been able to present my numerous readers with many excellent *jeu d'esprits*, or *bon mots*, from the lips of this amiable man ; but I hope the following sketch of our day's sport will make some atone- ment for the omission.

" The meet was on Bumpmead Heath, a choice fixture, but though it has the reputation of never failing to show sport, I could discern on mine host's countenance, as we rode along, an evident anxiety for the result. His conversation at first was strangely monosyllabic, and seeing little probability of getting ' a rise ' out of him, I trotted on to have a little chat with his huntsman, a fellow of the appropriate name of Hogg. But what an example of a man was he ! A great, lanky, hungry, ill- conditioned, raw-boned Borderer, speaking a language formed of the worst corruptions of Scotch and English, intelligible only to a master of languages like myself—a man devoid of the slightest idea of civility or respect, and whose manner would have baffled any one who was to be borne down by impudent assurance. Thank God, however, such is not the case with Pomponius Ego !

'Yet if my name were liable to fear
I do not know the man I should avoid
So soon as that spare Cassius.'

Still fame will work its way, and even this illiterate loggerhead, for I question if the fellow can write his own name, knew and venerated the name of Ego. May not I, then, without incurring the charge of vanity, exclaim with the ancient philosopher—

'Quæ regio in terris nostri non plena laboris?'

I think I may !

" From the appearance of early morning I feared we should not have been able to hunt so keen was the frost at the dawn; but the genial influence of an extremely powerful sun dispelled all fears, and before we reached the place of meeting, the country had quite laid aside its coat of white. I thought, what language can elevate the charms of Nature, and exclaimed, with the Tuscan poet—

'Difficile est propria communia dicere.'

Prior to throwing off, Mr. Jorrocks presented the principal members of his hunt to me, by all of whom I was received with marked respect, and, I am sorry to add, that he was also thrown off himself, by his horse pitching him over its head—an accident which I saw once occur to my friend Count Pitchinstern, at his *château* one morning, when I was chatting, with the charming Countess on my arm. I also remember, many years ago, as my readers may suppose it is, when I say it was in the days of Mr. Corbet, in Warwickshire, seeing Will Barrow, his huntsman —and a better never cheered hound—get precisely a similar fall, at the same time of day, just as he was turning his horse's head for the cover, and strange to say, I observed Mr. Jorrocks acted just as Will did on that occasion—he scrambled up as quick as he could, and remounted his horse.

"Now, then, for the sport ! We quickly found our fox, and the scent being good, he soon saw it prudent to leave the cover and try his fortune in the open. The hounds got well together, and every thing seemed indicative of sport, when one of those 'untoward events,' to which all countries are liable, occurred, and completely changed the aspect of affairs. The fox was shamefully headed by a man at work, forced from his line—one of the best he possibly could have selected—and driven upon ground all foiled with the stain of sheep and cattle. Seeing what had occurred, I pulled up in perfect despair, and almost vowed I would never come out hunting again. How strange it is that men will hoop and holloa when they see a fox, as though their lives depended on this exercise of their lungs ! I have often meditated a paper upon holloas, and the events of this day made me more resolved to execute the intention than ever. The readers of this lively publication may now look for its appearance.

"All prospect of sport being unhappily annihilated, I complacently resigned my place of leader of the front rank, and contented myself with trotting quietly on, and observing the performances of the others. Of those who went well, I may particularly mention a Cheshire gentleman, of large fortune, by the name of Barnington, whose acquaintance I had the pleasure of making some years since in Oxfordshire, when the late Sir Thomas Mostyn hunted the country Mr. Drake now has, and I was happy to see that the fine hand and nerve he then possessed, had matured, with experience, into the formation of a good sportsman. Mr. Barnington asked me to dine and stay all night at his house, which, I was given to understand, is the best in Handley Cross—every thing done in the most elegant style, which I so greatly admire—and kindly accompanied the invitation with the offer of a mount the next day the hounds went out ; but the duties of preparing this article imperatively recalled me to my desk, at home. But did Mr. Barnington do nothing else for me ? I answer yes ; he gave me some gingerbread-nuts !

Unexampled kindness! He would seem to havé sat for the picture so felicitously hit off by the ancient bard,—

'Impiger, iracundus, inexorabilis, acer !

" But I fancy I hear some of your readers exclaiming ' *Get forrard, Ego ; get forrard ;* or you will be having Oxoniensis,* or some of the saucy critics flanking you.' I answer, I do not care a *sou* for Oxoniensis or any critic on the face of the earth. I will, however, dismiss this subject in a few words. After a good deal of cold and slow hunting, we at last worked up to our fox, and Mr. Jorrocks most politely presented me with the brush, in terms far too flattering and complimentary to admit of my repeating it here. We then returned home. Arrived there, my most enthusiastic friend, who was evidently bent on showing off to advantage, proceeded to introduce me to his bet won hats, accompanying each castor with an account of how he got it. 'This,' said he, balancing a fine Jolliffe punt on the point of his finger, 'I won by the Water-Witch beating the Weazel from Wapping to Margate. This,' said he, producing a cream-bowl shallow, 'I won at my great Maid of Honour match at Richmond—eat eighteen maids of honour while Billy Buttonhole was tucking in ten;' an appalling feat, my myriads of fair friends would exclaim, were I not to add, that said ' maids' are a species of cheese-cake made at that beautiful locality on the Thames. Then a woolley whitey-brown hat was the product of prowess at the ' Cope ;' a shaved drab, the fruits of his gun at the Red House; a green wide-awake was won at Hornsey Wood, and a horse-hair drab felt at Jemmy Shaw's rattery, somewhere in Windmill Street. Having got through the history of these, he out with his foxes' brushes, and proceeded to expatiate on them, each brush furnishing an account of the ' finest run that ever was seen !' At length he talked himself out of breath, blew himself, in short; and as he proceeded to arrange the brushes becomingly in the hats, and set them out on the side-board, like racing-cups, against dinner, I retired to the privacy of my apartment, there to ruminate o'er the doings of the day, and think how best I could furnish an account that would delight my anxious readers, and maintain the lustre of a glorious name.

" *The Dinner.*—At five o'clock precisely, for no man is more punctual than Mr. Jorrocks, I found myself comfortably seated with my legs under his mahogany, in a delightful little party, formed of my estimable host and his lady, a very Venus, and suggesting, by her complexion, the words of the Poet of Love, ' *ut flos,*' &c. Miss Belinda Jorrocks, their niece, a most lovely and fascinating young creature, the Diana of private life,' rosy, with dew,' as Moore says. Mr. James Stobbs, a Yorkshire gentleman—heir, I understand, to a pretty fortune, and who was evidently making love to Miss Belinda, and another gentleman of the name of Smith,† or Smyth, but which it was, I regret exceedingly to say, I am unable to state.

* " Whipper-in to 'Bell's Life.' "

† " Being always most anxious for the accuracy of my statements, I have written twice to Mr. Jorrocks, to inquire which it was, but regret to add, that up to this time, the 25th of the month, I have not yet received an answer. Should it not arrive in time for insertion in the ' Heavy Triumvirate' this month, my readers may rely upon its appearing in the next number.—P. E."

"We had an excellent repast, in the old English style, of abundant profusion, which I so greatly admire—pig at the top, pig at the bottom, and myself on one side—turkey to remove one and a couple of hares to supplant the other. For side dishes, there were what I never saw before in any country—a round of beef, cut in two, one half placed on each side of the table; on inquiry, I found it was done to get the real juicy part of the beef, without the salt. In addition to these, there were two pork-pies.

"But my readers will naturally inquire, 'Had you, Ego, with all this eating, any thing like drinking in proportion?' Oh, indeed, I answer yes—*Oceans of Port !* We drank 'Fox-hunting' again, and again, and again. In short, whenever my inestimable host found himself at a loss for a joke, a toast, or a sentiment, he invariably exclaimed, 'Come, Mr. Ego, let's drink Fox-'unting again!' Particulars I will not enter into, but I may be allowed to speak of myself. I paid such devotion to Bacchus, that I fancied I became the God myself! Ego's forehead fancied the vine-crown around it! But he trusts he never, in his moments of deepest hilarity, forgot what was due to beauty and moral worth! Yet, the wine in—well may we say with the Augustan classic—

> 'Cereus in vitium flecti, monitoribus asper
> Utilium tardus provisor, prodigus æris,
> Sublimis, cupidusque, et amata relinquere pernix.'

"Any particulars of the establishment of so celebrated a gentleman as Mr. Jorrocks, will, I am sure, be interesting to the innumerable readers of the 'Heavy Triumvirate,' I may, therefore, mention the first thing that occurred to me on returning to sensibility on the following morning. I was lying tossing and tumbling about in a very nice French bed, with white dimity furniture, with a splitting headache from my over-night's Anacreonism, as Moore would elegantly call it, when a gentle tap at my door first drew my attention to the fact that I was not, as I fancied, in the Calais packet, off Dover. 'Come in!' at length I cried, after the knock had been more than once repeated, and in obedience to the order, little Benjamin, Mr. Jorrocks's 'buoy' of all work, presented himself at my bed-side. His whole person was enveloped in an old faded green baize apron, but there was no mistaking the rogueish *ginnified* countenance that appeared above it, even if he had suffered his tongue to lie dormant, which was not the case.

"'I say, guv'nor!' exclaimed he, in the slangy, saucy dialect, peculiar to the lower orders in London, 'I say, guv'nor, Betsy complains!'

"'Sirrah! Remember what the Latian said!—

> 'Syllaba longa brevi subjecta vocatur iambus,
> Pes citus.'

"'Hold your tongue!' cried I.

"Benjamin was struck with the language.

"'What business have you here?'

"'Vot business have I here? I'll tell you vot business I have here,' said he. 'The old 'un' (meaning his master) 'says, if your coppers

are 'ot, you may have one of his Sizeley (Seidlitz) pooders,' producing a
box as he spoke.

"Mr. Jorrocks, however, I suppose, gets Ben on such terms as makes
it convenient for him to put up with his impudence, as on no other score
can I reconcile the idea of his keeping such a scoundrel. One word
more relative to Mr. Jorrocks, and, for the present, I take leave of my most
respected friend, of whom none but himself can be his parallel. It may
not, perhaps, be generally known, that prior to Mr. Jorrocks becoming
master of the Handley Cross Fox Hounds, his amiable lady and he did
not live upon the most amicable terms, and frequent feuds disturbed the
serenity of Great Coram Street. Since he got them, all goes on smoothly
and well. Mrs. Jorrocks identifies herself with the sports of her husband,
and not unfrequently graces the field in a fly. Is not this a compliment
to hunting; and may not I, the chosen, the only *real* historian of the
chase, take some little credit to myself for the accomplishment of so
desirable an object?

"I think I may!

"POMPONIUS EGO!"

When Mr. Jorrocks, who had anticipated all sorts of flattering encomiums and agreeable comparisons—that would place him in the front
rank of sportsmen, and astonish the chaps in the city—read the foregoing,
he was half frantic with rage, and kept dashing the Heavy Triumvirate
about the room, until he knocked all the number to pieces. He then
deliberately kicked it together, and, taking the tongs, burnt it before a
slow fire under a heavy discharge of depreciatory anathemas and declara-
tions that it was as much out of date as an old six inside coach.

The following is his entry in his Journal respecting the account, to hear
which he had summoned a select party to dinner:—

"Read Pomponius Hego's account of me, my missus, my miss, my
'ats, my pork pyes, and my 'ounds. Never was such nonsense. This
sort of hoiling won't answer. Always one word for his host and two for
himself. All nonsense payin' chaps for butterin' one when one can do it
so much better oneself. Will take a leaf out o' the Blackmore Wale
chap's books another time. Spoiled the best dinner that ever was
cooked—turtle soup and turbot—haunch o' doe wenison and Stilton—
couldn't eat a bit."

And there leaving him to recover, we will take another peep at his
huntsman.

CHAPTER LIII.

THE PIGG TESTIMONIAL.

"Yis :—Resolved that James Pigg is evidently desarvin' of a testimonial—is evidently desarvin' of a testimonial,—yis—is evidently desarvin' of a testimonial." Such were the words that escaped the lanthorn jaws of friend James at the end of a long carouse at the sign of the Salmon in Handley Cross (beds 1s., breakfasts 1s. 6d., dinners with ale 2s. 6d.), where a sporting or perhaps gambling conversation had gradually turned into an enquiry as to the best means of raising the wind. Owen Sherry, the landlord, suggested one thing; Boltem, the billiard-table keeper, suggested another; Tom Taws, the schoolmaster a third;—but at length it was unanimously agreed that there was nothing like a testimonial. It required no capital; fourpence for books, a penny for pens, and a like sum for ink, would cover the expenses of any amount they could gather. It only wanted a popular character to testimonialise, and where would they get such a man as Mr. Pigg? They would give it a start, so Duncan Nevin being, as the most respectable man, voted into the chair, it was moved and seconded—"That James Pigg was eminently deserving of a testimonial, and that a committee, consisting of the present party, with power to add to their number, be appointed to carry the same into effect."

And, after a glorious evening, James went hiccuping home, bumping against pillar and post, vociferating—"Resolved! resolved that James Pigg is evidently desarvin' of a testimonial!—yis—*evidently* desarvin' of a testimonial!" adding, as he nearly came over on his nose, "had up 'ard boy, or ye'll be brikin' your knees. Sink! they dinna mak' their streets hafe wide enough," continued he, taking his bearings for another lamp post. Then, as he reached the top of Hill-street, he steadied himself awhile, and after shouting at the top 'of his voice, "*Whativer ye de keep the tambourine a roulin!*" he gave such a series of shrieks and view holloas, as brought a night-capped head to almost every window in the street.

"What's the matter!" demanded one.

"Police!" roared another.

"Thieves! fire! murder!" screeched a score.

"Sink ye! brandy and baccy 'ill gar a man live for iver!" hiccupped Pigg again; whereupon a fresh volley of yells arose, which Pigg seasoned with view holloas, who-hoops, and other hunting noises.

At length heads gradually withdrew, windows closed, and lights disappeared, and Pigg went lurching down the street, singing, "Sommer's comin' on, and ar shall roul i' riches, and ar will buy mar fancy man a pair o' leather breeches."

When Porker, the policeman (No. 9), was making his round some half-hour after, he stumbled over Pigg, lying in the gutter in Duke-street, muttering, as the dirty water trickled under his nose, "Not another drop,

I thank ye. No, not another drop." Porker then got a shutter, and, aided by a comrade, shot Mr. Pigg down in Mr. Jorrocks's back kitchen.

The next number of the "Paul Pry" newspaper contained a neatly-worded paragraph, stating that their numerous readers would be glad to see by an advertisement in their first page that a subscription had been set on foot by certain influential parties, for the purpose of presenting Mr. Jorrocks's excellent Highland huntsman with a becoming testimonial, which would afford all well-wishers of their unrivalled Spa, who did not partake of the exhilirating pastime of the chase, an opportunity of testifying their admiration of a man who contributed so much to the prosperity of the place; while the great "we" said he was sure all sportsmen would eagerly rush to do honour to one whose keenness was only equalled by his success.

The paragraph, which of course was paid for, concluded by saying, that in addition to Mr. Pigg's eminent qualifications as a huntsman, he had a claim upon their sympathies, as a gentleman of ancient lineage, and the chief of his clan, who had been unjustly defrauded of his rightful inheritance, which was very considerable.

The following is a copy of the advertisement referred to, which occupied a conspicuous place in the paper, along with Holloway's Pills, Dredge's Heal-All, Cockle's Antibilious, and similar stock announcements :—

" PROPOSED TESTIMONIAL TO MR. JAMES PIGG, HUNTSMAN TO THE HANDLEY CROSS (MR. JORROCKS'S) FOX-HOUNDS.

" Many of the sportsmen in the habit of hunting with this well-known and highly efficient pack having expressed a desire to present Mr. Pigg, their able huntsman, with a testimonial of respect, as well for his civility in the field as his general private worth, the following gentlemen have consented to act as a committee to receive subscriptions to effect that object, and they earnestly request the co-operation of all true lovers of the noble sport.

" DUNCAN NEVIN,
OWEN SHERRY,
ALFRED BOLTEM,
SIMON HOOKEM,
JUDAS TURNBULL,
MICHAEL GRASPER,
THOMAS TAWS,
JAMES BLASH,
JOHN DE PLEDGE."

The committee having agreed to sup together twice a week out of the proceeds of the subscription, did not think it necessary to add to their number, and went to work vigorously, aided by the chieftain, who did not consider it derogatory to his dignity to canvass for subscriptions; on the contrary, he went about urging people to "beave 'andsome," intimating to some that he would "ride o'er them," or "jump a top on 'em" the first time he caught them down, if they didn't.

Of course they went to our master first, who did not take the sanguine view the gentlemen anticipated. Indeed, he threw cold water upon it altogether, and gave the deputation a good lecture on the " wice " of insobriety, which he assured them was the root of all evil,—adding that he had seen drinkin' tried in warious lines of life, but had never seen it answer in any, and hinted that he thought his Pigg would be quite as well without the " 'quaintance o' certain gen'lmen in 'Andley Cross," looking significantly at Blash and De Pledge as he spoke.   Finding there was nothing to be got out of Mr. Jorrocks in the way of cash, they proceeded to coax him into being a decoy, by representing how injurious it would be to Pigg if his master didn't appear to sanction the proceeding ; and ultimately Mr. Jorrocks put his name down for a guinea, our master paying the shilling, and making them mark him down " then and there," as he said, as having paid the whole.

They then went to Captain Doleful, who, appalled at the amount Mr. Jorrocks had given, would fain have backed out of it altogether, on the plea of not being a fox-hunter ; but the committee urging the same arguments upon him that they had upon Mr. Jorrocks, he at length consented to write himself down for a sovereign, on the assurance that it would " never be called for," a delusion in which he indulged until a county-court summons enlightened him on the subject.

Testimonials, though nominally voluntary, being in reality almost compulsory—a non-subscriber being looked upon, if not in the light of an enemy, at all events not in that of a friend—money came flowing in from all quarters, especially from the townspeople, who did not like to be dunned face and face, taunted with being " shabby fellows," and " no gentlemen," as Pigg taunted them.

The country people were more difficult to move, and treated their circulars very small ; some putting them in the fire, others lighting their cigars with them ; and our active committee were obliged to issue a second circular, drawing attention to the fact of their not having been favoured with an answer to the first, saying " what the party intended to give," an ingenious device well worth the attention of the promoters of these nuisances.

They also inserted the following advertisement in the Handley Cross " Paul Pry :"—

" TESTIMONIAL TO MR. PIGG.

" At a highly respectable and influential ADJOURNED MEETING of the friends of MR. PIGG, held at Mr. Owen Sherry's, the sign of the Salmon, in Handley Cross, It was resolved,—That the list be kept open for a fortnight, to enable the outlying members of the hunt and others, to assist in honouring a gentleman who deserves so well at their hands, for his cheery affability and unremitting exertions in the noble cause of fox-hunting."

And so, leaving the testimonial to the benefit of its fortnight's grace, we will return to our notices of the pack.

CHAPTER LIV.

THE WANING SEASON.

THE season was wearing out apace.

An unusually dry spring brought the country forward, and set the farmers to their fences and their fields. Ploughs and harrows were going, grain was scattering, and Reynard was telegraphed wherever he went.

"You bain't a comin' this way again, I s'pose," observed each hedger, as he drove his stakes into the ground to stop up the gaps.

The hazel-drops began to hang from the bushes, the larch assumed a greenish tint, and the groves echoed to the sound of minstrelsy. The wood pigeons had long been exhorting Davy to take two cows, when he was about it—

"Take two ooos Davy,
    Take two coos,"

as some ingenious gentleman has interpreted their mild melody. The rooks, indeed all the birds were busy—primroses opened their yellow leaves, and the wood anemone shot into life and wild luxuriance. The broom was parched and the gorse sun-burnt.

After many days of declining sport, including two or three after the old customer, the following ominous paragraph at length appeared in the " Paul Pry," under the head of

" Hunting Intelligence."

" Mr. Jorrocks's hounds will meet at Furzy Lawn Turnpike, on Wednesday, at nine o'clock precisely." Significant notice! Another "last day" about to be added to the long list of "last days" that had gone before. The old stagers sighed as they read it. It recalled many such notices read in company with those they would never see again. The young ones said it was a "pity," but consoled themselves with the thoughts of a summer in London, a yachting or a fishing season. The would-be sportsmen who had been putting off hunting all the winter began to think seriously of taking to it next, and to make arrangements for November.

The morning of the last day was anything but propitious. The sun shone clear and bright, while a cutting east wind starved the sheltered side of the face—horses' coats stared, the hounds looked listless and ill, and men's boots carried dust instead of mud-sparks. Fitful gusts of wind hurried the dust along the roads, or raised it in eddying volleys on hills and exposed places. It felt like anything but hunting; the fallows were dry and parched, the buds on the trees looked as if they thought they had better retire, and all nature yearned for rain—rain would be a real blessing.

Still there was a goodish muster of pinks, and the meet being on the road, sundry flys and other sporting equipages contributed their quota of dust. Great was the moaning and lamentation that the season was over. Men didn't know what they should do with themselves all the summer. What wild resolutions they might have pledged themselves to is uncertain, for just as the drawing up of vehicles, the cuttings in and out of horsemen, the raising of hats, the kissing of hands, and the volleys of dust, were at their height, Walter Fleeceall's ominous visage appearing on one side of the gate, and Duncan Nevin's on the other, caused such a sensation, that (to avoid the dust) many of the gentlemen got into the fields, and never came near the gate again. Added to this a great black cart stallion, with his tail full of red tape, whinnied and kicked up such a row, that people could hardly hear themselves speak.

At nine o'clock, half blinded, half baked, and quite bothered, Mr. Jorrocks gave the signal for leaving the meet. It was a wildish sort of try, and every farmer having recently seen a fox at some distance from his own farm, James Pigg just run the hounds through turnip-fields, along dike-backs as he called the hedge-rows, and through any little spinneys that came in his way, till he got them to Bleberry Gorse. What a change had come over the hounds since last they were there! Instead of the eager dash in, they trotted up to it, and not above half the hounds could be persuaded to enter.

"*Eleu in, mar cannie hinnies!*" holloaed James Pigg, standing erect in his stirrups, and waving his cap; but the "cannie hinnies" didn't seem to care about it, and stood looking him in the face, as much as to say so. "Hoic in there, Priestess! Hoic in!" continued he, trotting round the cover, and holding them at the weak places, in hopes of striking a scent. "Ne fox here," said Pigg to himself, watching the waving of the gorse as the hounds worked leisurely through it. "Ne great odds, either," continued he; "could mak nout on him if there was."

* * * * * * *

"Where will you go to next, James?" inquired Mr. Jorrocks, coming up, horn in hand, preparing to call his hounds out of cover.

"A! ar dinna ken, ar's sure," replied Pigg; "mak's little odds ar think—might as well hunt o'er a pit-heap, as i' seck a country as this," looking at the baked fallows round about.

"Well, never mind," replied Mr. Jorrocks, "this is our last day, and high time it was; but we mustn't let it be blank, if we can 'elp it—so let's try Sywell plantation—the grass at all ewents will carry a scent, and I *should* like to hear the Jenny Linds again afore we shut up, if it was only for five minutes."

Out went the horns—Mr. Jorrocks determined to have a blow, if he could have nothing else, and the hounds came straggling out of cover, some lying down at his horses' heels, others staring listlessly about.

"Never saw such a slack pack in my life," exclaimed Captain Shortflat, eyeing them as he spoke: "I wonder what Scrutator would say if he saw them! Never saw such a listless lot of animals—glad I've not wasted my season by hunting with them."

Captain Shortflat's opinion was caught by Master Weekly (at home for the measles), who immediately sported it as his own to his school-fellow, Master Walker (at home for the hooping-cough); and it at length coming to Mr. Bateman's ears, he immediately attributes their slackness to the fact of their being fed on meal before hunting, which of course he considered was done to save flesh, and thereupon Mr. Jorrocks is voted an uncommon great screw. Meanwhile our master, unconscious of the verdict, goes on at a very easy pace, feeling that a hot sun and a red coat are incompatible.

Sywell plantations are blank, Layton spinney ditto; then they take a three-miles' saunter to Simonswood, where they find a hare, and at two o'clock Mr. Jorrocks announces that he will draw Warrington Banks, which is the last cover in his draw, and then give in. Some sportsmen go home, others go on, among the number Captain Shortflat, who meditates an article in "Bell's Life" on "Slackness in general, and Handley Cross slackness in particular."

The sun is very powerful, and Mr. Jorrocks gives his hounds a lap at a stream before putting them into cover. Warrington Banks are irregularly fringed with copsewood, intermixed with broom and blackthorn: lying warm to the sun, the grass grows early, and Old Priestess and Rummager feather across a glade almost immediately on entering. Presently there is a challenge—another—then a third, and the chorus swells. Mr. Jorrocks listens with delight, for though a kill is hopeless, still a find is fine—Captain Shortflat turns pale.

The hounds work on, bristling into the thick of the cover. Now they push through an almost impenetrable thicket, and cross a ride beyond. The chorus increases, but the hounds move not. *" Who-hoop ! it's a kill."*

Now Pigg jumps off his horse, and leaving him to chance, bounds over head among the underwood. His cap-top is just visible as he scrambles about in search of the place. " To the right ! " exclaims Mr. Jorrocks, seeing him blindly pushing the wrong way—" make for the big hash a top of the crag and you'll have 'em."

On Pigg goes, swimming, as it were, through the lofty gorse and brushwood, and his well-known who-hoop ! sounds from the bottom of the crag.

" Bravo ! " exclaims Mr. Jorrocks, chucking his hat in the air. (He could not afford to kick out the crown.)

" Delightful ! " lisps Captain Shortflat, wringing Mr. Jorrocks' hand.

" A glorious finish ! " rejoined Mr. Jorrocks, pocketing his wig.

" Charming, indeed ! " exclaims Captain Shortflat, resolving to call it twenty minutes.

" Catch Pigg's horse ! " cries Mr. Jorrocks to a boy, the animal having taken advantage of the commotion to make his way to the well.

After a longish pause, during which there appeared to be a considerable scuffle going on, Pigg's voice is at length heard calling his hounds out of cover ; and as his head pops above the bushes, Mr. Jorrocks exclaims, " Is't a dog, Pigg ! "

" Yeas," replies James,—" a banger tee."

" Capital, indeed ! " lisps Captain Shortflat ; " I'll take a pad, if you please."

" There arn't none ! " exclaims James Pigg, appearing with his purple-tailed coat torn in three places, and several of the hounds bleeding about the mouth. " Hounds were sae desp'rate savish, thought they'd eat me ; " adding, with a wink, in an undertone to his master, " *It's nobbut a hedgehog, and ar's gettin' him i' my pocket !* "

Captain Shortflat, however, is so delighted with the kill and with his own keenness in having stayed, that he forthwith lugs out five shillings for James Pigg, declaring it was perfectly marvellous that hounds should be able to run on such a day—let alone kill ; that he never saw a pack behave better in his life—" Uncommon keen, to be sure ! " repeated he ; " declare the tips of their tails are red with blood."

The last day closes—Mr. Jorrocks lingers on the ride, eyeing his hounds coming to the horn, till at last all are there, and he has no other excuse for staying ; with a pensive air he then turns his horse's head for Handley Cross.

CHAPTER LV.

PRESENTATION OF THE PIGG TESTIMONIAL.

THE Pigg testimonial became the fashion at Handley Cross. Every subscriber, no matter how little he had given, wanted to control the total expenditure. One thought a silver salver with a suitable inscription would be the thing, another thought a highly-mounted silver horn, a third a silver cup with the Pigg arms emblazoned thereon, a fourth suggested a portrait of Pigg by an eminent local artist, while a fifth inquired if there was a Mistress Pigg, in order that they might present her with a bracelet, an armlet, or some such suitable tribute. The trading subscribers were anxious to turn the tide of benevolence into their own peculiar lines. Selvage, the tailor, thought it was of no use sharing the subscription with Frostwork, the silversmith, who would charge them nobody knew what for pattern, and fashion, and fiddle-stick ; while a good suit of clothes—say a blue coat with bright buttons, a Berlin vest, with a pair of Oxford diagonal rib trousers with black stripes down the sides— would be a far more useful and sensible present than a cartload of plate to a man without a sideboard. Bunion, the bootmaker, thought a pair of new tops, or a pair of tops and a pair of Wellingtons, would be more in character for a huntsman ; while De Pledge, the pawnbroker, who had a very elegant ormolu eight-light candelabrum up the spout, wanted to make the payment of his half-crown contingent on their taking it. Then Frostwork, on his part, insisted that the correct testimonial to a huntsman was a coffee and tea-pot, sugar basin, and cream-ewer, with some sporting emblematical device engraved thereon, and spoke of a very nice set he could let the committee have very reasonable, and which was fit to grace the table of the first nobleman in the land.

Unfortunately, however, for all their schemes and calculations, the money melted almost as fast as it was collected.

The two suppers a week ran away with nearly all that the active committee didn't run away with themselves, the usual allowance of twenty per cent. for non-paying subscribers being taken into account.

This was rather an awkward circumstance, no testimonial being perfect without a presentation ; and Handley Cross of all places being the last that could afford to dispense with any excitement-giving proceeding.

As usual, those who had given the least made the most noise, and it very soon became evident that nothing but a public presentation would satisfy the expectations of the place. The " Paul Pry " had inadvertently magnified our huntsman into a hero, and as it was rumoured that he was likely to recover the money his " fore elder John " had deprived him of, he began to be looked upon, by the fair sex in particular, as a gentleman in disguise. Some even hinted that he was the rightful owner of Balmoral. The more the thing was talked about, the more impossible it became to avoid letting people see to the application of their money;

and at length it was settled that the testimonial, which the committee insisted on selecting themselves, should be presented at a half-crown six o'clock meal, which would serve the aristocracy for a dinner, and the democracy for a supper.

Mr. De Pledge, the pawnbroker, who had the care of a very extensive assortment of first-rate jewellery, agreed to job a handsome gold watch with a Watherston and Brogden chain, provided he were allowed to strip Pigg of the same when the party broke up; and these preliminaries being arranged, they began to look about for a chairman. This was rather a difficult point, it requiring a gentleman, while the "Salmon," though extremely comfortable, was only, as its tariff shows, a second or third-rate house. Many gentlemen were named, but there were objections raised to them all. One couldn't speak, another couldn't drink; a third, Pigg or some of them had insulted; while a fourth was so entirely a townsman, that he would be sure to keep the country people away. At last they hit upon Puppy Cackler, as he was improperly called, a sort of social bat, hovering between town and country. The country people wouldn't have him, and he wouldn't have the townspeople, so between the two he was badly off for society. Before Handley Cross became what it is, his place, Vernal Court, was in the country, and he had no notion of losing *caste* because the town had chosen to build up to it.

At first he demurred to taking the chair, because, though the hunt might be considered a country thing, yet the testimonial was a town one.

However, his great natural love of a let-off prevailed, and he consented to preside, first informing himself as accurately as he could, for he was no sportsman, of Mr. Pigg's habits and antecedents.

The walls of Handley Cross then became alive with red-lettered bills, announcing that

HORATIO CACKLER, ESQUIRE,

OF VERNAL COURT,

would present the

PIGG TESTIMONIAL

at the

SALMON HOTEL,

at six o'clock on Thursday evening, and forthwith the dandified Horatio began to comb out his words, and string together his sentences in his usual inflated much-ado-about-nothing style.

The committee had then to bestir themselves to prepare Pigg both outwardly and inwardly for the occasion—outwardly in the way of clothes, and inwardly in the way of a speech expressive of his gratitude. As they thought to catch a few more subscribers by making out that there was still a slight deficiency in the price of the Watherston and Brogden chain, it was at first proposed to dress Pigg up as a Highlander; but our friend rebelled and libelled the costume in terms not fit to be reproduced. His own wardrobe, consisting of the clothes in which Mr. Jorrocks hired him (*vide* p. 148), being clearly inapplicable, his hunting ones were then canvassed; but considering that he was to appear in the character of an out-of-luck gentleman, it was determined to draw on De Pledge's ample stores for a becoming suit.

The speech was the most difficult thing to manage, for though Taws, the schoolmaster, wrote him out several most appropriate ones, Pigg could never be induced to get one by heart, relying, like many untried orators, on the occasion supplying the needful.

Whenever Taws came to get him to recite, he was always too busy to attend to him.

MR. JAMES PIGG.

On the appointed day, Batsay having borrowed one of Mr. Jorrocks's best frilled shirts, and Mr. Barnington's washerwoman having supplied him with one of that gentleman's orthodox collars, Pigg was seen turning out of De Pledge's side-door in an uncommon "get up." Blash, the barber, had cut and curled him, at least what there was of him to curl, while the imposing-looking frill was further developed by a much amplified lace-tipped Joinville, and a broad roll-collared white waistcoat, with imitation blood-stone buttons. From his roomy-sleeved blue dress-coat pocket peeped a cambric kerchief—a thing altogether beside Pigg's wants, as were the braces that now preserved the equilibrium of a pair of candle-light kerseymeres over his red-legged patent leather boots. A damaged Gibus hat sat at an uneasy sort of half-cock on his head, while he flourished a pair of eighteenpenny lemon-coloured kids in his hand. Thus attired, he proceeded along Columbine Street through Larkspur Crescent to Longpod Lane, eliciting the grinning laughter of the grown, and exclamations from the little boys of "*L-a-u-k*, that's Pigg!" "Did you ever?" "No I never!" and so on.

Arrived at the Salmon Inn, there was such a crowd about the door, that De Pledge and Taws, who had agreed to walk at a respectful distance behind Pigg—near enough of course to prevent his bolting with the clothes—now came up, and with their authoritative "*make way there, make way!*" informed the starers that the gaunt elbower was the hero of the night. Pigg then pushed through the doorway, and was presently in the bar at the end of the passage, where, finding a couple of glasses of gin on a tray ready for serving, he just swigged them off, and then demanded where he was to gan? His keepers, who were close upon him, now took each an arm, and led him up the crowded old-fashioned stair-case, for the "Salmon" was Roger Swizzle's old original Handley Cross house, to the low reception room—his supporters urging him to mind his P's and Q's, and "be'ave like a gentleman."

Mr. Jorrocks, though rather jealous of the whole proceeding, had arrived sky-blued and canaried all the same, and was forming part of a select circle round the intense swell of a chairman, when "Mister Pigg!" came towering in after his name.

The sea of society dividing as Pigg approached, the chairman and he were presently *vis-à-vis.*

"Ho'o ist, canny man? ho'o ist?" exclaimed James; "give us a wag o' thy nief," tendering his horny fist to the thin-skinned Mr. Cackler. Then turning to his astonished master, he added, "Sink, thous' beat me here then, 'ard man!"

The chairman hearing this, rather recovered the shock of his own salute, and attributing the roughness of Pigg's manners to the ruggedness of his country,

"Caledonia stern and wild,"

proceeded to try and ingratiate himself with him notwithstanding.

"Beautiful weather," said Mr. Cackler, rubbing his hands as if he was washing them.

"Varra," replied Pigg, with a hitch of what he thought were his brace-less breeches.

"Hope you've got a good appetite," observed the chairman, as the smell of dinner came mounting up stairs.

"Can't say ar hev," replied James, fumbling about for his baccy box. "Can't say ar hev," adding—"ar's ne greet eater at ony time—drinkin's better for the teeth nor eatin'. Sink," continued he, still fumbling about for his baccy box, which he had left in his own coat pocket, and catching a sight of himself in the opposite mirror. " Sink, ar wonder what mar coosin Deavilboger would say gin he were to see me rigged out like a squeire, toppin' arle corled, and sark lap stickin' out ahint," Pigg ducking and bending and turning about to examine himself as he spoke.

" What sort of weather have they in the north—do you hear, Mr. Pigg ? " asked the chairman, thinking to fix his exact locality.

" A, grand weather ! grand weather ! " replied Pigg ; " its arleways grand weather there. Sink," continued he, speaking full gallop—" Ar wish ar was there—gin ar had me reets, ar de believe ar'd been a gen'lman this day, and hontin' my own hunds, only you see mar fore elder John you see, John Pigg you see, willed arle wor brass to the formary ye see, and left me wi' fairly nout—gin ye gan to the formary ye'll see it arle clagged up i' great goud letters gin the warll," Pigg fibbing away at the chairman until he got him " clagged up 'gin the warll " too.

At this critical moment, Owen Sherry, the landlord, announced that dinner was served, whereupon a bowing match took place between Pigg and the chairman, Pigg not understanding what Mr. Cackler's motioning towards the door meant. The latter at length put an end to the controversy by running his arm through Pigg's, and leading him out of the room—presently bringing him to anchor on the right of the chair, with a round of beef under his nose. Jorrocks followed, closely pressed upon by the company at large, who soon filled the not very long, long room of the Salmon. After the usual rushing, and scrambling, and fighting for seats, silence was at length obtained, when grace being said, they fell to with the voracity of fox-hounds.

The delicate-feeding Pigg astonished the chairman by asking for a third help of beef, after he had had what appeared to Mr. Cackler two most sufficient ones, together with an inordinate quantity of winter cabbage, carrot, and peas pudding. The half-crown only affording eatables, the company were soon invited to give their orders for fluids, and the table presently became dotted with pint decanters, which in a more aristocratic house would have done duty for bottles. The guests then began challenging Pigg to take wine, upon which our friend desired them to send up their bottles, observing " that it was ne compliment to a man to ax him to drink at his own expense." Thus Pigg, who had bargained for a bottle of rum to himself, got a very considerable quantity of other liquor to the saving of his spirit. Not that he did save it much, for he kept applying to it pretty freely between times, drinking nearly a pint during dinner. So the entertainment proceeded amidst great clamour, and the astonishment of Mr. Cackler, at the manner in which the chieftain eat with his knife. At length the most vigorous appetite was appeased, the clatter gradually died out, and the guests began puffing, and wheezing, and ruminating on what was to follow.

The cloth being drawn, and grace said, the chairman prosed through the usual loyal and patriotic toasts, and then paused for the grand let-off of the evening. Having duly received the gold watch with the glittering Watherston and Brogden chain at the hands of Mr. De Pledge, and examined it carefully inside and out, he coiled the chain becomingly round the watch on the table, and clearing his voice with a substantial "*hem*," stood well erect, with his right hand extended and his left reposing in his emerald green velvet vest, to pour the vial of his eloquence upon our curly-pated Pigg.

"Mr. Pigg !" said he, in a sonorous voice, amidst general applause; "Mr. James Pigg," repeated he, correcting himself, for he liked to do everything by the card.

"Aye," interrupted James, chuckling and laughing, "that's just what they carl me i' the smarl debts coourt."

"Mr. James Pigg," continued Mr. Cackler, amidst laughter from the interruption. "The pleasing—the extraordinarily pleasing and interesting—I may say exciting task of presenting you with this glittering memorial of our appreciation and approval," taking up the watch and showing the sparkling chain full length as he spoke, "has been entrusted —unworthily entrusted I fear (applause, with cries of 'No, no,') to the 'umble individual who now stands before you; but Mr. Pigg—that is to say, Mr. James Pigg—let not the inefficiency of the spokesman be to you a measure whereby to judge of the estimation in which you are held in this great county—a county second to none in the kingdom, whether we regard its agricultural properties, or the wealth and respectability of its inhabitants. (Applause from the country section of the party.) No, Mr. Pigg, let the merits—demerits rather of the spokesman be no more to you a measure whereby to judge of the estimation in which you are held than is this trifling present," again flourishing the testimonial, "richly jewelled though it be (applause), a criterion of the value the country sets upon your services. (Renewed applause.) Never was a call more heartily responded to than the suggestion that we should mark the approbation in which you are held by all ranks and conditions of her Majesty's subjects. (Great cheering.) Your courtesy, your urbanity, your true gentlemanly ease and polished politeness, are the universal theme of approval on every tongue."

"*Sink ! noo thous mackin' gam on me !*" roared Pigg, striking furiously on the deal table with his doubled fist.

"*Hush, James ! hush !*" exclaimed Mr. Jorrocks, kicking him under the table, fearing he would pitch into the chairman.

"Permit me to say, Sir," continued the chairman, looking rather foolish at his butter not being swallowed, "Permit me to say, Sir, that your private worth is equalled only by your public prowess. As a huntsman, you are unrivalled ! (Great applause.) For charging a bullfinch or negotiating a brook, I am told there is not your equal in her Majesty's wide dominions. (Renewed applause, with a 'Keep the tambourine a roulin' !' and clapping of hands from Pigg.) But these considerations," continued the chairman, shirking the ground on which he was weak as soon as possible; "but these considerations sink into insignificance compared to the excellent moral example your good and orderly conduct has set to all ranks and conditions of people in this rising and important town. (Applause, mingled with laughter, from Pigg's more intimate friends.) You have indeed shown that the highest sporting enterprise is not incompatible with the gentlest and most exemplary private virtues." (Renewed laughter and applause.'

"On behalf then of the subscribers," continued Mr. Cackler, again taking up the testimonial, "permit me to beg your acceptance of this gold watch and appendage." Mr. Cackler proceeding to invest Pigg with them as he spoke, much in the manner of a mayor investing his successor with the badge and chain of office. Having placed the watch in the left-hand pocket and arranged the chain becomingly over the white waistcoat, he rubbed his delicate hands together, and thus resumed :—

"Long sir, long may you be spared to enliven the woods and dales of this country with your melodious spirit-stirring voice, and should kind Providence decree, which I, which we all, most fervently pray may be the case—should, I say, kind Providence decree that you be again restored to those ancestral honours of which you have been so cruelly, so unjustly deprived, then amid the wild solitudes of your mountain grandeur may the mild notes of that repeater recall the warm hearts that beat responsive in Handley Cross."

Mr. Cackler bowed low to Pigg and the party, and resumed his seat amidst loud and long continued applause. As it gradually died out, all eyes became turned upon James, who kept winking and nodding in his seat as if going to sleep. At length the cry of "Pigg! now Pigg! James Pigg!" became so general that our master was obliged to kick him under the table, backing the application of his foot with an authoritative, "*now then!*" which caused Pigg to start and stare wildly about.

"*It's the speech,*" now whispered Taws, who had slunk along at the back of the guests, in his ear. "*The speech, returning thanks, you know.*"

"Aye, aye," replied James, preparing to rise, which at length he did with some difficulty, and stood with his honours around him, receiving the plaudits of the company. As they in turn subsided, he was observed to sway to and fro, so much so that it was even betting whether he fell backwards or forwards.

"Sink!" exclaimed he, sawing the air with his right hand, and then clapping the two violently together, "Sink, but *James Pigg's a brick!*" whereupon he went back over like a ladder.

Great then was the confusion. All rushed to the aid of the fallen chieftain. One sluiced him with water, another took off his Joinville, a third opened his vest, a fourth suggested he'd be better for some brandy, while Mr. Jorrocks hinted that perhaps he'd had enough.

In the midst of the confusion, the anxious Mr. De Pledge alone looked after the testimonial, and under pretence of taking care of it, proceeded to strip off the Watherston and Brogden chain, with its substantial appurtenance.

Mr. Jorrocks, who had eyed the watch as it lay on the table, with the look of an old acquaintance, now begged leave to examine it, and finding the name and number as he expected—"Green, Ward, and Green, No. 1157," he coolly claimed it,—his fair friend of the frying pan having pawned it at De Pledge's a few days after the Pinch-me-near forest day. So whatever happened to others, Mr. Jorrocks at least came in for his own.

Pigg was then conveyed home in a fly, and the refined Puppy Cackler disgusted at having been called upon to do honour to such a tiger—left too, whereupon Duncan Nevin was called to the chair, and with a somewhat shortened table the conviviality of the meeting was prolonged to the little hours of the morning. As Taws and he at length steered their way home in a very blind leading the blind sort of way, the glimmering lights in the " Pry " printing office reminded them that the paper then printing off would contain an account of things as they ought to have been and not as they were. However it was too late to alter it even if they had been in a fit state to do it. So the absentees were treated to a very different version of what happened, to that which we have given. After expatiating on the excellence of the entertainment—an excellence peculiar to Owen Sherry and the Salmon Hotel, it proceeded to give the opening speeches much as we have given them, and concluded with the following, which Mr. Pigg was stated to have delivered with much feeling and marked emphasis as soon as the cheering caused by his rising subsided.

Pigg loquitur. " Mr. Chairman and gentlemen, I rise under feelings of no ordinary difficulty to return you my most heartfelt and grateful thanks, as well for the superb and valuable testimonial you have been pleased to present me with, as for the flattering terms and cordial enthusiasm with which the presentation has been accompanied and received. (Applause.) Gentlemen, splendid as this testimonial is (producing it as he spoke) its real and intrinsic value to my feelings is the assurance it conveys that the exertions I have made in the furtherance of your sport and in promoting the prosperity of this Queen of watering places have not been in vain. (Great applause.) But gentlemen, I do not arrogate to myself the whole of the success that has attended these exertions. I have the honour and good fortune to serve under a gentleman whose name is closely associated with everything that is great, liberal, and patriotic. (Immense applause.) It is only for me to suggest anything either in the way of hounds, horses, or hunting, and it is sure to be responded to by my most excellent and liberal master. (Renewed applause.) Gentlemen, I could expatiate without fear of wearying either you or myself on the merits of our most popular master, were it not that his fame is universal, and his humility equal only to his fame. (Immense applause.) Long, I say, may the town of Handley Cross profit by the presence of such a sportsman ! (Renewed cheers.) For myself I may truly say I look upon it as the happiest incident of a somewhat chequered life, (applause) that my lot has been cast in such waters. (Renewed applause.) And now gentlemen," continued Mr. Pigg, dashing a tear from his manly eye, " again let me thank you for this memorial of your friendship and esteem, infinitely more valuable from that feeling than in money's worth, great as that undoubtedly is, (loud cheering), a memorial that I will hand down as an heirloom in the Pigg family to the latest generation."

The report stated that Mr. Pigg resumed his seat amid loud and long continued applause, far different to falling back over like a ladder, as he did. But we dare say the report was not a bit more exaggerated than the generality of the reports of these daily increasing outbursts of spontaneous coercion.

CHAPTER LVI.

SUPERINTENDENT CONSTABLES SHARK AND CHIZELER.

NEXT day as our Master was labouring away at his great work, the "Life of Johnny Gilpin," Betsey came to say that the Pollis wanted to see him.

"Pollis!" exclaimed Jorrocks, dropping his pen with evident alarm; "Pollis! wot can the Pollis want wi' me?" thinking he had come to take him up for stealing the watch. And in an instant our Master saw the whole paraphernalia of the law, from the inquisitiveness of the Justice to the disagreeable familiarity of Jack Ketch paraded before his eyes.

"Shall I send him in, then?" asked Betsey, surprised at her master's perturbation.

"*In then!*" ejaculated Jorrocks. "*In then!*" repeated he, staring out his eye-balls. "Yes—no—yes—that's to say, prisently;" thinking if he was rid of Betsey he'd bolt the back way.

The gentleman, however, who had followed close upon Betsey's heels, here made his appearance, and Mr. Jorrocks found himself confronted with the man of law. He was a hairy, seedy, well set-up, military-looking man, dressed in a shabby hook-and-eyed braided blue frock coat, which concealed as well the deficiency of linen as of waistcoat. His trousers were very broad, badly washed cords, strapped under a pair of boisterous badly-soled boots. Altogether, he was a sort of cross between a serjeant and a circus-master. He was a draft from the rural police in an adjoining county, where his dissolute habits had procured him a hint that his "resignation would be accepted," an arrangement that enabled the chief Constable to give him high testimonials for his present situation, to obtain which, of course, he represented to the innocent Justices he had resigned his former appointment. He was now Superintendent Constable, and he who couldn't control himself, was placed in authority over others.

He had a capital berth of it, having no one to look after him, and took his salary as a sort of retaining fee, looking upon "incidentals," as he elegantly called his extortions, as the real emoluments of his office.

He was a sharp fellow, too, and could twist and trim facts so as to inveigle people into prosecutions who would never have instituted them if left to themselves. In these cases, he had his fling at Sessions or Assizes, where, with always fresh victims to work upon, he preyed upon their generosity with considerable advantage, besides having his "reglers" from the reprobate lawyer with whom he confederated. If he could not manage a commitment, then he would have a little snug bill of costs drawn out so as to exhibit great activity, though his researches were generally directed to parts of the country where he wanted to visit rather than to where he was likely to catch the offender. His horse—like most of those worthies' horses—was a *Phantom* one, for he rarely had one, never if he could turn a penny by selling it.

His activity was unbounded. He would drink in any company, no matter how low, for the purpose, as he said, of worming out secrets, though the quantity of drink he took generally made the information of very little value on the morrow. No offence was too trifling for his vigilant eye. Indeed, he showed his activity chiefly in trifles, and in drawing out bombastic reports of his wonderful exploits. Omar Pacha himself, at the head of a victorious army, was not half such a hero as Superintendent Shark marching triumphantly along with a few shivering stick or turnip-stealers, whose fluttering rags scarcely concealed their poverty-stricken nakedness. But we will let his interview with Mr. Jorrocks speak for his general performances. We will suppose him entering the sanctum.

Having advanced right into the middle of the room, he drew himself bolt upright, and putting himself in the first position, gave our Master a full military swing of a salute. This rather comforted our friend, who expected a different sort of commencement.

" Your servant, Sir," said the Superintendent, dropping his arm straight down his side with a sound.

" Yours," bowed our Master, still full stare.

" I have made free, Sir, to call, Sir," said the Superintendent, elevating his voice to witness-box pitch ; " I have made free, Sir, to call, Sir, respecting the very daring and outrageous robbery that was committed upon your person on the——"

" What robbery ? " interrupted Mr. Jorrocks, still thinking there was some mistake, and that the Superintendent would be collaring him after all.

" The robbery of the watch, Sir ; the gold watch and seals, Sir ; ' J. J., St. Botolph's Lane ' on a red cornelian seal ; ' J. J., Great Coram Street,' on a white cornelian seal, with a gold fox-head key and ring ; " referring to a large clasped volume, like a regimental orderly book, as he spoke.

" Oh, ah," replied Mr. Jorrocks, dry-shaving his chin. " I did lose my ticker," thinking perhaps the less stir he made about it the better; especially now that he had got it safe in his fob.

" From information, Sir, that I received, Sir," continued the Superintendent, " I had reason to suppose that the parties who robbed you of your very valuable property, Sir, were part of a most daring gang of burglars and smashers, who have taken up their quarters at East Poppington, on the borders of the country, Sir, and immediately I heard of the robbery, Sir, which was not until the Monday afternoon, Sir, at two o'clock, Sir ; yes, at two o'clock, Sir, I immediately proceeded to Superintendent Chizeler's, for it is not in my district, and consulted with him as to the expediency of applying to Augustus Frederick Emanuel Smith, Esq., of East Rosemary Hall, the nearest magistrate, for a warrant, Sir —yes, Sir, for a warrant, Sir—but, Sir, Superintendent Constable Chizeler, Sir, who is an officer, Sir, of great ability and experience, Sir, thought the case was hardly sufficiently ripe, Sir, for a warrant, Sir, and recommended that we should pursue our enquiries and investigations conjointly together a little longer, Sir, which we did, Sir, and I——"

" Then you didn't grab 'em ? " interrupted Mr. Jorrocks, thinking how well they had run a false scent.

" No, Sir ; that is to say, not yet, Sir ; but from information I am now in possession of, Sir, I have little doubt, Sir, that the parties may be got, should you direct us to follow them up, which, of course, Sir, for the sake of example a gentleman in your position will do."

"*Humph!*" grunted Mr. Jorrocks, thinking they had better leave them alone.

"Only," continued the Superintendent, drawing up to his point; "as the investigation has lasted a considerable time, and been attended with some little expense, I considered it my duty to consult you before incurring any further cost."

"*Humph!*" grunted Mr. Jorrocks again, beginning to see through the object of the mission.

"The charges," continued the Superintendent, producing a bill from the important-looking book, opening and laying it before our Master, "are merely the usual charges for money out of pocket, money absolutely expended in the necessary prosecution of the enquiries."

"*Humph!*" grunted Mr. Jorrocks, preparing to peruse it.

It was a large, lawyer-like bill, a delicacy with which most of our readers, we dare say, are familiar. Thus it ran:—

" Account of Expenses boney fidey incurred by Jonathan Shark, Superintending Constable for the Hundred of Hungerlaw, in prosecuting an enquiry into a most daring and aggrivated robbery committed on the person of John Jorrocks, Esquire, Master of the Handley Cross Foxhounds :—

Superintendent Shark proceeding from Nutfield to Gilderdale to advise with Superintendent Chizeler respecting the above daring robbery, and as to the characters of certain part.es residing in his district, and as to the propriety of apprehending a certain party on suspicion of being the culprit, having to remain at the Dun Cow at Gilderdale all night	0	10	6
Personal expenses to East Poppington along with Superintendent Chizeler, to make further inquiries, one night and day, 7s. 6d.; gig hire, including ostler and horse's keep, 11s. 6d.	0	19	0
Having received information that the suspected party had gone to Merryweather fair, proceeding there by gig and horse with Superintendent Chizeler, gig hire and horse's keep, 12s.; personal expenses, Superintendents Shark and Chizeler, 12s.	1	4	0
Expenses incurred by Superintendent Shark going to Blatherfield to see Mr. Jaw in the case	0	4	0
Mr. Jaw not being able to attend to it, Superintendent Chizeler proceeding to Hurlington to see Mr. Law . .	0	5	0
Gig hire, including ostler and horse's keep . . .	0	12	0
Paid conveyance from Nutfield to Rushton to see and try to get up evidence, including ostler	0	11	6
Gig hire for Superintendents Shark and Chizeler from Gilderdale to Airylane, making inquiry after a certain witness, including ostler	0	11	6
Personal expenses for that day and night for Superintendents Shark and Chizeler	0	7	6
Extra expenses for Superintendent Shark's horse at Gilderdale, 4 nights, he having to use it occasionally in making inquiries into the above very serious and aggrivated case, including ostler	0	12	6
Total . . .	5	17	6

"Well," said Mr. Jorrocks, with a chuck of his chin, after reading it: "I dessay it's all right—at least I doesn't know nothin' to the contrary —you'd better take it to the chap who employed you, and see wot he says."

"O, this, Sir," replied the Superintendent, putting on a bold face; "this, Sir, is the mere preliminary charge that is always borne by the prosecutor, Sir; that is to say, Sir, by the party, Sir, losing the property, Sir; even, Sir, if it had gone before the magistrate, Sir, Augustus Frederick Emanuel Smith, Esquire, of East Rosemary Hall, no part of these costs would have been allowed in the certificate of expenses, under the seventh of George the Fourth, Chapter sixty-four, Section twenty-two," the Superintendent thinking to floor our Master with a redundancy of law.

"Well, but," replied Mr. Jorrocks, dry-shaving his chin; "well, but s'pose the party likes to lose his property, there's no law 'gin his bein' 'commodated, I s'pose."

"Why, no, Sir; certainly not, Sir;" replied the Superintendent, looking rather blank: "only that, Sir, is a case, Sir, the law does not contemplate, Sir."

"Well, but neither does the law contemplate keepin' you and your quad, and then havin' you joltin' 'bout wi' Chizeler in a 'ired gig, livin' at inns and places, as if you 'ad nothin' from the county."

"Ah, that you see, Sir," replied the undaunted Shark; "that you see, Sir, was in consequence of my having to go out of my own district, Sir, you see, Sir, in consequence of information I received, Sir, I proceeded at once into Superintendent Constable Chizeler's district, and——"

"Well! but surely you can follow your fox, that's to say, your thief, into another man's country, and take 'im, prowided you don't dig 'im," retorted Mr. Jorrocks, indignantly, reasoning by analogy to foxhunting.

"Yes, Sir; exactly so, Sir;" replied the complaisant policeman. "Yes, Sir; exactly so, Sir; only you see, Sir, it is necessary, Sir, to have the original warrant backed by a magistrate of the county into which you follow him."

"But if you haven't got a warrant. If you're takin' a bye on your own 'count; 'ow then?" asked Mr. Jorrocks.

The policeman was posed.

"Well, I don't know nothin' 'bout nothin' o' the sort," resumed Mr. Jorrocks, twisting and turning the bill about, to see if he would like it better in any other position. "Well, I don't know nothin' 'bout nothin' o' the sort—it may be all right and proper 'irin' gigs and 'osses when you are paid for keepin' your own, and chargin' pussonal expenses, you and Chizeler, when you're paid for keepin' yourselves; but I doesn't goinside i' that 'pinion. Wot I says is this, that if a man likes to be robbed, it's werry 'ard if he mayn't be indulged, but a man had better be both robbed and murder'd than 'ave sich a bill as this sent in to 'im. Zounds, Sir! You do take my life when you take the means whereby I live," exclaimed Mr. Jorrocks, boiling up, as he doubled up the bill, and thrust it back upon his visitor.

And the disgusted Superintendent, who had arranged for having a lark with Superintendent Chizeler at Jollyfield hiring, retired very much disgusted at our Master's spiritless parsimony, declaring that it was utterly impossible to expect Superintendent Constables to do their duty, if they were not properly supported.

CHAPTER LVII.

THE PROPHET GABRIEL.

"THAT was Gabriel Junks!" exclaimed Mr. Jorrocks, rising from his seat, and rushing to the window.

Sure enough it was Gabriel Junks; and after a short pause, another scream, more shrill and piercing, confirmed Mr. Jorrocks's surmise. Seizing his hat he rushed into the garden.

It was a misty sort of morning, and the sun was labouring through the flitting clouds that obscured its brightness. The wind, too, had got into the south, and there was a fresh, growing feeling in the air that spoke of spring and returning vegetation. The peacock again screamed, and sought the shelter of a laurel.

"As sure as my name's John Jorrocks, there's goin' to be rain," observed our worthy master, scrutinising the bird. "As sure as my name's John Jorrocks, there's goin' to be rain," repeated he. "*Pe-pe-pe-pe-pe-pe!*" exclaimed he, scraping the crumbs from the bottom of his pockets and throwing them to his prophet.

Gabriel Junks rushed from his retreat, and having picked up the crumbs, stood eyeing Mr. Jorrocks with a head-on-one-side sort of leer, which he at length broke off by another loud scream, and then a rattling spread of his tail. Mr. Jorrocks and the bird were thus standing *vis-à-vis* when James Pigg made his appearance.

"I'll lay a guinea 'at to a 'alf-crown gossamer, there's goin' to be rain," said Mr. Jorrocks to his huntsman, pointing to the bird.

"Deil bon me if ar care," replied Pigg; "ar hasn't getten ne seeds, nor nothin'—may be Deavilboger wad like a sup," his mind harking back to "canny Newcassel."

"Well but, don't ye see, if it rains we can have an 'unt," said Mr. Jorrocks, astonished at his huntsman's stupidity.

"*Se we can!*" exclaimed Pigg, all alive; "dash it! ar niver thought o' that now—another bye-day—sick a one as the first—ay?"

"Vy no—not exactly," said Mr. Jorrocks, not relishing an entire repetition; "but s'pose we have another turn at the old customer—go out early, and drag up to the warmint, find him when he's full—may be a cock, or a hen, or a Gabriel Junks aboard," looking at the bird still strutting about with his tail spread.

"Sink it, aye!" said Pigg; "let's gan i' the morn."

D D

Mr. Jorrocks.—"If it comes wet we will. We can feed th' 'ounds at all ewents, and be ready for a start."

*　　*　　*　　*　　*　　*　　*

The day continued hazy, but still no rain fell. Junks, however, persisted in his admonitions, and Mr. Jorrocks felt so certain it would rain, that he had Pigg into the parlour in the evening to make arrangements for the morning. Mrs. Jorrocks, Belinda, and Stobbs, had gone out to tea, and Mr. Jorrocks was left all alone.

Master and man had an anxious confabulation. Mr. Jorrocks was all for Pinch-me-near, while Pigg recommended Hew-timber Forest.

MR. JORROCKS AND PIGG DRINK "FOX HUNTING."

Of course Jorrocks carried his point.

About nine Betsey brought the supper-tray, and Jorrocks would treat Pigg to a glass of brandy-and-water. One glass led to another, and they

had a strong talk about hunting. They drank each other's healths, then
the healths of the hounds.

"I'll give you old Priestess' good 'ealth!" exclaimed Mr. Jorrocks,
holding up his glass. "Fine old betch, with her tan eye-brows—thinks I
never saw a better 'ound—wise as a Christian!" Pigg proposed Manager.
Mr. Jorrocks gave Ravager. Pigg gave Lavender; and they drank
Mercury, and Affable, and Crowner, and Lousey, and Mountebank, and
Milliner—almost all the pack, in short, each in turn being best. A, what
a dog one was to find a fox. A, what a dog another was to drive a scent.

The fire began to hiss, and Mr. Jorrocks felt confident his prophecy
was about to be fulfilled. "Look out of the winder, James, and see
wot'un a night it is," said he to Pigg, giving the log a stir, to ascertain
that the hiss didn't proceed from any dampness in the wood.

James staggered up, and after a momentary grope about the room—for
they were sitting without candles—exclaimed, "Hellish dark, and smells
of cheese!"

"*Smells o' cheese!*" repeated Mr. Jorrocks, looking round in astonishment; "*smells o' cheese!*—vy, man, you've got your nob i' the cupboard
—this be the vinder;" continued he, rising and opening some shutters
painted like the cupboard door in the other corner. Mr. Jorrocks undid
the fastening and threw up the sash.

The night was dark—black as pitch—not a star was visible, and a soft
warm rain was just beginning to fall.

"*Didn't I tell you so?*" exclaimed Mr. Jorrocks, drawing in his hand,
and giving his thigh a hearty slap; "didn't I tell you so?" repeated he,
"I was *certain* it was a goin' to rain, that Gabriel Junks was never
wrong!—Is better than all your wanes, and weathercocks, and Aneroid
glasses wot ever were foaled. We'll drink his 'ealth in a bumper!" So
saying, Mr. Jorrocks and Pigg replenished their glasses, and drank to "the
health of Gabriel Junks."

Pigg then would treat his master to a song—a song about ard Squier
Lambton and his hunds; so, ejecting his quid and filling a bumper, he
chaunted the following, our Master chiming in, and substituting the name
of Jorrocks for that of Lambton in the chorus :—

> * "Though midnight her dark frowning mantle is spreading,
>   Yet time flies unheeded where Bacchus resides;
> Fill, fill then your glasses, his power ne'er dreading,
>   And drink to the hounds o'er which Lambton presides.
> Though toast after toast with great glee has been given,
>   The highest top-sparkling bumper decides,
> That for stoutness, pace, beauty, on this side of Heaven,
>   Unrivalled the hounds o'er which Lambton presides!
>   Then drink to the foxhounds,
>   The high mettled foxhounds,
> We'll drink to the hounds o'er which Lambton presides.
>
> "Let Uckerby boast of the feats of the Raby,
>   And Ravenscar tell what the Hurworth have done,
> But the wide-spreading pastures of Sadberge can swear to
>   The brushes our fleet pack of foxhounds have won

* Tune—" Weave a Garland."

Then that Sedgefield, *our country*, all countries outvies, sir,
  The highest top-sparkling bumper decides,
That we've foxes can fly, sir, or sinking must die, sir,
  When pressed by the hounds o'er which Lambton presides.
    Then drink, &c.

"Of their heart-bursting ' flys ' let the Leicestershire tell us,
  Their plains, their ox fences, and that sort of stuff,
But give me a day with the Sedgefield brave fellows,
  When horses ne'er flinch, nor men cry, hold, enough.
Whilst the blood of old Cæsar our foxes can boast, sir,
  May Lambton their only dread enemy be,
And the green waving whins of our covers my toast, sir,
  Oh ! the hounds and the blood of old Lambton for me.
    Then drink, &c."

And Jorrocks did drink, and did whoop, and did holloa, and did shout, till he made himself hoarse. His spirits, or the brandy spirits, seemed to have fairly run away with him. At length he began to cool down and think of the morrow.

"Now you and I'll have an 'unt," observed Mr. Jorrocks.

"Squier Stobbs 'll gan te, ar's warn'd," observed Pigg.

"Oh, never mind him," replied Jorrocks, with a chuck of the chin, "never mind him ; no sayin' when he may be 'ome—gone fiddlin' out with the women."

"He's aye ticklin' the lasses' hocks," observed Pigg.

"You and I, at all ewents, will have an 'unt, and see if we can't pivy that tormentin' old customer. Never was sich a fox in this world. Do believe he'll be the death o' me, if I don't finish him.—Shall never get through the summer, for thinkin' on 'im. So now we'll start at six—or call it 'alf-past five, and see if we can't do the trick afore breakfast. My vig ! if we do, wot a blow-out we'll have—you shall have a gallon of XX, and a werry big-bottled gooseberry-tart for your breakfast."

"Ar'd rayther have a ham-collop," replied Pigg, replenishing his mouth with tobacco.

"So you shall," rejoined Mr. Jorrocks ; " and poached heggs into the bargain."

The other arrangements were soon made—and the brandy being finished, master and man separated for the night.

CHAPTER LVIII.

ANOTHER LAST DAY.

IGG having curled himself up in his clothes on the kitchen-table, awoke with the first peep of day. He was at the stables betimes, and dressed and fed the horses himself. Mr. Jorrocks was equally early, having been greatly tormented by the old customer, who had appeared to him in his dreams in a variety of ways—now running between his legs and upsetting him, now nearly blinding him with a whisk over his eyes from his sandy brush, again, as the chairman of a convivial meeting of foxes who did nothing but laugh and make finger fans to their noses at him, crying, "Ah, cut his tail! Cut his tail!" and mimicking his holloas and hunting noises; next sitting on a high stool, in his own counting-house, writing a letter to "Bell's Life" and the "Field," declaring he was the worst sportsman and greatest humbug that ever got upon a horse; anon, as a bull, with a tremendous fox's brush, charging him, as Gollarfield's bull charged him on the Hardpye Hill day, which ended as usual in our master flooring Mrs. Jorrocks, who vowed she would appeal to Dodson and the court for the protection of injured ribs. Altogether Jorrocks was sadly put out and was full of envy, hatred, malice, and all uncharitableness against the old customer. Charley Stobbs, to whom Pigg had sent word by Betsey, appearing just as our master got down, rather encouraged him to hope for the best, and sent him stumping to the door in better spirits.

It was a lovely morning! Mild and balmy—the rain had ceased, and the sun rose with unclouded brilliancy, drawing forth the lately reluctant leaves, and opening the wild flowers to its earliest rays. The drops hung like diamonds on the bushes, and all nature seemed refreshed.

"This be more like the thing," said Mr. Jorrocks, hoisting himself into his saddle with a swag that made old Arterxerxes grunt again; " if there arn't a scent this mornin', there arn't no hallegators ; " with which wise observation he turned his horse towards the kennel.

"Turn 'em all out," said he to Pigg, adding aloud to himself, " We'll 'ave a good cry at all ewents."

The hounds partook of the general hilarity. Out they rushed with joyous cry, and set the horses capering with their frolicking.

The dry and dusty roads were watered—the hedgerows were filled with the green luxuriance of spring, and the golden poplar stood in bright relief among the dark green pines and yews. If a fox-hunter can welcome spring, such a day would earn his adoration. All nature was alive, but hardly yet had man appeared to greet it. Presently the labourers began to appear at their cottages. The undressed children popped about the doors, cocks crew lustily, the lambs gambolled about the ewes, and indignant ganders flew at the hounds' and horses' heels.

"Sink them goslin's ! " said Pigg, eyeing a whole string of them ; " ar wish fox had ivery one o' you."

Our friends' frequent visits having made them well acquainted with the way to the valuable forest, they popped through gates and gaps, and made short cuts through fields and farms, that greatly reduced the distance they travelled on the first occasion. After a couple of hours steady butter and eggs bumping, they found themselves on Saddle-combe-hill, overlooking an oak-clad ravine that gradually lost itself in the general sterility of the wide forest. A slight change was just visible on the oak-buds ; the young birch had got its plum-coloured tinge, while here and there the spiry larch in verdant green, or the dark spruce or darker fir, broke the massive heaviness of the forest.

Jorrocks pulled up, as well to reconnoitre as to see if he could hit off the smuggler's cave, which he had never been able to do, though he made as diligent search as the agitation of pursuing the old customer would allow. He now eyed the sun-bright forest far and near, north, south, east and west, but identifying feature he saw none. It might be anywhere.

The hounds presently interrupted the reverie, by setting up the most melodious cry; and our master, awakening to a sense of what he had come out for, proceeded to distribute his forces as he thought best for circumventing the old customer.

"You take the far side, and cross by the crag," said Mr. Jorrocks to Pigg ; " Charley will keep on this, and ven I hears you twang th' 'orn, I'll throw th' 'ounds into cover ; " saying which, Mr. Jorrocks turned short round, and Stobbs assumed the place that Pigg had just occupied in the rear.

*   *   *   *   *   *   *

"Dash it, wot a mornin' it is ! " exclaimed Mr. Jorrocks, turning up his jolly face, beaming with exultation ; " wot a many delicious moments one loses by smooterin i' bed !—dash my vig ! if I won't get up at five every mornin' as long as I live ! Glad I've got on my cords 'stead o' my shags, for it's goin' to be werry 'ot," continued he, looking down on a pair of second or third-hand whites. "*Yooi over*, in there ! " to the

hounds, with a wave of his hand, as Pigg's horn announced he had taken his station.

In the hounds flew, with a chirp and a whimper; and the crack of Pigg's whip on the far side sounded like a gun in the silence around.

"Yooi, spread and try for him, my beauties!" holloaed Mr. Jorrocks, riding into cover among the stunted underwood.

The pack spread, and try in all directions—now here, now there, now whiffing with curious nose round the hollies, and now trying up the rides.

"There's a touch of a fox," said Mr. Jorrocks to himself, as Priestess put her nose to the ground, and ran mute across the road, lashing her sides with her stern. A gentle whimper followed, and Mr. Jorrocks cheered her to the echo. "The warmint's astir," said he; "that's jest where we hit on him last time." Now Priestess speaks again in fuller and deeper notes, and Ravager and Lavender, and the rest of the pack rush to the spot. How beautifully they flourish—eager, and yet none will go an inch without the scent.

"Vell done, old 'ooman! speak to him again!" exclaimed Mr. Jorrocks, delighted to hear the old bitch's tongue; "a fox for a pund; *ten* if you like!"

* * * * * * *

The pack have now got together, and all are busy on the scent. The villain has been astir early, and the drag is rather weak.

"Dash my vig, he's been here," says Mr. Jorrocks, eyeing some feathers sticking in a bush; "there's three and sixpence at least for an old fat 'en," wondering whether he would have to pay for it or not.

The hounds strike forward, and getting upon a grassy ride, carry the scent with a good head for some quarter of a mile, to the ecstatic delight of Mr. Jorrocks, who bumps along, listening to their music, and hoping it might never cease.

A check! They've overrun the scent. "*Hie back!*" cries Mr Jorrocks, turning his horse round; "gone to the low crags I'll be bund—that's the way he always goes; I'll pop up 'ill, and stare him out o' countenance, if he takes his old line;" saying which, Mr. Jorrocks stuck spurs into Arterxerxes, and, amid the grunts of the horse and the rumbling of the loose stones, succeeded in gaining the rising ground, while the hounds worked along the brook below.

The chorus grows louder! The rocky dell resounds the cry a hundred fold! The tawny owl, scared from his ivied crag, faces the sun in a Bacchanalian sort of flight; wood-pigeons wing their timid way, the magpie is on high, and the jay's grating screech adds wildness to the scene. What a crash! Warm in the woody dell, half-circled by the winding brook, where rising hills ward off the wintry winds, the old customer had curled himself up to sleep, till evening's dusk invited him back to the hen-roost. That outburst of melody proclaims that he is unkennelled before the pack!

Mr. Jorrocks, having gained his point, places himself behind a gnarled and knotted ivy-covered mountain ash, whose hollow trunk tells of ages long gone by, through a hole in which he commands a view of the grass ride towards the rising ground, upon which the "old customer" generally wends his way. There, as Mr. Jorrocks sat, with anxious eyes and ears, devouring the rich melody, he sees what, at first sight, looked like a hare coming up at a stealthy, stopping, listening sort of pace; but a second glance shows that it is a fox—and not only a fox, but his .dentical old friend, who has led him so many dances, and whose lightening fur tells of many seasons' wickedness.

Mr. Jorrocks can hardly contain himself, and but for his old expedient of counting twenty, would infallibly have halloaed.

The fox comes close up, but is so busy with his own affairs, that he has not time to look about; and before Mr. Jorrocks has counted nine, the fox has made a calculation that the hounds are too near for him to break, so he just turns short into the wood before they get a view. Up they come, frantic for blood, and dash into the field, in spite of Mr. Jorrocks's efforts to turn them, who, hat in hand, sweeps towards the line the fox has taken. A momentary check ensues, and the hounds return as if ashamed of their obstinacy. Now they are on him again, and Mr. Jorrocks thrusts his hat upon his brow, runs the fox's tooth of his hat-string through the button-hole of his roomy coat, gathers up his reins, and bustles away outside the cover, in a state of the utmost excitement—half frantic, in fact! There is a tremendous scent, and Reynard is puzzled whether to fly or stay. He tries the opposite side, but Pigg, who is planted on a hill, heads him, and he is beat off his line.

The hounds gain upon him, and there is nothing left but a bold venture up the middle, so, taking the bed of the brook, he endeavours to baffle his followers by the water. Now they splash after him, the echoing banks and yew-studded cliffs resounding to their cry. The dell narrows towards the west, and Mr. Jorrocks rides forward to view him away. A countryman yoking his plough is before him, and with hat high in air, "TALLIHO'S" till he's hoarse. Pigg's horn on one side, and Jorrocks's on the other, get the hounds out in a crack; the countryman mounts one of his carters, the other runs away with the plough, and the three sportsmen are as near mad as anything can possibly be. It's ding, dong, hey away pop with them all!

The fallows carry a little, but there's a rare scent, and for two miles of ill-enclosed land Reynard is scarcely a field before the hounds. Now Pigg views him! Now Jorrocks! Now Charley! Now Pigg again! Thirty couple of hounds lengthen as they go, but there is no Pomponius Ego to tell. The fox falls back at a wall, and the hounds are in the same field. He tries again—now he's over! The hounds follow, and dash forward, but the fox has turned short up the inside of the wall, and gains a momentary respite. Now they are on him again! They view him through the gateway beyond: he rolls as he goes! Another moment, and they pull him down in the middle of a large grass field!

"Hooray! Hooray! Hooray!" exclaims Mr. Jorrocks, rolling off his horse, and diving into the middle of the pack, and snatching the fox, which old Thunderer resents by seizing him behind, and tearing his white cords half-way down his legs. "Hooray!" repeats he, kicking out behind, and holding the fox over his head, his linen flying out, and his enthusiastic old face all beaming with joy.

"Oh, dear! oh, dear!" exclaims he, dancing about with it over his

head, "if ever there was a warmint properly dusted it's you," looking the
fox full in the face; "you've been a hugly customer to me, dash my
vig if you havn't;" and thereupon Mr. Jorrocks resumed his capers,
singing,

"Unrivalled the 'ounds o'er which Jorrocks presides!
     Then drink to the fox-'ounds,
     The 'igh-mettled fox-'ounds,
We'll drink to the 'ounds o'er which Jorrocks presides."

"Sink ar's left mar Jack-a-legs ahint," says Pigg, wanting to cut off
the fox's brush. "Has ony on ye getten a knife?"

The cart-horsed countryman has one, and Jorrocks holds the fox,
while Pigg performs the last rites of the chase.

With whoops and holloas Jorrocks throws the carcass high in air,
which, falling among the baying pack, is torn to pieces in a minute.

Joy, delightful joy, is theirs, clouded by but one reflection—that that
was the last day of the season.

They re-enter Handley Cross by half-past nine, and at ten sit down
to breakfast, Pigg getting such a tuck-out as he hadn't had since he left
his "coosin Deavilboger's."

THE OLD CUSTOMER.

CHAPTER LIX.

ANOTHER SPORTING LECTOR.

M R. JORROCKS now began sorting and righting his hunting
clothes, seeing what boots and
things would patch and come
out again, and what might be
condemned as no use keeping.
Among the condemned were
the memorable old customer
whites, which, independently
of the tear they got on that
day, were in a somewhat perish-
ing state from their over frequent visits to the washing tub.
Two pair of shags he thought
would do again, and he would
give a pair of old moleskins the
benefit of a doubt. One pair
of boots—the Pinch-me-near-
Forest ones—were a good deal
gone at the toe, but he would
consult Welts the cobbler before he cast them. Then as he
sat in judgment on his coats,
folding up No. 1 with the care
and respect due to the best one, regarding No. 2 as werry good when not
beside a better, and saying that No. 3 would do "werry well for a wet
day;" Betsey came to say that some gents. wanted to see him.

It was a deputation from the Handley Cross Infirmary, come to ask
him to give a sporting lecture in aid of their funds, which, as usual, were
very low.

Mr. Jorrocks hesitated at first, for he wanted to ease the steam of his
hunting enthusiasm down to business-like pitch before he returned to
Great Coram Street and the City. However, as they were very pressing,
and flattered him agreeably, he at length consented, and the lecture was
duly announced, as well by placards and hand-bills as by sending the bell-
man about. Our Master resuscitated his "Beckford" for inspiration,
thinking to dwell on the delights of the chase. The Infirmary scheme
answered, and tickets were in great demand, many parties coming up from
the country to hear our worthy Master hold forth.

Precisely at eight o'clock, on the appointed night, Mr. Jorrocks entered the lecture-room (the long room of the Dragon) by the president's door, and ascended the raised platform immediately on the left. He was dressed in the full evening costume of the hunt—sky-blue coat, lined with pink silk, canary-coloured shorts, white waistcoat, aud white silk stockings, and looked uncommonly spruce—his pumps shone with French polish. Several members of the hunt, some in morning dress, others in evening, followed; and James Pigg and Benjamin, in scarlet coats, black caps, and top-boots, brought up the rear. The room at this time was as full as it could possibly hold, not less than three hundred and fifty persons being assembled; among whom, of course, " we observed" several elegantly dressed females. Mrs. Jorrocks, we are sorry to say, had the tooth-ache, and could not come ; neither were Belinda nor Mr. Stobbs there, it being supposed they were availing themselves of Mrs. Jorrocks' indisposition. Immediately as Mr. Jorrocks entered, the whole company rose and greeted our hero with a volley of most enthusiastic cheers, which continued for some minutes, and appeared greatly to affect the worthy gentleman, who stood bowing and grinning like a Chinese monster on a mantel-piece. Silence being at length obtained, and all the attendants having settled themselves into their places on the platform, and the company having resumed their seats, he advanced to the front, and spoke as follows :—

"Beloved 'earers, behold your old frind John (cheers). John! old in years, but young in mind and body, and dewoted—oh *dewoted,* to the noble cause of 'unting. Oh, my beloved 'earers! I repeats, for the 'underd and fifty-fust time, that 'unting is the sport of kings, the image of war without its guilt, and only five-and-twenty per cent. of its danger (cheers). Do not think I say so for the sake of gainin' your most sweet applause, for, believe me werry sincere when I declare I'd rayther 'ear the cry of 'ounds, or even the lowest whimper whatever owned the scent, than have all the cheerin' your woices can bestow (laughter, with slight hissing).

" Great 'eavens ! " continued Mr. Jorrocks, with up-turned eyes, " wot a many things are wantin' to 'unt a country plisantly—things that would never enter the 'ead of a sailor !

"First and foremost, there should be the means o' praise—all labour's lost if the world's not well told. The finest runs are lost, the largest leaps over-looked, the 'ardest falls forgot, if an efficient record's not preserved. Every 'unt should have its trumpeter as well as its 'untsman—some nice easy-writin' cove to exhibit its bright pints; butterin' without bedaubin'—praisin' without besmearin'—jest as a barber hoils a customer arter a sixpenny clip. Oh, gen'lemen, gen'lemen," continued our Master, " I've been sufferin' severely from the effects o' clumsy soapin' (cheers and laughter)—hawkward hoilin'—havin' things told that I wanted kept snug, and havin' things kept snug that I wanted told. Gen'lemen, take my adwice, and never employ a reg'lar butterer. Do it yourselves, or get a kind frind wot knows your likin's and weak pints to do it.

" But enough of that—p'raps too much—let's to the business of the evenin'.

" Gen'lemen, this is the werry age of balderdash and 'umbug—balderdash the grossest, and 'umbug the greatest, that the most imaginative eye

of the liveliest intellect can possibly conceive (applause). There was a
poet, I think his name was Brown,—John Brown, who said,

> 'We think our fathers fools, so wise we grow,
> Our wiser sons no doubt will think us so.'

And well they may, for we do our best to merit the opinion. See 'ow we
treat 'unting! Dear, delightful 'unting, the werry mention of whose
name kivers me with the creeps, and thrills me all over with joy. We
must now 'unt by book, forsooth : fox and 'ounds must be alike under
our subjection, and if they don't do jest wot is laid down in print, reynard
is all wrong, and the 'ounds good for nothin' (cheers). Oh, my vig! to
think I should ever live to see a fox 'unted on mathematical principles
(cheers); to see the problem ' vich vay has he gone?' worked without
the aid of 'ounds!

"But gently, old buoy, gently," continued he, in a more subdued tone,
" your wehimence has got the bit between its teeth, and with borin' 'ead
is runnin' clean away with you—*steady there, steady*. Now, my beloved
'earers, I've brought you here to tell you *all* about the chass—to teach
you to enjoy that sport,

> 'For the weak too strong,
> Too costly for the poor.'

Aye, *too costly for the poor*, and more's the pity that it is too costly, for
there is more real genuine fox-'untitiveness, more of the innate genuine
hardour and dewoted affection for the chass in the poor man wot sacrifices
a day's pay for the sake of a 'unt, than in all your wauntin' cover-canterin'
swells wot ride forty miles to the meet for the sake of the boast, and the
plisure o' ridin' forty miles back. But that's beside the question, or
another pair of shoes, as we say in France. The chass!—the chass! or
the *noble science*, as the swells now call it, is to be the subject of my
discourse; but oh, my beloved 'earers; it's werry 'ard to turn one's
'tention to things that are fit to brik one's 'eart to think on—werry 'ard
indeed. There was a man wrote a book, and, among other intelligent
things he put in, was an obserwation that one cannot do an act not in
itself morally evil for the last time without feelin's of regret; and if that
be true with regard to indifferent things, 'ow much more tellin' must
it be when applied to what may be called the liver and bacon of one's
existence! To that noblest, sublimest, grandest, best of all sports, the
gallant, cheerin', soul-stirrin' chass " (cheers). Mr. Jorrocks paused for
some seconds, as if overcome by his feelings.

*   *   *   *   *   *

At length he resumed : " Here," said he, " we have closed a most
beautiful season. Though I says it who should not, never did a pack give
more universal satisfaction than mine,— satisfaction the most boundless, and
gratification the most complete. No 'ounds in England can 'old a candle to
mine for the sport they've shown. Summer is now drawin' on, at least it
did ought to do, if it is a comin' at all, leavin' us a long season of repose to
contemplate the past, and spekilate on the futur'—that uncertain futur' to

which we all look forward with such presumptuous certainty. Oh, my beloved 'earers, summer is a dreadful season. Whoever talked o' the winter of our discontent, talked like an insane man, and no sportsman. Summer is the season of our misery! Long days, short nights, and nankeen shorts. Contemptible wear!—but oh! genl'men, genl'men, top-boots delight me not now, drab shags nouther. Wot a change is comin' o'er the spirit of our dream! I knows no more melancholic ceremony than takin' the string out of one's 'at at the end of a season, foldin' hup and puttin' away the old red rag—a rag unlike all other rags, the dearer and more waluable the older and more worthless it becomes. Every rent, every stain, every patch, every darn, has its story and 'sociation. The large black patch all down the right side was got in Swallerton Bog, which I charged like a troop of 'oss, jest as the darlin's were viewin' the warmint, and I thought to pick him hup on the far side. Crikey, vot a flounder I had!—old Arterxerxes bogged up to the werry tail, plungin', and heavin', and groanin', and snortin', and sweatin', with every appearance of being 'stablished for life. Oh, my beloved 'earers, a bog is a werry rum thing to get into, and is so werry enticin' withal, that I don't wonder at people bein' cotched. Quiet, sly, soft, green, omelette-soufflée-lookin' things, so stuffed with currants as to be perfectly black below, and as holdin' as a stick-jaw puddin' at a charity school. I doesn't mean to detract from the merits of other bogs, but that Swallerton Bog, i' my mind, is the biggest bog whatever was seen, and as 'ospitable as man can desire, for once in, it is in no hurry to part with you again.

"Then the great double stitched rent right across the back! 'Ow well I remembers doin' o' that! We were goin' like beans over Harroway Fleets, with sich a crack scent as only comes twice a year. I viewed a fox or a dog, I couldn't say whether, risin' the 'ill by Hookem-Snivey Church; and wot with keepin' my eye on him, and gallopin' like blazes, I never saw a bulfinch that Arterxerxes was preparin' himself for on the sly until it was too late, and he charged a thing so big and so black, that if a lanthorn had been 'eld on the far side you couldn't have seen it; well, I say, he charged it with such wicked wigour and determination, that he left me stickin' like a sweet little cherub aloft right atween two strong 'olders, one of which had to be sawn off afore ever I could get out; and when I did, I found I had lost one coat-lap, and the other was 'angin' by a mere thread (laughter and applause). Delightful recollection! Shall I ever forget the joy I experienced, as, stickin' tight in the 'edge, I saw the darlin's take up the line on which I viewed the warmint travellin'? A delicate compliment to the brightness of my wision! Oh, never! My too sensible 'eart sickens at the thought that the joy of life is over for a season. Oh, the long summer months that are about to succeed are truly appallin' to the 'eart of a sportsman! True, each season brings its hoccupation, but if that hoccupation is no enjoyment, wot matter does it make there bein' such a thing? Oh," groaned the worthy lecturer, "but we are enterin' upon a most melancholic, sea-kaleish, buy-a-moss-rose season. 'Ow we are ever to get through it, I'm sure I don't know. I'm thankful 'owever to think that I pivied the old customer. Blow me tight if I 'adn't pivied the old customer, I really believe the old customer would ha' pivied me. Never suffered so much from a fox i' my life. He 'aunted me day and night. Seemed as if he was 'pointed to revenge the wrongs of all the foxes i' the world. Certainly he was a saucy sinner— a werry saucy sinner—wakin' and sleepin', he was always at me. 'Owsom- ever he's settled." Mr. Jorrocks again made a long pause, and appeared lost in thought.

At length he resumed.

"Great Coram is a lovely street," said he " the trees within the rails, and the wines within the areas, flourish and expand with all the wigour of foliage and wegetable life in the purest and most salubrisome spots. But sweeter, dearer far is the wild bleak heath,

> 'Where man has ne'er or rarely trod,'

with a good strong 'olding goss-cover, lyin' on a gentle slope, catchin' the rays of a mid-day sun, out of which one may reasonably calkilate upon findin' old reynard at home any hour of the day. But I can't pursue the subject. It is too much for me—painful to a degree. Pigg, get me some brandy-and-water—strong without—for I feels all over trembulation and fear, like a maid that thinks she's not a goin' to be married."

Mr. Jorrocks retired to the back of the platform, and Pigg presently brought him a stiff tumbler of brandy-and-water, which considerably revived our old friend, but still he did not feel quite equal to the resump- tion of his lecture. He therefore announced that his Pigg would favour the company with one of his national melodies, after which he had no doubt he should be able to go on, and Pigg, after a few minutes confab with his Master, who wanted him to sing,

> " Unrivalled the 'ounds o'er which Jorrocks presides !"

advanced to the front of the platform, and with a bob of his head and a kick of his heel, said, " Gen'l'men, wor 'ard Maister's gettin' the gripes, and ar's gannin' to sing ye a sang till he gets better." So saying James rubbed his sleeve across his nose, and turned his quid in his mouth. " Now," continued he, " what ar'll sing ye 'ill be yen o' the bonniest sangs that iver was sung, arle aboot ard Squier Lambton and his h'unds, and a grand hunt that they had fre Fox-hill, afore mast o' ye were born ; and when ar stamps wi' my foot, ye mun all join chorus." So saying our huntsman struck up with the following, which we give, like the former, as it was written, and not as Pigg sung it :—

> Descend ye chaste Nine. strike the chord you love best,
> I've a theme that will put your high notes to the test ;
> I've a chase to describe that assuredly will
> Rouse the dead from their graves with huzzas for Fox Hill.
>   Ballanamona ora
>   The hounds of RALPH LAMBTON for me.
>
> We must ever remember the glorious day
> When to Long Newton Village we rattled away,
> Each hound seem'd that morning instinctive to know,
> That the Long Newton Country would give them a go—
>   Ballanamona. &c.

Burn Wood was drawn blank—we cared not a rap—
Though we all thought it smel't hellish strong of a trap,
For we knew that a rallying point we could make,
Where a thoro' bred Son of Old Cæsar must break.
    Ballanamona, &c.

Scarce the pack crack'd the furzen, away the Rogue stole,
How high beat each heart, how transported each soul !
Every hound in his place, and to give them their due,
Over Newbiggin pastures like pigeons they flew.
    Ballanamona, &c.

By Sadberge and Stainton he now bent his way,
Old Elstob affording no shelter this day,
Little Stainton he gained—but durst not look back
So close at his brush lay this brilliant pack
    Ballanamona, &c.

Next pointing to Whitton by Stillington Mill,
One or two boasted clippers were fain to stand still,
But remember, my boys, with a Long Newton Fox
It won't do to *flash* when y're up to the hocks.
    Ballanamona, &c.

O'er the famed Seaton Hills with what vigour he flew !
Determin'd to prove himself thoro' *true blue*,
Sterns down, bristles up—'twould have done your heart good
To have seen the Dog Pack running frantic *for Blood !*
    Ballanamona, &c.

By Fulthorp and Grindon we rattled like smoke,
The hounds gaining on him at every stroke !
Disdaining Thorp Wood should his destiny mark
Dropp'd his brush and died varmint in Wynyard Park,
    Ballanamona, &c.

Fill, fill ye brave spirits that rode in the run,
May the pack add fresh laurels to those they have won ;
At my toast—how each bosom with ecstacy bounds,
Long life to Ralph Lambton ! ! success to his hounds ! !

When the enthusiastic applause, produced by the foregoing, had subsided, there was a general call for Mr. Jorrocks, who advancing to the front of the platform thus addressed the company :—

"Beloved 'earers, you must 'scuse my pursuin' the subject o' the chass —it's too much for my feelin's. I meant to have enlightened you on the management of 'osses and 'ounds at 'ome and in the field, glanced at the 'ard meat and the 'ard work systems, and taken a wide range o'er the realms of sportin' generally, but, somehow or other, I feels unequal to the task,—the excitement is too much for me. I feels as though my stomach was a biler, a throwin' red-'ot words up into my mouth. With your permission, therefore, we'll drop the subject till the arrival of the next 'unting season, when I will finish wot I've left unsung, as the tom-cat said when the brick-bat cut short his serenade. (Laughter and applause.)

"Let us turn to matters more seasonable, though less plisant, and consider the summer department of our lives. We are now about to

disperse, some to the north, some to the south, some to the heast, and
some to the west.   Many on you, I makes no doubt, will think it necessary to go to town, though I cannot but say that you are great fools for
your pains.   There are more people punish themselves annually once
a-year, by goin' to London, than the unthinkin' portion of the community
would credit.   If a man has plenty of blunt, it's all werry well.   London
is an undeniable place for gettin' rid of it in.   Frinds abound there for
rich men.   The kindest, the accommodatingest frinds, wot will do anything to serve you as long as your money lasts.   To London let the rich
man go.   Whatever is gay, or grand, or expensive, will be his; he will
mount his thorough-bred, with a bang-tail down to the 'ocks, put his
grum on another, in a dark frock-coat, leather-breeches, and a belt round
his waist, to strap on his master in case he tumbles off; they will hamble
down Bond Street and hup Regent Street, 'prowokin' the caper wot they
seem to chide'—master pretendin' to be short-sighted, with a quizzin'-
glass stuck in his eye."   Here Mr. Jorrocks put a half-crown piece over
his, and suiting the action to the word, proceeded amidst universal
laughter and applause,—" Meets an acquaintance.   ' 'Ow do ? ' ' Been
long i' town ? ' ' When do you leave ? ' For gen'lemen," continued
Mr. Jorrocks, " I'll lay a guinea 'at to a gooseberry, when two men meet
with little to say, that that is the conversation wot passes.   Six o'clock
comes and he's in the Park.   Wot a crowd about the gate !   It's to see
Wictoria pass.   Carriage and four—out-riders—equerring dust-catching
—Wictoria smilin'—Prince Halbert ditto, and touchin' his 'at to the
cheerers—*whisk*, and they are out o' sight.   Carriages break hup and
scatter over the Park.   The band plays at the gardens—up our rich man
canters, without knowin' why he breaks from a walk, throws the rein to
his grum, and lounges in to lisp to the ladies.   ' Oh ! 'pon honour—
exquisite—delightful band—Second Life Guards—Star and Garter—
Crown and Sceptre—Charmin' weather—Looks like rain—'Ow's your
mother ? Sister better !—So, Lady ——'s eloped at last.'   Back then he
goes by the Serpentine.   Kid gloves are kissed to him, feathers nod,
eyes ogle, and Johns and Jehus touched their laced-daubed 'ats.   Now he
reins hup at the foot of the Achilles, and, as the late accomplished
Mr. Truefit, the Harcadian 'air-dresser, or some other talented gen'lman
sung—

> ' Pride in his look, defiance in his eye,
> He sees the lords o' 'uman life pass by.

Dinner time comes, and Lord Cut and Shuffle has the rich man on the
box of his drag—four spankin' bays, tigers be'ind, frinds on the roof,
gals inside.   Away they bowl to Greenwich—best room, dinner two
guineas a-'ead, iced fizzey—fish of all sorts—Yarrell done up in dishes—
every sort but the one you went down for—should have ten stomachs
'stead of one—back at eleven.   Hopera—Time for ballet—squizzin'-
glass—gauze petticoats—or hup Windmill-street to the sparklin' French
Casino, or down heast to the British 'bomination of a dingy underground
kidney-shop.   These at length bein' swept out and closed, away they
go to some sham billiard room of a fortified gambling 'ouse, with scouts
on the watch, where they have some cureasore to digest the kidney—

iced champagne to correct the cureasore—lobster salad to keep the iced champagne company. Then iounge into the gamblin' apartment—large round table—strong light. Man with a green shade over his eyes and a hoe in his hand! Old rakes all round him. Fathers sittin' hopposite sons—the famine of play ragin'—then sudden noise—clean sweep—down the pipe—rush o' pollis—seize the party—away to the lock-up—in wi' false names—hup i' the mornin'—discharged for want o' gamblin'-tool hevidence, and all that sort o' gammon. All this may be called plissur, &c., but some'ow it never lasts. It's the pace that kills the finances as well as the fox. It's all nonsense men spendin' wots to keep them a lifetime in a single night's lark (applause). Ax any old member o' Crocky's if it is'nt.

"London's a grand place, to be sure," continued the worthy lecturer; "but oh, my beloved 'earers, there is no misery like that of solitude in a crowd, or inconwenience like that of livin' with men without being able to afford to partake o' their plissurs. London's the rich man's paradise, the poor man's puggatory? yet how many fools, who can ill afford it, think it necessary to make a hannual pilgrimage once a-year to the shrine of her monstrosity. Hup they come, leavin' their quiet country 'omes just as their sparrowgrass is ready for heatin', and their roses begin to blow—neglectin' their farms—maybe their families—leavin' bulls to bail themselves, cattle to get out of the pound, and wagrants into the stocks, as they can; hup, I say, they come to town, to get stuck in garrets at inns with the use of filthy, cigar-smokin', spitty, sandy-floored, saw-dusty coffee-rooms, a 'underd and seventy-five steps below, at a price that's perfectly appalin'. Vot misery is theirs! Down they come of a mornin,' arter a restless, tumblin', heated, noisy night, to the day den of the establishment, with little happetite for breakfast, but feelin' the necessity of havin' some in order to kill time. A greasy-collared, jerkin', lank-'aired waiter, casts a second-'and, badly-washed web over a slip of table, in a stewy, red-curtained box, into which the sun beats with unmitigated wengeance. A Britannia-metal tea-pot, a cup, a plate, a knife, and a japanned tea-caddie make their appearance. Then comes a sugar-bason, followed by a swarm of flies, that 'unt it as the 'ounds would a fox, and a small jug of 'sky-blue,' which the flies use as a bath durin' their repast on the sugar. A half-buttered muffin mounts a waterless slop-bason; a dirty egg accompanies some toasted wedges of bread; the waiter points to a lump of carrion wot he calls beef, on a dusty sideboard, and promises the 'Post' as soon as it is out of 'and. Sixteen gents sit at sixteen slips of table, lookin' at each other with curiosity or suspicion, but never a word is exchanged by any on them. Prisently they begin to wacate their slips of wood. One paces hup and down the coffee-room, with his thumbs in the harm'oles of his veskit; another takes a coat-lap over each arm, and lounges against the fireless fire-place; a third looks at his watch, and lays his legs along the bench for a nap; while a fourth flattens his nose against the winder, or reads the witticisms of former town captives, or the hamorous contributions of jaded waiters to buxom chambermaids on the panes. Carriages begin to roll; lords, dukes, captains, cockneys, jostle together, and the coffee-room is gradually emptied into the crowded streets.

E E

"Vot a sight! All the world compressed into Bond Street! carriages blocked, cabs locked, 'ossmen driven on to the footway, and the foot-people driven into the shops. But wot boots it to ingenuous Spoony if there were twice as many? He doesn't know one carriage from another, and hasn't got nobody to tell him whose they are. There he stands gapin' like a stuck pig, now starin' his eye-balls out at a carriage, now bringin' his body to bear upon a print-shop window, now fancyin' a lady in feathers on the footway to be a duchess that has taken a fancy to him, who he follows up to the suberbs, and comes away under the impression that it is their country willa. But wot a relief to have some one to whom he can speak! Talk of dull dogs! Live in London for a week without an acquaintance, and the stupidest lump of lead that ever was moulded into the shape of a man will be a perfect god-send at the end of the time. Well, hup and down the street poor ingenuous Spoony goes, round squares, into crescents, through parks, until his feet are swelled double their size, and the toes of his boots look up into his face, as much as to say, 'Wot *has* come over us now?' Still no one greets him, and Squire Spoony, who is a werry great man, and knows every body at once, is 'stonished that no one 'ails him in London.

"Now for a chop-house or coffee-room dinner! Oh, the 'orrible smell that greets you at the door! Compound of cabbage, pickled salmon, boiled beef, saw-dust, and anchovy sarce. 'Wot will you take, sir?' inquires the frowsy waiter, smoothin' the filthy, mustardy, cab-bagey cloth, 'soles, macrel, vitin's—werry good, boiled beef—nice cut, cabbage, cold 'am and weal, cold lamb and sallard.'— *Bah!* The den's 'ot to suffocation—the kitchen's below—a trap-door womits up dinners in return for bellows down the pipe to the cook. Flies settle on your face—swarm on your head; a wasp travels round; everything tastes flat, stale, and unprofitable. As a climax, he gets the third of a bottle of warm port as a pint, and, to prevent jealousy between body and mind, gives the latter a repast on second-hand news, by goin' through the columns of an evenin' paper. This, too, from a man wot can hardly manage a three-days-a-week one in the country.

"Nine o'clock at length comes, and he is at the theatre; and were it not for the excessive 'eat and confounded crowd, he might enjoy himself. As it is, the curtain drops, a welcome release, and after half an hour's solitary stroll, he finds himself smokin' some painted Jezabel, who sits to be fumigated by all wot buys cigars at her shop. Thus he goes on day after day, week after week, in a melancholy state of existence, and all that he may have the pleasure of sayin' when he returns to the country, that he has 'jest *come from town*'—that town was werry full—werry gay or werry dull—talk of high people in a low-lived style, and pretend to have been where he never was. No captive released from gaol—no bouy let free from school—no starlin' escaped from cage, hails with more 'eart-felt joy the arrival of that hour which restores him to wot the immortal Mr. Fieldin' (I thinks) calls

'Fresh fields and pastures new;'

and not all the pliability of a flexible mind can coax him into believin' that he feels one longin' lingerin' pang of regret, as he turns his back upon the crowded, 'eartless, busy, bustlin', jadin' city. (Great applause.)

" 'Well, but,' says a sportin' reader, 'I must see the Darby and Hoaks run for ! '

"Darby and Hoaks run for ! " exclaimed the worthy lecturer. " Wot matter does it make to him who wins the Darby and Hoaks ! Why can't he content 'imself wi' readin' on it i' the paper, or in seein' a neighbourly donkey race on a common ? He may know summut 'bout the donkeys, but he can know nothin' 'bout 'osses, the owners of which werry likely know nothin' themselves. Then bother their bettin' books, and the 'ole tribe of trickey, lynx-eyed circumwenti'n knaves wot would rob their own fathers if they could, and who set hup to bet thousands with a farthin' capital ! O that the noblest of hanimals should be soiled with the contamination of such reptiles ! O that the 'ighest and the noblest should be found jostlin' and helbowin' for hodds 'mong the werry scum and scourins o' the stews—fellers that no decent tradesman would touch wi' a pair o' tongs (applause). On the turf and under the turf all men are obliged to be equal," mused our Master. " But let us leave the gloomy subject," continued he, " and gather hup our points for a finish. Some on you will p'raps ax wot has racin' and livin' i' London to do wi' 'unting ? I say it has a great deal. There is an old sayin' and a true one, that you carn't eat both your cake and 'ave it, and by the same rule, or one werry like it, you carn't both spend your money and have it. Now, if ingenuous Spooney comes to London on a gallivantin' expedition, with nothin whatsomever at all to do, the chances are that he gets rooked. ' Idleness ' has been werry well described as ' the papa of all mischief ; ' and assuredly Satan, as Mrs. Barbauld beautifully expresses it in her ' Pleasures of 'Ope,' is always busy in London, findin' work for ' idle 'ands to do.' Walk along Jermyn Street of an evenin', and see how many beautifully illuminated doors stand ajar inwitin' the passer-by to enter ; go—and you're done. It is not here,

'All ye what enter abandon 'ope ;

but wot I say is, all ye wot enter, leave your pusses at home, or assuredly you will have werry little call for them when you come out. In short, if you waste your money i' summer, you can't expect to have it to spend i' winter, and then wot comes of your 'unting ?—ay, then wot comes of my 'ounds ? That's the question put in a familiar form (cheers). Ah, now I see you twig, and go along with me. Oh gen'lmen, gen'lmen, there's nothin' so difficult as gettin' a subscription to a pack of hounds. Chaps that would give a 'undred a-year to a cuk, grudge a fi pun note to a pack that would keep them in 'ealth, and save them all the money i' Seidletz pooders (laughter and applause). Which then will you have ? 'Unting i' winter, or street-strollin' i' summer ? I'll diwide the meetin' on the question, and take the sense of this assembly. All then who are for the sport of kings, the image of war without its guilt, with only five and twenty per cent of its danger, 'old up their 'ands."

A forest of hands were held up for hunting ; on the other question

being put, no one was found in favour of it, whereupon Mr. Jorrocks
concluded amidst loud and long-continued applause, by complimenting
them on their choice, calling on every man to put his shoulder to the
wheel, and do his possible in support of himself and the "HANDLEY
CROSS FOX HOUNDS."   A large party sat down to supper after the
lecture ; and we are happy to add that a subscription was opened for the
purpose of presenting Mr. Jorrocks with a solid token of esteem in the
shape of a silver steak dish, with a model of himself on Arterxerxes on
the cover.   More gratifying still it is to add, that the subscription was
immediately filled.

TESTIMONIAL TO JOHN JORROCKS, ESQ.

CHAPTER LX.

THE STUD SALE.

THE following was the strength of Mr. Jorrocks s stud at the close of the season.

There were our old friends Xerxes and Arterxerxes; also a great raking, bony, cock-throppled, ragged-hipped, shabby-tailed, white-legged, chestnut, fired all round, that had belonged to a smuggler, and was christened "Ginnums;" a little jumped-up, thick-set, mealy-legged, sunken-eyed bay, with a short tail and full coarse mane, whose unhappy look procured him the name of Dismal Geordy; a neatish brown, that our master bought of young May, the grocer at Handley Cross, and christened Young Hyson; and the cut 'em down Captain's quad, six in all. Arterxerxes did most of Mr. Jorrocks's work, and Xerxes could carry half-a-dozen Bens every day in the week, so that Pigg and Charley came in for most of the work of the others, Charley never having gone to the trouble of getting any more horses than the one he brought with him.

Xerxes and Arterxerxes (capital feeders) were both desperately troubled with the slows, and the latter puffed and blew in a way that made ill-natured people say he was going broken-winded.

Having long stood together, they had contracted a friendship, that displayed itself in constant neighings and whinnyings when separated, and rushings together and rubbings on meeting, to the derangement of the dignity and convenience of their riders. Thus, if Mr. Jorrocks was yoicking on one side of a cover on Arterxerxes, and Ben all hot-ing* it on the other side on Xerxes, there would be such a neighing and whinnying, and exchanging of compliments all the time, as greatly to interfere with our master's attention to his hounds, and when the horses caught sight of each other, Xerxes would take the bit between his teeth, and rush to his friend Arterxerxes, making a rubbing-post of him and his rider in defiance of resistance on the part of Benjamin, and remonstrance on the part of Mr. Jorrocks.

Ginnums was quite the reverse of the preceding. He had commenced life as a leather-plater, and done hard service on some country courses, and after experiencing the vicissitudes of fortune in the hands of various masters of different callings, had descended into the hands of a smuggler, when he was seized by the Excise, well weighted with contraband goods, and publicly sold to Mr. Jorrocks for fourteen pounds ten shillings. He was a raking goer, but a nasty wriggling beast to ride, continually throwing his head in the air, to the danger of his rider's countenance. His mouth, too, was deadened on one side, and he had a careless rushing sort of way of going at his fences, but he never tired, and could go through heavy ground with wonderful ease to himself.

Dismal Geordy was of the hot and heavy sort,—a better hand at

---

* " 'Yo hote,' to make hounds hunt."—*Diary of a Huntsman.*

trotting than galloping. He used to jump and squeal with a cow-like action at first going out, and could gallop pretty well for a mile or so, after which he would shut up, and be dull and heavy the rest of the day. He was a dull, under-bred brute, with very little taste for hunting.

Young Hyson was a neat horse, and a good goer, but quite unmade when Mr. Jorrocks bought him.—Pigg and he used to roll about tremendously at first.

" Gin ar were ye," said James to his master, as the latter took his usual stroll through the stable, " gin ar were ye, ar'd get shot o' some o' these nags—they'll niver de ye ne good."

" Why so, James ?" inquired Mr. Jorrocks in a more amiable mood than usual when his stud was abused.

" Because ar thinks there's ne use i' keepin' sick a lot through the summer; ye that have ivery thing to buy and nothin' for them to de. Ye arn't like ma coosin Deavilboger, that can work them i' the farm a bit, and gar them pay their keep."

" True," replied Mr. Jorrocks; " 'ay's dear—so is corn—but how's one to get rid of these sort of animals, think ye ? No demand for them now that the rallys have dished all the coaches."

" Why, but it's just the same thing, if ye sell cheap now, ye'll buy cheap i' the autumn, and save all the summerin'. There's Ginnums, now, his near foreleg's verra kittle—ar'd get shot o' him while it stands. Arterxerxes, tee, is queer iv his wind,—ye'd better be rid o' him while it lasts. Geordy, tee, is nabbut fit for the pits ;—ye canna get worse ! "

" I doesn't know that," said Mr. Jorrocks who had rather an affection for the Dismal, and thought he would do for his Boobey Hutch. " Besides, we shall want a couple, at all ewents, to exercise th' 'ounds during the summer."

The close of a watering-place season generally produces some change among the studs. Gentlemen have got to the end of their tethers, spring captains have to join their regiments abroad, and some always make a practice of selling at the end of a season (or at any other time). Handley Cross formed no exception to the rule, and Mr. Palmer, the auctioneer, having canvassed the town, persuaded the owners of some eighteen or twenty horses to entrust them to his persuasive eloquence in the shape of a sale by auction. Mr. Jorrocks having considered Pigg's suggestions, and being up to all the tricks of horse-auctions, agreed to send his six, on condition of the sale being well advertised, and his stud especially mentioned as being sold in consequence of his wishing to remount his men on horses more suitable to the country.

Accordingly advertisements were inserted in all the papers and lists distributed far and near, headed " GREAT STUD SALE," and describing Mr. Jorrocks's horses as masters of great weight, that had been regularly hunted all the season with the Handley Cross Fox-hounds.

The publicity thus given had the effect of causing all the curious-looking, cut-away coats and extraordinary top-boots in the country to drop into the town of Handley Cross on the morning of the sale. Some people cannot stay away from a horse-auction ; and men that can hardly keep themselves will appear, and sometimes undergo the spasm of putting in a horse at a low figure, for the momentary *éclat* of being taken for

purchasers. Luckless wights if in an evil moment the hammer drops
with the fatal fiat, " *Yours, sir !* "—— But to our sale.

At an early hour the horses were brought from their respective stables,
and arranged in numbered stalls in the Dragon Yard, according to their
classification in the bills. All the hand rubbing was done at home, so
that they had only to receive the finishing touch from the clean waist-
coated grooms, who, with plastered hair, were charged with their
respective lies as to their qualifications. James Pigg arrived first, and so
well done were his horses, that Mr. Jorrocks almost hoped they might

THE STUD SALE.

return as he saw them pass along the street to the yard. Ben and Pigg
had on their top-boots, striped waistcoats, and brown frocks, which latter
were taken off, carefully folded up, and put into a corn bin in the stable
where their horses stood. It was a nine-stall one, and there were two

horses belonging to two fast-going foot-captains, and a mare the property of a water-drinker, along with Mr. Jorrocks's.

At twelve o'clock the stables were thrown open, and fussy gentlemen in taglionis, macintoshes, siphonias and reversible coats, &c., whips and bills in their hands, began their examination.   There was Captain Shortflat admiring Arterxerxes, and abusing Dismal Geordy, that he wanted to buy; young men feeling old horses' legs, and rising from the operation as wise as they stooped ; some bringing all their acquaintance to assist in finding faults, and others pumping grooms to tell what they were paid for keeping secret.

James Pigg gave his horses the very best of characters, which Ben as quickly counteracted by telling every thing he knew to their disadvantage. This, of course, Ben did in confidence, and in the hopes of a *douceur* for his honesty.   Pigg kept protesting as he patted them ; "that they were just the best husses he had ever seen, and he didn't ken what could make his 'ard feuil of a maister think o' parting with them," while Ben, with a leer and a wink, declared it was "all his eye, and they were only fit for the knackers." *

Towards one, most of the inquisitive gentry having satisfied their curiosity, the motley group began to congregate in the stable-yard, and some began to look at their watches and inquire for the auctioneer.   The assembly at a sale of this sort exhibits every link in the chain of sporting life, from the coronetted peer to the broken-down leg.   There is a good deal of equality, too, in the scene, the generality of the company being strangers to each other; and as many people consider it knowing to dress differently to what they generally do, the great men are not easily distinguishable from the little ones.   A stud-sale is a sort of fox-hunters', hare-hunters', prize-fighters', dog-stealers' *réunion*, for which people pull out queer-cut, and flash-coloured coats, and dress themselves in drab breeches with knee-caps, or moleskins with gaiters.   All have whips, even the pedestrians.

Mr. Jorrocks launched an uncommonly smart new taglioni for the occasion, a brown-striped leopard's skin looking duffle, all decorated in front with tassels and cords, with pockets of various size and position, bound with nut-brown velvet : the standing-up collar and pointed cuffs were of nut-brown velvet also, and it was lined and wadded throughout with rustling silk.   Thus he swaggered into the yard, his hands stuffed into the lower tier of pockets, and his great tassels pattering against his Hessian boots as he walked.   There was an easy indifference in his air which plainly said he didn't care whether he sold his horses or not.

His appearance was the signal for Mr. Palmer, the auctioneer, to quit the Dragon bar, where he was sipping a glass of cold brandy and water, and forthwith he emerged with a roll of catalogues and his hammer in his hand.   He was a rosy-gilled, middle-aged, middle-sized man, who had failed twice in the hosiery line, once in the spirit-way, and once in the Temperance Hotel line.   He was sprucely dressed, as most auctioneers are, wearing a superfine velvet-collar'd great-coat, open in front, dis-

* Horse-slaughterers.

playing a superfine black coat and waistcoat, with a clean white neck-cloth, and small shirt-frills, secured by a handsome brooch.

Having saluted Mr. Jorrocks with becoming respect, they paired off for a few minutes, to arrange the puff preliminary for his horses.

This being done, Mr. Palmer repaired to the end of the yard, where, under the clock, a temporary rostrum had been erected, formed of short planks placed on four beer-barrels, on which stood a table, and there was a desk below for the clerk to take the deposits upon. At the back was a short step-ladder, upon the top stair of which Mr. Palmer mounted, and Mr. Jorrocks perched himself on the one immediately below. The crowd, with the usual follow-my-leader propensity, were soon ranged round the rostrum, and, a slight shower beginning to fall, umbrellas went up, and Mr. Palmer unfolded a catalogue, and cleared his voice for an oration.

"Gentlemen! ' said he, "may I request your attention while I read the conditions of sale?"

"Throw us a catalogue!" cried half-a-dozen voices; and forthwith a shower of half-crumpled catalogues began to fly about, to be scrambled for by the gentry below. The demand being satisfied, Mr. Palmer again cleared his throat, and requesting attention to the conditions of sale, proceeded to read about "the highest bidder being the purchaser; and if any dispute arose," &c., which was listened to with the usual patience bestowed upon such "I know it all" sort of orations. After some very inferior rubbish had been passed or disposed of, Mr. Jorrocks's turn drew on, and Arterxerxes' great Roman nose was seen peeping out of the stable-door, when at the word "*Out!*" Ben gave him a cut behind, and forth flew the horse, kicking and squeaking from the combined effects of the whip and the ginger. Pigg ran him up to the hammer, which the horse approached with such energy as to threaten demolition not only to the crowd, but to the rickety fabric of a rostrum.

Having got him stopped without a more serious injury than upsetting the clerk's uncorked sixpenny bottle of red ink, and scattering the crowd right and left, the spectators formed an avenue on each side of the horse, while Pigg tickled him under the knee with his whip, to get him to stand out and show himself.

"Now, gentlemen," said Mr. Palmer, with a preparatory hem, looking the horse full in the face, "this is lot one of Mr. Jorrocks's stud, *The celebrated horse, Arterxerxes!* familiar to every one in the habit of hunting with the celebrated hounds over which his distinguished owner has the honour to preside."

"*Presides with such ability*," growled Mr. Jorrocks, in the auctioneer's ear.

"Over which his distinguished owner presides with such ability," repeated Mr. Palmer. "He is, as you see, a horse of great power and substance, equal to the ——"

"Say *speed!*" whispered Mr. Jorrocks.

"He is, as you see, a horse of great power, speed, and substance, equal to any weight ——"

"How can we see his speed?" inquired a drunken-looking groom, in an out-of-place costume, covered buttons, and so forth.

"Hold your tongue, sir, and listen to me!" said Mr. Palmer with an air of authority.

"He is, as you see, gentlemen," resumed the auctioneer, "a horse of great power, speed, and substance, up to any weight, and quiet——"

"Quiet enough," observed a bystander, "if you hadn't figged him."

"And is only sold," continued the auctioneer, "because his owner has no further use for him."

"Highly probable!" exclaimed a voice.

"No one else, I should think!" rejoined another.

"*He's an undeniable leaper!*" whispered Mr. Jorrocks.

"As a leaper, this horse is not to be surpassed!" observed the auctioneer,

"*Temperate at his fences,*" prompted Mr. Jorrocks, adding, "Vy don't you go on, man?"

"Because you put me out," replied the auctioneer, turning snappishly round, and saying, "*Do hold your jaw!*"

"*Blast your imperance!*" roared Mr. Jorrocks, an exclamation that produced a burst of laughter, during which Mr. Palmer turned again, and had a conference with Jorrocks behind. After a few seconds' parley, during which Mr. Jorrocks assured the auctioneer that he'd set to and sell the "osses" himself, if he didn't take care, Mr. Palmer resumed, in a more submissive tone,—

"I was going to observe, gentlemen," said he, "that as you are not all

in the habit of hunting with the celebrated hounds in this neighbourhood, that this horse is the property of the renowned Mr. Jorrocks, and
has been ridden by him during the whole of the past season, and is equal
to any weight you can possibly put upon him."

" *Aye is he !* " exclaimed Pigg, rubbing the horse's great Roman nose :
" top huss ! best we have, by far."

" Now 'bout Surrey," whispered Mr. Jorrocks.

" And, gentlemen," continued Mr. Palmer, looking sadly disconcerted,
" before coming here, this horse was a distinguished performer in the
Surrey Hunt—a hunt that beats all other hunts, except the Handley
Cross Hunt, for intensity of ardour and desperate conflixion."

" Well done ! " exclaimed Mr. Jorrocks, patting the orator's back.

" Keep the tambourine a rowlin' ! " growled Pigg, turning his quid,
and patting the horse's head.

" All round my 'at ! " squeaked Benjimin in the crowd.

" Now 'bout the cut-me-downs," whispered Mr. Jorrocks.

" And gen'lemen, he is favourably known in the cut-'em-down and 'ang-
'em-up-to-dry countries, where his distinguished owner has frequently
shown them the way."

" Werry good," said Mr. Jorrocks, chuckling and rubbing his hands.
" So I do—so I do—the way to open the gates at least."

" He is quite in his prime," continued the auctioneer, " fresh, and fit
for immediate work. Now what will any gentleman give for this celebrated hunter ? Put him in at whatever you like : he *is* to be sold !
Shall I say a hundred and fifty for him ? "

" Shillin's ? " exclaimed one of the auctioneer's tormentors.

" Will any gentleman give a hundred and fifty guineas for the horse ? "
continued Mr. Palmer, without noticing the interruption ; " a hundred
and fifty guineas ! No one say a hundred and fifty ? A hundred and
forty, then ?—a hundred and thirty ?—one hundred guineas, then ?—
throwing him away ! "

" *Deed is't !* " exclaimed Pigg.

Still no one was sensible enough to see the matter in this light, and
after a pause, during which a seedy-looking little fellow, in a very big
bad hat, a faded green kerchief, and a long dirty, drab great-coat, that
concealed a pair of nearly black top-boots, requested to see Arterxerxes
run down ; and, having visited him with a severe punch in the ribs
on his return and a nip in the neck, coolly observed that he was
a bull.*

" No more than yourself ! " roared Mr. Jorrocks.

" Will you warrant him, then ? " inquired Drab-coat.

" *Varrant him !* " repeated Mr. Jorrocks, " I *never varrants*—wouldn't
varrant that he's an oss, let alone that he's sound."

" You knows better ! " replied Drab-coat, examining the horse's eyes
as he spoke ; adding, " I'm not sure but he's a-goin' blind, too ! "

" You be d—d ! " growled Pigg, doubling his fist as he spoke.

" Pray keep order, gentlemen ! " interposed the auctioneer.

" What teeth he has ! " exclaimed Drab-coat— " *long as my arm !* "

* A roarer.

"You must have length somewhere ; and I'm blow'd he harn't got it nowhere else," rejoined a confederate.

"Come, gentlemen, let's have no more of your chaffing, but proceed to business," interrupted the auctioneer. "What will any one give for this valuable——"

"Dray-horse !" exclaimed some one.

"*Hunter !*" continued the auctioneer, without noticing the interruption.

"Fifteen pund," said Drab-coat.

"Fifteen pund !" exclaimed the auctioneer, in disgust. "You must bid in guineas, sir."

"Then fourteen guineas !" replied the man.

"Fourteen guineas," said the auctioneer. "Come, gentlemen, please to go on—*quick.*" Fifteen, sixteen, seventeen, eighteen, eighteen in two places, nineteen, and twenty, were bid, without any further persuasion. "Twenty guineas are only bid for this beautiful animal !" exclaimed Mr. Palmer, flourishing his hammer. "Why his tail's worth all the money."

"For a hat-peg !" exclaimed some one.

"His head would make a fine fiddle-case," observed Drab-coat, with a sneer.

"He's up to any weight with any hounds," observed Mr. Palmer.

"He'll be more at home with millers' sacks," rejoined the confederate.

"'Ard as iron," whispered Mr. Jorrocks.

"Very stout !" exclaimed the auctioneer.

"'Deed is he !" rejoined Drab-coat, punching his fat sides.

"Confound your imperance !" muttered Mr. Jorrocks, over the rostrum : "I'll skin you alive !"

"Ar'll tan your hide enow !" said Pigg, looking indignantly round.

"Now, gentlemen, please keep order, and go on," urged the auctioneer. "Twenty guineas are only bid for this valuable hunter, and I can't dwell. Are you all done at twenty guineas ?"

"One," nodded some one.

"Two !"

"Three !"

"Four !"

"Five !" and again the biddings came to a pause. Drab-coat retires, his commission being exhausted.

"Twenty-five guineas !" recapitulated the auctioneer. "Five-and-twenty guineas only bid for this splendid hunter—master of great weight —great cut-'em-down powers—giving him away—but I can't dwell. Are you all done, at twenty-five guineas, gentlemen ? *Going !* for the last time," lifting his hammer as he spoke.

Just as the fatal blow was about to be struck, Jorrocks's conscience smote him at parting with a faithful old animal that had carried him triumphantly through many a glorious chase—the model, too, of his mount on the silver steak dish handle—causing him to blurt out " *three 'underd !*" which had the effect of saving the lot and spoiling the sale of the rest, people grumbling and saying they didn't come there to be made fools of by him, and so on. Arterxerxes then returned to his stable, and was replaced at the hammer by Xerxes, who came with his great switch tail sticking up like Gabriel Junks'.   Again Mr. Palmer's persuasive powers were put forth to induce the audience to look favourably on the horse's pretensions; all the good qualities ascribed to his late comrade were freely transferred to him; indeed, if anything, Xerxes was *rather* the better horse of the two.   Drab-coat puts him in again at a low figure, and the same scene of complimentary politeness ensues that marked the course of Arterxerxes.

The biddings being languid, and the auctioneer seeing little chance of *bonâ fide* ones, took up the running himself at a brisk pace, and knocked the horse down at sixty guineas, announcing Mr. Scroggins as the buyer. This gave the thing a fillip, and Dismal Geordy was knocked down to Captain Shortflat for eight-and-twenty pounds, ten more than Mr. Jorrocks gave for him.   The captain then received the usual compliments on his purchase, one man asking him if he was "fond of walking;" another observing that he supposed the captain had purchased the horse for his farm, to which latter the captain replied, with a growl, that he had bought him to go in a bathing machine—a retort that had the effect of suppressing the rest of their chaff.   The other lots were then proceeded with; some being sold, and others retained.   Thus closed the Handley Cross hunting season.

Mr. Jorrocks having instructed James Pigg what to do, and taken an affectionate leave of Gabriel Junks, set off for London, leaving Mrs. Jorrocks and Co. to follow as soon as Mrs. Jorrocks had paid her bills and left her P. P. C.'s.

Then, as she drove from house to house, knocking and ringing and leaving of cards, significant looks and knowing sentences passed respecting Belinda.

Disappointed mammas, who had risked the season in vain, "supposed they *ought* to congratulate Mrs. Jorrocks.   For their parts, they saw little cause for rejoicing in losing an object both near and dear, and they hoped they might never know the affliction."

Mrs. Jorrocks 'oped they never might.

Ladies who had gentlemen in tow were more amiable, and thought it was an exceedingly nice thing.   Others, whose pretensions to beauty were eclipsed by Belinda, were sincerely glad to hear she was going to be married.   Hoped she meant to come a good deal amongst them after.

Mrs. Jorrocks heard all they had to say, and kept bobbing, and bowing, and muttering something about "much obleged—werry gratifyin' —not settled—let *them* know *first*," which being construed into an admission, the old women set to and abused both Belinda and Charley, while the young ones sought out their threads and their worsteds to work her a collar or a piece of crochet work each.

CHAPTER LXI.

THE PRIVATE DEAL.

AN usually good season having crowned Captain Doleful's exertions, and things altogether wearing an upward aspect, he entered into a deep mental calculation, whether it would not be quite as cheap keeping a horse altogether as hiring the town hacks, which he found were not so safe as was desirable for a great official character like himself. The idea originated in the circumstance of Mr. Jorrocks' horse Xerxes being unsold, which Captain Doleful thought might be got for a trifle, and seemed to have been put to all the purposes a horse is capable of performing. Having weighed the pros and cons, and inquired the horse's character of every body about the town, our cautious M.C. at last ventured to write the following letter about ten days after Mr. Jorrocks's return to London :—

"Dear Mr. Jorrocks,—I regret much to learn that your horse Xerxes still remains on hand. I was in hopes some of the indifferent judges would have taken a fancy to him, and relieved you of an animal confessedly unsuited to your purpose; but that not being the case, I trouble you with this, to say that Miss Lucretia Learmouth is in want of an animal to draw her four-wheeled chaise about, and make himself generally useful, and I should be happy to be of any service in recommending him to her. Price, I should observe, will be the first consideration, therefore please put him in at the lowest possible figure. Of course I presume he is what they call 'all right.' On a close examination of his countenance, I perceive sundry grey hairs scattered about :—is not this symptomatic of age? With compliments to the ladies, who, I hope, arrived safe, believe me, dear Mr. Jorrocks,

"Yours, very sincerely,
"MISERRIMUS DOLEFUL, M.C.
"*Handley Cross Spa.*

"To John Jorrocks, Esq.,
"Great Coram-street, London."

The following was Mr. Jorrocks's answer :—

"Dear Doleful,—Yours is received, and note the contents. Xerxes may not be first-rate, but he is a good enduring quad, well calkilated for much honorable exertion in many of the minor fields of oss enterprise. He can go a good bat, too, when he's roused; and though I says it who should not, Miss Lucretia may go a deal farther and fare worse. What say you to five-and-twenty guas? If Lucretia's young and 'andsome, I'll take punds, if not I must 'ave the guas. Let me hear from you, as to this, always

"Yours to serve,
"JOHN JORROCKS, M.F.H.

"P.S.—Grey 'airs is nothin'. I've seen 'em all grey afore now."

The following was Captain Doleful's rejoinder :—

" Dear Mr. Jorrocks,—Your polite letter merits my warmest gratitude. Miss Lucretia is young and beautiful! Left an almost unprotected orphan, I feel deeply interested in her welfare, which I am sure will be participated in by you when you have the pleasure of her acquaintance. Twenty-five pounds seems a great sum for a horse confessedly not first-rate—could you not soften it a little? Fifteen, I should think, considering the circumstances, ought to buy him. He is not handsome—Lucretia is *beautiful!* Believe me, ever, dear Mr. Jorrocks,

" Yours, very truly,
" MISERRIMUS DOLEFUL, M.C.
" <i>Handley Cross Spa.</i></div>

" To John Jorrocks, Esq.,
" Great Coram-street, London."

The same post brought the following letter from James Pigg :—

" Honnor'd Sir,—The ard dancin'-maister has been in and out o' wor stable varry oft, and seems sweet on ard Xerxes. He says he's for a lady, but his Miss Jelly tould a woman I had for the season, who tould me, that he wants him for hissel'; so mind your eye, and no more from

" Yours, humbelly,
J. PIGG.
' <i>Handley Cross.</i></div>

" H'unds be main well—so be sel'. "

Mr. Jorrocks took the hint, assumed the indifferent, and wrote as follows, for the delay of a post or two :—

" Dear Doleful,—Handsome is wot handsome does. If Xerxes arn't a beauty, he's uncommon useful. Five per cent. seems discount enough between ' beauty and the beast.' If you like to fork out 25*l.* he's yours, if not, say no more about it.

" Yours to serve,
" JOHN JORROCKS, M.F.H.

" To Miserrimus Doleful, Esq., M.C.,
" Handley Cross Spa."

The captain did not exactly like this letter, but not being easily choked, he returned to the charge with the following answer :—

" Dear Mr. Jorrocks,—At the risk of being thought importunate, I again venture to intercede very respectfully on behalf of the young and beautiful orphan who has sought my assistance in the matter of a horse. Under no other circumstances could I venture to intrude myself further upon your valuable time. You, like all high-minded men, disdain two prices. I admire your independence, but in expressing my admiration, may I venture to hope that some little relaxation from so meritorious a rule may be allowed in a case so peculiarly interesting as the young and beautiful Miss Lucretia Learmouth's. Could we not put it thus :—I'll give you twenty-five pounds for Xerxes, on the understanding that you return me five. That, I think, seems *very fair*. Hoping you will accede to a proposition so reasonable, believe me, dear Mr. Jorrocks,

" Ever yours, very faithfully,

" MISERRIMUS DOLEFUL, M.C.

" To John Jorrocks, Esq.,
 " Great Coram-street, London."

The following was Mr. Jorrocks's answer to the proposition :—

" Dear Doleful,—I doesn't see the wit of your offer. If to give a high price is the object of your ambition, I'll give you a receipt for 100*l*., and throw you back 75*l*., but I cannot throw back nothin' out of 25*l*. Make up your mind—and let's have no hagglin'.

" Yours, to serve,

" JOHN JORROCKS, M.F.H.

" To Miserrimus Doleful, Esq., M.C.,
 " Handley Cross Spa.'

Finding Mr. Jorrocks was not to be worked upon in his way, and that there was nothing to gain by personating Miss Lucretia, Captain Doleful determined to come forth in his own character, and wrote as follows :—

" Dear Mr. Jorrocks,—I have just received yours, and regret to inform you that Miss Lucretia Learmouth has been suddenly called into Scotland by the alarming illness of a beloved relative, whereby all occasion for a horse is, of course, done away with. The difficulty of making this announcement is, however, relieved by the circumstance of my willingness to place myself in her shoes; I therefore beg to say, I shall be glad to take the horse, provided, of course, he is all right, &c., and will send you the money on hearing from you. Dear Mr. Jorrocks,

" Yours, very truly,

" MISERRIMUS DOLEFUL, M.C."

Mr. Jorrocks thus closed the bargain :—

" Dear Doleful,—I'm sorry Lucretia's gone. I should have liked to have had a look at her. I'm a great admirer o' beauty in all its branches, and would always rayther give a shillin' to look at a pretty woman than at a panorama. Howsomever, never mind, the 'oss is yours, and you may hand over the dibs to James Pigg, who will give you a receipt, and all that sort of thing. Charming weather for bees. Do they make much 'oney about you?

" Yours to serve,

" JOHN JORROCKS, M.F.H.

" *Great Coram Street, London.*

" To Miserrimus Doleful, Esq., M.C.,
 " Handley Cross Spa."

Armed with this authority, Doleful repaired to James Pigg's, and, after a desultory conversation, parted with five-and-twenty sovereigns in exchange for the celebrated Xerxes.

Like most young horse-masters, Captain Doleful did not give his new purchase much rest. Morning, noon, and night, he was on its back, or driving it about in a job-fly. The Captain felt it his duty to call upon everybody in the town, and poor Xerxes was to be seen at all hours, either fastened by the bridle to a lamp-post, or pacing melancholily up and down the street in charge of some little dirty urchin. Sometimes a party of them would take him into a by-street, and bucket him up and down

POOR XERXES.

till they thought the "Capt'in would be a comin'." This with indifferent grooming and very indifferent keep, soon reduced the once sleek and pampered hunter to a very gaunt, miserable-looking dog-horse.

The Captain marked the change with melancholy bodings. He had hoped to sell him with advantage, so as to ride for nothing, and now he seemed more likely to lose by him than anything else. The horse grew

F F

daily worse, and a cough settled upon him that seemed likely to finish him. A more unfortunate-looking couple were never seen, than the cadaverous Captain and the poor coughing quadruped. Still he went on working him as long as the cough would let him walk, but, it soon getting past that, the Captain was thrown on his wits for getting out of the purchase. The following correspondence will show how he attempted it:—

"Dear Mr. Jorrocks,—I am sorry to say your horse is very ill, labouring, we think, under pulmonary consumption. He is dreadfully emaciated, and labouring under a hooping-cough, that is distressing to himself and his hearers. I thought he looked queer when I bought him, as I remarked a nervous quivering of the tail after a slight gallop over Bumpmead. It is unfortunate, but you, as a great horse-master, know these sort of accidents will happen, and it is well the loss falls on one so well able to bear it as the wealthy Mr. Jorrocks. With compliments and best wishes to Mrs. and Miss Jorrocks, who, I hope, are both well, believe me to remain, dear Mr. Jorrocks,

"With great sincerity, yours very sincerely,
"MISERRIMUS DOLEFUL, M.C.

"To John Jorrocks, Esq.,
"Great Coram-street, London."

Mr. Jorrocks was rather puzzled how to act on receipt of this. His first impulse was to tell the Captain that he was a dirty fellow; and, indeed, he wrote a letter to that effect, but, with praiseworthy prudence, he kept it over night, and his wrath being somewhat appeased by the operation of writing, the old adage of "least said being soonest mended" came to his assistance, and induced him to concoct the following:—

"Dear Doleful,—Yours is received, and note the contents. Mrs. Jorrocks is misfortunately rayther indisposed, but much obleged by your purlite inquiries. She went to Sadlers' Wells the night before last, and the house being full, and consequentially 'ot, she was imprudent enough to sit with the box-door open, which gave her the ear-ache. In other respects, howsomever, she is as lively as usual. This is fine weather for the country. It's a pity but you had Xerxes right, as toolin a young 'oman about in a buggy would be unkommon nice sport. I have no news. Town is very full and 'ot. Wenus, I see by my Almanack, is an evenin' star till the 13th, and arterwards a mornin' star. Jupiter is a mornin' star till about the 15th. Adieu.

"Yours to serve,
"JOHN JORROCKS, M.F.H."

This, as may be supposed, was not at all satisfactory, so the captain immediately fired off the following:—

"Dear Mr. Jorrocks,—I fear I was not so intelligible as I ought to have been in my last hurried communication. My object was to inform you that *your* horse, Xerxes, is very bad—dying, we think; and as it appears he had the seeds of consumption at the time you sold him, I think it right you should have the earliest intelligence, in case there is any particular mode of treatment you would like adopted. I feel assured you only require to be acquainted with the untoward circumstance to make you rescind what appears to be an untenable bargain. Wishing you every happiness, I remain, with compliments to the ladies, dear Mr. Jorrocks,

"Ever yours very faithfully,
"MISERRIMUS DOLEFUL, M.C.

"To John Jorrocks, Esq.,
"Great Coram-street, London.

"P.S.—Please to send me a pound of pretty good tea, in ounce packages."

Still Mr. Jorrocks was determined not to take the hint, and, after the delay of a post or two, concocted the following :—

"Dear Doleful,—I am werry sorry to hear so bad an account of my old frind Xerxes. It's a bore to lose the services of a quad jest at the time one wants them. I certainlie considered him a consumptive hanimal when I had him, but it was an 'ay-and-corn consumption. I am werry much obleged by your communication. In course I feels an interest in the prosperity of a hanimal wot has carried me, with such unruffled equinimity, through many a glorious chase : but in the hands of a 'umane and discriminatin' cock like yourself, I feels assured he will receive every attention his pekoolier case can require, and therefore must decline all recommendation. I 'opes you'll be able to patch him up to do much good work yet. S'pose you try cod-liver hoil.

"Yours to serve,
"JOHN JORROCKS, M.F.H.

"To Captain Doleful, M.C.,
"Handley Cross Spa.

"P.S.—I send the tea, and 'ope you will like it. The market has been heavy to-day, owin' to the reports in circulation of the arrival of the overland mail. Little has been done in the article since the 11th inst. : About twelve chops of congou have recently arrived, common quality, for which high rates are asked. Sugar's riz. Mrs. J. has gone for change of hair to Shepherd's Bush, but I don't know that I shall follow her. Coram for me. Pleasantest street in London."

Captain Doleful was very angry when he received this. He saw Mr. Jorrocks was laughing at him, and determined to show fight :—

"Dear Mr, Jorrocks,—I wish to state to you, very plainly and explicitly, that the horse Xerxes is unsound, and was so when you sold him, and that I mean to return him. If there is any stable in particular you wish him sent to, please to let me know by return of post, as he now stands at your expense.

"Yours very truly,
"MISERRIMUS DOLEFUL, M.C

"To John Jorrocks, Esq.,
"Great Coram-street, London."

Then as Doleful read it over, and thought it rather tart, he softened it with the following *plaisanterie* :—

"P.S.—The tea is very good. I wish I could say as much for the trotter."

Mr. Jorrocks was equally determined, as appears by his answer :—

"Dear Doleful,—I thought you'd have been more of a conjurer, than to s'pose I'd take back a 25*l.* 'oss wot I never warranted. You took him for better or for worser, jest as I took Mrs. J. P'raps he may not be quite so good a ticket as you could wish; it werry seldom 'appens that they are; but that's no reason why you should be off the bargain. Make the best on him. ' Be to his wirtues ever kind : be to his faults a leetle blind,' as I told you in my second lector.

"Yours to serve,
"JOHN JORROCKS, M.F.H.

"To Captain Doleful, M.C.,
  "Handley Cross Spa.

"P.S.—Perhaps he's got worms; if so, linseed hoil him."

The following was the captain's ultimatum :—

"Sir,—When I opened the negotiation with you respecting your rubbishing good-for-nothing horse, I thought that in dealing with the Master of the Handley Cross Foxhounds, I had some guarantee that I was dealing with a gentleman. I grieve to find I was mistaken in my conjecture. I now demand a return of the money I paid for your nasty diseased horse, which an honest English jury will award me in the event of a refusal. Waiting your answer, I remain, sir,

"Yours obediently,
"MISERRIMUS DOLEFUL, M.C.,
"Captain, Half-pay.

"Mr. Jorrocks, Grocer,
  "Great Coram-street, London."

Mr. Jorrocks's answer was very short :—

"Dear Doleful,—I doesn't know nothin' wot an honest English jury may do for you, but this I knows, *I'll do nothin*'. Zounds, man! you must be mad—mad as a hatter!

"Yours to serve,
"JOHN JORROCKS, M.F.H.
"*Great Coram Street.*

"To Captain Doleful, M.C.,
  "Handley Cross Spa.

"P.S.—Let's have no more nonsense."

And Doleful, seeing that all negotiation was hopeless, rushed off to that last consolation of the injured—a lawyer,—who advised that he had a capital case if he took it to the superior courts ; and Doleful assenting, he immediately prepared for having a pop at friend Jorrocks.

While all this was going on, Handley Cross became quite a different place. The winter legion of semi-sporting invalids passed away, and were replaced by a spring detachment from the various seats of unhealthiness—pimply aldermen, plethoric and purse-plethoric millowners with their radiant ladies, anxious mammas with their interesting daughters making the grand round of the matrimonial watering-place markets.

Still we regret to say that our famous Spa, though abundantly supplied with every thing else, was but indifferently well off for eligible young men. Not but that there were plenty of idle, cane-sucking, wide-sleeved, flagrant neckclothed youths, but the real woodcocks of life if we may so term them—men who could say to a lady, " I can keep you as you ought to be," were scarce—very scarce indeed. Most of the youths were mere hobbledehoys—hanging about home till they got something to do—hopeless for anything but flirtation, and even then they could only be worked on the reciprocity system; Miss de Glancey favouring her brother's "appreciation" of Miss Glow on the understanding that Miss Glow encouraged their Tom to "think well" of Miss de Glancey. Under these circumstances, it will be readily imagined how welcome, how exciting was the advent of a gentleman unfettered with females, and unencumbered with the protection of all friends and relations of this life —an occurrence so unusual, that we should ill evince our gratitude for the dispensation were we not to devote a separate chapter to the announcement.

CHAPTER LXII.

WILLIAM THE CONQUEROR; OR, THE A.D.C.

EVERY one who has visited—and few there are, we take it, who have not—our delightful watering-place, must have observed the fine gilt-wired letter-cage in the entrance-hall of the Turtle Doves Hotel, in which are arranged the letters of expected visitors, proclaiming as well the coming greatness, as acting as advertisements of the house's custom. Here, as regular as swallows in the spring, or as the horse in the little roundabout at a fair, have appeared, year after year, the letters of Major-General Sir Thomas Trout, the letters of Captain Hely Hobkirk Smith, the letters of Lady Maria and Miss Muff, the letters of John Brown and Mr. Lamb, the letters of Mrs. Sharp and Miss Flint, the letters of we don't know who besides. It is from this and similar sources that our respected "we" of the "Pry" compiles his weekly bulletin of the rank, fashion, and beauty that visit this most celestial of all sublunary scenes.

The entrance-hall is well adapted for a watering-place lounge, being a fine, lofty, airy apartment, flagged with black and white diamond-patterned marble flags; while the walls are done in such good imitation of various marbles, that many a one feels them, to be satisfied that they are not in the real marble halls of the song. On the south, the hall opens into a public billiard-room; on the right is the spacious coffee-room, where

wax-lights are supplied without charge—or "free gratis," as the waiter
says; while on the left are the private apartments of the hostess,
Mrs. Mendlove; through the large plate-glass window of which, commanding the aforesaid letter-cage and hall, her lovely daughter Constantia,
may afternoonly be seen reclining elegantly on a rose-coloured sofa, in
the full-blown costume of a Bloomer. The sash of the window is then
up, and while the sill forms an agreeable resting-place for the arms of
an admiring lounger, the letter-box below is a convenient excuse for
being there if any one happens to come in unawares. Then Constantia
goes on with her knitting or needlework, and the swain drops upon his
light reading of " Major-General Sir Thomas Trout," " Captain Hely
Hobkirk Smith," or whoever happens to be in the " lock-up," just as
if the improvement of his mind was his sole and whole object.

The hall of the Turtle Doves Hotel forms a sort of centre of attraction
for the visitors at either end of the town; and, being on a level with the
street flags, invalids having the *entrée* can be wheeled in in their garden-
chairs through the bright-folding mahogany sash-doors, where, in addition
to the benefit of a well-framed railway time-table and the sight of a
weather-glass, they have the run of the letter-cage, of a couple of country
papers, a second-hand copy of the " Post," a guide to the Wells, and the
use of a hat-brush—all very attractive things in their way. High
'Change is generally about noon, when the Bloomer, having got herself
becomingly up, and the letter-box arranged, throws up her window, and
subsides in easy elegant attitude on her sofa. Sir Thomas Trout, who always
arrives with the punctuality of the soldier, is the self-elected great gun
of the place, and to him are referred all matters of pedigree, etiquette,
points of honour—of warfare and military discipline generally. What he
says is law. Sir Thomas, who is a peripatetic *gourmand*, always feeds
into a severe fit of the gout towards spring, and comes to Handley
Cross to be cured—than which, we need scarcely say, there is no
better place.

Last summer, however, we grieve to add—for we have a share in it on
the sly—the Turtle Doves had not its fair share of company. Whether
this was owing to undue and, perhaps, unfair competition, or to the
Boniface castigation by the " Times," or to whim, or to fashion, or to
caprice, we know not; but such was the case, as we know to our cost.
That it was not owing to any falling-off in the management of the hotel,
we are in a condition to speak; for we were there the greater part of the
autumn, and never saw better management, better cookery, better wine,
better beer, better tea, better butter, better anything, or a more beautiful
Bloomer; and, despite what the " Times" may say as to hotels generally,
the charges were by no means exorbitant. Not, of course, that we paid
anything, but we saw and helped to inflame the bills of those who did.
That, however, is not the point, and is only thrown in by way of giving
the house a lift. Our business is with a guest.

It was just as the spring was setting in with its usual serenity that the
drooping spirits of the Bloomer were cheered by the arrival of three
portentous-looking letters, headed,

" On Her Majesty's Service,"

Sir Thomas Trout & The Bloomer.

and addressed—

> " To William Heveland, Esq., A.D.C., &c., &c., &c.,
> " Turtle Doves Hotel,
> " Handley Cross Spa."

" My wor—rod ! " exclaimed the Bloomer, clutching them, and admiring the great seals—the royal arms; and then turning to the directions—" my wor—rod," repeated she, " but this is something like," reading—

> " ' On her Majesty's Service,
> " ' William Heveland, Esq., A.D.C.'

A.D.C." repeated she—" A.D.C.—what's A.D.C., postman ? "

" A. B. C. D. E. F. G. H. I. J.," replied the postman, hurrying off, saying the alphabet.

" Well," said the Bloomer, turning one of the letters upside down, " he's somebody, that's quite clear—on Her Majesty's Service—well, I think ! If this isn't the making of the house, I don't know what will."

She then turned it upright again, as if in hopes that a fresh view would help her to decipher it, but with no better success. The A.D.C. fairly puzzled her. She would like to know what it meant. K.C.B.'s, LL.D.'s, F.R.S.'s, D.C.L.'s she had severally caged, but had never had an A.D.C. through her hands before. " What could A.D.C. mean," thought she, as she run her eye over the bed-room book, considering where she should put so important a personage. " It must be a good room—low down, too. Ah, there was No. 3—nice airy room, three windows, two looking to the street, and the other to the Buttermead meadows."

" Mary ! " exclaimed she, ringing the housemaid's bell, and applying her lips to the ivory-mouthed communicating pipe in the wall.

" Mary ! " repeated she upwards.

" Mem ? " answered a voice downwards.

" No. 3 ready ? " replied the Bloomer, upwards.

" Yes, mem," answered the voice downwards.

" Put on the pink toilet-cover, clean muslin curtains, and the new counterpane, and I'll give you some fine towels when I come up-stairs," said the Bloomer.

" Yes, mem," replied the voice.

The Bloomer then had another look at the letters, in hope of inspiration; but none coming, she took down the key of the lock-up, and proceeded to place them in custody. Very conspicuously she arranged them, too, one above the other in the very centre of the long gilt-wired box, keeping all the insignificant Browns, Jones, and Robinsons, at a respectful distance from them. After taking a lingering look, she resumed her place on the sofa, " Punch " in hand, to watch the impression the large letters made upon the comers.

The first to visit the gay scene on this auspicious day were the three Miss D'Oyleys. They generally accompanied their brother to the billiard-room, and after conning the fashionable column in the "Post," informing themselves what was doing in high life, they glanced their lustrous eyes through the letter-box, and then proceeded on their travels. They were all struck with the important A.D.C. letters, but made no demonstration in the presence of the Bloomer. When they got outside, however, it was different.

"Who can Mr. Heavytree be?" "What's A.D.C.?" exclaimed Anna Maria and Jane Sophia in the same breath.

"Heavytree! it's not Heavytree," replied Miss D'Oyley, who had taken a more deliberate read than her sisters.

"Who is it then?" asked Anna Maria.

"*Heveland*, I read it," replied the elder sister.

"Well, but what's A.D.C.?" asked Jane Sophia.

"Don't know," replied Miss D'Oyley.

Next came Mrs. and the Miss Bowerbanks. They lived at Raspberry Tart Lodge, but having seriously damaged a ten-pound note at the Turtle Doves on their coming, had arranged with Timothy, the head waiter, to have their letters directed to the Turtle Doves, instead of to the less aristocratic mansion they occupied. Great talk, too, it made in the little country town from whence they came, that they should be sojourning so long at such a first-rate hotel, accompanied with the usual significant shrugs and wishes that they "mightn't be going it." Mrs. Bowerbank, however, not coming up to the Bloomer's idea of a lady—chiefly, we believe, because she gave her cast-off clothes to the poor of her village, instead of to her maid—the Bloomer just contented herself with exclaiming from the back of "Punch," as she contemplated the party over the top,

"Nothing for you to-day, mem."

"Oh, indeed!" replied Mrs. Bowerbank, who had brought her gold-chained eye-glass to bear on the all-absorbing letters: "William Heveland, Esq., A.D.C. Who can he be, I wonder? On her Majesty's Service, too;" and thereupon she turned into the hall to take up the "Post," in hopes that some one would come in to expound.

Little old Miss Gaby followed, but being a lady who professed to be quite destitute of curiosity, she never looked into the letter-box while there was any one there to see her; so she immediately entered into a most cordial disquisition with Mrs. Bowerbank about the weather, expressing the most sanguine hopes as to the result, just as if she had three hundred acres of wheat, and two hundred acres of barley, to say nothing of green crops, dependent upon its caprice, though all the soil she possessed was what she had brought in on her dirty thick shoes.

The overpowering Mrs. Flummocks, known in the matrimonial market as "the Crusher," from the summary way she settles little gentlemen's pretensions who make up to her towering daughters, then forced the barrier of both doors, and sailed into the hall like a tragedy queen, leaving the folding-doors flopping like condor's wings behind her. Mrs. Flummocks held herself high, and only vouchsafed a gentle inclination of the head to the Bowerbanks, while she honoured Miss Gaby who could in no ways interfere with her daughters, with the tips of her fore-fingers. This done, she sailed majestically round to the letter-box, and was soon struck with the imposing-looking documents in the middle.

" On Her Majesty's Service.
" William Heveland, Esq., A.D.C."

read she, slowly and deliberately. "William Heveland," repeated she, looking up. "Wonder if he's any relation of the Hevelands, of Heveland Hall—very old friend of our family's if he is. Oh, good morning, Miss Mendlove," continued she, addressing the Bloomer, as if she now saw her for the first time; "good morning, Miss Mendlove. Pray can you tell me what county this Mr. Heveland, whose letters I see in the case, is from?"

"Are there any letters in the case for that name?" asked the Bloomer, with an air of the utmost innocence, for she hated Mrs. Flummocks, whose maid gave the worst possible description of her meanness, particularly in the tea-and-sugar department. Moreover, though Mrs. Flummocks "Miss Mendlove'd" her to her face, she knew that she "young person'd" her behind her back, and laughed at her "ridiculous costume," as she called the Bloomer attire. "Are there any letters in the case for that name?" replied the Bloomer, in answer to Mrs. Flummocks's inquiry.

"Yes, three," replied Mrs. Flummocks, looking them over. "Can you tell me who he is?"

"No, mem, I can't," snapped the Bloomer, returning to her "Punch."

"What does A.D.C. mean, Martha?" asked the Crusher, turning to her eldest daughter, who, with her two strapping sisters, had now entered the hall, while mamma was looking into the letter-box, and making her attempts on the Bloomer.

"A.D.C., A.D.C.," repeated the gigantic Martha; "I'm sure I don't know, mamma. A B C one understands, but I don't know what A.D.C. means."

"It's on a letter—something Heveland, Esq., A.D.C." observed the Crusher, adjusting her front.

"Can it have anything to do with the Company's service?" suggested the second strapper, whose name was Sarah.

"Company's service," repeated the Crusher, who had had one or two of that breed of suitors through hands—"Company's service—no—that is H.E.I.C., Honourable East India Company, isn't it?"

"The Geographical Society, perhaps," suggested the youngest, Miss Margaret, who, being last from school, might be reasonably supposed to have her learning fresher than the others.

"No; that's F.R.G.S., Fellow of the Royal Geographical Society," mouthed the eldest, in her usual knock-me-down way, silencing the sister, and settling the disquisition.

The hall now began to fill. Mr., Mrs., and three Miss Softeners, came stealing in, and before the door closed on their entry, Mrs. and the Miss Holloways followed. Then came Mr. Biddle and Mr. Dawes, Mr. Dixon and Miss Hat, Mr. Rap and Master Paine, Mr. Slade and Miss Corner, Mrs. Corner following judiciously with old Mrs. Fisk, whom she had assisted last year to capture the slippery Mr. Prance. Ladies, however much they may dislike each other, and which, by-the-by, they almost all do, will always combine to catch a man. They don't know how soon they may require similar assistance themselves. That, however, by way of parenthesis.

Well, as the hall filled, the box was visited, and fresh inquiries arose what A.D.C. meant. "What does A.D.C. mean?" superseded the state of the weather, or "What do you hear of the war?" One said it meant one thing, another another, but each fresh suggestion was disposed of almost as quickly as it was made. At length, as ingenuity was about exhausted, a cockaded footman, in a coat of many colours, was seen manœuvring a garden-chair outside, and a rush being made to either folding-door, the great Major-General Sir Thomas Trout was wheeled into the hall. The usual salutations over, and inquiries made as to the state of his dear hand, and his dear arm, and his dear foot, and so on, the question was soon put,

"What does A.D.C. mean, Sir Thomas?"

"A.D.C.," replied he, with a mingled smile of pity and contempt— "A.D.C. Why, don't you know? *Aide-de-camp* to be sure—what I was to my Lord Bullywell."

"Oh, to be sure!" exclaimed half a dozen voices; "how stoopid not to know it! Aide-de-camp, to be sure! so it is."

"Why do you ask?" inquired the great man, as the exclamations subsided.

"Oh! only there are some letters directed so to a gentleman here, or coming here."

"Indeed!" replied the major-general, raising his eyebrows; adding, "I have no information on the subject."

Just as if no military man had any business at Handley Cross without consulting him.

"Indeed!" repeated Sir Thomas. "What's his name?"

"Heveland, Sir Thomas," replied the Crusher, who was very ambitious of the great man's notice; indeed, at one time, fancied she was to be Lady Trout.

"Heveland—Heveland—Heveland," repeated Sir Thomas. "Know the name—know the name;" adding to his coach-horse footman, "Jeremiah, tell Miss Mendlove I want to speak to her."

"Yes, Sir Thomas," replied Jeremiah, touching his hat most obsequiously, and moving away to inform the Bloomer through the window.

This brought the fair lady, in her silver-buttoned light-blue silk vest, with a flowing jacket of a darker blue above a lavender-coloured tunic and white trousers, fingering her cambric collarette and crimson silk neck-tie above her richly-figured shirt, with mock-diamond buttons scattered freely down the front.

"Good morning, Miss Constantia," exclaimed the old knight, gaily. "Good morning, Miss Constantia. So you've got an aide-de-camp here, have you? No wonder you're so smart," added he, looking her over.

"A *what*, Sir Thomas?" asked the Bloomer, not exactly catching what he said.

"Ah, you know, you naughty one!" exclaimed the major-general, archly; adding, "Tell me, my dear, is Mr. Heveland at home?"

"He's not come yet, Sir Thomas," replied the fair lady, now putting that and that together, and reckoning she had done well to order the best bedroom to be got ready.

"Not come yet!" replied Sir Thomas. "Not come yet!" adding, after a pause, "Well, I must notice him—I must notice him. Tell him, when he comes, that Major-General Sir Thomas Trout has called upon him—or stay," added he, "Jeremiah," appealing again to the coach-horse footman, "give Miss Constantia a card out of my case. Whereupon Jeremiah dived into the pocket of the coat of many colours, and fishing up the mother-of-pearl card-case, handed the all-important pasteboard to the Bloomer, who placed it above the "A.D.C." letters in the box.

Sir Thomas's card clenched the business. There was no further speculation or inquiry as to who or what the stranger was. The thing now was to get a sight of the great A.D.C. In this our friends were doomed to a good deal of tantalisation; for, though the next day brought two more letters "On Her Majesty's Service," and several others sealed with crests and many-quartered coats of arms, all of which were duly paraded in the letter-cage, yet neither the Bloomer nor any one about the place could give any information as to the man himself. Sir Thomas Trout shook his head mysteriously when appealed to, and said he was "not at liberty to mention"—a course the knight generally adopted when he wanted to conceal his ignorance.

Great excitement was the consequence; the title "aide-de-camp" representing to most minds a dashing young officer, full of giggle and conversation, with a great aptitude for love-making, dancing, and singing. We don't know how many young ladies were set out for him; half the town, in short; for women like playing at appropriation, let the chance of success be ever so remote. It is their castle-building in the air in fact.

However time and the hour against the longest day, and excitement like other things comes to an end.

The shades of evening were drawing on, lady parties were settling to their tea, and gentlemen to their wine, when the tit-tupping tramp of a horse's hoofs drew all eyes to the street, and a déshabilleishly dressed gentleman, looking like a man going to bathe or shoot wild ducks, was seen cantering in an easy toe-in-the-stirrup way, with a slack rein and a smart silver-mounted whip under his arm. It struck almost everybody who saw him that it was the A.D.C. Nor were they wrong in their conjecture, for pulling up at the door of the Turtle Doves Hotel, he threw himself carelessly off the half cover-hack, half shooting-pony's back, and leaving it to stand by itself, swung into the hall with a noisy flourish.

"Any letters for me? (haw)," exclaimed he, in a throaty, consequential sort of way—"any letters for me? (haw)," cracking his whip jockeywise down his very loud-striped brown trousers' side, as he straddled to the still open window.

"Oh, yes, sir!" exclaimed the beautiful Bloomer, not behind the rest in sagacity—"oh, yes, sir—a great many, sir," continued she, unlocking the cage, gathering together all the documents, great and small, and placing them in his hand.

"Haw!" continued he, pompously, from his throat, as he sorted them like a hand at cards, placing "Her Majesty's Service" ones unopened in the little outside pockets of his queer pepper-and-salt-coloured jacket, along with Sir Thomas Trout's card, and tearing open the seals of those he was not acquainted with, scattering the crumpled envelopes freely about the floor. "Haw!" repeated he again, having mastered their contents. "Now," continued he, feeling his sky-blue ariel tie, "send the (haw) ostler to take moy (haw) hack, and order me a (haw) bedroom with a (haw) sitting-room adjoining, or near at hand (haw); and let me have some (haw) dinner. What (haw) soup have you? (haw)," pulling away at his painted gills as he spoke.

"I'm afraid we've no hare soup, sir," replied the Bloomer, modestly.

"(Haw) I don't mean haw soup—but what (haw) soup have ye?" said he, fumbling at his shirt front.

The Bloomer then, better comprehending his dialect, recited the usual inn varieties—giblet, ox-tail, mulligatawny, and so on; and the great man, having chosen ox-tail with a sole, and a rump-steak with oyster-sauce to follow, swaggered across the hall, and up the light cork-screw staircase after the waiter, to inspect his rooms and prepare for the repast.

"(Haw) that will do (haw)," said he, glancing at the dimensions and furniture of the Mitre; adding, "Now let me see the (haw) bedroom (haw)."

That he also said would "do," but he said it as if it was not the sort of thing he was accustomed to; but having made up his mind to put up with it, he forthwith proceeded to unpack himself. From his drab felt wide-awake he drew out half a quire of clean dickeys and a front; from the breast-pocket of his jacket he produced three pair of socks, a razor, a toothbrush, and a comb; while out of the back pockets came a shirt, a dark blue Joinville, some pocket-handkerchiefs, no end of letters and papers, with a cigar-case and a case of instruments. Having deposited the clothes and dressing things on the table, he bundled the letters, papers, and cases back into his pockets, and finding that dinner would not be ready for half an hour, descended to make the better acquaintance of the Bloomer, whose appearance had struck him greatly as he entered, and in whose agreeable society he spent the greater part of the evening. Our business at present, however, is more with his out-of-door conquests, and to them we will now devote our attention.

The "A.D.C." letters appended to his name, coupled with the extreme commonness, not to say vulgarity, of our present style of morning dress, caused what in other days would have been thought "queer" to be overlooked, or attributed to fashion or the whim of travelling incognito. Military men like making "guys" of themselves out of harness, some said; others made no doubt he would be a great swell in the evening. Great were the hopes entertained for the morrow. Here, however, our friends were doomed to disappointment, for our hero studiously kept to his room; nor could all the giggle and chatter of high 'Change, or the important rumbling of Sir Thomas's wheels, or the audible tone in which the great man inquired if the Bloomer had given Mr. Heveland his card, induce him to show himself. Sir Thomas, indeed, looked rather disconcerted when, in reply to his inquiry, what the A.D.C. said when she gave him it, the Bloomer replied that " he just put it in his pocket." Sir Thomas had hoped he would have made such a demonstration of gratitude as, when told, would have enhanced Sir Thomas's consequence in the eyes of the company.

Nor could Timothy, the waiter—a genius possessed of all the easy inquisitive impudence of the brotherhood—throw any light upon our friend's movements, beyond that he seemed very busy, whenever he went into the room, with compasses and pencils and tracing-paper, which being communicated from one person to another, at length resolved itself into a very plausible story—namely, that he was aide-de-camp to the inspector-general of fortifications, down on a secret mission from the government in connection with the war. Some said the inspector-general was coming too. This idea seemed to receive confirmation from Sir Thomas Trout, who, being questioned about it, replied, with a solemn shake of the head, that he was " not at liberty to mention." The interest greatly increased with the mystery. It became all-absorbing.

Next day brought partial relief. Towards noon the great man was seen sauntering along, cigar in mouth, staring idly at horses and carriages, and into shop-windows, giving both ladies and gentlemen ample opportunity of looking him over—a privilege that he seemed equally disposed to partake of himself.

We may candidly admit that there was a difference of opinion with regard to his looks; but what young gentleman ever appeared on the stage of public life without raising adverse opinions as to his appearance? It does not, however, follow, that because young ladies proclaim a man a fright, an object, a horror, or anything of that sort, that they really think so. They have a useful way of running men down, in hopes of preventing each other from entering for them; a trick that we should think they are all too well up in, ever to impose on each other with.

As praise, however, is always more agreeable to a well-disposed Bramah pen than censure, we may commence by stating that both the Miss Sheepshanks and their mamma thought our friend very handsome. They admired the rich jet-black luxuriance of his hair, also the stiff inward curl of his regular all-round-the-chin whiskers, above all, his beautiful billy-goat imperial. Their sagacious eyes, too, saw in the deep-blue outline of his upper lip evidence of his self-denial in not growing the now degraded shop-lad appendage of a moustache. Altogether they thought him very, very handsome; and miss it was who christened him "the Conqueror!"

The Miss Trypperleys, too, thought him good-looking—rather more colour, perhaps, than was strictly aristocratic, but that looked as if he kept better hours than the generality of young men, and as if that " nasty smoking" didn't disagree with him as it did with many.

The Miss D'Oyleys thought he would have been better if he had been a little taller, though, to be sure, he would look different in uniform; and wondered whether he was in the lights or the heavies, or the artillery or what. The Miss Bowerbanks, too, liked his looks; and the Softeners were as enamoured of him as the Sheepsbanks. Mrs. Flummocks passed no opinion in public, priding herself upon her discretion; she, however, thought well of him in private. The Miss Sowerbys (oldish) couldn't bear him; they thought they never saw such a great, staring, impudent, vulgar-looking fellow, and only wished they had a brother to horsewhip him; while the poor Conqueror had never looked at either of them. He furnished abundant conversation for the town that day.

Meanwhile, the A.D.C. letters poured in apace; not a post arrived but some came, either "On Her Majesty's Service," or in the smaller form used by ordinary mortals; and the importance of the Conqueror's mission swelled with the exclusiveness of his retirement. Though many people called, all anxious for an interview, the unvarying answer was, "Not at home," though the waiter, on his cross-examination, could not but admit that our friend was up-stairs. Indeed, we may observe that the A.D.C. had completely overpowered the otherwise communicative waiter's loquacity, and from having nothing to tell, he assumed a sort of mysterious gravity that greatly assisted the A.D.C. interest. The Conqueror was so throaty and important, so peremptory in his orders, so stern in his censures, that Timothy, who is rather free and easy, given to the *persi-flage* of matrimony, pretending to get heiresses for young gentlemen, and so on, stood awed in his presence, and bowed lowly and reverentially before him. Moreover, as Timothy afterwards said, he was satisfied the Conqueror was a gent, because he always took a glass of sherry before he began his port after dinner. But though the Conqueror evidently did not court—nay, rather seemed to avoid society, he was not above conforming to the ordinary rules that regulate its dealings; and having got the fair Bloomer to sort his callers' cards, and tell him where each lived, so that he might not go over the same ground twice, he shot meteor-like through the place, knocking at this door, ringing at that, putting in his pasteboard, "Mr. William Heveland, A.D.C.," but firmly resisting all the reiterated assurances of both Johns and Janes that their mistresses or the young ladies were at home.

"Dear me, Mary!" exclaimed the Crusher, taking the card off the silver salver on which it was brought up, "how *stoopid! Didn't I tell you we were at home!*"

"Please, mum, the gen'l'man didn't ask;" or "Please, mum, I told him so, and he just gave me that."

"Oh, don't tell me! It's one of your stoopid mistakes; you are the stoopidest girl I ever saw in my life."

Nor did the Conqueror make any exception in favour of the great Sir Thomas Trout, though the man of the coat of many colours insisted that his master was at home to *him*—as if a special exception had been made in his favour.

"Then, give him that," said the Conqueror, presenting his card, and blowing a great cloud of smoke right past the man's face into the anti-tobacconist major-general's very entrance-hall.

This disgusted the great man. The ladies, however, are not so easily put off a scent as the men, and the preliminaries to an acquaintance being now accomplished, they proceeded to clench it with invitations to dine. Cards came pouring in from all quarters, some in envelopes, some open, some printed, some written, some embossed, some plain, requesting the honour of Mr. William Heveland's company to dinner on Monday the 10th, or Tuesday the 11th, or Wednesday the 12th, just as their larders or previous engagements favoured the speculation.

The Crusher, thinking to steal a march on the rest, drew a short bill upon him for a tea, which the Bloomer, who had firmly established herself in the A.D.C.'s confidence, had great pleasure in recommending him to put in the fire, which he did accordingly. The rest of the cards he just bundled into his queer jacket-pocket, to answer at his leisure.

One great beauty of Handley Cross—indeed, of all small idle places is, that everybody knows what you are about. It isn't like London, where you may die and be buried without your next-door neighbour being any the wiser; but at a watering-place, all your in-comings and out-goings are watched and accurately noted—where you dine, who there is to meet you—nay, what you have for dinner—and you feel as if you didn't stand quite alone in the world.

Some people—generally those who take plenty of time themselves—are often desperately anxious to get answers to their invitations, and wonder others don't answer—so idle not answering—what *can* they be about they don't answer; and so it was on the present occasion. Our friend, not intending to accept of any of the invitations, just let them remain in his jacket pocket, along with " Her Majesty's " and other letters, until it suited his convenience to have a general clearance; and as cards and crested notes still kept dropping in, he kept putting off and putting off till he had all the senders in a state of excitement. Great were the gatherings in the hall of the Turtle Doves, and numerous the whispering inquiries that were made of the Bloomer, if there was anything for Mrs. Softener or Mrs. Sheepshanks, or Mrs. Bowerbank; and then if the Bloomer was *quite sure* Mr. Heveland had got a certain card or a certain note, or whatever it was. Little satisfaction, however, was to be obtained from the Bloomer, who seemed rather to take pleasure in their mortification, and in increasing the mystery that enveloped our hero.

All things, however, must have an end: and on the fifth day, as the crowd was at the greatest, and Major-General Sir Thomas Trout was indulging in his usual ominous shakes of the head, and "not-at-liberties-to-mention," a stentorian voice, proceeding from a dirty dog-cart, with the name, "JOHN GOLLARFIELD, FARMER, HARDPYE HILL" painted in honest legible letters behind, was heard roaring,

"TIMOTHY! TIMOTHY! TIMOTHY!" drawing all eyes to the vehicle.

In it was seated a little round-about red-faced man, whose figure might have been drawn with a box of wafers—a red wafer for the face, a brown one for the body, four drab ones for legs, and so on; the little man being then in a terrible state of perturbation, appearing as well by the red wafer as by the white lather in which he had brought his rough-headed, curly-coated brown horse.

Timothy at length appearing, napkin, or rather duster in hand, the man of the dog-cart thus addressed him, speaking as before at the top of his voice,

" Is Mr. Heavyland in?"

"Heavyland, Heavyland," repeated Timothy, quickly: "no such gen'l'man here, sir."

"Oh, yes, there is," roared the voice, confidently.

"There's a Mr. *Heveland* here, sir—a Mr. *Heveland*, sir—aide-de-camp to the Right Honourable the Inspector-General of Fortifications," thinking to flabbergaster Gollarfield with his greatness.

"No! no!" roared the little man, peevishly; "it's Heavyland I want. *I know he's here.* Had a letter from him yesterday, sayin' he'd be at my place, Hardpye Hill, at ten o'clock this mornin', and he's never come."

It then struck Timothy that he had posted a letter headed "On Her Majesty's Service," for Mr. Gollarfield, Hardpye Hill; and he began to think whether Heavyland and Heveland could be one and the same person.

"What 'un a lookin' gen'l'man is he, please, sir?" asked Timothy.

"Oh, a queer black-and-red-lookin' beggar—all teeth and hair, like a rat-catcher's dog," replied Gollarfield, shaking with vexation.

"What is he, sir, please, sir?" asked Timothy.

"An ASSISTANT DRAINAGE COMMISSIONER!" roared Gollarfield. "Puts A.D.C. on his cards, like an ass as he is. Promised to be at my house, Hardpye Hill, at ten this mornin', to pass my drains, and he's never come;" adding, "if he thinks to get three guineas out o' me, he's DEUCEDLY mistaken."

If a hand-grenade had fallen among the assembled company, it could not have caused greater consternation than this proclamation. There was such shrugging of shoulders, such bateings of breath, such frowning from those who had invited our friend, and such giggling and laughing from those who had not; while the unfortunate Conqueror, who now came bounding down stairs three steps at a time to appease the choleric Gollarfield, was regarded with very different eyes to what he had been before. However, there was no harm done; for, on returning from Mr. Gollarfield's, who now carried him off in his dog-cart, he placed his invitations in the hands of the Bloomer, who set all minds at rest by politely declining the whole of them.

And our fair friends at Handley Cross speedily relapsed into their former state of anxious excitement, ready to be hoaxed by any body who would be at the trouble of doing it.

CHAPTER LXIII.

MR. JORROCKS'S DRAFT.

LTHOUGH we have hitherto refrained from mentioning it, such mishaps procuring little sympathy, Mr. Jorrocks's hounds were not quite so steady as they might be, and sundry sheep had been laid to their charge during the season, with more or less appearance of probability. To be sure, most of these accusations Mr. Jorrocks had combatted successfully, vowing that it was "downrightly ridicklous to charge his 'ounds wi' nothin' o' the sort; that they wouldn't *look* at ship, let alone touch 'em;" an assertion that Pigg always backed by declaring his readiness to fight anybody who doubted it. As, luckily, the hounds had never been caught, by the owners of the sheep at least, *flagrante delicto*, with the mutton in their mouths, our master escaped the inconvenient responsibility of paying for them.

On the memorable "old customer" morning, however, as Mr. Jorrocks was making all sail round the road by the green fields of Primrose-side Hill, hitting and holding, and grinning and scolding as usual, what should he see but his skirting friends, Limner and Sultan—some of the Bugginson lot—nip up a young lamb and pass on as if nothing particular had happened, and Mr. Jorrocks's aphorism being, as he told Ego, "'andsome is wot 'andsome does," he determined not to keep such dainty customers, who wanted to have lamb before their master. Lightning and Bluebell, too, presently deviated after a hare, not an unusual occurrence with either of them, Lightning having once led off the pack at a very critical cold-scenting moment of the chase, when it required the united experience of master and man to keep the pack on the line of the fox over Sandyfield Moor.

These and similar mishaps set Mr. Jorrocks a-thinking, after the enthusiasm of the victory was over, whether there weren't others that he would be as well without, and considering that there were many mere "show partners," as he called them, hounds that did little or nothing in the way either of finding or trouncing a fox, and that meal was werry dear and flesh scarce, he determined to rid himself of some of the sleeping partners of the chase.

Ranter was a resolute, headstrong brute, all very well on a good scenting day, but a hound that a man might holloa and roar at till he was hoarse, if there was an unjumpable wall or impossible ravine between them. He used to treat Ben's "Ranter! *Ranter!* RANTER!" with the most marked contempt.

Resolute, a very handsome, rich-coloured hound, with as good legs, loins, depth of chest, and general points, as eye could desire, ran mute, and would go away at score with a scent, leaving the pack to hunt him and the fox as best they could. Mr. Jorrocks, who was well up to his tricks, had often vowed "he'd 'ang 'im when he got 'ome," but had always relented when he came to see 'ow 'andsome he looked on the flags, and felt his coaxing winning ways. Resolute, indeed, was Jorrocks's model hound. "Take his 'ead atween your knees," he used to say to judges or would-be judges who came to wile away an hour in the kennel; "Take his 'ead atween your knees, and see the width of his ribs be'ind the shoulders. Now stand sideways," he would exclaim, "and look at his legs—see 'ow straight they are! straight as harrows!" Indeed, Resolute had but one fault, though that was undoubtedly a great one— running mute. Jorrocks had consulted Pigg about splitting Resolute's tongue with a sixpence, to try to make him musical, just as boys try to make their magpies talk by a similar expedient.

Clamorous was a dweller, and insisted upon throwing his tongue and hunting every yard of the line, though his comrades might be fields before him with the scent. He was a crooked-legged, flat-sided, loose-loined beggar, that Jorrocks had made sundry ineffectual attempts to get rid of by riding over. Then Limner and Sultan had rather corrupted the good manners of some others; a skirting hound, like a skirting rider, being always sure to have a good many followers; and altogether Jorrocks decided that there were five or six couple he would be just as well shot of.

These, of course, came to Mr. Pigg, who received them under the injunction that he was to get rid of them as soon as possible, and James "kennin' a chap," as he said, "whe had jist sich another lot," the two laid their heads together, and advertised them in the sporting papers as a very superior lot of hounds, parted with solely on account of the owner reducing his establishment, and well worthy the attention of any one wanting hounds, as they were not drafts, but hounds that had been regularly hunted together, and were some of the best blood in England.

Now it so happened that young Mr. Barege, son of the late head of the firm, Barege, Tissue, and Caps, whom some of our fair readers will

Mr Bareye & The Draft.

perhaps remember occupying the beautiful plate-glassed premises, Nos. 21, 22, and 23, Threadneedle Street; either fired with noble emulation of Mr. Jorrocks, or of his own proper accord, thinking perhaps to advance himself in society; had taken the Gambado country, vacant by the retirement of Mr. Slack, and, with all the generous ignorance of a beginner, as soon as ever he read the advertisement, he thought it was the very thing for him : so filling his *porte-monnaie* full of five-pound notes, he railed down to Handley Cross, in a desperate stew lest any one should be there before him. Arrived at his destination, he made straight for the kennel, expecting to find at least half-a-dozen M.F.H.'s wrangling for the lot.

Mr. Pigg, having taken his usual drain, his custom always of an afternoon, was about half-seas over when his mincing, dandyfied, clean-stepping customer came; and thinking it was just one of the idle, watering-place set, come to do the knowing among the hounds, he was not disposed to give himself much trouble; a tack that he very soon abandoned when Mr. Barege, with a flourish of his scented cambric 'kerchief, announced himself as a master of fox-hounds come to look at Pigg's draft. James was then all zeal and activity, all praise of the pack and the draft in particular, which, he said, were just as good as any they'd kept; and really, if he'd been choosin', he thought he'd have prefar'd many of these to some they'd put back; but of course their ard maister was the best judge, and had a reet to please hissel, and it was not for him to find fault—cartainly not—he was nabbut a sarvent, and had te de what he was tell'd, and a man what didn't de what he was tell'd wasn't a sarvent, and so on; all very sound doctrine, though not exactly what our friend acted up to.

Mr. Barege took exception to one or two of the hounds as being rather short in the neck and throaty, but Pigg immediately overruled it, by declaring that they were of "undeniable blood, and first-rate line hunters, huntin' and drivin' a scent without dwellin' on it," though Pigg knew no more about what they could do, than they knew what Pigg could do, these being some of "t'other chap's" lot.

In short, Pigg was too many for the mercer, who not wishing to show his ignorance, began to talk about price. Pigg then took a comprehensive survey of him, noted his hairy lip, his pudding face, and vacant eye, inwardly resolving that a man who would wear such a flowing tie and funny boots, must have a good deal of the goose in him.

"Why noo, sor," replied Pigg, scratching his head and turning his quid, with a hitch of his braceless breeches, "Why, noo sor, ar doesn't want to be hard 'pon ye 'bout them—not ar, indeed, only ye see, sor, ye see," rubbing his nose across the back of his hand, "this isn't like a young draft, that may be good for summut, or good for nout, just as things chance, nor yet is it like an 'ard draft, that may have arl sorts o' 'fenders, sheep-worriers, skirters, babblers, dwellers, and what not 'mang it, but this is like hafe a pack o' good h'unds as it were, that you may tak' into ony country with the certainty o' sport, and of their dein' ye credit; in fact gin ar had me reets ar'd gan down te the Morpeth country wi' them mysel', only ye see, sor," continued he, boiling up as he spoke, "only ye see, sor, mar foreelder John, John Pigg ye see, willed arl wor

brass to the 'Formory, ye see, and left me wi' fairly nout—gin ye gan to
the 'Formory, ye'll see it arl clagged up i' great gou'd letters 'gin the
warll," Pigg flogging away at the kennel wall with his whip till he drove all
his draft away.

Mr. Barege, to whom both the sporting and the grievance part of the
foregoing was Greek, now essayed to edge a word in sideways.

" Well," said he, twirling his cane-coloured moustache, and throwing
back his little conceited coat—as he stood in consequential attitude—far
different to the way his father used to stand behind the counter, showing
his ribbons—and " wot's the next article, mam "-ing the ladies ? " Well,"
said he, " say the word—*How.much ?* "

" Why, arl tell ye 'i twe words," replied Pigg, now rubbing his nose
the reverse way, on the back of his hand, " arl tell ye 'i twe words—ar
doesn't want nothin' but what's reet and fair—nothin' but what's reet
and fair—ar's as honest a man as iver was shaved—though ar hasn't
'zactly getten me Sunday claes on "—Pigg looking down at his tattered
purple coat-laps, drab breeches, and continuations—" and gin ye fancy
these h'unds, ye shall hev them at a varry fair, moderate figure, for when
wor 'ard maister's made up his mind te part wi' a thing, he doesn't like
te see it 'bout the place, and ar's warned ye, if he was to come down
now, he'd be readin' the riot act, for he's a rum'un when he's raised, and
ar might ha' selled them to 'ard Mr. Dribbler, o' the Daddyfield hunt,
only he's sic a fond 'ard chap—parfect lunattic ar may say—that ar
said ar'd sooner knock 'em on the head than he should hev them, and so
ye see they're here now, and though ar say it, who shouldn't, any gen'l'man,
either settin' oop a pack, or addin' to one, couldn't be better suited, for a
more valuable lot were never sorted. Ar wadn't tell ye a lee 'bout them,"
continued he, now rubbing his nose upwards. " Ar wadn't tell ye a lee
'bout them, ar assure you, for wor 'ard maister's a most particklar man
'bout the truth—leers and drunkards bein' things he can't abeer, and if
iver he catches a man either drunk or tellin' a lee, he off's wi' 'im at yence,
and if arl gen'l'men would de the like, and give true and proper c'ara*c*ters
of sarvents, they'd be far better sarved, and we shouldn't hev a lot of
nasty, idle, druuken dogs fillin' the places o' good men, and ye may 'pend
upon it, if ar was to tell ye out but the 'zact truth, and wor 'ard maister
were to ken, he'd gi me the sack, se its ne use me sayin' nothin' but wot's
the real truth, and no mistake—"

" Well, well," interrupted Mr. Barege, who was too well up in the
puffing art, not to see through it, " Well, well, that 'ill do, that 'ill do—I
dessay the hounds are good—Mr. Jorrocks, I know, is a pretty good
judge ; and you say he's only parting with them because he's reducing his
establishment—what I want to know is the price—the neat unadorned
price, without any superfluous flourish or *badinage*." Mr. Barege, taking
a diminutive gold watch out of his flashy waistcoat pocket, and holding
it as if to time Pigg.

The admission, that Jorrocks was a good judge, encouraged Pigg, and
knowing that a purchaser would have no opportunity of trying the hounds
before autumn, he determined to, what he calls, " lay it on."

" Well then," said Pigg, nerving himself for the announcement, " Well
then," repeated he, " ye mun just gi' me five guineas a coople for them."

" Five guineas a couple," mused Mr. Barege, knitting his brows, though in reality he was pleased, it being less than he expected. " Five guineas a couple—ten couple at five guineas a couple—five times ten, is fifty, and fifty shillings, is two pun' ten—fifty-two pun' ten."

" Give you forty," resumed he, turning short upon Pigg.

" Could'nt tak' it," replied Pigg, with a shake of his head, " couldn't tak' it. They're worth just as much again, gin the season were on. Ard lay ony money," continued Pigg, " ard gan down to Tilton wood wi' nabbut them ten couple and kill the 'ard Cottesmore* customer for them."

And Barege, to Pigg's astonishment, produced his beautiful green and gold *porte-monnaie*, and told out ten clean, crisp, raspberry-tart-marked

---

* Pigg here alludes to the famous Cottesmore fox, that gave the Leicestershire swells such a drubbing last season. This run being quite out of the common is well worth a place in our pages. We take our account from the " Field," which agrees with that given us by a friend who was there, save that our friend lays the time at two hours (up to Glen Gorse, one), and the distance twenty instead of five-and-twenty miles; from point to point fourteen, the whole over grass with the exception of five ploughed fields, scent first-rate, though the ground was desperately hard and dry. Now for the newspaper version:—

" Tuesday, the 21st of March proved one of the most extraordinary days ever known, and competent authorities have no hesitation in asserting that it was even superior to the celebrated Billesdon Coplow day in Mr. Meynell's time, or to the run from Ashby Pastures, recorded by Nimrod in 'The Chase;' and, indeed, when the whole extent of country traversed over in an hour and a half is taken into consideration, it does almost seem fabulous to state that one fox could have lived so far. The meet was at Launde Abbey; the field was not numerous at all, because of the dryness of the ground. Tilton wood was drawn, and this gallant fox immediately went away for Halstead, leaving Tilton village on the right; he bore straight to Skeffington Hall; leaving that also on the right, he went to Rolleston, and through the plantations, pointing his head for a few seconds towards Allexton; he then leaned to the right over the best line of country in the world for Shangton Holt, which he did not enter; then on to Illston-on-the-Hill and Norton Gorse, the pace almost racing, and many of them shook off. Mr. Lloyd was here leading on The Felon—the fox then went straight as an arrow by Burton Overy, and on to Glen Gorse, running bang through which, he pointed to Wistow House, and leaving that on the right he went to Fleckney, and straight away to Countesthorpe, doubling then again and bearing for Shearsby Inn. He was lost for the simple reason that the hounds could go no further; they were without a huntsman the last four miles, and for a long way the fox was on one side of a fence, and the hounds on the other, and they had not strength left to go over, nor could they get through. The distance, according to the Ordnance map, is about twenty-five miles. This is an occasion when we shall be justified in departing from a general rule, and state, that the first flight consisted of Mr. Lloyd, Mr. Ainsworth, Mr. Wood, Colonel Campbell, Mr. T. Heycock, Captain Hawkesley, Hon. H. Coventry, Lord Gardiner, &c.; all were, however, dead beat, and it was with considerable difficulty the hounds could be got to Leicester, where a special train was chartered, and hounds, horses, and gentlemen were carried along the Syston and Peterboro' line, the Meltonians being dropped *en route*, and the others taken on to Oakham.

" The same hounds met at Tilton wood on Saturday, the 25th, and not the least doubt exists but that they found the very same fox again, for he went over exactly the same line of country, and gave them an excellent run, until he got to Illston-on-the-Hill, where he was headed by a shepherd's dog, and run into Norton Gorse, from which place a fresh fox went away, and a most excellent day's sport ended by his being lost at Somerby, a distance of twelve miles at the least."

five pound notes, and handed them over in exchange for this very valuable
lot of hounds, combining amongst them about every vice and deficiency
that hounds are capable of.   Pigg at first was so struck at the possession
of such wealth, that he kept fumbling and turning the notes about in a
stupified sort of way—neither counting them nor putting them right for
counting, quite different to the way old Barege used to deal with his
darlings when he sold an Indian shawl, or any expensive article of raiment
to the ladies; and our embryo master of hounds, thinking James was
going to haggle for the shillings, demanded in a peremptory tone, "if it
was a deal?"

"Cartainly, sir, cartainly," replied Pigg, with another hitch of his
braceless breeches, "Cartainly, sir, cartainly, but we mun hev a glass
tegither oot on't ar's warned."

This Mr. Barege declined, intimating that he was not addicted to
glasses, whereupon Pigg tendered him his hand, saying—"Giv us a'
wag o' yeer nief then, giv us a wag o' yeer nief," at which Barege seemed
equally disgusted.

And Pigg was so petrified at the acquisition of such unexpected wealth,
that he did not know what he was about, and Mr. Barege, after thrice
telling him how he wanted the hounds sent, was obliged to write it down,
and having done so, he left Pigg to decypher his instructions at his
leisure.

When Pigg came to his senses, he went straight to the Salmon hotel,
and astonished Sherry by paying off his score, after which he remitted
the balance of his share of the plunder to his coosin Deavilboger, in the
north, to invest in the Jarrow docks, in hopes that it might lay the founda-
tion of a fund for the future redemption of the "ould ancient Pigg
property."

And when Pigg saw the hounds depart in charge of Barege's feeder, he
chuckled and laughed outright, saying to himself, "Sink, but ar'd be the
death of a guinea to see them divils hunt."

CHAPTER LXIV.

DOLEFUL *v.* JORROCKS.

IN due time the great suit of Doleful *v.* Jorrocks reached maturity. The Captain feeling deeply injured, and cocksure of winning, lured perhaps by Lord Campbell's assertion, that theirs was the "cheap shop," determined to trounce his quondam friend in Westminster Hall, instead of availing himself of the honest rough-and-readiness of the county court.

Accordingly one fine sunny morning a brace of brandy-nosed trumpeters, on long-tailed black cart-horses, dressed in silver-laced cocked hats, yellow coats, striped waistcoats, red plush breeches, and top-boots, with the quarterings of many generations on their bugle-banners, were seen preceding a lofty coach-and-six, in which were seated Barons Botherem and Funnyfile; Mr. Marmaduke Muleygrubs, and his under sheriff, Mr. Jeremiah Capias, of Walsington. The coach, jobbed from London, and newly done up for the occasion, was dark claret, or Queen's colour, with a flaming red hammer cloth, and a coat of arms, under a sort of red petticoat, on the panel, that nearly filled the whole of the door. Behind, were stationed our two footmen friends in the costume we have seen them in at home, stiff neckcloths and all, with the addition of cocked hats and silver-headed canes with red and yellow worsted tassels in their hands.

A large body of vaguely dressed, white wanded constables, under the command of superintendents Shark and Chizeller, both pompously drunk, surrounded the coach to prevent the cargo being stolen. Two grooms in cocked hats, yellow frocks, plush breeches, and top-boots, brought up the rear. In this order the cavalcade proceeded, at a foot's pace, up the High Street of Walsington; the shaking of Baron Funnyfile's cauliflower wig, from the inequalities of the pavement, striking terror into the minds of evil-doers as they eyed him through the coach window. Just as they passed the end of Cross Street, Mr. Jorrocks, who had driven his solicitor, Mr. Fleeceall, over from Handley Cross in his dogcart, fell in behind; and what with the coach, the liveries, the brazen trumpets' sound, the crowd, and the gig with John Jorrocks, M. F. H., painted up behind, things wore a very imposing appearance.—Mr. Marmaduke Muleygrubs was the first high sheriff who had sported six horses.

Great was the rush as the coach drew up at the venerable Saxon archway of the county courts, and it was not until the police had formed a double line that the under sheriff gave the stiff-necked foot-boy the signal to open the door. Out he popped; next came little Marmaduke himself in a full court dress, with an Elizabethan ruff, or what, in former times, was called "three steps and a half to the gallows," from the size and number of its folds. Marmaduke had borrowed the idea from a portrait of one of his ancestors, wherein that worthy sporting moustachios, he had very appropriately added a pair to his own countenance.

Having descended the flight of steps from the coach with great caution, as well for the purpose of exhibiting his person as to prevent his tripping over his basket-handled sword, the judges followed and entered the building amid a prolonged flourish of trumpets.

This, and the rushing in of a white-wanded bailiff, exclaiming, "Gen'le-men of the grand jury wanted i' *Kurt !* " startle a room full of rosy-gilled, John Bull-looking squires, in full cry after various subjects—hay, harrows, horses, hounds—who forthwith hide their hats and canes, hoping they'll be forthcoming when wanted, pull on their buckskin gloves, and scramble into a spacious pen of a box just as the judge, Baron Funnyfile, is bowing to Messrs. Briefless, Dunup, Drearyface, and other ornaments of the "rope walk," before taking his seat for the day. Silence being at length obtained, the commission of the peace is called over, and her Majesty's most gracious proclamation against vice and immorality openly read, the loose hands nudging each other at appropriate passages, and saying, "That's a hit at you, Smith!" or, "What a thing it is to be a loose fish, Jones?" The magnates of the grand-jury box then answer to their names and are sworn, the florid verbiage of the foreman's oath contrasting with the bald plainness of the "you say ditto to that" of the rest.

His lordship then turns side-ways in his richly carved crimson velvet chair, and glancing a laughing eye along the line of looming waistcoats, thus addresses the upright men inside them : "Gentlemen of the grand (hem) inquest—(hem) it is extremely gratifying (hem) to see such a full attendance of gentlemen of your (hem) figure and substance in the county "—his lordship thinking he never saw so many fat men before,— "many of you, I make no doubt, have left your (hem) homes at great personal sacrifice and inconvenience "—(and to himself, "perhaps injury to your hay"). "The benefit of a resident magistracy," continues he, "fulfilling all the (hem) duties of their (hem) station in the exemplary way they do in this (hem) county is abundantly testified by the lightness of the calendar before me "—(or, *sotto voce*, "it may be from not having a rural police to hunt up your (cough) crime "—aloud : "your experience as magistrates "—(to himself, "a nice set of Solomons you are, I dare say ")—aloud again : "will enable you to deal with any cases that may be brought before you, but if there are any that you feel any difficulty about, I shall be most happy to render you any assistance in my power—(to himself, "unless you prefer skying a copper yourselves")—

aloud again : " as you are not encumbered with depositions, or anything to distract your attention, you will, perhaps, soon be able to favour me with a commencement of those valuable (hem) services for which a grateful (cough) country can never be sufficiently (hem) thankful." Whereupon his lordship makes a solemn bow, which the grand jury return, each man after his own dancing-master's fashion, and away they all scuttle to the place from whence they came, hoping to find their hats where they left them, declaring that his lordship is a most agreeable, sensible man, and believing that they are going to be uncommonly useful. Presently they all get settled to a long green baize-covered table, plentifully garnished with pens, ink, and paper, which each man appropriates as if he was going to make a full note of everything. This idea gradually subsides into a drawing of heads, a scribbling of notes, or a making of mems of things forgotten at home, to mend the gap between the seeds and the turnips, to send to Yarrowfield to borrow the haymaker, to tell Lovelock the keeper to have an eye on Tom Brown, &c., &c. In due time they get up as general hum of conversation—much such as prevails at a race ordinary on the removal of the cloth; Mr. Girths asking Mr. Buckwheat what he will take for his brown mare; Squire Screecher wondering whether Captain Dips will want a subscription if he takes the hounds ; Mr. Larkspur inquiring after some lupins he had sent Mrs. Lettuce; Captain Couples declaring he won't vote for young Lord Longbow, unless he'll subscribe to the coursing club; another asking about the dinner hour; a second about the luncheon hour—a general hum of conversation, we say, is interrupted by the loud knocking of Sir Thomas Tenpence, the foreman, on the table, followed by cries of " Silence, silence! order! chair!" from those who have been making the most noise.

The worthy baronet, assisted by a few friends on either side of the chair, has been endeavouring to grope his way to the truth through a long list of witnesses, on the back of a formidable-looking bill of indictment, against the celebrated Lucifer Crowbar, the London cracksman, for burglary, and which, though bolstered up with a fine array of circumstantial evidence, is deficient in the main proof. The fact is, that Tom Tripper the great thieves' attorney, has palmed the principal witness, Joseph Hobnail, whose farmhouse was broken into, and Joe's memory has failed him. Tripper knows well that grand juries have no depositions to guide them, and always marks his sense of their services by drinking their healths first at his thieves' ordinary, thus :—" The grand jury! the magsman's best friend!" Tripper has operated successfully this time.

What Hob swore to point-blank before the magistrate he only *thinks* now; and altogether he is painfully conscientious. He " wouldn't like to swear nothin' he's not certain of." There's an earnest honesty about his wrinkled sunburnt face, shaded with venerable snow-white locks, that looks like truth. Sir Thomas Tenpence is puzzled. " Pray attend to this, gentlemen!" he exclaims, from the top of the table.

" What's the number?" asks Mr. Buckwheat, referring to his calendar.

" Six," replies Mr. Screecher, across the table.

" Is that the assault on the woman?" asks Mr. Badlad, from below.

" *No,*" growls Mr. Prettyman, with a frown.

Sir Thomas, in a clear business-like way, then states the difficulty, observing that he does not think a petty jury will convict on the evidence, while if they ignore the bill, and any fresh evidence be afterwards procured, Crowbar can then be put on his trial.

"That's to say if you can catch him again," observes Mr. Screecher.

"Wish you may get him!" exclaims Mr. Larkspur.

"Bird in the hand's worth two in the bush," suggests Mr. Buckwheat.

"Precious little chance of getting any further evidence if he's in the hands of any of the great perverters," observes Mr. Girths. "Alibis, five pund; suppression of evidence, two pund ten; witnesses to character, seven and six each." (Laughter.)

"Well, gentlemen, what do you think?" asks Sir Thomas.

"O! give him a squeak for it now," says Captain Couples.

"Cost no more," observes Mr. Buckwheat.

"No doubt he did it," says Mr. Snoreem.

"Or something quite as bad," joins Mr. Boreem.

"Or he wouldn't be here," asserts Mr. Floorem.

"His name's enough," adds Mr. Quorum.

On a show of hands, however, the bill is thrown out, and, on the application of Mr. Drearyface, his lordship allows the cost of the judicial farce.

The filthy Tripper reels off with the prisoner, vowing that he will bring an action on behalf of his *most* respectable and *much*-injured client!

But we have made a mistake and gone into the wrong *Kurt*, Mr. Jorrock's business is in the other one. Let us look at him, as Sterne did at his captive.

Few are ignorant of the miseries of hanging about a court of justice,—either they have appeared in the characters of injured plaintiffs, or the still less enviable one of unwilling defendants, or they have been subpœnaed as witnesses, summoned as jurors, or waited for those who were. Unlike other crowds, the fever of excitement never flags.—Crowds rush in to supply the place of those whom victory sends rushing out, or those whom blighted hopes send stalking unconsciously through the throng.

In the box on the judge's right are the "specials,"—men who have little to do in court, and less at home, and yet think themselves desperately oppressed by being called on at all. Opposite are the common jurors—tradesmen, mechanics, farmers, and so on, drawn from their homes at a great inconvenience, for four-pence, a verdict, and no thanks. The bench is sprinkled with pretty faces, ranged like milliners' bonnets for sale. Below is the bar-table, round which are wigs and gowns, whose owners could tell fearful tales of hope deferred and disappointed expectations.

There is a leader, with a bag full of briefs; not a cause is called on but he is engaged; the judge lends his ear, and the fawning juniors flutter at his frown. Next him, with whiskers matching the colour of his wig, is one whose day is gone by,—whose well-stored bag has dwindled to a single brief, the winter of whose discontent is sharpened by the recollection of the prosperity he once knew. The rosy-gilled gentleman on his left is a country practitioner, who reaps a small harvest at assizes and sessions, without enduring the pangs of Westminster Hall, the turmoil of the circuit, or the confinement of inn-chambers. Another great leader

follows on; sallow, solemn, and care-worn;—and then come a long file
of juniors, with health ripening on each brow, until we come to the pink-
and-white youth with the wig and gown of yesterday.

Some judges consider special jury cases, which Doleful's was, peculiarly
the property of the rich, consequently have no compunctions about letting
them remain to the last, and Baron Botherem was of this opinion.   Four
mornings did Mr. Jorrocks fall into the rear of Mr. Marmaduke Muleygrubs' coach, each morning showing the fading finery of the set-out : the
trumpeters' boots grew less bright, the harness lost its polish, Marmaduke's ruff began to droop, and on the fourth morning the stiff-necked
flunkies appeared in black cravats.   Still, despite all the worthy high
sheriff's assurances to Mr. Jorrocks, that he would *make* the judge take
his cause out of order, Baron Botherem went pertinaciously through the
list according to the order in which they had been set down.   The fourth
day was the last, and there were four special jury cases to be tried,
Doleful *v.* Jorrocks being the third, the briefs in those before it being
of such a size as to make the trials appear well calculated to last for ever.
The first, however, went off unexpectedly ; and at half-past ten the cause
immediately before that in which our worthy friend was to figure came
on before a full special jury, with a string of witnesses that occupied the
court till eight o'clock at night.   It was a dull, uninteresting affair,
respecting the liability of an insurance office, and the verdict was heard
with apparent indifference by a crowded court, all anxious for Doleful *v.*
Jorrocks to be called on.

The jury-box was at length cleared, the judge supplied with fresh pens
and a few green-shaded block-tin-standed compos scattered promiscuously
about the bar-table, while the crier made proclamation for all special
jurors in the action of Doleful *v.* Jorrocks to appear and answer to their
names.   This was a signal for a general commotion in the court ; jurors
fought their ways out, while others fought their ways in ; and a messenger having been despatched to the Criminal Court, for both judges
were working double tides in order to get away in good time to dine with
the Lord Lieutenant next day, the high sheriff entered in such a hurry
that he tripped over his sword and blobbed headforemost into court at
the back of Baron Botherem, who was sadly discomposed by his
awkwardness.

Order was at length restored, and five top-booted and five trousered
esquires having answered to their names, two gentlemen in drabs and
continuations (described in the panel as merchants), fill up the jury,
who, having taken the oath by threes to a book, settle themselves into
their box, looking both solemn and wise.   Mr. Jorrocks, having the *entrée*,
plants himself behind the judge's chair, and Captain Doleful confronts
him below, near the witness-box.

Our old friend, the Hon. Mr. Lollington, having muttered something
beginning with " My Lud " and ending with " issue," sits down, and
Mr. Burley Bolster, a large pasty-faced gentleman, in silver-rimmed
spectacles and a patent wig, presents his ample front to the jury.   Clearing
his voice, he leans with his thumb on the table and scrutinises the jury as
he thus addresses them :—

" Gentlemen of the jury, the plaintiff in this case, as my learned friend has told you, in somewhat more technical than intelligible language, is Captain Miserrimus Doleful, a gentleman, not only holding her Majesty's commission in the army, but also the important and highly honourable office of master of the ceremonies of Handley Cross Spa, a watering-place with which, I make no doubt, you are all more or less acquainted ; and my distinguished client comes into court this day to seek at your hands that reparation which one John Jorrocks refuses to afford him out of it. Jorrocks, he understood, was manager of the Handley Cross fox-hounds, a situation that enabled him to obtain all manner of information relative to horses ; and he regretted to see a man whose appearance was respectable so far losing sight of all honour and gratitude, as to avail himself of his superior knowledge to the injury of a friend, to whom he was under the greatest obligations, and who had fought and bled for his country.

"Captain Doleful, as he said before, was an officer—one whose life had been devoted to the service of his country, and who now, applied his energies to the promotion of the happiness and hilarity of the public. Jorrocks, in another line, was also a servant of the public, and he could not but regret that services so dissimilar should have been unfortunately brought in collision by the misconduct of either party. He would not trouble the jury, at that late hour of the night, with a detailed account of the obligations Mr. Jorrocks was under to the plaintiff, not only for obtaining him the mastership of the Handley Cross hounds but also for introducing him to the *élite* of the aristocratic society frequenting the celebrated Spa ; but he would content himself by showing how Jorrocks now sought to kick down the ladder by which he had risen to fame by injuring the man to whom he was under such onerous obligations." (Mr. Burley Bolster shook his head, as though he felt it desperately, and referred to his brief. Doleful grinned with delight.)

"Towards the close of last hunting season, gentlemen," continued Mr. Bolster, "the defendant, for reasons best known to himself, offered the whole of his stud for sale by public auction, but, among other horses that were not sold, was one called Xerxes, which was afterwards purchased by my client by private contract of the defendant's servant, who, by the direction and consent of his master, warranted the horse sound,—*warranted the horse sound*, I say. It was a long and troublesome negotiation, carried on sometimes by letter with the principal, at other times by conversation with his servant, whom I shall call before you ! but, ultimately, a bargain was concluded, and the sum of twenty-five pounds paid to the defendant as the price and value of the horse.

"*Value*, did I say, gentlemen ?" exclaimed Mr. Burley Bolster, suddenly checking himself ; "I made use of an erroneous expression, for he was absolutely *valueless ;* but the sum of twenty-five pounds was paid as the price of the animal. Well, gentlemen, the plaintiff immediately removed him to a most comfortable and commodious private stable, where he had every attention and accommodation that a horse can require—corn the soundest, hay the sweetest, water the purest, grooming the most elaborate and scientific, but, somehow or other, he throve not. My client's amiable and unsuspecting nature never allowing him to imagine that he had so long fostered a viper in his bosom (casting a contemptuous look at Mr. Jorrocks), went on, day by day, and for several days, in the hope that the change was merely occasioned by a difference of treatment or of food, and that the horse would speedily resume his wonted appearance; but, alas! 'hope,' as usual, 'told a flattering tale.'   He went on, from bad to worse, and when at length the consuming fever had worked deeply into his constitution, my unsuspecting client, awaking from the trance of confidence in which he had been so long enthralled, wrote to the defendant, representing how matters stood; that individual, so far from expressing his regret at the inconvenience he had caused my client, and offering to take back the horse, actually treated the matter with levity, and added insult to injury, by laughing at the man he had so basely defrauded.   My client, then, has no alternative, but presenting himself before a jury of his country, and I am happy to see that the defendant has empanelled a special one, at whose intelligent hands, I feel no manner of doubt, my defrauded client will receive that reparation which John Jorrocks so unjustly denies him.

"Were it not for the appearance of the defendant in court, and the voluminous brief I see before my learned friend Mr. Chargem, I should have imagined that judgment would be suffered to go by default, as in the case of an undefended action; and even now, gentlemen, I am at a loss to imagine what defence my learned friend's ingenuity will enable him to offer; for I submit, under the guidance of his lordship, that it is clear law, that where an article is asked for to answer a particular purpose, the seller impliedly warrants that it is fit for that purpose, so that even should I fail in my proof of actual warranty, which, however, I do not anticipate, I shall still be entitled to your verdict on the general construction of the agreement; for, had my client been in want of a coughing, consumptive horse, he would have asked this defendant, Jorrocks, if he had such an animal, instead of which, throughout the transaction, he goes on the principle of obtaining a useful, though not a handsome horse.

"And now, gentlemen, one word with respect to a person of the name of Pigg, whom I shall presently call before you, though, perhaps, he will appear rather in the nature of a reluctant witness. This Pigg is huntsman and general stable manager to the defendant Jorrocks, and seems to be a convenient sort of person, on whom Jorrocks foists such jobs as he does not like to take upon himself, and Pigg will be placed in the witness-box to show that he was the accredited servant of the defendant, from which a legal axiom arises, laid down by the great Lord Ellenborough himself, in the case of Helyear v. Hawke (Espinasse, page 72); that if a servant is sent with a horse by his master, and gives directions respecting his sale, that the servant thereby becomes the accredited agent of his master, and what he says respecting the horse is evidence.

"And in another place his Lordship adds, 'I think the master having intrusted the servant to sell, he is intrusted to do all he can to effectuate the sale, and if he does exceed his authority, in so doing he binds his master.' Now, gentlemen, I shall prove by a letter, in the hand-writing of the defendant, that Pigg was authorised by the defendant not only to receive the purchase-money, but also to warrant the horse; and having established that point, I shall proceed to prove, by competent witnesses, that the horse was labouring under a mortal disease at the time of the sale. That done, I feel assured you will arrive at the only conclusion open to sensible men, and find a verdict for my client."

The letters, as already given, being admitted, were put in, and read amid much laughter, and Mr. Burley Bolster then desired the crier to call James Pigg.

"James Pigg! James Pigg! James Pigg!" sounded all around the building, and passed outside.

"Ar's here!" exclaimed a voice at the back of the witness-box, where he had been sleeping; and presently James Pigg made his appearance in front.

A solitary mould-candle placed on the crier's desk at the side shed a dim light over James's person, showing the lustre of his eye and the care-worn character of his countenance. He was dressed in a dark coat, with a striped waistcoat, and white neckcloth, upon the tie of which was a large stain of tobacco-juice, which in the gloom of the court looked like an extensive brooch.

"Now, Pigg?" said Mr. Bolster, in a familiar tone.

"Now, Wig!" responded James, in the same way.

"Mind what you are about, sir!" said Baron Botherem, with a frown.

"You are, I believe, huntsman to Mr. Jorrocks, the defendant in this action?" observed the learned counsel.

Pigg.—"Yes ar is," replied James, brandishing his hat over the brass rail of the witness-box, "but ar de believe gin ar had me reets, ar'd be a gen'l'man this day, and huntin' me own h'unds, only ye see, mar foreelder John—John Pigg, ye see—"

"Well, never mind about your foreelder, John," interrupted Mr. Bolster, "We want to know about Mr. Jorrocks; and you say you are huntsman to him. Now, tell me, do you remember a horse he had, called Xerxes?"

Pigg.—"Nicely!"

"Now, what became of that horse? Raise your voice and speak out, so that the gentlemen of the jury, many of whom are deaf, may hear you," pointing to the jury-box.

Pigg.—"HE DEE'D!" roared Pigg.

"He died!" repeated Mr. Bolster. "Ah, but before he died, whose hands did he pass into?"

Pigg.—"Ard Doleful's."

"Now, then, Pigg, you seem an honest, intelligent sort of man," continued Mr. Bolster, smoothingly, "try if you can recollect what passed between Captain Doleful and you as to that horse."

"A! ar ken nicely—'twas just twenty-five pund."

Mr. Bolster.—"No, that's not what I mean—I want to know what inducement you held out to Captain Doleful to buy him."

Pigg.—"Sink ar said nout."

"What *does* the witness say?" exclaimed Baron Botherem, who had been fidgetting about ever since Pigg appeared.

Mr. Bolster, very obsequiously.—"He says, my lord, that there was nothing the matter with the horse."

"No, I beg pardon," interposes Mr. Chargem, "I understand him to mean that he said nothing to Captain Doleful."

" Precisely, what I say," rejoined Mr. Bolster ; " Captain Doleful asked him what was the matter with the horse, and he said, ' nothing.' "

" The question, as I understand it," said Baron Botherem, " was, what inducement he held out to Captain Doleful to buy the horse ? But what answer he gives, I cannot for the life of me make out."

Mr. Chargem.—"Precisely so, my lud. My learned friend asks what inducement the witness held out to plaintiff to buy the horse, and the witness in the language of the colliery country from whence he comes, replies, ' Ar said nout ;' meaning, I did not say anything. Perhaps your ludship would have the kindness to put the question yourself."

" Witness—*Pigg!*—attend to me ! " exclaimed his lordship. " Tell the gentlemen of the jury what you said in praise or commendation of the horse to induce Captain —— What's his name, to buy him."

Pigg.—" Ar said *nout*—T'ard man was aye comin' to wor stable, and he axed me yen day gin hus had had meazles."

" I can't understand a *word* the witness says ! " exclaimed the judge, shaking his head in despair.

Mr. Bolster.—" He says, my loord, that the plaintiff inquired if the horse had had the measles—Now what did you say to that ? "

Pigg.—" ' Measles ! ' said I—' aye hoopin'-cough tee ! ' "

" Measles and hooping-cough too," repeated Mr. Burley Bolster, with great gravity, to the convulsion of the jury.

Cross-examined by Mr. Chargem.

" I suppose, Mr. Pigg, you are a pretty good judge of a horse ? "

" *Pigg.*—" Top judge."

" What sort of a judge is that ? " exclaimed Baron Botherem in despair.

" My lud, he says he is a *good*, or *supreme*, judge ;" adding *sotto voce*, though loud enough to be heard by the bench, " Much such a judge as your ludship, in fact."

Baron Botherem.—" Humph !—really we ought to have an interpreter. Well, now go on."

Mr. Chargem.—Now, Mr. Pigg, will you have the kindness to tell the gentlemen of the jury, if, in the course of your experience, you ever knew a horse have the measles ? "

Pigg.—" Niver ! "

Mr. Chargem.—" Or the hooping-cough ? "

Pigg.—" Niver ! "

Mr. Chargem.—" So that, when you told Captain Doleful that this horse had had both, you meant to say that he had had neither ? "

Pigg.—" T'ard gouk was aye axin' me about the hus, whiles if he slept well, whiles if he had the lumbago, whiles if he liked eatin', and ar was tied to tell him summut."

Mr. Chargem.—" But what you said was merely loose, off-hand conversation, and not intended as an inducement to get him to buy ? "

Pigg.—" Diel a bit ! It was nout to me whether t'ard sinner bought him or no, se lang as he held his gob, and didn't keep fashin a ' me about him."

" Oh, dear, this subterranean language puzzles me exceedingly ! "

exclaimed the judge, weary in mind and body; " I didn't catch *one* word of that sentence."

Mr. Chargem interprets.—" He did not care, my, lud, whether Captain Loleful bought the horse or not, so long as he held his gob—which, I presume, means his tongue."

Benjamin Brady was the next witness.

"Now, Mr. Brady," said Mr. Burley Bolster, eyeing him through his spectacles; " you are, I believe, a servant with Mr. Jorrocks?"

" I'm first vip," replied the boy, with great dignity.

Mr. Bolster.—" You remember the plaintiff in this action, Captain Doleful, coming to your master's stable about a horse called Xerxes?"

Ben.—" Yes; he came werry often."

Mr. Bolster.—" Well, what did he say?"

Ben.—" The first time he came, he inquired most about the other 'osses, and only axed the pedigree of Xerxes."

Mr. Bolster.—" And what answer did Pigg give him?"

Ben.—" He gave him **our** usual pedigree—said he was by President, out of a Vaxy mare."

Mr. Bolster.—" Your master keeps but one pedigree, then?"

Ben.—" One for 'osses; he has another for 'ounds."

Mr. Bolster.—" Then all your horses are by President, out of Vaxy mares."

Ben.—" Yes, sir."

Mr. Bolster.—" Now you say the plaintiff came very often to your stable; can you tell the gentlemen of the jury how many times, on the whole, he might be there?"

Ben.—" Perhaps ten or a dozen times."

Mr. Bolster.—" Did he come alone?"

Ben.—" No; he always brought one or two chaps with him,—Miss Jelly came once."

Mr. Bolster.—" And what used they to say?"

Ben.—" Oh, they would look, first at one horse, then at another, and ax about them."

Mr. Bolster.—" And Mr. Pigg, I suppose, was very glad to see them?"

Ben.—" No, 'deed wasn't he! He used to swear very hard."

Mr. Bolster.—" He's a heavy swearer, is he?"

Ben.—" Uncommon! "

" Very improper," remarked the judge, with a shake of the head.

Mr. Bolster.—" And what questions, in particular, did the plaintiff ask?"

Ben.—" Oh, why, he used to ax if this orse was a good 'un, and that a good 'un; and Pigg used to swear they were all good 'uns, there wern't no choice among 'em."

Mr. Bolster.—" Was that said of any horse in particular, or generally of the stud?"

Ben.—" He said it of whatever horse the captain was axing about."

Mr. Bolster.—" Can you remember the words he made use of?"

Ben.—" ' Best 'orse goin',' he used to say; ' best 'orse goin'.' "

Mr. Bolster.—"Do you remember the captain inquiring if a horse called Xerxes had had the measles ? "

Ben.—" I can't say I do,—remember his axin' if he had been innoculating him."

Mr. Bolster.—" What made him ask that ? "

Ben.—" The horse had been bled, and there was the mark on his neck."

Mr. Bolster.—" Now do you remember the plaintiff coming to the stable for Xerxes ? "

Ben.—" Yes."

Mr. Bolster.—" What did he say ? "

Ben.—" That he had come for Xerxes."

Mr. Bolster.—" And what said Mr. Pigg ? "

Ben.—" He axed for the brass—he could not let him gan without."

" He asked for the what ? " inquired the judge.

" My lord, witness says that Pigg asked for the brass, which is a north country corruption of the word money."

" Oh ! " said the judge, who thought it was part of the bridle.

Mr. Bolster.—" Now, when Pigg asked Captain Doleful for the brass, what took place ? "

Ben.—" The captain paid him five-and-twenty golden sovereigns, sayin', ' I s'pose he's all right;' and Pigg said, ' Sound wind and limb.' "

Mr. Bolster, repeating after the witness, eyeing the jury all the time, " And Pigg said, ' *Sound wind and limb.*' You give your evidence very creditably," observed Mr. Bolster to the boy.

" Yez-ir," replied Benjamin.

Cross-examined.—" Is not on the best of terms with Mr. Pigg, Pigg has given him too much of what he calls ' cobbler's-wax oil '—thrashing with a strap. Was not in the stable when the sale of the horse took place,—was in the loft, playing cards with Tom Turnbin, Mr. George Smith's helper, and Joe Haddock. Saw what took place through a hole in the floor. Is certain Pigg said, ' Sound wind and limb '—heard him say it twice."

John Scott is a helper and occasional groom.—" Remembers accompanying Captain Doleful to Mr. Jorrocks's stables, when he bought the horse.—James Pigg was there. The captain said he had come for Xerxes. Pigg asked if he had brought the brass for him, as he could not let him gan without. The captain produced twenty-five sovereigns. Pigg was very angry, swore that his master was an ard gouk, and had sold the best horse in the stable. The captain said, Mr. Jorrocks would soon pick up another. Pigg swore very much. The captain paid the money, saying, ' I suppose he's all sound.' Pigg swore he was sound wind and limb, and it would be lucky for the captain if he were half as sound. Witness then led the horse away. In going along he coughed."

Cross-examined.—" Witness has lived in several situations, but has been out of place for three years or so,—maybe for want of a character. Looks after six horses and two flys. Servants in place think two horses and one fly enough at a time.—Makes a great difference whether a servant is in place or out as to the quantity of work he can do. Had a blow-up

with James Pigg about the merits of their masters—that is to say, about
Mr. Jorrocks and Captain Doleful. Pigg complained that the captain
had not given him a glass when he bought the horse. Witness told him,
perhaps the captain didn't know the custom. Pigg said it was all his
eye, and that he was a nasty, mangy beggar. Witness replied, that the
captain was as good a man as h s master, and that he, witness, wouldn't
stay in a place to be 'bused as he understood Mr. Jorrocks 'bused his
servants. Pigg said, he'd rather be d—d by his master than dine with
mine. Then he said, he wouldn't borrow half-a-crown to get drunk with
mine, that he was fit for nout but a Dorm (Durham) farmer, and a great
deal more wulgarity of that sort.

"Will swear positively that the horse coughed on his way from
Mr. Jorrocks's stable to Captain Doleful's. When he got him to the
latter place, Captain Doleful borrowed a saddle and bridle, and rode the
horse to Bumpmead. Had him in harness the same evening to take him
to a tea-party. The night might be wet, but witness does not remember.
Does not know how long he waited for the captain,—might be half-an-
hour,—might be an hour,—does not think it was two hours. The captain
rode the horse to Deepdeene Park the next day,—fifteen miles, and back.
Had him in the fly again at night. There was a party at Miss Fribble's,
and the captain conveyed all the young ladies from Miss Birch's seminary,
there and back, by ten at a time."

Mr. Horsman, veterinary surgeon.—"Has been in practice three years.
Remembers being sent for to attend a horse that Captain Doleful had
bought of Mr. Jorrocks. Found him labouring under idiopathic fever
in its most malignant form, which soon turned to inflammation of the
lungs. Did what he could for him, but without avail. The horse had
then been some time in Captain Doleful's possession, but from the
appearance he presented on his being first called in, witness has little
doubt but he had the seeds of the disease upon him at the time he was
sold."

Cross-examined.—"Is not a member of the Royal Veterinary College,
—is a self-dubbed doctor. Found the horse in a stable along with a
monkey and bear belonging to a travelling showman. The stable was
cold, perhaps damp, and witness will not say that the horse might not
have caught cold by his removal from a warm to a cold stable. Horses
soon catch cold, inflammation quickly follows, and death soon comes after.
Is certain the horse is dead,—knows it, because he skinned him." This
was the plaintiff's case.

Mr. Burley Bolster having resumed his seat with great self-complacency,
Mr. Chargem gave the front of his wig a pull, and his gown a hitch at
the right shoulder, and turned to the "specials."

"May it please your Ludship,—Gentlemen of the jury," said he, "I
hardly know whether I am justified in trespassing upon your valuable
time, particularly at this late period of the night, by rebutting a charge
so feebly sustained as the case my learned friend, Mr. Burly Bolster, has
laid—has presented to your notice. I hardly know whether I should not
be best discharging my duty to my client, by closing my brief, and sub-
mitting to your verdict, which I am satisfied will be for the defendant,
instead of exposing those fallacies that carry a too palpable conviction

along with them. But, gentlemen, lest by any chance it might be inferred that I have not the satisfactory evidence invariably required by a British jury, I will hazard a brief trespass on your time while I glance at the evidence now before you, and call a few witnesses in disproof of the statements of my learned friend.

"The case, gentlemen, I take to be simply this. Captain Doleful, no great conjuror in horse-flesh, treats for a horse in Mr. Jorrocks' stud. There is a good deal of haggling, as you have seen, about the transaction, Captain Doleful offering Mr. Jorrocks less than he asks, and Mr. Jorrocks, on the other hand, insisting on his price. And here let me draw your attention to the fact, that, throughout the transaction, the plaintiff is the anxious party. Mr. Jorrocks holds out no temptation to get him to buy; on the contrary, he admits the horse is not first-rate; but, speaking of him in the language of friendship, Mr. Jorrocks says he is calculated for much honourable exertion in many of the minor fields of horse enterprise, which, I suppose, is a figurative mode of saying, that if he is not fit for a hunter, he will make what the defendant would call a werry good 'chay-'oss' (laughter.) And again, when the plaintiff hesitates about the price, does my client evince any anxiety to get him to give it? Surely not! So far from that, he says, in one of the letters you have heard read, that if the plaintiff does not like to give the twenty-five pounds, he is to 'say no more about it:' and again, when the plaintiff bothers him to take fifteen pounds, and give a receipt for twenty-five, he scouts the idea, and desires 'the plaintiff will make up his mind one way or other, as he hates haggling.' Does all this, I ask you, bespeak the man anxious to foist a bad horse off upon a friend, or a man anxious to get rid of a horse at all? I need not tell you who the defendant in this action is. Despite my learned friend's sneering ignorance, and talking of him in the disrespectful way he did as this Jorrocks and that Jorrocks, he could not conceal from himself,——still less from you, gentlemen of the jury, that he was keenly alive to the celebrity and importance of my most distinguished client,—a gentleman whose name precludes the idea of his being mistaken for any other, and who, in every relation of life, has worn the broad arrow mark of probity and honour!"

"Keep the tamborine a rowlin'!" exclaimed James Pigg, causing a roar of laughter throughout the court, and procuring James the promise of a commitment from his lordship.

"And now, gentlemen," resumed Mr. Chargem, as order was restored, "we come to the gist of the action, as regards the plaintiff. Captain Doleful says he will take the horse, 'provided, of course, he is all right, *et cetera.*' That *et cetera*, gentlemen, was once described by Lord Mansfield as the largest word in the English language, and assuredly the plaintiff is of the same opinion, for he intends to make it cover a most comprehensive range over an unlimited period. That *et cetera* is to guarantee the horse from all illness and infirmity, not only at the time he was sold, but for ever after, under whatever treatment he may be subjected to, or to whatever vicissitudes exposed. It is to guarantee his safe career over Bumpmead Heath by day, his health in harness at night, and his convalescence in that comfortable abode which he enjoyed in common with the monkey and bear belonging to a travelling showman. (Laughter.) All this is meant to be covered by this little *et cetera* !

"My learned friend, well knowing his weak point, anticipated the failure of his evidence of warranty, and bespoke your verdict on the supposed terms of the agreement; but I also submit, under the guidance of his lordship, that, in an action on a breach of warranty, distinct and positive evidence of an undoubted warranty must be given to entitle a plaintiff to recover, and no constructive evidence will supply the place of clear and distinct warranty. I grant, that if the plaintiff had wanted a diseased horse, he would probably have asked for one; but, then, you must also take this along with you, that if he had applied to my client for a horse that would stand all the racketing that this poor beast was exposed to, he would have said that nothing but an iron horse would stand such work, and have recommended him to an engine-builder. So that, even supposing my learned friend had made out a case of distinct warranty, still I would submit that the plaintiff's treatment of the animal was not such as a prudent man would adopt, and that so far from the result being matter of surprise, it would have been much more singular if it had not happened. My learned friend places Mr. Pigg, the huntsman, in the witness-box to prove his warranty, with what success I need hardly say. I think his evidence went as much against the plaintiff as for him. Next, we have the boy whipper-in, who seems to come in for a share of the whip himself, who speaks to a conversation he overheard while playing cards in the hay-loft; and you are expected to believe that this boy could distinguish which horse Mr. Pigg was praising, when, upon his cross-examination, he admits that Pigg was in the habit of praising them all.—'Best horse goin'!' he used to say of them all.

"After the boy Brady comes one of those questionable creatures,—a servant out of place, who is the only witness that at all goes to the second point—supposing the warranty to be proved—of the horse being unsound at the time he was sold. And what does he say? Why, that the horse coughed on his way from Mr. Jorrocks' stable to that of the travelling showman. Such evidence, I feel, will have no weight with you, gentlemen. A hundred things might make him cough. Perhaps the occasional groom had been trying his wind by the usual pinching of the windpipe, or a bit of hay might have lodged in his throat; but if the horse had such a violent cold upon him, do you think it could have escaped all the lynx-eyed witnesses the plaintiff had to inspect him? Is there none of all that numerous host to come forward and say that the horse was unsound at the time he was sold? None but this gentleman, who, it seems, Mr. Pigg would prefer being damned by to dining with. (Laughter.)

"Such evidence is not worth rebutting. It would be an insult to your understandings to suppose so. Mr. Horsman alone requires contradiction. He has been in practice for the long period of three years, and says, from the appearance of the horse, he has little doubt but he had the seeds of the disease upon him when sold. To rebut that, I propose placing another veterinary surgeon in the witness-box; and although by so doing, I shall entitle my friend to a reply, yet I feel his case is so hopelessly weak that I shall not injure my client's cause by throwing him the chance, confident as I am of obtaining your verdict."

Mr. Castley, a veterinary surgeon of ten years' standing, deposed that he made a *post-mortem* examination of the horse. The lungs presented one confused and disorganised mass of blackness. The appearance would lead the inexperienced to imagine that long inflammation had gradually broken down the substance of the lungs. Proves no disease of long standing, but inflammation, intense in its nature, which had speedily run its course. The horse died from suffocation, every portion of the lungs being choked up with this black blood, which had broken into and filled all the air-cells, by means of which it should have been purified.

Two other witnesses spoke to the healthy appearance of the horse at the time he was sold.

John Brown was the next witness. He deposed that he was pad-groom to Mr. Barnington, a Cheshire gentleman of large fortune, who kept a good stud of hunters at Handley Cross. Was well acquainted with James Pigg and with all Mr. Jorrocks' horses. Their stables adjoin. Was at exercise on the morning of the sale with James Pigg, who rode Xerxes and led Ginnums. Never heard the horse cough all the time. Was out two hours. Would have been sure to have noticed it if he had coughed. Grooms are always on the look-out for coughs.

Joseph Haddock, a lad of fourteen, being sworn, deposed that his mother was a washerwoman, and he turned the mangle and sought the dirty clothes in a donkey-cart. Is well acquainted with Mr. Benjamin Brady the whipper-in. Was playing cards with him in the hay-loft on the morning of the sale. Mr. Brady lost one and ninepence, and was very angry. The game was blind hookey, and Mr. Brady played without intermission till one o'clock. Is quite certain Mr. Brady never stopped playing to see what was going on below or to listen. Brady is a desperate gambler. Will play at any thing, or swear to any thing.

Cross-examined.—"Witness remembers the day, because Mr. Brady had not paid him. Believes Mr. Brady had the money, but insinuated that witness had cheated; quarrelled in consequence. Had been very intimate before. Mr. Brady used to let him ride his led horse when Mr. Pigg was not at exercise. Used to gallop and race along the road. Owes Mr. Brady money on the balance of their racing account. The largest stake they ever run for was five shillings, four miles along the Appledove Road. Mr. Brady on Xerxes and witness on Arterxerxes. Mr. Brady won, but witness afterwards heard that he had given Arterxerxes a pail of water before starting, and he refused to pay. Had tossed for choice of horses the night before the race. The case is referred to the editor of 'Bell's Life,' who has not yet given his decision. Expects it in the notice to correspondents. Been before the editor since the spring. Should say that Mr. Brady is what they call a 'sharp hand'—not much the gent."

Bolster replied at great length, during which process Baron Botherem went through his notes, preparatory to charging the jury. He began almost before Bolster got sate down, as if to reprove his unseasonable prolixity. Thus he instructed them :—

"Gentlemen of the jury," said he, "this action, as you have heard, is brought by Captain Doleful against Captain Jorrocks, both of them filling distinguished offices at Handley Cross Spa, one being master of the ceremonies, the other master of the blood hounds; and it is much to be regretted that gentlemen in their exalted stations should not be able to arrange their differences without the intervention of a judge and jury; however, as they come here, we must endeavour to do justice between them. The action is brought to recover the price of a horse, and the points you will have to consider will be, first, whether there was any warranty at all or not, and if you think there was a warranty, then you must consider to what extent it went.

"The evidence, as usual in these cases, is very conflicting, one witness swearing point blank the reverse of what another one swears.

"First, you have James Pigg, the huntsman, who informs us, in his subterranean language—if, indeed, it can be called a language—that he said 'nout,' which, I suppose, is meant to imply that he did not warrant the horse; the word 'nout' doubtless being one of extensive signification in the colliery country, from which this witness comes.

"Then you have Mr. Benjamin Brady—the whipper-in, I think he is called—who says, ' I was lying in the hay-loft, and heard a conversation between Pigg and the plaintiff, when Pigg distinctly stated, two several times, that the horse was sound wind and limb. Then, on his cross-examination, he admits that the plaintiff was in the habit of coming into the stable, and asking all sorts of questions, and that Pigg was in the habit of giving the same character to every horse; so that, you see, he might be talking about any of the others, for anything Mr. Brady knows to the contrary. All this is very perplexing, to say nothing of the flat contradiction given by the last witness, Mr. Joseph Haddock, to the material point of Mr. Brady's evidence. I may be wrong, but they appear to me to be what would be—hem, hum, haw,—not exactly what they ought to be.

"Indeed, the only undisputed point seems the death of the horse. One veterinary surgeon says that he has no doubt he had the seeds of disease upon him at the time he was sold; and the other, that the symptoms he saw on the *post-mortem* examination prove nothing of the sort. The plaintiff's occasional groom swears the horse coughed on his way from the stable on delivery. Counsel for the defendant cross-examined him as to his present servitude; but I do not think anything was elicited that should throw discredit on the witness's testimony. To contradict him, then, I should observe, you have John Brown, who describes himself as '*bad* groom to Mr. Jones." It seems an odd character for a man to give himself," chuckled his lordship, " but I suppose we must take his word for it."

A titter ran through the court, which the judge, attributing to his wit, proceeded.

"This witness says he was at exercise on the morning of the day of sale with Captain Pigg, and the horse never coughed: ' I should have been sure to have noticed it if he had,' he adds. So there again, you see, the evidence is at direct variance.

"Altogether, it is a most perplexing case, and one that we, who have passed our lives in courts of law, are but ill calculated to unravel. I would rather try ten insurance cases than one horse cause. All I can do is to put the points that you will have to decide, and leave you to judge of the worth of the evidence. The points are, whether or not there was a warranty, and, assuming you find there was a warranty, then you must consider whether the horse had the seeds of disease upon him when sold, or acquired them after he passed into the plaintiff's possession. On the other hand, if you are of opinion there was no warranty, then the second point will not arise, and your verdict will be for the defendant.

"In the event of your finding for the plaintiff, the measure of damages will be the price paid for the horse; and haw, ha, hem, I think, gentlemen, that is about all the assistance I can give you." Saying which, Baron Botherem bowed, and threw himself back in his throne.

The jury immediately seized their hats and coats, and while the usher is swearing the bailiff to keep them in some safe place, without meat, drink, or fire—candle-light only excepted—till they agree upon their verdict, they betake themselves from the heated atmosphere of a suffocating court, to the chilly, vault-like dampness of the retiring-room; a rough deal-table, with a bench on each side, is all the accommodation that greets them, while a single candle, showing the massive gratings of a lofty window, and the dull clank of the lock, as the bailiff turns the key upon them, reminds them of the importance of an early agreement of their verdict. Twelve strangers are thus left to make each other's acquaintance by arriving at the same conclusion.

* * * * * *

"Well," said Mr. Strong, throwing himself on the table below the window, "I suppose we shall have no difficulty about this case. We must find for the plaintiff, of course."

Mr. Strong was one of the three gentlemen described in the panel as merchants, and was under obligations to Captain Doleful for getting partners for his plain daughters.

"I don't know that," replied Mr. Heartley, one of the top-booted gentry; "I am neither satisfied that there was a warranty, nor yet that the horse was unwell when he left Mr. Jorrocks' stable."

"That's my view of the case, too!" exclaimed half-a-dozen voices, glad to follow a leader.

"Nay, then," exclaimed Mr. Strong, "I think it seems clear, by the evidence, that Pigg warranted the horse; and, that being the case, the law says, the owner is bound by the representation of his servant."

"I think so too," observed another.

"The evidence on that point is very unsatisfactory," exclaimed two or three.

"I'm afraid we can't make it any better," replied Mr. Strong.

"If there was no warranty, there can be no damages; perhaps we had better divide on that point first. Those gentlemen who are of opinion that Mr. Jorrocks warranted his horse will have the kindness to hold up their hands."

Mr. Strong then took the candle, and waving it round the gloomy room, found he had three in his favour. That was not very encouraging, but he had been in a worse situation, and carried his point after all, so he deliberately set down the candle, and pulled a book out of his pocket.

That looked ominous.

The conversation was then taken up promiscuously, the jurymen huddling in groups, with their hats on, talking to keep themselves warm.

"Perhaps we had better have some more candles," observed Mr. Strong, looking off his book; "I suppose we arn't stinted as to them."

"I should hope we won't want them," observed a shivering youth, who had left his hat in the jury-box.

"Don't know that," responded Mr. Strong, pulling a night-cap out of his pocket.

Again they huddle into groups, or walk hurriedly about, stamping, and clapping their arms.

After some half-hour consumed in this way, a knock at the heavy door arrests their attention, and the bailiff announces that the judge desires to know if they are likely to agree on their verdict.

"Yes!"—"No!"—"Yes!" respond half-a-dozen voices, which, the bailiff understanding, informs his lordship that they are not; so, arranging that the verdict shall be taken by the officer of the court, his lordship awakes the dozing under-sheriff, who rouses the drowsy trumpeters, and as the Town Hall clock chimes twelve, his lordship arrives at his lodgings.

The dying notes of the shrill trumpets fall with clear and melancholy cadence on the ears of the pent-up jurymen, and again the most tractable attempt an accommodation. Mr. Strong only replies by winding up his repeater, and striking the hour.

"It's as cheap sitting as standing," observes one of the jurymen, taking his place at the table, an example followed by the rest, to the ejectment of Mr. Strong from the end, and the whole party sit down as if to a meal.

They now begin the case anew, going through the evidence with an accuracy considerably promoted by hunger. One o'clock strikes—two—three—and yet they are as far from agreeing as ever. Day begins to dawn, and at length finds its way even through the iron bars of the dingy prison window.

The jury eye each other like through railway passengers eye those who have got in during the night, and Mr. Strong puts out the candle.

Mr. Heartley has a pocket-full of horse-beans, which he begins eating, offering them liberally to his friends, with the assurance that he has enough for a week. Mr. Strong produces a cold tongue, which is in more demand, and he gets little himself. Cold and hunger tell upon his supporters, and at four o'clock he stands alone.

At half-past he gives in.

The joyous jury almost break the door in awakening the sleeping sentinel, and they rush into court to deliver their verdict.

How changed the scene! The heated hall is cleared—Mr. Jorrocks sleeps in the judge's chair, his wig is awry—James Pigg and the crier are nodding, back to back, in the witness-box—Benjamin is curled up on the bar-table—and the attorneys and their clerks are huddled together at opposite corners, lest they should fight in their sleep. A crier is found in the bottom of the reporter's box—and the officer left to take the verdict, being summoned from his coffee in the gaoler's house, hurries in with Captain Doleful, and hears a verdict for the defendant.

The crier dissolves the court, and James Pigg, frantic with delight, hoorays, and hoops, and yells, and proclaims that he'll be *the death of a sovereign* !

CHAPTER LXV.

THE CAPTAIN'S WINDFALL.

THE verdict sank deep into the heart of Captain Doleful.

He returned to Handley Cross long before people were stirring; but Miss Jelly's watchful eye "traced the day's disaster in his morning face." Taking to his bed, the captain obstinately remained there for two whole days, impervious to the call of friends and foes. The verdict was one of the severest blows that had befallen him in a somewhat eventful life. The price of the horse was nothing compared to the long lawyer's bills that were sure to follow,—a hundred and fifty pounds, perhaps. Dreadful! But for the pleasure of trouncing Jorrocks, he could have had the thing tried quite as well in the county court for 5*l.*

Consolation, however, came on the third day, and an important change commenced in the fortunes of our captain. Sitting in moody stupor, with a last week's " Paul Pry " in his hands, Miss Jelly's little girl presented herself before him with a deep black-edged letter, bearing the Clifton post-mark. The Captain started at the sight, for though almost alone in the world, the sign of mourning shook his shattered nerves.

He broke the seal with nervous hand, and read as follows:

" Sir,—We have the honour to acquaint you, that your good friend, and our excellent client, Miss Louisa Crabstick, is no more;—she expired this morning at half-past six, without pain or struggle. As her confidential advisers, we are in a situation to acquaint you, that a few days since she executed a will in your favour, and it is highly important that you should forthwith repair to the spot, and take upon yourself the direction of affairs. Her property is considerable, and we believe there is a large sum of money and valuables in the house, all of which should be looked to without delay. In making this melancholy announcement, we beg to offer our congratulations on your justly merited good fortune, and to add, that any instructions you may honour us with will be carefully attended to. We have the honour to subscribe ourselves, dear sir, your most obedient and very humble servants,

"PIKE, LAMB, AND LAMBRO,
" *Keen Street, Bristol.*"

What a state of excitement Captain Doleful was thrown into on reading this! A new world seemed opening before him, and he felt himself hurrying away from the cares, the contentions, and the disappointments of the old one.   For once a lawyer's letter conveyed a charm.   For some moments he was perfectly childish.   He looked at the letter, then he looked at himself; then came the recollection of former days, with a slight twinge of regret that one, to whom he had poured forth his whole soul in mercenary adoration, should now be no more.   That was quickly followed by wonderment at getting the money, and a hasty speculation as to the amount.   His head was in a complete whirl, and he ordered and ate half-a-dozen calves'-foot jellies with apparent unconsciousness.

That evening saw him off to Clifton, and surprise at the unexampled extravagance of his conduct having tempted Miss Jelly to cast a hasty glance at the letter as it lay on the table during the captain's absence, sorting his clothes, the confectioner's shop spread the news like wildfire, and half-a-dozen candidates for the office of M. C. sprung up before the captain was well out of the town.

Captain Doleful's acquaintance with Miss Crabstick was one of those intimacies that frequently arise where people are thrown together in watering-place idleness, and though considerably older than himself, he had no hesitation in making the excess of money balance the excess of years.   Miss Crabstick, however, conscious of her wealth, and not despairing of her charms, determined upon trying another season or two elsewhere, before yielding to the captain's solicitations.   That season or two had been protracted into eight or ten, and the captain had almost ceased to think of her.   Brighton, Cheltenham, Hastings, and Clifton, had all been tried since first they met at Willoughby Baths, and still Miss Crabstick thought a season at the German Spas would supply the *quid pro quo*, or "equivalent," that she deemed essential to connubial happiness.   She died.—Her wealth was great,—more than people imagined, and the captain, with the assistance of Pike, Lamb, and Lambro, soon discovered he might swear the property under twelve thousand pounds, without defrauding himself.

He was now a great man.   The M. C. card-plate was thrown aside, and a flourishing new one struck, on which Captain Doleful alone appeared, in the midst of a broad melancholy-looking black border.   The captain was well up in the world.   His own wealth, added to Miss Crabstick's, made a man of him.

Poor Miss Jelly's lodgings were deserted, and he returned to Handley Cross to occupy the best apartments at the Dragon Hotel.   He brought with him the dear deceased's baboon, three Angola cats, a parroquet, and a silver squirrel, all especially provided for by will, and charged with his attention, on forfeiture of a certain sum.

Great was the change in the manner of the people.   Instead of the captain running about the town leaving cards on new-comers, and refreshing the minds of the old ones with his name, notes, cards, and invitations poured in apace, and he sat in his rooms considering who he should honour, and who not.   His wealth was magnified into treble and quadruple its amount, and the old ladies were astonished that so attractive a young man should so long have remained single—"Not that they wished for anything of the sort now," looking at their daughters, "but before he got all the money, they would have liked it well enough;" just as disinterested old ladies will talk, though they know nobody believes them.

So Doleful set up to be cock of the walk, and longed for old Jorrocks back, that he might snub him.

CHAPTER LXVI.

JORROCKS IN TROUBLE.

DOLEFUL's day of triumph soon arrived, the monotony of Mr. Jorrocks' summer life seeming likely to be more than compensated by the busy incidents of the autumn.

Scarce were the rejoicings for his victory over Doleful finished ere our worthy friend found himself involved in a more delicate and difficult dilemma than he had ever yet known. The report of the action about the horse having done good service to the London papers in the dulness of autumnal news, Mr. Jorrocks' conduct and career had been greatly canvassed by cautious citizens, and among others by his next-of-kin, with whom our worthy friend had long been on indifferent terms, or rather no terms at all.

To the uninitiated, the idea of keeping a pack of hounds is looked upon as the surest proof of riches or ruin; an opinion that is periodically confirmed by the papers, in announcements of the great expense certain establishments are kept up at, Leicestershire and Northamptonshire being represented as hunted at an expense of five or six thousand a-year, though we dare say the present worthy masters would be glad if they got off for that.

The expense of Mr. Jorrocks' hounds was estimated in a like ratio, though they did not perhaps cost much above as many hundreds. There are two ways of doing everything.

Without impeaching the motives of the parties, or indeed alluding to them in more than a general way, we may briefly state, that our worthy friend's jollities or eccentricities at length earned for him a commission of lunacy.

After the necessary preliminaries, the Commission was opened in the long room of the Gray's Inn Coffee-house, in Holborn, where the following highly respectable jury were sworn to inquire into the merits of the allegation :—

Mark Stimpson, Starch-manufacturer, Pimlico;
John Brown, Greengrocer, High Street, Borough;
Henry Hobbs, Feather and Court Head Dress Maker, Hatton Garden;
Richard Jones, Dustman, Edgeware Road;
John Lotherington, Shoemaker, Margaret Street, Cavendish Square;
Thomas Coxon, Poulterer, Hadlow Street, Burton Crescent;
William Smith, Islington, Toy-shop-keeper;

James Rounding, Minories, Cheesemonger;
Albert Dunn, Sweeting's Rents, Newsman;
John Cook, Pentonville, Milkman and Cowkeeper
George Price, Long Acre, Gin-shop-keeper and Distiller;
John Shaw, Covent Garden, Fruiterer;
Thomas Boggon, Whitechapel, Nightman.

The Commission having been read, Mr. Mark Stimpson was elected foreman of the jury.

Mr. Martin Moonface, the celebrated Chancery lawyer, and Mr. Percy Snobb, appeared as counsel for the inquiry; Serjeant Horsefield and Mr. Coltman, as counsel for Mr. Jorrocks. Mr. Jorrocks appeared in court, taking his seat beside the learned sergeant, with two papers of Garraway's sandwiches before him, one labelled "beef," the other labelled "ham."

The long room was crowded to excess, the greatest possible interest and sympathy being manifested by the numerous auditors who thronged every part of the house where hearing room could be obtained. An immense number of persons arrived from Handley Cross, and the revenue of the Lilywhite Sand Railway was considerably augmented in consequence. The usual preliminaries having been observed, and silence obtained, Mr. Percy Snobb briefly opened the proceedings, during which Mr. Martin Moonface kept inflating his cheeks, preparatory to his own "let-off." Mr. Snobb having finished and sunk into his seat, and a proper time having elapsed, Mr. Martin Moonface rose with great solemnity, and addressed himself, promiscuously as it were, in a very deep and sonorous voice, thus:—

"I do not know that I can call to my recollection," said he, "ever rising to address twelve honest Englishmen with such mingled feelings of gratification and regret as I experience at the present moment." Here he paused, and ran his eyes along the jurymen to catch a soft one, to whom he could more particularly address himself.

Having selected Mr. Rounding, the Cheesemonger, whose ample bald head and staring blue eyes gave sufficient evidence of vacancy, he proceeded:—"Gratification that I should have the advantage of so intelligent—so enlightened—so conscientious a jury, to weigh with poiseless balance the niceties, the delicacies, the subtleties, the intricacies, of this complicated case; and regret—deep and poignant regret—that such a step as the present should be found necessary against so meritorious and amiable an individual as the unfortunate gentleman against whom I now appear." Here Mr. Martin Moonface heaved a heavy sigh, and looked at the back of his brief, on which was marked "50 guineas."—"Believe me when I say, that nothing but that high sustaining power, the moral consciousness of doing right, could induce me to undertake so thankless—so ungracious, a task. No feeling of personal ambition, no consideration of worldly aggrandisement, could tempt *me*—I may say (and the learned gentleman said it with the most dignified emphasis) could tempt any member of the honourable profession to which it is my pride and glory to belong, to enter upon a case where his own honest, conscientious opinions did not convince him of the propriety—I may say, *necessity* of the step." Mr. Moonface then unfolded his brief, and proceeded to pick out the first passage marked with a score in the margin.

"Gentlemen," said he, "my learned friend, Mr. Snobb, has stated to you the nature of the business that has called us together this day, and in doing so, he properly confined himself to the simple outline usually confided to young gentlemen entering the profession, leaving to me the duty of substantiating the case and filling up the narrative in detail. The name of the gentleman whose state of mind you are this day called upon to consider, as my learned friend has already told you, is Jorrocks, head of the firm 'Jorrocks and Co.,' tea-dealers and grocers, in the City of London; and in his commercial relations, I am free to admit, that his character and conduct are not only irreproachable, but exemplary in the highest degree. Still, as is generally found to be the case in these inquiries, the blameless tenor of his grocer's life is mixed up with a strong undercurrent of eccentricity, which has long been observable; and as the murmuring rill, strengthened by tributary streams, rolls on with growing strength until its force attracts the notice of the world, and calls for measures to restrain the torrent of its impetuosity, so Mr. Jorrocks' oddity has gone on increasing until the present inquiry has become absolutely and indispensably necessary. And let me here observe, gentlemen of the jury, that the more futile and absurd the chimera that obtains possession of a man's mind, the stronger and more forcible is the argument in favour of the restraining measure; for, assuredly, the farther an unhappy infatuation removes a man from the occupation of trade and the pursuits of a rational being, the stronger and more urgent is the necessity for supplying, through the medium of a next-of-kin, the deficiency that calamity has occasioned.

"I may at once admit that the delusion under which the unfortunate gentleman labours, is one of great novelty, and one that I have experienced very considerable difficulty in making myself sufficiently acquainted with to enable me to describe to you. You, gentlemen, if I mistake not, are tradesmen, living in the heart of this great metropolis, and, like myself, have passed your lives in honest, industrious callings, in perfect ignorance of the way that men remote from towns contrive to waste that time which to us is so valuable and productive. You will hardly credit me, I dare say, but I speak under the correction of my learned friends on the other side, who will put me right if I err in the detail—you will hardly credit me, I say, when I tell you, that in some counties of England large assemblies of dogs are annually made, sometimes as many I am told as fifty or sixty dogs——"

"'Ounds, you fool!" roared Mr. Jorrocks, from the opposite side of the table, indignant at the unsportsmanlike appellation.

"Gentlemen!" exclaimed Mr. Martin Moonface in astonishment, "I call your attention to the unfortunate gentleman. I think his conduct might warrant the closure of the business, even at this early stage of the proceedings, but if you, gentlemen, are not so fully satisfied in your minds of the situation that he is in as to render the further prosecution of the case needless, I must call on the Commissioners, in the exercise of the power with which they are invested, to afford me the protection and freedom from interruption to which I am entitled in the discharge of this most painful and difficult duty." [Mutual shakes of the head and nods having passed between the gentlemen at the end of the table and Mr. Moonface, and Serjeant Horsefield having remonstrated in an under tone with his client, Mr. Moonface smoothed down his feathers and harked back to the point at which he was interrupted.]

"I was observing, gentlemen of the jury," said he, again eyeing the cheesemonger, "that in some parts of the country annual hunts take place, for which large gatherings of dogs are made, and assemblies of people are to be found. How long this custom has prevailed, is immaterial to the present inquiry, but I believe I am instructed to say, that so far back as the year 1812 Mr. Jorrocks took an active—I may say, a prominent part, in the festivals—for such, I believe, is their character, that have been held in the county of Surrey.

"I should further inform you, in relation to these fêtes, or festivals, that a master or manager of the revels is annually chosen by ballot or otherwise, and the person so elected has the absolute government of the dogs and their doings during the period of his elevation. Accompanying Mr. Jorrocks onward then from his prominent though subordinate situation in the county of Surrey, we at length find him—I think it was in the course of last winter—elected the premier of a festival (here Serjeant Horsefield intimated in a whisper that the technical term was hunt)—I thank my learned friend," continued Mr. Moonface,—"hunt is the term—elected the premier of a hunt, called the Handley Cross Hunt, and it is, gentlemen, his doings in that capacity that you are more particularly called upon to examine, to form an opinion of the soundness or unsoundness of his understanding.

"I do not know that I am in a situation, nor is it perhaps material to the present inquiry, to explain the nature of the duties connected with the office of a hunt-master; but it must be apparent to you all, that if a person accepts a situation so totally dissimilar to his usual avocations, considerable detriment must arise to his private affairs; and, perhaps, it is not possible to imagine two things more unlike than the calm, reflective genius of a grocer's business, and the noisy, boisterous, clamorous—*riotous*, I may say, accompaniment of a hunt management. Not only are the two occupations totally incompatible, but their natural consequences are utterly dissimilar; for one is the honest course of sober industry, pointing, with cheering hand, to that brightest, noblest summit of all mercantile ambition, the possession of the lord-mayor's gilded coach and six, with glittering trumpeters and men in armour, while the other points downwards upon unhallowed scenes of riot and confusion, days made horrible with yelling, and nights spent amid the wildest, the most unprofitable debauchery.

"Thus, gentlemen of the jury, arises the cause of the present inquiry. The promoters of it say that Mr. Jorrocks is neglecting his business, and dissipating his means in mad and unnatural pursuits; while the law says, and wisely does it say it, that a man is not to be permitted to waste his substance in idle, wild, and unprofitable speculations; and when acts are committed which militate against good sense, it becomes the duty of those who are interested in the preservation of a family to call twelve honest, enlightened, conscientious men together to consider the acts that have been committed, and to ask of themselves whether they are the acts of a man blessed with sound discretion, or the acts of one who, though shrewd and intelligent in many respects, is yet visited with some unfortunate weakness that tends to nullify and destroy all the other faculties of which he may be in possession.

"Now, gentlemen, it becomes my duty to explain that there are two sorts of idiots; one the natural-born fool, that hath no understanding from his nativity, and therefore is by law presumed never likely to attain any ; and the other a lunatic, or one *non compos mentis*, who hath understanding, but who, from disease, grief, brandy-and-water, or other accident, hath lost the use of his reason. That great man and commentator, Judge Blackstone, says, 'A lunatic is one who hath lucid intervals ; sometimes enjoying his senses, and sometimes not, and that frequently depending upon the change of the moon.' Sir Edward Coke, another great legal luminary, places under the head of *non compos mentis* not only lunatics, but all persons under *frenzies*. I would particularly direct the attention of the jury to that term, conveying, as it does, a nicer definition of what may be considered sufficient to deprive a man of the custody of his affairs than any other that I am acquainted with. 'Not only *lunatics*,' says the learned judge, ' but all persons under *frenzies*,'—all persons, in fact, suffering from distraction of mind, alienation of understanding, or any violent passion, for such, I take it, is the meaning of the word frenzy.

"In all times, under all circumstances, the preservation of a man's property has been considered worthy the attention of a civilised government. By the Roman law, if a man by notorious prodigality was in danger of wasting his estate, he was looked upon as *non compos*, and committed to the care of curators, or tutors, by the prætor : ' Solent prætores, si talem hominem invenerint, qui neque tempus neque finem expensarum habet, sed bona sua dilacerando et dissipando profundit, curatorem ei dare, exemplo furiosi : et tamdiu erunt ambo in curatione, quamdiu vel furiosus sanitatem, vel ille bonos mores, receperit.' And by the laws of Solon such prodigals were branded with perpetual infamy.

"Gentlemen, the promoters of this inquiry are actuated by none but the purest, the best of motives ; they do not seek, by a long retrospective search, to expose the foibles of the unfortunate object of the inquiry, to brand him with idiotcy from his birth, or to disturb those commercial transactions with which his name, in connexion with the firm to which he belongs, has blended him : all they ask is to dissolve the ridiculous establishment of which he is the head, and to cancel the obligations that may have arisen out of it.

"I have already stated, that in the autumn of last year Mr. Jorrocks allowed himself to be dubbed the Master of the Handley Cross Hunt ; and it is from that period that we seek to annul his transactions, and to declare his incompetency to manage his affairs. A violent, a sudden, an uncontrollable frenzy seems to have seized him at the time ; for not only did he neglect his warehouse, but absolutely shut up his house in Great Coram Street—a house that I am instructed to say is superior to any in that street—and took one in the town of Handley Cross, in order, as he said, to be nearer the Hunt. His acts there became of the wildest and most eccentric description : he arrayed himself in a scarlet coat with a blue collar, something like a general postman's, and rode about the country, surrounded by dogs, whooping and holloaing, and blowing a horn : he converted the festivals, which had formerly been few and of periodical occurrence—something, I presume, like the Epping Hunt, of which you all have probably heard—he converted them, I say, into a regular downright matter of daily business, and whoever did not join him was treated with contempt, and if any one over whose land he trespassed in riotous confusion dared to remonstrate, he was laughed to scorn, or threatened with violence.

" I can hardly expect you to credit the assertion, that men moving in the higher walks of life,—men to whom the public are wont to look for precept and example, abandoned their lawful callings and the elegances of life, and joined the infatuated train of this unfortunate gentleman. Train bands of men in scarlet moved about the country, striking terror into the minds of elderly ladies, and disturbing the peaceful course of husbandry and trade. Wherever it was known that one of these field-meetings was to be held, it was made in open defiance of the statute against ' riots, routs, or unlawful assemblies ; ' trade was suspended, and the plough stood still. If any one were inclined to censure the present proceedings, or stigmatise it as an act of harshness and severity, I would here entreat him to pause and consider the position in which this deluded,—this unhappy individual has been placing himself and his followers. So far from continuing of that opinion, I think, he will hail it as one of the brightest, most beautiful blessings of our jurisprudence, that the law steps in through the medium of a next-of-kin, and rescues a man from the consequences of his own unhappy rashness. The wasteful, profligate expenditure of his substance is not the only charge against Mr. Jorrocks ; he has outraged the law of the land, and sought the vengeance of offended justice.

" Gentlemen of the jury," continued Mr. Martin Moonface, very slowly and deliberately, " Jorrocks is, to all intents and purposes, a rioter. So far back as the year 1797, if there is any truth in Chitty's Criminal Law, a person was indicted for the ancient and apparently harmless custom of kicking about footballs on Shrove Tuesday at Kingston-upon-Thames ; and surely that will bear no comparison with the military spectacles that this gentleman's eccentricity has lately presented to the astonished county in which they took place. The law upon the case I take it to be quite clear. It says, when three persons or more shall assemble themselves together, with an intent mutually to assist one another in the execution of some enterprise of a private nature to the manifest terror of the people, whether the act were of itself lawful or unlawful—mark that, gentlemen, I pray you—whether the act were of itself lawful or unlawful, if they only *meet* to such a purpose or intent, although they shall after depart of their own accord, without doing anything, this is an unlawful assembly ; and if after their first meeting they shall move forward towards the execution of any such act, whether they put their intended purpose in execution or not, this, according to the general opinion, is a *rout ;* and if they execute such a thing indeed, then it is a *riot.* In Clifford *v.* Brandon, 2 Campbell, page 370, Chief Justice Mansfield laid it down, that if any person encourages, or promotes, or takes part in riots, whether by words, signs, or gestures, or by wearing the badge or ensign—mark that, gentlemen—by wearing the badge or ensign—which assuredly all the followers of this unfortunate individual did—to wit, scarlet coats with blue collars—he is himself to be considered a rioter; for in this case all are principals. So that you see Jorrocks has not only placed himself in jeopardy, but all those whose wildness, weakness, or wickedness, induced them to join the phalanx round his standard.

" What was the cause of its supineness I know not, but government certainly permitted these outrages; and during the whole of last winter, up to the very outburst of spring, Mr. Jorrocks continued this extraordinary career, without let, suit, molestation, hindrance, or interruption.

During the whole of that time he never once visited the city of London, or his commercial concerns in St. Botolph's Lane, or seemed to recollect that he had anything to attend to but these hunt-festivals or meetings.

" The expense of the establishment is wholly incalculable, embracing, as it does, items of most miscellaneous and extraordinary description—hay, straw, corn, beans, bran, curry-combs, dandy-brushes, brooms, balls, pails, pitchforks, whipcord, coals, wood, oil, nitre, sulphur, Epsom salts, oatmeal, horse-flesh, farrier, saddler, wheelbarrows, soap, linen, and a hundred other items.

" Nor were Mr. Jorrocks's eccentricities and extravagances confined to the day-time. I am instructed that public dinners were held, at which he was in the chair, avowedly for the purpose of promoting and organising

I I

these illegal meetings; speeches were delivered in praise of them, songs were composed in honour of their doings by day, and night brought no rest to the unquiet spirits that reigned triumphant at Handley Cross.

"Spring, it appears, puts an end to these hunt-festivals or meetings ; and one would naturally infer, that with the close of them would end the tom-foolery of the business. Not so with Mr. Jorrocks. He convened a public meeting of all the disorderly inhabitants of Handley Cross, and delivered a speech or lecture in praise of himself and his doings, and in eulogy of the unaccountable amusement that has brought him into this unhappy position. It is true that other matters were mixed up in his speech; but the very jumble of which it was composed bears evidence of a highly disordered imagination, and he stated that his feelings on the point were too acute to admit of his adhering closely to the text he had prescribed for his oration.

"After this, Mr. Jorrocks returned to his house in Great Coram Street, and resumed his attendance in St. Botolph Lane with his former punctuality, to the great joy of his friends, who began to flatter themselves that he had fairly got over his frenzy ; when, unfortunately, it broke out with redoubled violence. The first symptoms of it were visible on the morning of the 2nd of October. He had been taking his usual ride in the Regent's Park, when the sight of some black and blighted dahlias, hanging their heads, and drooping in all directions, completely upset his philosophy. It was not the sudden destruction of these bright and many-coloured beauties that struck the feeling chord of a too sensible imagination, and conjured up mournful reflections on the precarious tenure of all earthly endearments, for far different, I grieve to say, were his thoughts on that occasion. 'Hurrah! blister my kidneys!' exclaimed he in delight, 'it *is* a frost !— the dahlias are dead !' Gentlemen of the jury," continued Mr. Martin Moonface, throwing up his arms, and putting himself in the attitude of a spread eagle, "can you imagine a sane man indulging in such an exclamation on such an occasion? 'Hurrah! blister my kidneys! it *is* a frost ! —the dahlias are dead !' And so, because Jenkins's dahlias were cut down by the frost, Jorrocks saw cause to rejoice at the circumstance— unfortunate individual ! "

"You are another indiwidual !" roared Mr. Jorrocks, in a rage at being considered a subject for Mr. Martin Moonface's pity.

[The commissioners interpose with great gravity, amid the uproarious laughter of the spectators ; and Mr. Jorrocks eyes Mr. Martin Moonface as though he would eat him.]

"Well, then, gentlemen of the jury, as I was observing, the sight of these weather-stricken dahlias had such an effect upon his imagination— and awful, indeed, is it to contemplate such a visitation—that instead of pursuing his ride, as he was wont to do, one-and-twenty times round the inner circle, he immediately turned his horse's head towards home, ate a hurried breakfast, and set off by the Lilywhite-sand Railway for Handley Cross, without giving the slightest intimation to his poor distracted wife, whose feelings may be imagined but can never be described, and without sending any notification whatever to his partners in St. Botolph Lane. Three bills of exchange, to a large amount, were presented for payment that day, one being for oatmeal supplied at Handley Cross, of which his partners knew nothing; and the consequence was that a protest became necessary, to the injury alike of his private character and his mercantile reputation. True it is that the following day he wrote a few hurried lines, ordering his servant, Benjamin Brady, to be sent down; and I will now proceed to relate the purpose for which he wanted him, and it is hence that the present inquiry more immediately originates. It appears, that by some unaccountable mystery the sight of these withered dahlias had conjured up recollections of the hunt-festivals of the previous winter, and, determining to eclipse all his former doings, he had gone down to Handley Cross to inspect a numerous progeny of puppies that he had had scattered about the country, which he intended to add to the extensive retinue of the previous season, and which a man he has in his pay, called Pigg, had been left in the charge of.

"On his arrival at Handley Cross, it appeared that a disease had broken out among the horses of that place, which ended in the deaths of very many. Among others, Mr. Flasher, the gentleman coachman of the Handley Cross 'True Blue Spankaway,' lost eighteen; Mr. Giles Eden, a post-master, lost ten; Mr. Duncan Nevin, four; and various other people lost smaller numbers, amounting, in the aggregate, to fifty-three. Now it would appear, so far as any deduction can be drawn from the conduct of individuals in the unhappy state of this unfortunate gentleman, that on leaving home it was his intention to return either the same or on the following day; but, hearing of the deaths of these horses had altered his determination, and he resolved to endeavour to turn the misfortunes of others to some advantage to himself; and, certainly, he adopted a system that no one but himself would ever have thought of. He commenced a negotiation with the owners of the dead horses—fifty-three in number, I beg you to remember—and bought up the whole at an average of nine shillings and sixpence a-head, hide and all. And, gentlemen of the jury, what do you think he did with them?—buried them under apple-trees? —retailed them to cat's-meat mongers?—dragged them away to distant places to rot without tainting the air? No such thing! He skinned and stacked them for winter use!—actually *stacked* the dead bodies of fifty-three horses that had died of disease in the precincts of the town of Handley Cross! Was there ever such a thing heard of? I ask, was it likely such a thing could be tolerated? Certainly not! The authorities —the churchwardens, overseers, constables, &c., interfered—a fracas took place between them and Mr. Jorrocks and his men, while in the act of stacking, which ended in the stackers being captured and taken before the magistrates of Handley Cross. The sequel of the story it is needless to trouble you with. Your intelligent minds cannot require more than evidence of the facts I have imperfectly laid before you to enable you to arrive at the only conclusion that is open on such an occasion. Remember, gentlemen, this is not a case entailing on any party the infliction of punishment from the law; it is a simple question of domestic policy, performed in public, for the safety of the subject. We ask you to save this unfortunate gentleman from himself, and from the consequence of his own acts —in fact, to save him from ruin, and keep him in affluence. After the patient attention with which you have honoured me, I cannot for a moment doubt that the circumstances I have related have made the impression on your minds that they must have made on the minds of every one open to conviction ; and though you might not consider the exhibition he made of himself as master of the hunt revels, the profligate expenditure of his substance in support of his fictitious dignity, the tenor of his lectures, taken singly, of sufficient weight to warrant you in depriving him of the management of his affairs, yet, collectively, that they are amply sufficient, even without that great, that crowning feat of all—the stacking of dead horses —to the danger of the lives of Her Majesty's liege subjects.

"With your permission, then, I will proceed to call witnesses to substantiate the statements I have made."

The commissioners here intimated they would like to retire for a few minutes ; and during their absence, the court became a scene of great uproar, Mr. Jorrocks protesting at the top of his voice against the whole proceedings, inquiring most emphatically—" 'Ow vas I to know, wen I stacked the 'osses, that it was a goin' to turn 'ot weather again ? " The return of the commissioners restored silence, who having got settled in their seats, Mr. Moonface, with great dignity, exclaimed, "Call Tony Lumpkin ; " whereupon a diminutive apology of a man skipped into the witness-box, and, being sworn, proceeded to give evidence, of which the following is the material outline :—Is a tailor at Handley Cross and Cranbourne Alley, London ; has had an establishment in the former place about three years. Remembers Mr. Jorrocks's entry into Handley Cross when he came to take possession of the hounds, and heard his speech from the balcony at the Dragon Inn—understood the general purport of it, but not the detail. Made him a sky-blue coat lined with pink silk, and two pair of canary-coloured shorts ; also changed the green collar of a scarlet coat into a blue one—understood the green collar was the costume of some other hunt. Often saw him going out with the hounds, but never accompanied him—has no curiosity that way. Might have forty or fifty dogs with him at a time, of different colours—prevailing colour, he thinks, was drab—there might be some buff ones among them.

Cross-examined.—Had a quarrel with Mr. Jorrocks after he made the clothes ; not because Mr. Jorrocks considered them ill-made, but because he insisted on witness going out to hunt. Cannot ride. Was paid for the clothes, less the discount. Did not consider Mr. Jorrocks insane because he paid for them. Never said he was cracked or insane. Made sky-blue coats and canary-coloured shorts for many other gentlemen. Perhaps thirty or thirty-five others. Some paid, some didn't—lived in hope. Some of the hounds might be blue. Thinks there were no green ones among them, but is not sure.

Re-examined.—Might have said Mr. Jorrocks was flighty. Meant that he rode fast ; not that he was mad.

Miss Sniffle, a maiden lady, was next sworn.—Lives at Handley Cross, and has done so for the last twelvemonth, for the benefit of the waters. Keeps a pony chaise and a boy to drive it. Boy wears a gold band, and a red stripe down his trousers ; many buttons like peppermint-drops. Remembers the 13th of December ; was coming along the Appledove Road, and met an immense procession ; many men in scarlet, some in black, but most in scarlet ; was dreadfully alarmed. There might be an hundred horsemen · never saw such a sight in her life. Mr. Jorrocks

Pigg in the Melon Frame.

rode second in the procession. A man in a black velvet cap and a scarlet coat rode a little in advance of him. Mr. Jorrocks wore a broad-brimmed hat. Did not see the hounds; might have been there without her observing them.

Cross-examined.—Was staying at Handley Cross for the benefit of the waters, she said, not for the benefit of a husband; does not want one. Is on her oath, and swears she was dreadfully alarmed. Was alarmed at the whole thing, not at Mr. Jorrocks's winking at her as she passed. Did wink at her certainly. Swears she did not drive in that direction to meet the hounds. Could have turned back when she saw them coming, but her presence of mind forsook her. Would not say whether she had ever been forsaken before or not. Never said Mr. Jorrocks was mad. Came there to state her alarm. Would be alarmed at a herd of cattle. Open to alarm generally.

Re-examined.—Had heard Mr. Jorrocks was deranged. Thinks her maid told her first. Believes Miss Dumpling's maid told her maid, or Miss Freezer's maid told Miss Dumpling's maid, who told her maid. Might have said she thought his attics badly furnished. Meant it in the literal sense, if she did say so.

Peter Savoy, market-gardener and green-grocer, sworn and examined. —Lives at Mountjoy, five miles from Handley Cross, where he occupies garden ground and a field or two. Remembers the 24th of December. Mr. Jorrocks's hounds met at the toll-bar on the Cadby road. Witness was working among his winter cabbages, when his attention was attracted to the cry of dogs, which grew louder and louder; presently three or four entered the garden at the east end, near where there is a watering-place for cattle, and almost at the same moment a loud crash among the glass at the other end attracted his notice, and he saw a man in a black cap and scarlet coat, and a brown horse, over head in a melon-frame. Ran to take the man for the trespass, and seized him by the collar, when the man struck him a violent blow in the face and made his nose bleed. Mr. Jorrocks, who had come up in the meantime, stood erect in his stirrups, looking over the fence just by the melon-frame, encouraging the man, and blowing a horn to drown his cries for assistance. Has no doubt whatever he would have been killed but for the timely arrival of help.

Cross-examined.—The man was not on the horse when he saw them in the melon-frame. Would appear to have thrown a somerset, and parted company in flying over the fence. Will swear it was a man and not a boy. The blow was heavy and stunned him. Mr. Jorrocks appeared to be encouraging him, crying, " Have at him my beauty! have at him, my darling! " and blowing his horn. Never told Tom Straw, the ostler at the Dragon, that Mr. Jorrocks kept crying, " Go it, Binjamin! Go it, Binjamin! " Was not present at the meet of the hounds in the morning. Never was at one. Had never either hunted or gambled in his life. The melon-frame was much injured. Had not been paid the damage in full. The account was disputed. If it had been discharged, does not know that he might have been there. Will not swear that he was in fear of his life. Had had many conversations with Mr. Jorrocks on the subject of the melon-frame, but never could

obtain any final satisfaction.   Does not know what the hounds were
after, or that a fox had passed through his garden.   One of the objections Mr. Jorrocks made to pay the price he set upon his melon-frame
was, that the witness had lost them the fox by stopping his man.   Should
say Mr. Jorrocks was not "all there," though he would not go so far as
to say he was mad.

James Greenwood.—Is one of the keepers of the Regent's Park.
Lives at the Park Crescent Lodge, and the inner circle is within the

bounds of his jurisdiction.   Knows Mr. Jorrocks well, and has been
acquainted with him for many years—perhaps ten or a dozen.
Mr. Jorrocks has been in the habit of riding in the inner circle all that
time, almost every morning throughout the summer season.   Generally
comes in about seven o'clock, getting on a little later as the autumn
advances.   Canters round and round, perhaps eight or ten times, and

then walks his 'oss away. Witness has often conversed with him; generally before he began cantering, or after he was done. The canter might have been a gallop. Does not know the difference. Had never received any complaints against Mr. Jorrocks for furious riding. Once had a complaint against him for winking at a nursery-governess. Believes he winks at the nursery-maids; but witness does not consider it any business of his. Their conversation is generally about dogs and 'osses. Understands he has a great collection of dogs somewhere. Once offered witness a mount to go out with the Surrey; but witness cannot ride. Considers Mr. Jorrocks a very agreeable gentleman. Remembers him once riding his 'oss into the ring with a blanket under the saddle. Told witness the 'oss had the tic-douloureux. The blanket was folded when he entered the ring, but Mr. Jorrocks let it down about the 'oss's sides before he began to canter. Remembers the morning of the 2nd of October. There had been a sharp frost during the night, and the leaves of many of the shrubs had changed colour in consequence. It was a fine bright morning, and Mr. Jorrocks overtook him on the bridge by the Archery ground, as witness was on his way to the inner circle. They began talking about the frost. Mr. J. thought it had not been so severe as witness represented. Witness showed him a cherry-tree, the leaves of which were quite red, also a purple beech that had turned copper colour. Mr. Jorrocks seemed much pleased, and as they entered the circle he exclaimed, as he looked over the nursery-ground palings, "Hurrah! blister my kidneys, it *is* a frost! the dahlias are dead!" Did not continue his ride, but after a pause of a few seconds gave witness half-a-crown, and cantered away. Had not seen him again until he met him on the stairs of this court.

Cross-examined.—Many gentlemen canter their 'osses round and round the Regent's Park, but not many round the inner circle. Never thought there was any thing odd in Mr. Jorrocks doing so. When witness told Mr. Jorrocks the nursery-governess had complained of his winking at her, he said he did it to clear the circle of her, for she was so hugly she frightened his 'oss. The nursery-maids are all fond of Mr. Jorrocks,— he generally carries barley-sugar in his pockets for the children. Does not know whether it is in the shape of kisses or not. Many old gentlemen wink at the maids—some pinch them in passing. Does not know that pinching is altogether right, but should not interfere without a complaint. Witness thinks it was a reddish-coloured 'oss that Mr. Jorrocks said had the tic-douloureux. Grooms are not allowed to exercise 'osses in clothing in the Regent's Park. Thinks it probable an 'oss would sweat sooner with a blanket about it than without one. Does not know the object of sweating an 'oss. Mr. Jorrocks never talked to witness about dahlias,— has heard him inquire after the potato-tops,—asked whether they were black or not. Seemed always very anxious for winter—has heard him say, if he had his own way, he would strike summer out of the almanack. Once proposed to witness that they should publish an almanack between them, and omit summer altogether,—said, in a general way, summer was merely inserted as a sort of compliment,—three 'ot days and a thunder-storm being the general amount of an English summer. Never considered Mr. Jorrocks mad—mad gentlemen generally walk in cloaks,—some ride, and have their keepers on 'oss-back in livery after them,—those are of the richer class. Does not suppose every gentleman he sees with a groom insane, but considers it suspicious. Sets every man he sees in the Regent's Park in a cloak, down for mad, and no mistake. Sees a good many mad gentlemen in the course of the year—they chiefly live in the Alpha Cottages on the west side of the Park. Considers Mr. Jorrocks quite the reverse of insane.

John Strong.—Is constable, and one of the churchwardens of the parish of St. James, Handley Cross. Remembers the 3rd of October, ———. Michael Brown, one of the churchwardens, called upon him, and told him that Mr. Jorrocks of London was down, and employing carts to collect all the dead horses, and that they were leading them to Grant's paddock, just at the back of the Methodist chapel. Went together to inspect the premises—found carts coming in from all quarters with dead horses, and three or four men skinning them. Mr. Jorrocks was not present. Witness returned to his house, and after a consultation with the other churchwardens, wrote Mr. J. the following note :—

"The churchwardens of the parish of St. James, Handley Cross, present their respectful compliments to Mr. Jorrocks, and having heard that you have bought all the dead horses in Handley Cross, desire to be informed what purpose you intend putting them to.

"Your humble Servant,
"To J. Jorrocks, Esq."   "JOHN STRONG.

Sent the beadle in his gold-laced coat, cocked hat, and staff, with it. He found Mr. Jorrocks in the paddock, superintending the stacking of the carcasses, which were placed one upon another like a stack. Mr. Jorrocks having read the note, took a pencil out of his pocket-book, and wrote at the bottom :—

"Soup! soup!

"Yours, &c.,
"J. J."

and re-directed the note to the churchwardens. Witness and the other churchwardens made a second visit of inspection, about three o'clock, and finding the stack was getting very high, wrote a second note, headed :—

"VICTORIA REX.

"The churchwardens and overseer of the parish of St. James, Handley Cross, hereby require you to desist and abate the nuisance you are now creating in Grant's paddock, by stacking sundry dead horses, or he will proceed against you according to the form of the statute in that case made and provided, and against the peace of our Sovereign Lady the Queen, her crown and dignity.

(Signed)   "JOHN STRONG,
                         "M. BROWN,
                         "T. HOGGINS,
"To Mr. J. Jorrocks."   "Churchwardens.

Witness sent this note per beadle, in state, as before, who found the stack nearly finished, and a man and a boy dressing off the top with horses' heads. Mr. J. took the note as before, and wrote at the bottom :—

" You be ——

"Yours, &c.,
"J. J."

saying, as he handed it back, " Peace of our Sovereign Lady the Queen, indeed! Wictoria must have a werry good nose if she can wind this at Windsor."

The special constables were then called out, and after a desperate conflict, succeeded in capturing Mr. Jorrocks, James Pigg, and Benjamin.

Cross-examined.—There had been a sharp frost at Handley Cross for two or three days before Mr. Jorrocks's arrival,—seemed as if we were going to have an early winter. The mortality among the horses was very sudden, they all died within a short time of each other. Had an idea that Mr. Jorrocks was buying the horses up to feed his hounds upon. Don't understand about hounds. Does not know how many hounds he keeps, or whether they could eat a horse for breakfast, another for dinner, and another for supper. Will not swear that Mr. Jorrocks bought the whole fifty-three horses that died—knows that there were a great many by the size of the stack. It was in the usual form of a corn-stack, and the slope of the top was formed of horses' heads put lengthways, so that the rain might run off down their noses. Was very cleverly made. Had a novel appearance. Many people came to see it. Flesh may keep a month or six weeks, but witness does not know that it will. Supposing the hounds to consume three horses a-day, and the flesh to keep for a month, does not know that Mr. Jorrocks's act was otherwise than prudent.

Sebastian Mello, whose name had been called, and bellowed, and vociferated up-stairs and down, and along the passages after the examination of each witness, having announced his arrival by sending his card up-stairs by a powdered footman, vacated his brougham, and, proceeding up-stairs, tendered himself for examination on behalf of the promoters of the inquiry. Sebastian was got up with uncommon care, and the most scrupulous nicety. His yellow silken locks flowed over his coat-collar, exhibiting the boldness of his forehead and the regularity of his features. He was dressed in studied black, with a snow-white cravat, whose tie entwined among the four lace-frills of a curiously-wrought shirt-front. He wore lace ruffles at his wrists, and a massive diamond ring on his right-hand little finger, and a beautiful pearl one on his left, while the corner of a richly embroidered cambric handkerchief peeped from the breast-pocket of his coat.

Mutual salutations being exchanged between Mr. Moonface and Mr. Mello, the former began his examination with the following inquiry,—

" You are, I believe, Mr. Sebastian Mello, a physician in very extensive practice at Handley Cross Spa ? "

"I am," replied Mr. Mello, with a slight inclination of the head.

"And you have, I believe, resided there for a considerable length of time?" continued Mr. Moonface.

"I have," answered Mr. Mello.

"In short, you are the principal resident, or head of the place, I believe?"

"I am," said Mr. Mello.

"Now, then, sir, would you have the kindness to tell the jury what you know respecting the unfortunate gentleman, Mr. Jorrocks, whose case we are met here to inquire into?"

"Excuse me, sir, if before I answer your inquiry I take the liberty of correcting your description of the person referred to. If the individual you allude to is John Jorrocks, whom I see sitting there," looking at Mr. J. with great disdain, "I should say, a person conducting himself as he has done is unworthy the flattering appellation with which you have honoured him."

"True," observed Mr. Moonface; "but, for the sake of brevity, perhaps you would condescend to waive that point, and inform us what you know about him."

"Know about him!" replied Mr. Mello, with a toss of his flowing head and a curl of his lip; "I really know nothing about him, further than that he is a great nuisance. He came to Handley Cross the beginning of last winter, ever since when the place has been in a state of tumult, and the religious portion of the community sadly scandalised and terribly annoyed. For my own part, I have suffered all sorts of indignities at his hands. Besides his ravenous hounds, he keeps a pugnacious peacock that kills all the poultry in the place.

"He took it into his head to stroll every day with his flock of dogs and servants into the open immediately below the front of my house, where he would stay for hours, surrounded by all the riff-raff and irreligious people of the place. Because I stated that my piety was outraged, he got a wild beast-show established there, and paid the band five shillings for every hour they played after nine o'clock at night. The anonymous letters I received were extraordinarily numerous, and full of the most insulting expressions; and when I refused to take them in, baskets and boxes began pouring in by the railway and coaches, containing dead-cats, donkey-haunches, broken dishes, and other rubbish. I never saw John Jorrocks out hunting, but I understand his general conduct is of the most extraordinary and extravagant description, and his proceedings subversive of morality and true religion—only to be palliated on the score of downright insanity. I consider him a mischievous maniac."

"You're a warmint!" growled Mr. Jorrocks, stuffing a ham sandwich into his mouth.

"Go it, Ned!" continued he in the same strain, as Mr. Moonface, having extracted as much as he wanted out of the doctor, sat down, in order to let his "learned friend" endeavour to counteract what he had said, by cross-examination.

"And so you are a physician in a great way of practice, are you?" drawled Mr. Coltman, through his nose, in a careless, colloquial sort of style, as if he meant to have a good deal of conversation with Mello before he was done.

"I am," replied Sebastian Mello, with a slight tinge of red on his countenance.

"You are sure of that?" asked Mr. Coltman, carelessly turning over the pages of his brief, as if he were thinking of something else.

A PRESENT TO DR. MELLO.

"I am," replied Mr. Mello.

"*You are!*" rejoined Mr. Coltman, looking him full in the face. "Now, sir," said he, very slowly, "do you mean to *assert that?* Do you mean to say you have ever taken a degree?"

"I mean to assert, sir, that I am a physician in full practice."

"Will you, *on your oath, sir*, say that you are a regularly qualified and admitted physician? *On your oath, sir*, will you say it?"

Mr. Sebastian Mello was silent.

"Will you, sir, swear?" continued the inexorable Mr. Coltman, "that you have any diploma, save what your own assurance and the credulity of your patients has conferred upon you?"

Mr. Mello was silent.

Mr. Coltman, throwing out his hands, made a pantomimic appeal to the jury with his eyes, and then, with a waive of his head, motioned Mr. Mello to retire.

"Werry good," growled Mr. Jorrocks, thrusting the last ham sandwich into his mouth.

This was the case of the promoters; and a waiter, with a napkin twisted round his thumb, having whispered something in the ear of the chief commissioner, the learned gentleman looked at his watch, and immediately adjourned the court.

CHAPTER LXVII.

THE COMMISSION RESUMED.

THE court resumed its sittings next morning at nine o'clock precisely, and as soon as the doors were open such a rush of people forced their way in, that every seat and place was occupied, and some time elapsed ere room was obtained for the counsel and professional gentlemen engaged in the inquiry. Mr. Jorrocks was accommodated with a seat in the reporters' place, immediately behind his counsel. The jury having all answered to their names, and silence being at length obtained, Serjeant Horsefield rose to address the jury. He spoke in so low a tone of voice at the commencement, that it was with difficulty the reporters could catch what he said; but, with his usual urbanity, he obligingly supplied the deficiency by revising their reports.

"Gentlemen of the jury," said he, "if my learned friend, Mr. Martin Moonface, with his splendid talents and vast acquirements, rose under circumstances of difficulty and embarrassment, how much greater must be my perplexity, in introducing myself to your notice, to attempt to grapple with and rebut the grave and voluminous charges with which his speech has loaded the inquiry, standing as I do without the manifold advantages of which my learned friend is so pre-eminently possessed? The learned gentleman well observed, that nothing but that high sustaining power— a moral consciousness of right—could induce any member of our profession to undertake the conduct of a case, and I claim for myself the same degree of credit for a similar assertion that my learned friend bespoke for himself. I ask—I implore you, gentlemen of the jury—I beseech you, as enlightened—as able—as conscientious citizens, to regard my assertions and my protestations of sincerity in the same light—and give them the same weight that you have given to the assertions and asseverations of my learned friend." Here the learned gentleman made a long pause.

At length he resumed. "In opening this great and important case— great, I may call it, for it involves the liberty of many of the aristocracy of this country, and important it most certainly is, as regards the position of my most respectable client—my learned friend, Mr. Martin Moonface, introduced Mr. Jorrocks with an exordium upon the singularity of his name. I will not imitate the example of my learned friend, or speculate on the difference a change of name might have produced, but I will endeavour closely and sedulously to apply myself, and the best energies of which I am possessed, to the real merits and peculiarities of the case. As mercantile men, you are doubtless, many of you, acquainted with the exalted position occupied by my client in the commercial world; and if I can show—as show I believe I undoubtedly can—that the amusement which he now follows is not incompatible with the honest, industrious habits and occupations of a British merchant, I feel confident I shall receive a verdict at your hands. My client, as you may see," pointing to Mr. Jorrocks in the reporters' place, " is one, whose hey-day of youth has been succeeded by the autumn of maturer years ; and shall I surmise for one moment in the presence of a jury, drawn from the very heart of this, the first city of the world—that a man entering trade binds himself irrevocably to the counter—with no bright prospect of affluence and ease to gild the evening of his days, flitting in the vision of his mental horizon ? Is a ' youth of labour ' no longer to be crowned ' with an age of ease ? ' Are the toils, the cares, the speculations, the enterprises of a British merchant to end but with his death ? Is trade, in short, to be regarded as but another name for perpetual slavery ? That, gentlemen, is the real question in its pure, unadulterated form, divested of the technicalities— freed from the mystifications and jargon—with which my learned friend's logic and eloquence have attempted to envelope it. How stands the matter ?

" Five-and-thirty years ago, my client, John Jorrocks, entered the firm of Grubbins, Muggins, Potts, Crow, and Tims, wholesale grocers in St. Botolph's Lane. Mr. Jorrocks was then, gentlemen, just out of his apprenticeship, which he had served with such credit to himself and satisfaction to the firm, that they took him into partnership the moment they were able, and the firm then became Grubbins, Muggins, Potts, Crow, Tims, and Jorrocks. Gentlemen, Grubbins and Muggins shortly after paid the debt of nature ; but so great was the attention and ability of my client, that, instead of adding the number these deplorable events deprived the firm of, by fresh partners, Crow and Jorrocks divided the duties of one partner between them, and took in Mr. Simpkins, who had long filled the office of western traveller, and the partnership deed was then drawn out in the names of Potts, Crow, Tims, Jorrocks, and Simpkins. I need not follow my respectable client through the long labyrinth of years that followed, or through the weary mazes of commercial transactions and speculations which throve under his auspices ;—suffice it to say, that revolving years found Mr. Jorrocks constant and sedulous at his warehouse, until the man who entered as the junior partner of the house stood at the head of a firm so long and so extensive, that it became necessary to condense its name under the title of Jorrocks & Co. I will give my learned friend the benefit of the admission, that for many years my client was in the habit of devoting his Saturdays to what Mr. Moonface calls hunt-festivals, and I will also give him the benefit of the admission that the county of Surrey was the arena of his operations. So far back as during the management of Mr. Maberly, my client's name appears as a subscriber to the Surrey hunt, and the same punctuality of payment characterises this matter that characterises all his other transactions. My learned friend commenced with a broad general rule, that any man following a pursuit at variance with trade must necessarily follow it to the detriment of the former, forgetting all the while, that though in trade, Mr. Jorrocks is so far independent of it as to be able to recreate himself, how and when he pleases, just as though he never had anything to do with it. But, gentlemen of the jury, though you, and I, and Mr. Martin Moonface, may not be aware of it, I am instructed to state that hunting is not only compatible with trade, but may even be followed with advantageous results."

" So it may ! " exclaimed Mr. Jorrocks ; " so it may ! werry good ! say it's the sport of kings ; the image of war, without————" " *Order, order, order !* " cried all three commissioners at once. " Really, Mr. Jorrocks," observed the chief, " we shall have to order you out of court if you persist in interrupting counsel." " Now do, Mr. Jorrocks," interposed the learned Sergeant, very mildly, " let me argue your case for you, or else take it in hand entirely yourself ; for between us we shall make nothing of it."

" True," replied Mr. Jorrocks, " true ; too many cooks always spoil the broth ; but just say now that 'unting is the sport of kings, the image of war without its guilt, and only five-and-twenty per cent of its danger."

" But though I make this statement broadly and unequivocally," continued the learned Serjeant, without noticing Mr. Jorrocks's suggestion, " I take a still higher ground, and say that my client's means entitle him to follow what pursuit he pleases, regardless of all pecuniary considerations. He is a wealthy man ; and unless the promoters of this inquiry can show that he is spending such a sum upon the maintenance of his dogs as involves a probability of injury—injury of such an extent, mind you, as to amount almost to utter ruin—unless they can do this, I say, the success of their case is absolutely hopeless. This, gentlemen, I defy the promoters of this inquiry to do. I hold in my hand a number of an able work, by Mr. Blaine, who says, ' that the practice of field-sporting is both convenient and useful we presume may be made evident, and it is only when these rural amusements are followed so unceasingly as to rob us of that time, wealth, and energy, which were given us for other purposes, that the pursuit of them can be censured.' *Censured*, gentlemen, you observe, is the term ; so that even if Mr. Jorrocks had devoted both day and night, and the whole of his income and energy, to the amusement of hunting, *censure*, and not a commission of lunacy to deprive him of the management of his affairs, would be all that he merited.

" But let me proceed a little farther with this author. ' The severest moralist must allow,' says Mr. Blaine, ' that worldly wealth is a desirable possession ; but when the miser brings upon himself premature decay, by the extent of his daily toils and nightly speculations to amass riches which he neither uses himself nor permits others to enjoy, the impartial observer sees in his conduct a flagrant abuse of wealth :—warped by his cupidity, he is poor in the midst of his plenty, and remains fast locked in the embraces of Want, that very fiend he supposes himself to be ever flying from.' So that you see, gentlemen, so far from Mr. Jorrocks's pastime being fitting subject of censure, it even becomes matter of encomium and recommendation. My pursuits, like those of my learned friend's on the other side, have been of such a nature as to afford me but little insight into the detail of these hunting proceedings. I believe, however, my learned friend was right in describing a hunt-establishment to consist of a multitude of dogs, over which the head or chief reigns supreme. It is, I believe, the business of the establishment to muster at a certain hour of a morning, and then find a fox or other wild animal, who leads the mounted field a gallop across a country ; and those who know the pleasure there is in being proudly borne on the back of a noble generous horse can appreciate the sensation of delight that must be experienced in riding at the head of a vast assembly, composed of all the choice and gallant spirits of the land. The very thought is exhilarating ! The clear sky above, the wide expanse of country around, the refreshing air, the jovial spirits, the neighing steeds and chiding hounds, all in one rush of indescribable joy ! Who does not exclaim with Shakspeare,

> 'I was with Hercules and Cadmus once,
> When in the wood of Crete they bayed the bear
> With hounds of Sparta: never did I hear
> Such gallant chiding; for, besides the groves,
> The skies, the fountains, every region near,
> Seem'd all one mutual cry : I never heard
> So musical a discord, such sweet thunder ! ' "

" Bravo ! " exclaimed Mr. Jorrocks, " werry good indeed—werry good indeed ; say it's the sport of kings, the image of ——." The commissioners again interpose, and vow they will turn Mr. Jorrocks out, or commit him for contempt of court. The sergeant again acts as mediator, Mr. Jorrocks growling something about " werry 'ard that a man mightn't kick up a row in his own court ! "

" But shall it be," continued the learned Serjeant, " because a man enters into and enjoys the enlivening scene,—because for a time he casts off the cares of the counter, and ' this every-day working world,' and roves unfettered in Nature's wildest, most sequestered scenes, that he is to be declared insane and incompetent to the management of his affairs ? Forbid it, reason ! Forbid it, ye nobler and more generous feelings of our nature ! Rather let us suppose, that, with mind refreshed and body strengthened, he returns to the peaceful occupations of his trade, grateful for the exercise he has enjoyed, and thankful for the means of partaking of it."

> " Better to rove in fields for 'ealth unbought,
> Than fee the doctor for a nasty draught ; "

observed Mr. Jorrocks to himself, in one of his whispers, which produced a roar of laughter, during a long pause the learned Serjeant made.

" My learned friend's feelings were shocked at Mr. Jorrocks's exultation at the sight of the drooping dahlias, and would fain draw a conclusion that a person who rejoiced at the return of winter must necessarily be insane ; but consider, gentlemen, before you adopt such an idea what might be your situation if the sight of the snowdrop or crocus, drawing from you an exclamation of delight at the sight of returning spring, was to deprive you of the management of your affairs, and, perhaps, of your liberty !

" All you have heard, the evidence of Lumpkin, the evidence of Sniffle,

—Miss Sniffle I should say, the evidence of Savoy, and the evidence of Greenwood, prove nothing but the devotion of Mr. Jorrocks to a highly popular pleasurable sport; and even the constable Strong, when detailing the act which principally caused the issuing of this commission, admitted that, for aught he knew to the contrary, the purchase and stacking of the horses was a prudent and commendable act. Fortunately, however, I am in a situation to prove that whatever Mr. Jorrocks has done in the way of management has been prudent and cautious, that his character is humane and moderate, and his uniform conduct all that can be desired of an honest grocer and a good man. My fervent hope is, that my excellent client may not suffer through the deficiency of his advocate. I am aware that I have not acquitted myself to the unfortunate gentleman—unfortunate in being placed in such a situation—in the manner I could have wished; but I feel confident, when you have heard the evidence I shall now proceed to offer, that you will come to the only conclusion open from the premises, namely, that Mr. Jorrocks is not only a rational, but a highly talented man."

A buzz of applause followed the close of the learned Serjeant's address, of which the foregoing is merely an outline, and the Court availed itself of the break in the proceedings to retire for a few minutes.

Mr. Jorrocks, whose spirits rose thirty per cent. with the eloquence of his advocate, now mounted upon the table, and, dancing about on one leg, declared he would "beat them arter all,"—offering to lay any one a guinea 'at to a sou'-wester that he did; upon which Pigg, seeing the Jury eyeing him, exclaimed, "Had the gob thou ard gouk." Whereupon nothing would serve Jorrocks but Pigg should sing them one of his national melodies,—should sing them,

"Unrivalled the 'ounds o'er which Jorrocks presides."

but Pigg was impervious, telling his master "he'd desarve arl he gat gin he went ramin' on that way."

CHAPTER LXVIII.

THE COURT RESUMÉS.

Mr. Serjeant Horsefield, having refreshed himself with a glass of sherry and a water biscuit, now rustles back into court; and all parties being again prepared, he glances at his brief and exclaims, "Call William Bower!" whereupon our versatile friend Bill emerges from a side room, or rather a closet, in which he had been ensconced, attired in the incongruous habiliments that theatrical people and cockneys consider peculiar to sportsmen. What a sight it is to see a fox-hunter put upon the stage! Mr. Bowker, who has come to assist his great patron out of trouble, by assuming the character of a fox-hunter at short notice, has got himself, as he thinks, becomingly up. He has on a pair of Mr. Jorrocks's drab shags and top-boots; and, as a red coat would be inappropriate in a court of justice, he preserves the character in a bright green one, with a black velvet collar, and a hare on a dead gold button, with a burnished rim. His capacious chest is covered with foxes' heads on a double-breasted, worsted-worked, brown waistcoat, and his green cashmere neckcloth is secured in front with a gilt coach-and-four brooch. He has a cane-whip stick in one hand, and a hat with a red cord to it in the other.

"You are, I believe, Mr. Bowker,—a great merchant?" said Serjeant Horsefield, eyeing him intently, as one does a person we think we have seen before.

"Head of the great house of Bowker and Co." replied Bill with a slight bend of his body, as he dived his forefinger and thumb into a massive gilt snuff-box set round with brilliants, and a huge mock diamond in the centre of the lid.

"And a great sportsman, I believe?" continued the Serjeant.

"And a great sportsman," repeated Bill, drawing the immense pinch off his thumb up his nose with a long and noisy sniff.

"You have hunted in many countries, I believe?" continued the Serjeant, "and are well acquainted with the minutiæ of the management of a pack of fox-hounds?"

"Perfectly so," replied Bill, twirling his hat-string round his forefinger.

"You are well acquainted with Mr. Jorrocks, the gentleman respecting whom we are met together this day?"

Mr. Bowker.—"Have known Mr. Jorrocks long and intimately."

"Then would you have the kindness to state to the Court your opinion generally of that gentleman?"

"My opinion generally," said Bill running his many-ringed fingers through his sandy locks; "my general opinion is—is—is—that he is *quite the gent.*"

"Ah! but the Court would like to know what you consider of him in relation to general life?"

"In relation to general life," repeated Bill; "I should say he is a very *good relation,*—good as a grandmother to me, I'm sure,—liberal— hospitable—dines at five and never waits for any one."

"I think you do not exactly understand the point I wish to arrive at. I wish you, as an old and intimate friend of Mr. Jorrocks, to state the impression that gentleman's general conduct creates in your mind."

Mr. Bowker.—"Mr. Jorrocks' general conduct, I should say, is very much the conduct of opulent merchants generally,—he takes care of the pence and lets the pounds take care of themselves,—he's very rich."

"Then you consider him a good man of business?"

"Capital man of business—double entry—cash at Christmas, bill-book off by heart, and so forth."

"And in his amusements you consider him sober and rational?"

"Oh, quite! He's president of our free-and-easy, chairman of the incorporated society of Good Fellows, and recorder of the Wide-awake Club."

Serjeant Horsefield.—"Are those high offices?"

"Undoubtedly so."

"And conferred on men of talent and standing?"

K K

"Undoubtedly so. A fool would never do for recorder of a wide-awake club."

Serjeant Horsefield.—"And in these clubs is he considered a wit ? "

Mr. Bowker (with emphasis).—"*Premier wag !* "

Serjeant Horsefield.—"Does he ever favour them with any of his literary performances ? "

"Frequently. Ode to April-fool's day; elegy on a giblet-pie that was smashed in coming from the baker's ; ode to the Lumber Troop, in most heroic measure; odes to—I don't know how many other things."

"You are, I believe, acquainted with his establishment at Handley Cross, and having, as you say, had considerable experience in hunting matters, will you favour the Court with your opinion of his set out ? "

"Certainly," replied Bill, tapping his boot, or rather Mr. Jorrocks' boot, with his Malacca cane-whip stick. "His set out is very good— *quite the go,* I should say."

"Is it larger or smaller than you have been accustomed to ? "

Mr. Bowker.—"Oh, smaller, decidedly. It's what we fox-hunters call a two-days-a-week establishment. Melton men hunt six days a-week, and think that too little.

"And a five or six-days-a-week establishment is larger than a two-days-a-week one."

Mr. Bowker.—"Undoubtedly so; more boots, more breeches—more breeches, more boots."

"And requires more horses and hounds ? "

"Undoubtedly so; more hounds, more horses—more horses, more hounds."

"And the larger the establishment, the greater the consumption of food ? "

"Of course; more hounds, more food—more food, more hounds."

"You have heard, I suppose, of Mr. Jorrocks's purchase of horses,—will you tell the Court your opinion of it ? "

Mr. Bowker.—"My opinion as to the merits of the bargain or the prospects of remuneration ? "

"No, your opinion of the policy of the step."

"Upon my word, it is a difficult question to answer. Speculation is the soul of commercial life, and it is only by ventures of this sort that men get rich. If Mr. J. bought the horses to sell as sausages, there is no doubt he would have cleared a considerable sum by the spec."

Serjeant Horsefield.—"No ; but confining it to the simple question of buying them for the purpose of feeding his hounds upon, what would you say of the prudence of such a step ? "

Mr. Bowker.—"Oh, I should say it was a very prudent step ; the war was sure to raise the price of horse-flesh, and Mr. J. was making himself independent of fluctuations and foreign markets."

"And you think there would not be more flesh than his hounds would require ? "

Mr. Bowker.—"Certainly not ; suppose they had half a horse for breakfast, a whole horse for dinner, and half a horse for supper. Let me see—one horse a-day is seven horses a-week, two horses a-day—two horses a-day is fourteen horses a week, fourteen horses a-week is fifty-six horses per calendar month, and fifty-six horses per calendar month is ——"

Serjeant Horsefield.—"Never mind any further calculation. Am I to understand, then, that you consider buying and stacking the horses was a prudent step on the part of Mr. Jorrocks?"

Mr. Bowker.—"Undoubtedly so;—war and all things considered, he must either have stacked or potted them."

"Pray, Mr. Bowker," inquired Mr. Smith, the Islington toy-shop-keeper, looking uncommonly wise, "may I inquire if Mr. Jorrocks is a Poor-law guardian?"

"No he's not," replied Mr. Bowker, with a sneer.

Mr. Martin Moonface now proceeded to take Bill in hand.

"I think I understood you to tell my learned friend that you are a great sportsman?" observed he.

"Right!" replied Bill, taking a huge pinch of snuff.

"Pray do you keep hounds yourself?"

Mr. Bowker (flattered by the supposition).—"No, sir, not at present at least."

Mr. Moonface.—"Then you *have* kept them?"

Mr. Bowker.—"Why, no, not exactly—thinking of it."

Mr. Moonface.—"It will depend, perhaps, upon the verdict of this case?"

Mr. Bowker (nodding).—"Perhaps so."

Mr. Moonface.—"Then you merely hunt with other people's hounds?"

Mr. Bowker.—"Merely hunt with other people's hounds."

Mr. Moonface.—"Pray whose hounds do you hunt with?"

Mr. Bowker.—"Oh, just any that come in the way,—the Queen's, Prince Albert's—Prince Albert's, the Queen's."

Mr. Moonface.—"Then you are not speaking from your own knowledge when you say Mr. Jorrocks' hounds would eat a brace of horses a-day?"

Mr. Bowker.—"Not of my own knowledge exactly."

Mr. Moonface.—"Then what made you say so?"

Mr. Bowker (looking rather disconcerted).—"Why, I suppose they must eat—couldn't hunt if they didn't eat."

Mr. Moonface.—"But might not they eat more than a brace of horses a-day?"

Mr. Bowker.—"Undoubtedly they might."

Mr. Moonface.—"Now might they not eat three just as well as two, for anything you knew to the contrary?"

Mr. Bowker.—"For anything I know to the contrary."

Mr. Moonface.—"Ah, but say yes or no."

Mr. Bowker.—"Yes or no?"

Mr. Moonface.—"Come, sir, don't fence with the question. I want you to give a direct negative or a direct affirmative to that question,—whether, for anything you know to the contrary, Mr. Jorrocks's hounds might not eat three horses a-day, as well as two."

"What! *five* a day?" replied Bill.

Mr. Moonface.—"No, sir;—might not Mr. Jorrocks's hounds eat three horses a-day for anything you know to the contrary?"

Mr. Bowker.—"Perhaps they might."

Mr. Moonface.—" Well now, sir, having got that question answered, let me ask you another."

" Certainly," interrupted Bill.

" What would be the value of each horse ? "

Mr. Bowker.—" Value of each horse!—how can I tell without seeing them ?   I give a couple of 'undred for some of mine."

" I'm talking of dead horses."

" I know nothing about dead horses—I'm not a Whitechapel knacker ! "

Mr. Moonface.—" Well, sir, but you talked just now of horseflesh rising in price in consequence of the war."

" That was *beef*ologically considered," replied Bill, with a smile.

Mr. Moonface.—" You say Mr. Jorrocks is a good man of business— takes care of the pence and leaves the pounds to take care of themselves, —I suppose from that, you mean to say he is penny wise and pound foolish."

Mr. Bowker.—" Pardon me ; no such thing—pounds are supposed to be better able to take care of themselves than pence—Mr. Jorrocks has a very proper respect for a sovereign—*very loyal !* "

" You mentioned some clubs, I think, Mr. Bowker, that Mr. Jorrocks belongs to ; pray what is the nature of them ? "

" Nature of them, sir—nature of them, sir,—convivial, intellectual, musical—musical, intellectual, convivial ! "

Mr. Moonface.—" The free-and-easy, for instance, what is that ? "

" Convivial, musical—musical, convivial ! "

Mr. Moonface.—" Where does it hold its sittings ? "

" Sky-parlour of the ' Pig in Trouble,' Oxford Street ; sign, ' Pig in the Pound ;' motto,—

> ' Self-praise, we know, is all a bubble,
> Do let me out, I am in trouble !' "

" Never mind the motto—tell the Court now what are the rules of that society."

" Certainly,—sir, certainly.   Fundamental rules of the ' Sublime Society ' are, that members eat nothing but chops and Welsh rabbits ; drink nothing but port wine, porter, or punch, and never take offence at what each other say or do."

Mr. Moonface.—" The members may take all sorts of liberties with each other ? "

" Undoubtedly ! cut all sorts of jokes ! "

Mr. Moonface.—" Call each other names, play tricks, and practical jokes—like the officers of the Forty-Sixth ? "

" Undoubtedly so — undoubtedly so ; jokes, tricks, names — names, tricks, jokes !—just like the officers of the Forty-Sixth."

" And Mr. Jorrocks is the president of this society ? "

Mr. Bowker.—" Mr. Jorrocks is the president of this society."

" And what are the distinguishing characteristics of a president ? "

Mr. Bowker.—" All the distinguishing characteristics in the world— sits on a throne—wears the crown and robes—collar, grand order of Jerusalem—passes sentence on offenders—month in a muffin-shop— bucket of barley-water—kiss the cook—no appeal."

Mr. Moonface.—" And what offences do you try ? "

Mr. Bowker.—" Anything—not particular—anything to make fun—try a man for saying a good thing—try a man for saying a bad thing,—whatever comes uppermost."

" And this you consider intellectual ? "

Mr. Bowker.—" Pardon me, *convivial.*"

" Do you admit strangers to the ' Sublime Society ? ' "

Mr. Bowker.—" On certain days—grand days, in fact, when the regalia is used—bishop's mitre, caps and bells, and so on."

" And do you proceed on the free-and-easy principle with strangers ? "

Mr. Bowker.—" Undoubtedly so."

" Then you must astonish them a little."

Mr. Bowker (with a wink).—"*Galvanise them !*"

Mr. Moonface.—" And pray what is the collar with the grand order of Jerusalem like ? "

Mr. Bowker.—" Gold and enamel — enamel and gold, like my lord mayor's."

Mr. Moonface.—" And the order of Jerusalem, what is it like ? "

Mr. Bowker.—" Simply a Jerusalem, suspended to a collar."

Mr. Moonface.—" But what is a Jerusalem ? "

Mr. Bowker.—" Jerusalem—jackass !—jackass—Jerusalem ! " (Roars of laughter.)

Mr. Moonface.—" And the club has a button, I believe ? "

Mr. Bowker.—" Jerusalem button—motto, ' Ge-o, Neddy ! " (Renewed laughter.)

Mr. Moonface.—" And where does the Wide-awake Club hold its sittings ? "

Mr. Bowker.—" At the ' Cauliflower,' in Cateaton Street."

" And what are the distinguishing features of that club ?—What style of men, in fact, is it composed of ? "

" All stylish men—velvet collars, Hessian boots, kid gloves ! "

" No, I mean what class of men is it composed of ! "

Mr. Bowker.—" First-class men—merchants, bankers, private gentlemen."

" And Mr. Jorrocks is recorder of that society ? "

Mr. Bowker.—" Mr. Jorrocks is recorder of that society."

" Does he sit in state there also, in a crown and robes, with a Jerusalem round his neck ? " (Great laughter.)

Mr. Bowker.—" No ; the president is chosen every evening. After a constitution is obtained, the first member that says a good thing takes the chair, and it is the duty of the recorder to enter the saying, and the circumstances that led to it, in the book."

" And then what do you do ? "

Mr. Bowker (after a pause).—" Drink brandy and water ! "

" And that is intellectual ? "

Mr. Bowker.—" Pardon me ; *convivial*—convivial decidedly.

" Then what is the intellectual portion of your entertainments ? "

Mr. Bowker.—" Oh ! why when somebody sings or spouts, that is both musical and intellectual."

" And then you all get very drunk, I suppose ? "

Mr. Bowker.—"Pardon me; drunkenness is forbidden."

"Then how far may you go with impunity?"

Mr. Bowker.—"By the twenty-first canon of the 'Sublime Society' of the free-and-easy club, it is enacted, that no member shall be considered drunk or liable to the pains and penalties contingent upon intoxication, if he can lie without holding."

Mr. Moonface.—"Then after he is incapacitated from walking, if he can lie still on the floor he is considered sober?"

Mr. Bowker.—"He is not considered drunk."

Mr. Moonface (eyeing the jury).—"He is not considered drunk." To Mr. Bowker, "You may stand down."

"With all my heart;" adding as he went, "never had such a wigging in *my* life."

Our old friend Roger Swizzle was the next witness. Time, we are sorry to say—and perhaps port wine—had done little towards improving Roger's figure and complexion. His once roseate face had assumed a very ripe mulberry hue, while his snub nose bore some disfiguring marks, called by the florists grog-blossoms. His bristly, brushed back hair was still strong, but sadly bleached, and his bright twinkling eyes were about the only features remaining as they were. Neither was his costume more becoming. His puddingy neckcloth was more clumsy, his brown coat more uncouth, his black waistcoat more stained, his drab trousers shorter, and his high-lows thicker and more developed.

Serjeant Horsefield received him with a bow. "You are, I believe," said he, "a medical gentleman in extensive practice at Handley Cross, and well acquainted with Mr. Jorrocks?"

"I am," replied Mr. Swizzle.

"Then will you have the kindness to favour the Court with your opinion of that gentleman?"

Roger Swizzle.—"Certainly, sir. He's what I should call a very good fellow."

"No, I mean with respect to his intellect. Do you consider him of sound mind?"

"Sound as a bell."

"And capable of managing his affairs?"

"No doubt about it.—Why shouldn't he?"

"*That's a trump!*" observed Mr. Jorrocks aloud to himself, adding, "*No doubt about it.*"

Mr. Moonface then proceeded to cross-examine Roger Swizzle:—

"You say, Mr. Swizzle," said he, "that you are in a great way of practice; pray is it among gentlemen afflicted with Mr. Jorrocks' infirmity?" (Mr. Moonface putting his finger to his forehead.)

"Why, no," replied Mr. Swizzle, "principally among gentlemen afflicted with this infirmity," (poking his finger against his stomach).

Mr. Moonface.—"Just so; you are what they call a diet doctor."

Roger Swizzle.—"I don't know I'm sure what they may call me."

Mr. Moonface.—"Suppose they were to call you a 'lushy cove,' would there be any truth in that?"

Roger Swizzle.—"None whatever!"

"And yet you like your wine?"

Roger Swizzle.—" *Good* wine."

" And what do you consider good wine."

Roger Swizzle.—" Two bottles of port is the best of all wine."

James Pigg was the last witness.

" Now ; Pigg," said Serjeant Horsefield, " you are, I believe, huntsman to Mr. Jorrocks, and as such, have the management of his hounds and horses ? "

" Ar has," replied Pigg, with a sniff of his hand across his nose, and a hitch of his braceless brecches.

"And as such you have frequent opportunities of seeing and judging of your master's conduct at home and abroad ? "

" Yeas," drawled out Pigg. " Out a-huntin' that's to say."

" Will you now favour the Court with your opinion of it generally ? "

Pigg.—" Why, noo, ar should say he's a varra good ard man, baith at hyeam and abroad—he gives me monny a shillin', and monny a glass o' brandy i' card weather, and sic like times."

Serjeant Horsefield.—" Ah, but I want to know more about his headpiece, you know—more how you think he manages his establishment in-doors and out."

Pigg.—" Why, noo, ar should say he manishes 'em all gaily well, barrin' that bit bowdekite, Ben; but sink him ! gin ar had him, ard soon manish him."

Serjeant Horsefield —" And his hounds, how do you think he manages them ? "

Pigg.—" Why, noo, ar think the hunds 'ill be just 'bout the warst thing he does. He's all for stuffin' of their bellies till they're not fit to gan, and his back casts are parfect*lie* ridicklus."

Serjeant Horsefield.—" Well, but that is mere matter of opinion, isn't it ? "

" *Ar, but ar say it isn't matter o' pinion!* " roared Pigg. " Ye gan and ax Payne, or Goodall, or any on 'em, if iver they mak back casts first, unless they see it fox has bin hidded."

Serjeant Horsefield.—" But you don't mean to say that, because a man makes back casts first, he is necessarily mad ? "

Pigg.—" Mad, aye ! ne doot ! what else could he be ? "

The Serjeant looking sadly disconcerted, sat down.

" Well, Mr. Pigg," commenced Mr. Moonface, in a familiar tone, " and so you fill the distinguished post of huntsman in this celebrated hunt, of which Mr. Jorrocks is the head ? "

" Ar does," replied Pigg, wondering what they were going over the same ground again for.

Mr. Moonface.—" And if I am rightly informed, you were selected on account of your great knowledge and experience in these matters ? "

" Ar's warn'd ye," replied Pigg; " it wasn't like they'd chose me because ar was a feul ! "

Mr. Moonface.—" Well, now, you told my learned friend something about back casts. Will you allow me to ask you if you think any man in his senses would make back casts ? "

" Niver such a thing ! Not at first hand like ; always make the head good first. Sink it ! ar's talked, and ar's battled, and ar's cussed wor

ard maister, till ar's been fairly aside mysel'; but the varry next time—
may be, afore iver the hunds have cast theirsels—up he's com'd, blawin'

his horn, and taken them back o er the varry same grund, while the fox
all the time was gannin' straight away."

Mr. Moonface.—"And that you consider very ridiculous?"

"Parfect*lie* ridicklus!"

Mr. Moonface.—"And what no man that knew what he was about
would do?"

Pigg (vehemently).—"Niver sec a thing! Niver sec a thing! Ax
ard Sebright, or ony on 'em. Whativer ye de, always cast forrard for a
fox;" saying which, Pigg hitched up his breeches again, and rolled
frantically out of the witness-box.

The Commissioner proceeded to address the jury :—

"This was a case of great peculiarity," he observed, "but he thought of little difficulty, inasmuch as the main question—the existence of a most extraordinary establishment—was admitted, and the only question for them to decide was whether such an establishment was compatible with their ideas of rational life and the steady course of mercantile pursuits. If he mistook not, they were all merchants; and it was for them to say what effect one of their body, arraying himself in a scarlet coat with a blue collar; or a sky-blue coat with pink-silk lining and canary-coloured shorts; or, again, in the crown and robes of a member of the Sublime Society, with the grand order of Jerusalem round his neck, would have upon their minds. The evidence, though slightly conflicting in some parts, was, he thought, very clear; nor did he think either Mr. Bowker or Pigg had done anything towards lessening the force of it. Indeed, the latter seemed to consider the very way in which the unfortunate gentleman managed his extraordinary establishment of hounds was strongly symptomatic of incompetence.

"There was no doubt that a man might be mad upon hunting as well as upon any other point. It was for them to consider whether Mr. Jorrocks had carried the thing so far as to amount to insanity. It was immaterial that other men were equally enthusiastic. It was no reason for permitting one madman to remain at large, that there were many others equally mad. The Court would consider their cases, and deal with them if their next of kin thought proper to bring them before it. It certainly did appear a most extraordinary pursuit for a rational being to devote himself to, in the manner Mr. Jorrocks appears to have done; and with that observation he should leave the case in the hands of the jury."

The jury thereupon retired, more for the sake of appearances or for having a parting crack, than from any difference of opinion as to the state of our friend's mind.

If indeed any doubt had existed, it would have been speedily dispelled by Hobbs, the court head-dress maker, putting himself in attitude, distending his great flobby cheeks, and exclaiming—"Fancy me in a red coat and cap ridin' about 'Amstead 'eath, with a pack of 'ounds at my 'eels!"

"Aye, fancy him!" exclaimed Coxon, the poulterer, who kept a trotting pony and called himself a sportsman.

They then talked Jorrocks over.

One knew his face, another his figure, a third his "fist," having had a bill of his once.

It was generally admitted that he was "respectable," indeed, as Mr. Rounding observed, if he hadn't been his friends wouldn't have troubled a commission, and as Rounding's feeding time was then long past, he got them to return into Court, where he delivered a verdict of "Insanity," adding that "Mr. Jorrocks had been incapable of managing his affairs since he took the *Handley Cross Hounds.*"

CHAPTER LXIX.

BELINDA AT SUIT DOLEFUL.

GREAT was the astonishment, both at Handley Cross and in London, at the intelligence of this verdict.

It was viewed and commented upon, according as the tastes and inclinations of the parties inclined towards mirth or took a serious turn. Some thought it quite right; others, that the jury were mad themselves. The Swizzleites and the Melloites divided, as usual. The annoyance of such a thing as a commission of lunacy is enough to drive a sane man mad; and Mr. Jorrocks's indignant outburst and threatening conduct were construed into violence, and a removal for quiet insisted upon by the promoters of the commission. To Hoxton then he went, to the large brick house, with the pond behind, and the tall poplars before it, which stands so gloomily secluded as almost to mark itself out for such an asylum.

Among the earliest visitors that called upon Mrs. Jorrocks from Handley Cross was Captain Doleful. Hearing of the verdict, he bethought him that something might be done in the matter of the horse, either by way of total or partial refunding; and, accordingly, he took a second-class fare by the early train of the Lilywhite-sand railway, and sought the "lovely retirement" of Great Coram Street.

Mrs. Jorrocks received him with fervour, for she remembered his attention at the fancy-ball, and, moreover, had an idea that " Jun " had been *ray*ther too many for him in the matter of the 'oss.

Both sat silent for some time, Mrs. Jorrocks heaving heavy sighs, and the captain playing with the broad crape that enveloped his newly lined old hat.

"Sad business this, captin," at length observed Mrs. Jorrocks, with a groan.

"Melancholy in the extreme," replied the captain.

"Poor Jun! it's a pity but he'd stuck to the Surrey—might have gone on with them for long."

"I don't know that," rejoined the captain, recollecting that he was the man who got Mr. Jorrocks to take the Handley Cross Hounds; "it would have broken out some other way—set fire to his house, perhaps, or some such thing."

"Oh, dear!" exclaimed Mrs. Jorrocks, who dreaded fire; "it seems like a hinterposition of Providence, that he did take them then."

"Been better for me if he'd set fire to his house," observed Captain Doleful, with a ghastly smile.

"'Ow so?" inquired Mrs. Jorrocks.

"I shouldn't have been done with the horse," replied he.

"Ah, true!" recollected Mrs. Jorrocks; "that 'oss business was a bad 'un; Jun understands 'osses rayther too well; but, howsomever, you are rich, and well able to bear it."

"Mr. Jorrocks is rich, too," observed Captain Doleful.

"He was afore he took the 'ounds," replied Mrs. Jorrocks.

"Oh, but the hounds couldn't hurt him—small establishment—large subscription."

"I doesn't know; it's the 'ounds that have done the mischief, howsomever," replied Mrs. Jorrocks.

"They might turn his head, but they couldn't hurt his pocket—at least, if he has what people say."

"Well, I doesn't know nothin' about that," replied Mrs. Jorrocks, heaving a sigh.

* * * * * * *

"I suppose there'll be no difficulty in the way of an equitable arrangement about the horse," observed Captain Doleful, after a pause; "it's hard for me to bear the whole of the brunt."

"I'm sure I should be werry 'appy to do wot's genteel," replied Mrs. Jorrocks: "but I s'pose the Chancellor's the person that must be applied to—he's to keep the cash-book, I hear. Doesn't know how he's to understand about mexin' the teas, I'm sure."

"Then you'll give me your good word?" inquired the captain, still harping on the horse.

"Indeed I will," replied Mrs. Jorrocks; "I'm sure you were always most purlite to me; that fancy-ball I never shall forget."

Doleful grinned, and thought how good sometimes came of evil.

* * * * * * *

"And how's your lovely niece?" at length inquired Captain Doleful, with a feature-wrinkling grin. "This business will not defer her nuptials, I hope?"

"Oh, I knows nothin' about nuptials!" exclaimed Mrs. Jorrocks, an idea suddenly striking her that will develop itself as we proceed. "I s'pose you allude to Charles Stobbs?"

"Exactly so," replied the captain.

"*He von't do*," replied Mrs. Jorrocks, with an ominous shake of the head.

"Indeed!" exclaimed Captain Doleful; "I'm surprised to hear that—thought he was rich."

"*Rich*, certainly," replied Mrs. Jorrocks; "at least he will be; but we must look to somethin' besides riches in these matters. *Stobbs von't do*."

Captain Doleful wondered how that was.

"It's a hawful responsibility wot dewelopes upon me now that poor Jun is 'non compus,'" sighed Mrs. Jorrocks.

"It must be," replied Captain Doleful.

"I'm sure I've no wish but for Belinda's welfare, and have neither mercenary nor hambitious views; but that 'are-brained Yorkshireman can never do. Indeed, her uncle's malady seems like a hinterposition o' Providence on her be'alf. Fancy what a sitivation hers would a' been had she married this Stobbs, and he'd gone 'non compus' down in Yorkshire!—wild, out-o'-the-way country, scarcely inhabited, and nobody to lock him up."

"Dreadful!" ejaculated the M.C., half laughing at her ideas of the country.

"No," observed Mrs. Jorrocks, thoughtfully; "if she marries at all, it must be a different sort o' man—some nice, steady person, wot will keep her right, and be kind to her when her poor huncle and I are gone."

Mrs. Jorrocks burst into tears at the idea of her dissolution. "Had Jun been dead, she'd have looked out for another investment before she thought of that."

*   *   *   *   *   *   *

"I wonders *you* don't think o' marryin', captin?" observed Mrs. Jorrocks, after a pause.

"Time enough for that!" replied he, with a grin, running his fingers through his straggling hair.

"True," observed Mrs. Jorrocks, "but youth, you know, don't last for ever. Howsomever, I'm sure," added she, "you are lookin' uncommon well; I always said black was quite your become."

The captain grinned, and thought a flirtation with Belinda might not be amiss.

"Then Mr. Stobbs is gone?" inquired he casually, thinking perhaps Charles might cast up and kick him.

"Gone, *decidedly*," replied Mrs. Jorrocks; "at least, he don't show here no more."

"Belinda seems a sweet girl," observed Captain Doleful, thoughtfully.

"She's a hangel!" exclaimed Mrs. Jorrocks; "so affectionate, so tractable, and so engagin'! Whoever gets Belinda, gets a treasure. She'll have a nice fortin'," added Mrs. Jorrocks, casually.

"Will she?" observed Captain Doleful, brightening up.

"Oh, yes," said Mrs. Jorrocks; "her father left summut 'andsome."

(It was "an 'andsome" amount of debt, for, poor man! he died insolvent.)

"Two or three hundred a-year, perhaps?" observed Captain Doleful, carelessly.

"I dare say," replied Mrs. Jorrocks, "besides wot *we* leaves her."

"It's worth thinking of," thought Captain Doleful.

"You, who are so rich, fortin' makes little matter to," observed Mrs. Jorrocks; "but Belinda's a beautiful figure—all nattural, and not a heap of feathers, like a Jinney Howlet, as some gals are. If Exchequer Bill, as my poor dear 'usband used to call 'im, had put the bustle-tax on, that folks talked about, he'd a' got nothin' out o' Belinda."

"How nice!" grinned Captain Doleful, thinking what a contrast she was to Miss Crabstick.

"Oh, she's a sweet gal," rejoined Mrs. Jorrocks; "you couldn't 'elp likin' of her if you know'd her."

"I'm half in love with her already," quoth the captain; "she wouldn't be difficult to come over, I suppose?" inquired he, pulling up his gills, and fingering his straggling whiskers.

"Not by *you*, I dare say," said Mrs. Jorrocks. "The gals can't stand captins."

"Is her fortune in the funds?" inquired Captain Doleful, after a pause.

"Partly," replied Mrs. Jorrocks, "partly in somethin' else; but I really doesn't understand these matters, Jun used to do them all; but Belinda's a treasure in herself. S'pose you come and dine with us some day, and see her to adwantage."

"Most happy, I'm sure," grinned the captain.

"Then come to-morrow at four," rejoined Mrs. Jorrocks; "just we three—*you understand!*"

"*Perfectly!*" replied the captain, dropping on his knee, and imprinting a kiss on Mrs. Jorrocks' mutton-fist.

That was carrying a sudden thought out quickly, and the captain having taken his departure, Mrs. Jorrocks began considering how she should manage matters with Belinda.

CHAPTER LXX.

BELINDA AT BAY.

"I HAVE had your old friend, Captin Doleful, here," observed Mrs. Jorrocks to Belinda, as they sat at their early tea.

"Indeed!" replied Belinda.

"Lookin' so well and so 'andsome; I really think you'd have been smitten with him."

"*Me, aunt!*" exclaimed Belinda, with unfeigned astonishment.

"And vy not, miss?" inquired Mrs. Jorrocks.

"Why, in the first place, he's quite an old man, and——"

"*Old!*" exclaimed Mrs. Jorrocks, "men are never old!"

"Well, but he's anything but good-looking, and is such a horribly mean wretch; I——"

"Fiddle his meanness! no meaner than other folks. He's werry rich—a thousand a-year, paid quarterly."

"So much the better for him," observed Belinda.

"Now don't be perwerse—you know what I means jest as well as I do myself," observed Mrs. Jorrocks, looking irate.

"Indeed I don't, aunt!" replied Belinda, turning frightened.

"Well, then, stoopid! I thinks he's worth you settin' your cap at."

"*Me, aunt!*" exclaimed Belinda, blushing deeply; "you know I can't—*I'm engaged!*"

"Fiddle, engaged! soon get off that,—nothin's finished till it's done."

"Oh, aunt!" exclaimed Belinda, burying her face in her hands, "don't—*pray don't* talk to me in this way—*I cannot bear it!*"

"Foolish gal!" rejoined Mrs. Jorrocks; "don't know what's good for you. The captin's worth fifty of your fly-away, break-neck fox-'unters,—nice, agreeable, quiet gentleman, wot'll take his tea with you of an evenin', instead of snorin' and sleepin' as your huncle does, or startin' up, thinkin' he's gettin' run away with or kicked over a wall."

"You are not in earnest, aunt?" replied Belinda, turning her beautiful blue eyes, with their silken lashes suffused with tears, upon her aunt as she spoke.

"Vy not?" inquired Mrs. Jorrocks.

"Oh, aunt! you *cannot* be in earnest—*you*, who have always encouraged Charles, and encouraged me to like him; and——"

"It was your huncle wot encouraged him!" exclaimed Mrs. Jorrocks, "*not me!*"

"And you, *too*, aunt," replied Belinda, calmly, but firmly; "don't you remember the night uncle and he were benighted, and I sat anxiously waiting their coming, trembling for their safety, how you consoled me by praising Charles, and talking of what a nice husband he would make me, and how pleasant it would be visiting us in Yorkshire, and——"

"No doubt," replied Mrs. Jorrocks; "no doubt—and now that a better chance turns hup, I encourages you to think of it,—a gal should

MRS. JORROCKS ADVISING BELINDA.

never be without an admirer; but it's a reg'lar rule always to take the best,—nothin's done till it's finished, as I said afore."

"I want no better!" exclaimed Belinda; "Charles is my first—my only love, and I'll *never* marry another!"

"*Fool!*" ejaculated Mrs. Jorrocks; "that's the way all gals talk!—got your 'ead stuffed full of boardin'-school, novelish nonsense."

Belinda was silent—the eloquent tears chased each other rapidly down her beautiful cheeks.

"Now, don't be foolish!" said Mrs. Jorrocks, in a milder tone; "consider wot hobligations you are under to me and your huncle—brought you hup, and edikated you, and hintroduced you to people of the first extinction, and all the return I ax is, that you'll oblege me by makin' a helligible match. There isn't a gal in 'Andley Cross but would jump at such a chance. Charles may be a werry respectable young man, but he's wild and thoughtless; besides, we doesn't know wot he has, and it's werry imprudent, to say the least of it, for a gal to fall in love with a man till she knows wot he has,—*I* didn't do so, I knows."

"He will have enough for me," replied Belinda; "money alone will not constitute happiness."

"Provokin' gal!" exclaimed Mrs. Jorrocks; "you are just one of those silly, romancin', love-in-a-cottage sort o' gals that one sees in the plays;" and Mrs. Jorrocks vented an inward malediction on Mr. Bowker, and all patrons and frequenters of the drama.

*   *   *   *   *   *   *

"Oblege me now, Belinda," continued she, after a pause, "by thinkin' of the captin."

"Aunt, I *couldn't for the world!* I know the gratitude I owe—and Heaven knows the gratitude I feel, for all you have done for me, but this can never be;—I should detest myself could I think myself capable of entertaining the idea."

"There, again!" exclaimed Mrs. Jorrocks, reddening up! "stage-players again! Wish you would be a little rational. Tell me, now, in plain English, why can't you entertain the idea?"

"Because you know, aunt," replied Belinda, slowly and calmly, "that I accepted Charles with the full approbation of you and my uncle."

"And wot of that?" inquired Mrs. Jorrocks.

"Simply that my word is pledged, and I am precluded from thinking of another."

"No such thing!" rejoined Mrs. Jorrocks; "'appens every day,—sayin' you love each other is nothin' towards a match. I tells you, no prudent gal accepts a man till she knows wot he has. Look at Mrs. Wrigglesworth! She was engaged to Walter Leigh, and her acquaintance congratilated her, and made her bags, and said nothin' could be nicer, when Wrigglesworth turned hup with just double Leigh's fortin', and she chopped over to him, and her friends congratilated her again, and said nothin' could be nicer, and made her duplicate bags, slippers, scent-'olders, and I don't know wot."

"Sincere their congratulations must have been," observed Belinda; "I'm sure I should not like to be talked of as people talk of her,—pointed out as the lady who cheated the government by not paying the auction duty on herself, and I don't know what else."

"Let them laugh as wins," replied Mrs. Jorrocks; "she has a futman—and would only have had a Betsy with Leigh. But there's no puttin' old 'eads on young shoulders," sighed Mrs. Jorrocks. "Take my word for it, howsomever," continued she, "if you live, you'll see these things in a werry different light;—if you kicks the ball away, you may never 'ave it at your foot again."

"I don't wish for such a ball as Captain Doleful, I'm sure," replied Belinda, smiling.

"And tell me, Miss Pert, wot's the matter with the captin?" inquired Mrs. Jorrocks, tartly.

"I'm sure I don't know what is the matter with him, exactly," replied Belinda; "but I should not think he was a man that any woman would ever take a fancy to."

"Fiddle *fancy!*" exclaimed Mrs. Jorrocks; "it's your fanciful marriages wot breed misery—foolish, moon-struck, stage-play sort of botherations, that breed bastiles, and I doesn't know what;" for Mrs. Jorrocks had only got the smattering of that idea. "I tells you," continued she, "*that you're a fool!*"

Belinda was silent.

*   *   *   *   *   *   *

"I do wonders," observed Mrs. Jorrocks, "that any gal can be so ungratefully hobstinate as persewere, in spite of the adwice and hadmonitions of her friends—wot good can you get by it? If you doesn't like partin' with the books and things Stobbs gave you, I'll tell him you prefers keepin' of them, so you'll lose nothin' by the transaction."

"Oh, aunt!" exclaimed Belinda, "*don't* torture me thus—*don't* make yourself appear little by insinuating that such an idea could enter *your* head."

"And vy not?" inquired Mrs. Jorrocks. "It's nattral that you should like keepin' the things."

"Indeed no, aunt, it isn't. If I could bring myself to think that the connexion on which I have set my heart was not to be, the greatest favour you could do me would be to remove from my sight every trace, every recollection, that could remind me of my loss."

"*Loss, indeed!*" exclaimed Mrs. Jorrocks, sneeringly. "Pretty loss, forsooth! It's wot I should call gainin' a loss—gettin' a nice, steady captin, with a large fortin', to a young harum-scarum scamp of a boy, that nobody knows nothin' about—nasty, 'oss-copin', ditch-jumpin' beggar!"

Belinda was silent.

"Well, you may be perwerse and hobstinate, too; but, take my word for it, you'll get nothin' by it. I'm missus here, and I'll be hobeyed; and my horders are that you receive the captin at dinner to-morrow, and be'ave like a lady. Put on your Hindia muslin, or I'll let the Chancellor know;" so saying Mrs. Jorrocks flounced out of the room.

CHAPTER LXXI.

DOLEFUL PREPARED FOR THE SIEGE.

HAVING returned to his quarters at the George and Blue Boar, High Holborn, Captain Doleful reconnoitred his wardrobe, for the purpose of seeing how killing he could make himself on the following day. He had on the suit of black he had turned for Miss Crabstick's funeral; a patent tubular tie, a finely flowered front with two rows of little frills, and a pair of cheap, open-work black silk socks, with French polish on his old pumps, would make him a very respectable candle-light swell.

Passing down Holborn, he was struck with the display in Mr. Frizwig the advertising hair-dresser's window—such wax-busts, such wigs and ringlets! "HAIR CUT FOR SIXPENCE." The captain thought he would have a clip.

*   *   *   *   *   *   *

L L

The obsequious "perruquier" ushered him into the cutting-room through the shop, and Captain Doleful, divesting himself of his coat and seedy Joinville, got his person enveloped in a buff cotton wrapper.

Taking a hard brush out of his apron-pocket, Mr. Frizwig proceeded to brush the captain's lank locks over his flat head. He then produced a comb and scissors.

* * * * * * *

"'Air getting rayther thin on the crown, I'm sorry to *per*ceive," observed Mr. Frizwig, as though he were a partner in the concern.

"That's no news," growled the captain, eyeing his unbecoming appearance in the unflattering mirror against the wall.

* * * * * * *

"Your 'air requires a good deal of moisture," observed Mr. Frizwig, nothing daunted by his customer's gruffness.

"Does it?" growled the captain.

"Thin in parts—strong in parts," continued the perruquier, snipping, and clipping, and combing. "The grand Scandinavian extract of Patagonian cream would restore it all;" adding, half to himself and half to his foreman, "Must have had a fine 'ead formerly."

The captain grinned. "What is it a bottle?" inquired he.

"All prices," replied the hairdresser, wondering the extent of his customer's gullibility—"all prices, from two-and-six up to ten shillings. The largest pots cheapest in the end."

"How long is it in acting?" inquired the captain.

"Depends upon how you use it: well rubbed in twice a day, it would begin immediately. Renovates what's gone, and imparts a beautiful healthy gloss to what remains."

"A *leet*le off the whiskers?" inquired he.

"A *little*," replied the captain, with an emphasis, thinking there was not much to spare.

"Just the pints off," observed the hairdresser, pretending to be very exact.

* * * * * * *

"If I might take the liberty, sir, I would recommend one of my patent, self-ventilating, porous zephyr scalps with invisible spring d'Orsay whiskers—the most surprising deception ever witnessed!—Impossible to detect!"

Captain Doleful was silent, for he thought they would be dear.

"Sell an immense number of them," continued Mr. Frizwig, still trimming the whiskers. "Perhaps you know Captain Orlando Smith, the gentleman who stood for Taunton at the last election?"

The captain said "No."

"Indeed! s'cuse the liberty, but you are so like, I thought you might be brothers. Well, his 'air was just like yours—thin at the top, strong be'ind, and I rigged him out with a scalp and whiskers, so neat and so natural that he won all the gals' 'earts in the borough. If they'd had votes he'd have been returned. Gals like whiskers. You never see a newly married man but his whiskers have always increased."

"And what is the price of them?" inquired the captain, recollecting how Miss Jelly had admired him in his fancy-dress moustache.

"All prices, sir! all prices!—Twenty shillings upwards. Allow me to show you some. Enoch!" calling to his foreman, "bring half-a-dozen patent zephyr scalps, dark, with invisible spring d'Orsay whiskers."

While the apprentice was looking them out, Mr. Frizwig took a pair of large scissors and cut a great patch off the captain's thin-haired crown.

"What are you after now, man?" exclaimed he, jumping off the chair.

"Only preparing a place for the spring to act upon," replied Mr. Friz-wig, coolly. "You are exactly like Captain Orlando Smith, the gentleman who stood for Taunton at the last election. He would have that I had spoiled him when I did so, but, my word! when he saw himself in his new ornaments, I heard no more of that.—*Allow me* now, sir," continued he, bowing most obsequiously, and pointing to the chair, "to have the honour of rigging you out the same way."

Captain Doleful, somewhat testy, but hoping for the best, then resumed his seat, and Mr. Frizwig, with the aid of Enoch, proceeded to exhibit sundry scalps and whiskers. "Too light," said Mr. Frizwig, rejecting three or four in succession. "Too dark," continued he, holding one to Captain Doleful's head. "Haven't you one with a shade of grey in it?"

"There is a *slight* tinge of grey in your 'air," whispered Mr. Frizwig confidentially, as Enoch returned to the shop, "which, I have little doubt, the grand Scandinavian extract of Patagonian cream will entirely remove; but, as you only intend wearing the scalp until your own 'air gets strong, it will be better to match it now, than to get a scalp of the colour your 'air will be 'ereafter."

"But I haven't made up my mind to have one at all yet," observed the captain, snappishly.

"Ah, you're exactly like Captain Orlando Smith, the gentleman who stood for Taunton at the last election," repeated the audacious perruquier. "Nothing could persuade him that I was not cheating him, and, indeed, he threatened to call the police; but, when he saw himself, he was so delighted that, in his 'urry to show himself, he left his new alpaca umbrella and cotton gloves on the counter. Ah, now this'll be the ticket!" added he, taking an iron-grey scalp out of Enoch's hand—"Allow me, sir," to the captain, putting the scalp on his head and expanding it over the crown.

* * * * * *

"Delightful!" exclaimed he getting in front and looking the captain full in the face.—"A *lee*tle farther back, Enoch. That'll do. Now fasten the clasp. Charming match! Don't think I ever saw a better."

"Now down with the d'Orsays," continued he, proceeding to lower his side of the bushy whiskers under the Captain's chin; adding, as they fell by the sides of his cadaverous countenance, "beautiful indeed! the very man himself.—D'Orsay, sir, was the greatest swell, sir, the world ever saw, sir. Yes, sir, the greatest swell, sir, the world ever saw, sir; and you are amazingly like 'im, sir; yes, sir, *amazingly* like 'im, sir."

L L 2

"But I don't look a bit like myself," exclaimed the captain, tartly, eyeing his hirsute appearance in the glass.

"Paradoxical as it may appear, sir, my motto is 'art before nature,'" replied Mr. Frizwig. "This scalp and whiskers possess an elegance and gracefulness of contour almost unattainable. Stop till you're used to them a little," added he, giving the horse-hair-looking beard an inward twitch. "There may be a *lee*tle fulness round the chin, but that is easily remedied," added Mr. Frizwig, taking the large scissors and cutting about half-an-inch off. "Now," said he, "how do you like it?"

"Why, it's more like the thing," replied Captain Doleful, grinning through the great collar of horse-hair; "but I should say it is still much too full."

"You *must* have it full, you know, or where would be the use of having a porous zephyr scalp and d'Orsay whiskers at all? I should say you look now as you ought to do, and as you did before your 'air got so thin. Wouldn't you, Enoch?" Enoch thought it a charming match and fit, too.

"The hair matches well enough, perhaps," observed the captain; "but it is the whiskers I object to. They are too large—too bushy, and look altogether too much like what one sees on a barber's block."

"That's the perfection of the thing! They look like art naturalised. Nobody would even suspect that they were not your own whiskers. They're too large to be false. As you walk up street now, you'll hear the ladies exclaim, 'What beautiful whiskers!' Just as they did to Captain Orlando Smith, when he stood for Taunton."

The captain twitched and pulled the whiskers and beard, and scanned himself minutely.

"If you would allow me to cut off the remnants of your own whiskers," observed Mr. Frizwig, "these new ones would sit much closer and have a more natural air;" saying which he gently lifted a whisker, and with his large scissors laid one cheek bare before the captain had time to say nay.

"*Confound* it, I wish you wouldn't be *quite* so handy with your scissors," observed the captain with a frown.

"Beg pardon," bowed the obsequious barber, "but I think you'll agree with me, that that's a *de*cided improvement—Isn't it, Enoch?"

"Looks uncommon well now," replied Enoch, grinning. "Does'nt the gen'leman think so himself?"

Doleful did not deign a reply. He sat twisting and turning and examining himself first in the mirror, then in the hand-glass, then in the hand-glass and mirror conjointly, trying if he could make himself believe he looked as he did when he came in. The whiskers certainly were tremendous—strong, coarse, black hair, with a uniform inward curl. Still we do not mean to say that we have not seen as big a pair, though certainly not on so unhealthy a soil as the captain's cheeks.

*   *   *   *   *   *

"What's to pay?" at length inquired he, adjusting his embroidered collars over his mohair stock, and putting on his coat: "you'll not charge for *cutting*, of course?"

"Let me see," replied Mr. Frizwig, rubbing his hands—"any 'air-brushes, tooth-brushes, sponges, soap, wanted?"

"*No*," said Captain Doleful, dryly.

"Just a ten-shilling pot of Scandinavian extract.—No curling fluid, tooth-powder, lavender water? Got some uncommonly genuine Eau de Cologne."

"*No! No!*" interrupted the captain; "I only want a half-crown pot of extract, that, and a shilling discount off the sovereign, will be a guinea and sixpence—say a guinea."

"Beg pardon, scalp, six-and-twenty."

"How's that? you said a sovereign."

"*From* a sovereign."

"I understood you to say that *a* sovereign was the price, or I wouldn't have had one."

"Beg pardon, sir, you quite misunderstood me. No doubt you could have one for a sovereign, but it would be a thing like a door-mat, without the invisible spring d'Orsay whiskers."

"Invisible spring d'Orsay fiddle-sticks!" growled the captain. "I wanted nothing of the sort."

"Beg ten thousand pardons, sir,—shall be happy to take it back, I'm sure."

"And what am I to do without my own whisker that you cut off?" inquired the captain angrily.

"The Scandinavian extract 'ill soon restore it!"

"Scandinavian devil!——Well, come, six-and-twenty," repeated the captain, producing his old leather purse.

"Scalp, six-and-twenty; invisible spring-whiskers, ten—one pound sixteen."

"*Hold!*" cried the captain, "I won't be imposed upon!"

"Sir!" exclaimed Mr. Frizwig, in a tone of dignified astonishment, drawing himself up. "We are not accustomed to such language here."

"I tell you, sir," said the captain, "that you gave me to understand the scalp and whiskers were a pound."

"I don't know what your comprehension may be equal to," replied Mr. Frizwig, rubbing his hands, "but I assure you, one pound sixteen shillings is my price, and one pound sixteen shillings I mean to have, or you may doff your head-dress as soon as you like. Enoch, mind the door!" giving his foreman a wink.

*   *   *   *   *   *   *

"*Take it then!*" screamed the captain, dashing the money on the counter; "and if ever I set foot in your —— shop again, I hope I may be ——."

"Shut up shop, Enoch!—shut up shop!" exclaimed Mr. Frizwig to his apprentice. "It's all over with us: this venerable ourang-outang says he won't come back;" saying which master and man burst into a loud guffaw, in the midst of which Captain Doleful hurried away.

CHAPTER LXXII.

MRS. JORROCKS FURIOUS.

MRS. JORROCKS received the captain as a lady would her intended nephew. She was somewhat struck with the change in his appearance, but said nothing; and Belinda, not having seen him for some time, and not understanding the management of whiskers, thought nothing of it.

Dinner being announced, Mrs. Jorrocks motioned the captain to take Belinda, while she complacently followed in the rear, admiring Belinda's beautifully rounded form, set off by the simple drapery of Indian muslin, and the captain's gaunt figure—the handsomest couple she had ever seen —seemed made for each other—the usual "common form," in fact, as Bill Bowker would say.

They had mutton-broth and mackerel for dinner, roast-beef, boiled chickens, and tongue; and the captain, having only had a second-class coffee-room breakfast (bread with one egg), played an uncommonly good knife and fork—rather better, perhaps, than might have been expected, considering the delicacy of his situation. Belinda trifled with her dinner, for the sake of drowning the comparisons that every moment arose between her death's-head-looking neighbour and he who so long had sat at her side.

Immediately after dinner, at least immediately after her second bumper of port, Mrs. Jorrocks had arranged to be called out by Betsy; and answering the summons, she desired Belinda to entertain the captain until her return.

Our hero now began to take fright, and wrinkling his face like a man with a very tight shoe, he attempted to force a conversation about indifferent things : "Did she like Handley Cross or London best? Great Coram Street was certainly a very charming situation, airy and clean. But nothing could be nicer than Diana Lodge. Supposed she knew the Barningtons were not going to return—had gone to live at Boulogne, where they were quite the head people of the place. Hoped the hounds would not be given up at Handley Cross, and had she heard of Mr. Stobbs lately? "

This last was too much for poor Belinda. Her utterance became choked. She rose from her seat, and hurried out of the room.

* * * * * * *

" Is that you, Belinda? " inquired Mrs. Jorrocks, in a suppressed tone of anger, hearing a light footstep pass the drawing-room door and proceed up-stairs.

Without waiting for an answer, our hostess hurried out to see, and caught a glimpse of Belinda's petticoats whisking round the landing-place.

* * * * * * *

" Didn't I tell you to sit with the capt'in till I came down? " inquired Mrs. Jorrocks, in a voice stifled with rage, "and here, you minx, you have the unmannerly imperance to leave him all alone—*Vot do you mean?* " screamed she, closing the door.

"Aunt," replied Belinda, firmly, "you can't frighten me. Where no hope is left, is left no fear, and I tell you most decidedly, that sooner than marry—oh! sooner than *think* of, that horrid man, I'll throw myself out of the window? "

" FOOL! " ejaculated Mrs. Jorrocks, hurrying down-stairs to the captain.

* * * * * * *

" And 'ow do you get on? " inquired she, entering the parlour with a smile on her countenance.

"Oh, pretty well, I think," replied the captain, who had taken advantage of Belinda's absence, to fall foul upon a preserved orange, with which he had his mouth plentifully crammed. " She's shy, you know, but I make no doubt she'll soon come to."

" All gals are shy at first," replied Mrs. Jorrocks; "indeed they wouldn't be fit for wives if they weren't. Bless us! I remember how frightened I was the first hoffer I got. You must be gentle with her, poor thing!—she's never been used to no 'arshness," continued Mrs. Jorrocks, as the captain scraped up the syrup with a spoon.

"That I will," said he, licking his lips; " she shall have everything she wants—sable tippets, chinchilla muff—phaeton—footman——"

* * * * * * *

Tea followed, and Mrs. Jorrocks having apologised for the absence of Belinda on the usual plea of headache, and the captain and she having played at cross purposes about the relative fortunes until each was tired, he at length took his departure, promising a speedy return.

Mrs. Jorrocks then applied herself seriously to the consideration of Belinda's case. She was sadly bothered how to manage her.

The captain evidently was to be had, but how to get rid of that " 'orrid Yorkshireman " was more than Mrs. Jorrocks could devise.

She had certainly encouraged Belinda to like him, and there, perhaps, she was to blame (without knowing what he had), but then Mr. Jorrocks was the great promoter of the thing, and she had only now acquired the power of putting a *veto* upon it. That power she was determined to use.

Mrs. Jorrocks was a woman without personal friends; all her acquaintance being the acquaintance of her husband, and partaking more or less of his honest integrity. Long and anxiously did she ruminate who she could call to her counsels, and who would be most likely to aid her. Mrs. Barker would blab; Mrs. Brown would rather hurt her than aid her; if she let Mrs. Flower into the secret, she would try to get Charles for one of her own "ugly gals;" and altogether Mrs. Jorrocks was very much puzzled.

The only person to whom she thought she could with safety apply was Mr. Bowker, and to him she addressed the following note :—

"Mrs. Jorrocks's comp^ts. Mr. Bowker, and I will thank you to come and see me as soon as you can.

"Great Coram-street."

*　　*　　*　　*　　*　　*　　*

"Curse your impudence! what do you mean by knocking that way, you little brazen beggar!" exclaimed Mr. Bowker, opening the door of old Twister's chambers to a long and loud *rat-tat-tat-tat-tan* from our friend, Mr. Benjamin Brady, whom Mrs. Jorrocks had reinstated in his pagehood.

Mr. Bowker was deeply engaged, looking out "common forms" for a settlement for parties "in a desperate hurry," and Mr. Brady's summons startled both him and old Twister.

"What an audacious little rascal you are!" continued Bill; "you knock, I declare, just as if you were a Queen's counsel."

"And so I am a *Queen's* counsel," replied Benjamin,—"counsel to the old gal in Great Coram Street; and here, I've brought you a brief," presenting Bill with the note.

*　　*　　*　　*　　*　　*　　*

"Curse the old fool! what can she want with me?" muttered Bill, as he read it. "*Mischief*, I'll be bound,—ungrammatical old jade! 'Compliments Mr. Bowker'—Mr. Bowker wants none of her compliments!"

*　　*　　*　　*　　*　　*　　*

"Make my compliments to your mistress," said Bill, with great dignity, "and say I'll be with her at dinner-time—that's to say, one o'clock, or a little after; and see, the next time you come, that you knock a little quieter, or I'll knock your head off your shoulders!"

"Vill you?" rejoined Benjamin; "you'll find yourself in the wrong box, if you do," said he, spitting upon Bowker, and running down-stairs as hard as ever he could go.

*　　*　　*　　*　　*　　*　　*

"Nasty little beast!" exclaimed Bowker, returning from the chase, and wiping his tights as he ascended the stairs; "that boy'll be hung as sure as a gun!" with which comfortable assurance Bill returned to his office, and busied himself with his common forms, and in thinking what Mrs. Jorrocks *could* want.

* * * * * *

When one-o'clock came, instead of repairing to " The Feathers," or to any of his familiar dining-houses, Mr. Bowker wended his way to Great Coram Street. Many were his conjectures as to the cause of his summons, his ideas partaking of the character of the streets through which he passed—gloomy when in narrow ones, and brightening as he entered upon the wider expanse, and purer atmosphere, of the Foundling Hospital and Brunswick Square. At length he stood at Mrs. Jorrocks's door—that door at which he had so often stood in sadness and in joy, but which he had never re-passed uncomforted.

* * * * * * *

Mrs. Jorrocks was alone in the front drawing-room. The chintz covers were on the chairs and screens, and a blue cloth covered the round table at which she sat, with a pile of bills, letters, papers, and memorandum-books before her.

" Good mornin', Mr. Bowker," said she, in a melancholy tone, motioning our friend to a vacant chair on the opposite side of the table.

Bowker pulled a long face, and, unbuttoning his leopard-like Taglioni, sidled a respectful portion of his person on to the chair, and, bending forward, rested his right hand on his gold-headed cane.

* * * * * *

" Sad business, this, Mr. Bowker," observed Mrs. Jorrocks, with a sigh.

" *Very sad, indeed,*" replied Bill.

" You never suspected nothin' of the sort, did you, Mr. Bowker ? "

" Oh, never, indeed ! "

" Werry shockin'," continued Mrs. Jorrocks ; " don't know what's to become on us."

" I should hope there's no fear of your being well provided for," observed Bill.

" Oh, it arn't myself that I cares about, Mr. Bowker," replied Mrs. Jorrocks ; " but what's to become of that poor dear child—she who has lived with us so long, that I looks upon her in the light of a darter ? "

" Oh, I should hope there will be no difficulty about her," replied Mr. Bowker.

" They won't allow nothin' for her keep," continued Mrs. Jorrocks, wiping her eye.

" Indeed ! " replied Mr. Bowker.

" They say the Chancellor's to manage matters, both here and in the Lane, and I shall only have as much as will keep myself genteel."

" Indeed ! " replied Mr. Bowker ; adding, " But what is Mr. Stobbs about ? Why doesn't he marry her ? "

" *Don't mention his 'orrid name !* " screamed Mrs. Jorrocks. " I werrily believes he's been the cause of all the mischief."

" Indeed ! " repeated Mr. Bowker, wondering what had happened.

" Idle feller ! " exclaimed Mrs. Jorrocks.

" He certainly was not a worker when he was with us," observed Mr. Bowker ; " but he'll have a nice fortune, won't he ? "

"Oh, I knows nothin' about fortin'," replied Mrs. Jorrocks; "money alone won't make 'appiness."

"True," observed Mr. Bowker, thinking it went a long way.

"I should like to see her marry some nice, quiet, respectable person, wot would be kind to her when her poor huncle and I are gone," sobbed Mrs. Jorrocks, covering her face with a dirty linen handkerchief.

Mr. Bowker was beat for an answer; he couldn't see his way.

"Such a man, now, as Capt'in Doleful," resumed Mrs. Jorrocks, finding Mr. Bowker remained silent: "any religious, quiet, charitable person, rather than that hare-brained Yorkshireman. Fox-'unters are all queer," added she, putting her finger to her forehead; "get shook out 'unting."

"Captain Doleful's a very nice man, I suppose," observed Mr. Bowker, looking at his Hessian boots.

"Oh, he's a *charmin'* man," responded Mrs. Jorrocks; "you don't know what a comfort he was to me at the Spa."

"Indeed!" observed Mr. Bowker, "very genteel, too, isn't he?"

"He's quite the go at 'Andley Cross," replied Mrs. Jorrocks.

"Then he'd be the go anywhere, I should think," observed Mr. Bowker, tucking the ends of his blue satin neckcloth into his red tartan waistcoat, and contemplating his drab stocking-net pantaloons and Hessian boots.

*   *   *   *   *   *   *

"Mr. Bowker," said Mrs. Jorrocks, after a long pause, during which she shuffled among some papers, and applied a large blue smelling-bottle to her nose,—"Mr. Bowker," repeated she, "in lookin' through Jun's drawer's, I find some mems, about some money you owes him."

"Indeed!" said Bill, colouring up to the redness of his waistcoat.

"A hundred pounds and interest," continued Mrs. Jorrocks, eyeing him intently.

"One year's interest on fifty, and half a year's on the same sum; I have it all down in my cash-book, in Eagle Street. I'll give you a check for it now," continued Bill, diving into his back pocket in search of his cheque-book—a search that he might have continued some time, had not Mrs. Jorrocks relieved him by observing that she didn't want the money, she only wished to know that all was right.

"*Quite right!*" repeated Bill, in his usual off-hand way; "interest on fifty, for a year, two pund ten; on fifty, for half a year, one pund five—three pund fifteen, and principal, a hundred—a hundred and three pund fifteen—you can have it any day for sending for. We always have as much in the till as will answer that."

"Mr. J. 'ill be a great loss to society," observed Bowker, in a melancholy tone, anxious to turn the conversation.

"*Poor man!*" responded Mrs. Jorrocks, with a sigh.

"Don't know who we shall get for a chairman of our Free-and-easy, or president of our incorporated society of Good Fellows; the recorder-ship of the Wide-awake Club will be vacant, too. Do you think Captain Doleful would take office?" inquired Mr. Bowker.

"Not of them sort of things, I should think," replied Mrs. Jorrocks, with a toss of the head; "the capt'in's more a tea-and-Terpsichore sort of man—*werry genteel*."

"True," observed Mr. Bowker; "but just for the sake of popularity, I thought perhaps he might lend us a hand. The recordership's a high office."

"He cares nothin' for poppilarity now," replied Mrs. Jorrocks; "wot should a man with a thousand pounds a-year care for poppilarity?"

"True," assented Mr. Bowker, wishing he had half of it. "Why shouldn't *he* make a good match for Miss Belinda?" inquired Bowker, willing to help Mrs. Jorrocks to her point.

"That's just what I've been a plannin' of," replied Mrs. Jorrocks, with a knowing leer,—"that's just what I've been a plannin' of. Now," continued she, after a pause, during which she scrutinised Mr. Bowker and bagged her dirty pocket-handkerchief, "it's no use you and I 'umbuggin' each other."

Bill bowed assent.

"Well, then, I may as well tell you at startin' that I knows all about the money and the shop—*you can no more pay me than you can fly!*"

Bill coloured brightly.

"But if you can't pay me in cash, you can pay me in kind," continued Mrs. Jorrocks, anxious to relieve her visitor's uneasiness. "You think Capt'in Doleful will do for Belinda?"

"Undoubtedly, if he has what you say, and will keep her a gig." (The possession of a gig was the summit of Bill's worldly ambition.)

"A *fe-a-ton!*" replied Mrs. Jorrocks, with a look of exultation.

"*He must be had!*" observed Bill, with a wink and a nod.

"So say I," replied Mrs. Jorrocks; "the thing is how to get him."

"There can't be any difficulty, I should think," observed Bill "Beautiful blue-eyed girl—nice foot and ankle—swelling figure—just leave them together a bit, he'll soon come to, I warrant."

"Oh, *he's* all right," said Mrs. Jorrocks. "It's Belinda that bothers me."

"She'll surely take your advice," observed Bill, in a tone of confidence—"at least, if she wont, you can make her."

"But there's that confounded Yorkshire scamp in the way!" said Mrs. Jorrocks; "and she vows nothing shall make her marry another so long as he remains faithful."

"Silly girl!" exclaimed Bowker; "that's the way with them all—just as if there weren't as good fish in the sea as ever came out of it. She should be whipped for throwing away such a chance. Far better to ride about town in a Fe-a-ton than pad the hoof in the country," observed Bill, looking at the slanting heels of his Hessians.

"Far!" exclaimed Mrs. Jorrocks.

* * * * * * *

"Girls are queer cattle," observed Bowker, after a pause. "Lucky when they have older heads than their own to keep them right."

"'Deed is it!" said Mrs. Jorrocks; adding, with a shake of her head, "Belinda's werry obstinate."

"Pity!" said Mr. Bowker, who was a great admirer of beauty. "I always thought she was very amiable."

"*Fiddle hamiable!*" exclaimed Mrs. Jorrocks, angrily. "Hugly girls are hamiable."

"Well, but I thought she'd have done what you liked," said Mr. Bowker. " I'm sure she ought, after all your kindness."

"Well; but it's not never of no use speckilatin' on wot she ought to do," rejoined Mrs. Jorrocks, anxious to make her point, " I tells you she *won't*, and that's poz ! "

"Then we must see if we can't make her," said Bill, somewhat reluctantly ; for, rogue as he was, he had still a tinge of kindness left in his composition.

"And you'll help me ? " said Mrs. Jorrocks, inquiringly.

Bill bowed again.

"Well, now, I'll tell you wot," said Mrs. Jorrocks, turning Bill's I. O. U's. over in a careless sort of way, "if you can manage to choak Stobbs off, and get the capt'in on, I'll put these writin's in the fire."

" I'll do my best, I'm sure," said Bill, delighted at the prospect of a clearance.

"It must be managed gingerly," observed Mrs. Jorrocks.

> " ' Love may die by slow decay,
> But by sudden wrench believe not
> Hearts can thus be torn away,' "

replied Mr. Bowker, flourishing his right hand as he spoke.

" *You'll* manage it, I think," said Mrs. Jorrocks cheerfully.

" If she's of womankind," replied Bill.

"Get Stobbs off, and there will be little difficulty in gettin' the capt'in on," said Mrs. Jorrocks ; "only you know," added she, "a woman never gives hup a man short o' the church door."

" No," mused Bill—" no, but I think I can choak her off—make her believe he's married already, how would that do ? "

" Capital," exclaimed Mrs. Jorrocks, clapping her hands, "nothin' could be better. That would settle the business at once "—added she, "for a man that's married is as good as dead to any other woman."

"But my hour is almost come ! " observed Bill, starting up, as he drew a richly chased pinchbeck watch from his waistcoat-pocket, and saw it wanted but ten minutes to two, at which time he had "to render up himself" to old Twister and present him with a ship-biscuit for luncheon. He bid Mrs. Jorrocks a hasty adieu, and half happy, half wretched, retraced his steps to Lincoln's Inn.

"Needs must when the devil drives ! " said Bill, as he hurried along ; "but I'd rather do anything than injure that poor blue-eyed beauty. Nice little thing, with her pretty taper fingers, that used to shake hands with me so kindly ; " and the more Bill thought of his task, the less he liked it. Still he saw no way of helping himself, for well he knew that Mrs. Jorrocks was merciless, and having got him in her power, she would grind him to the ground.

He wanted no dinner, for his appetite had fled ; added to which, old Twister was in the sulks, and did nothing but abuse him for bringing the wrong common forms.

Difficult was Mr. Bowker's task. He paced round his little cage of an office like a wild beast on the fret. No settled plan of proceeding occurred to his inventive genius. We question if he could have succeeded singlehanded ; but wisely judging, that where women are concerned women would be the best advisers, he enlisted Mrs. Bowker's cunning in the cause, by the lure of a long wished-for ring.

A third person was afterwards added in Miss Slummers, or rather Miss Howard, of Sadlers Wells Theatre, with whom it ultimately was arranged a sham register-office marriage should be concocted, the certificate of which should be handed to Mrs. Jorrocks, who was so delighted with the scheme and with Bill's sagacity that she presented him with a five-pound note for his trouble. It was just what Bill wanted to enable him to purchase a beautifully carved Prince Le Boo nigger he had seen down in Shadwell, which he thought if he only could get for his shop door it would be the making of him. He therefore immediately slipped on his old broken-down bargain-making clothes, and partly by walking, and partly by bussing, arrived at the "marine store," where the object of his errand stood. Prince Le Boo was a magnificent nigger, six feet high, stout, and well formed. He had a splendid diadem, full of parti-coloured feathers, and wore the dress of a savage chief. He had been the property of some East-end Bowker, who, in classical language, had "gone to the wall;" and Bill, in his nautical perambulations, had often admired the stately ease with which the Prince faced the street, offering the contents of his snuff-box to the world. When the owner failed, Bill traced the Prince to his purchaser, and often, on a Saturday afternoon, he would stroll down to see if he was safe, and envy the possession of him. The reader may judge with what joy Bowker placed his prize in a cab, and drove up to Eagle Street, as proud as though he were riding alongside the Prince of Wales. The new purchase threw the blue-jacketed, red-stripe-trousered predecessor into the back-ground, and Bill spent 10*l*. in advertising his establishment as Bowker's "Splendid Prince Le Boo Snuff and Tobacco Warehouse, and Cigar Divan, &c. The Trade supplied."

A sparkling paste necklace propitiated Mrs. Bowker for the apparent extravagance, and Bill replaced Stobbs' wheat earrings, with a coral necklace, and added a false-diamond bandeau as an equivalent for Susan's share in the venture and prize-money.

That no man is a match for a woman till he's married, is an axiom most Benedicts will subscribe to, and Mrs. Jorrocks plied the "marriage lines" so skilfully and successfully that there was little occasion to follow up Belinda's ultimatum with the following production of her own :—

"Mrs. Jorrocks' Comp^ts Mr. Stobbs, and, sir, I am shocked and 'orrified beyond all mensuration at his onprincipled conduct to my niece, which must be extremely painful both to Mrs. Jorrocks's pride and delicacy; and, sir, Mrs. Jorrocks begs to say most implicitly, that upon no consideration at all can she admit Mr. Stobbs into my house in Great Coram Street again any more.

"Mrs. Jorrocks considers it an interposition of Providence that has disclosed Mr. Stobbs' wickedness, and saved Mrs. Jorrocks' niece from Mr. Stobbs' rascality. Mrs. Jorrocks considers Mr. Stobbs far worse than Mr. Carden.

"P.S.—The hat and trousers you left with her are left at Mr. Bowker's; and the books and things Mr. Stobbs gave Belinda, Belinda will prefer keeping if you have no objection."

CHAPTER LXXIII.

MR. BOWKER'S REFLECTIONS.

"Thus conscience does make cowards of us all," muttered Mr. Bowker;

> " And thus the native hue of resolution
> Is sicklied o'er with the pale cast of thought;
> And enterprises of great pith and moment,
> With this regard their currents turn awry,
> And lose the name of action,"

continued he, pacing home from Lincoln's Inn to Eagle Street.

The shades of night were drawing on. The gas men hurried from pillar to post; early shops were shutting up; and it was time to illumine the cigar-divan for the genteel young people they were letting loose.

Mr. Bowker was unhappy—Prince Le Boo had not brought him the comfort he expected. The snuff-merchant was conscience-striken—he had had no peace since he sold himself to Mrs. Jorrocks. Still he couldn't help himself, nor could he help repeating the lines already quoted. Belinda, as he had often seen her at Mrs. Jorrocks', appeared before him —so young, so graceful, and so agreeable,—

> " Sweet as the dewy milk-white thorn ;
> Dear as the raptured thrill of joy."

Then he thought of Stobbs—recalled his first coming to chambers —his open, hearty manner — and, above all, how differently Charles treated him to the generality of old Twister's pupils. What might he be doing then ? Perhaps brooding over his misfortunes—racking his brain, to remember anything that had passed that could be construed into a promise of marriage.

"Why have I done all this ? " asked Bill. "Oh, curse the day that saw me in the clutches of that old hag ! " continued he, as his interview in Great Coram Street came to his recollection. " ' Who would fardels bear to groan and sweat beneath a weary life, but that—' B— boy's shoved the corner of the shutter right into the pit of my stomach ! " exclaimed Bill, breaking off, and doubling himself up ; " Cursed little scamp ! " added he, straightening himself, and seizing the boy by the cuff of the neck, and bastinadoing him with his cane. " What do you mean by flourishing your shutter about in that way ? " whereupon Bill gave the boy two or three more hearty whacks, and then kicked him into the hosier's shop.

" Little unmitigated scamp ! " continued Bill, hurrying on, muttering as he went, " By Jingo ! it would have been just the same thing if I'd been the lord-mayor."

Fearing he might be followed, Bill cut on as quick as he could. He kept close to the wall, and rounded the corner into Red Lion Street at something between a walk and a run. Unfortunately, a gentleman had just stepped aside to tie his shoe-string, and Bill went a somerset over him with his face and hands in the kennel.

* * * * * * *

Great was the hubbub! Women screamed — dogs barked — men stood and laughed — and boys jumped about, cheered, and clapped their hands.

Bill was sadly damaged; both hands and one cheek were covered with mud, and his drab tights were split across the knees.

* * * * * * *

"Confound you, sir!" roared Bill, gathering himself up, and addressing the gentleman; "what the d—l did you do that for?"

"I was only tying my shoe-string!" replied a timid-looking little powdered man in black, eyeing Bill with unfeigned fear.

"TYING YOUR SHOE-STRING!" roared Bill; "d—n you, sir, you're *always* tying your shoe-string. I've a deuced good mind to commit you for an assault!—*Con*founded good mind to commit you for an assault! By Jove, I *will* commit you for an assault! Hanged if I *won't* commit you for an assault! *What's your name?* I'll *send* you to Newgate!"

* * * * * * *

Mr Bowker's temper was sadly ruffled. His neighbour Bullpit's apprentice shouted and roared, and Mrs. Bowker even was graceless enough to laugh at him, as he entered his shop fresh from his fall; added to which, she had done no business during the day, and Mrs. Jorrocks had sent to say she wanted to see him again.

* * * * * * *

As he was purging himself from his contempt, as he called it, and beginning to regain his usual equanimity, a Hansom cab, as these ugly things are called, rolled rapidly up the street, and, passing his door, pulled up short with a skate before his window.

"*That's here!*" exclaimed Bill, from the back shop, where he was washing; "why don't you light up, woman, and let our clients see where we live?" inquired he of his wife, hurrying on his night-coat, and bustling behind the counter.

A youth in a dark macintosh jumped out of the cab, and entered the shop. The collar was up, but Bowker immediately recognised the hat and eyes.

"Did you get a letter from me?" inquired Charles, hastily, undoing the collar of his macintosh as he spoke.

"No—yes—no," replied Mr. Bowker, confusedly, "all right."

"*All right!*—but it's not all right," repeated Charles,—"I think it's all wrong. Who told Mrs. Jorrocks this confounded lie?"

"Mrs. Jorrocks!" repeated Mr. Bowker; "Mrs. Jorrocks—Mrs. Jorrocks—the old girl in Great Coram Street! 'Faith, I don't know."

"Real Havannahs, those, sir," turning to a customer who had just entered the shop. "The ship only arrived the day before yesterday, and

I took the whole cargo—two hundred ton in my warehouse. Thank ye, sir—want a case to put them in—great variety in the window—all prices. New one there!—Prince Albert in kilts, Shooting in Scotland—most popular pattern—sold three dozen to-day—*only* five shillings. Thank you, sir. You don't snuff, I suppose?—got some of the purest Lundyfoot I ever received —forty barrels—four hundred pounds worth, in fact !''

The customer did not, and therefore took his departure.

"Now, Bowker, tell me candidly," said Charles, as soon as he was gone, " what all this means—tell me the worst at once."

" 'Faith, I have no *worst* in the matter," replied Bill; "you seem to know just as much about it as I do, if not more."

"Nay, don't say that—don't deceive me—you've seen old mother Jorrocks—you've some idea what she's driving at."

Bill was silent.

"You know the story about Susan's all made up."

"Indeed I don't," replied Mr. Bowker, confidently—" Indeed I don't —I've no reason to doubt my wife's sister—none whatever. Quite the contrary."

"Nay then!" exclaimed Charley, subsiding into a seat.

"Why, really," replied Bill, looking very solemn, "I should be very happy to befriend you in any way in my power, but there's an old saying, blood's stronger than water; and I must consider my wife's sister first. Matrimony's not so easily got over as a cane and rice fence, as poor old Jackey would say."

"Stuff and nonsense," growled Charles in disgust.

"Aye, stuff and nonsense, indeed," retorted Mr. Bowker, "stop till you've had your nose at the matrimonial grindstone as long as I have, and you'll know it's not stuff and nonsense."

"Come, old Bill," exclaimed a well-musked youth in a blue Spanish cloak, with a profusion of ringlets and rings, " sarve me out a couple of your confounded dried cabbage-leaves, you brandy-faced, big-looming beggar."

"Certainly, sir," replied Bill, strewing a handful along the counter— "there's no standing your insinuating manner ! Your politeness exceeds your beauty. Those cigars, sir,—though I say it,—are not to be equalled."

The youth lit one of them, and sticking his back against the counter, proceeded to draw long respirations, puffing out volleys of smoke at intervals. His great unmeaning eyes rested first on Prince Le Boo, then on the other nigger, next on Charles, then back on the Prince, then again on the nigger.

Mr. Bowker lighted the revolving fan-light in the window, which, with the gas on the counter, made a goodly illumination. He leaned with folded arms against the well-canistered shelves, and Charles seated himself on the make-believe snuff-barrel in which Mrs. Bowker kept her muff.

Bowker eyed Charles intently. Anguish had bleached his cheek, and there was a subdued melancholy in his dark eye that told of intense suffering.

"Rot it, Bill!" exclaimed the smoker, taking the cigar from his mouth, " what's that rakish old nigger got his fisherman's boots on for ?"

"They're not boots, they're his black legs," replied Mr. Bowker, snappishly. "Don't you know that a nigger has black legs?" inquired he, in a tone of contempt.

"They look uncommon like boots by this light," replied the smoker, "I wonder you don't gild his toes to let people see what they are."

"He's not a candle-light beauty," replied Mr. Bowker, carelessly.

The smoker threw open his cloak, and jumping up, seated himself on the counter.

"You're *flat* old chap!" observed he to Bill, after a long puff—"no *jump* in you to-night—what's the matter?"

"Bad tooth-ache," replied Mr. Bowker, putting his hand to his cheek.

"Poor beggar!" replied the customer, "why don't you smoke one of your own cigars? It'll either cure you or make you sick—come, accept the Chiltern Hundreds, and let's off for the night—Coal Hole, Cider Cellar, Offley's, or somewhere."

"I think not, shall return myself for *Bed*fordshire before long," replied Mr. Bowker, yawning and stretching his arms—most heartily wishing his customer gone.

In vain Mr. Bowker tried to get rid of him; the smoker was evidently one of those who consider tobacconists public property—bound to find conversation and house-room.

* * * * * * *

At length he went.

"Mr. Stobbs," said Bowker hurriedly, as he passed round the counter where Charles sat, and laid his hand upon his arm. "Lend me your ear—I mean, let me have a word with you. You'll think me a scoundrel, I dare say," said he, his utterance almost choked, "but if you knew my necessities you'd pity me: I can't bear to see the misery I'm creating. *I know the story about Susan's all my eye.*"

Bill burst into tears.

"You don't say so!" exclaimed Charles, brightening up; "what's the meaning of it, then?"

Bowker, more composed, proceeded to tell him all. When he came to the end he got so excited, that seizing a wooden roll of pigtail off the counter, he aimed such a blow at Prince Le Boo's head, as sent it flying through the milkman's window on the opposite side of the street.

CHAPTER LXXIV.

MR. JORROCKS TAKING HIS OTIUM CUM DIGGING A TATY.

NEXT day saw Mr. Bowker and Charley Hansoming it to Hoxton to see Mr. Jorrocks, for it was the unanimous opinion of all the common law clerks with whom Bowker associated, that the verdict could not be sustained. Indeed, Mr. Shoestring, Serjeant Mustymug's clerk, contended that all people were more or less mad on some subject or other, and that it would be quite as consistent to shop Mr. Catchball for constant cricketing, or Mr. Troller for fishing, as Mr. Jorrocks for .nunting. Altogether, this great legal luminary, a far greater man than his master, was of opinion that the verdict would not hold water. An application to the Chancellor was recommended.

After much parleying and bullying from Mr. Bowker, and liberal allusion to Mr. Perceval, and the Lunatics' Friend Society, they at length got admission, and found our old friend much as a pent-up fox-hunter might be expected to be. He had been digging potatoes in the garden, and as they had deprived him of his wig, he had supplied its place with a red pocket-handkerchief.

"Now this is werry kind o' you!" exclaimed Mr. Jorrocks, running to receive them, "werry kind indeed," continued he, jumping about on one leg, exhibiting a pair of clogs in which he had been digging; "these are most comfortless quarters. I've had nobody to talk to," continued he, "since I came here, except yon poor booby among the cabbages, and a most uneasy companion he is. Thinks he's made o' glass, and that the buoys are shyin' stones at him. I tells him, he'd better be mad upon 'unting than mad upon such nonsense as that—haw! haw! haw! But come, sit down—make yourselves at 'ome, in fact, and tell me the news o' the willage.—Trade brisk or only middlin'?"

Thus Mr. Jorrocks rattled on in his usual strain, first on one subject, then on another, and not always waiting for an answer to his questions.

Of course Dr. —— maintained he was mad. He had lucid intervals certainly, but as soon as ever the subject of hunting was mentioned, off he went at a tangent. Charles said he had seen many men that way, and the doctor's eyes glistened, for he thought he'd like to fill his house with them: call it the "United Fox-hunters' Asylum," or some such name.

Mr. Bowker rather disconcerted him, when he hinted that he would like the Chancellor to see Mr. Jorrocks; and when he proclaimed himself to be a gentleman of the law, and talked about a "habeas corpus," the doctor's countenance fell amazingly.

After much shuffling backwards and forwards work, many protestations from the mad doctor, that the indiscretion of his friends would very materially retard, if not altogether prevent, Mr. Jorrocks's recovery, the solicitors at length agreed upon requesting a private examination by the Chancellor, which was kindly vouchsafed, his lordship having been struck by the perusal of the proceedings as published in the newspapers, and having, moreover, some little curiosity to see the distinguished subject of the inquiry.

Accordingly it was arranged that Mr. Jorrocks should wait in his lordship's private room for the rising of his court. Thither our friend went, accompanied only by his partner, Mr. Simpkins, and Charley Stobbs. Mr. Bowker presented them with great dignity to the usher, and returned to old Twister. The court sat late. His lordship's train-bearer lent them a newspaper, and, stirring the fire, advised them to sit round, and make themselves comfortable.

Accordingly they did.

Several people looked in upon them ;—a footman, an usher, a laundress, but nobody seemed inclined to stay.

Towards dusk a gentleman, with a singularly pleasing expression of countenance, who seemed more at home in the apartment than any of his predecessors had been, entered the room.

" Is Mr. Jorrocks here ? " asked he, after surveying the party by the fire.

" Mr. Jorrocks *is* here ! " replied our hero, getting up.

"Don't let me disturb you, pray," rejoined the gentleman, bowing, and motioning Mr. Jorrocks to be seated. Our friend, however, being up, took a coat-lap over each arm, and turning his back to the fire confronted the enterer.

"Coolish evening, this, Mr. Jorrocks," observed the gentleman, rubbing his hands as he approached the fire; "I hope your accommodation is comfortable at Hoxton ? "

" Any thing *but*," replied Mr. Jorrocks; "at least I shall be werry glad to let you have it if you like. Can't even get a seidletz-pooder without an order from the Chancellor."

The gentleman smiled. " Rather be in the City, perhaps, among your bills and your books ;—do you know how the funds are ? "

" Indeed I don't, replied Mr. Jorrocks; " consols were at ninety-two and a quarter when they shopped me; don't know what they may be now, wot with the weather and Nicholas Rumenough's wagaries," adding half to himself and half to his interrogator, " wish I could send Pigg over to fight him."

" You understand money matters, I suppose," observed the gentleman. " Can you tell me the difference between discount and interest ? "

" I should think so," replied Mr. Jorrocks. " Catch a merchant not understandin' that. Discount's a premium paid in 'and for the loan of money for a time yet to come, and the chap wot gets the discount can lend the discount out again, while the chap wot gets the interest has to wait his time afore he has it to lend."

" They feed you pretty well where you are, I suppose ? "

Mr. Jorrocks.—"Tol-lol—*mutton ! mutton !—toujours* mutton, as we say in France."

" What ! mutton every day ? Can you tell me how many legs a sheep has ? "

" Dead or alive ? " inquired Mr. Jorrocks.

"They say you are mad about hunting, I understand," observed the gentleman after a laugh at Mr. Jorrocks's acuteness.

" Ah,—'unting's the thing "—exclaimed Mr. Jorrocks—" the sport ot
kings—but, however, never mind, we won't talk about that," added
he, checking himself, and saying, "I wish the old gentleman would
come."

"I suppose hunting's a fine amusement," observed the gentleman,
after a pause. " Did you ever hunt with the stag-hounds ? "

" *Once,*" replied Mr. Jorrocks. " *Once,* I should think, would be
enough for any body."

" How so ? I thought they were popular."

" They may, but I thinks nothin' of them. The *fox* is the thing !
Confound it ! *There goes,*" observed Mr. Jorrocks aloud to himself.—
" Well, never mind, I'll tell you something," continued he, after a pause
—" 'Unting exemplifies wot the grammarians call the three degrees of
comparison :—stag-'unting is positively bad, 'are-'unting is comparatively
good, and fox-'unting superlatively so. There's a wrinkle for ye !
Haw, haw, haw. I'll give ye another," continued he, "as you seem
a goodish sort o' chap. If ever you keep 'ounds," said he putting his
forefinger to his nose, and winking his right eye, " if ever you keep
'ounds, always 'ave a year's meal in advance. Old goes 'alf as far again
as new."

" Your lordship's carriage is at the door," announced a footman in
undress livery.

" My vig ! " exclaimed Mr. Jorrocks, starting ; " have I been talking
all this nonsense to the Chancellor ? Oh, dear ! oh, dear ! " continued
he, wringing his hands and stamping, " wot a confounded old jackass I
am ! Dash my vig ! I don't think I shall ever grow wiser."

" Don't alarm yourself, my good friend," observed the Chancellor,
mildly ; " I am glad to have seen you in this way, for it has given me an
opportunity of judging how you are. You may be an enthusiast ; but I
think, sir," turning to the doctor, " Mr. Jorrocks seems perfectly able to
do without your assistance, and I should recommend your letting him
go home quietly from here," so saying, his lordship bowed and retired.

*   *   *   *   *   *   *

" Dash my vig ! but that's somethin' like a Chancellor ! " exclaimed
Mr. Jorrocks, as his lordship got out of hearing ; and seizing the mad
doctor with one hand, and desiring Charley to take him by the other,
they danced three reels with him till the mad doctor could dance no
longer. Mr. Jorrocks then having kicked out the mad doctor's hat-crown,
politely placed the remains on his head and shoved him out of the door.
Joining arms with Bowker, who had now returned, and Stobbs, he then
strutted away most consequentially for Great Coram Street—just as they
did on the first night of Charles's introduction.

*   *   *   *   *   *   *

" Now," said he, when he got to the Hunter Street turn, producing
his sneck-key as he spoke, " we'll give 'em an agreeable surprise."

Having arrived at the Great Coram Street door, he gently opened the
latch, and motioning them to enter on tiptoe, as quietly closed the door
after him.

There was a solitary candle in the passage, and a strong smell of dinner
below. Knives and forks were going in the parlour.

Mr. Jorrocks's Return to his Family

He gently opened the door. There sat Mrs. Jorrocks, in a fine red and gold turban, at the top of the table, Belinda with her back to the door, and Captain Doleful in the host's chair, in the act of diving a fork into the breast of a boiled turkey.—" *Holloa ! you old bald-faced baboon !* " roared Mr. Jorrocks, an exclamation that caused Captain Doleful to drop his fork, his whiskers to fall from his face, and Mrs. Jorrocks to swoon on the floor.

*   *   *   *   *   *   *

Jorrocks then installed himself in his rightful position, and insisted on Doleful staying to see " ow 'appy they would all be." And werry 'appy J. got, so 'appy that he didn't know when Doleful went away, or how he got to bed himself.

Doleful was desperately dejected and took to his bed at Handley Cross as if he would never leave it again. At last he got up, but only to fall into another snare. Let us take a fresh chapter to detail it in.

CHAPTER LXXV.

DOLEFUL AT SUIT BRANTINGHAME.

Mr. Jorrocks's early, but unseen friend, Sir Archy Depecarde, had a sister, one Mrs. Brantinghame, for whom he was anxious to do something at somebody-else's expense, and hearing of Doleful's disappointment, he bethought him it was the very time to fix a wife upon him, knowing that when a man has made up his mind to commit matrimony, he will often take up with the next best chance that offers, rather than go without a wife. Accordingly, Sir Archy despatched the following laconic to Droppingfall Wells, where Mrs. Brantinghame was staying :

" Try Miser*. Doleful, at Handley Cross."

And as soon as ever her week was up at the Wells, she flew on the wings of steam to our renowned Spa, accompanied by her only remaining unmarried daughter, Louisa Letitia Carolina Jemima, for Mrs. Brantinghame had been most particular in loading all her daughters with names, well knowing the agreeable expectations such repletion engenders.

To Captain Doleful, Sir Archy wrote as follows :—

"Pluckwelle Park.

" Dear Captain Doleful,

" My sister, Mrs. Brantinghame, purposes paying a visit to your Spa, to consult our friend, Dr. Mello, and any attention you can show her will be gratefully acknowledged by

" Dear Captain Doleful,

" Your's, very truly,

" Archibald Depecarde."

And the captain, albeit out of humour with the sex, on receipt of the note, began perking and simpering himself up, and when he heard of the widow's arrival at her nice six guinea a-week house, in Acacia Crescent, having given her time to shake out her feathers and get settled, he put on his best grin, and went mincing and picking his way, taking care of his Molière shoes, to pay his respects.

We may here mention that Sir Archy had furthered the design, by lending Mrs. Brantinghame his butler and footman, who were out at grass on board wages, at his expense, while he reconnoitered some minor watering-places, *incog.*, in the west, a country that he knew the wise men did not come from, so that, what with the six guinea a-week house, the butler, the footman, the powder, the plate, Mrs. Brantinghame's three hundred a year, looked like as many thousands. We say plate, for Sir Archy lent a becoming quantity of that too, together with some most unimpeachable looking linen and glass, for a gambler always has the best of everything, everything at least that contributes to outward show and adornment. We will now suppose our innocent captain approaching the well-set snare.

His resolute ring at the visitors' bell, was speedily answered by a smart well powdered, well put on footman, in brown and black plush, who was quickly seconded by a portly £50-a-year-at-least looking butler, who politely bowing an admission that his mistress was at home, proceeded to conduct our hero up the gaudily carpetted stair-case, to the presence chamber.

"Capting Doleful, I b'live," smiled the obsequious butler, who had taken in and let out many a gambling victim for his master. "Capting Doleful, I b'live," repeated he, in the most deferential tone, as he paused upon the flossy pink sheepskin mat, on the landing outside the door, that as yet shut out the view of the *terra incognita*, upon which our adventurous traveller was about to enter. What a region is that same matrimonial wilderness of undiscovered connection, of which no man's imagination has ever depicted the reality!

"Captain Doleful," assented our visitor, as the man opened the cream-coloured door by its flowered handle.

"Capting Doleful, Miss," announced he, softly, over the swelling bust of a lady, apparently engaged at her writing-desk; but in reality arranged so as to show the luxuriant rolls of her double-banded brown hair, and the delicate whiteness of her swan-like neck, before her face and general features. All women have some point on which they more particularly pride themselves, and Miss Brantinghame went on her figure and complexion. She had carried Rapin's quarto edition of the History of England, with Marco Polo's travels atop, on her head, till she was as straight and erect as a dairymaid, or a Fulham strawberry-carrying woman.

Having kept her position sufficiently long to enable her to finish the sentence she was writing, she now arose and turned round, when, in lieu of a crumbey old lady, in a cap and false hair, Doleful found himself confronted with a pleasant looking woman, if not an exact beauty, or in the full freshness of youth, at all events one good to look at, who, with a sweet smile, and a stick-out-behind curtsey, begged him to be seated, while she intimated her connection with the house, by an aside, "*Tell mamma,*" to the butler.

Doleful was dumbfoundered, and wished he had put on his best Poulson and Co. suit, instead of the second-best one he had come in. He required a second smile, and a second stick-out behind curtsey, to induce him to venture on an Elizabethan India japanned chair, that stood appropriately near where the fair lady sat. Miss then put up her papers, glanced at the opposite mirror, felt her side hair, elongated her nose, and arranged her features generally to what she considered captivating pitch, as she turned in her Jenny Lind chair, to do the agreeable to the caller.

The captain noted a pretty foot, a taper hand, and saw a delicately white well-turned arm up the accommodating width of her sky-blue jacket sleeve. He didn't care if mamma didn't come for an hour. Miss, on her part, though she thought the captain older and more wrinkly than she expected, and not to be compared, in point of looks, either to Peter Bullock, to whom she was then engaged, or Captain Capers, whom she had jilted in Peter's favour, felt that Doleful was infinitely their superior in point of wealth and station, and that a pair of proudly-stepping greys would amply compensate for the few envious gray streaks she saw scattered through his straggling hair. She therefore pointed a toe, arranged the heavy manacles on her arms, and placing her pretty hands becomingly on her smart blue spotted muslin dress, opened volubly upon him about the weather. The captain chimed in, and having speedily exhausted that interesting subject, they adjourned to the Crystal Palace, at Sydenham, whose magic wonders soon afforded our fair friend an opportunity of expressing a regret that she had not a brother to take her there, adding, with a half suppressed sigh, something about "only children," which fell very gratefully on the grinning captain's ear. She would like to go to Sydenham every day—Oh! she *should* so like to go to Sydenham every day—She would like to go through all the Courts, and all the galleries, and all the walks, and all the lobster-salad places, and she soon talked herself into a perfect glow of animation. The captain sat in ecstasies, thinking how much pleasanter it was to be courted than to have the up-hill game he had had with Belinda—Belinda be hanged, thought he. Here was a lady infinitely her superior, and not much behind her in looks, at least, not when the looks were directed at him. She was more of a woman, too. Her figure was fuller and more developed, her hair as bright and glossy, her teeth as pearly, while her animated conversation soon imparted a lustre to her greyish blue eyes, and threw a gentle flush o'er her otherwise pallid cheeks, that chased away what ill-natured people would call lines. Altogether Doleful soon began to think he had lit on his legs. The scars of his old heart began to heal. Miss Brantinghame for ever! chuckled he. Now for mamma.

That experienced and judicious old lady, always easy at the outset, but most urgent towards the end, was busy with her only maid, Martha, in the dining-room, putting away groceries, when the Captain came, and receiving for answer to her enquiry, as the maid peeped through the green trellis blinds, whether the ring proceeded from "petticoats or legs," that it proceeded from "legs;" she had little difficulty in appropriating them, and, like a prudent matron, deliberately finished her work 'ere she adjourned to her bed-room, to make those little adjustments, or perhaps

additions to her dress, that we will leave to the imagination of the
reader.

And now, as our grinning friend sat lost in ecstasies, listening to the
silvery notes of the syren, the door gently opened, and in sidled Mamma,
the smiling autumn of her voluble daughter.

"My dear Captain Doleful," said she, advancing, and extending her
hand as she spoke, "My dear Captain Doleful," repeated she, in a tone
of mournful resignation, "this is indeed most kind—most considerate—
my dear brother, Sir Archy, will be deeply grateful, when he hears
of your early compliance with his wishes." And thereupon she shook
the Captain heartily by the hand, not a fine fore-finger shake, but
a genuine confiding greeting, that spoke of confidence of the most substantial and inexhaustible order.

The Captain, who was up on the instant, to make one of his most
elaborate bows, was now invited to occupy a berth by mamma, on the
spring-cushioned sofa, instead of the ricketty fabric on which he had been
getting mesmerised. Having subsided by her side, he harked back upon
the weather, which he reviewed under various aspects, Harvest-ically—
Turnip-ically — Potatoe-ically — Promenade-ically — Invalid-ically, and
Handley Cross-ically.

They then went to the war, and just as Mrs. Brantinghame was making
the unfortunate enquiry, if the Captain was at Waterloo, the noiseless
butler announced luncheon (in reality dinner, the servants dining after),
which saved our hero the humiliation of stating that he was only a militia
captain, and had never been out of England. The announcement, however, stopped all this, and even if the Captain had been inclined to confess,
we dare say the answer would have been lost upon Mrs. Brantinghame, so
intent was she in hoping that Partridge, the butler, and Frederick, the
footman, and Martha, the maid, had arranged everything, comme il faut,
in the dining-room. After the lapse of a few seconds, for Mrs. Brantinghame was now quite on the "take-it-easy tack," she hoped the dear Captain
would come down stairs and take a little luncheon with them, whatever
there was, for she feared it would only be of the scrambling order, not
having either her cook or her housekeeper, and only one footman with
her, but she was sure he would excuse any little deficiency. So saying,
she arose, and, taking the grinning Captain's arm, conducted him
down stairs, leaving his eight-and-sixpenny hat and twopenny cane to
take care of themselves. The Captain went hugging himself, thinking he
would save a dinner at home, for he had one of those convenient appetites
that could be made to bear upon a dinner, whenever one came in the way.
Thus they reached the lower apartment.

Upon the snowy, well got up cloth, of an elegantly set out table, stood
a couple of beautiful cold Dorking fowls, a tongue, mashed potatoes, and
greens, an uncut apricot tart, a shape of pastrycook's blancmange, a
bottle of pale Sherry (brown, watered), and as much of a bottle of
Malmsey Madeira as Partridge could spare in the decanting, while the
sideboard exhibited Seltzer water, a bottle of Allsop, and a quart of
"Dobbs and Co.," which Partridge intended for himself. Mamma took
the top of the table, Miss the bottom, and Doleful the side opposite the
fire. Partridge carved the fowls from the sideboard. Frederick handed

them round, and the party were soon in the enjoyment of eating made easy. As Doleful sat munching away, he made a mental inventory of what he saw; bright plate, beautiful creaseless linen, crystal-like glass, noiseless butler, powdered footman, everything quite genteel; couldn't be done under two thousand a year—no not for a halfpenny under two thousand a year—and he contrasted it with old Jorrocks's rough and ready style, his bustling Batsay, bubbly Binjimin, and duplicate dishes. Then Partridge was so attentive, so anxious to draw the "Allsop," so discouraging in his offer of the "Dobbs," that Doleful was quite taken with him, and, after the third glass of wine, felt as if he could give him half-a-crown. Partridge, we are sorry to say, did not reciprocate Doleful's admiration, for on getting down stairs, he declared to Martha, that Miss must be desperately in want of a husband, to take up such a death's-head looking man, and thinking that Mrs. Markham, Sir Archy's housekeeper, to whom he was privately married, would not have had him if he had been such a "guy." The appetites of the parlour party being at length appeased, they return to the drawing-room, where Miss enchanted Doleful with her execution of " Vilikins " on her harp, an instrument she never travelled without, being admirably adapted for showing off her fine swelling figure. And after a long protracted sit, Doleful at length took his departure, feeling that Sir Archy was not half a bad fellow, and vowing that he would return without fail on the morrow.

Mamma and Miss then talked him over, Mamma observing that she thought he " would do," Miss, who always liked to run counter, replying, she " didn't know."

<hr>

CHAPTER LXXVI.

THE GRAND FIELD DAY.

THE morrow came, and with it came Doleful—Doleful, no longer an indifferent duty visitor on behalf of Sir Archy Depecarde, but Doleful, a very cock-a-hoopish caller on his own account, got up with uncommon care and circumspection. He sported a sixteen-shilling hat, with a flexible silk band instead of a rusty draggling crape, while a black and white watch-ribbon-like tie encircled his stiff round-about collar, with as much end floating over his machinery-worked shirt-front as could reasonably be expected for two-and-sixpence. A Regent Street registered Pardessus was thrown gaily back, to show as well its rich quilting as his new wide-sleeved coatee with a red silk cuff lining, his twelve-and-sixpenny vest to order, and his black clerical riding-trousers falling becomingly upon his bright Molière shoes. Thus attired, he led himself gaily to the charge, causing no little sensation as he passed through the streets.

Behold him entering Acacia Crescent, and now at the door of his charmer. The house never looked so attractive before. He could almost have kissed the scraper.

Visitors' bells certainly are a great improvement upon the time when a man

had to mark his own claims to consideration by an appeal to the knocker.
It was all very well for ladies, with twelve or thirteen yards of powdered
impertinence to act as their heralds, and pound at the panels, but for a
humble pedestrian to have to indoctrinate the servants into his claim to
attention by the number and freedom of his raps, was rather a nervous
undertaking for gentlemen unaccustomed to public knocking. And yet,
if one didn't make a noise, they would often let one stand till one starved.
So thought Doleful, as he turned the ivory-knobbed handle at the right of

THE TAKING OF CAPTAIN DOLEFUL.

Mrs. Brantinghame's door, and faced the sun as if for a wait.   Quick as
thought, the door opened—opened, not in a doubtful, hesitating sort of
way, but flew wide open, as if there wasn't a doubt upon the subject of
the ladies being at home.   Lowly bowed the smiling Frederick, who was
powdered to perfection, and starched and ironed out down to his very
shoe-ties.   Partridge, too, was in full feather, and never did the horse-shoe
breast of one of the winged tribe look more bright than did his ample

chest in a rich blue, green, yellow, red, all the colours of the rainbow
reflecting, cut velvet vest, set off with steel buttons. Indeed, he should
rather have been called Pheasant. He had also a splendid velvet-collared
blue coat, made of far better cloth than Doleful's, decorated with hiero-
glyphical buttons, B. P. A. entwined (Butlers' Perquisite Association),
and superfine drab trowsers, with broad brown stripes down the sides.
Thus attired, he received our suitor at the hands of Frederick, and as he
helped him out of his registered Pardessus, woman-like, Martha the maid-
of-all-work flitted in the background, arrayed in one of her young
missus's cast-off silks, enacting the character of upper servant. For the
wages of one servant and a half, she did the work of three, eating only
the victuals of one.

The Captain being now ready for presentation, Partridge preceded him
up-stairs, making a mental bet with himself—for he was a bit of a
wagerer—on the double events of something winning the Derby, and
Miss capturing the Captain. Mrs. Brantinghame, who was arranging
matters in the parlour, peeped up at her son-in-law's legs as they ascended
the stairs, and knowing that all was right above, resumed her occupation,
like a nice, discreet old mouser as she was.

And now the drawing-room door opens, and in stalks the gallant
Captain, bowing and grinning, and capering as usual. Miss receives him
most cordially, as well with a shake of the hand as a stick-out-behind
curtsey, and the Captain at once subsides upon an ottoman full of the
usual odds and ends, and non-company things.

Miss is most carefully got up for the important occasion. Martha has
had a good hour and a half's spell at her toilette, between making the
beds and preparing the lunch, and, by dint of careful sitting since, not a
single hair is displaced. She has on a light blue barège dress, the body
and flounces trimmed with plaited blue ribbon, and on her well turned
arms she wears her first-class manacles, the product of many an ardent
courtship, for she always made it a rule to confiscate the offerings of her
suiters when the matches went off. She begins by apologising for the
absence of Mamma, who had lain down to try to sleep off a sick headache,
a statement that Mamma subsequently contradicted by saying she had been
poring over her steward's accounts for the last quarter, which was quite
as agreeable a hearing to our Captain, who thought he would like to
relieve her of that trouble in future.

Mamma has got on her best bib and tucker, and everything wears a
holiday aspect. She is all smiles and serenity. The luncheon, too, was
of the elegant order, without any make-weight dishes, or apparent eking-
out from any other quarter. Indeed, Partridge took better care of the
scraps than that, and already his onslaughts on the cold tongue, and his
refusal to share the overplus of the " Dobbs " with Martha, had led to
unpleasant bickerings between them. To-day, however, they seem to
have merged their differences for the common weal, and play into each
other's hands in the most praiseworthy manner. Everything is cold,
except the vegetables and game, which latter Mrs. Brantinghame would
have insinuated came from her own manor, were she not afraid that the
ever-watchful Partridge, who brought it from Sir Archy's, would contradict
her. Miss, however, did the fine by desiring Frederick to tell her maid

to bring her a pocket-handkerchief; and Mrs. muttered something about the inconvenience of only having one footman, as Partridge followed Frederick out of the room for a bottle of Allsop, in which he hoped to get Doleful to give him a reversionary interest by having it opened. In fact, the ladies rather over-did the thing, as pretenders often do when they want to cut it fat. Doleful, however, was too much mixed up with them to see anything of the sort, and munched and eat, and munched and eat, with the greatest apparent satisfaction. At length, after a hearty repast, and a long *téte-à-téte* with Miss after (the affairs of the estate requiring Mamma's attention elsewhere), the old grinner took his departure; and as Mamma surveyed the wreck of luncheon, above all, the greatly diminished Malmsey, and thought of the blabbishness of servants, she came to the conclusion that the sooner she got out her landing-net the better.

CHAPTER LXXVII.

A SLOW COACH.

CAPTAIN DOLEFUL was so extremely well satisfied as well with the fare as the fair, that he did not feel at all inclined to press his suit to a termination, which he felt he could do at any moment he liked. He therefore just dropped in every day at luncheon time, and stayed till the shades of evening began to draw on, when he adjourned the High Court of Hymen until the next day, instead of letting the clock of courtship run down, and having to wind it up again. Thus he went on for above a week, much to the edification of the opposite neighbours, who, for " serious people," were more curious than discreet.

Mrs. Brantinghame, on the other hand, waxed very impatient. She disliked the expense, and dreaded the information afforded by electric telegraphs, penny postage, Bernard Burkes, and busybodies generally. Partridge, too, was anything but tractable, and wanted to have everything as they had at Sir Archy's, prigging included, which did not at all accord with Mrs. Brantinghame's ideas of housekeeping. She was therefore all for pressing her daughter on, just as old J. pressed his hounds on after a fox. A council of war was held every evening, after the Captain's departure, to hear as well how Miss had got on that day, as to arrange proceedings for the next. Miss always reported that she saw the offer was coming, but Mamma very wisely observed that " Christmas was coming too ; " a season that conjured up all sorts of disagreeable associations,—" To bill delivered," " Bill to deliver," " Bill if not paid on or before," &c., &c.—and then to think how ill she was providing for the future, by the expense she was then incurring. She wished the thing was settled, one way or other.

She gradually lowered the standard of entertainment, and instead of Dorking fowls and roast game, she jobbed a joint from Saveloy's beef and sausage shop in Grudgington Street, which was weighed in and weighed out, to stop the unreasonable incursions of Partridge. The Sherry,

and Malmsey Madeira too, were replaced by Marsala, and some of
Walker and Walton's Tent, one-and-sixpence a bottle (one-and-three, if
the bottle was returned), and the Allsop supply was cut off altogether.
Still the old Captain plodded on at his own pace; neither Mamma's
broad hints, nor Miss's variously decorated charms nor wants of a brother,
could get him beyond kissing her hand. This, as Mamma said, might
mean anything. The servants began to see through the thing, and
Partridge no longer took the trouble of appearing at the door, while
Frederick gave himself up to fancy trowsers and flash ties, instead of the
decorous apparel in which he had at first appeared. Mamma soon waxed
dreadfully nervous, that is to say, desperately out of temper. Every time
she saw Partridge's broad back looming along the Crescent, she pictured
to herself the stories he would be propagating at the Dun Cow, the Load
of Hay, the Fox and Hounds, or whatever house he frequented, and she
fancied she saw them all going to the Captain bound up in a sheaf. Still
she was too wise to attempt to bribe the job butler to secresy, well knowing
that the course of servitude is to keep the bribe and tell the secret.

She thought the Captain desperately slow. Mr. Cowmeadow hung off
a long time with Catherine Christian Clementina Constance, and Captain
Cushet was anything but as quick as he might have been with Winifred
Rebecca Leonora Lucretia, but then they had other things to attend to,
whereas Captain Doleful had really and truly nothing whatever to do or
to think of, but to court and eat, and still he couldn't be brought to book.
It was very provoking. He was the slowest suitor she had ever seen, and
she had had nearly a score through her hands, to say nothing of her own
experience in that line. Why didn't he propose?

CAPTAIN DOLEFUL'S MOTHER-IN-LAW.

CHAPTER LXXVIII.

THE CAPTAIN CATCHES IT.

ONE fine morning, as our hand-kissing friend came hopping, and grinning, and bounding up-stairs, without giving Frederick the trouble of announcing him, what should he find, instead of dear smiling Letitia sitting at the receipt of custom, but stiff old Mamma, with her front well down over her care-worn, wrinkled brow, and her once smiling lips compressed into a very firm, resolute-looking mouth. Doleful started at the sight. He saw there was mischief. She didn't look like herself.

"Good morning, my dear Captain," said Mrs. Brantinghame, extending her two forefingers for a salute, a sort of instalment of what he might get if he was a good boy; "Good morning, my dear Captain. Louisa Letitia will be down presently. But before she comes," added she, in a lower tone, "I should like to have a few words with you," motioning the taken-aback Captain to a seat on the sofa by her side. "You see, my dear (hem) Captain," re-commenced she, *sotto voce*, as soon as he got settled; "you see, my dear Captain," repeated she, with one of those nasty dry coughs with which old women generally preface their unpleasantness, "you see, my dear (hem) Captain," added she for the third time, "though of course I'm extremely (hem) happy and (cough) pleased to see you (hem) here whenever you (cough—hem) like to come, yet the (hem) world is censorious, and when a (cough) young gentleman comes so often to the house where there is a (hem) young lady, ill-natured people will (cough) talk, and "—here she had recourse to her kerchief.

The Captain was non-plussed, for he had not calculated on overhauling time coming so soon; but, with the comfortable consciousness of having the wherewithal, he soon recovered his composure, very different to a young gentleman who feels that overhauling and kicking-out time will be all one.

Mrs. Brantinghame marked his countenance with satisfaction, and felt encouraged to go on; indeed, she had never known Sir Archy's information fail, though she had not always been able to realise it. "Of course (hem)" continued she, smoothing out the corner of her kerchief, "Of course I need not (hem) say that my (hem) daughter is very much (cough —hem) flattered and (cough) gratified by the (hem) partiality you have (cough) shown her, and I'm sure (cough—hem—cough)" simpered she, "I have every reason to show you (cough) confidence and esteem, as well on my brother Sir Archy's account as on that of my poor dear child, but, considering the difficulty (hem) and the delicacy (hem) of my (hem) situation, I feel assured you will excuse a mother's (hem) and (hem) "—the old lady checking herself, in the hope that the Captain would now take up the running.

In this, however, she was disappointed; for the Captain, having taken a careful survey of the ceiling during the earlier part of her discourse, and seen what he was almost sure was a spider's web in the cornice above the door, now took to studying the roses, lilies, and convolvuluses of which the light-grounded carpet was composed.

In the course of his floricultural pursuit, the following ideas came to his assistance :—

First, that he was a very great man.

Secondly, that the old lady was in too great a hurry.

Thirdly, that he wouldn't be bullied.

As he seemed likely to increase his stock of ideas, Mrs. Brantinghame resumed the appeal, *ad misericordiam.*

"People," whimpered she, pretending to brush away a rising tear, "People may blame (hem) me for allowing my (hem) daughter's (cough) affections to be (hem) engaged before the (cough—hem—cough) preliminaries are all arranged, but really, my dear (cough—hem) Captain, I have been placed in a very trying and difficult situation, and my great regard for my brother, Sir Archy, prompting (hem) me to show you every (cough) attention, without p'r'aps thinking or (cough—hem—cough) considering the great (cough) risk and (hem) danger I was exposing my poor dear child to." Whereupon she went off full cry, burying her sobs in her kerchief.

During this second performance, the Captain's thoughts had time to take another turn, and they served him thus :—

First, he recollected his ignominious expulsion from Great Coram Street.

Secondly, he thought he would like to show Belinda how soon he could suit himself, and that, too, with a great heiress.

Thirdly, he considered that the not having a brother was always as good as a thousand pounds to a girl, as sooner or later the brother would be sure to do him out of that sum.

Fourthly, that the old lady could not live for ever, and, in addition to a very lady-like wife, he would come in for no end of property—plate, and china.

Accordingly, by the time Mrs. Brantinghame was done heaving and sobbing, the Captain was gifted with the following powers of speech :—

"I'm sure, marm, (hem)—I'm sure, marm, (cough)—I'm sure, marm, (sneeze)—" now looking up to the cornice for the spider's web, "I am certainly—I may say undoubtedly—deeply—that is to say sincerely— sincerely, that is to say deeply—attached—to your very elegant and amiable, that is to say, amiable and elegant daughter, and," looking at his rather ragged nails, "I flatter myself—that is to say—I have reason to believe—that your lovely and beautiful—that is to say amiable—and (cough) accomplished daughter is equally attached to me," now looking down at his Molières.

"That I have no doubt of, my dear Captain," interrupted Mrs. Brantinghame, glad to have got that admission from himself; "that I have no doubt of, my dear Captain," repeated she. "If I had not been satisfied on that point, I should not have thought of troubling you to day; but, standing almost alone in the world, and knowing the danger of allowing these sort of (cough) intimacies to ripen into (hem) friendships, without a little (hem) understanding, I felt it my duty as a mother to satisfy myself that your (cough) feelings are reciprocal, so that my (cough) child's (hem) affections might not be (sneeze) sacrificed."

The Captain grinned assent, whereupon a game at cross-purposes ensued between Mamma and himself, each wanting to find out what the other had ; but, Mrs. Brantinghame having determined to make her daughter Mrs. Doleful at all hazards, she did not go so close to the wind as she would otherwise have done.   They were both in a good deal of debt, and Mamma was determined to saddle the Captain with her daughter's share.

This exciting discussion was at length interrupted by Frederick (who had been listening at the door for some time) entering the room, to announce that luncheon was ready, whereupon, Mrs. Brantinghame having gathered herself together, tendered Doleful her hand, saying emphatically, as she eyed his slightly flushed face, " *Then we understand each other.*"   And the gallant officer having answered " Yes ;" she replied, as she took his arm to go down stairs, " *Then you shall have an opportunity after luncheon.*"

CHAPTER LXXIX.

THE CAPTAIN IN DISTRESS.

THE luncheon that day was rather better than usual.   In addition to a nice piece of cold sirloin of beef, Saveloy sent in a dish of hot sausage-rolls, and some pork-pies, on " sale or return," as the booksellers say, and Martha had tried her hand, not altogether unsuccessfully, at a sweet omelette.   The decanters, too, were replenished, though we are sorry to add that Partridge was so exasperated at Mrs. Brantinghame's meanness in locking away the wine, that he had infused a very strong dose of jalap into the Tent.   He had just had time to shake it well up, as Captain Doleful and Mrs. Brantinghame descended.

Ere they had got settled in their seats, Miss entered the room, looking the very essence of innocence, though most carefully got up, and rustling in a new drab and pink shot watered silk.   Doleful was up on the instant to receive his intended, whose smiling features had just been regulated at the looking-glass. Notwithstanding the wigging our old friend had just had, he played a pretty good knife and fork, and though he thought the first glass of Tent tasted rather queer, he did not hesitate to take a second, in which Mrs. Brantinghame joined him. So they beefed, and sausaged, and Tented, as if there was nothing particularly astir.

Mrs. Brantinghame, however, retired earlier than usual, giving a significant *hem* and look at her daughter, and no sooner did the door close than Doleful, instead of finding himself in the delightful elysium young gentlemen anticipate on such occasions, began to experience all sorts of queer qualms and disagreeable sensations. Miss, who was under orders to bring the affair to a termination, one way or the other, seeing his perturbation, thought to assist his courage by Marsala, which proving more like liquid fire than wine, he again had recourse to the jalaped Tent. He still thought it queer, and sipped and tasted, and turned it over on his palate, wondering if it could be the sweet omelette that made it taste so.

Miss, knowing Mamma's sanguine temperament, and that she would not rest long, now that she was fairly raised, tried to get him into conversation as soon as she could. She first broached that convenient autumnal subject, the court-martial on Lieutenant Perry, and censured the naughty officers who tried him. Doleful, who was still lost in meditation on the wine, merely replied between sips, that soldiers generally made as great a mess when they played at lawyers, as lawyers would if they played at soldiers. He then sip, sip, sipped, till he finished the glass, and set it down, thoroughly satisfied there was something wrong about it. He wondered where they had got it. Miss noted his abstraction, and also her Mamma's hurried footsteps pacing over head. She tried to get him into the warlike line—the Crimea—then into the Baltic—to Helsingfors, Bomarsund, Revel, saying she thought it was almost better to be as she was, without a brother, than have him exposed to such terrible dangers. This observation, with the falling of a worsted-work weight above, drew Doleful's attention from certain inward qualms he was feeling, to the subject on which Mamma had been sounding him. It was a great nuisance the old woman being so pressing. What could make her change her tactics so suddenly? She, who had been all ease and confidence before. Could another suitor have turned up? Oh dear! what a twinge that was—wish he mightn't have got the cholera. And he incontinently took another pull at the Tent. It was decidedly nasty; and he set his glass down, determined to be done with it. He would give his ears for a little brandy.—There again!—Wished he was at home.—Believed he would have to take a cab.—Would cost him a shilling.—Could have dined at home for ninepence.

Miss, little thinking what was going on internally, but dreading her Mamma's impetuosity, who, not over comfortable herself, was fretting and fidgetting about in the drawing-room, counting the minutes as hours, venting her spleen on Doleful and all dilatory sweethearters, and wondering how much he had cost her in the way of victuals and drink. Miss, we say, little thinking of what Doleful was suffering, and anxious to give him a lift, tried him personally, by asking what he thought of her new dress, getting up to show it, and just as he was paying the old compliment to her fair hand, after admiring the dress, Mamma, who had stolen noiselessly into the room, exclaimed, " Well, I'm *glad* you've got it *all* settled.   I'm *glad* you've got it all settled," seizing Doleful's hand as it dropped from her daughter's; "for really I was getting very nervous and uncomfortable. And, oh, my dear child!" continued she, giving her a strong hug, " I *hope* you'll be happy! " adding, as she turned again to the now teeth-grinding Captain, " I'm sure if she's not, it will be her own fault, for I never saw a sweeter disposition than yours. And now," inquired she, in the same breath, "will you take any more luncheon," pointing to the still well-stored table, and thinking the servants would be wanting their dinners.

Doleful declined any more luncheon.

" Or wine? " asked she.

Doleful would have no more of that either.

" Then let us go up stairs, and communicate the joyful intelligence to your sisters by this post," continued Mrs. Brantinghame.

" Sisters! " exclaimed Doleful, sickening, " I thought you were an only child ! "

" *Only child I have left*," replied Mrs. Brantinghame, with the utmost effrontery.

" Only child you have left," gasped Doleful.

" Yes, only child I have left," continued Mrs. Brantinghame, volubly. "Only child I have left; but we have a charming family circle to introduce you to, and shall have more as soon as ever this weary war is over."

" War ! " ejaculated Doleful, turning livid.

" Yes; my sons are with their regiments in Turkey, but—"

" Why, I thought you wanted a brother ! " interrupted Doleful, appealing imploringly to Miss.

" So I do," replied Miss, calmly. " So I do. These are only half brothers, as mamma will tell you, and a half-brother is never like a whole one, you know."

" Yes, their name is Honeyball," explained Mrs. Brantinghame, accepting her daughter's invitation; "my first husband's name was Honeyball. P'r'aps you may have heard of him. My eldest son, Archibald, called after my dear brother, Sir Archy, is in the Hot and Heavy Huzzars, and my second son, Humphrey, is in the Royal West Highland Practical Jokers."

Doleful thought he saw their nasty naked swords gleaming before him, and was fairly overcome. Rushing out of the room, he seized his hat and left the house, running out of Acacia Crescent, up the back lane, through Short's Gardens, and Milkington Street, like a man possessed, and took to his bed like a dormouse.

CHAPTER LXXX.

WHO-HOOP!

THE sequel is soon told. Three days after, Sir Archibald Depecarde's travelling chariot, drawn by four smoking posters, was seen rolling, hurriedly, into Handley Cross, with the pinion-folded Partridge lolling consequentially in the rumble, and to draw up with a dash at Captain Doleful's door. What took place between them, of course we are unable to state, but an adjournment was presently moved to Acacia Crescent; and almost immediately after, bales of haberdashery, and piles of cap and bonnet-boxes began to arrive, and Martha had a busy time of it, taking in and letting out the counter-skippers, and genteel young people bringing them. In due time, white favours flourished through the town, Sir Archibald Depecarde giving away the lovely bride.

Concerned, however, we are to add, that just as Mrs. Brantinghame and Martha were clearing out of the Crescent for Bath, Mrs. Doleful cast up at her mother's, looking so wretched and haggard, that no census-taker would have booked her at fifty. She declared she could not live with that " 'orrid man" another day, though for what cause, we, as Sir Thomas Trout would say, are not at liberty to mention. Mamma tried Jorrocks's famous horse recipe upon her, advised her to be to his faults a little blind, and to his virtues ever kind; but Mrs. Doleful declared, she would rather do anything than return to him, and thought, with bitter anguish, of Peter Bullock and Captain Capers, and the other gentlemen she had jilted.

On that very day, James Pigg was seen turning out of the Marquis of Cornwallis's bottle department into Great Coram Street, with a huge tobacco-stained favour under his nose, holloaing out, as he got staggered into the middle of the street, *"Keep the tambourine a rowlin! Whativir ye de, keep the tambourine a rowlin!"* Then having got himself steadied, he went lurching along, holloaing out, "B-r-r-a-andy and baccy 'ill gar a man live for iver! Sink ar say b-r-r-a-andy and baccy 'ill gar a man live for iver!" So he proceeded down Great Coram Street, tendering his nief to every body he met, declaring he'd been the death of a guinea, and would be the death of another when young Stobbs was born, until losing his head in the open, he finally subsided under the pump in Brunswick square. Then, just as the little boys were preparing to sluice him, the tall lobster merchant with the big calves, who was going his evening rounds of "Buy LoB-*ster-r-r!* fine LoB-*ster-r-r!*" came to the rescue, and restored him unhurt to Great Coram Street, where the lobster merchant was speedily made as drunk as his friend.

On that very day, too, our elegant Bloomer having captured the Conqueror, and found out what day Belinda was to be married, entered into the happy state also, as appears by the following paragraph extracted from the Paul Pry: "On the 29th ult., at St. Mary's Church, by the

Rev. Simon Pure, assisted by the Rev. Arthur Lovejoy, William Heveland, Esq., A.D.C., to Constantia, youngest surviving daughter of the
late Michael Mendlove, of Handley Cross Spa. The lovely bride, who
was dressed as a Bloomer, was attended by six beautiful bridesmaids
similarly attired."

The Conqueror very handsomely settled himself, not quite so good an
investment as Charley Stobbs made with pretty Belinda, Mr. Jorrocks
having come down with what old Miss Freezer described as "something
v—a—a—ry handsome," and promised them a thousand every time she
has twins. They were now down at old Stobbs's place in Yorkshire, but

BENJAMIN AND HIS FRIEND EXERCISING MR. JORROCKS'S HUNTERS.

purpose being back at Handley Cross by the hunting season. They are
accompanied by that eminent sportsman Ben, who has been glad to retire
from the agonies of hunting and subside into a buttoney-boy for
Belinda. This metamorphosis was somewhat accelerated by the following
contretemps.

Pigg having gone out in the gray dawn of morn to meet his friend Whiskey Tim and recruit his stock of mountain dew, saw Joe Haddock and Ben having a trial of speed with two of their horses along the south turnpike, and not all Pigg's frantic yells and gestures, though he knocked his hat crown out in the effort, could overpower the clatter they made on the road. Pigg therefore made the best of his way home and providing himself with a cutting whip, surprised Ben in the parlour in the act of refreshing himself with some of Mr. Jorrocks's marmalade, which he was scooping out of the pot with his thumb. Taking him as he would a hound by the ear, Pigg pitched into him, exclaiming at the top of his voice,

"Ar'll teach ye te gallop mar h'ussus, it will 'e (whack)—it will 'e (crack)—it will 'e (smack)."

Squeak, squeal, writhe, wriggle, roar, went Ben, throwing himself on to the floor.

"Ar'll teach ye te steal t'ard maister's marmelade," continued Pigg, now taking Ben by the cuff of the neck; "Ar'll teach ye te steal t'ard maister's marmelade, it will 'e (crack), it will 'e (smack), it will 'e (whack)."

Writhe, roar, wriggle, *murder!* shrieked Ben.

"Aye, *morder* aye," repeated Pigg, turning him deliberately over and taking him by the other ear. "Aye, *morder* aye, ar'l morder ye, ye bit brazen bowdekite, whe d'ye think ill stand sic wark as this," (whack, crack —whack, crack—whack, crack)—and altogether Pigg gave him such an elaborate licking as perfectly disgusted Ben with whips and every thing belonging to the chase.

Mr. Jorrocks therefore being without a whip, and in order as he says that they may all break their eggs at the same end, has allowed Pigg to choose his own, who, kennin as he says, "Jist sic another chap as hissel, what used to whop in to the Tynedale," he has written to engage him, character being no object with Pigg, and Mr. Jorrocks and Pigg have entered into a compact that master and man are not both to get drunk on the same day.

Moreover, Mr. Jorrocks has offered to increase Pigg's wages if he will make Batsay, who we are sorry to say has had to get her stays let out again—an honest woman.

And now for our jolly old master himself. He says their people have "be'aved so un'andsome in tryin' to shop him," that he's determined to give a loose to pleasure the rest of his life, and is getting hounds together for four days a week—three and a bye at least, which latter he means to have in Pinch-me-near Forest. This is to be permanently added to his country, and the Right Honourable the Lords Commissioners of her Majesty's Treasury having very properly dismissed the Honourable the Commissioner in charge of her Majesty's Woods and Forests, together with his Scotch Sylvan oracle, Mr. Prettyfat is again pretty comfortable and able to turn his attention to his poultry, of which he has appointed Mr. Jorrocks grand protector. Pigg and he are to have their breakfasts and a glass of brandy a piece every time the hounds meet there.

Mr. Jorrocks's country is full of foxes, many of which he hopes to make cry "Capevi," and as the ordnance hedge-hashers have made hunting comparatively easy where they have carried on their operations, he anticipates being able to scramble about in tolerable safety. He has begun greening his breeches knees among the hazel bushes, cub hunting, and arranged his meets for the first week in November, of which he has kindly sent us the following card :—

MR. JORROCKS'S FOX-HOUNDS
MEET

Monday, Nov. 6th, at Handley Cross.

Tuesday,   at_____

Wednesday, Nov. 8th, at Hardpie Hill.

Thursday,   at_____

Friday, Nov. 10th, at Pinch-me-near Forest (at eight).

Saturday, Nov. 11th, at the Rest and be Thankful.

EACH DAY AT HALF-PAST TEN O'CLOCK

BRADBURY, EVANS, AND CO., PRINTERS, WHITEFRIARS.

LIST OF SUBSCRIBERS

M.J. Abberton
J.S. Abbott
A.G. Adams
G.N. Adams
R.G. Adams
Robin Addison
Major J.W.
　Aggleton,M.B.E.
H.W. Aidley, M.F.H.
I.R. Scott Aiton
D.T. Allan
Lt.-Col. J.H. Allason
D.J.R. Allen
Edward Allen
Frank Allen
J.A. Allen
J.H. Allen
James Allen
G.A. Allsop
P.H.B. Allsop
J.R. Allt
Mrs. M.R. Ambrose
A.G. Amos
P.T.K. Anderson
D.S. Andrew
Miss D. Andrews
G.A.N. Andrews
G.P. Andrews
R.E. Ansell
Mrs. Antrobus
F.H. Armitage
H.E. Armitage
C.J. Armstrong
K.W. Armstrong
D.A. Ashley
P.R. Ashley
R.S. Ashwood
J.P. Asquith
Angela Auckland
Mrs. Delia Averns

Major R.I. Bailey
Mrs. F. Bain
David Baker
Mrs. V. Baker

A.J.C. Balfour
B.A. Banfield
Nigel Banham
D.I. Barker
John Barker
Thomas L. Barker
C.J.M. Barlow
Thomas Barlow
Robert D. Barnard
Simon J. Barnes
C.G. Barnett
C.J. Barnett
R.A. Barnett
F.J. Barratt
H.L. Barrett
A.G.S. Barstow
F.B. Barton
D.S. Bass
W.G. Bate
A.A. Bati
Peter Batty-Smith
Miss W.R. Baughan
Michael Baxandall
Mrs. F.K. Bazley
The Duke of Beaufort,
　K.G., M.F.H.
Hon. Mrs.
　M.H.Beaumont
P.A. Beddows
A.F.L. Beeston
Mrs. S.M. Beetles
Diana Lady Beith
N.J. Belcher
J. Bellchamber
G. Bennett
J.M. Benzie
Mrs. M.D. Berger
Sigi R. Bergmann
C.P.A. Bertie
M. Ide Betts
R.T. Betts
Cmdr. G.E. Bingham
D.A.L. Birrell
R.J. Bird
Lt.-Col. A.L. Birt
R.J. Birts

K.C. Bishop
Peter Bissmire
L.C. Blaaberg
P.J.W. Black
Dr. B. Black
W.T. Blackband
Mrs. Jill Blackbourn
Roger Blackburn
Peter Blacklock
E.C. Blake
Lt.-Col. E.P.T. Blake
M.D. Blake
Mrs. P. Blake
The Revd. Michael
　Bland
C.T. Bletsoe
T.R.C. Blofeld
Miss K.I. Blunsden
A.H. Boddy
Richard Body, M.P.
T.E.T. Bond
H.L. Boorer
D. Boot
Col. R.G. Borradaile
L.A.F. Borrett
Stanley W. Botterill
Mrs. Robert Boucher
Miss J.D.T. Boultbee-
　Brooks
Lt.-Col. M.C. Bowden
Mary J.E. Bower
Dr. J.R. Bowers
James T. Bowie
W.H. Bowker
L.F. Bowyer
G. Boxall
J.M. Bradley
Mrs. K.P.M. Bradley
Adrian Bradshaw
Maj.-Gen.
　D.H.Braggins
J.B. Braithwaite
Mrs. R. Braithwaite
The Hon. P.E. Brassey
G.W. Brazendale,
　C.M.G.

Dr. O.B. Brears, O.B.E.
Miss S.M. Brien
Lt.-Cmdr. G.A. Briggs,
  R.N.
Mrs. M. Briggs
D.C. Bright
Frank Brightman
John E. Brindle
M.J.L. Brodrick
Mrs. P. Brooke
C.J. Brookes
K.C. Brookes
Sam Brooks
Col. J.M. Browell
Mrs. Alison Brown
C.N. Brown
F.A. Brown
J.F. Brown
John N. Brown
Mrs. P.M. Brown
Sue Browne
R.C.W. Brownsdon
D.W.K. Bruce
M.G. Bruce-Squires
D.S. Bull
James D. Bunney
Richard Burge
J.S. Burgess
Miss A.L. Burhouse
T.F.J. Burland
Lieut. A.G. Burns, R.N.
John D.C. Burridge
Philip Burrows
Dr. J.D.R. Burton
Mrs. M.W. Burton
R.S. Burton
Mrs. M.C. Butler
J.W.A. Butler-Sloss
Mrs. B.B. Buttenshaw
Dr. D.I. Butterworth
Edward Button
His Honour Judge J.H.
  Buzzard
J. Byles
Brendan Byrne

A.J. Cairns
Dr. K.V. Calder

Dr. J.A. Calvert
Mrs. P. Cambray
Capt. E.G. Cameron
Neil Cameron
J.P. Camp
Alexander J.C. Campbell
Mrs. J.A. Campbell
J.D. Campbell
L.R. Campfield
R.J. Canning
Capt. P.B. Cannon
The Revd. W.R.D.
  Capstick
A.R.P. Carden
R. Carew
M.I. Carpenter
A.G. Casewell
James E. Cashmore
J.A. Caslaw
P.A. Cattermole
Mrs. W.E. Catto
W.T. Cavey
Mrs. E. Cawkell
E.S. Cazalet
Lord Charles Cecil
Major J.P. Chadwick
Philip Chadwick
C.L. Chafer
D.J. Challen
T.J. Chapman
Lt.-Col. J.E.S.
  Chamberlayne
G.M. Chambers
P.M. Charles
Capt. L.W.L. Chelton,
  R.N.
Dr. Max A. Chernesky
D.M. Child
Mrs. G.S. Ching
E.F. Choppen
N.Christie
J.R. Clack
D.L. Clarke
I.D. Clarke
K.M. Clarke
A.M. Clarkson
A.M. Clayton
Michael Clayton
W.A.M. Clayton

Harry Cockburn
M.A. Cockrell
A.L. Cole
B.E. Cole
R.H. Collard
Miss A. Colliass
F.L. Collins
Major C.W.E. Collins
Ken Collins
Carl B. Cone (U.S.A.)
Mrs. C. Conway
Charles N. Compton
Mrs. S.P. Conan-Davies
M.L. Congdon
F.A. Connelly
J.C. Conner
J.H. Cooch
E.J. Cooper
W.H. Cooper
Mrs. Pauline Cooper-
  Reade
John Cope, M.P.
Mrs. R.A. Corby
M.D. Corke
D.J. Corlett
John Cormack
H.L. Cottrill
M.H. Couchman
M.G. de Courcy-Ireland
J. Cowen
Col. J.A. Cowgill
Major W.D. Cox
S.R. Craddock
Col. J.F. Cramphorn
J.W. Crawford
M.G. Cripps
John H. Cross
J.P.O. Crowe
John J. Crown
Mrs. J. Crowther
Roy Culver
Major G.J.P. Cummins
Geoffrey Cuttle

T.L.A. Daintith
Miss J. Dakin
A.G. Dale
R.D. Dalraine

Miss J.S. Nicholson
John Nickels
The Nickerson Group
Stuart Nicoll
Mrs. A.C. Nicolle
Jonathan S. Nield
Col. G.W. Noakes,
 O.B.E., T.D., J.P.,
 D.L.
Lady C. Noel
Brigadier J.A. Norman,
 D.S.O. (France)
Dr. T. St. M. Norris
A.H.W.P. Norton
 (Malaga)
R. Norton
P.H. Northen

Mrs. I.F. O'Brien
D.L. O'Byrne
E.J. O'Grady
Major-Gen. Odling,
 C.B., M.C.
J.A. Ogilvie
Miss Susan Okell
Mr. and Mrs. Openshaw
B.D. Orchard
Roseanne O'Reilly
K.G. Orme
M.J. Orr
M.W.M. Osmond
A.T. Osborn
R.D. Ottley
C.D. Outred
G.J. Over
Barry Owen
B.J. Owen
R. Elwyn Owen
D. Owen

D.J Palmer
G.H. Paris
E.B. Park
Anthony Parker
H.M. Parker
G.A. Parker
Mrs. C.M. Parker

Rear-Admiral R.W.
 Parker
G.N. Parkes
Dr. M. Parkes
I. Parkinson
Mrs. C.H. Parlby
Mrs. Susan A. Parry
Miss G.M. Partridge
K.G. Pates
Dr. H.O. Paton
C.T. Payne
Mrs. V. Paynter
D.F. Pearl
N.F.K. Pearse
Mrs. J.E. Pearson
J.R.H. Pearson
Margaret A. Pease
Dr. J.D.W. Peck
Mervyn R.C. Peckham
Mrs. M.C. Peek
J.F. Penley
R.S.L. Penn
D.W. Pennell
Robert Perfitt
A.B. Perry
Jane Perry
D.J. Peters
Mrs. R. Peters, M.F.H.
Mrs. B.W.B. Pettifer
Mrs. J.A. Pettinger
Peter Petts
Mrs. A. Philips
J.H. Philips
M.H. Pibworth
Dr. David Pick
Sir Charles Pickthorn,
 Bt.
James Pickthorn
M.V. Piddocke
J.L. Pigg, M.B.E., J.P.
A.O. Piggott
D.S. Pinney
B.G. Pirie
Frank Pitt
C.M. Plumbe
A.J. Plummer
Michael J. Plummer
Robert Plumridge
George Pocklington

David Pollard
Brian Pomeroy
Major the Hon. R.W.
 Pomeroy
The Hon. Mrs. Pomeroy
J. Derek Poole
P.M. Potter
Dennis R. Poulson
C.J. Powell
E.S. Powell
M.F. Powell
Dr. Vincent Powell-
 Smith
N.F. Pratt
R.J. Pratt
P.J. Preston
Col. R.F. Preston
R. Preston-Jones
J.M. Price, Q.C.
Mrs. S.E.R. Price
John Pringle
R.F.D. Pritchard
S. Pritchard
Simon Pritchard
Timothy Proctor
Miss S.J. Profit
B.G. Purdey
Mrs. Gwennyth Pye

Dr. T.J. Quaite
W.B. Quarmby
J. Quayle
Elsie Lady Quilter

M.F. Race
Donald Rae
John W. Rae
Cyril Ralton
G.H. Ramage
Kim Randall
Leonard Rangeley
A.E. Ranson
J.R.S. Raper
J.H. Ratcliff
H.L. Rawnsley
Cyril Ray
Mrs. Helen Raybould

Peter Read
H.S. Read
Dr. E. Reddy
A.P.S. De Redman
P.F. Rednall
J.L. Reed
Peter J. Reed
Prof. H. Rees
R.C.D. Rees
Lt.-Cmdr. C.G.L. Reid, R.N.
Brig. D.W. Reid
Dr. R.W. Reid
W.F. Rendall
Dr. R.E. Rewell
B.K.K. Richards
Mrs. D. Richards
E.J. Richardson
William Richardson
C.W. Richmond-Watson
Lt. Cmdr. Rickards, R.N. (Retd.)
Andrew W.G. Rickett
R.R. Riddle
H.W. Riddolls
Miss N.A. Ridley
Marianne E. Rifat
Mrs. R.H.D. Riggall
R.L. Ringrose
Mrs. A.M. Roberts
Mrs. S. Roberts
T.J. Roberts
R.F. Roberts
W.I. Roberts
Mrs. G.V. Robertson
J.W.F. Robins
Miss L.D. Robinson
Lt.-Col. R.B. Robinson
Wing-Cdr. S. Robinson (Rtd.)
A.W. Robinson
Mrs. M. Robinson
Mrs. A.L. Rook
Mrs. Genevieve M. Rose
Joseph Rosenblum (North Carolina)
D.R. Rosevear
C.M. Ross

W.N. Ross
R.H. Rowbottom
Mrs. Pamela Rowe
John Rowley
Miss J. Roy
Mary E. Rubie
Viscount Runciman of Doxford
J. Rushin
Maurice Russell, M.C.
J.F. Rutherford
S.J. Rutherford
P.L.G. Rutland
Dr. Josephine Rutter
J.P. Rycroft
L.E. Rydings

Mutsuo Sakata (Japan)
John Samuel
Mrs. Sam Sandbach
D.P. Sandeman
Roy Sanders
C. St. J.D. Sanders
D.G. Sandlin
F.W. Saunders
Basil Savage Bookseller
Robert Sawers
J.J. Saxby
J.D.M. Sayers
E.M.P. Scott
L.R. Scott
Miss J.V. Scott
J.D. Scouller
Sarah Screen
Dr. J.P. Scrivener
Mrs. Philip Scrope
A.J. Scruby
J.H. Scrutton
John Seabrook
J.C. Sedgwick
Lady Sells
Col. J.W. Sewell
J.A. Seymour Jones
M.M. Shannon
M.E. Sharp
M.E. Sheard
Richard G. Sheard

Frank Sheardown
Mark Sheardown
S.R. Shearman
A.J. Shears
Mrs. A. Sheehan
Lt.-Col. F.W.L. Shepard, M.B.E.
Mrs. C.A. Shephard
T.R. Shepherd
N.E.C. Sherwood
Mrs. M.N.H. Short
Dr. P.W. Shillito
Stuart Sillars
R.E. Silvey
Mr. and Mrs. A.C. Simmons
J.T.H. Simms
G.H. Simpson
A. Singer
J.H.J. Slater
Douglas A. Sloan
B.W. Small
Major M. Smalley
Mrs. D.A.R. Smallwood
F.J.R. Smith
Mrs. D. Smith
N.L.H. Smith
Mrs. P.A. Smith
R. Smith
J.M. Smithells
J.C.S.F. Smithies
Mrs. J. Smyth
S.M. Smyth
W.J. Soden
Mrs. I.J. Barclay Sole
G.H. Southern
I.P.G. Southward
Dr. P.Q.M. Spaight
J.A. Spalding
John Sparrow
Major B.L. Speegle (Virginia)
M.J. Spencer
Shaun Spencer, M.H.
A.J. Spillane
Mrs. P. Spiller
Mrs. Arthur Spiro (Malta)
H.N. Sporborg

C.G. Squance
Mrs. M. Stables
S.C.C. Stacey
Robert Stanier
Mrs. Suzanne M.
  Stanley
W.B. Stanley
Mrs. J.M. Stannah
Mrs. B. Chetwynd
  Stapylton
Miss Lesley Stark
Peter Starr
E.W. Stearn
David Steeds
B.G. Steff
Mrs. D. Steiner
Leonard Stephenson
Miss B. Sterry
Miss A.J. Stevens
T.F.G. Stevens
C. Walter Stewart
Ben Stimpson
Mrs. G.M. Stoddart
G.E. Stokes
J.S.R. Storer
Mrs. J.R. Strange
J.H. Stratton
J.R. Strong
G.M. Stubbs
W.J. Studdert
F.S. Stych (Italy)
Irene Suffield
D. Sullivan
D.B. Sumpter
Conyers A. Surtees
Major R.E. Surtees
P. Surtees
S.J. Surtees
Richard Suter
Miss M. Sutherland
Dr. R.N.P. Sutton
I.F. Swain
E.T. Swarbrick
M.C.C. Swift (Portugal)
Dr. P. Swinson
C.R. Syckelmore
M.A. Syddall
Mrs. Annette Syder
Malcolm Sykes (Ontario)

Lt. R.M. Sykes
Lt.-Col. G. Symonds

David J. Tallentire
K.G. Tanner
Mrs. T.C. Tanner
G.G. Tarlton
Mr. & Mrs. J.R. Tate
Alec I. Taylor
Mrs. A.J. Taylor
Miss Anne Taylor
Mrs. M.E. Taylor
Mrs. R. Taylor
Maurice Taylor
D. Teesdale
C. Templeman
R.G. Terry
R.G. Tetley
E.H. Thomas
L.C.T. Thomas
Peter C. Thomas
A. Thomas
G. Thompson
J.W.M. Thompson
M.G.Thomson
R. Thomson
W.G. Thorn
R.M. Thorpe
Eric A. Tidy
Michael John Timms
E.H. Tindall
C.H. Tinsley
H.J. Titley
A.G. Todd
Maj.-Gen. D.A.H. Toler
M. Toll
J.P.L. Tory
L.E. Trafford
J.J. Trapp
Mrs. J.M. Trippier
P.J.M. Trollope
R.W. Trollope, M.F H.
  (Canada)
R.M. Trounson
John Tucker
David Tudor-Pole
E. Tully
I. Turner

P.D.H. Turner
S.J.E. Turner
Mrs. K.A. Turney
C.H. Tutton
P.T. Tweddle
William J. Twibill
Francis E. Tynan
Capt. F.J. Tyrwhitt-
  Drake

Col. A.C. Uloth
F.A. Underwood
R.J. Unwin

Capt. M.J. Vacher
D.B. Vale
P. Van Ufford
Mrs. Susan
  Verberkmose
Stewart Varney
I.A. Vere Nicoll
The Lord Vestey
Fiona Vigors
D.J. Viveash

Michael Wace
Justin Wadham
G.C. Wagstaff
T.J. Wainwright
Dr. Peter Wakeley
M.J. Wake-Walker
Brig. A.G. Walch
C.P.Walker
J.H. Walker
Mrs. P.M. Walker
Major J.S.M. Walker,
  K.O.S.B.
Major P.J.R. Waller
D. Walley
B.J. Wallis
Edward Walsh
John H. Walton
H.F. Warburton
R.W. Warden, M.F.H.
Jean Wardrop
Susan M. Warren
Mrs. J.S. Warrington

A.T. Warwick
H.A. Waterson
D.W. Wates, M.F.H.
K.J. Watkins
C. Watson
Dr. D.H. Watson
Dr. D.J. Watson
Ian R. Watson
Mrs. P.S. Watson
Dr. W.W. Watson
R.K. Watson
M.A. Watt
Mrs. J. Watts
R.H. Waugh
E.D. Way
E.D.B. Way
I.H. Wear
M.J.R. Wear
The Rt. Hon. B.
   Weatherill, M.P.
M.J. Webb
Mrs. A.J. Webb
The Rev. W.P. Webb
Mrs. D.H. Webb
W.R.B. Webb
A.H. Webber
S.G. Weber-Brown
G.R. Weddell
R.E. Wellman
John H. Wendelboe
G. Westall
Col. L.H.M. Westropp
E. Davan Wetton,
   C.B.E.
George A. Weatley
R.T. Wheeler
Dr. W.F. Wheeler

Lt.-Col. W.E.S.
   Whetherly
M. Whitaker
E.H. White
James W. White
M.R. White
Ralph White
Mrs. Alan Middleton
   White
J.L. White-Hamilton
A.P. Whitehead
J. Whitehouse
D. Whiteley
I.C. Whitfield
H. Whyte-Melville
   Jackson
H.H. Wicks
T.F. Wilder
Mrs. Pamela Wiles
J.N. Wilkinson
Dorian Williams, O.B.E.
Dr. E.T. Williams
John Williams
K.E. Williams
R.M.C. Williams
Mrs. W. Willis
T.M. Bent-Willson
C.N. Wilmot-Smith
S.N. Wilshire
B.R. Wilson
Herbert Wilson
Patrick Wilson
Miss Ann E. Wilson
John Winch
E. Windsor-Clive
K.R. Wing

Barone R. Winspeare
   (Italy)
John Winter
David Witt
Harry Wolton
Douglas J. Wood
Douglas Wood
Stuart Wood
Miss B. Woodcock
Major M.G. Woodhams
J.A. Woodhouse
Miss S.M.W.
   Woodman-Smith
J.G. Woodrow
J.G. Wooldridge
Miss R.H. Woolley
C.A. Worsley
M.A. Wright
Patrick W. Wright
W.D. Wright
E.A. Wrighton-Edwards
C.P. Wykeham-Martin
Major N. Wylie-Carrick
R. Wynn-Williams
L.R.W. Wysock-Wright

John H. Yarroll
A.G. Yates
Clifford W. Yates
Ian B. Yeaman
Col. J.L. Yeatman
Mrs. G.W. Young
Anthony
   Younghusband,
   M.F.H.

PUBLICATIONS OF
THE R. S. SURTEES SOCIETY

HANDLEY CROSS;

OR,

MR. JORROCKS'S HUNT.

Further copies of *Handley Cross* are available at **£14·95,** packing and postage included.
Instructions for ordering are on page 570.

JORROCKS'

JAUNTS AND JOLLITIES.

Pre-publication prices:
Until 28th February, 1984, **£11·75** for books which are collected and **£12·70** for books which are posted.
For full information, see the Advertisement at the beginning of this book.

SOME EXPERIENCES OF AN IRISH R.M.

by E. Œ. Somerville and Martin Ross

The R. S. Surtees Society's edition of *Some Experiences of an Irish R.M.* is a facsimile of the first (1899) edition. It includes the 30 black and white illustrations by **Miss Somerville** in the first edition. The pictorial stamping on the cover ("blocking") is the same as that of the first edition.

Molly Keane, who wrote the best-seller *Good Behaviour*, and who has lived most of her life in Southern Ireland, wrote the Introduction.

Price **£7·95**, packing and postage included. Instructions for ordering are on page 570.

FURTHER EXPERIENCES OF AN IRISH R.M.

by E. Œ. Somerville and Martin Ross

Further Experiences, like *Some Experiences*, contains twelve episodes in which Major Yeates recounts his discomfitures with quiet and sober dignity, humour and tolerance (Molly Keane's words). Flurry Knox, Philippa, old Mrs. Knox of Aussolas, Sally Knox and Slipper re-appear. And, as in *Some Experiences*, there is a wealth of lesser characters, natives of south-west Ireland whose rhetorical variations from normal English usage provide the wit and drama.

The R. S. Surtees Society intends to publish a facsimile of the first (1908) edition of *Further Experiences of an Irish R.M.*, to be available by the end of June, 1984. Its format will be similar to, though not exactly the same, as *Some Experiences*. It will include the 35 black and white illustrations by Miss Somerville which appeared in the first edition.

A minimum of 1500 subscribers must be obtained by 28th February, 1984.

Pre-publication prices

For those who subscribe for *Further Experiences* before 28th February, 1984 the prices are:

(*a*) **£5·75** for books which are collected from J. A. Allen & Co. Ltd., 1, Lower Grosvenor Place, Buckingham Palace Road, London, S.W.1.

(*b*) **£6·50** for books which are posted, the price including packing and postage.

A list of those subscribing before 28th February, 1984 will be printed at the end of the book. Although the period of pre-publication prices may be extended for a few weeks after 28th February, 1984, it will not be possible to record the names of subscribers after that date.

The post publication price will be **not less than £7·95.**

Ordering

A leaflet, which includes an order form, has been enclosed. If no order form is available, write to **the Hon. Mrs Robert Pomeroy, R. S. Surtees Society, Rockfield House, Nunney, Nr. Frome, Somerset.** Your order should be accompanied by a cheque for the appropriate amount, made payable to the R. S. Surtees Society. Please show your name and address clearly.

All cheques will be acknowledged. All subscription money will be kept in a separate *Further Experiences* bank account and will be returned in the event of publication not going ahead.

MR. SPONGE'S

SPORTING TOUR.

Mr. Sponge and the Missess Jawleyford

Mr. Sponge, or Soapey Sponge, as his good-natured friends called him, was devoted to fox-hunting. His remedy for impecuniousness was free hospitality and selling unmanageable horses at prices which reflected their performance on their good days, and when he was riding them.

His dexterity in getting into people's houses was only equalled by the difficulty of getting him out again. His long-term objective was to marry an heiress, until at Sir Harry and Lady Scattercash's he met the beautiful Lucy Glitters, of Astley's Royal Amphitheatre.

When *Mr. Sponge's Sporting Tour* was first published in 1853 it was an immediate best seller. It was the favourite reading of subalterns serving in the Crimean War.

Sponge was the B.B.C.'s 'Book at Bed-time' in December, 1982.

The R. S. Surtees Society's edition is a facsimile of the 1853 edition and reproduces in colour the 13 full-page hand-coloured plates in the 1853 edition, which were printed from engravings on steel by **John Leech**. The text, slightly enlarged, includes 90 black and white illustrations from wood engravings, also by **Leech**. The cover is of the same design and has the same pictorial stampings as the 1853 edition. In size and format (though not in colour) it is uniform with the Society's editions of *Mr. Facey Romford's Hounds*, "*Ask Mamma*" and *Handley Cross*.

Auberon Waugh wrote the Introduction.

Over 4,500 copies have been sold since October, 1981.

Price **£14·95**, packing and postage included. Instructions for ordering are on page 570.

MR. FACEY ROMFORD'S HOUNDS.

Facey and the Lady Whipper-In

It was lucky for our friend Mr. Romford—or Facey Romford as he is sometimes familiarly called—that there was another Mr. Romford in the world of much the same pursuits as himself. We don't mean to insinuate that Facey went about saying "I am the rich Mr. Romford, owner of Abbeyfield Park, patron of three livings, J.P., D.L." and all that sort of thing; but if he found he was taken for that Mr. Romford, he never cared to contradict the impression.

Facey, having constituted himself heir to his bachelor, cattle-dealing Oncle Gilroy, followed no occupation other than his sporting amusements. The first intimation of his rich uncle's death was the arrival from London of his widow, together with "a perfect sliding scale of children".

Facey extricated himself from his predicament by becoming an M.F.H. The immense respect accorded to this office, and sealing his letters with a seal which was very similar to the *other* Mr. Romford's seal, procured hounds, house, horses and credit. Lucy Sponge (*née* Glitters) was a wonderful co-adjutor.

Mr. Facey Romford's Hounds is the sequel to *Mr. Sponge's Sporting Tour*. **Enoch Powell** writes in his Introduction "I personally have always thought *Facey Romford* the cream of Surtees."

The R. S. Surtees Society's edition of *Romford* reproduces in colour the 24 full-page hand-coloured plates from the first (1865) edition. These were printed from engravings on steel, of which 14 were by **John Leech** and 10 by **'Phiz'** (Hablôt K. Browne). The text is a facsimile of a somewhat later edition and includes 50 black and white illustrations by W. T. Maud and Dawson. The cover is of the same design and has the same pictorial stampings as the 1865 edition. In size and format (though not in colour) it is uniform with the Society's editions of *Mr. Sponge's Sporting Tour*, "*Ask Mamma*" and *Handley Cross*.

Over 3,000 copies have been sold since July, 1982.

"This fine edition . . ."—David Holloway in *The Daily Telegraph*.

"The R. S. Surtees Society's facsimile edition of *Mr. Facey Romford's Hounds* was the best new book of 1982. The combination of prose, pictures, 405 pages and stamped binding would be hard to beat . . ."—Eric Christiansen in *The Spectator*.

Price **£14·95**, packing and postage included. Instructions for ordering are on page 570.

"ASK MAMMA;"

OR,

THE RICHEST COMMONER IN ENGLAND.

Miss Willing and Billy Pringle get acquainted

Billy Pringle had booked a preference seat in the cramped inside of the old True Blue Independent coach "comin' hup". He found himself opposite a smiling, radiant young lady wearing a black terry velvet bonnet with a single ostrich feather, a dark Levantine silk dress, with rich sable cuffs, muff and boa, and (though you can't see them in the picture) a pair of well-fitting primrose-coloured gloves, which if they ever had been on before had not suffered by the act. Billy was quite struck in a heap.

"*Ask Mamma*" is an hilarious account of mid-Victorian social climbing, against a sporting and rural background. The ruthless progress of Miss Willing, from shop-girl to Mrs. Pringle and on to Countess of Ladythorne, scandalised contemporary readers. It is vintage Surtees—"His Lordship indeed was a well-known general patron of all that was fair, fine and handsome in creation, fine women, fine houses, fine horses, fine hounds, fine pictures, fine statues, fine everything. No pretty woman either in town or country ever wanted a friend if he was aware of it."

The R. S. Surtees Society's edition of "*Ask Mamma*" is a facsimile of the 1858 edition and reproduces in colour the 13 full-page hand-coloured plates in that edition, which were printed from engravings on steel by **John Leech**. The text, slightly enlarged, includes 70 black and white illustrations, also by **Leech**. The cover is of the same design and has the same pictorial stampings as the 1858 edition. In size and format (though not in colour) "*Ask Mamma*" is uniform with the Society's editions of *Mr. Sponge's Sporting Tour*, *Mr. Facey Romford's Hounds* and *Handley Cross*.

The late **Dame Rebecca West** wrote the Introduction a few months before her death.

Price **£14·95**, packing and postage included. Instructions for ordering are on page 570.

Illustrations available separately

Complete sets of the full-page plates which appear in the Society's Surtees publications are offered at the following prices, which include packing and postage:

Mr. Sponge's Sporting Tour. 13 coloured plates by John Leech. Price £5.

Mr. Facey Romford's Hounds. 24 coloured plates, 14 by Leech and 10 by 'Phiz'. Price £8.

"Ask Mamma". 13 coloured plates by Leech. Price £5.

Handley Cross. 17 coloured plates by Leech. Price £6.

Jaunts and Jollities. 31 plates of which 21 (coloured) are by Henry Alken, 1 (coloured) by W. Heath and 9 (uncoloured) by 'Phiz'. Price £8.

Jaunts and Jollities plates will not be ready until the end of June, 1984. Meanwhile all money received in respect of them will be kept in the separate *Jaunts and Jollities* bank account.

Ordering

Send your order to **the Hon. Mrs Robert Pomeroy, R. S. Surtees Society, Rockfield House, Nunney, Nr. Frome, Somerset.** Please show your requirement, name, and address clearly. Your order should be accompanied by a cheque for the appropriate amount, made payable to the R. S. Surtees Society. If you are ordering more than one item, it would be helpful if you would include a note showing how the sum on your cheque is made up.

Books to be collected

Pre-publication subscribers for *Further Experiences of an Irish R.M.* and/or *Jorrocks' Jaunts and Jollities* who choose to collect their books must collect them from J. A. Allen & Co. Ltd., 1, Lower Grosvenor Place, Buckingham Palace Road, London, S.W.1. They will be notified when their books are ready for collection.

J. A. ALLEN & CO. (THE HORSEMAN'S BOOKSHOP) LTD.

1 LOWER GROSVENOR PLACE, LONDON, SW1
(Adjacent to Royal Mews, Buckingham Palace).

**For Over Half a Century we have
Specialised in Books Old & Modern
On Hunting and all Equine and
Equestrian Sports**

Catalogues Issued

Telephone 834/5606 (3 lines)

J.R. Dalton
T.A. St. M.V. Daly
M.R. Dampier
H.R.M. Daniel
Major N.H. Daniel
John H. Daniels
Mrs. R.E. D'Arcy
Margaret Darley
Mrs. G. Darling
Mrs. D.M. David
Marshall David
Miss Brenda Davidson
J.H. Davidson
K.R. Davies (Swaziland)
Dr. M.L.R. Davies
E.J.T. Davies
Miss Olwen Davies
J. Davies
R.I. Davies
R.W. Howard Davies
Mrs. Davis
Simon Daw
Mrs. E.J. Dawkes
Clarissa Dawson
Peter A.J. Day
G.R. Deacon
G.J. Dear
Martyn J. Dearden
E. Dearing
G. De Bethune
Lewis De Fries
Rowland P. Dell
Simon Dell
Paul Denholm
Mrs. R.D.W. Derby
John Devaux
Robin De Wilde
Dr. A.M. Dixon
Glyn D. Dixon
Nigel Dobbins
Dr. William Dodd
Julia M. Dolby
Mrs. M.A. Donnelly
R.G.T. Dorsett
Nigel T. Doxat
Mrs. P.M.E. Drane
W.B. Draper
Dr. H.W. Drescher
John E.S. Driver

J.M. Dudley
J. Duncan
Major N.G.F. Dunne
L.S. Dunning
C.D. Dunstan
P.G. Durrans
Daniel J. Dwyer
A.M. Dyer
Martin Dyke

A.C. Eaton
Mary Eaton
Mark John Edis
R.C. Edgell
E.F. Edwards
J.M. Elder
E.T. Eley
Kenneth Charles Elkins
Mrs. B. Ellington
A.G. Elliott
Brig. A.S. Ellis
Douglas D. Ellis
Wray Ellis
Mrs. M.P. Elmes
D.M. Ely
James Emmet
Mrs. Elaine Emmott
Dr. H. Emson
M.N. Enfield
Miss M. Esher
M.G. Esther
L.E.C. Evans
L.J.C. Evans, O.B.E.
G.F. Evans-Vaughan
Mrs. Evelyn
R.H. Everard
R.M. Everett
B.M. Ewbank

J.C. Fareham
T.C. Farmborough
Major A. Farrant
James Farrer
Dr. F.C.J. Fawcett
D.W.L. Fellowes
R.V. Fenton
Mrs. M.R. Ferens

Dr. J.B. Ferguson
Major R.S. Ferguson
J.J.F. Field
Miss J.M. Field
G.Findley
Reginald Finn
J.A. Fishbourne
J.S. Fisher
Mrs. Peter Fitzgerald
J.E. Fleeman
R.J.C. Fleming
G.J. Fletcher
A.M. Florey
Miss V.T. Foley
K.R. Foot
Geoffrey Ford
Roy Foster
Mrs. D. Foster
Mrs. B. Foulds
Lieut. J.G. Fountain
Charles Fox
A.V. Fox
K.M. Fox
G.G. Fox
Arthur J. Foxton
Lieut. D.R.K. Francis,
    R.A.
R. Francombe
S.J. Fraser
Miss M.M. Fraser-
    Roberts
R. Frears
Mike Freeman
Mrs. R. Fremantle
M.J. Frost
J.C. Fuller
Lt.-Col. S.J. Furness
Dr. M.J.P. Furniss

R. de V. Gaisford
E.A. Gamba
O. Gardener
John Gardner
Peter Gargett
Audery Gardham
A.F. Garnett
C.J. Garnett
C.P. Garnett

W.J. Garnham
Ivan Gault
N. George
A.A. Gibbs, M.B.E., T.D.
Dr. Hugh Gibbs
A.L. Gibson
A.R. Gibson
Mrs. R.I. Gilchrist
Professor R.W. Gilliatt
Dr. Richard A. Gilman (California)
W.A. Gilmour
Ian Girvan
I.A. Glover
Leslie Gobey
John Godley
Capt. W.E.B. Godsal, R.N.
Harley Godsall
C.A. Gold
J.A.H. Gold
Mrs. H.B. Goldsmid
Paul Goodlet
Mrs. B.A. Gordon-Cranmer
H.P. Gordon-Jones
Mrs. D.W. Gorton
Terence F. Gostling
Brig. G.F. Gough
Mrs. J.R. Gough
Andrew Gould
Mr. and Mrs. J.H. Gould
G.B. Graham
Reginald Graham
R.I. Graham
Dr. Rod Graham (Australia)
D.I.P. Granger
J.C.P. Granger
G.D. Grasby
R.C. Grassley
B.T. Gray
G.A. Green
J.M. Green
Harry Greenway M.P.
J.G. Grice
Major R.V.E. Grieve
Mrs. V.J.H. Grieve

Mrs. M. Griffin
Mrs. A. Griffiss
Brian R. Griffiths
Professor D.A. Griffiths (Hong Kong)
Gordon Griffiths
His Honour Judge B. Griffiths
Brig. E.L. Griffith-Williams
K.W. Grimsley
J.F. Grimwood
Mrs. M.P. Groom
J. Grossart
Sheena Grosset
A.D. Gunner
Miss N.D. Gutch
P.L. Guy

C.S. Hadfield
Mrs. P.R. Hadfield
A.G.L. Hale
A.D.R.S. Hall
E.J. Berney Hall
H.C.S. Hall
G.G. Hall
J.A. Hall
Mrs. A.B. Hall
Mrs. Garnet Hall
Dr. N.M. Hall
Wing-Comdr. N.G. Halliday
N.K. Halliday
C. Halsall
J.A.L. Hamilton
C. Hamilton-Miller
David E. Hammon
D.A. Hampson
D.G. Hannah
R.J.K. Hannington
Donald R. Hanson
J.I. Hardwick
T.G.G. Hardwick
G.N.A. Hardy
G.M. Hardy
K.M. Hardy
Mrs. G. St. J. Hardy
Lady E.J. Harman
Mrs. J.D. Harper

R.O. Harris
C.E. Harrison, M.H.
J.P. Harrison
Mrs. V.A. Harrison
Dr. N. Hart
Mrs. Rita Hartwell
Charles Harvey
T.D. Harvey
Jason Hassard
G.A. Havell
Count John H. Havenaar Kazimirski (Switzerland)
Dr. P.W. Hawkes
A.W. Hawkins
C.H. Hay
Dr. Bernard Hayes
M.E.J. Hayman
I.S. Haynes
J.K. Hayward
Jiro Hazama (Japan)
John Heald
Sqn.-Ldr. N.V.O.P. Healey
G.I. Heath
J.E. Heath
Lt.-Col. M.L. Heathcote
David Hebb
Mrs. I.A. Hebditch
J. Hefford
Mrs. K.B. Hellens
B.E. Henderson
Sir James Henry, Bt.
Mrs. V.M. Herd
Robin Herdman
Michael Herman-Smith
A. Herriott
Mrs. A. Hesketh
Mrs. S.E. Heyworth
Brian Hicks
Anthony Higgins
S. De Premorel Higgons (France)
J.A. De C. Hill
Mrs. A.E. Hill
David Hill
Mrs. K.A. Hill
Miss Sophie Hill
G. Hiller

C.F. Hingston
J.F.M. Hislop
M.R. Hoare
J.H. Hobbiss
James G. Hobden
J.A. Hock
P. Hodgkinson
C.J. Hodgson
T. Hodson
Ivan Hoffe
Mrs. K.M. Hogg
Graham Holdsworth
P.J. Hole
David C. Hollis
Mrs. E.M. Holloway
R.I. Holman
M.E. Hook
Dr. J.N. Hope
Mr. and Mrs. R.W.J. Hopkins
A.A.H. Hopkinson
H.L. Hoppe
M. Hord
R.G. Horsnell
J.H.R. Hosford
Lt. M.A. Houghton, R.A.
E.N. Houlton
Mrs. M.J. Howard
J. Howard-Jones
D. Howcroft
Mrs D.J. Howe
Miss Wendy Howes
Major F.C. Howlett
John Vivian Hughes
Mrs. E.J. Hughes
Mrs. Joan Hulme
Capt. H.J.C. Humfrey
T.D. Humphris
James Hunter Blair
I.W.M. Hurst
Mrs. R.J. Hutchings
G.J. Hyatt, M.F.H.

A. Iliff
N.V. Ince
N.R. Innes
Mrs. P. Innes

G.W. Iredell
J.G. Irving
Mrs. J. Irwin

Mrs. J.M. Jachim
Mrs. P.A. Jackson
P.G. Jackson
Lt.-Col. J.M. Jago
R.H. James
D.A.S. James-Griffiths
Geoffrey W. Jarman
D.M. Jarvis
David Jeffcoat
C.P. Jenner
J.D. Jennings
Mrs. J.B. Jewell
R. Johnston
Cdr. B. Joinson
H. Thomson Jones
W.D. Jones
Ronald Jones
Terry Jones
Mrs P.A. Jordan
P.K. Jordan
M.D. Joslyn
Frederick H.J. Jukes
H.L. Jukes

James Kane
G.H. Keable
Michael Leo Keane
Mrs. M. Keeling
David Kellett
Francis Kelly
J.E. Kelly
V. Kelly
Dr. A.J.I. Kelynack
Simon M. Kemp
J.H. Kemple (Zimbabwe)
B.J. Kennedy
Callum S. Kennedy
Miss P. Kennedy
J. Kenneth
H.R.H. The Duke of Kent
F.C. Kent
M.B. Kent

D. Kenward
Robert Kerby
N. Kerman
Allan Kerr
Dr. D.F. Kerr
W.R. Kewley
Mrs. Archie Kidd
Maurice G. Kidd, W.S.
T.W. Killick
A.E. Kindred
Hon. Mrs. John King
Jonathan G.N. King
Peter B. King
Miss S.R. King
Lt.-Col. R. Kinsella-Bevan
M.E. Kitler (Switzerland)
Miss J.A. Kneale
David A. Knight
S. Knight
S. Knowle
Andrew Knox
A.J.S. Knox
Miss T. Kynaston-Jones

Mrs. B. Lake
G.A. Lakin
Mrs. C.M. Lambert
R.E. Lambert
S.N. Lane
Mrs. V.A. Langridge
Mrs. V. Lantin-Plant
H.T. van Laun
Arvin Law
The Hon. Hugh Lawson-Johnston
Mrs. Mary G.L. Lawton (Las Vegas)
Mrs. C.F.A.B.J. Le Vay
J.L. Leach
M.S. Ledger
John Leigh
J.W.P. Lewis
R.V. Lewis
Walter Lilley
G.M. Lilly
J.W. Linfield

George Linfoot
William Ling
Dr. C. Lipp
C.S. Lippell
Robin J. Lipscombe
T. Lisney
William Lister
M.R. Little
A. Littlejohn
H.G. Llewellyn
The Earl Lloyd George
  of Dwyfor
Dr. T.L. Lloyd
Mrs. J.C. Lodge
Anthony D. Loehnis
Terry Logan
G.A. Longbottom
J.V. Lonnen
Thomas Lonnergan
E.H. Lord
Roger Losa
A.A. Loudon (Holland)
Mrs. C.E. Lovejoy
Mrs. Mary S. Lovell
Mrs. Ian Lowe
Mrs. S.J. Lowe
Dr. S.B. Lucas
Dr. Richard Luckett
J.D. Lucock
Oliver Lynas
Dr. P.F. Lynch

Mrs. O.H. MacDonald
Iain Macfarlane
Lt.-Col C.H.T.
  Macfetridge
A.J. Mack
The Revd. Hugh
  Mackay
R.D. Mackay
Lt.-Col. R.M. Mackie
N.G. Mackinlay
  Macleod
J.G.H. Mackrell
K.M. Macleod
Mrs. Macleod
R.N. Alington Maguire
M.V. Malyon
C.D. Mann

N. Mann
P.R. Mann
R.D. Mann
G.R. Mannell
Mrs. P.M. Manning
Mrs. C.E.D. March
A. Marchant
J.W. Martin
Mrs. T.L. Martin
Dr. Martyn-Johns
P.J. Maslen
R.J. Mason
Stephen Mason
Mrs. Evelyn Masterman
Robin Mathew
A.A. Mawby
Mrs. J.G. Mayers
H. Maynard
Denis J. McCarthy
  (Brazil)
Wing-Cdr. C.E.
  McCullagh
P.O. McDougall
Dr. Ewen McEwen
D.J. McGlynn
Major C. McInnes
W.A. McIntosh
Stuart McKeever
Mrs. Sheila McKinley
Mrs. S. McClymont
J.A. McNeish
Mrs. McWilliam
M.A. Meacham
W.J.B. Meakin
C. Mears
William Meek
Paul Mellon, K.B.E.
  (Virginia)
David C. Mellors
T.J. Mercer
K. Messenger
R.G.C. Messervy
R.J. Michel
John Millar
L.A. Miller
C.H. Millin
T.W. Millson
R.J. Milton
Peter Mimpriss

Robin Minnis
A.L.W. Minns
Mrs. G.M. Mitchell
N.H. Mitchell
A. Moger
Mrs. H.E. Monteith
Catherine Moody
E.G.H. Moody
Mrs. E.G. Moon
Mrs. Kathleen Moore
Mrs. Wendy Moore
P.D. Moorhead
Miss A.J. Mooring
D.J. Morgan
B.T. Morgan
I. John Morgan
J.G. Morgan-Owen,
  M.B.E., Q.C.
Mrs. H.F. Morison
  Maidment
G.E. Morris
L.F. Morris
Major Douglas C.
  Morris
Dr. E. Morrissey
Mrs. G.T. Morton
E.D. Moylan
Mrs. D.K. Moyle
Mrs. A.M. Mumford
Dennis J. Murphy,
  M.F.H.

Mrs. S.J. Nash
J.W. Naylor
P. Naylor
P.E. Neal
W. Keith Neal
David Negus, F.R.C.S.
Major A.J. Nettleton
Basil Newall
Mrs. C.A. Newby
Diana Duchess of
  Newcastle
Mrs. M. Newcomb
D. Newell
D.A. Newton
M.J. Nicholas
C.B.Q. Nicholls
M. Nicholson